# Fancy's Way

# Fancy's Way

Walter A. Turner

Writers Club Press
San Jose  New York  Lincoln  Shanghai

Fancy's Way

All Rights Reserved © 2000 by Walter A. Turner

No part of this book may be reproduced or transmitted in any form or by any means, graphic, electronic, or mechanical, including photocopying, recording, taping, or by any information storage retrieval system, without the permission in writing from the publisher.

Writers Club Press
an imprint of iUniverse.com, Inc.

For information address:
iUniverse.com, Inc.
620 North 48th Street, Suite 201
Lincoln, NE 68504-3467
www.iuniverse.com

ISBN: 0-595-12815-7

Printed in the United States of America

# 1

The bright red, or bright orange, (depending on who was looking at it) 240 Z cruised along Miramar Road toward the entrance to the Naval Air Station Miramar. Of course it was better known throughout the Navy as simply "Fighter Town". The driver tapped out the rhythm of a Beach Boys' favorite—"Surfin' U.S.A." So far, thought Lieutenant Dan "Gator" Fancy, I like California. The weather, the music, the new duty station—a chance for a whole new start.

The entrance to the main gate popped up on the right. The 240, without slowing down too much, hung a sharp right and screeched to a halt in front of the guard shack. The Marine Sergeant on duty seemed not the least bit amused. Smart bleepin' Navy officers he thought to himself. "Good morning sir," he intoned, somewhat just to the left of insubordination.

"Good Morning Sergeant. I'm reporting in to VF-124 this morning. Can you give me some directions, please?"

"Yes sir, I can. If I can get a quick look at your orders?"

Almost immediately a thick sheaf of papers were thrust out the window. "Here you go."

"Thank you sir. If you could please park over there in the visitors' section, I'll check these and make a call to your squadron."

"Thank you, Sergeant."

As Sergeant Diganci made his call to 124, he observed the Lieutenant as he got out of his car. Being what he thought a good judge of character, he watched the man stretch and walk around his car. He seemed kind of old to be an O-3. He wasn't tall but he wasn't exactly what you consider short either. Not exactly well built, but not a wimp. Hair, a little too long. He had noticed the blue eyes that seemed to be on the verge of twinkling as if he knew what the joke was and who it was on. His uniform wouldn't pass a Marine inspection, but the license plates on the car were from Virginia, so maybe the guy's been driving. But why would anyone drive across country in his uniform? He decided he would probably like the lieutenant, but he couldn't put his finger on exactly why.

After what seemed, to Fancy, a very long time, , but what was in reality only a few minutes, a long, black '65 Cadillac tore up the road, sliding to a halt in a cloud of dust and noisy brakes. The driver flipped a U and got out bringing a smile to Fancy's face. "Bagger! I didn't know you were here. Man, it's good to see you."

"Gator, I heard you were comin' and I wanted to be the first one to welcome you to California, where the real fighter pilots live. Babe, it's good to see you!."

Scott Bailey, call sign Bagger, had crossed paths with Fancy when they were at NAS Oceana. Bagger was a tall Texan who seemed to always be one step ahead on the power curve. If he wasn't flying he could be found climbing rocks, mountains, or even sometimes up buildings. A good many people had mistaken his Texas drawl and down home ways for someone who wasn't the brightest bulb in the house, and had later paid the price for that miscalculation. Bagger was sharp on the ground and in the air. He just didn't advertise it.

"Follow me. You still got that Z? Man, out here everybody drives Porsches or four-wheel drives."

"Hey, this car is part of me, it's a classic. Besides, it brings back some good memories."

"Yeah, I heard you and Janice split up. I couldn't believe it at first. I thought that was one marriage made in heaven."

"Yeah, well, so did I," said Fancy, with a far away look in his eyes. "After the baby died we just sort of drifted apart. I wasn't there for her as much as I should have been I guess. She wanted me to get out and go to work for some airline. One day I came home and told her I wasn't going to leave the Navy and the next day she was gone."

"What'd her old man say about that? I mean, wow! Duke Cross's daughter?" queried Bagger.

"Shoot, at first I guess he was pretty brassed off and wanted to kick my butt all over Oceana. He even came down there lookin' for me. Luckily, we were down at Key West playing with VF-45. I guess he talked to some people and found out it was her idea and some of the things she told him about me weren't quite true."

"So you're still friends, so to speak?"

"More or less. I still think the world of him. The guy can still flat out fly and he's showed me some things."

"Well," grinned Bagger, "it's really great to have you here. We're going to have some fun! Let's get down to the squadron and get you squared away."

Building 145 was the home of VF-124, the Gunfighters. Actually it was part hanger, admin offices, gymnasium, and hang out for the squadron.

Fancy pulled in and parked by the Caddy, noticing for the first time the fake foot extending from the gas tank. Taking a deep breath he got out.

Bagger bounced out of the Caddy. "Leave your stuff in the car and we'll get you squared away later. Let's go see the skipper."

"What's he like?"

"Commander Robinson? Good guy. Heck of a stick and rudder man. Goes pretty much by the book most of the time, but seems to know when to cut people some slack. The XO, Lt. Commander Matsen, is pretty easy going—that is until you screw up. Then he's all over you like ugly on an ape. The squadron is up at "Strike U", you know, at Fallon. The skipper and I came back yesterday and Commander Matsen's coming back with the rest of the guys tomorrow. We're about ready to hit the boat for carrier quals and then we say good-bye to our loved ones for a six month cruise."

The two aviators went in the cavernous building. Fancy was drawn immediately to the two F-14's parked inside, noticing they were the D models. They looked dangerous just sitting there. However, they seemed to be saying, "Come on, let's go, let's have some fun."

After climbing the stairs and walking down the hall, Bailey paused before a door marked, Commanding Officer, VF- 124, Commander Richard Robinson. "Good luck. I'll meet you downstairs in the ready room."

"Okay, I'll see you in a while." Fancy knocked on the door.

"Come in," barked the voice on the other side.

Fancy entered, walked to the desk in front of the door, came to his best Boot Camp attention and said, "Lieutenant Fancy reporting aboard, sir."

Commander Richard Robinson looked the newest addition to his squadron up and down for what seemed an uncomfortably long time. "At ease Lieutenant. Have a seat."

"Thank you, Sir, as he eased himself into the chair in front of Robinson's desk.

"Well Lieutenant, you made good time all the way from Oceana. It looks like you drove nonstop."

"Uh—I'm sorry about my appearance, sir. I drove straight through from Denver. I wanted to get here as ASAP."

"That's commendable, Fancy. I'd rather have someone who is anxious to get going rather worrying about spit and polish, to tell you the truth. Welcome aboard," said Robinson, as he extended his hand across the desk.

Fancy rose to meet his hand. He noticed the handshake was firm, seemingly friendly. He also noticed that when Robinson smiled, he did it with his whole face, even his ears seemed to get involved.

"So, you're coming over from VF-84, are you?" he queried. "That's a good outfit. Commander Hammeras and I went through Pensacola together. How is he, anyway?"

"He was fine when I left, Sir. I enjoyed serving with him."

Robinson held Fancy under a steady gaze before he spoke again. "You had the "B's" back there didn't you, Lieutenant?"

"Yes, Sir, we did. They had the GE F-110 engines, same as the "D's. It made a world of difference to have all that power. We could fly right up to the limits of the air frame."

"Well then, you're going to feel right at home. We've got the "D's". What do you know about the D model?"

"I've heard nothing but good things, sir. There were some guys from VF-31 passing through a couple of weeks ago, flying the D. They say it's like a whole new plane. Everything digital, more power, better software. They couldn't say enough. The only thing they didn't like was the fact that they were probably going to be lugging some iron around."

Robinson smiled, leaned back at this desk. "Nobody is crazy about that, but if we have to, and we will, we'll do it better than anybody else."

"Understood, sir."

"Tell me Lieutenant, are you ready to go to work? The word I got from Commander Hammeras was that you had lost your focus, somewhat. What was going on? I'm not usually the nosy type, but I want to get the past in the past and move on. Commander Hammeras thinks you're a heck of a pilot, but…" his voice trailing off. Again the steady gaze.

"Well sir, I did lose it for a while. My wife left me after the death of our baby daughter. I wasn't there for her and when I tried to make it up to her, I wasn't where I should have been for the skipper or the rest of the squadron. For a while I was drinking more than I should have." *Might as well lay it right out on the table* he thought.

Robinson's eyebrows raised. "I'm sorry about your daughter. I've got two of my own, plus a son. It would be tough not to lose it. However, I'm not looking for excuses, and I'm sure you're not looking to give me any. How about the drinking?"

"That's right, sir. I feel like I'm back. If I'm not mistaken, Commander Hammeras seemed to think a new squadron would help me out. Looks like he figured a new coast wouldn't hurt either. I'm glad to be here, sir. As for the drinking, I've quit. Period, Sir."

"In effect, that's what he told me. I was on the phone with him about thirty minutes ago. He said to tell you hello and you still owe him $20 bucks." Robinson grinned.

Fancy shifted uncomfortably in his chair. "I think it's the other way around, sir. But I appreciate what he's doing for me."

"That's good enough for me. Why don't you take the rest of the day to get settled in and squared away. I can recommend a good barber by the way." Robinson was grinning again—the whole face. "I'll let that criminal Bagger help you get settled. How long have you known Bagger?"

"We go back to when we were going through the RAG squadron at Oceana. You know, we kind of helped each other over the rough spots."

"He seems to always be in the thick of things—one way or another." Again the whole face smile. "All right, get settled in and squared away and report back tomorrow by 0730."

"Yes, sir," said Fancy enthusiastically, as he came to his feet. "It's nice to meet you, sir, and I'm glad to be here."

As Fancy walked out of Commander Robinson's office and down the stairs, he noticed a plaque and he paused to read it.

*Only the spirit of attack borne of a brave heart will bring success to any fighter aircraft, no matter how highly developed it may be.*

Amen to that thought Fancy.

Bagger was at the foot of the "ladder" or stairs as Fancy descended. "Don't you look happy," he remarked. "It looks like you got off to a good start with the old man?"

"Not too bad. How come he thinks you're some kind of criminal?"

"Me!" exclaimed Bagger in mock horror. "Hey remember, I'm the guy that sticks to the straight and narrow. I mean—you know me. You probably won't believe this, but I have not come up before the old man for anything, at least officially."

"Yeah, I know you and it's good to see that you haven't changed a bit. It's the unofficial garbage the skipper has to worry about—right?"

"Right," smiled Bagger. "Say, what are your plans to camp out until we hit the boat? If you haven't thought that far ahead, why don't you plan on staying with me, uh, well, us. Big Wave Dave, Poncho and I are renting this great place down at Ocean Beach. Man, its got hot and cold running babes all over the place. We just had a guy move out. He's going to some kind of school and won't be back."

"Hmmmmm, that sounds better than the BOQ. Are you sure the other guys won't mind?"

"Nah. Big Wave and Poncho are great guys. You'll like 'em. They're j.g.'s so we outrank 'em anyway. Not that I'd ever pull rank you understand."

"Oh, no, you'd never do anything like that."

"Come on and follow me. The skipper gave me the rest of the day to help you. Let's get the admin garbage out of the way and then we'll head on down to the beach."

After a mind numbing two and a half hours of signing and initialing what seemed mountains of papers and forms at buildings that seemed be as spread out from each other as possible, the two aviators headed for Ocean Beach.

Fancy was surprised when he started to follow Bagger down the 805 Freeway. He had expected something more like a 1 v 1, a down and out furball, with Bagger playing bumper tag with anyone who got in his way. Instead, he drove like any sane driver would, driving just at the speed limit with no weaving in and out. It was actually easy to keep up and follow him. Of course, maybe the volume of traffic had something to do with it.

They arrived at a large yellow house facing directly on the Pacific Ocean after a quick twenty minute drive. The house was trimmed in white and had a large front porch. It reminded Fancy of his grandparents' house in Maine.

Bagger jumped out of his bright red Porsche, with the license plates "Chek Six". Fancy wondered how Bagger managed to wind his lanky frame into the car.

"I was really worried about keepin' up with you, Bagger."

"Oh man, I've had to change my driving habits. The cops are really tough out here and you can't talk 'em out of a ticket. I even promised one guy I'd give him a ride in the back of my Tomcat. No sale. The old man says if I get another ticket, my rear end is grass and he's going to be the lawn mower."

"Another ticket? How many have you had?"

"Only two. They had to chase me for a while to give me the second one. I had to spend most of a day in the gray bar hotel before Matsen came down to get me out. Was he brassed off."

"How do you stand with Matsen now?"

"I think we're okay, but if any stuff rolls downhill, I've been the guy to catch it. The old man found a place where I could get my insurance . Good old State Farm decided I wasn't good for their bottom line and sent me a "Dear John" letter. Come on in and lets find a place to dump your gear."

"How'd you find this place?"

"When I first reported in the BOQ was full up and somebody I knew invited me to stay. The lady that owns it is Captain Ault's widow. You know the Frank Ault of the Ault Report that told the Navy what they needed to do to improve the shoot down ratio in Vietnam. That of course led to Top Gun. She takes pity on poor wayward fighter jocks. I guess this place got too much for her to take care of and she moved to a condo over on Coronado. Everybody who stays here has to pitch in and take care of the place. She'll throw you out if you're not helpin' with the chores. It's kind of like being back in high school, but it's a great place to live."

As they entered the spacious house, Fancy noted right away that widow Ault must have made an impression on Bagger. The house was immaculate—no clutter, no muss, no fuss. "Jeez Bagger, you've turned over a new leaf. I can't believe you live here."

"It's home sweet home, Gator. We all try to keep the mess down by ordering out or eating on base before we come home. That leaves just the yard work to do," Bagger sighed. "Really, it's not too bad. Mrs. Ault will show up sometimes and take a look around. If we've been really good, she might leave us some of her chocolate chip cookies. I can't get enough of those and she knows it."

Fancy laughed. "Where do you want me to put my stuff. I'd like to shower and clean up. Robinson strongly suggested I find a barber. Is there one close?"

"There's one just up the street not too far. Get freshened up and we'll go on up there and then grab something to eat. Are you up for that?"

"Just lead the way, babe."

The two men carried the contents of the Z up to a sizable room on the second floor that overlooked the Pacific. Fancy immediately noticed a pretty blond bicycling in front of the house. *Bagger must think he's in heaven,* thought Fancy.

The room contained a large closet, a chest of drawers, large bed, and two night stands, with lamps. It was clean and Fancy thought he could get to enjoy this. "Say, this is all right. How come one of you didn't want this room?"

"Nobody wanted to move all his stuff. Big Wave's got so much stuff it would take a week to move it. It just wasn't worth the hassle."

"I really appreciate this, Bagger. One more time, I owe you."

"What are friends for? Get cleaned up and we'll go get something to eat. I'm starved."

Three hours later after one trip to a barber, a fairly short line at the DMV, and two burgers, the duo returned to, what as Fancy thought of as, the big yellow house. They parked Fancy's car in the biggest garage Fancy had ever seen. There was room for at least four other cars beside the Z and Bagger's Porsche.

A few minutes after entering the house, Fancy heard the sound of someone coming in the back door. The someone turned out to be two. The first to enter the room was a short, somewhat stocky, maybe on the chubby side, flier still dressed in his flight suit. After the initial look of surprise he extended his hand. "Dave Schwartze. VF-124, fighter pilot, surfer, dog tired person." Fancy's hand was immediately enveloped in a beefy paw with a sure, friendly grip.

"I'm Dan Fancy. Call me Gator. It looks like I've taken over your spare room."

"That's cool man. We're glad to have you. Not to mention that it makes it easier to pay the rent and keep up with the yard work."

The second of the two men was taller, darker, and had deep set black eyes. Coupled with his hawk-like nose and strong jaw, he was also one of the best looking men he'd ever seen. Right out of central casting, a poster boy for fighter pilots. "I'm Rodrigo Barnes. Call sign Poncho. Nice to meet you Gator. Bagger's been talking about you. It'll be nice to have you. Welcome to our humble abode." His grip was likewise firm and friendly.

"It's good to be here I hope I'm not going to inconvenience anybody."

Poncho grinned. "Are you kidding. It'll be nice to get some new blood around here. We don't get to spend that much time here anyway."

"How was the flight back? Everybody get home okay?"

"No problems," chimed in Dave. "We took the scenic Owens Valley tour on the way back. Two plane sections, with one of three. Straight shot home. I'm pooped and I'm headed for the sack. Skipper wants us back at 0730 sharp."

"Sounds like a plan," said Poncho. I"ll see you guys in the morning."

"Big Wave, how about if we all go up with you in the morning," asked Bagger.

"Fine with me, but you guys will have to do my share of the dishes tomorrow," grinned Big Wave as he headed for the stairs and what he hoped was a good night's sleep.

"Well Gator, what do you think? Are you going to like it here?" asked Bagger.

"I don't see why not. These guys seem like they've got their acts together. Now if I can ease into the routine of the squadron and drive that "turkey" around to keep up with the high standards of the west coast, I'll be okay," replied Fancy.

"Let's hit the sack then, we've got a big day manana," grinned Bagger.

Going through the Main Gate the next morning was a great deal quicker than the day before. The four fliers rolled right on through with hardly a glance from the Marines on duty. As they drove down to building 145, Fancy noticed that the base was already alive with the whine of jet engines being started and planes moving toward the active runways.

By 7:28 they were seated in the Gunfighter ready room. The walls were covered with pictures of planes and aviators who had been part of the history of VF-124.

At 07:30, on the nose Commander Robinson and his executive officer, Lt. Commander Matsen entered the room. "Attention on deck," someone in the back of the room boomed out and the entire room of pilots and radar intercept officers (RIO s) jumped to their feet.

"As you were," snapped Matsen. Lt. Commander Jeff Matsen was a little taller and heavier than the skipper, Fancy noticed. He had a flat top with just a few flecks of gray starting to show. "I wonder if Bagger contributed to that," thought Fancy.

"Good morning, gentleman. Welcome home, not that we're going to be here that long." Many groans chorused through the room.

"I'd like you to welcome Lt. Dan Fancy, fresh from the east coast and the Jolly Rogers. He'll be a permanent part of our little family. His call sign is Gator."

"How did you come up with something like that?" a voice came from the back.

Fancy recognized the voice immediately. There was only one voice like that in the Navy—probably in the entire world. It sounded like a frog playing a French horn. Only Moose Milwood could be connected to that voice. Immediately Fancy turned in his chair to find the speaker. He didn't have to look far. Sitting in the next to last row sat the Moose. In addition to having the most distinct voice anywhere, Moose was also the Navy's shortest pilot, probably the shortest pilot anywhere. Rumor had it that before he was allowed to join the service, several of Moose's friends had had to stretch him to make sure he made the minimum height requirement. Even then everyone was sure that the recruiters, doctors, and anyone else who had anything to do with Moose getting in the Navy must have taken something. To say Moose was short was one of the understatements of the twentieth century. Fortunately, that never stopped Moose—from anything.

Fancy grinned at Moose. "As I recall, I had to save someone who was about to be a snack for an alligator, down in Key West."

What a night that was thought Fancy. VF-84 had been undergoing some DACM (dissimilar air combat maneuvering) with VF-45, the East Coast adversary squadron. At day's end most everyone had hit Duval St., Key West's main drag. Most everyone headed for a place called P.J. McCarthy's, where it was rumored, the place was wall- to- wall beautiful women. The rumor was mostly true. Where else would fighter pilot's go? An additional feature was Amanda, the house alligator.

As things heated up during the evening, most everyone was feeling no pain. It was Friday, and flying wouldn't resume until the following Monday. It was soon evident that not only was the Navy represented, but the Air Force as well. The blue suiters were from Seymor-Johnson in South Carolina, flying F-16's. They were presently doing TDY (temporary duty) at Homestead Air Force Base.

One thing had led to another about who had the best planes, who had the better pilots, and who had the biggest "cajones". Moose, never one to back down from an argument, had stated that the Navy had the best and the biggest. Naturally, several of the Air Force gentleman took issue, mostly with Moose. Subtlety was never one of his strong points. Moose made the mistake of taking a swing at one of the F-16 drivers. It was said Moose looked him right in the kneecap and swung away. Things proceeded to go south in a hurry.

Before anyone really knew what was happening, Moose was being held upside down over Amanda's pit by two burly Falcon drivers. As Fancy remembered, he had asked them, politely, to please put the struggling Navy pilot down. They did. Right in the pit. Without too much hesitation, Fancy charged the now laughing pilots and knocked them over the railing into the pit where Moose was struggling to get out. The muck inside the pit was not helping any as Moose slipped and slid toward the railing to get his body away from Amanda, who by now smelled dinner. By then the friends of the two Air Force pilots started to flail away at anyone who even looked like they were in the Navy. Chairs, tables, people, and assorted items that weren't nailed down soon became airborne. As a brawl, everyone agreed later, the event was at least a nine on the Richter Scale.

Another voice chimed in, "So how'd you get the handle Gator."

Fancy took a deep breath. "Well, when the two blue suiters went in the pit, I wound up there too, with that big, ugly mother closer to me than anyone else. I just barely got out."

"You should have let him have Moose," someone else said. "He could have been swallowed whole and nobody would have known the difference."

"Ha, Think of all the broken hearts I would have left behind!"

The cat calls and hoots of derision fell on Moose like a heavy rain shower. Robinson ended the torment shortly and everyone came back to the business at hand. "Gator, we're glad to have you."

"All right, you all know we're going to hitting the boat next week to get everybody qualified. Enterprise is going out today to shake down and see if the guys at the shipyard put everything back together right. Gator, you're going to have to go through a little bit of survival training at the FASO, (physiology) outfit. Lucky, you."

Fancy groaned inwardly. The Navy requires recurrent survival training for everyone who flies its aircraft. Only a smattering of VIPs get to miss out. Everyone else is expected to get that ticket punched.

Robinson continued, "It'll take you the better part of two days and most of that will be lectures. After that you need to get some simulator time in over at the RAG (Replacement Air Group), to get you up to speed on the differences between the B and the D. See Chief Tomsha after we get done here and he'll get you all squared away and let you know where you have to be. Any questions?"

"No, sir. I'll be ready to hit the boat."

"Good. Killer, you're scheduled to go back to FASO too. You and Gator might as well go together."

"What?" came a startled voice from down the row. "Skipper, I just went through that garbage."

"As I remember, Killer, you almost drowned too. You've got to pass the course before we hit the boat."

"I got a cramp, " came the somewhat weak reply.

"Cramp or no cramp, you're going."

Fancy met the eyes of someone who was not happy about the turn of events so far in the day. He was a tall, solid looking fellow, with short black hair. Fancy grinned and said, "Looks like we hit the jackpot. This is not my favorite part of being in the Navy."

The tall pilot extended a hand in greeting. "Desmond Stevens. It's definitely not my favorite part. Who knows, maybe

they'll cancel it." The weak smile again, then a resigned shrug.

Robinson began speaking again. "The rest of you need to get your affairs in order, wills, insurance, and all that stuff. Chief Tomshaw has a roster of who needs to do what. XO, any further words of wisdom?"

Commander Matsen stood and faced the group. "We did some pretty good work up at Strike U. We really seem to be getting all our stuff in one bag. The "Desert Boggies" had all they could handle up there, I was pleased with the way things went. Even the attack pukes had some good things to say about us, particularly the way we were able to cover their behinds. Although we didn't drop any iron, that day is coming. Those of you who aren't going to FASO will get some simulator time and we'll start to do some day and night bounce practice. Gator, after you finish up with FASO and the simulator time, I'll arrange some time with you out on Whiskey 294."

A few chuckles and groans met that pronouncement.

Fancy leaned over and asked Killer, "What's Whiskey 294?"

"That's the local restricted air space. Looks like Matsen going to see how well you represent the east coast."

Gee, thought Fancy, good news comes in bunches.

After a few more announcements, the squadron broke up and headed for their various assignments for the day. Fancy caught Bagger and Poncho as they were walking out.

"We'll my man, it looks like you're going to get your feet wet—so to speak," chuckled Barnes. "I'm always glad when those two days are over. Have you ever had to ditch?"

"No, and I don't plan on it either," Fancy answered.

"Let's meet back here about 14:30, and we'll drag your wet butt home. Good luck," chimed in Bagger.

"Ok, 14:30, I'll see you guys later."

He saw Killer Stevens waiting and walked quickly toward him. "Let's go and get this over with."

The two pilots drove over to building 2134 where the FASO unit was housed, right next to the mammoth base pool.

They were ushered into an auditorium where about two dozen other, somewhat glum looking pilots and flight officers were waiting for the class to begin.

Almost immediately after they were seated, an athletic officer, dressed in navy blue shorts and white T-shirt climbed the stairs to the small stage and began addressing the assembled men. "Good morning. My name is Commander Duehr, call sign Krank. I'll be giving the lecture part of this class and assisting in the water part of the class. Today we will start by covering hypoxia, or oxygen starvation or narcosis, spatial disorientation, effects of diet on vision and cockpit performance and comfort."

Gator knew that oxygen-starved pilots have been known to fly right into the ground, laughing all the way down, not paying one bit of attention to the frantic calls of their wingman to pull out.

The next two hours went quickly and Fancy was surprised that he was so focused and in tune with CDR Duehr. He was pleased with himself that he was able to answer several of the questions that were thrown out to the group from time to time, and made several comments that added to the lecture.

After a working lunch, where diet was discussed, the group was taken down a flight of stairs. Most of the basement room was taken up by a large cylinder that looked somewhat like a section of a wide-body airliner.

Another officer, a very pretty blond, Fancy noted, greeted them. "Good afternoon, gentleman. I'm Lieutenant Hamilton. This afternoon you're going to take a short hop. You will be taken to an altitude of 35, 000 ft. On the way up, I'm going to ask you to remove your oxygen masks and write your names."

After another 30 minutes of safety instructions and answering questions, the aviators were ushered into the chamber. Lt. Hamilton's metallic voice came over a speaker. "Can everyone hear me okay? Give me a thumbs up if you can. Good. On the pad in front of you, write your name as neatly as you possibly can."

Fancy complied in his best schoolboy script.

"Now," said Lt. Hamilton, we're going to start up to altitude by removing the oxygen in the chamber. I'll let you know what to do next."

Fancy could hear a faint hissing sound. He looked over at Killer, who seemed much more resigned to his fate. Killer gave him a thumbs up.

After a few minutes, Lt. Hamilton asked them to write their names again and then take off their oxygen masks. Fancy was feeling pretty good.

In another few minutes they were asked to write their names again. By this time, Fancy felt absolutely wonderful, not a care in the world. He felt he could do anything, and feel good while he was doing it.

After what seemed like a very short time, the melodic, beautiful voice came over the speaker. "We're at 35,000. How's everybody doing? Give me a thumbs up if you're okay." All the thumbs went up, accompanied by giggling and laughing. "Okay, write your name one more time, for me please."

No problem, thought Fancy. I'll even do it twice for you baby.

What happened next got Fancy's and everybody else's attention—all at once. A tremendous **bang** brought everybody down to earth literally and figuratively and not without some pain. The rapid decompression had brought everyone down to sea level in one big hurry.

"Everyone, please exit the chamber," came the voice.

"Judas priest, that scared the bejesus out of me," growled Killer. "Man, I keep forgetting they're going to do that!"

Fancy answered, "Shoot, back on the east coast they just bring us down gradually. That's painful."

"The things we do in defense of our country," grinned Killer, rubbing his ears.

"Gentleman, if you will please look at the papers you wrote your names on.

Fancy looked at his and was not surprised. The first time he had written his name it looked perfectly normal and very neat. Something his third grade teacher would have been proud of. In progressive stages, the name took on a horrific look until the last name couldn't be read at all. It brought the point home that oxygen starvation could kill you while you laughed all the way to your death. He also realized the real thing would be a great deal more violent and a heck of a lot more frightening.

"Gentleman," Lt. Hamilton continued, "we hope our little demonstration has brought to your attention the several problems that hypoxia can cause. We wanted to end it with a bang, so to speak."

After the groans and laughter had died down the pilots and flight officers were offered a brief respite before they reported upstairs for a lecture on the part of FASO that everyone detested, the dreaded day in the water.

As Killer and Gator walked up the stairs, Gator said, "That Lieutenant is quite a package."

"She sure is, and she's dating Matsen."

"Oh. Enough said."

At the lecture upstairs, they found out what they already knew and dreaded. Day two FASO gets rough. They could plan on a full, tiring day in the water. Lieutenant Humphreys, who looked more like a large frog to Fancy, told them to get a good night's sleep and report back to the room they were in now at 08:00 with a pair of old boots and a flight suit. He grinned maliciously and told them the FASO unit would furnish the rest.

As Fancy and Killer walked back to VF-124, Fancy noticed a slight southern drawl when Killer talked, which he did all the way back.

"Do I detect a southern boy?" Fancy asked.

"You bet," replied Stevens. "I'm from Alabama, Mobile. My dad teaches at the University of Alabama and my mom teaches high school. And they both warned me there would be days like this."

Fancy grinned. "Hey, one more day, we can hack that."

"Actually, I'd rather kiss a dead moose's butt than go through that garbage tomorrow, but you're right."

By that time they had reached the squadron hanger where Big Wave, Bagger, and Poncho were waiting. "Let's go home, I know you're going to want to turn in early, Gator."

"You know it. That decompression chamber took all the starch out of me for today. I just want to log some rack time and then get tomorrow behind me."

08:00 came all too soon. After a good night's sleep, Fancy figured he could get through the day in pretty good shape. He and Killer stood in the knot of men looking at the base pool. "I bet they haven't had the heat on," mused Fancy. "Is it my imagination or does this pool look cold, Killer?"

"Are you kidding, man. Why would they make it easy, when they can freeze our nuts off and play games with us. That's just not the Navy way."

"Listen up, men," barked Lt. Humphreys. "We're going to start today's festivities with a swimming test. On the sound of my whistle, I want you to jump off from this end of the pool." He indicated with his hand, the deep end. "You'll do this in full gear, helmets for everybody. Get one off the rack there as you go to that end of the pool. You prop and helo people, grab a survival vest off the next rack. Attack and fighter guys, you put on the g-suits down at the end. You'll swim three full laps or seventy-five yards. Any questions? If anyone gets in trouble, my able assistants will fish your lifeless bodies out of the pool."

Gator and Killer shuffled down the line toward the deep end, getting a helmet and the g-suit. Soon enough Humphrey's whistle pierced the air like a knife and they jumped in.

At first the cold water took Fancy's breath away, but he started to get used to it as he started to swim. He started to swim in a lazy free-style toward the other end. This isn't too bad he thought as he turned and started the second lap. By the time he had turned and started the third lap, the g-suit and his flight suit were starting to slow him down. Fancy kept on plugging watching the end of the pool get slowly nearer. At last he was able to reach the end and hold on to the side of the pool, taking deep ragged breaths.

Again Humphrey's whistle sounded when all the water logged swimmers had finished the three laps. There was no conversation, just the sound of heavy breathing. "I'm glad to see we haven't lost anyone. Anybody with cramps?" There were none and Humphreys continued. "When I blow the whistle again, I want you to push off the side and swim toward the center of the pool. Once everyone is there, I'll blow the whistle again. You will then tread water or do the dead man's float for fifteen minutes. Any questions?"

The whistle blew and Fancy swam to the center of the pool. Fifteen minutes, he thought. Fifteen minutes isn't that long. He started to tread water very slowly to conserve his strength. After what seemed an hour he felt a cramp begin to assert itself in his right calf. "Oh, oh," he thought, "I don't need this." Around him, the sound of breathing was growing louder. Fancy reached down and tried to pull up on the big toe on his right foot. The steel toed boot made that impossible. He then tried to push his toe up toward the top of the boot, again without success. The cramp started to grow worse and he felt a momentary stab of panic. It can't be much longer, at least he hoped not. This was not fun. As the pain started to grow and deepen, Fancy tried to will himself to think about something else. However, it seemed that the pain had other ideas. Just when he thought he might have to ask for help, the blessed sound of Humphrey's whistle ripped the air. Barely, just barely, he crawled over to the side of the pool where Killer had just pulled up. Killer didn't even look like he was breaking a sweat, if you could break a sweat in a pool.

"Gator, you look like you're on your last leg. Are you okay?"

In deep, ragged bursts, Fancy answered, "I got a cramp. That whistle sounded just in time. I was just about ready to go down for the count."

"I can't believe it. This was a no sweat deal," said Killer. "I hope this doesn't mean the Dilbert Dunker is going to be my undoing. That thing is a royal pain in the butt."

"All right, gentleman," yelled Humphreys over the gasping of the aviators who looked more like drowned rats than Naval officers, "I'll give you a ten minute break before we go next door.

Next door resided the "Dilbert Dunker", an old F-8 cockpit on a track that was angled down 25º degrees. After going ten feet down in the water it rolled over inverted. At this time the unfortunate passenger had to unhook and get to the surface. Doing it twice just added to the fun. The second time you got to do it blindfolded—chances being that in a real crash, visibility would be zero.

Killer and Fancy slogged to the pool with Dilbert waiting for the sacrificial lambs.

"Men," growled Humphreys, are there any questions?"

"Yeah," came a voice, "is this really necessary?" That brought nervous laughter from the assembled group.

"Only if you want to live if your bird goes down," shot back Humphreys. "Any volunteers?"

Fancy stepped forward. The only thing that was worse than doing this, he thought was waiting to do it.

"All right, Lieutenant, mount up."

Fancy squished his way to the cockpit, and with the assistance of an enlisted man, climbed in. He fastened and unfastened each koch fitting making sure each fit and came apart as advertised. They seemed to be working and he snapped off a salute to indicate he was ready.

Almost immediately the cockpit started its slide into the water. Fancy waited until the last possible moment to take a huge gulp of air. At the bottom, the F-8 cockpit rolled over and Fancy reached for the koch settings at his shoulder. Working immediately, he felt himself come free. With one kick he was out and headed toward the surface. Breaking free of the water, with air to spare, he swam over to the edge of the pool and hoisted himself out to the cheers of his fellow pilots.

"Way to go, Gator," he heard Killer call out.

"Well done, Lieutenant," he heard Humphreys say. "First-timers get to get it over with if they want to. You ready to try it blindfolded?"

"I'm good to go, let's do it."

After climbing in the second time, a blindfold was placed over his eyes, and his helmet put on. "Ready, sir?" asked the enlisted man.

"All set, just let me try these fittings again." One more time they worked. He fired off what he hoped was a snappy salute and felt the dunker start to move. His timing for getting that last breath was a little late and he swallowed some water. I can cheat just a little he thought, and began to feel his way toward the koch fittings. Just as the conpit rolled inverted, Fancy flipped the settings, gave one kick, and was out headed toward the surface. Piece of cake, he thought, as he broke the surface of the water and swam toward the side of the pool.

The rest of the time spent with the Dilbert Dunker went smoothly. Everyone took their two turns without mishap.

After a brief respite, Humphreys led the way inside to another, smaller pool—home of the even more dreaded "Helo—dunker, often referred to as panic in a barrel. The Helo-dunker is a large cylindrical drum that represents the fuselage of the CH-46 helicopter.

"Gentleman," said Humphreys, "our last round of fun will take place in this simulation of a "Frog", or CH-46 helo. As you know, the Navy uses many types of helicopters. Many of you will be passengers or you're here because you already fly one. Any time blue water ops are taking place, you're going to find helos. Due to their high center of gravity, if you have to ditch at sea, that helicopter is going to turn turtle very quickly. If this happens, crew and passengers have to make a rapid exit, usually from under water, while you're sinking. I've gone through this and it is not a pleasant experience, particularly when the sea is rough.

"I want you to form groups of six. There will be four trips in the helo-dunker. The dunker will be dropped from about twelve feet up, as you can see. Upon hitting the water, it will begin to sink to about a depth of twelve feet. Then it will invert, and at that time you will make your exit from the window you are sitting by. The second time you will exit by the front door. After that, we will repeat the process—blindfolded. A word of advice, wait until the motion stops before you try to make your exit. Any questions?" Humphreys took his time, looking at each individual before moving on. "Good, let's form up and get started."

By now the soggy fliers were anxious to get this particular part of the day over with and the pairs of six were formed quickly and without much discussion.

Killer and Gator formed their group of six with an F-14 RIO and three CH-53 crewman. "Man," Killer whispered, "I try to stay away from helos as much as possible. They're just not safe. Besides that, they're ugly. I just don't like to be around anything that ugly and unsafe."

"Careful," answered Fancy, "you don't want to insult our fellow aviators."

"Humph," Bagger replied, "the truth is the truth. A lot of those CH-46's have gone down."

"F-14's forever, babe," grinned Gator.

Killer and Fancy's group was the last to get in the "dunker". Each group of six went through the exercise, doing one before moving on to the next, more difficult problem.

As Fancy and Stevens climbed in they moved toward the back of the cylinder. They were ordered to strap in. Without warning, the tube dropped to the surface of the water and started to sink. There was more motion and movement than Fancy had bargained for and he was only just able to gather in a huge breath of air. Finally, the dunker reached a point where it started to slowly roll over. Fancy felt a moment of panic and then released his harness and pulled himself through the window and again headed for the surface. Breaking the surface of the water he heard one of the enlisted men, acting as lifeguards call out, "Six out and at the surface!"

Fancy pulled himself up and out of the pool as the other five men of their party came out of the pool. "Well, Killer, three more times and we're finished."

"Yeah man. Three more times. I can do it."

"Like we have a choice," Fancy replied with a grin.

Everyone seemed to have the idea of how to get out, both blindfolded and sighted.

As the sodden aviators made their way to the far end of the pool, Fancy noticed Humphreys opening a door into another building. He motioned them to follow him.

In the room they entered was a pool, smaller than the one they had just exited. Immediately Fancy noticed the huge fan like contraptions at either end of the pool. His eyes traveled upward to a parachute, complete with harness. "Killer, if this doesn't finish us, nothing will."

"Kemosabe, we have come too far to be turned back now. Let's press on."

Another instructor took over from Humphreys. The Lieutenant got everyone's attention right away. She was dressed in a pair of tight blue shorts and a white t-shirt. Her black hair was cut short and her pouty lips expressed seeming displeasure at the assembled group. "Good afternoon, I'm Lt. Andrews. This afternoon, you'll wrap things up by making a simulated bailout."

Your parachute can be your best friend if you have to punch out. It can also be your worst enemy, especially if you have to ditch over water, which is mostly preferable to risking capture over land. As you know there are no practice ejections. Once you do it, it's for real. Today, you're going to put on the harness and be hoisted up into our wild blue yonder. The fans will give you enough relative wind to balloon your chute. Once you hit the water, get out of the chute and into the seven man raft or the helo rescue lift."

Fancy knew all too well that the chances of having to bail out were a distinct possibility. Nobody ever thought it would happen to him—it was always the other guy, but just the same…"

"Any volunteers?" Andrews shouted. "I'll go," said one of the F-18 pilots. He walked over to the edge of the pool where an enlisted man helped him into the harness. Immediately he was hoisted up into the blackness of the building. Fans came on and then the chute was coming down, almost full blown. Upon hitting the water, the other fan came on and started to blow the unfortunate aviator away from the raft. After struggling for what seemed a long time, he was able to make his way to the raft. After another few seconds or was it minutes of struggling, he was able to climb into the raft, clearly a little the worse for wear.

After their experience with the helo-dunker, everyone was tired and ready for the day to end. Two people had to be helped out after they had managed to disengage themselves from their harnesses.

At last it was Fancy's turn. After being helped into the harness, he was hauled upwards, probably 80 feet he thought. It was always hard to judge distance over the water, but the edge of the pool gave him some prespective. He was only slightly startled when he suddenly started to descend. If this was real, he remembered from earlier lectures, his life raft would deploy about twenty feet below him. When that hit the water, he would release the kotch fittings and drop into the water, and wouldn't have to worry about the parachute. That was the theory anyway.

This time he hit the water with a thud. Funny how water could be so hard. Maybe California had harder water than back east, he mused. Right away the chute ballooned out and started to drag him through the water. Then the fans went off and the chute started to sink. I hope this pool isn't very deep he thought. He was surprised at how quickly he was being dragged down as he gropped for the koch settings. The first one opened without a hitch, but the second one wasn't budging and he was starting to run out of air. It seemed the more he struggled the less movement there was on the fitting. If you don't calm down he told himself, you're going to be in real trouble. Willing himself to stop struggling, Fancy gave one last tug and almost breathed a sigh of relief as the fitting came open. With his lungs at the bursting point be came up gasping and sputtering. One of the enlisted swimmers came over and gave him a hand to the edge of the pool.

As he looked up he noticed the long, shapely legs of Lt. Andrews. "You had us worried for a minute, Lt. Are you okay?"

"Oh, just peachy keen," he gaped. "Nothing a week in Hawaii wouldn't cure. No make that a week in the desert, I don't even want to get a drink of water—ever again.

"Let's all hope this is as bad as it ever gets," she said. Then she turned around and walked back to the class.

Finally, they were finished. After changing and turning in the FASO issued gear they headed back to the squadron, going right to the ready room where Bagger, Poncho, and Big Wave were waiting.

"Ahh, the survivors are back. How'd everything go. You guys don't look too much the worse for wear," said Big Wave.

"Yeah, it wasn't nearly as bad as I remember the last time I did it," replied Killer. "Of course, Gator might not think so."

"Not too bad," chimed in Gator. "I sure wouldn't want to go down at sea. This was nothing compared to how that'd turn out. Can you imagine being hurt, using the great nylon let down, getting in that little dingy. Shoot, let's keep our fingers crossed."

"Are you holding out on us, Gator?" querried Bagger. "What does he mean, 'Gator might not think so?'"

"I had a little difficulty with the parachute drop. One of the koch fittings wouldn't open up. It was closer than I would have liked it to be. It definitely got my attention."

"Remember that guy from 213 that had to step out last year. Chute deployed, he got down, and then the chute filled with water and started to go down. He about bought the farm, just barely got the shroud lines cut. Then they never found his RIO. That got everybody's attention. Six weeks after he went down and was cleared to fly, he turned in his wings. Said one close call was enough," Poncho intoned.

Everyone was silent, each thinking, *it wouldn't happen to me.*

"Well, hey dudes," said Big Wave, breaking the silence. "Let's get out of here. You may actually get to sit in a plane tomorrow, Gator."

"I hope so, I'm starting to feel a little bit edgy. It's been too long."

"Man, I get that feeling too when I haven't been up for more than a day or two. Suckin' rubber just bugs the hell out of me."

Everyone nodded in the affirmative.

"Skipper says we need to be here by 0:730, " said Bagger. "Gator, he wants me to take you over to the simulator building for a quick and dirty rundown in the morning. In the p.m. I guess you're going to get your feet wet in the "D". You and Matsen will be heading out to Whiskey-294. A little getting acquainted party I suppose."

"Sounds good to me," grinned Fancy. "I can't wait to strap that baby on."

"And I know the first two words that will come out of your mouth once you bring those big GE F-110 engines up too," grinned Poncho.

"Oh, you can read minds now?" said Fancy.

"It's easy, no problem," said Poncho, winking at the others, who in turn grinned and nodded back.

"Okay, I'll take your word for it, Poncho," said Fancy as he got up out of the chair.

"Let's get goin'," said Big Wave. "I want to catch a few sets before the sun goes down."

# 2

0730 would come quickly, but not quickly enough for Fancy. He was getting itchy. In fact he hadn't been able to sleep so he had gotten up early and had taken a walk across the street to check out the now peaceful waters of the Pacific. The sounds of the waves crashing seemed to only make him more anxious and he turned and went back to the house. Haviing showered, shaved and dressed in record time, he left a note for his three compatriots telling them he was leaving early. By now he knew the way and he and the Z had the road mostly to themselves.

Arriving at the squadron an hour early he went into the ready room and found the pile of literature on the F-14D, that Bagger said would be there. He turned on the rest of the lights and settled down to read and familiarize himself with the plane. It wasn't really new, it was after all the same airplane, but with some improvements that made it so much better than its brother, the B.

Starting with the engines. At 27,000 pounds of thrust per engine, the plane could be flown to limits of the airframe, which were considerable, instead of the limits of the engine. The TF-30's had only been a little more than adequate at best.

Another big improvement was the installation of the Hughes AN/APG-71 radar. With its high speed digital processing capability it offered a six fold improvement over the Hughes AWG-9 system. The newer system offered monopulse angle tracking and a digital scan control. Monopulse is able to locate the target precisely within the radar beam, while the rest of the system retains its look-down, shoot-doown pulse doppler scan/track capability. He found it reassuring to know that this system can track up to twenty-four targets while guiding six missiles to their individual targets at an engagement range of over 100 miles, with target altitudes between 80 and 80,000 feet. Bad news for the bad guys, thought Fancy.

Another big plus for the D, was that the older analog type equipment was replaced with state-of-the-art digital equipment, making the majority of avionics in the D compatible with what was installed in the newer F/A-18's. Other avionics improvements included two AYK-14 mission computers, programmable digital controls and displays, such as the ASN-139 digital inertial navigation system, as well as a digital stores management system and an infrared search and track system (IRSTS) housed in the same pod as the television camera set (TCS). A tactical Data Recording System (TDRS) is installed in conjunction with the TCS; the TDRS) is basically an on board video cassette recorder (VCR) tied to the TCS.

Systems that were improved and updated from the A and the A+'s were the ALR-67 Radar Warning Receiver, and the ALQ-165 Airborne Self Protection Jammer as well as The Joint Tactical Information Distribution System (JTIDS) and the Naval Aircrew Common Escape System (NACES). The JTIDS is the secure fighter to fighter data link for both voice and radar information. The system allows on F-14D to pass radar information to another F-14 so that these aircraft could remain radar silent. Another advantage is that other aircraft in the vicinity such as F/A 18s or E2Cs could receive radar information while operating their radars in a standby mode (not transmitting).

Alternatively, the F-14D can receive data link information from the E-2C while remaining radar silent.

Fancy kept reading, if he couldn't fly yet, this might be, at least for the moment, the next best thing. The F-14D is cleared to carry a number of advanced air-to-air and air-to-ground weapons, including the Hughes AIM-120 Advanced Medium Rmange Air-to-Air Missile or AMRAAM. This formidable weapon would replace the AIM-7 Sparrow, or as it is comonly referred to as the Great White Hope. (I hope it hits something.) AMRAAM can be launched at a target that is beyond visual range. It then can receive midcourse correction targeting information updates from the aircraft that launched the missile by data link. In the later phases, the AMRAAM's own on board radar seeker guides it independently to the target without any further asistance from the launch aircraft.

*"Buck Rogers, Buck Rogers" thought Fancy*, shaking his head. He read on coming upon what he thought was the biggest improvement of all. The Super Tomcat is powered by the same general Electric F-110-GE-400 engines used in the F-14A (Plus). These engines not only increase the available thrust significantly and provide significant improvements in operation, reliability, maintainability and fuel consumption. 80% of the parts in the engine are compatible with the Air Force F-110-GE-100 engine used in the F-15 and F-16. As if the blue suiters would ever let the Navy borrow anything, he mused.

He was startled by the sound behind him of someone entering the room and he turned around quickly to see who it was. Jumping to his feet he said, "Good morning sir."

"Morning Gator," replied Commander Robinson. "What brings you in so early?"

"Well, uh, I'm just anxious to get back in the air, sir. I've just been brushing up on the D. I've got some simulator time scheduled this morning before I go up the afternoon."

"What do you think of the D?"

"Just before you came in I was thinking this is something right out of Buck Rogers. The idea of being able to shoot without having to give yourself away is really something."

"Yeah, that JTIDS got everybody's attention. While we were up at Strike U everyone got to try it out and work with it. It drove the guys in VF-127 nuts."

"I can believe that, sir.

"Well, I'll let you get back to your browsing. Someone will be in shortly to put the java pot on if you want some. What time are you scheduled in the simulator?"

"Bagger's going to go over with me around 07:30, Skipper."

Robinson shook his head and grinned. "Bagger," he muttered. "Sounds about right. The simulator won't give you much of a ride. You'll be mainly just getting acquainted with the new radar and the 'Buck Rogers' stuff. There isn't much difference in the cockpit between the A plus and the D. I'll see you later." Robinson turned to walk out and then turned around again. "Lt. Humphreys called and said you had a little trouble at the pool yesterday. Are you okay?"

"Yes, sir. The koch setting was a little on the stubborn side about opening. I managed not to panic, and as you can see, it did come open."

"Good, I'd hate to lose anybody in that pool." With that he turned on his heel and walked out.

Fancy listened to Robinson's footsteps receding down the hall. Looking at his watch he was surprised that it was almost 07:30. Getting out of the chair, he put the materials down where he had found them and walked out to the front of the building. After stretching and pacing for a minute or two Bagger pulled up in his Porsche.

As he jumped out he called, "Man, I didn't hear you go out this morning. Why don't we go down to the mess hall and grab something to eat. I'm starved. Mainly because I slept in of course."

Fancy suddenly realized that he was more than a little hungry and nodded in agreement. "Sounds like a plan. How far is it?"

"Just down the this street and we hang a left and we're there. Hop in, I'll drive."

The morning passed quickly. Breakfast was tasty and the time in the simulator was well spent. Robinson had been right about the cockpit layout, no big surprises, everything was where it was supposed to be. Fancy noticed that everything seemed much clearer and just a little easier to use. Pilot friendly Bagger had said.

After what seemed an eternity of signing still more forms and tending to assorted Navy BS, Bagger and Fancy walked down to the ready room where they proceeded to go over the afternoon hop with Matsen. Fancy, at last, got to meet his RIO, Lt. j.g. Tony "Rhino" Miribal. Miribal was a short, gregarious Puerto Rican with a short compact build, who seemed to be endowed with a permanent smile. Coal black hair, close cut, framed his face. He thrust out his hand saying, "Glad to meet you sir. It looks like we'll be kicking some butt this afternoon."

"Nice to meet you, Tony. You sound pretty confident for someone who's never flown with me before."

"Begging your pardon, sir, I just know with me in the back seat, we're going to win. If you can get that big beast in the air and in the same galaxy, I'll find 'em and you can shoot 'em, sir."

Fancy grinned and said, "You're talking my kind of language, Rhino. Immediately Fancy knew he had found a kindred spirit.

Matsen who had been listening, smiled as he shook his head and remarked, "Rhino, someday your mouth is going to get you in a fix you won't be able to get yourself out of."

Rhino winked at Fancy and smiled that supremely confident grin and said nothing.

Matsen spoke up again. "Okay, Gator, this afternoon we'll be going out to range Whiskey 294. You fly my wing out there and then we'll separate and come at each other from an altitude of 21,000 feet. The hard deck will be 4,000 feet. If you hear Knock It Off from anybody, the fight's over. Any questions?"

"Yes, sir, what weapons are we going to carry or simulate?"

"We'll simulate guns and winders (AIM-9 Sidewinders). If that's all, lets get down to the equipment room, get dressed and go have some fun."

"I'm all for it, sir. Let's go."

At the ready room, Fancy found his locker to keep his valuables and personal possession in, as well as his helmet, green bag, (flight suit) g-suit consisting of chaps and a vest like affair that held his life pre-servers, a compass, whistle, PRC-112 survival radio, smoke, signal flairs, sun block, chap stick, bug repellent, water-purification tablets, matches, malaria tablets, global positioning system receiver, signal mirror, first-aid kit, face-camouflage paint and a map of the local area, as well as the 9mm Beretta and two fifteen round clips. There were even more goodies in the chute pack that was built into the Martin-Baker ejection seat.

After much grunting, considerable, wriggling, and shrugging, Fancy was suited up He and Rhino followed Matsen and his RIO, Lt. Cmdr. Jeff, "Smash", Johnson out to the flight-line. Fancy and Miribal were assigned to Desperado, the squadron tactical call sign, 204.

It never failed. As Fancy approached the plane he felt his heart quicken. It was all he could do to run to it and jump in. He supposed there was something to be said for decorum and made himself walk the remaining distance. Matsen was assigned to Desperado 208, parked right next to Fancy's plane.

A young petty officer was busily closing up panels. At Fancy's and Rhino's approach he came to attention and barked out, "Good afternoon, sirs. Your bird is up and good to go!"

Fancy and Miribal returned the salute. "Good afternoon. I'm Lt. Fancy. She looks good, Shrader."

Petty Officer Randy Shrader positively beamed. "Sir, this is the best plane in the squadron. She's up and ready."

Fancy and Shrader took a quick look around. He never expected to find anything amiss and in his short time in the Navy had never found anything wrong. The preflight was more of a courtesy to the maintenance folks who worked long, long hours to keep the Tomcats mission ready. It was no easy job and Fancy always figured the maintenance guys were worth their weight in gold. The Tomcat was a great airplane, but it was maintenance heavy. The F-14A took 8 to 10 hours of maintenance on the ground for every hour it flew.

After the preflight Fancy was satisfied that the bird was up and ready. All the panels were closed, no hydraulic fluid was dripping, no JP-5 or hydraulic fluid were leaking and the blue practice AIM-9's weren't going to come off.

Right away Fancy spotted the only real external difference between the A's and the D's. That would be the dual optical/electronics chin pod which houses both the standard TCS system and the Infrared Search and Track System (IRSTS) and the deletion of the wing glove ECM fairings. Man, what a beast he thought.

Petty Officer Shrader continued giving them the gouge on the Martin-Baker ejection seats. He was not shy about telling Fancy that it never hurt to sit calmly at the end of the runway, just before beginning the take-off roll, and mime the procedure one more time: things like all loose articles stowed, straps super-tight, good body position, head back with both hands feeling one more time the overhead handles. "You never know, sir, this could be The Day."

True enough, thought Fancy as climbed into the cockpit. He and Rhino, after pulling on their helmets, quickly ran through their checklists and start-up procedures. Finally, they were granted permission to start engines. Battery on, master switch on, fuel on, and hit the start button. I think I could do this in my sleep and frequently do, Fancy thought to himself. The port engine came to life with a rumble that Fancy felt immediately. "Jesus Christ," he murmured, "this is too good."

He could feel the power. Bringing the starboard engine up, Fancy felt that this baby could do anything, anywhere, anytime.

Rhino came up on the intercom and said, "Did you say what I thought you said, Gator?"

"Yeah, that was what I said. Why?"

"That's what everybody says. Instant religion."

An instant later, Fancy looked to his right and noticed Matsen looking over at him. Before he realized quite why he was doing it, he made the international signal for a machine gun, left hand making the gun, while the right hand turned an imaginary crank like the old gatling gun. At first Matsen didn't get it, then a grin spread over his face, and he gave the okay sign with his thumb and forefinger in acknowledgement that the fight would be guns only, no missiles.

"Rhino, how's everything look back there? Are you ready?"

"Gator, 'I was born ready'. Everything looks perfect for bringing everything on line." Normally, the powerful radar was brought from standby to active just as the plane started its takeoff roll. There was no sense frying some poor unsuspecting person on the ground.

At last the chocks were pulled and the young petty officer gave Fancy a snappy salute and directed him to pull out of the space. Fancy returned the salute and eased the throttles ahead ever so slightly, pressing the right rudder pedal for a brake. He followed Matsen down the taxi way. They would have to taxi the length of the flight line in order to take off on runway 24 right.

Fancy realized how big Miramar actually was. He noticed the huge hanger that said FIGHTER TOWN, U.S.A. on it and realized once again how glad he was to be here, doing what he was doing. Absolutely no regrets.

Finally, after what could have been a long drive to downtown San Diego, they were lined up on runway 24 right. After completing their final cockpit checks, he saw Matsen pull onto the active runway and start his takeoff roll.

Fancy was then cleared to the active runway. "Tower, this is Desperado 204, requesting permission for take off."

"Roger, 204. Permission granted. Wind is 12 from 270, squawk at 10,000. Good day, sir."

"Rhino, time to pull the pins." It was now time to pull the safety pins on the ejection seats.

"Roger that," said Rhino. "Final checks completed and the pin has been pulled." Now both officers knew that the word "eject" would not be uttered in any context unless they really meant EJECT.

This was part of the contractual agreement between pilot and wingman and between the front and back seat of the Tomcat and any other multi-crew birds. The idea is to know what your buddy is going to do, particularly in a fight or an emergency. The middle of a 500 knot furball is not the place to initiate a discussion of appropriate tactics on the radio. Given that the Russians and many of their clients are big on jamming communications, it can be impossible for a pilot to talk to his wingman even when they are only a wingspan apart. The contract covers essential things like code words and prodedures, such as the understanding that once the canopy is closed, the word eject is not to be uttered.

"Thank you tower, squawk at 10,000, roger." Fancy pushed the twin throttles slowly forward and felt the big Tomcat start to move, slowly at first then gathering momentum as Fancy advanced the throttles. He had noticed that Matsen had not gone to afterburner on his take off. Another advantage for the Tomcat, save all that fuel for where you really needed it—in the air. V-1 and V-2 came and went quickly as Fancy pulled back ever so gently back on the stick. The big plane brought her nose up and they were airborn. Bringing the stick back and continuing to advance the throttle, the F-14 came into its element. Gear up, flaps up, all up and clean. Looking at the HUD, he noticed that he was at 4,000 feet already and still accelerating. San Diego quickly disappeared and they headed out over the Pacific.

"Miramar, Desperado 204 squawking 10,000," Fancy called as they passed 10,000.

"Roger, Desperado 204. You are cleared to Whiskey 294. Good day and good hunting, sir."

"Thank you, Miramar. Cleared to Whiskey 294, roger."

"I have Desperado 208 about two degrees starboard off our nose, Gator."

"Thanks, Rhino. Coming right two degrees." Fancy started to retard the throttles as they slid along Matsen's port side, stepped down with about two hundred yards of separation.

Matsen's voice crackled in his ear. "Desperado 204, we'll fly out to 294 together. We'll be there in about six minutes. Once we're there we'll separate and head in opposite directions for two minutes. When I call, "fights on", we'll come 180 degrees and have at it. Any questions?"

"Desperado 204, separate on the range, when "fight's on" is called, do a 180 and have at it, roger," Fancy answered.

Six minutes and sixteen miles later the two big fighters separated and Fancy headed further out over the Pacific. "Okay Rhino," called out Fancy, "as soon as we come back 180 I want you to find Matsen, give me a steer, and as soon as I've got him locked up I'll shoot a winder."

"What? I thought this was guns only? Matsen's going to be really pissed."

"This is true," smiled Fancy.

"Fights on," came the call from Matsen.

Fancy brought the Tomcat around to come back to the original heading and put the nose down in a shallow dive to lose just a little altitude to put Matsen, he hoped, above him. All the better for the AIM-9 to acquire and hold the target against the colder sky.

"Come ten left," said Rhino calmly. "He'll be right on our nose."

"Coming left," replied Fancy, hoping he was as cool as Mirabal sounded.

"I've got him. The winder's giving off a good tone." He could hear the rattlesnake tone of the AIM-9 getting stronger. "Fox 2," he called and mashed down on the "*trigger*" on the stick. Calling Fox 2 told friend and foe alike that a heat seeking missile was in the air.

"We got him! We got him! shouted Rhino. "Whoeee!"

"Geeze Rhino, calm down. You're going to break my eardrums."

Seconds later the two planes flashed past each other. "Gator, what is this Fox 2 garbage! This was supposed to be guns only, remember!"

"Sorry sir," Fancy said in what he hoped was a voice of contriteness, "it was just such a perfect set up, I couldn't pass it up, sir. It was just a perfect shot."

"All right," said Matsen, in a somewhat exasperated voice, "lets try it again."

"Okay, sir," said Fancy, hoping he still sounded contrite.

"Rhino, get ready, we're going vertical." Fancy pulled the stick back into his gut and pushed the throttles to the stops. The Tomcat shot straight up. At 21,000 feet, he pushed the stick forward, rolled left, and brought the plane down the same path he had so recently traveled. "Find him Rhino! Let's get him locked up!" Fancy grunted. Six G's tended to make it hard to talk in any kind of normal voice. More often it sounded like a wrestling match when things got hot and heavy.

"I've got'im. He's off our nose 15 degrees left!" Rhino managed to croak back.

"Coming left 15. I've got a tone! I've got a tone!" Fancy didn't even try to sound calm now. The adrenalin was flowing. The tone was even stronger now, not unlike the warning of a rattlesnake. "Fox 2! Fox 2!" he sang out.

Fancy was closing with Matsen at a rate of over 1,400 miles per hour and just when it seemed he picked him up visually, he was flashing past him. His gut told him he would have scored another kill. Again Fancy rolled left bringing the Tomcat on what would be Matsen's nose. Matsen would be trying to start things on at least a neutral footing and would come back toward Fancy as soon as he could.

"He's on our nose. Come port five degrees and we've got him nose to nose," said Rhino in a more controlled and less stressed voice.

"I've got him. Going to guns." Fancy could well imagine the devastation the M61-A1 20mm Gatling gun could cause, and he who shoots first, usually wins, he thought, as he mashed down on the "*trigger*" on the stick. "Bang, bang, Ratchet, you're dead!" he called.

The two Tomcats flashed past each other at over 1,300 miles per hour. Immediately Fancy turned as far around as he could to try and pick up Matsen's plane, and at the same time started to reef the big plane around 180° to face Matsen again. As he came around he saw and then heard Matsen. "Desperado 204. I've got a rough port engine. Join on me and we'll RTB (return to base)."

"Roger, Desparado 208. Joining on you to RTB." Fancy retarded his throttles and went to a slow rolling scissors so he wouldn't over shoot his XO. He slid smoothly on Matsen's right wing about 400 yards and stepped down another 50 yards.

"Desperado 204," look me over to see if I'm losing anything. She feels okay, but let's be sure."

"Desperado 208. Commencing quick visual. I'll come from your starboard and slide under you to your port side."

"Roger, 204," answered Matsen.

Fancy continued to play with his throttles as he slid under Matsen's plane. "Rhino, look carefully. Do you see anything?"

"Negative Gator," answered Mirabal. "He looks okay."

"208, you look okay. I'll take one more look and rejoin on your starboard wing."

"Roger 204."

Seeing nothing loose, hanging, or leaking, Fancy rejoined on Matsen's wing.

Fancy immediately swept his panel, even though all the important information, as far as he was concerned, showed up on the Heads Up Display (HUD). Everything looked good and in the green. The plane swept through the sky as smooth as silk. He kept glancing at Matsen's plane out of the corner of his eye, keeping a loose duce formation on his XO. Glancing at the chronometer on the instrument panel, he noted that the entire action had taken place in less than eight minutes.

As they neared the Southern California coast, Fancy heard Matsen inform the tower at Miramar of his situation and request a straight-in approach to land. Permission was granted and the two planes were cleared to land. Fancy kept looking over at Matsen's plane and nothing seemed amiss.

"204", called Matsen.

"204", replied Fancy.

"204, I'm going to land first. My port engine is starting to heat up and it feels like it's running rough."

"Roger, 208. I'll slide back. Good luck, sir. You still look okay, nothing falling off or leaking." He tried to keep his voice light. Everything seemed okay, but with any type of flying there were never any guarantees.

Matsen's plane pulled ahead as Fancy retarded the throttles and Desperado 204 fell back a quarter of a mile.

Fancy and Mirabal quickly went over their landing checklists. The landing gear and flaps were lowered and the outer marker was soon in sight. Matsen's plane passed over the fence and settled onto the runway. It was the worst part of the day, Fancy thought. There was never enough time in the air.

Fancy greased the big fighter onto the runway, holding the nose up and settling on the main landing gear. Preserve that nose gear, he mused. The nose gear came down slowly and the plane eased down and began to lose speed. As the plane began to slow, Fancy eased the throttles forward in order to taxi back to the flight line.

As he taxied to their parking space, he saw that Petty Officer Shrader was there, looking anxiously at the plane as he pulled into the parking space, under the direction of one of the ground crew. When he got the signal to cut the power, he sighed as he heard the engines wind down.

The plane was chocked and Fancy raised the canopy. As he released the koch fittings, Shrader's head appeared above the canopy rail.

"How'd it go, sir? Didn't I tell you she was the best plane in the Squadron. What happened to Commander Matsen's plane." It all came out in about a two second rush.

"You've got to show a little more enthusiasm, Shrader. Come on, get interested in what's going on here," Fancy said with a straight face.

"I'm sorry, sir. I just wanted to…" his voice trailed off and what had been an ear to ear grin faded away.

Fancy immediately realized that Shrader actually had taken his tone and demeanor seriously. "Relax, Shrader. I only trust people with your brand of enthusiasm. You were right. This is one sweet airplane. We got three kills out of three go arounds—thanks to the flawless performance of this plane and the even more flawless performance of Lt. Mirabal, who deserves all the credit. Mr. Matsen's plane lost an engine—no doubt due to the lack of attention to details by people no where near as dedicated to their job as you are, Shrader."

Shrader's grin came back immediately even larger that it had been before. "Thank you, sir. Is there anything we need to write up, sir?"

"Nothing in my end. Rhino, how about it? Anything back in the pit that wasn't up to snuff?"

"Zero, zilch, nada," replied Rhino.

Fancy unfastened his kock fittings and handed his helmet to Shrader, who climbed down as Fancy followed. Rhino joined them, obviously very pleased with himself.

"Gator, we were really hot out there. Matsen doesn't loose three time in a month, much less three in one day. With losing that engine, he's going to be one unhappy camper."

"Do you think he's going to be too bent out of shape?"

"Nah, Matsen's a pro. He'll just come at you that much harder next time he gets the chance though."

By then a van had appeared to take them back to the equipment room. They boarded and drove down the line to where Matsen had parked Desperado 208. He seemed to be in an intense discussion with his plane captain. The enlisted man looked very unhappy. Matsen waved them on and the van took them back to the squadron area.

After a quick shower and a change of clothes, Fancy and Mirabal headed for the Officer's Club. Upon their arrival Bagger and Big Wave motioned them over to their table. With them was another officer, whose lapel trappings identified him to be a doctor.

"Well," asked Bagger, "how'd it go?"

Before Fancy could answer, Mirabal took the lead. "Man, we did a number on Mongo. Three out of three. My nose gunner here did everything–just as I directed."

"Three out of three," gasped Big Wave. "Give me a break. Nobody goes three out of three with Matsen."

"Hey, man, we just did," continued Mirabal. "We locked him and shocked him." Mirabal turned to Fancy to give him a high five.

"Gator, Rhino has been known to embelish the facts at times. What really happened?" demaded Bagger.

"Actually, Rhino's not embelishing, at least not today. We got lucky and got him with two 'winders and one gun shot. Tony had me on him and locked up like ugly on an ape. Of course he lost an engine."

"Before or after the third time?" asked Bagger.

"Uh, the third time," replied Fancy.

"Well Lieutenant, allow me to buy you a drink."

The offer came from the third man sitting at the table. For the first time Fancy noticed that he was Asian. He had close cropped black hair and a face that seemed, what Fancy would call, inscrutible.

Bagger chimed in, "Gator, this is Doc Su, the Air Wing Flight Surgeon. He naturally hangs out with the top squadron because we're just a better class of people."

Fancy extended his hand. "It's nice to meet you, Commander. A soft drink would be great about now, thanks."

"Just call me Doc," replied Su. He motioned for a waitress to come over and ordered Fancy's Dr. Pepper.

In a minute or two the soft drink arrived along with something with an umbrella for Rhino.

Rhino raised his glass and called for a toast. "Gentleman, and you too Big Wave, a toast to 124's newest pilot, Gator!"

The rest of the men raised their glasses in a solemn salute. Big Wave let out a tremendous belch and any resemblance of decorum immediately disintegrated.

About that time Lt. Commander Matsen stomped into the club. Upon spying the happy group of aviators he launched himself in their direciton. "Fancy, what the hell happened to credibility," he fumed.

The silence was immediate as if someone had brought down the curtain on the last act of a play.

Fancy stood up raised his glass and said, "Sir, credibility is down and kills are up." Fancy didn't know if Matsen was going to have a fit, heart attack or what, becuase Matsen just stood there as if he was trying to say something and he just couldn't spit it out.

Finally, Matsen said, "You're right! You're right! Kills are up and that's the name of the game!"

Everyone in the group raised their glasses and shouted, "Credibility is down and kills are up!" With that everyone made room for Matsen. A drink appeared and Matsen sat down next to Fancy. "Fancy, you mudsucked me good and proper. That's going to be the only time though." He laughed and shook his head as he said it.

"Listen up you jokers. It looks like we won't be hitting the boat next week. Enterprise had to return to port. Seems like the catapults aren't working as advertised. They tried to launch a

T-2. It just dribbled off the pointy end of the boat. Both crewman were killed. They ejected too late and went straight into the water."

Another silence shrouded the group. Finally, Poncho spoke up. "XO, what does that mean for us as far as hitting the boat and carrier quals?"

"I just talked to the skipper for a couple of minutes before I came down here. He says some of us will probably go up to Nellis. They've got a Red Flag exercise starting up there this coming week. He thinks we can get in on it and play some of the bad guys."

"Who gets to go?" asked Bagger.

"I'm not sure right now. Anybody here want to go?"

Almost as one the four aviators shouted, almost as one "Yeah, where do we sign up?"

Matsen smiled like a Cheshire cat. "What's in it for me if I put in a good word with the skipper?"

"You won't have to go 1 v. 1 against Gator," chimed in Big Wave. Waves of laughter washed over Matsen. Fancy was glad to see that he was laughing too. In that moment, Fancy gained a great deal of respect for "Mongo" Matsen.

As the hilarity died down, Bagger leaned in toward Fancy and said, "What's with the Dr. Pepper? You haven't turned over any kind of new leaf have you?"

"That's it exactly. I decided on the drive out here that I'm not going to imbibe anymore. Drowning my sorrows back at Oceana got to be a little too easy. There were a couple of days back there when I was a real menace in the air." Fancy shook his head, "No more for me, man."

Bagger just kind of looked at him in disbelief for a second before answering. "You've got my support. Are you really giving up everything that has to do with drinking?"

"That's my plan. I haven't had anything to drink for about a month, and I feel really good. At first I thought I was going to really miss it, but I don't."

"Is there anything else you've given up?"

"I'm taking that one day at a time," said Fancy. "I'm not really interested in anyone. Janice is pretty much behind me. She's someone I'll always be fond of, but as an item, it's over."

Bagger just starred at him for a few moments and then grinned, "Yeah, let's just see what happens."

A few minutes later, Commander Robinson and Moose Milwood joined the group. Robinson was immediately bombarded with questions about the delay with the Enterprise and about the detachment that would go to Nellis for the Red Flag exercise. "They figure Enterprise will be in port for a week, ten days at the outside. The wheels at Nellis and here, want us to send eight planes and ten pilots and RIOs up there on Monday. Since it looks like it could be a long deployment once we're on the boat, I'd like to send the unmarried men to Red Flag. So far I haven't heard any objections from the married guys or the unmarried guys. Don't get me wrong, I'm not turning this squadron into any kind of democratic decision- making institution, it will still be a dictatorship, with me as your friendly neighborhood dictator."

"Si, commandante, your highness, sir," croaked Moose, in his best Spanish dictator impersonation. "This is an excellent plan."

Big Wave chimed in. "Does this mean we go up Monday or Sunday?"

"They want you to go up Sunday, so you're all in place for the briefings first thing Monday morning. The exercise kicks off that afternoon. Naturally, we'll be Orange. It's most likely that you'll brief in the morning and fly out to one of the satellite fields in the country you'll be defending or attacking from. There should be a lot of DACM (dissimilar air combat maneuvering). If the infomation I got was right, the Brits should be there with Tornadoes, maybe even the Frogs with their Mirage 2000."

"Well, dudes," sighed Big Wave, "this should be one fine week. But I hate spending it so far from the water."

"Wave," chortled Matsen, "just look at Nellis as one big beach."

"Okay," said Robinson, "Bagger, Killer, Big Wave, Poncho, Gator, Moose, Animal, and my peerless XO, report in 0900, Sunday morning. Plan to launch for Nellis at 1130."

Friday night and Saturday came as welcome days off. Of course part of Saturday was spent doing yard work around the big yellow house. After the chores were finished everyone adjourned to the beach to soak up some sun and watch Big Wave ride the waves. He surprised Fancy by how well he could handle a surfboard.

"Wave," asked Fancy, as Schwartz came out of the water, set his board down, and flopped down on his towel," think you could teach me to do that?"

"I'm really still learnin', but if you want to try, just let me know. Do you want to go out now?"

"Not right now, I'm still recovering from FASO. I would like to give it a try some time, it looks kind of fun."

"It really is," answered Wave as he polished off a Coke.

"What about the time the board hit you in the head, and they had to drag your carcass out of the water?" asked Poncho.

"Yeah, how about the time that riptide had you headed for Hawaii?" chimed in Bagger.

"They were just speed bumps in the road of life," sighed Big Wave, as he closed his eyes against the afternoon sun. Besides, I've met some pretty awesome women down here. Let's see, there was Annette, whom you squired around town, Bagger. Poncho, you saw that blonde, what's her name?"

"Molly," grinned Poncho. "You better keep this up Wave, it's been a good deal for everyone."

# 3

"Come on Dan, it's time to get up. It's not a good idea to show up late when the XO is going to be running things."

"Man, what time is it? I just hit the pillow," groaned Fancy.

"It's 0730 and time to rise and shine," prodded Bagger. "We want to get a bite to eat on the way to the base."

"Oh, man, I feel stiff as a board."

"That's what you get for spending all that time in the water and the sun. Come on, let's get a move on."

Fancy willed himself to get out of bed and move toward the bathroom where he hurriedly shaved, showered, and collected his gear for the week at Red Flag. Next time he promised himself, not quite so much surf and sun. Thank God he hadn't had a drink.

The trip to Miramar in Big Wave's jeep was interrupted only by a quick bite to eat at Denny's. Fancy didn't know about anybody else, but he was excited about the upcoming week. He knew the flying would be fast and furious, the next best thing to combat a pilot could get.

Matsen was waiting for them in the ready room. He too seemed anxious to get going. Hunter "Animal" Schott, Moose Milwood, and

Killer Stevens joined them several minutes later, followed by the RIOs, who took seats in front, while the pilots seated themselves in their customary seats in the back. No doubt about it, everybody seemed wired and ready to go. "Listen up," said Matsen. "We're still set to launch at 1130. The maintenance guys have the birds tweaked and ready. We're going to be part of the Orange forces defending Redland. As far as I know, we will be opposed by F-16s, F-15s, for sure, and probably anything else the blue suiters have up there that's handy. Make sure you have all your gear. Suitcases and that garbage will go up with the maintenance detachment. Make sure you have enough money with you. It seems like every time we go up there, somebody's always bummin' money from me."

"That's cause you make the big bucks, XO," Bagger said.

"Bagger," grinned Matsen, "the big bucks, as you say, goes with the enormous amount of responsibility I carry. Need I say more?"

"No, sir. You know me, fiscally responsible and very conservative. I'll be the very model of decorum."

"That'll be the day. I'm going to keep an eye on you, Bagger."

Killer leaned over to get Fancy's attention and whispered, "How much are you takin'? I've only got about $140." Fancy fished out his wallet and was relieved to see three hundreds, two fifties, and several twenties. "I've got about $500. We should be okay." He realized that not drinking any more was paying off in more ways than one.

"Thanks, man," sighed Killer as he slid back to an upright position.

"If there are no further problems or questions, let's finish so we can suit up and preflight the birds. Gator, you'll fly my wing, Bagger and Big Wave, Killer and Animal, Moose and Poncho. We'll launch in that order in section take offs."

Moose raised his hand and asked, "Do we get to take any E-2s?"

"Are you kidding," growled Matsen. "Blue forces will have their E-3, (AWAC) but they don't want to make the playing field level, so to speak. In other words, no."

"Can we take out the E-3 if we get the chance?" Hunter Schott asked.

"I doubt it, but I sure would like to try. Let's see what they say about it. Don't ask about it. If they don't mention it, let's see what happens. Taking that big eye out of the sky would put those guys in a world of hurt."

Poncho asked, "What's our route up there. The usual, George Air Force Base Corridor?"

"That's right. Getting back to the E-2, our friends, the Screw Birds, are going to launch an E-2C at 1100 hours. We're going to go up there zip-lip, no radar. They're going to orbit over the desert for us and feed us any useful information. Remember, the last time, we got bounced going up there? The skipper just wants everything to get off to a good start. Last time up there it seems like we were behind the eight-ball after that little run in. We might as well get used to the JTIDS system. This is an ideal time to get some practice using it again. As I mentioned, it will be section takeoffs. After we get out past George, we'll get down on the deck and stay there until we're fifty miles from Nellis. Then we'll pop up to 5 grand (5000 ft.) and land in the same order we took off. No fancy stuff on recovery, just a nice little tuck under break and then we're on the ground. In case we do get jumped, have at 'em. Flame 'em and then land as quick as you can Anything else?"

"Will we have tankers?" croaked Moose.

"No, are you kidding?" said Matsen.

With that final question, the RIOs and pilots started to file out and head toward the equipment room. Rhino fell in step with Fancy. "Are you ready for this, Gator? You ever been to Red Flag before? This is one great time, I can hardly wait."

"In answer to your questions, yes, no, and neither can I," grinned Fancy.

As they exited the briefing room, Matsen called out, "Gator, what's the NATOPS departure drill for the Turkey?"

Fancy stopped and turned, "Sir, stick forward, neutral lateral, lock harness. Rudder opposite turn needles or yaw. If no recovery, stick into direction of spin. If engine stalls, throttles to idle. If rcovery indicated, neutralize controls and recover at seventeen units angle of attack. If spin confirmed due to flat attitude, increasing yaw rate, eyeballs-out G, lack of pitch and roll rate—jettison canopy and RIO will command eject prior to 10,000 feet AGL."

"See you on the flight line Gator."

It wasn't unusual at the end of a brief for anyone to call for the departure drill, on the F-14 or any aircraft, including those on the other side.

After getting their equipment on the aviators walked out to the flight line. The eight F-14s sat like great birds of prey also seemingly anxious to get into the air. Enlisted personnel busied themselves making last minute checks, closing up panels, or in two cases, wiping down the canopies. Fancy was assigned to Desperado 207. Petty Officer Shrader was not there, having gone on to the waiting C-130 with the rest of the men who were going to maintain the planes at Nellis. A young, a very young, Fancy thought, enlisted man came to attention. "Good morning, sir. She's already to go."

Fancy noted that his name tag said Whitlock. "Good morning. She looks good from here. Let's take a look around."

"Very well, sir."

Again, the plane was ready to go. Today there would be two fuel tanks, one hung below each wing, and one centerline tank hung under the fuselage. Instead of the AIM-9s and AIM-7s, there were eight blue missiles that looked like the two missiles, but were actually lacking motors and warheads. Instead their noses contained electronics for more realistic simulated firing. Who got shot down, or who didn't, wouldn't go to the pilot with the loudest voice. They could now replay entire fights on the big screens at the control center called Blackjack. The gee- whiz electronics were able to keep track of every aircraft over or even near the entire Nellis range.

Rhino was busy storing their personal gear. Neither of them completely trusted the baggage handling of the C-130 crews. In a plane as big as the F-14, there was always some place to store the two small bags of personal effects the two men were taking. Fancy didn't think he would need very much. If he lived in his green bag, that would be fine with him. He didn't plan on playing the tourist.

By now it was 1120 hours and the time to finish up the checklists and start engines. Both engines spooled up as advertised. Fancy still marveled at all the power as it seemed to travel up his spine. "How 'bout it, Rhino, everything okay back there?"

"We're clean and in the green. Let's go to Las Wages."

After scanning the gages one more time he received the hand signal the chocks had been removed. Fancy snapped off a salute to Petty Officer Whitlock, and advanced the throttles. Matsen was two plane lengths ahead of him. Due to a favorable wind change they would not have to taxi to the other end of the field, but would instead take off on runway 6. Desperado 207 turned onto the active runway just slightly aft of Commander Matsen's 208.

"Okay, Rhino, let's pull the pins."

"Pin pulled, Gator, let's go have some fun."

"Desperado 207, commencing takeoff roll."

"207, roger that. We're with you."

Fancy wished that Matsen was his wingman and he got to be out in front on the seciton takeoff. He didn't like that little buffeting he would get, but he wasn't about to complain. Both planes moved as though joined by a string. As V2 flashed by Matsen started to lift his nose and Fancy did likewise. The big planes came off the ground as though they had been shot from a gun. *Man, it just doesn't get any better than this thought Fancy as he raised the gear and flaps and tucked in on Matsen's starboard side.*

Matsen started a gentle turn to port and Fancy increased power just slightly to stay in formation. He knew that the other three sections would be in the air by now. They headed inland toward George Air Force Base, or what used to be George. It had been shut down several years ago in the first round of base closures that had hit California particularly hard. It was a CAVU day, clear and visibility unlimited, a perfect day for flying.

It didn't take long to get to the George Corridor. Since the flight was zip-lip, Matsen indicated by a downward pointed finger that they would descend to 300 feet. As Fancy scanned his instruments he noted the radar console showed few flights in the air. It was hard to imagine that the information was coming from the E-2C, over a hundred miles away.

"Gator, everything looks good. I've got a good scope and there doesn't seem to be anything out there except commercial traffic."

"I've got the same picture. Going down to 300 feet and 350 knots. Fancy had to pull power slightly to keep from leaping out in front of Matsen. At 400 miles an hour, the ride was somewhat rough. As the hot desert air rose, it wanted to lift the big Tomcat up with it. It wasn't difficult flying thought Fancy, but it wasn't time to gawk around at the scenery either. Actually, Fancy rather enjoyed being down low and going fast. *The faster the better* he thought.

"Gator, take a quick look at your screen. Do you see what I see?" said Rhino a few minutes later, almost in a whisper.

"You mean those little blips that appear to be coming toward us?" Those little things?"

"Very funny. What do you think Mongo's going to to do?"

"I don't know, but if it was up to me…"

Fancy's voice was cut off suddenly. "Desperado 207, we've got a little change in plans. We're going to stay low. As soon as the boggies are back of our 39 line we're going to climb and reverse into their six, take one shot, and do a quick 180º and head back toward Nellis. The rest of you will cover Gator and me. We'll fall in back of you. Bagger, you take the lead. Make sure we look good when we land. Give me two clicks of your mikes if you understand."

Fancy clicked his mike twice to signal that he understood. With a closure rate of nearly 850 miles an hour it wasn't long until he saw Matsen's plane start to pull ahead as he increased speed and began to climb.

The two boggies were at 12,000 feet on a heading of 260°, almost due west. Fancy widened the distance between his and Matsen's plane until they were nearly three quarters of a mile apart. It wasn't long before he had visual contact, if you could say two things with wings were a visual. He could tell they definitely weren't F-14s. Matsen continued to close the distance on the two planes. *Man, are those guys out for a Sunday drive or what?* thought Fancy. "Rhino, keep your head on a swivel, I don't want anybody driving up our six."

"Roger, that Gator. We're okay. What are these guys thinking about?"

"They're not," replied Fancy.

"Desperado, 207," came Matsen's voice, "we're in range, lock 'em up and shoot."

"Roger, 208. Fox-2, Fox-2 on unidentified aircraft on heading 260. You're dead, boys." Fancy noticed each aircraft, not identified as two F-16s give a little shudder as if the two pilots had been shaken out of their lethargy. Boy what a way to end the day mused Fancy as he banked the Tomcat away from the chagrined Falcon pilots. *Ignorance kills, boys,* he thought as he reefed the fighter back onto its original course.

He pulled onto Ratchet's starboard side and gave him the okay sign with his thumb and forefinger. Matsen returned the okay sign with a clenched fist.

"Desperado 207, we may as well go to radar and find the rest of the brood. I don't think we're much of a secret anymore."

"Roger that, 208. Looks like we're off to a good start."

"Don't pat yourself on the back just yet, Gator. Those guys were asleep at the switch. That was too easy. Keep your eyes peeled so nobody springs any surprises our way."

"I've got a six pack at six zero degrees. Come left five degrees gentleman and we'll be at their six," chimed in Rhino.

"Coming left five degrees," said Mongo.

Gator followed suit and found the rest of the Desperados.

"We got two F-16s he heard Matsen tell the rest of the flight Bagger, take us in and make it look pretty."

"Rog that," replied Big Wave.

The eight Tomcats flew down the length of the flight line. Fancy took a quick glimpse at the bustling field. He was impressed by the number of aircraft he was able to get a look at.

Bagger executed a break at the numbers. Four seconds later Big Wave did the same. At four second intervals the Tomcats turned into their final approach. Fancy slapped the gear handle down and felt the plane slow as the gear dropped into place. A quick scan of the board told him it was down and locked. Flaps thirty degrees, crossing the fence, and on the ground. He held the plane in a nose up attitude to slow it down. Five seconds later he dropped the nose wheels down as the plane slowed. As he touched the rudder pedals gently the plane slowed even more. He watched as the line of Tomcats turned off the active runway and taxied past, what he guessed was at least a hundred planes—F-15s, F-16s, A-10s, F-111s, F-117 Night Hawk. Wow, it's all here, he thought. He almost felt like a kid again when he had been taken to his first air show.

He followed Matsen and was directed into a space. He looked out and saw Shrader in his Mouse ears to protect his hearing. Shrader looked relieved to see his baby again.

Fancy shut down the engines and raised the canopy. He immediately felt the heat grasp him like a rag doll. Boy oh boy, maybe FASO wasn't so bad after all.

"Welcome to Nellis, Sir," beamed Shrader. "How was the flight up, sir?"

"Oh, you know, just routine."

"Routine? Routine? declared Rhino, as he climbed down. "Are you kidding! We jumped two F-16s and hosed 'em down. Winders right up the wazoo. Man oh man, they never knew what hit 'em," he exclaimed.

"Two, sir?" asked Shrader.

"Yeah," answered Fancy. "They were just motoring along and we took unfair advantage of them I'm afraid. It'll never get any easier than that, I tell ya."

Matsen joined them a few seconds later with the rest of the aviators.

"Way to go sir," blurted out Killer. There was a chorus of YESes and way to goes. Everyone was up.

"Don't get carried away. They were sloppy and we just did it the way it's supposed to be done. You know things will get a lot more difficult before we're through here."

At that moment, a blue air Force van pulled up. The doors opened and the airman driving inquired if the pilots and RIOs would like a lift to their quarters. "Beats walkin," volunteered Moose. Bags were retrieved and the men crowded into the van.

They were driven to the visiting BOQ. They were assigned two to a room. He and Bagger carried their gear to room 305. the room while not luxuriant had two beds, dressers, a TV, a small refrigerator, two desks, and a closet. "Not bad," drawled Bagger. "Not the Ritz, but comfortable. What bed do you want?"

"Hey take the one you want. They both look okay."

"Bagger flopped down on the bed nearest the door. "I'll take this one, they're not bad. The Air Force lives too well." Bagger was interrupted by the ringing of the phone. Fancy picked it up, "Room 305, Desperado 207 speaking, sir."

Matsen's voice crackled in his ear. "Fancy, we've got a briefing in half an hour, at 1400. We'll meet in the lobby and a van will pick us up. You guys all squared away?"

"Yes, sir. Bagger has proclaimed the accommodations satisfactory."

"Well, I'm glad to hear that," chuckled Matsen. "See you in the lobby at 1400." The phone clicked dead.

"That was Matsen. Briefing at 1400."

"Just when I was getting comfortable," yawned Bagger. "We gotta stock that fridge. Man, the heat here is something else."

At 1400 the pilots met in the lobby of the BOQ. Their ground transportation was waiting. Mercifully, it was air conditioned. The van took them to building 201, also known as Blackjack. From there all the activities at Red Flag are monitored in real time.

The Naval aviators disembarked from the van and went as quickly as they could into a large auditorium. As soon as they were seated, an Air Force Major came to the podium that was at center stage. "Good afternoon, gentleman. Welcome to Nellis and Red Flag. We're glad you could join us on such short notice. Even though you will be here for only a week, we hope both you and the Air Force will benefit from your presence. My name is Major Oldeorp. First, I would like to know if your accommodations are okay? Any complaints?" Before anyone could raise their hand he moved quickly to the next part of his introduction.

As you know, you will be part of the Orange force. You will be defending the country of Redland. Even though Redland attacked the friendly country of Suter first, Redland forces are being pushed back and the Orange forces are trying to gain control of the air so our valiant Orange forces can once again go on the offensive.

"I hate being lumped in with those Communist bastards," croaked Moose, who was sitting next to Fancy. "Why do they go through this crap anyway?" he groused.

"There's got to be be some kind of scenario," whispered back Fancy.

"Well, this is a bunch of crap. Mrs. Milwood didn't raise her kid to be a Commie."

"Geez, Moose, it's just to set things up, don't take it so seriously," replied Fancy.

"It's just the idea, you know?"

"Pipe down you guys," growled Matsen.

Oldeorp looked down in their direction. "Questions, gentleman?"

"No, sir," said Milwood. "Sorry, sir."

"I hope you didn't get unpacked and too settled in. We've arranged a new wrinkle we hope you'll like. A large map flashed on the screen, showing Nellis and its various ranges. "If you will look at the map, you can see there is a satellite field up at a place we call Coyote North . We want you to take your F-14s up there today and remain there the whole week. In addition to your eight planes, the 64th Aggressor Squadron will also be there with fourteen F-5s. The accommodations are not luxurious, but they're comfortable and the air-conditioning really cranks out some cold air. This way you won't have to fly all the way out and back again to refuel. In addition, it adds reality to the scenario."

"Will we have full maintenance support?" asked Matsen.

"Yes, you will. There will be a C-130 on stand-by to take anything out there you might need, any time of the day or night."

Matsen asked, somewhat cautiously, "Will we be defending against standard western air assets and doctrine?"

"That's correct, Commander. No doubt you'll be seeing the full first string lineup of NATO aircraft, pilots, and doctrine."

Fancy noticed that Matsen was careful not to look at anyone. He also bet that all of the pilots and RIOs were thinking the same thing: get the E-3 Sentry AWACS plane.

"I'd like to go over some of the rules of engagement now if there are no further questions. To date, since the inception of Red Flag, there have been thirty-four aircraft losses. Four of those hit the ground doing poor pop-up maneuvers, three hit the ground evading the video threat. We know cause we've got the video to prove it. Twenty-three of them flew their airplanes into the ground. That makes me real mad—wrong set of priorities. I'm going to tell you now that the first priority threat out here has two subcategories and it'll kill you both times: running into another airplane and hitting the ground. Now that's number one priority for everything you do out here, recognizing that the biggest threat in this Redland territory out here is the ground or hitting another plane. If, and I emphasize if, you get priority number two, three, four, five, or six confused with number one, you'll get sent home in a body bag. It is still simulated war, and there is nothing, I repeat nothing, at

Nellis worth dying for! Rule number one: all pilots will not be scheduled for sorties or maneuvers beyond their ability. This is no place for check rides, gentleman. Am I clear?"

"Yes, sir," answered sixteen voices, sounding more like boot camp Marines than Naval aviators.

"If I sound somewhat passionate about this, gentleman, it's because I am. I've lost friends out here and it just wasn't worth it!"

The rest of the discourse went on to explain such things as: the defender must assume an aircraft chasing anyone into the sun has lost visual contact and he is responsible for maintaining separation; if visual contact is lost during setups for engagement, the flight leader will assure that altitude separation is provided until there is a Tally-ho; if two aircraft approach head-on, each fighter will clear to the right and the fighter with the higher nose position will attempt to go above the opponent, and, this really got Fancy's attention, no front quarter gun attacks, unless you are an A-10 driver, who depends solely on the massive 30mm cannon for air-to-air protection.

"Another problem, gentleman, is the AIM-9L and AIM-9M. The Sidewinder in the Lima and Mike versions are causing us some problems as we write the ROE. With their expanded envelope and all-angle, all-aspect capability, the Lima and Mike can be used in some ranges and angles that were only possible with air-to-air cannons. So, AIM-9, Lima and Mike shots on the front quarter are allowed only to a minimum range of 9,000 feet."

Oldeorp finished up with rules of separation and maybe one of the most important of the ROEs, "Knock it off", enabling any member of a flight to end an engagement at any time because of mechanical or any other kind of trouble. At that time all participants will cease maneuvering and acknowledge with their call sign.

Just when Fancy thought things might be winding up, Oldeorp added, "Remember we still use the universal sign for NORDO, meaning the aircraft has lost radio communications, by rocking your wings. The nearest aircraft will then escort you back to base. With those final words of wisdom gentleman, and if there are no further questions, I'll let you get back to your quarters. Plan on launching at 1500 hours. Enjoy your stay here at Nellis and Red Flag."

The pilots and RIOs filed out. Killer laughed and said, "Well, there goes our time at the gaming tables."

"What a bunch of crap," snapped Moose. "I can hardly wait to see Coyote North."

"Hey, Moose, join the Navy and see the world," said Poncho. "How bad can it be?"

"Poncho, you know how bad. Remember when we went up to Mountain Home, we froze our butts off! Now, we're going to fry!"

They boarded the waiting blue bus and headed back to what were looking like better and better, quarters. Packing their belongings took just a few minutes and they reboarded the bus to get back to the flight line.

As they rolled down the line Moose gave a strangled cry and stood up, his mouth wide open with no intelligible sounds coming out. It didn't take long until they did though. "What in the hell is going on here?" he managed to spit out before he jumped off the still rolling bus, and ran toward his plane. By the time the rest of Navy contingent had waited for the bus to roll to a stop and get off, Moose was literally jumping up and down. To say he was angry, was a gross understatement. "Look! Look at this crap! Look what some bastard has done to my plane!" Fancy noticed that Moose's angry voice cut through all the noise on the flight line.

Painted on the nose, extending back toward the intakes was EAGLE MEAT. DIE YOU COMMUNIST FAGGOTS. By now Moose had quit jumping up and down and was slamming his fist against the side of the plane. "By God, who ever did this is going to be in a world of hurt! I'm going to put my boot right where the sun doesn't shine! Who did this?" he roared."Man oh man, this is the CAG's plane. I'm going to kill somebody!"

The rest of the pilots and RIOs stood there not quite sure what to say, Moose seemed to be saying it all—in spades. When he finally calmed down, somewhat, he started to call for his plane captain, Petty Officer Shehade. "Shehade! Where the hell are you?"

The enlisted men were nowhere in sight. Fancy figured they had been taken to chow. As he looked around he noticed several Air Force pilots standing by their F-15s starring at them. Moose spotted them at the same time. Before anyone could stop him he was racing toward them with what looked like to Fancy the intent to inflict great bodily damage. "Moose!" he yelled, as he started running after him. "Wait a minute!" Moose only seemed to pick up speed.

Moose must have realized he was vastly outnumbered and screeched to a stop. "All right, who's the wise ass that did the paint job on my plane?"

"Why do you think any of us would bother with that sorry looking Tomcat, swabby? We've got better things to do."

By that time Fancy and Bagger had raced to Moose's side. He sure could scoot for a little guy, thought Fancy as he tried to regain his breath. "Wait a minute guys," he wheezed, all he wants to know is if you saw anything, right, Moose? Nobody's looking for any trouble. Right, Moose?"

"Wrong!" Moose bellowed. "Did you guys have anything to do with that, or know who did?"

A tall Captain, wearing his green bag and a straw cowboy hat, with the name Katzenberger on his name tag, smiled, "Like I said, we don't have time for those kinds of games, do we guys?" The four men standing behind him all nodded in acknowledgement, all the while looking as innocent as lambs.

"Yeah, well, what's this can of spraypaint doing here?" asked Animal Schott, as he walked up behind them. As one they turned to look in his direction. "I 'spose this just happened to be hiding behind your landing gear and you don't know anything about it, right?"

"That's right," Katzenberger replied. "How do we know you just didn't bring it with you? I don't know where that came from."

"Come on, Moose, let's go, these bozos don't know anything," said Matsen.

"Who you calling a bozo, swabby?" Katzenberger blurted out.

"What I'm saying is that if you didn't see anything, as close as you are to that plane, you must be as dumb as you look." With that he turned on his heel and walked away.

"We'll see who's calling who dumb!" Katzenberger called after the retreating aviators. "We'll see!"

By the time the angry aviators had walked back to the Moose's plane, the enlisted personnel had returned from eating. Petty Officer Shehade was standing by Moose's plane. "I'm sorry, sir. I had no idea something like this would happen. We'll get it right off, sir."

"It wasn't your fault, Shehade. Get some rags and I'll help. Round me up some paper, a pen, and some tape too, please."

"Yes, sir, right away, sir."

"All right Moose, you get this cleaned up. Fancy, you wait here with him and we'll see you two up at Coyote North. I'll make a quick call to Major Oldeorp to get what ever you need to take care of this."

"Moose, no problems, I don't want you going ape-shit and starting anything. These things have a way of working themselves out. Know what I mean?"

"Aye-aye, sir," barked Moose. "No trouble -yet," he replied with the last word just under his breath. Again under his breath, he muttered, "I'd like to jam that cowboy hat somewhere."

By the time the supplies to clean off the plane arrived, Matsen and the other five F-14s were taxiing toward the active runway. "Come on, Moose, let's get started," said Fancy.

It took an hour of rubbing and some repainting to get the F-14 looking like Moose thought it should. Even then it didn't look as good as when it had landed. "Shehade, you got that paper for me," Moose demanded.

"Yes, sir," answered Shehade, handing him the paper and what looked like a magic marker.

Moose began to write:

Yankee Imperialist Pig,

**It has come to the attention of the Motherland** that you are, how do we say, KING KONG amongst your apple-pie-eating colleagues. We therefore challenge you to meet our Hero of the People's Republic of Redland. we look forward, after our bullets have ventilated your cockpit of your large twin-tailed tennis court you call an airplane, and sipping Margaritas along your coastline, with your wives and girlfriends as our companions. Nothing will please us more than to toy with your inept abilities and obliterate your pitiful, obsolete airplanes. In fact we are looking **forward to taking a dump on your graves. My call sign is**

Moose, tactical call sign is Desperado 200.

Moose held up his masterpiece for Fancy's inspection. "Gee, Moose, you're so subtle. Why don't you really say something that will piss 'em off?"

"Are you kidding? I'm restraining myself." With that he grabbed the tape from Shehade and stalked off toward the F-15s, whose pilots had grown tired of watching the Navy men clean up the F-14. Moose taped his message right on the canopy rail where it couldn't be missed. He yelled to the enlisted Air Force men who had begun moving toward the F-15. "Make sure your boss sees that message. If he can't read, I'm sure one of you can help him out."

"All right, let's saddle up and get out of here." he crowed as he returned to his plane.

"I'm good to go," replied Fancy.

Fifteen minutes later they were climbing out of Nellis heading toward Coyote North, both planes in full burner hoping to make as much noise as they could.

Climbing to 12,000 feet they headed northwest on a course of 345. Fancy was amazed at how barren this part of the United States was. "Rhino, you think anything lives down there?"

"Would you believe that over 5,000 wild horse manage to live on this base. What's more amazing is that they've never found the circus of one of those horses. Did you know Las Vegas means the meadows in Spanish? Most of the life down there is scaly, you know, stuff like horned toads, gopher snakes, spiny lizards, desert iguanas, bull snakes, king snakes, rattlers, sidewinders, and tarantulas. But, surprisingly enough, the Great Basin is also home for the largest water bird wildlife refuge in the United States. Hey there's even mountain lions skulking around out there."

"Where'd you hear all that?"

"I picked up some little panphlet one time when my parents were traveling through here."

"How'd you remember that?"

"I've got a porongraphic memory, I guess," laughed Mirabal.

Fancy laughed too. "This certainly looks like Wily Coyote country to me. Good place to train. There can't be many people who would want to live in this part of the world."

"Desperado 200," Fancy called, "let's go to a combat spread."

"Roger that, Desperado 207."

Fancy saw Moose slide out to his port side about three-quarters of a mile. The big Tomcat stuck out like a sore thumb against the cobalt blue sky. No place to hide out here, he thought.

Both planes were weaving and changing altitude, four pairs of eyes scanning the sky for anything that might be closing on them. It seemed however that they had the sky all to themselves.

"I've got Coyote North, dead ahead, at 20 miles," said Rhino.

"Let's get ready to bring 'em home then," replied Fancy. "Desperado 200, bring her back in close, tighten it up. Let's look good."

Moose tucked in close on Fancy's starboard side.

Fancy radioed the tower, "Coyote North, two Tomcats, requesting permission to land, after a quick look at the field."

"Coyote North to two the Tomcats. Permission granted for one quick look. Winds are from 340 at 8. There is no other traffic in the vicinity. The runway is clear."

"I'm beginning to like this place already. They're not quite so stuffy about taking quick looks around. I like that."

"It's cool," replied Rhino.

"You ready, Moose?"

"I'm clean and in the green, Gator."

"Okay, we'll make one low pass over the field, come back, show 'em the tuck under break, and break at the numbers."

"Roger that, 207. One low pass, come back, and show them the tuck under break."

The two planes picked up speed as they descended toward the field. Fancy could make out the planes already down, the almost toy like F-5s and the big Tomcats. Both planes streaked down the right side of the runway at 500 miles an hour, at an altitude of 200 feet. At that moment Fancy felt he and the plane were one single entity. After going out about three miles, the two planes pointed their noses at the sky and began to turn back toward the field. The wings of each plane going from the swept back position of 68 degrees to the fully swept position of 20 degrees. As he dumped the nose slightly, the wings automatically began to sweep back again. Picking up more speed, he headed back toward the runway. Turning again he came back down the runway, wings fully back now, as he roared down the runway, he rolled the big plane 270 degrees, while turning to a course of 90 degrees, on the downwind leg of the landing pattern at the numbers of the runway, 27, and immediately Rhino started to call out the landing configuration. Gear down, flaps down, all down, turn on final, and they were on the runway. Smooth, thought Fancy, that was smooth.

They taxied to the end of the runway, turning off the taxiway back toward the flight line. Fancy saw Shrader using hand signals directing him toward his parking place. When Shrader signaled that they were choked, Fancy, reluctantly shut down the engines and raised the canopy.

"Everything okay, sir?" queried Shrader as his head suddenly appeared above the canopy rail.

"She's sweet, Shrader."

"You and Mr. Milwood sure looked pretty when you came in sir."

"Thanks, Shrader. We looked good because you've got this baby tuned to the max."

The praise immediately caused Shrader to break out in a grin that covered his face. Fancy also thought he saw a slight blush. It was then that Fancy noted the intense heat. "Man, this place is warm. How are your quarters, Shrader?"

"Fine, sir. Air-conditioning works like a champ, sir."

"Good. Is there anything you're going to need to keep her up and running?"

"I think we're pretty well set, sir. Does she need any attention right now, sir?"

"No, like I said, she's sweet. She handles and flies like a dream. Get her refueled and she's ready to go again."

"Yes, sir." No sooner than the sir had come out of Shrader's mouth, than an Air Force tanker truck rolled up alongside.

"We're going to stick with JP-5 aren't we, Shrader?"

"Yes, sir, that's my understanding."

"Make sure, Shrader. And make sure you check the oil."

Shrader grinned, snapped off a salute and went to oversee the refueling. As Fancy turned to Rhino, Shrader, turned, held up five fingers and gave the OK sign with his thumb and forefinger.

"I'm so happy this is dry heat," smiled Rhino as he retrieved their gear.

"Yeah, this isn't near as bad as Florida in the middle of summer. I won't be sorry to get back to cooler climes though," answered Fancy, as he wiped his forehead with the sleeve of his flight suit.

A blue Air Force pick-up pulled up and a tall Air Force Lieutenant Colonel climbed out. "Welcome, gentleman to Coyote North. I'm Colonel Winkleman, 64th Aggressor Squadron. Glad to have you aboard. Can I offer you a lift?"

"Good morning, sir, said Fancy as he and Rhino came to attention. I'm Lieutenant Fancy, this is Lieutenant Mirabal. A lift would be much appreciated, sir"

"Hop in. I'm afraid we don't have a great many amenities, but this will beat walking."

By this time Moose and his RIO had joined them and after further introductions had been made, the four men jumped in the truck. "Nothing but the best," Moose grumbled. "So far I'm really not too impressed by the Air Force."

After a short drive the truck pulled up at a long, low barracks type building.

"The quarters here are somewhat spartan, but the air works and the chow is outstanding," Winkleman said as he helped them get moved into what Fancy supposed were Coyote North's BOQ.

As they entered the building the rest of the detachment gathered around them. "Did you get everything cleaned up okay, Moose?" asked Matsen.

"Yes, sir, she looks good," replied Moose.

"There weren't any further problems after we left were there?"

Moose looked at Fancy as if to say, "Let's not tell him everything." "Uh, no sir. I did leave them a short note thanking them for their co-operation."

Matsen studied Moose for several seconds. "I just bet you did. Are they going to be very brassed off?"

"No," interjected Fancy. "He was the very model of decorum."

"He doesn't even know what decorum is, do you Moose?"

"Oh, yes sir, I do sir."

"What happened?" asked Winkleman.

"Someone left a little message written in spray paint on Moose's plane," answered Matsen. "It seems to have cleaned up pretty well, right Moose?"

"Man, that happens all the time when we hit the road."

"What do you do about it?" asked Moose.

"Clean it up, ignore it, get on with what we have to do. We try to be as professional as we can. Sometimes we don't stick to standard Soviet Frontal Aviation tactics though."

"Hear that Moose, we stay professional and get on with what we have to do."

"Listen, why don't you guys get settled in and come on over to the Coyote North Officer's Club. It's the best game in town, in fact it's the only game in town," laughed Winkleman.

"Sounds good to me. What do you think, guys."

A chorus of confirming "yeses" and "allrights" left little doubt about the answer to that question.

"Thanks for the welcome," said Matsen as he again extended his hand to Winkleman.

The BOQ looked more like a boot camp barracks to Fancy. The pilots and RIOs would all be housed in one large rectangular squad bay. There were simple metal lockers to hold their gear. Even the shower area would be communal. Mercifully, though it was cool and the bed was fairly comfortable. In one corner was a large screen TV and VCR in front of some chairs and two couches that looked like they had seen better days.

"Come on Gator, let's get over to that O Club," grinned Killer Stevens.

"Sounds like a plan," said Fancy. "Come on Bagger, let's get a move on."

"Hold your horses, I'm coming. I just want to make sure all my belongings are properly put away." With that, Bagger tossed his overnight bag into the metal locker and slammed the door shut.

"Always the neatnik," croaked Moose.

The pilots and RIOs walked across a parking lot to a building that Fancy thought was called a double Butler hut. As they entered they were greeted with calls of welcome from the 64th Aggressors. "Welcome, comrades, the first round is on us!"

"I just hope these guys aren't hiding any spray paint," growled Moose.

"Let it go, Moose," said Fancy. "I think we're among friends."

The club was sparsely furnished. There were several tables, but the highlight of the room was a long bar complete with a brass rail. The mirror behind the bar resembled, Fancy thought, something out of the old west. All that was needed were some swinging doors and John Wayne coming through them.

"Step up gents," said a blond pilot with curly unruly hair and somewhat Slavic features. "Ian Mattox, XO of the 64th Aggressor Squadron," he bellowed for all to hear. "Drinks are on the house today."

"Devil!" someone called, "go easy on the booze, we've got to fly tomorrow—early!"

"Who said anything about booze, all we've got are soft drinks anyway."

Boos met that pronouncement. "Devil, I'm Gator, this is Killer, Bagger, Moose, Animal, Ratchet, Big Wave, Rhino, and Poncho, and we'll take anything that's cold and free."

Another pilot with coal black eyes and a hawk like nose, turned and extended his hand to Gator. "I'm Adam Steel, Bird to most of these clowns. Welcome aboard."

Fancy shook his hand and said, "Glad to be here, I think. We're all looking forward to some good flying and having some fun."

"You came to the right place. The flying is outstanding, even with some of the Mickey Mouse rules they hang around our necks."

"We got the run down back at Nellis. I gather Coyote North is something that's fairly new?"

"It's been up and running for about four months. Saves us a lot of time and gas and it really adds to the realism. We fly the fighter pilot's dream missions- lots of CAP (combat air patrol.) Although you guys will probably fly it as a BARCAP. Of course that's just a bunch of b.s., we just mostly roam around at high speed looking for anything that's on the other side."

By now Devil had all the Navy pilots' attention.

"Of course," he continued, "it's called ADF or Air Defense Forces, or the Bad Guys CAP."

The rest of the afternoon and evening was spent talking planes and tactics—big lies and little ones. No one ever lost or was about to.

Morning came early- earlier than most of the pilots believed was real. Of course, there were no hangovers so it didn't take long before everyone was up and running. Breakfast at the mess hall, was filling, if not tasty .

"Listen up, a minute," Matsen said, as Fancy was just about to spoon some eggs into his mouth. "Briefing is in ten minutes in the operations building, that's building 201, just in back of the O club. Don't be late."

Fancy and the rest of the pilots shoveled down the rest of their food and made their way to building 201. It too was sparse with folding chairs and a stage with a large map of the Nellis ranges. Winkleman and Matsen arrived and mounted the stage. "Good morning, gentleman," said Winkleman. "It looks like we'll have an interesting week ahead of us. Redland forces are poised to resume their offensive against the Yankee Imperialist dogs as soon as we take back control of the air. We anticipate air strikes by F-15Es and F-16s. In addition we'll probably see some B-1s and B-52s. Our Navy brothers will take off first this morning at 0730. They'll fly sections, we want to CAP the gap with one section at what we call Student Gap." He pointed Student Gap out with a long pointer. "Other sections we want to CAP are at Cedar Peak, The Farms, Caliente East. We figure these will be the major tap points. Keep your eyeballs peeled. Since our side has no AWACs, we want the Tomcats to use their more powerful radar to let us know what's coming. We'll scramble about ten minutes after you launch. With our shorter range, we can make better use of our assets that way. More bang for the buck so to speak. Any questions?"

Fancy had been taking notes on his knee board. He liked the casual no nonsense way things had been going. Right to the point, keep it simple and straight forward he thought. They seemed more like the Navy than the Air Force. He wondered if Matsen still had any ideas about going after the E-3 Sentry AWAC plane.

"Fancy and Schott, you'll cap Student Gap, Matsen and Milwood, you take Cedar Peaks. Bailey and Schwartze, the Farms, Stevens and Barnes, Caliente East. As soon as you're airborne, Ground Control Intercept will vector you into position. As soon as you have a tally ho, give us the word and we'll converge and join up on whoever has the tally. It wouldn't surprise me to have to split our forces though. The devious imperialist dogs have been known to run a feint," continued Winkleman. Our call-sign will be "Pintail."

At the personal equipment room, as the Air Force called it, everyone dressed in silence. Each pilot having his own routine, his ritual procedure for wiggling into the Nomex armor of the modern knight. Fancy remembered when as a newly minted pilot he made more of a show of it, buckling up his G-suit like Jesse James strapping on his guns, smoothing down his hair before screwing on the astronaut style skull cap. Now as an old head, he dressed in silence with no wasted motion or chit chat.

Since Coyote North was built on such a small scale, Fancy, Bagger, and Rhino walked out to their planes. Shrader, Fancy, and Mirabal made the walk-around. As usual nothing was amiss. Desperado 207 was ready to go. Fancy noted the blue inert AIM-9 Sidewinders and AIM-7 Sparrows. They did not have warheads or motors, but were stuffed with electronics for realistic simulated firings.

Fancy and Rhino, once buckled in, ran quickly and with a minimum of talk through the pre-engine startup. They were quickly becoming a team.

Immediately after the big General Electric engines were up and running and the last items on the checklist had been completed, they received permission to taxi. Four minutes later they were in the air with Animal, in a loose combat spread headed for Student Gap on a course of 105 degrees.

"Whatcha got on those mysterious black boxes and screens back there, Rhino?

"Nada," came Rhino's clipped reply. "But, you'll be the first to know when something pops up."

"You're a prince, babe," replied Fancy.

It didn't take long for them to arrive at their assigned position. The sky remained empty.

"Desperado 201, Let's bring it around and head toward Crystal Springs," Fancy suggested.

"Desperado 201, coming to course 190, Crystal Springs," answered Schott.

The two planes weaved and bobbed, much like two prize fighters, never presenting a predictable course or target.

After another few minutes Fancy's radio announced the first contact of the day. "Desperado and Pintails, we have contact," Moose announced calmly. We have eight Eagles at 19,000 at 80 miles, eastbound. Repeat 19,000 at 75 miles, now. Come on and join the party."

"Desperados 207 and 201 headed your way from Crystal Springs," said Fancy as he pushed the throttles to max military power. The big plane leaped ahead, seemingly eager to join the fray. Again Fancy could feel the surge of power right up into his backbone.

"I have bogeys at 285, 19000, at 95 miles, headed east" said Rhino calmly.

By now the Tomcat had accelerated to 675 knots and was rapidly eating up the distance to Cedar Peak.

"Looks like a couple of 'em are breaking off and are heading our way. Two at 18,000, climbing at two eight zero, coming hard and climbing," advised Rhino.

"Okay, let's lock them up, we'll shoot two AIM-7s at max range." Fancy willed himself to be as calm as possible, but he could feel his heart start to pick up some steam inside his chest. He could see that the two bogeys were still climbing and he raised the Tomcat's nose ever slightly to compensate. He guessed the closure rate was close to 1600 miles an hour.

"I've got 'em locked! Shoot! Shoot! Shoot!" yelled Mirabal.

"Shooting! We've got 'em locked!" At that moment Fancy wished the AIM-7s could come off the rails. Electronically it just wasn't going to be real enough. He quickly glanced over to port to see Animal's plane tearing through the sky. At the same time he started to bob and weave to throw off any AIM-7s or AIM-9s that would no doubt be headed his way.

"We've blown by them," blurted out Rhino. "They're behind our 3-9 line!"

"Keep an eye on 'em," commanded Fancy. "If they don't do a quick one-eighty, that means they were hit and have to go out to the regeneration line." So far their RAW gear was silent which was a good sign.

"I can't see them and there's nothing on my RAW gear. Come to zero eight five. I have a whole bunch of air planes at 55 miles, between 15 and 23,000 feet," said Rhino.

"Coming to zero eight five," grunted Fancy as he brought the plane to its new course. A quick sweep of the panel showed him they had plenty of gas and everything was in the green.

"I've got something big down on the deck," called Rhino. Could be a BUFF (Big Ugly Fat Fellow). Come to zero seven zero. He's low, probably no more than 500 feet. Range 30 and closing. Did anyone say hard deck?"

"If he can, we can. Animal, do you have the Big Ugly?"

"Uhh, yeah, he's clogging up my whole scope. "We goin' down to get him?"

"Roger that. Let's keep our eyes open!" Fancy immediately lowered the nose and a quick look told him Animal was right with them, 500 yards to port and stepped up about 100 yards.

"Come left a tad. Do you see him?"

No more were the words out of Rhino's mouth than Fancy picked up the B-52 visually. "Going guns, guns." Again Fancy imagined what the 20 mike mike shells would do to the giant bomber. "You're gone, big guy!" he yelled, as they flashed past the B-52.

"Anything else for us to play with, Rhino?"

"The scope is clean. It's like everything just disappeared," answered Rhino.

Just then Fancy heard the warble of the RAW gear. Just like that they had gone from the hunter to the hunted. "Animal, are they getting the same news we are?"

"My RAW gear is getting active. So far no threat."

"Rog that, let's reverse and climb into them. They'll be a better target than we will. Let's go vertical." Fancy brought the nose up to start an outside loop. As he came to the vertical, he rolled left and and at the top of the loop the Tomcat had reversed into their attackers.

"Talk to me Rhino!"

"Come to two five five. They're high, 17,000 feet, range 20 miles and closing. I've got 'em locked."

"Animal?"

"Same picture," said Schott. "We've got 'em bore sighted."

"Let's go zone five and climb into them. Fox-1! Fox-1!" Fox-1 signaled that there were radar guided missiles in the air. Both planes climbed into the cobalt blue sky. Again Fancy had to wonder, who shot first or was there even any point in wondering about it? If they were hit, wondering would probably not be an option.

"Passing through 12,000, range 15 miles. What was that with the Sparrows, Gator?"

"I just wanted them to think about something else. Let's close and we'll go to the winders."

"I've got no tone."

"Not yet," Fancy replied. "We're about 10 degrees angle off, best as I can see. Coming left. I've got 'em visually."

"We're in range! Do you have a tone?"

"Negative, negative, no tone, no tone! Damn!" complained Fancy.

"18,000, they're behind our 39. I've got them visually."

"Coming left, hang on," Fancy grunted as he reefed the Tomcat to port in what pilots often referred to as a bat turn. Fancy could see the two F-15 also starting to reverse their course. *Knife fight* Fancy thought. "Coming out of burner." He hoped Animal was still with them. Right now he wasn't going to take his eyes off the F-15s.

"We've got two Winders left," cackled Mirabal.

"Desperado 201, how you doin'?" asked Fancy.

"Hangin' on your starboard side, loose duce. I see the Eagles. I have a tone."

"We have no tone, no tone, shoot, shoot," growled Fancy.

"Fox-2, Fox-2," came the immediate response.

"All right, Animal. I think it's time to RTB. We've got 1,7 00 pounds."

"Desperado 207, we're getting on the light side too. It looks like the Eagles are headed home."

"Coming to course zero seven five. Let's keep our heads on a swivel. Keep moving around. Let's not become sitting ducks," sighed Fancy.

The two Tomcats headed back to Coyote North, at a somewhat reduced speed.

Upon landing the two Tomcats taxied into the flight line where they were directed to their parking spot. It seem as if they were the last section to land. All the F-5s and F-14s were being fueled and serviced at breakneck speed.

As soon as the canopy was open, Shrader's head immediately appeared above the rail and he asked, "How'd it go Lieutenant?"

"I think we did some damage. We were engaged with a couple of Eagles and we couldn't get a tone from the 'winders. Lt. Schott was in the same engagement as was able to shoot. Check it out. Otherwise everything was real good."

"Sure thing, Lieutenant. Is there anything else?"

"No, like I said she was a dream."

By then Mirabal had climbed down and was about to say something when Fancy turned around. "Rhino, when I say shoot whether it's with the Hope, Winders, guns, rocks, or bows and arrows, I don't expect to be questioned about it. We've got no time for that crap. If you've got a problem or question about what's going on, stow it until we get back here. Got it!"

For once Mirabal was speechless. He wanted to say something, but even though his mouth was moving, nothing would come out. At last he managed to answer, "Yes, sir. No offense, Gator. I'm just the curious type, that's all."

Fancy relaxed and looked at Mirabal, who looked like a puppy that had had an accident on the new carpet. "I just want to make the point that airtime is not the time for debate, second guessing, or anything else. We're still getting to know each other, but now you know how I feel about it. I've had my say, so let's see what's going on."

By then a fuel truck had pulled up and was pumping JP-5 into the Tomcat's depleted tanks. Shrader and another enlisted man had a panel open and it looked like they were running down the problem with the Sidewinder.

An Air Force pickup pulled up and the driver asked if they wanted a lift to the operations building. Fancy put his helmet in its bag and he and Mirabal jumped in the back.

Fancy grinned at Rhino and said, "That wasn't a bad morning's work. You had those guys locked up and ready to shoot. I'm impressed."

Rhino could only grin. Fancy's words let him know that there was no problem between them. He liked that. *Get it out and over with,* he thought.

At the operations building they thanked the enlisted driver and went in. Fancy realized how hot it had been out on the flight line, but hadn't noticed it because of the excitement of the mission. Now that he was winding down, he realized how thirsty he was. For the first time he noticed the somewhat battered soft drink machine. Then he cursed himself because he remembered he didn't have any change with him.

"Just push the button, it's free. Just think of it as Air Force hospitality. Actually, we all pitch in to keep it filled up," said Winkleman, as he walked over and demonstrated. "Everybody was taking their frustrations out on this poor old machine, so we figured if it was free, they wouldn't destroy the machine. So far it's only been marginally effective."

Fancy retrieved a drink. "Thanks, I really need this. What a morning! How'd we do?"

"We did some damage. The tale will be played out when they send us the tapes from Blackjack. How do you think it went?"

I think we got a couple of Eagles and a BUFF for sure. On the way home we hassled with two more Eagles. We couldn't get a tone to shoot, but Lt. Schott did. Close call. Who knows," he shrugged.

"Well pull yourself together. There will be a quick brief and then it's back up." Winkleman's grin spread from ear to ear when he mentioned going back up.

It wasn't long before he and Mirabal were strapped back in the cockpit, running through the preflight check list.

"You ready, Rhino?" asked Fancy.

"I'm right behind you, Gator."

Shrader and his enlisted cohorts had found the problem with their Sidewinders. It turned out to be only a loose connection. Desperado was buttoned and ready to go.

They had been assigned to cap Cedar Peak. It was felt by the powers that be, that the blue forces would come that way. All the planes at Coyote North were going to launch at once, the F-5s first.

Fancy watched the smaller F-5s start up, taxi out to the active runway, and take off. He marveled at how small they were, betting that their wingspan was about the same or smaller than the horizontal stabilizer on the F-14. They were great MiG simulators. As the last F-5 cleared the runway, he gestured to Animal to come up on button six. "Animal, why don't you fly lead? We'll fly your wing." Unlike their Air Force friends, they could, and were encouraged, to think independently, and plan their operations. Making changes was just part of the process that was encouraged by higher ups in the Naval aviation community.

"Thanks, Gator," came the immediate reply. "I can dig it."

They got the word to start engines. Although he should be used to it by now he thought, those engines were still sending tingles up and down his spine.

Schott's F-14 started down the runway, slowly gathering speed. As Schott brought her off the runway, Fancy advanced the throttles. 207 rumbled down the runway. Fancy was tempted to go afterburners, but thought better of it. Why waste fuel on the ground for a momentary high. "*A little joke*," he chuckled to himself.

After they were in the air, Fancy flew a loose deuce, with Schott off his port wing at a half mile spread and stepped up about 500 feet. The two planes climbed to 20,000 feet. Visibility was unlimited. After arriving in the Cedar Peak area it didn't take long for things to start happening. "Desperados, over Cedar Peak," came the voice of Baron Control or the GCI—ground control intercept, "bogeys incoming, 190, at twenty." Fancy noted that Schott's Tomcat was already coming to the new heading.

"Gator, coming around. Did you copy?"

"Roger the copy, Animal. We're with you."

"Rhino, have you got incoming?"

"I've got 'em. My scope's all lit up. There's a bunch of 'em. They're comin' fast—closure is 900 knots. Range is 40 miles and closing."

"Well, that's what we came for." Fancy swept the instrument panel one more time. Everything was in the green.

Rhino's voice broke into his thoughts. "I have one, no make it two contacts down on the deck, probably a pair Weasels bearing 190, for 12 miles."

"We're goin' down, boys," came Schott's broken up voice. "It looks like they're jamming today. Be sharp. Let's take 'em head on. I'll take the guy on the left, Gator."

"Roger, going after the Weasels. Take'er down, Animal."

Both Tomcats pushed over. "We're closing fast," grunted Rhino as the big plane began to unwind and pick up speed. "They're right on the deck!"

"I've got 'em. They're splitting up. Take the guy on the right!" I'm getting a tone! Shooting! Shooting! Fox-2! Fox-2!"

The words were no more than out of Fancy's mouth when the four planes shot past each other.

"Weasels at Cedar Peak," came the disembodied voice of Black Jack. "You're both morts. Take yourself out to the regeneration point—then get back in the war."

Fancy thought, those two F-16 drivers were going to be pissed.

"Gator, let's close up a little and climb."

"Closing on you, Animal. What's out there Rhino?"

"It looks like a flight of four Eagles at uhh, 30, eastbound. Oh oh, four more at 27, eastbound, eight miles. The lower guys are coming down and comin' hard."

Now they were the hunted. "Do you see what we see Animal?" Fancy called.

"We see four Eagles at 30 and four more at 24, range 10 miles, and closing. Those guys are coming after us. Let's stay low. At least we'll be a real crappy target."

"Roger, we'll stay low."

"Tomcats at Pahute Mesa. You're toast. Drive on out to the regeneration point and come back in."

"Well, it was quick and painless," Fancy grumbled to Rhino as they climbed out to 18,000 feet and took a course to the regeneration point at the point of range 75. After "regenerating" themselves they could jump back into the fray.

"Gator, do you want to fly lead," asked Schott.

"No, I would have probably done the same thing, Animal. You're fine," answered Fancy. Inside he was seething. He hated to lose—at anything. As far back as he could remember he had hated to lose. He chuckled to himself as he remembered going to school and losing his marbles, literally, to some older boys. When he arrived home hoping to get some sympathy from his parents. Of course there had been none. His father's advice had been to practice and get better or not play, but don't whine about it. and that's what he had done. Borrowing some money from his older sister, he had bought some more marbles and had practiced until his knuckles were almost raw. When he played again, unfortunately, he lost nearly all those marbles too. Again, more practice until his knuckles were actually bleeding and his thumb ached. Winning came slowly, but he did manage to wind up the spring with more marbles than he had started out with—and they weren't taken from the younger kids either.

Upon reaching the regeneration point, they were about to turn to their new course to get back into the battle when Black Jack announced, "F-14's at the regeneration point, you're both morts."

"What!" shouted Mirabal. "What is this crap?"

"They capped the regeneration point," muttered Fancy. "They're starting to get to me now!" But, he thought, turnabout is fair play—and if this was the real thing…there would be no regeneration point—period, just spots on the desert floor.

The two planes turned once again to the edge of range 75. By the time they had regenerated and had turned back to a course they hoped would get them back in the war, Mirabal had told him that there wasn't a plane, friend or foe to be had. Just like that it was over.

"Baron Control to Desperados coming in from the regeneration point, proceed back to base. We have no targets in sight. We're probably done for today."

Fancy fought down the urge to dip into his colorful language vocabulary. It was one thing to lose, but to lose twice in the space of less than six minutes was almost too much. He noticed the taste of oxygen in his mask and for the first time felt the mask on his face.

"Gator, I'm sorry. I guess I just wasn't paying attention, I didn't pick 'em up."

"Ah, don't worry about it. We'll just have to consider it part of the learning process. It happens. The good news is that we get to play again tomorrow."

"Man, I didn't have any indication we were being lit up. I'm always scanning, and I just didn't have any indications. The RAW gear wasnt making a peep. How about up there?"

"Nothin', I bet that AWAC plane is passing along the information to the Eagles, just like the E-2C s pass it along to us. Turn about is fair play."

"I guess," replied Mirabal. Rhino sounded really down.

"The Tomcat settled down on the runway, Fancy thought, somewhat heavily. *It's probably got its tail between its legs*, he thought.

When Shrader climbed up to get Fancy's helmet, the scowl on Fancy's face told the story—it hadn't been a good day. He wasn't quite sure what to say, so he did what he thought was the smart thing to do—say nothing. He retrieved Fancy's helmet and scrambled down.

Wearily, Fancy unstrapped, made sure everything was shut down and turned off, and then hoisted himself over the side of the plane and climbed down. "She seemed a little heavy when we recovered. The stick seemed a little stiff. Can you use your magic powers and make sure she's ready to go in the morning?"

"You bet, sir. She'll be ready. How'd she do today, sir?"

"The plane did just fine. I was piss poor," Fancy growled.

Shrader decided that it was still just not a good time to say anything and remained mute. He also noticed that Lieutenant Mirabal wore the same expression. It had not been a good day for the Navy.

Both men took one look around the the plane and then boarded the blue pick-up for a ride back to their quarters. Fancy turned in the direction of the runway as he heard two more Tomcats touch down. It looked like Bagger and his wingman. He hoped they had had more success than he had.

Schott and his RIO clambered aboard and the truck headed toward the BOQ. The usual light-hearted banter was noticeably absent and the short trip was made in total silence.

Fancy did not want to admit it, but the shower and shave had actually lifted his spirits somewhat. He wasn't giddy by any means, but he definitely felt more upbeat. After all, he got to go up again tomorrow. As he let the cold soft drink slide down his throat Bagger, Moose, Poncho, and Big Wave rolled in and grabbed something to drink. "Welcome home, valiant warriors," Fancy said, as he raised the can in a mock salute.

"What a day," sighed Poncho as he dropped into a chair. "I don't know about you, but I didn't exactly do the Navy proud today. How'd it go with you and Animal?"

In spite of himself, Fancy grinned and said, "Actually we were mortified, twice in about six minutes. Some Eagles hammered us and then we extended out to the regeneration point at Range 75 and got hammered again."

"Hey, that happened to us too," grinned Bagger. "Damn, that irked me. At least I was in good company," he said as he raised his can.

"You know it's got to be that E-3," fumed Big Wave. "It's time to take that big piece of aluminum overcast out."

"Amen to that," croaked Moose. "Who wants to do it?"

Everyone nodded in agreement. Ideas right now were in short supply as everyone drifted into his own thoughts.

"Good afternoon, gentleman," said Col. Winkleman as he entered the room. "Please, stay seated," he commanded as everyone started to come to their feet. "Somehow I get the feeling that things did not go well this afternoon. Don't let it get you down. This is the time when you have to fold up your egos and stick 'em in your pockets. By all means, don't look at it like you lost, chalk it up to the learning curve."

About that time Matsen clumped in. Any doubts about how his day had gone werre written all over his face. He was positively beaming, from ear to ear. "What a day! Man oh man, we put some hurt on a couple of Eagle drivers this afternoon. How'd you guys do?"

The silence hung like a dark cloud. "Oh, oh," sighed Matsen, "it couldn't have been that bad, could it?" More silence. "I know what it was, you got hammered at the regeneration point, right? That's probably my fault. We didn't talk about that little Air Force trick at all. Look, let's get cleaned up and get over to the club and forget today. There's not anything we can do about it anyway."

With Matsen taking some of the heat, the mood of the pilots and RIOs started to rise and it wasn't long before they were all at Coyote North's finest and only club. Shortly there after bantering and joking among the Air Force and Navy pilots was in full swing. The Gloom becoming a thing of the past.

Colonel Winkleman walked in, carrying a tape cassette. "Gentleman, here's the results of todays' go—rounds. If anybody's interested, you can take the tape and play it at your convenience."

"Have you seen it sir?" one of the aggressor pilots asked.

"I just got through, I kind of surfed through it. All the close calls went the other way. They were legitimate. By now you probably have figured out why they're getting the jump on us."

"AWACs!" chorused the Navy pilots.

Winkleman didn't reply, but instead raised the soft drink he had been handed in a mock salute to the assembled pilots. "This is true," he replied.

"What about taking it out?" asked Matsen, who had come in behind Winkleman. "That's the first thing the other side would do if things hit the fan. When they went over the rules of engagement, they didn't mention that would be a 'no—no.'"

"It's kind of an unwritten rule," sighed Winkleman. "Of course nobody's brought it up lately. Everyone's just kind of accepted it."

"Then it's time to start rewriting the rules," charged Fancy. "I don't mind getting hammered, if I have a chance to hammer back and put some hurt on the other guys."

Devil Mattox, XO of the aggressors chimed in, "You know, they're right. We just kind of accept some of this b.s. Let's throw a monkey wrench in their machinery."

Winkleman just grinned, "Why not? What have we got to lose, except our careers? I already know I'm not in line for a star. Anyone else?"

The resulting cheers quickly answered that question.

"Any ideas?" asked Winkleman.

"Do they CAP the E-3?" asked Bagger.

"As a rule they do. But they've been getting kind of sloppy. I think they release the CAP after things get hot and heavy."

"What's the CAP, a section or division?" someone else asked.

"It's usually a section, Eagle drivers who haven't been good and followed some of the rules," answered Winkleman.

"Who owns the C-130?" asked Big Wave.

"It's mostly ours. We put in a lot of time and effort after it bellied in, right here as a matter of fact. It was going to be surveyed out to

Davis-Monthan, in Arizona. We straightened some things out and got it running. It's got a weight limitation, but the old crate has been reliable and does what we need it to do. Why?

"Oh, just wondering," grinned Big Wave. "Maybe it could be our Trojan Horse."

"How so?" asked Mattox.

"Well, what if we launched the Herk on one of its legitimate runs back to Nellis or wherever it goes. At the same time, we could launch two Tomcats. They could tuck in real close so the radar paint is just the C-130. It gets as close as possible to where we could go after the E-3."

There was silence as the idea was mulled over.

"You know, it could work," hedged Winkleman. "Of course, what they would do is launch the back-up. How do we deal with that?"

"Let's put someone on the ground and sabotage the big mother while it's just sitting there," volunteered Poncho. "I think I know who would like that little job."

All the Navy pilots looked at Moose, who appeared to be in deep thought.

"I think I could handle that job."

"How are we going to get our "commando" back to Nellis to do the deed?" asked Killer.

"We need to get one of our birds back there. It's got some turbine blade problems. Moose, you think you could get it back there."

"No problem, I think," said Moose. "I've got a couple of hours in them. We've got some at Miramar."

"Of course Moose might be too well known back at Nellis after he got into that ruckus with those Eagle drivers," put in Animal. "He does tend to stand out at times."

"This is true," retorted Moose, as he stood and started to flex like a body builder. "I do tend to stand out."

"Or stepped on," chuckled Bagger.

After the chuckles and guffaws died down, Fancy said, "I think Moose is just the man to do it. The question is, how are we going to put that baby out of action without actually damaging it. If that happened, we might as well put our heads between our knees and kiss our collective asses good-bye. It's got to be something disabling or enough to let them know we were there and could have done it."

"You're right," chimed in Winkleman.

Big Wave put up his hand.

"Wave," said Matsen, "we're not back in fourth grade. Spit it out."

"Why don't we just leave an alarm clock with a note. The alarm goes off, they find it, and read the note."

"Yeah, and if that doesn't work, I'll just throw myself in front of the big mother," croaked Moose.

"Moose, that wouldn't even slow it down," said Poncho. "But that's not a bad idea. They'd know we were there. If they go along, great, if they don't, we'll shoot that one down too."

"What do you think?" asked Matsen, as he turned toward Winkleman.

"I like it, and right now, I can't think of anything better. Let's do it."

Moose raised his Coke in a salute, "I like these guys. Shoot, they're almost as devious as we are."

"When are they expecting that F-5 back at Nellis?" asked Fancy.

"They'd like it tomorrow, but there's nothing set in concrete," answered Winkleman. Of course, the more we stick to whatever routine we have, the better," said Mattox. "You know how the military loves routine."

"How are we going to get him on the plane?" asked one of the aggressor pilots. "You know how paranoid those AWACs guys are."

Mattox turned to Winkleman, "Herdman's back there, he's just coming off a thirty day leave. He's pretty chummy with everybody."

"Yeah, and he just loves to mudsuck anybody he has to fly against," grunted Winkleman. "Let me get on the horn and see if he has any bright ideas."

"Good idea," said Mattox. "I know he'll go for it in a big way."

Matsen said, "Okay, we launch the F-5 first, say at 0800. When Moose is almost back at Nellis, if we haven't launched, we'll put up the 130. Who wants the honor, I think, of going after the E-3?"

Fancy raised his hand, at the same time everyone else did. "Why don't we draw straws? That way nobody's going to get a case of the redass if they don't get to go."

A broom seemed to appear out of nowhere. Mattox broke off the straws and arranged them in his hand. "The two shorts get their choice, okay?"

Animal drew the first long straw, Poncho another. Bagger stepped up and got the first short straw. Matsen got another long one. Fancy reached in and drew the other short one. Immediately, he and Bagger high-fived each other.

"Great minds," grinned Bagger.

"And greater fliers," added Fancy.

"Amen to that," said Bagger, as they slapped hands again.

Winkleman, got up and said, "Let me get on the horn to Major Herdman and see what he can cook up."

"Sounds good," said Matsen. "Gator you and Bagger better put your heads together. Maybe we ought to get together with that C-130 crew to see how they feel about this madness."

"Uh, Colonel, where could we find the crew?"

Winkleman paused, "Probably over on the plane. I saw some people poking around there . Captain Kobayashi is the aircraft commander."

"Come on Bagger, let's go find Captain Kobayashi."

"Right, let me grab another cold one, and I'll be right with you."

Fancy wished he had grabbed something cold to drink as they walked across the field toward the parked C-130. This place is just too hot he thought as he trudged toward the plane. He could almost feel the moisture being sucked out of him.

Upon their arrival at the plane, there didn't seem to be anyone around. "Anybody home?" Fancy called. "Hello!"

From the front of the plane a voice answered, "Just a second, I"ll be right with you."

"Thanks," Bagger answered.

As they waited they looked over the big Hercules. The C-130 already had the reputation of being a great airplane, almost a legend in its own time. It had served with distinction in Viet Nam (and with newer models being introduced) it would be flying well into the next century.

"This is a great airplane," mused Bagger. "But, I'm glad I'm not driving one. I can't imagine myself anywhere but an F-14. How about you, Gator?"

"It's hard to imagine flying anything else. Would you rather fly this or something else if you couldn't fly the 'Cat?" asked Fancy.

"That's hard, man. I don't know. Flying means so much to me…"

"Good evening, sir," came the voice from the cavernous fuselage of the big plane. "What can I do for you, sir?" The voice belonged to a very tall airman first class.

"We'd like to find the aircraft commander, uh Captain Kobayashi?"

You just missed Captain Kobayashi and Captain Dodson, sir. They just went over to their quarters. That is their temporary quarters, they don't stay here much since they fly out of main side at Nellis, sir."

"Thanks," said Fancy. "Where are their quarters, uh…"

"Oh, sorry sir, Airman Allen. I'm the crew chief, sir. They're in building 205. It's just down the way from the officer's club, sir."

"Thank you, Allen. We'll wander over there."

As they walked back toward the buildings that made up Coyote North, Fancy wished again he had something cold to drink. The heat weighed on him like a heavy wool blanket. He felt he might melt and run down one of the cracks in the cement. I'll never return to this state for any other reason than to come to a Red Flag he thought. This place is just too hot.

They found building 205 and went in. Building 205 appeared to be more of a conventional BOQ. It also appeared to be deserted. Fancy looked at what seemed to be a check-in roster or at least appeared to be. He quickly located the names of Captains Kobayashi and Dodson. "It looks like they're in rooms 108. Let's go."

Room 108 was about three quarters of the way down the passageway, painted in that sickly government green paint. At least it's cool in here Fancy thought as he knocked on the door of room 108.

"Just a minute, please," answered a female voice."

"Oh oh, I think we've got the wrong room," Fancy said.

The door was opened by a stunning, diminutive Oriental woman, with coal black eyes, and long black hair that hung straight down her back. She couldn't have been much over the legal height limit. "I'm sorry, we were looking for the aircraft commander of that C-130."

"You can stop your looking," she answered. She extended her hand, "I'm Captain Kobayashi. Come on in," she said as she opened the door. The grip was firm, surprisingly so, considering her size mused Fancy, and what was the height limit for pilots in the Air Force?

As they stepped into the room, another woman got up the the desk, where it appeared she was filling out some sort of report. "This is my co-pilot, Captain Cassie Dodson. And this is…? she motioned toward Bagger, who seemed to be in some sort of trance.

"Oh, this is Lieutenant Bailey, first name Scott, call sign Bagger." Bagger was still in the trance. "Bagger!" said Fancy, somewhat louder than he would have liked.

"What? I'm tactical," growled Bagger.

He was tactical all right, thought Fancy. He's zeroing in on Captain Kobayashi.

"What can we do for you? Say, you must be two of the Tomcat drivers. We just came back from looking at those big beasts. They're something else."

Captain Kobayashi was talking to both pilots, but her attention was focused on Bagger, who still seemed to be oblivious to everything else except the Air Force captain.

"They belong to us," said Fancy. He was beginning to wonder if Bagger was ever going to be coherent again. "What we'd like to talk to you about is using your C-130 as kind of a decoy or a Trojan Horse in order to take out the E-3 that's been giving us fits. We figure it's payback time. Think you might be interested in helping us out?"

Kobayashi looked at her co-pilot. Dodson just shrugged and said, "Why not?"

"Well, we can at least listen to what you have to say. Why don't you give us a couple of minutes and we can talk things over down in the rec room at the end of the hall. It'll be more comfortable. When is this bit of mayhem going to take place?"

"We were thinking in the morning," replied Fancy. Am I going to have to do all the talking he thought.

Fancy turned to leave, taking Bagger none too gently, by the arm. "Come on, Bagger, let's wait down the hall."

"Uh, sure," said Bagger as Fancy walked down to the room at the end of hall. Like their quarters, the air-conditioning worked well. The furniture looked like early Air Force modern, pretty well worn, but functional. The two men cleared some old newspapers off the table and sat down to wait.

"Geez, that Air Force babe is something else," murmured Bagger.

"I didn't think you even noticed her by the way you were doing so much of the talking," responded Fancy.

"She's just so, so…"

"Exquisite," volunteered Fancy.

"Yeah, exquisite, that's perfect. Man oh man. She is something else.

"Hmmmmmm," said Fancy, sounds like it's love at first sight.

"It could be. Shoot, do you think she's married or engaged? I didn't see a ring, did you?"

"No, but I wasn't especially looking for one. I don't think so."

"There's no ring, gentleman," declared Captain Kobayashi, as she and Captain Dodson entered the room. Kobayashi was wearing slacks and a simple white blouse, with sandals. Cassie Dodson was wearing some denim shorts and a sleeveless, what Fancy thought was called a green shell. Oh, oh, thought Fancy, Bagger is going to zone out again.

Bagger stood up and pulled out a chair for Kobayashi and then one for Dodson. He said, "I'm glad to hear that, Captain, because I would sure like to see you sometime."

He didn't even stammer noted Fancy.

Kobayashi gave him a long look. A smile creased the corners of her mouth. "Lieutenant, I'm just coming off a relationship."

Bagger's face fell.

"However, if we can get through this," she continued, I think maybe we could work something out."

Bagger's face said it all, with a grin that could only be described as ear-to-ear.

"Well," Fancy broke in, "let's get on with it then."

"How come you just don't take a straight shot at it?" asked Dodson.

"We thought about it, for about a minute," grinned Fancy. Reality seemed to dictate that they would see us coming and would be able to stack the deck against us right away. The F-14 is not exactly what anyone would call stealthy. We want a better than even chance of taking it out."

Dodson looked at him for a moment, shrugged and said, "Seems like the way to go then. So the idea is to tuck in close to us and get as close as you can, right?"

"That's the plan, unless something better comes up. We're willing to listen if anyone can come up with anything better. We don't claim to have the last word in tactics."

"I don't have anything better right offhand, how about you, Rowdy?"

Kobayashi shook her head, no. "It seems that this is as simple and direct as anything. Keeping it simple seems like the way to go to me."

"You know there's another E-3 at Nellis. Won't they just launch the other one?"

Bagger spoke up. "We've got a plan for the spare. We're going to put someone on the ground and plant kind of a bomb. Actually, it's an alarm clock simulating a bomb. We decided to draw the line at any kind of damage to the plane."

The Air Force pilots laughed. "An alarm clock?" smiled Kobayashi. "Oh, boy. What next? Actually that's not a bad idea."

"Wait a sec," said Dodson, "let me get a map."

Dodson returned with a map showing Nellis and all its ranges. "Usually, they orbit around Lathrop Wells, right around here, just inside the Nevada—California border, flying a race track pattern between Lathrop Wells and the southeastern corner of range 76S. That puts them about 175 miles from Coyote North."

"We can't take a straight-in approach though," said Rowdy Kobayashi. "We'll have to skirt area 51 or what we call Dreamland, sometimes called the Ranch. Lots of hush-hush stuff goes on there and they're real serious about keeping wandering eyes at a distance."

"Are they going to wonder about the course or time you'll be on?" asked Fancy.

"No, not really, we're supposed to go in to Indian Springs to pick up some empty oxygen bottles, then go back to Nellis. It's not a real strict schedule. We can get lost in the shuffle. There's so much coming and going with so many planes here, they don't pay too much attention to us."

Fancy and Bagger bent over the map. "So, we take off, fly southwest down Kawich Valley, hit Pahute Mesa, and over Range 4808W," said Bagger, as he traced the proposed route.

Dodson, leaned over and put in, "Right here, just when we hit 4808W, we should change course and head for Indian Springs."

"Do you ever like to take that big bird down on the deck?" asked Fancy.

"We've been known to do that, although at this time of year it's a rough ride. What do you say, Razor, do you want to get down and dirty?"

"Oh, sure, why not," she shrugged. "Anything for a few laughs. Let's face it we've been in a rut lately."

"What's the terrain like?" asked Fancy.

"Kawich Valley is about two and a half miles wide, ground is pretty flat. The big deal is the updrafts. That desert heats up really fast, you can really bounce around out there. That could make it real interesting if we're tucked in close. Have you ever done something like this before?" asked Kobayashi.

"Nope," said Bagger. "But, we can do it."

"How low do you want to go?" she requested.

"What do think, Gator, three hundred feet?"

"I can live with that. How about you?" He nodded toward the two Air Force Pilots.

"That's about what I was thinking, what do you think Cassie?"

"Sounds good. Let's do it," she said, as she and Kobayashi high-fived.

They quickly firmed up the plans for take-off. Just before the C-130 rotated, the two F-14s would begin their take-off roll, Everyone agreed this would be the trickiest part of the mission. The wing vortex turbulence could cause some problems. Luckily, the runway would be wide enough, barely, for a section take-off. Something F-14s didn't do very often. Fancy and Bailey felt confident they could make it work, and work safely.

Fancy stood and said, "We'd like to thank you for the help, particularly with us just barging in on you like this. I hope you don't mind mudsucking your own guys."

"Like Cassie said, we've been in kind of a rut lately. It'll be nice to do something a little different. We like to mix it up as well as anybody. That's why we joined in the first place."

Dodson stood up and said, "I'm beat, I think I'll bid you a good night. When are you going to give us the launch time?"

"I'll go back to the club and try to find Colonel Winkleman and our exec. I'll call back as soon as I can. See you in the morning. Thanks again, we really appreciate it."

Fancy shook their hands, and had turned and walked down the hall several feet before he realized Bagger was still in the rec room. "Bagger," he called, "I'll see you back at the BOQ, okay?"

"That'll be great," called Bagger.

Fancy grinned to himself, shook his head and headed back to the O Club.

Upon entering the club he headed straight for the table where most of the pilots were still seated, talking among themselves. He noticed that neither Winkleman nor Matsen were among those seated at the table. "It looks like we have our decoy. Anybody know where Matsen and Colonel Winkleman disappeared to?"

"They said they'd meet you over at the BOQ," responded Animal. "They'd like you to get over there as soon as possible."

"I'm on my way then," said Fancy as he turned on his heel and headed back toward their quarters. He had a definite spring in his step as he anticipated the coming action.

Matsen and Winkleman were seated at a table in one of the cubbies that passed for an office for transient officers. "I just got off the phone with Major Herdman. He's in. He'll meet Lt. Milwood when he takes the F-5 back. In fact, he's so gung ho about this, he's on his way to get the "bomb". Did you find Captain Kobayashi, okay?"

"Did we," grinned Fancy. "Bagger may want to transfer to the Air Force and fly C-130s. He's still back there, working out some details with her."

"You mean he's trying to hustle her?" asked Matsen.

"No, I wouldn't say that, but he's definitely interested. She's really attractive."

"Rowdy's left broken hearts all over this base," said Winkleman. "The latest in fact, was mine, but not to worry. We parted friends. She's a very strong person as well as being a heck of a pilot. If your friend is planning on a wham bam, thank you, ma'am, he's strictly out of luck. She looked me in the eye and said she's saving it for marriage—part of her religious heritage. She's a Mormon, and makes no bones about it. Don't get me wrong, she's a lot of fun; she does things like rock climbing and even writes poetry."

Fancy gave Matsen a look and a shake of the head that said, "Another one?"

After an awkward pause Fancy said, "All we need to do is finalize the launch time."

"You've got the route all worked out," queried Matsen.

"Yeah, we'll launch as soon as the 130 starts to rotate. We'll head down Kawich Valley, over Pahute Mesa," He nodded toward Winkleman, "I hope I've got that pronunciation right. As soon as we hit Range 4808W, the 130 will head toward its intended destination, Indian Springs. At that time we'll break radar silence and look for the E-3, bore in, and shoot it."

Winkleman wrinkled his brow. "I don't think I'd try a section takeoff. The edges of the runway are a little on the dicey side."

Fancy shrugged. "Okay, we'll tuck in real quick and hope we don't get spotted."

"How about if we launch right after you and angle over toward the Farms and Cedar Peak. We can light up the E-3 and pass the information on to you via JTIDS. You can stay radar silent," interjected

Matsen. "You're not exactly stealthy, but you're not giving anything away either."

Fancy nodded. "Let's have some fun, sounds good to me. How about launch times?"

"We figure, Moose should launch about 0725. He's got to keep his gear down to show he's not a player if he gets jumped. that'll slow him up and probably put him on the ground about 0800," said Matsen.

Winkleman continued, Jeff will meet him on the ramp and take care of any inquisitive people. He figures by the time they get down to where the second E-3 is, it will probably be around 0815, maybe even 0825. I'm not sure what he's got up his sleeve to get you on board, but if I know him, he's already got something cooking. Figure on launching the 130 around 0755. We may even beat the E-3 into the air or at least to her race track station at Lathrop Wells."

"I'd better find Rhino and Bagger so we can get our stuff all in one bag," said Fancy, as he arched his back and stretched. He walked toward the hallway and turned around. "I think I speak for all of us when we say we appreciate what you guys are doing. Thanks."

Winkleman grinned. "Think nothing of it, after all we're really all on the same team."

"Get those guys up to speed, and if there's no further discussion or planning needed, let's plan on meeting in the club for breakfast at 0630," added Matsen.

Fancy, turned and continued down the hall, anxious to find Mirabal.

It was another hour before everyone had been brought up to speed and Fancy was more than ready for some rack time as he flopped on the bed. He immediately fell into a deep sleep, even while Bagger was going on and on about the new love of his life.

At 0530 an Airman First, announced to the slumbering pilots that it was indeed a new day and it was time to get the mattress of their collective backs.

After showering and shaving, Fancy, Mirabal, Bailey, and his RIO, Lt. j.g. Curtis Carpenter, call sign Walrus, headed for the club to get some breakfast and make sure nothing had changed since last night.

Moose Milwood was already seated when the four officers came in and sat down. "Moose, you all set?" asked Fancy as he settled into his chair."

"Ready, more than ready," he grinned. "I just hope that F-5 makes it back to Nellis."

Winkleman entered, followed a few seconds later by Ratchet Matsen and the rest of the F-14 pilots and RIOs. There were no changes in the plan that had been worked out last night and breakfast was eaten quickly. The easy banter of last night was replaced by a more serious, professional tone. Everyone was on the same page and ready to go. Much to Fancy's surprise, Bagger didn't say anything about Captain Kobayashi. Maybe, he thought, the short lived romance was over.

After putting on their equipment, they preflighted their planes. Bagger made a quick trip over to the C-130, just to make sure he said, that everything was still okay. It still was. Then again, maybe it wasn't, but this was not the time to get involved in Bagger's love life.

They all stopped what they were doing and watched the F-5 break the silence of the morning as Moose lifted off and headed to Nellis.

Fancy watched the C-130 start to come to life and it wasn't long before all four of its turboprop engines were up and running.

"Their call sign is Buick," Fancy reminded Rhino as they finished their pretakeoff checklist. "She's starting to roll."

Immediately Shrader indicated, with hand signals that the F-14 was unchocked. He signaled Fancy to pull forward out of the parking place. Fancy returned Shrader's snappy salute and inched the throttles forward. Desperado 207 moved out of the parking space and moved to the taxiway. In spite of himself, Fancy felt his heart beat faster.

Desperado 207 moved to one side of the active runway, behind Bagger, who in turn was behind the C-130. They had decided last night that Bagger would shoot the E-3, while Fancy would provide cover.

The C-130 began its takeoff roll, black smoke poured from the turboprop engines and it quickly gathered momentum. Kobayashi brought the big plane off the runway and leveled out at three hundred feet. Bagger was rolling as soon as the big transport broke free of the runway. Fancy, after pausing to give Bagger a little room, pushed the throttles forward to max military power. In spite of two planes taking off so close together, he was mildly surprised to find there was less turbulence that he had anticipated. It was there, but manageable. Easing back on the throttles he pulled almost even with Bagger.

It didn't take long to catch the C-130 and they pulled slightly aft and below the plane, Bagger to port and Fancy slightly back of Bagger on the starboard side. He'd refueled from Marine KC-130s before and was now surprised that there was more turbulence than when they had taken off. It was a bit of a jolt to find himself working harder than he had anticipated.

"How's everything back there, Rhino?"

"Everything's up and running just like they advertise in those shiny little brochures. It's a little bumpier than I thought it would be. But, hell, I shouldn't be surprised. Tucked in close, desert heating up... Par for the course."

Bagger and Fancy pulled in a little closer and surpsisingly the turbulence eased up somewhat. Fancy scanned the instruments finding everything in the green.

The three planes screamed across the barren desert floor, seemingly welded together, moving up slightly up or down as the small ridges and valleys passed beneath them. Information was now being passed to them from the F-14s that had launched just behind them. So far the only objects in the air were their three plane force.

Fancy took a quick glance over at Bagger, who gave him a quick thumbs up and then turned back to business in his cockpit. They were traveling at a liesurely, at least for the F-14, pace of only 350 knots or only 402 miles per hour. It wasn't very fast but it was enough to keep his attention.

Pahute Mesa was coming up fast. The buffeting was becoming more acute now. He motioned to Bagger to move aft a bit farther. It didn't seem to help much, if at all. Fancy began to wonder if this was the good idea it had seemed last night. Again he caught Bagger's eye and got a thumbs up.

"Uh oh," said Rhino. "It looks like we're going to have some company. It looks like we've got some Eagles coming up from Nellis. Uh, they're at our ten o clock, high, at 85 miles, course two nine zero. Looks like a flight of four. No indication that they've seen us."

"Bagger? Looks like we're going to have some company."

"Roger the flight of four Eagles," answered Bagger.

"Pahute Mesa called out Mirabal. RAW gear is starting to heat up. They've seen us. Range 80 miles and closing."

"I'm getting the same message. Buick is going to change course and head to Indian Springs pretty quick. Watch for them to rock their wings. When they do, we'll slide back, they'll go to port and we'll pull off to starboard. When we do, we're going to warp speed. You might as well bring up the radar as soon as we start to pull off to the right."

"Roger, that," replied Rhino.

"Okay, there's the wing rock."


Moose Milwood had put the F-5 on the ground and was taxiing to the 64th Aggressors parking area. It was a good thing, he thought that they had sent a follow-me truck out to greet him. Nellis was a huge base with an immense amount of planes launching and recovering. That's all I need is to get lost. *Excuse me, could you direct me to the 64th,* he smiled to himself.

The short flight had been no problem. Moose found the F-5 terribly underpowered. Of course it was about the most dirt simple thing he had flown since he had taken flying lessons in a Piper Cub in Nebraska.

*No thanks, I'll stick with the big cat,* he mused as he shut down the engines on the tiny fighter.

He had no sooner finished raising the canopy when a smiling face appeared just below the canopy rail. "You must be Lt. Milwood?" the face said. "How do you like the F-5?"

"To be honest," said Moose, hoisting himself out of the cockpit, "I am and I was just thinking to myself that I would stick with my Tomcat, thanks, anyway. You must be Jeff Herdman?"

"At your beck and call. Most folks call me Stretch."

"Moose," said the diminutive pilot, as he extended his hand. Man, this guy is tall, thought Moose, as he looked up at the still smiling face. I wonder if Bagger could climb this guy And, how does this guy fold himself up to get in an F-5?

"How was the flight in, she give you any trouble?" asked Herdman.

"No, it was a piece of cake, absolutely no problems, although, she felt a little rough when I took off."

"Great, here come the maintenance boys now. They're going to tear that engine out and slip in a new one."

For the first time Moose noticed the bag Herdman was holding. "Is that, the uh, bomb?" he asked in his best conspiratorial voice.

"This is it," grinned Herdman. "I picked it up at the base exchange. It's kind of a funny little thing. I tinkered around with it a little bit and it makes quite a loud bang when it hits the hour or for whenever we set it for. I also put some baby powder in it so it leaves a little bit of a puff of smoke, and I put in a note to tell then exactly who it's from and what its purpose is. What do you think? I've got it set to go off in two and a half hours."

Sounds marvelous to me. Any ideas on how we're going to get on the E-3?"

"I called in a favor from a guy I know in intel. He's arranged for a little tour for my brother and me."

"Your brother?" exclaimed Moose. "Yeah, I can see the resemblance."

"We can tell them we had two different fathers, if they get nosy."

"Hey let's give it a try, We've got nothin' to lose. I'm good to go."

"Come on, we'll get that follow-me truck to take us down the flight line to the E-3. Did you see it when you landed?"

"To tell you the truth, I didn't. I just wanted to make sure I got the scooter to where it was supposed to be."

The two aviators presented an odd pair as they walked over to the truck and climbed in. Mutt and Jeff were alive and well in Las Vegas.

Herdman told the driver to stop well short of the big E-3, a converted Boeing 707. Its large radome mounted on the top of the fuselage looked, to some, like two flying saucers mating.

The two fliers, package in hand, walked over to the big plane, which was guarded by a very serious looking airman toting an M-16.

"Good morning, sir," he asked seriously. "How may I help you this morning?"

"Good morning," returned Herdman. "My brother and I are supposed to get a little tour from Captain King. Unfortunately, my brother has to return to his unit this afternoon. He's always admired the work these folks do on this magnificent plane."

Moose began to cough.

The airman looked over the two men, with a somewhat bewildered looked on his face. "Yes, sir. A Captain King went on board a few minutes ago." He reached around his back and brought out a walkie-talkie. "Major Reigle, I have two officers out here that are expecting a tour by Captain King. Shall I let them on board, sir?"

Milwood couldn't hear the reply, but it must have been in the affirmative. The airman motioned them toward the plane.

"Excuse me, sir. I'll have to look in that package."

"Of course," said Herdman as he handed him the package. "It's a gift for my niece, I just picked it up at the base exchange."

The airman took a look in the package and handed if back as if he had been embarrassed by what was in it. "Sorry, sir, those are my standing orders. In fact I should keep it out here, but it looks pretty harmless."

Herdman extended him the package. "Listen if it will make you feel better, you keep it out here. We don't want you to have any problems. Right, Moose?"

"Right," croaked Moose, "no problems."

"That's okay, like I said, it's only an alarm clock. You can board now, sir."

"Thank you, Airman," they intoned and headed for the plane.

Brothers, thought the Airman as he followed their progress across the ramp and into the plane.

At the head of the boarding stairs they were met by Captain King and Major Reigle. After the round of introductions they were led into the E-3. "Gentleman, come this way. On your right…"

An hour and a half later they were climbing down the boarding stairs, only slightly the worse for wear, thought Moose.

"That's more than I ever wanted to know about that big piece of aluminum," sighed Moose.

"Me too," sighed Herdman. "Why'd you keep asking all those questions?"

"I wanted to appear interested, and, I didn't want to let the family down for crying out loud. I just didn't think he'd go on and on. They're really proud of it. Let's hope they find that package. That was a great idea, having that extra sack stuck up your sleeve. Come on, lets get something tall and cold."

They passed the Airman who was still guarding the plane. "Good afternoon, sir," he said as he came to attention, noting that the tall Major still had the package from the base exchange.

The two Tomcats throttled back momentarily as the C-130 commenced a shallow turn to the left. The two Navy fighters came right and Fancy pushed the throttles forward to max military. Both planes accelerated and began to climb, wings going to the full sweep position as they picked up speed.

"Gator, I've got a target, she's just turned back to course 295, 20,000, at 65 miles, the good news. Eagles are still comin', now at 55 miles."

"Bagger, I'll discourage the Eagles."

"Roger, I'll shoot the big guy and then come and rescue you."

Fancy stole a glance over at Bagger's Tomcat as he continued climbing on his course for the Sentry.

Fancy grinned. "Rhino, coming left, going zone five, hang on tight, and lock 'em up."

"Coming left and we've got 'em." Mirabal was immediately pushed back and down into his seat as the afterburner kicked in and the big plane accelerated like a rocket ship into the azure blue sky.

"I've got 'em on our nose, but they're still out of range," said Fancy, as he thanked the inventors of the heads up display. By this time the F-14 was accelerating like a run away freight train. Astonishingly, the four Eagles were still coming on, straight and level. "What's the matter with these guys."

"It looks like they're trying to make up their minds," groused Mirabal.

At that instant two of the Eagles broke away from the other two and started to accelerate away, toward Bagger and the E-3.

"We'll take those two going after Bagger!" Fancy said probably a bit louder than he intended. "I've got a visual—and a tone. It'll be a front quarter attack; we're at 20 degrees off- angle! I'm going with the 'winder! Got'im locked! Shooting! Shooting!" He envisioned the two AIM-9 Sidewinders coming off the rails and streaking toward their prey. In an instant the F-14 had closed the distance behind the two F-15s.

"We're coming right, coming right. He felt the weight of 7g's pushing him back and down into his seat, the "chaps" on his legs inflating, forcing the blood back into his upper extremities, or at least trying to. "Keep on him, Rhino, don't let him get out of sight." Now he sounded more like a wrestler in a hammer-lock applied by a three hundred pound gorilla. Things started to go to black and white, then they were out of the turn. Fancy shook his head trying to clear it, and his vision returned to normal—more or less.

"I lost him!" shouted Mirabal. "Damn!"

"Three—o' clock, high, he's comin' down! We're going vertical and coming right!" Fancy racked the Tomcat into a climbing right hand turn as he lit the afterburners—the two planes coming together at over 1,000 miles per hour. "I've got a tone! Shooting!" For the second time in just under three minutes, Fancy figured, he'd shot the Eagle down for a second time.

"Coming left!" he grunted as he rolled 270 degrees right and then turning left as he completed the roll. The F-14 picked up speed as he headed back down. the sky was empty. He leveled off at 10,000 feet.

"Let's go find Bagger. What have you got on the scope?"

"It looks like the E-3 range forty miles, twenty-five angels, at 500 knots. Uh, it looks like they'll be turning, they're almost at Beatty. Yeah, they're starting their turn."

"Any sign of Bagger?"

"Uh, yeah, there he is, I think, and if that's him, he's got company. Looks like two Eagles coming up on his six."

Fancy shoved the throttles forward.

"Bagger's turning into them, he probably took a sparrow shot at the E-3."

Fancy took a quick look at the fuel situation and wasn't thrilled with what he saw. Zone five sure ate into your fuel in a hurry, 9,000 pounds wasn't a lot.

"Twenty-eight miles," called Rhino. "The Eagles are going to squeeze him."

"Feel free to jump in any time," called a calm Bailey. "There's more than enough to go around."

" Twenty-four miles," announced Rhino.

"Okay, let's take the guy on the right," said Fancy. "I've got him at twenty-miles and closing." Now, thought Fancy, he's got to decide who he wants to dance with.

"Seventeen miles," intoned Mirabal. "Looks like he's going to come after us. Fourteen miles."

Fancy strained to get a visual, even though he knew it just wasn't possible—yet.

"Uh, you see anything yet, Gator?"

"Not yet, I've got 'em on the scope. Wait, maybe, yeah, I think I've got someting. Yeah, yeah, he's just off the nose not quite at one o' clock, level. I'm going to stay nose to nose."

The two planes hurtled toward each other at over 1,000 knots.

"Rhino, I'm going to pass as close to him as possible so we can take out as much lateral separaration as possible. That way he's going to have more trouble converting to our six." *But,* thought Gator *if this were the real thing both our noses would be lit up like Christmas trees—we'd definitely be going guns.*

"Rhino, going vertical."

Trying to imagine what that would be like Fancy pulled sharply up into the vertical to mess up his tracking situation. As the Tomcat went straight up he strained to see the F-15, hoping he had gone into a horizontal turn or had just run. Of course that was wishful thinking.

As Fancy looked over the back of his ejection seat he saw the F-15, canopy to canopy barely 300 feet away. Fancy found himself looking right into the Eagle driver's eyes. If I went to afterburners I would be right out in front of him and I would be giving him a predictable flight path thought Fancy, trying to stay at least one jump ahead in the game.

"This guy is pretty good," Fancy grunted to his back seater. "We'll get him now." Pulling down to match the Eagle's speed, Fancy watch and waited until the F-15 had committed his nose down. Immediately he pulled up into him and rolled over the top placing the F-14 at the Eagle's five o' clock. Even though they were too close to fire a missile and they were at an angle-off his tail, the maneuver had placed them in an advantageous position. Over confidence was beginning to replace fear.

Pulling down, holding top rudder, to press for a gun shot, the Eagle pulled into them. "Damn, this guy is good!" shouted Fancy. He had just used the same maneuver I used, pulling up into me and forcing an overshoot thought Fancy as he strained to keep the Eagle in sight.

Both planes were now in the classic rolling scissors. As the Eagle committed his nose Fancy pulled into him.

Good basic training thought Fancy. If my opponent had his nose too high, I could snap down, using the one G to advantage, then run out to his six o' clock before he could get turned around and get in range.

Both planes were slowing and Fancy knew it was time to get out. He remembered that Lieutenant Dave Frost, an instructor at Oceana, had told him to watch for his nose to raise, when he did get it just a bit too high, pull into him again. Then go zone five afterburner, Rhino and Fancy pulled out in front of the Eagle, Fancy figured it was at least two miles, out of range of guns, but not a Sidewinder.

"Going vertical," he said as the G forces pressed him back into his seat. With their energy back Fancy made a 60° nose up vertical turn back into the pressing Eagle. Again he climbed right after them.

"He's comin' hard, Gator!"

Fancy lit the afterburners again and the big Tomcat outzoomed the Eagle again. Again the the two planes went into a rolling scissors.

Once more they were forced to disengage as advantage and disadvantage traded sides. As the F-14 blasted away once again to regain energy, Rhino came up and said, "How you doing, Gator? You okay up there. This guy really knows what he's doin'. You think we ought to call it a day.

Fancy felt himself start to go into a blind rage. Just the idea of some blue suiter having stood off their attacks, let alone having managed to gain an advantage on them twice, was almost too much.

"Hang on, Rhino, we're gonna get this guy!"

"Go get him, Gator, I'm right behind you."

Rhino could tell that Mirabal was all over the pit trying to keep the F-15 in sight and I was really glad for that second pair of eyes.

Once again the two planes met head on, only this time the F-15 had a slightly different offset to take advantage of his guns. Fancy figured this was the time for something slightly different on his part, his mind just coming up with a last ditch idea. Fancy pulled hard toward his aircraft and yanked the throttles back to idle, popping the speed brakes at the same time. The Eagle shot out in front of them for the first time. Their nose was 60º above the horizon with with the airspeed winding down in almost no time. Again Fancy pushed the throttles past the detents into full burner in order to hold their position. The Eagle pilot attempted to roll up on his back above them. Using only the rudder to keep from stalling, Fancy rolled to the Eagle's blind side. The F-15 driver attempted to reverse his roll, but in doing so stalled the plane momentarily and his nose started to fall through placing the Tomcat at his six, but still too close for a missile shot.

"Going to guns! Shooting! Shooting!" Fancy called out.

The Eagle pitched over the top and started to go straight down. Fancy let him go and watched while the Eagle pulled out and headed back to Nellis or the regeneration point.

"Gator, check ten o' clock. Eagle rolling in on us."

It was a good thing Rhino had his eyes open. They had 600 knots now as Fancy pulled nose high into the attacking plane. "Let's get another one," he told Rhino.

The words were no more than just out of his mouth when he heard Bagger. "Gator, get out of there, there's two more on your tail at seven."

Just then Fancy glanced up to see another F-14 coming straight at them and then pass just over the top of their canopy. His wild flying must have done the trick because the two Eagles separated and got out of the way. They looked like fleas jumping off a dog.

Taking a quick look at their fuel gage, Fancy knew it was time for them to head back to Coyote North, and the sooner the better. Fancy rolled the big fighter and they headed for home.

Colonel Dean Woldfogel, Chief of Staff for the commanding officer, General Dennis Smith, of the vast Nellis Air Force Base, pushed himself back from his desk. He puffed out his cheeks and slowly let the air out. Cocking his head in the direction of the flight line, he ran his hand throught his receeding hairline, and listened to a departing F-16 as it blasted off into the hot Nevada air. Right now he would trade the eagles on his collar tabs to be able to strap in and go cheek to cheek with…shoot, anybody, he thought to himself. Flying a desk was harder than he thought it would be. However, it would be good for his career. Nuts, he thought. In choosing this career path he had been trying to save his marriage. Then she had walked out anyway. Some trade-off.

He turned back in the direction of his desk when he heard the phone on his desk buzz. He picked it up and growled, "Yes?"

His, aide, Captain Anne McCarthy answered, "Sir, Lieutenant Colonel Ellis, OIC with the two E-3s from Tinker, is on the horn. He sounds a little excited."

"Put him through Captain, thank you."

"Colonel Ellis, what can I do for you.?"

"Sir, I just got a message from the E-3 we have orbiting between Lathrop Wells and Beatty. It seems that two F-14s from the Redland forces broke through and got close enough to shoot it down. Are we considered out, sir?"

Colonel Woldfogel, in addition to his other duties, was the last word in disputes between the two forces. "When did you stop providing an escort for the Big Eye, Colonel?"

"Sir, it just hasn't been an issue for so long, so we decided we could use our assets in a more offensive posture. We got complacent."

"You did," grinned Woldfogel. "Yes, you're out. Are you going to launch your backup?"

There was a long pause before Colonel Ellis answered. "Uh, at the same time they were shooting down our E-3, someone placed a bomb on the backup. We're also wondering what the status of that plane is, sir."

"Bomb? What kind of bomb. What's the damage, Colonel!" barked Woldfogel, sitting straight up in his chair, fearing that he would have to explain milions in damage to one of the E-3s.

Another pause. "Colonel, there was no actual bomb or damage. Two visitors placed an alarm clock on board the backup. It went off with a little puff of smoke. It also came with a note letting us know what the function of the alarm clock was."

Colonel Woldfogel took a deep breath of air and let it out slowly, grinning to himself, actually almost laughing out loud. "Well, Colonel, it looks like your boys are out of action. How long would it take to bring in another E-3, say if you were operating in Saudi Arabia?"

"At least twenty-four hours, sir. Maybe a bit longer depending on the status of the birds, sir."

Woldfogel already knew the answer, but he wanted it confirmed. Ellis wasn't blowing smoke at least. "Okay, Colonel, they're out of action for thirty-six hours starting now."

"Yes, sir," Ellis replied, "thirty-six hours from now. Thank you for your time, sir."

"Good day, Colonel," replied Woldfogel, as he hung up the phone.

Fancy greased the F-14 on to Coyote North's runway. He was suddenly aware of the rubbery, oxygen mask taste in his mouth. Suddenly he felt very thirsty. That was par for the course. It seemed that after any ACM he felt as if he could drink a barrel of water. As he pulled in to the parking space and shut down the engines, he pulled off the mask and raised his visor.

Shrader's face popped up above the canopy rail. "How'd it go, sir?"

"Pretty well, we think." He twisted around in his seat. "Rhino, how'd we do?"

"Oh, man, we kicked some ass and we had some fun."

Shrader beamed. Their victory became his. Since their successes depended on how well the fighters performed mechanically, Fancy wanted to spread any success he and Rhino has as far as it would go and Shrader was a good place to start.

Fancy climbed out of the place and dropped down to the very warm flight line. Rhino followed pulling off his skull cap.

"Hey, I wasn't second-guessing you up there. I just wanted you to know I was with you, no matter what you decided to do. That Eagle driver was good, but not near as good as you were."

"I know, man. You did a great job. And that guy was good. You made all the difference," said Fancy as he slapped Mirabal on the back and put his arm around him. "We're a team."

Bagger and Walrus Carpenter walked up. "Boy oh boy, we did it. I hope I didn't pucker you up when I came after the guys that were on you. Nothing else came to mind."

"You got my attention okay, but the end justified the means. Thanks, one more time."

"It's the least I could do. Besides I may want you to be my best man in the near future."

"What?" responded Fancy and Mirabal together.

"You didn't pop the question when you went over to the 130 to make sure things were okay, did you?" asked Fancy.

"No, but I thought about it," grinned Bagger.

Just then the relative silence was broken by the arrival of the F-14s. They turned as one to watch them land. "Looks like everyone is back," remarked Walrus Carpenter to no one in particular. No matter what the mission it was always a relief to see everyone come home.

"Come on," said Bagger, "let's grab something to drink before we find out what's going on the rest of the day. I'm so dry I feel like I could spit dust."

"Maybe we can find out what's up with the E-3s," chipped in Mirabal.

With one last look at the arriving planes, the four aviators headed for the "O" Club, by way of the personal equipment room.

Upon arrival at the club, Carpenter volunteered to get everyone something to drink from the bar. Everyone else drew up chairs around one of the battered tables. "Man, that was fun," grinned Bagger. "I didn't think there would be that much turbulence though. How 'bout you Gator?"

"There was more than I thought there would be. I was beginning to think maybe we should pass on it. Losing three planes just wouldn't have been worth it, but…" his voice trailed off as he sighed, stretched, and put his hands behind his head.

"That was a nice move you put on those Eagles, Bagger," said Mirabal with a huge grin on his face. "What do you think they're going to say about the E-3?" he asked no one in particular.

Fancy shrugged. "Your guess is as good as mine. But, for my money, that's what the bad guys would do if they had the chance. It seems only right that they rule that it's down. It should be real interesting as to how they rule on the E-3 at Nellis though."

The quiet discussion was interrupted by Matsen and Winkleman. "We're going to head on over to my office and see what we can find out. Let me get something to drink and we'll get back ASAP." announced Winkleman, as he leaned over the table, resting himself on his hands. "Colonel Woldfogel, the referee, should have made his ruling by now." With that the two men turned on their heel and headed toward the bar.

By that time the rest of the 64th Aggressors and the F-14 drivers and RIOs were entering the club bringing a loud din to the here to fore quiet building. It seems everyone was dry and the bar was going to do a land office business.

Poncho and Big Wave brought their soft drinks over to the table pulling up chairs as they did so. "It looks like you two had yourself quite a morning. How was it?" asked Poncho.

"There was more turbulence than we figured on, and I didn't think they would pick us up that quick. Other than that…" Bagger shrugged.

Fancy and Bailey tipped their cans together in a mock toast. "Of course," continued Fancy, "Bagger and Walrus got some Eagles off our back when we were coming back to help him."

At the same time the pilots and RIOs at Coyote were congratulating themselves on a job well done, Moose and Stretch Herdman were walking down the flight line doing some congratulating of their own.

"I think we put some hurt on those guys," said Herdman.

"I do to," replied Moose. "Say, I've got to get back to Coyote North. Those guys can't get much done without me there, you know."

"Man, I believe it," said Herdman. I think we can grab a T-38 and I can run you out and get a little air time. Let's mosey down to our equipment room so I can get into something comfortable."

As the two pilots walked down the line, Moose noticed a large Air Force pilot break off from a knot of pilots in front of an F-15 and enter one of the heads located along the flight line. "Stretch, I need to take a whiz. If I come out of there on the run, can you buy me a little time?"

"Uh, sure," said Herdman, more than a little puzzled.

"I'll be quick. If we get separated, where shall we hook up?"

"Building 95, just up the line."

Moose started toward the latrine and noticed an airman, who must be on somebody's list, thought Moose, wielding a hose around the building.

"Excuse me, son," said Moose, did a large pilot type person just go in there?" This guy should stay out of the chow line—for about a month thought Moose.

The rotund Air Force enlisted man looked at Moose and answered. "Yes, sir, a pilot just went in."

"Great," said Moose. "Now, if you'll just loan me that hose for about two minutes..." he let his voice trail off. "And here's ten bucks, because you look pretty hungry to me. Okay?"

The man studied Moose for several seconds. "Okay, sir, he said as he handed Moose the hose.

Moose immediately kinked the hose, shutting off the flow of water. He walked quietly to the building and inched open the door. There were the usual urinal and three stalls. Only one stall had its door shut and the building was otherwise unoccupied. Bending down Moose could see a pair of steel toed boots, much like his own. Moving as quietly as he could, he moved stealthily toward the closed stall door. Taking a deep breath he kicked open the door and was met by the surprised face of Katzenberger who appeared stunned by the sudden intrusion. "Trash my plane will you!" shouted Milwood, as he turned the full force of the hose on the still surprised and immobile Air Force pilot.

By the time Moose figured he had done enough damage, he let go of the hose and tore out of the building passing a quizzical looking Herdman on the way out.

As the enraged Air Force pilot gathered his wits, clothes, and very little dignity, he started to run after his tormentor. Just as he reached the door, Herdman walked in, bashing Katzenberger square in the face, knocking him to the floor as he did so.

By now Katzenberger was not only wet, but his nose was bleeding profusely. Herdman bent down to help him up.

"Get out of my way! Where did he go? I'm going to kill that little bastard!"

"Major, what ever are you talking about? Why, you're all wet. What happened in there?"

"Geez, are you blind? Can't you see what that little mother did to me with that hose?" All this sounded a little muffled because by now Katzenberger was not able to breathe through his nose.

"Who was that, anyway?' questioned Herdman in his most interested voice. "He should be arrested!"

"Arrested my ass! I'm going to kill him!"

"Who is him?" asked Herdman again, all the while hoping that Moose was long gone. This guy was definitely pissed.

"He's one of those Navy fighter pukes. I'm really going to tear that guy a new asshole! Get out of the way!" With that the enraged Air Force pilot pushed his way past Herdman and raced out on to the flight line—looking both right and left for the recently departed Navy pilot.

By this time Moose, moving just slightly below the speed of sound, had reached Building 95. Finding a door he tore inside and looking for something he could use for a club if he was cornered.

By the time Herdman had excused himself from the bleeding and wet Katzenburger, and had directed him in the opposite direction from building 95, he had caught his breath and was wondering if he could wangle a transfer to the Navy. He definitely had concluded that he really liked their style. Open the door the building of refuge, he called out, "Moose, the coast is clear. That guy is headed in the opposite direction. We can follow the trail of blood if you want to."

Moose peered around the corner of a cubicle. "Bleeding? I only hosed the guy off. I never laid a glove on the guy." Herdman tried to look contrite. "Ah, the fact was that he seemed to have run into the door at exactly the same time I was coming in. To say the least, he's really bent out of shape." Moose extended his hand and started to laugh. "Oh man, I wish I could have seen that."

By now Herdman was beginning to see the humor, as well as the big picture, of what had just happened and he began to laugh too. It wasn't long before both men were laughing hysterically—the more they laughed the funnier the situation became.

At last, with tears of laughter streaming down their faces they staggered to a well worn government issue couch and collapsed upon it.

"Listen", said Herdman, "we better get you out to Coyote North. I don't think I can stand much more fun. And I know a certain Air Force pilot can't." With that, both men dissolved into laughter again.

Thirty minutes later both men were on the flight line looking over the T-38 Talon that would take them out to Coyote North.

"It seems to be altogether," smiled Herdman. "You ready to get back to the war?"

"Yeah," replied Moose, "but there's one thing I've just got to see."

"What's that," inquired Herdman, with a puzzled look on his face.

"I want to know how in the world you get all of your body into that cockpit. Personally, I don't think it can be done—at least without some pain involved."

Herdman immediately slapped Milwood on the back that all but sent him to the ground, laughing heartily, "It's no sweat." With that he climbed into the cockpit as an amazed Milwood watched Herdman fold himself into the cockpit. Ten minutes later they were airborne, headed to Coyote North.

"He's back," called out Big Wave as Moose and his new found friend and conspirator walked in the "club". "How'd it go at Nellis, Moose?"

"We planted the bomb," smiled Moose. "And," he paused for the dramatic effect, "even better, I…"

Herdman cleared his throat.

"I mean we," Moose hurriedly corrected himself, gesturing toward Herdman, and hoping Herdman wouldn't honor him with a whack on the back, "put the big hurt on that bleep that decorated my plane."

"Is this going to cost us anything, Moose?" growled Matsen. "I thought we had an understanding."

Moose drew himself up to his full height. "Sir, it was pure poetry. Pure poetry. Wouldn't you agree, Mr. Herdman?"

"Pure poetry, Mr. Milwood."

With that both men again dissolved into gales of laughter as they tried to tell the story. By the end of the tale, which had only been slightly embellished, even Matsen was laughing.

The remainder of the day consisted of two hops. The absence of the E-3 proved to be an advantage, albeit slight, for the forces of Redland. The powerful AN/APG-71 on the F-14s gave the aggressors somewhat of an advantage. The F-5s and the Tomcats were able to send more F-15s and F-16s out to the regeneration point than in the previous two proceeding days combined. Morale skyrocketed.

# 4

Fancy was reclining on his rack running over what had happened in the air that day. He felt he had flown well, maybe as well as he had ever flown in his entire career. *Don't get big-headed he thought, tomorrow is another day and things can go south in a hurry.*

Bagger came in and flopped down on his bunk. "I'm beat. A good kind of beat—but beat none the less," he sighed. Turning on his side he grinned at Fancy. "Wasn't she great today? Man, she can flat out fly. Can't she?"

"She can," Fancy intoned. "She is one sierra hotel pilot. You know, she can probably do things like climb mountains too. Nothing would surprise me about that woman."

Bagger sat quickly sat up and stared and his friend. "How did you know she liked to climb?"

"I just sensed that about her," Fancy said, trying desperately to keep a straight face. "She just seemed to be that kind of lady. Strong—yet feminine. A woman of the nineties. It wouldn't surprise me if she even wrote poetry."

"She does—both those things. How did you know that?" By now Bagger was sitting up staring intently at Fancy.

Fancy couldn't keep his straight face any longer and he started to laugh.

"Come on," pleaded Bagger, "how did you know that?"

Fancy stopped laughing. "I was talking to Winkleman. It seems they were somewhat of an item."

"Winkleman?"

"Yup, but it didn't go very far. She told him his intentions had to be strictly honorable. Did you know she was a Mormon? Your intentions better be honorable or you can forget about things going very far."

Bagger ran his hand throught his hair. "A Mormon? She doesn't look like a Mormon—does she?"

"Well, what does a Mormon look like?"

"I dunno know—kind of a withered pioneer person with more that one husband?"

"It's the other way around I think. Husbands had more than one wife."

"Oh, well, I knew that," grinned Bagger. "I guess I could learn to be a Mormon."

"Um-hum. No drinking, smoking, carousing around. You wouldn't last five minutes."

"Seriously," said Bagger, "

I think I could make some changes in my life for someone like her. She's so different from anyone I've ever known. It's way different than just meeting a good lookin' babe. How did you know about Janice. Maybe, I shouldn't bring that up. If I've stepped over the line…?"

"No, no, that's okay. I don't know how to explain it, I just knew. Hey, follow your heart and nothing else further south," said Fancy. "She could be the one. Geez, next we're going to talking about who's going to drive to the senior prom."

"What about you?" asked Bailey. You think you may give the great institution of marriage another try."

Fancy was silent for several seconds. "I don't think so. Before you came in I was thinking that when I was up today, it was probably the best flying that I had done—ever. Whether it's been no booze or maybe no other distractions, just flying, it just felt great, almost like I was in a zone. Everything just kind of slowed down and I could see the big picture. This is what I really want to do and there's no doubt in my mind about it. When I was married it seemed to be just distracting enough to keep me from doing my best. At least that's what I think. Nope, I'm going to concentrate on flying, period."

Bagger pushed himself up on one elbow, studied his friend, shrugged, smiled, and said, "Do you want to go back to the club and swap lies with the blue suiters?"

"No, I just want to get some shut-eye. You're not the only one who feels a little older."

"Actually, I was hoping you'd say that," said Bagger as he fell back down on the bed, stretched out, sighed, and shut his eyes. It wasn't long before they were both fast asleep.

Somewhere, Fancy thought, he had heard someone describe ACM, as a game of chess. "Bull," grunted Fancy as he tried to shake the F-15 Eagle of his six. It's like billiards—all angles, and lets face it, this guy's got the angle.

Funny how things can go delta sierra so quick. One second he had a perfect gun shot on an F-16 when Mirabal called out the present problem at their deep eight and coming hard. *I took the shot and that nano second is costing me—us* Fancy corrected himself.

"This guy's all over us," called Rhino.

"Yeah, tell me something I don't know," Fancy grunted back. Fancy continued to rack the big fighter hard to the right as he rolled into a rolling scissors trying to get away from the Eagle.

"Going vertical!" he called as he pulled the Tomcat up into the sun. "Might as well make it miserable for him too." He felt as if there were several large men—men hell, more like elephants trying to push him into one corner of the cockpit. The RAW gear was going absolutely ape now and Fancy knew that the Eagle had him on a platter.

"F-14 over Cedar Peak. You're a mort. Come level at 12 grand and head for the regeneration point, heading 280. Copy?"

Fancy willed himself to wait a few seconds before he replied. "Copy, Blackjack. Coming to 280 at 12,000. Roger that," he grumbled.

As they rolled wings level Fancy scanned the sky in front of him. What he saw in that instant brought an involuntary gasp of horror. The F-5 on his nose climbing from his starboard side suddenly hit almost nose to nose with another F-15.

"Knock if off! Knock it off! We've had a midair." Upon hearing Knock it off, all activity was to cease until whatever situation that caused the call in the first place was resolved.

Fancy scanned the sky as he followed what was now a tumbling mass of unrecognizable metal and…Fancy didn't want to think about it, what was trapped inside. There were no chutes. He thought he could hear Mirabal pounding on the instrument panel in the pit. Now other calls of Knock it off and Mayday were filling their headphones.

"Blackjack, to all aircraft over Cedar Peak. Return to base. I repeat, return to base."

With a heavy heart Fancy turned the F-14 toward Coyote North.

It was a somber group of Air Force and Navy pilots that gathered in the Coyote North O' Club. Small knots of pilots gathered around the battered furniture talking in hushed tones, about their fallen comrades. After something like a needless loss of life, it didn't matter what color uniform you wore. Everyone realized that death knew no boundaries.

Commander Matsen walked in and headed toward the pensive Navy pilots. He sighed as he sat down, running his fingers through his thick black hair. "You've probably heard it was the XO of the Aggressors, the guy with the blond hair, Devil Mattox. The wreckage came down more or less in one piece. Gator, you and Mirabal saw it happen so I guess you can appreciate that fact. All three bodies have been recovered—that Eagle was an E model. It's a hell of a way to wind things up here. It just makes me so damn mad." He pushed back his chair and rubbed his eyes. "I'm just glad it wasn't any of you."

Poncho replied, "Frankly, I'm glad too. It makes me ill that it had to happen at all, but that's the business we're in."

"Sometimes it's a pretty sick business, but I wouldn't be anywhere else doing anything else," said Killer.

"Is there going to be any kind of service?" asked Rhino.

"Yeah, on Sunday at Nellis. The Eagle drivers have some relatives that need to be flown in," answered Matsen. "I already talked to Robinson and he okayed a representative from our squadron to stay for the service. Any volunteers?"

Bagger started to say something, but thought better of it and drew back into the group of pilots. In the silence that followed, all eyes seemed to fixate on him.

After a few moments Matsen asked, "Well Bagger, I get the feeling you'd like to stay."

Bagger stiffened and stepped forward. "Yes, sir, I would, but not for what some of you may be thinking. If there's anyone else who wants to stay, say so. If not, I'd be proud to represent the Navy and VF-124—but I'd be lying if I didn't want to stay for an ulterior motive."

The silence told Matsen all he needed to know. "Okay Bagger, you've got the job. This of course was the last mission for us at Red Flag, accident or not. We'll let the maintenance department tweak the birds and we'll fly back to Miramar tomorrow at 0930. Make sure you've filled out the gripe sheet if there's anything wrong with your plane. Gator, someone's going to want to talk to you about what you saw. Be available."

"One other thing, there's going to be an air show going on on Saturday. We have to supply four crews to stand by a plane and answer questions from the folks that paid for 'em. Fancy, you and Mirabal are up for Saturday from 0800 to 1200 hours. Killer, you'll take the afternoon shift on Saturday, 1200 hours to to 1700. Poncho you get Sunday morning and Big Wave you finish up in the afternoon. Wear your green bags. The skipper and all the higher ups at the head shed want no problems, so look sharp. These folks are going to hold you up as role models for their kids—so don't let anybody down—especially this squadron. any questions?"

"So much for sleeping in," he said as he turned to Rhino.

"It's kind of fun. We can do a half day standing on our head," replied Mirabal. "Besides, sometimes you get to meet some babes."

Fancy snorted his disbelief, while shaking his head. "Uh—huh, right."

Matsen continued, "Take the rest of the day and go over the tapes that will be coming out from Nellis. take a good look at them and try to learn something from them. This isn't the first time or the last time something like this is going to happen. Let's try to make sure we put the odds in our favor. We've got a long cruise coming up. I want to make sure, as does the skipper that everybody comes back. We can start that process today by looking at those tapes."

Later that afternoon Fancy, Bagger, Rhino, and Killer Stevens walked outside into the inferno of the August heat toward their quarters. "Well, Killer, did you learn anything from watching all those tapes this afternoon?"

"I sure did," grinned Killer. "I'm keepin' my head on a swivel every time I step into that big beast. Shoot, I didn't even see it happen and it's scared the wee out of me. Any second thoughts for you, Gator?"

"It sure got my attention. I know I sure don't ever want to see anything like that again. It's somethin' I'll never forget, it was so quick, not to mention violent. That's the most violent thing I've ever seen."

Fancy turned to Bagger, "You seem pretty quiet, you okay?"

Bagger pursed his lips and let a good deal of air out. It was several more seconds before he spoke. "I never really thought that it could happen to me. Part of me is still telling me it won't, but another louder voice is starting to make itself heard. Living to a ripe old age is something I'm thinking about all of a sudden."

"Living to a ripe old age with anyone in particular or just you and your dog?" queried Fancy, probably more seriously than he meant to be.

Bagger stopped. "I don't think I want to grow old alone. Especially in the light of the events earlier today."

"You sound like your pretty serious about that Air Force Captain, Bagger," said Killer. "She really must be something. I never thought I'd see the day when you might go off the market. There'll be hearts breaking all over West Pac."

Bagger grinned, "You know, when you put it like that—, it, well, it just sounds right. Man, it's just unbelievable how quickly your life can change."

He paused. "I'm not making light of what happened up there today; I hope you know that."

"We do," replied Fancy, " and, yeah it can happen that fast, and, I'm glad it's happening to you."

All three of the men paused as they watched an F-5 touch down and start its roll out.

"But, I don't want to leave this either," said Bagger.

"Man," grinned Killer, "if you're talking about this place, you've got to get out more."

"Come on," said Fancy, "the soft drinks are on me."

The flight back to Miramar was uneventful. Matsen had reminded them that he didn't want to get bounced on the way back the way they had taken out the F-16s on the way to Nellis. No one else did either and the trip back was subdued and quiet. No one seemed to mind.

# 5

Fancy and Mirabal walked slowly from VF—124's hanger across the flight line. When they had departed for Nellis it had been wall-to-wall F-14s. Now there was a grandstand, for what Fancy thought, must be several thousand people at least. Instead of Tomcats, there was a myriad of planes and helicopters, from the very latest in Uncle Sam's arsenal to the relics of World War I.

"Shoot, I wish I'd brought my camera," grumbled Fancy. "This is really great. Look at that Forker triplane. The Red Baron himself."

"Who?" asked Mirabal.

"You know, Count Baron Von Ritchoven. The big stud in World War I. I think he bagged at least eighty planes."

"Good thing he didn't meet up with Snoopy," smiled Mirabal.

Fancy laughed. "Geez, look at that! An F-8. That's not from here is it?"

"Nah, belongs to some outfit in Arizona. It's probably one of the few fighters in private hands. They do a lot of testing of things."

"What kind of things?"

"Beats me."

"I wonder if they'd mind if we took it for a spin. Boy, I'd like to get my hands on that."

"That's all you hear about that bird. It's the most tits plane for air-to-air period. Last of the true gunfighters." continued Rhino.

After passing Mustangs, Hellcats, Phantoms, an A-10 Warthog, a pristine B-25 and a classic B-17, they came to their F-14.

Fancy stopped and took a long look at the Tomcat. Adjusting his sunglasses, he ducked under the yellow tape that separated the plane from the public. Those other planes had their place in history, he thought, but the studliest of them all was sitting right here. He did a quick walk around to make sure the engine intakes were covered and secure. Shaking the inert AIM-7s and AIM-9s to make sure they weren't going to fall off, he found he was actually looking forward to the day. People were starting to come in the gates. Somebody said people lined up in their cars as early as 0300 to get a good seat along the flight line to see the air show.

Smells from the many food booths were starting to permeate his senses. Now he wished he'd grabbed something to eat. *I'll slide over and get something later he thought to himself.*

The morning was passing quickly and he and Rhino had been busy dispensing information about their bird. "Is it fun to fly? How fast does it go? Which one of you has to sit in the backseat? Are those bombs?

Fancy found himself enjoying the give and take immensely. The public was proud of the armed services. More than a few people had thanked them for what they did and said how proud they were of the Navy and pilots in particular.

He and Rhino had just finished shaking the hand of an elderly gentleman who had told them he had flown off the carrier *Essex* during the Second World War. Fancy followed him as he was swallowed up in the crowd which had grown considerably. His stomach had just let it be known that it needed immediate attention, when he felt someone pulling on the leg of his flight suit. Looking down he found himself looking into a mouth full of braces and a big smile.

"Hi," he said. "What can I do for you?"

"Well, for starters, how about a ride in your plane. It is yours isn't it?"

"This plane belongs to our squadron. Nobody really gets to have their own personal plane."

"How 'bout it? Can I have a ride. Are you a pilot, or do you sit in the back?"

"First," demanded Fancy, "you have to tell me your name."

"Amanda, Amanda Thorn. Do I get a ride or not?"

"I'm afraid not. As much as I'd like to, we're just not allowed to do it. What I could do is bring you in here for a private tour," Fancy said as he bent down to meet the girl's solemn face. "Maybe, you had better ask your dad or mom if it's okay with them, though."

"I don't have a dad. But I have a mom and she's not married and she's really pretty. Are you married?" The answers and questions came out at machine gun pace.

"No..." Fancy started to say.

"Amanda, where have you been? You just can't go running off that way."

Yes, she did have a mother and yes, she was pretty, Fancy thought as he started to stand up, unable not to notice the very shapely legs. The shapely legs were part and parcel of a very attractive woman. As Fancy reached a standing position he was met by the largest, deepest, brown eyes he had ever seen, crowned by auburn hair pulled back in a simple pony tail. Only one word seemed to come to mind as he realized that this very lovely lady had been extending her hand toward him for several seconds.

"Hi, Cody Thorn," she said. "And no, we are not here trolling for men, are we Amanda?"

"Well, no, I'm sure, uh..." Fancy stammered. *Smooth*, he thought to himself, *real smooth*.

"Come on, Amanda, this nice gentleman has to get back to...?"

"As a matter of fact, I was just going to give Amanda a little closer tour of the plane. Of course, you're invited too," he said as he lifted the yellow tape.

"Are you sure it's all right? I wouldn't want to get you in any kind of trouble."

"Oh, you won't, besides that's what we're here for today."

She stepped under the tape and Fancy felt his heart beat faster.

Amanda was already over by the F-14 looking up at the names painted on the side under the canopy rail. "What's your call sign?"

"How do you know about call signs, anyway?"

"She's watched the movie Top Gun so many times I think she has it memorized," her mother said, shaking her head. "She's decided that she wants to fly Navy fighters."

"She is as smart as she looks," grinned Fancy. "My call sign is Gator."

"Gator? That's pretty funny. How'd you get that one?" asked Amanda as she came over and looked up at him.

"It's kind of a long story and it's not very interesting, really," Fancy shrugged.

"I'd like to hear about it," the girl demanded.

"Amanda, watch your manners, young lady." her mother scolded gently.

Fancy noticed that the relationship between the two was good—respectful with expectations. He liked the easy, but firm way that Amanda's mother talked to her.

"Gator," chimed in Mirabal, as he walked up to the tour group, "need any help here?"

"Amanda, Ms. Thorn, this is my RIO, Tony Mirabal, call sign Rhino."

Rhino shook hands with Amanda and her mother.

"You're the guy that sits in back. What do you do back there?"

"I'm glad you asked," replied Mirabal, "because I'm the guy that makes this whole thing work," he continued, drawing himself up to his full height. "Now, Gator gets us to where we need to be, with my help of course. Then I do everything else to shoot the bad guys down. Gator, is what we RIOs call, the nose gunner."

Amanda looked from man to man, squinting, trying to figure out whether Rhino was putting her on. Finally, she concluded, "Are you sure that's the way it works?"

Rhino recoiled in mock horror. "Gator, tell this young lady how important I am. How you couldn't do anything without me."

"Actually," said Fancy, "he is important. He empties out the ash trays, makes sure the windshield is clean, tires have enough air, those kinds of things."

"I'm hurt," groaned Mirabal, feigning the beginning of a heart attack. "Oh, the shame of it all. I get no respect."

Fancy stooped down in front of Amanda. "The truth is, without Rhino, not much would happen. We're a team and he's very good at what he does back in the pit."

Rhino gave Fancy a good natured punch on the arm, and a wink. "I'll go work the crowd while you continue with your tour. Nice to have met you Mrs. Thorn."

"Cody, please," she said as the shook his hand again. "It was nice to meet you."

"By the way," he said, as he walked away, "I can vouch for Gator if you're wondering about him. He's a very sweet boy."

"Come on," grumped Fancy, "I'll tell you all about the AIM-9s." *I'm going to throttle that boy*, he thought to himself.

Thirty minutes later Fancy found himself running out of things to say. Even Amanda had run out of questions. Somehow he didn't want it to end.

"What do you think, Amanda? Would you still like to be a pilot and fly one of these?" he said as he gestured toward the plane.

"You know it!" she gushed. "I can't wait! How old do I have to be?"

"You could think about going to the Naval Academy. That way you could get a great education and learn to fly if you can meet all the academic and physical requirements. How are you doing in school?"

Amanda looked at her mother who all of a sudden felt a need to clear her throat, several times.

"Oh, mom, I'm doin' okay," she said, not very convincingly.

"I didn't say a thing, did I," her mother said as she hugged her from behind.

"Amanda?" questioned Fancy. "How are you doing?"

"She has had a little trouble remembering to bring home all her books, and getting all her work in on time. Amanda is very bright, but kind of lazy at times. She attends a year round school."

"Mom, who needs all that stuff anyway. Pilots don't, do they?" she asked, looking to Fancy for some help. "I mean, pilots fly. They don't need English or History."

Again Fancy stooped down to eye level. "At one time, that's exactly what I thought. But, you'd be surprised at how much I have to write. It surprised me. I even had to write an essay about why I wanted to fly for the Navy. Doing well in school helps your discipline and you have to have a great deal of that to be a pilot. Also, you need to be pretty good in math."

Amanda wrinkled up her nose. "Math, yuck. I hate math."

"You'll have to kiss your dream good-bye without an education and discipline. I didn't like to write or do grammar very much, but I did it and it paid off. Here I am flying the most awesome plane in the world and working with guys like Rhino. It's worth every bit of it, believe me."

"Listen, I can't promise anything, but I'll try to get you a ride in something, maybe it won't be one of these," he gestured, "but then again you never know. If you really work hard and do well in school. How about it?" he said extending his hand.

Amanda looked down at the ground, pondering the offer. After thinking it over for several seconds, she looked up and extended her own hand. They shook. "Okay, I will. I promise," she said seriously. "How will you know I'm doing better?"

"As a future Naval Officer, your word should be unquestioned. I'll have to take your word on it. Fair enough."

Amanda shook her head in the affirmative. "Why don't we shake hands again, but before we do, let's spit on our own hands first to really seal the bargain."

Fancy wrinkled his nose in mock horror. "I haven't done this since I was a kid. All right, let's do it."

"And how are you going to talk to me to find out if I'm doing better?" Amanda demanded, after she wiped her hand on the side of her shorts, as her mother grimaced.

"I better leave that up to you and your mother," said Fancy as he looked at Cody Thorn. She wan't grimacing now he noted. "She probably just doesn't give her address or phone number out to anyone? The bad news is that my squadron is getting ready for a deployment. We'll be gone for about six months.

The girl's face seemed to drop right to the ground.

Her mother came to the rescue. "You know, I think we could give out our address and our phone number. Naval Officers have to be trusted. They are, after all, gentlemen, as well as officers. Isn't that right, uh…"

"Lieutenant, I'm a Lieutenant," he stammered, blushing slightly. *Lt. Commander would sound so much better,* he thought.

What am I thinking about, she's not interested in me. "I could give you my mailing address, you could write me and I could write back to you."

"Mom, could we, please?"

"Sure, why not," her mother answered looking straight at Fancy, who felt himself getting red.

Reaching in to her purse, she wrote down an address and a phone number. Handing it to Fancy, she extended her pen and he wrote down the mailing address that would eventually get his mail to them.

"You know," he said, you should go home and write down your goals. Then they're really goals and not just something you just happened to say. I did it and it works."

"Come on Munchkin, we need to get going and let Lt. Fancy get back to his job. We can't monopolize him all day."

*Why not*, thought Fancy, as he shook both their hands. He watched them until they disappeared into the growing crowd. In fact he continued to look in that direction for more than several seconds. Change, he thought, it can happen so fast. For the first time in a long time he thought he might like a drink. As quickly as the thought came into his mind, he pushed it out. Things had been going too well, he wasn't going to do anything stupid, and that would be stupid with a capital S.

Rhino walked over and put his arm around him. "Brother, that was one attractive lady. And if I don't miss my guess, she found you somewhat attrractive."

"Ah, I don't think so. She must have a line a mile long wanting to date her." He sighed, "I just don't need any complications in my life right now."

Killer Stevens and his RIO climbed under the tape and approached Mirabal and Fancy. "This is one heck of a crowd. How's everything going. More to the point, any babes?"

Mirabal looked at Fancy, getting a look that said, please, don't bring it up. "Oh, you know the usual. There was an elderly gentleman that flew off the *Essex* in W W Two. He was interesting to talk to. Other than that, pretty routine. Come on, Gator, let's get out of here."

Fancy started to saunter off toward VF-124's hanger, while Rhino grinned at Killer, shook his head in the affirmative, and mouthed the word babe.

Killer raised his eyebrows, but decided to say nothing, as he and his RIO looked over the crowd gathered around the F-14. *Who knows*, Killer thought, *maybe lightning would strike twice*.

Fancy and Mirabal continued to make their way through the mass of people along the flight line. His mind was no longer focused on the vintage airplanes they were walking by. He found himself thinking, rather more deeply than he had planned, about Cody Thorn.

When he heard the voice calling his name, he figured that someone in the squadron was trying to get his attention. Then he realized that it was a feminine voice. "Lt. Fancy, Lieutenant."

Fancy scanned the crowd but couldn't make eye contact with anyone. He continued to search and was about ready to chalk it up to a case of two people named Fancy, when he heard the voice again. After doing a quick 360, he took one stride and almost knocked Cody Thorn off of her feet. Instinctively, he reached out to keep her from falling backward.

"Hello again," he stammered. "I didn't think I'd get to see you again so soon. Where's Amanda?"

"She's over in line to get us a hamburger. Listen, I really appreciate you taking the time to talk to her. I could tell that really meant a lot to her."

"To tell you the truth, I really enjoyed it. She seems like a bright little girl. Who knows, maybe I've recruited a great pilot for the Navy."

"You really made an impression on her. Frankly, not many people have done that, particularly most of the men in her life. I know you're busy though and, well, if you're too busy for her, I'd understand, and I'll try to let her down easy."

Without realizing what he was doing, Fancy took her hand in his. "I meant every word I said and I intend to keep my end of the bargain, not because I have to, but because I really want to."

They stared at each other for a few seconds and Fancy suddenly realized what he had done and dropped her hand like a hot potato. "I'm sorry, I didn't mean to…"

She smiled, with what seemed to Fancy, a definite twinkle in her eyes. "Actually, that's what I hoped you would say, but I just wanted to make sure and leave you an honorable way out if you needed it."

"My dad always said, 'Finish what you start', and that's what I intend to do," he said, more seriously than he had intended.

She thrust a piece of paper into his hand. With that same twinkle showing no sign of disappearing, "If you're not busy and you don't find me too bold, why don't you come for lunch tomorrow. We live in Carlsbad, just up the 5 Freeway. Here's the directions and a phone number if you get lost. Amanda would love it…and so would I."

Fancy remained silent for a few seconds wanting to accept on one hand and wondering whether or not he needed to complicate his life right now. "Well, I, I…"

The smile faded. "I'm so sorry, I didn't mean to come on so strong. Please, forgive me."

"No, no, I'd love to come. I'm feeling kind of light headed right now, must be the heat." "Yes, I'll come. What can I bring?"

"It's no secret that we both have a craving for cream soda. I'll supply the rest."

"Okay, count me in. What time?"

"How about 10:00, or just whenever you get here. We'll plan to eat around noon."

"I'm in. I mean, I'll be there, thank you."

"See you tomorrow," she said as she turned on heel and was once again swallowed up by the crowd.

"Come on lover boy, we've got to get you out of here so you can rest up for your big day," Mirabal grinned slapping him on the back. "Some people…"

Fancy slipped on his sunglasses, gave a deep sigh, putting his hands behind his head. "You know, maybe she just wants a friend."

"Uh huh, give me a break. Look at her. She's the genuine article, not like some of these camp followers you'll see here today," he said as he gestured toward the sea of humanity they were presently engulfed in.

"As a good, no make that a great RIO, and the person who is really in charge of this team, this could be a really terrific thing."

"You know, you really have a way with words."

"Yes, yes, I do," Mirabal replied in his most sagacious manner.

Fancy shook his head. "Is this the way things work in California, just slightly faster than the speed of light. I'm out of my league here."

"Remember, this is not only California but it's California in the nineties."

"Of course. That explains it. I feel so much better now."

On Sunday morning, just about the time Fancy was pulling away from the big yellow house, Bagger Bailey was sitting in a memorial service for the three Air Force pilots who had died in the midair collision. Seated next to him was Captain Wendy Kobayashi, and next to her, Captain Cassie Dodson. All were decked out in their respective service uniforms. Bagger had to admit to himself that Rowdy Kobayashi made the Air Force uniform look good. He'd always thought they looked more like something a bus driver would wear.

There had been several speakers, representing the squadron the F-15 drivers had been a part of, the 64th Aggressors, as well as the command structure of Red Flag. Bagger was impressed that the service was dignified, yet upbeat.

As Colonel Winkleman, the 64th's CO, was concluding, he said, "As you know Devil's last flight was made in conjunction with some of our brothers from the Navy. The day before Devil and I were talking about working with the Navy. Devil said that he was so impressed with the detachment from the Gunfighters, VF-124. Today, one of VF-124's pilots is here, representing that squadron. Their XO assured me that the whole detachment would be here were it not for the fact that they are getting ready to deploy to WESPAC for a six months cruise. Lt. Bailey, call sign Bagger, we'd all appreciate it you would say a few words to conclude this program."

Bagger felt the breath go out him. Public speaking was not one of his strengths. Wendy reached over and gave his hand a squeeze and smiled encouragement at him.

Taking a deep breath, he rose and walked to the podium at the front of the massive hanger that was home for the 64th Aggressors. Next time he would not sit so far back. It seemed that it took forever to get to the podium.

When he finally arrived he looked out over the large audience. He gripped the sides of the podium tightly. "I feel very honored to be able to say a few words to you." Sighing deeply he continued, "What we do, no matter what uniform we wear, is dangerous. What we do is necessary. I didn't know Major Mattox very well, I just got to meet him this week. What impressed me about him was his dedication to what he was doing. He stood out as the consummate professional. Several of us remarked that Major Mattox, and the Aggressors are so much like us. Flying is our passion and Devil Mattox and the pilots from the 49th Tactical Fighter Wing, were passionate about what they did. We could see it in the way he talked about what we were all doing out there at Coyote North." Bagger stopped, feeling his throat start to get tight and tears welling up in his eyes. "Excuse me. We've all heard that old cliche that freedom isn't free. It's true. These men have paid the ultimate price for the freedom that we all enjoy in this country. No doubt there will be criticism and fault finding for this tragedy. There are folks that will moan and whine about the high cost in lives and probably, material. This country is so fortunate to have people like Devil Mattox, David Wilson, and Tom Courtney who put everything they have on the line day in and day out, not only here but all over the world." Looking down at the families of the deceased men, he felt lightheaded. He hoped he could finish without bawling. "There is no way I can explain your loss. I just have no words for what I feel right now, except to say that I'm so sorry, but also so proud of haveing been able to spend time in the company of these men." Stepping back he turned to the three flag draped caskets, came to attention, and snapped off a salute that would make a Marine DI proud. Turning on his heel he marched back to his seat, tears streaming down his face.

He gave a huge sigh as he settled once more into his seat. Wendy reached up and put a tentative arm around him. Smiling, she said, "I'm proud of you. That's not something I could do today."

Bagger let himself be drawn closer to her. He didn't trust himself to say anything just yet.

Ninety minutes later after a great many handshakes and promises to keep in touch, Bagger and Walrus were completing the walk around preflight inspection of their plane. A blue Air Force van rolled down the flight line and stopped. Rowdy Kobayashi hopped out of the driver's side. Dressed in white shorts, jogging shoes, and sporting a new Gunfighters t-shirt, she walked up to Bagger. Smiling, she thrust out her hand. "Lt. Bailey, it's been nice to meet you. I hope you have a pleasant flight back to Miramar."

Bagger, taken aback by the somewhat formal send-off, stammered, "Uh, well, it's been nice to be here."

Seeing his face fall almost to the cement of the flight line, she laughed and playfully punched his arm. "Oh, you big dufus, what I really want to know is when I can see you again?"

Bagger immediately pulled out of the funk he had been headed toward and in spite of himself, gave a big sigh of relief. "Oh, man, I was hoping I would hear something like that. I gotta tell ya, it's been real hard to concentrate on flying ever since I met you." Pausing, he plunged on. "Listen, I want to see you again so bad. In fact, I want to marry you!" he blurted out. "Look, don't say yes or no right now. I know we need to get to know each other better, but just think about it, please. I'm not such a bad guy, especially once you get to know me. Right Walrus?"

Walrus Carpenter, who had been standing back of Bailey, shook his head in the negative, stopping suddenly as Bagger turned around to get some support. He couldn't believe what he was hearing.

"Right, Walrus," Bagger demanded again.

"Well," drawing out the well, there was that time at Rosey Roads…"

Bailey quickly clamped his hand over his mouth. "Walrus, we're going to go low, real low, and real fast on the way home, man." Walrus didn't like the low level stuff at all.

"Ma'm, he's a great guy. He flosses twice a day, writes his mother once a week, and is a model United States Naval officer."

"See," said Bagger, turning back to Rowdy Kobayashi, you have it from a fine upstanding Naval officer.

"Do you really floss twice a day?" she asked. "That is something I've always looked for in a man. Someone who is really in touch with his teeth."

"Seriously," said Bailey, "I've never felt this way about anyone, ever." Walrus cleared his throat in the background.

"Lt. Bailey, I just about feel the same way. I really turned the corner when you got up and spoke today. It wasn't what you said, but it was the way you said it."

Bagger could contain himself no longer. He picked her up and spun her around and around, much to the delight of the crews and pilots on the flight line. When the spinning stopped, the kiss began. When it ended, Bagger Bailey could have flown home without the plane.

As they proceeded through their check list prior to take off Bagger told Walrus, "You better hang on babe, we're going to light up the loud pipes today."

"Roger that," sighed Walrus.

Of all of the thousands of takeoffs that took place at Nellis, there would be one that would be remembered, at least for a while. Bagger requested, and got permission for a high performance takeoff. Going to zone five afterburner he brought the big Tomcat off the runway just enough to retract the landing gear, held it along the runway in front of the flight line, and suddenly pitched the nose up almost into the vertical, all the while doing aileron rolls until he disappeared into the blazing

Nevada sky. Walrus Carpenter, much to his relief, had a smooth ride back to Miramar.

By the time Bagger had taken off, Fancy, after a stop at a supermarket, had found his way to Carlsbad. The directions were well written and he found his way to her front door in no time at all. Drawing a deep breath he rang the bell. Almost immediately the door was thown open. Amanda greeted him with a huge grin. "You found us. Mom! Mom, come quick Lt. Fancy's here!"

"For heaven sakes, I'm right here, you don't need to yell. Let him in," her mother said as she opened the door wider.

"Wow, is that your car? That's so cool. What kind is it? Can I have a ride?"

Walking in, Fancy said, "It's a 240 Z, and yeah, I bet you could cage a ride—uh, providing it's okay with your mom."

"That is a great looking car. 71, right?"

"Yes, it is."

"In fact that's considered a classic."

"Well, thank you. Most people just say, 'Hey that's a real old car'."

"Good thing I'm not most people," she said smiling, ushering him into the living room.

*Amen to that*, thought Fancy as he stepped in. *You're sure not.*

"Here's some cream soda I picked up."

She took the sack and gave it to Amanda. "Honey, could you please put these in the fridge?"

"Sure, mom."

"Come on in and sit down. I'm glad you could follow my directions. How was the traffic coming up from San Diego? Traffic questions are standard in California you know." She gestured for him to sit down.

Easing on to the couch, he answered, "Traffic wasn't bad at all. I think I spent more time in the market than I did on the road. Directions were great." He was struck by the tasteful decor and noticed for the first time the Indian artifacts that were placed around the room.

Amanda bounced into the room, announcing that her mother was going to BBQ hamburgers.

"What can I do to help?" he asked.

"Nothing," she answered. "Just relax and enjoy yourself."

"That won't be hard at all. It's been a long time since I've had a home cooked meal. I'm really looking forward to it, but I can be useful, especially lighting fires. Believe it or not, I used to be a Boy Scout."

"I do believe it." She said it with that mischevious grin that made Fancy's heart beat slightly faster. "Okay, you and Amanda light the fire and I'll finish up making the patties."

An hour and a half and three hamburgers later, Fancy pushed back his chair and sighed contentedly. "I never should have eaten that last slider, but, they're so good."

"What's a slider?" demanded Amanda.

"That's Navy slang for hamburger. Sometimes when we finish up flight ops real late that's about the only thing you can get to eat."

"I'm glad you liked them. Would you care for anything else? Beans, salad, cream soda?"

"Everything is so good. I would like all of the above, but I don't know where I'd put it. I don't want to go back to San Diego looking like Big Wave Dave."

"Big Wave Dave!" exclaimed Amanda. "Who's that anyway?"

"He's one of my roommates. We live down by Ocean Beach in a big old yellow house."

"Sounds like a perfect bachelor pad," interjected Cody.

"I don't know about that. I've only spent about three nights there. I just transferred into this squadron from back east. A Mrs. Ault owns the house and keeps everybody on a pretty short leash as I understand it. You certainly have a lovely home. This backyard reminds me of my folks house, where I grew up."

"Where was that?"

"Upstate New York. Little town of Evan Mills. It's just northeast of Lake Ontario."

"Are your folks still there?"

"Yes, they are, althought my dad threatens to go to Florida every time it snows."

"What does he do or is he retired?"

He retired a couple of years ago as the town's fire chief. My mom taught school and she retired the same time my dad did."

"Do you get to see them very much?"

"No, not that often. The Navy keeps us pretty busy. Never too much time in one place."

"Brothers, sisters?" she inquired.

"One brother, older. His name is Rodney. Of course everybody calls him Rod. He's working his way up the ladder on the fire department there. I imagine he'll be the chief some day. He's married and has two kids. Funny, he and I fought over the girl he married."

"Disappointed you lost?" she teased.

Looking straight at her Fancy said, "Not since last Saturday."

Amanda broke the lingering silence by asking, "Why don't we go down to the beach?"

Cody looked at Fancy, raising her eyebrows as if asking what he'd like to do.

"Sounds good to me. I'll drive. Maybe we can find some ice cream."

"Yeah, we can have it with the cake mom made after we get back."

"Cake? That's one of my many weaknesses, homemade cake."

"Don't get your hopes up, it came out of a box and Amanda helped me, so if it turns out okay, I'll give her the credit."

Cramming themselves into the 240 they drove the short distance to the state beach. Even though the day was bright and sunny, there was no problem finding a parking place. The three of them walked along the beach for a while with their shoes off, Amanda finding shells and exclaiming their beauty with every step she took.

"This is a nice beach. It must be great having it right at your doorstep. Do you come here often?"

"Every chance we get. You should see the shoe boxes full of shells we have out in the garage. Amanda's never met a shell she didn't like."

"She's a good kid isn't she?"

"Considering everything, yes I think she is. I think I'll keep her, not that I have a choice mind you."

Amanda had run off to join several of her school friends who were busy burying one of their brothers in the sand and at the same time building a rather large sand castle.

Fancy and Cody sat down on the sand just above the high tide line and watched the waves roll in, sitting in silence, enjoying the moment and beauty of the day. The cries of seagulls wheeling and darting through the sky seemed to punctuate the peace that Fancy felt. He couldn't remember when he had felt this at peace with himself.

Finally Cody broke the the silence. "Tell me some more about you and your family. How did you wind up in the Navy?"

"Life in Evan Mills was pretty ordinary. Looking back it was pretty idealistic. Kind of like a Norman Rockwell sort of town I guess. Everybody knew everybody else. People looked out for each other. Folks would let you know if you weren't doing the right thing. All my aunts and uncles lived in town or really close. It was a great place to grow up."

"And the Navy?" she inquired again.

"My brother got a job in high school working at the little airport, just one runway and no tower, on the edge of town. The man who ran it couldn't always afford to pay him, so he would give him a ride every now and then, let him take the controls, you know. Well, anyway, my brother kept getting sick, he just couldn't hack being up in the air. Finally, he let me go up and I just couldn't get enough. I'd hang around and just look for stuff to do so I could cage a ride. I was hooked. Mr. Veneble gave me some lessons when I worked there, taking Rod's place. One day he let me solo.

"My grades in school hadn't been the greatest so I went to the local junior college. One day a recruiter for the Navy set up a table by the science building. He and I got talking about what it would take to be a Navy pilot. It sounded good to me. He arranged for a regular pre- flight physical for me so I'd know whether to proceed or not. I passed."

"School took on a little more importance for me and I buckled down and did pretty well. The Navy recruiter told me that Syracuse University had a really good ROTC program. I was able to transfer there as a junior, kept working hard and eventually got selected for Officer Candidate School. After that flight training at Pensacola, Florida, more at Beeville and Corpus Christi, Texas."

"My first squadron was VF-84 at Oceana." Pausing for a few moments, he continued. "Unfortunately or fortunately, depending on how you look at it, it could have been my last."

"How so?"

Fancy stared at the sand, making a hole with his foot. Finally, he answered. "I really liked being in the Navy, and of course I really wanted to fit in—be one of the guys. It seemed like everyone drank so naturally I thought I should try to keep up. Then I got married." He drew in a deep breath.

"Look, if I'm making you uncomfortable or prying, I'm sorry. We can talk about something else. It's really none of my business."

"No, no. Actually it feels kind of good. I haven't really talked about it- out loud at least to anyone before. Where was I?"

"You got married."

"One day I was assigned to show a visiting congressman around, answer any questions, that kind of thing. This guy was an ex fighter jock, Duke Cross. In fact he represents a district around here. Ever heard of him?"

Cody shook her head no.

"Well, he brought his daughter along with him on what ever it was that he was supposed to be doing. Of course he introduced us and we seemed to hit it off. We started seeing each other and one thing led to another and we wound up having big a military wedding at the National Cathedral in D.C."

"Sounds impressive."

"It was. My folks were kind of on cloud nine. My brother's wife wasn't," he grinned. "Nature took its course and about ten months later we had a beautiful baby girl. A month after she was born, Janice, found her dead in her crib. It's called SIDS—Sudden Instant Death Syndrom. One of those things doctors know very little about, or didn't then. I was out on the boat and couldn't get back right away so she had to deal with that by herself for a few days. I don't think she ever forgave the Navy or me. My drinking got kind of out of control. I don't know whether it was grief or whatever...."

"Janice wanted me to quit the Navy and go to work for the airlines, who were recruiting rather heavily on base at the time. I wouldn't do it and one day she just left." Fancy sighed deeply and shook his head.

"I'm sorry about the baby. That must have been hard for her and you," she said. "I really didn't mean to pry."

He turned and smiled. "No problem. I kind of feel like I've unloaded some negative g's. I feel lighter—better in fact."

"I'm glad. Come on, let's collect Amanda and find some ice cream."

"Sounds like a plan, let's go."

Half an hour later they were sitting back on the patio eating their ice cream and cake. Fancy was on his third piece. "This is great cake. I haven't had anything like this in a long, long time. My mother makes great cakes and this is right up there with hers – even my dad would say so."

"I like the frosting the best," said Amanda, who was finishing up her second piece and was thinking about another. "It's my mom's special recipe. We call it the Red Cake."

"It's chocolate, isn't it?" inquired Fancy. Holding it up for further inspection he said, "Although I can see a bit of red. No matter what you call it, it's definitely sierra hotel."

"Sierra hotel?" said Amanda looking up with a quizzical look on her face. What's a sierra hotel?"

Fancy realizing he didn't want to tell her what sierra hotel really meant, felt himself blushing. "Well, uh, it it uh means just the very best there is. Take my word for it, okay."

Still looking at him, very intensely now, she asked, "Is that pilot talk or Navy talk. Is it secret?"

"That's it, it's Navy talk. It's not secret, but it isn't very nice, especially in front of a young lady like yourself." He looked to her mother for help.

"Let's not put Dan on the spot. I'm sure he knows best in this situation."

"Will you tell me when I become a Navy pilot?"

"If it's okay with your mother, yes, I will."

Cody raised her eyebrows as if mulling it over. "We'll see," she said. "You'll have to tell me first." Again the mischievous grin.

Amanda grumbled, "Adults get to have all the fun. Hey mom, can I show him what I did in my room? Please?"

"Sure, I'll clean up these dishes while you show him. I think he'll want to see it."

Grabbing him by the hand she pulled him up and toward the inside of the house. Her room was neat and tidy and there were two posters, probably purchased at the air show of F-14s. Taped to her mirror was a piece of paper. In girlish scrawl was written: I'm going to do better in Math, English, History, and Spelling, especially Math. And no more whining about homework. I'm willing to pay the price. Amanda Thorn.

"I did it right when we got home yesterday. How do you like it?"

"I'm impressed, I really am. That is another sierra hotel. Have you got a pen or pencil?"

Fishing around in a desk drawer she produced a pen. Fancy asked, "May I add to it?"

"Yes, please, yes!"

Fancy bent down and wrote: Go for it Amanda. This is Sierra Hotel. Lt. Dan "Gator" Fancy.

He stood up and turned toward the door. Cody was leaning against the door jam, wiping something out of her eye.

"Mom, did you get something in your eye?"

"No, sweetheart, I'm okay. Come on let's go to the living room."

As they entered the living room he again noticed the collection of Indian artifacts. He walked over to one that looked something like a net. It was almost two and a half feet in diameter, decorated with feathers and beads. He thought it was quite striking. "What's this? I've never seen one of these before?"

Cody came over and carefully lifted it off the wall, handing it to him. "It's called a Dream Catcher. It catches all your good dreams."

"Is this your hobby, collecting Indian artifacts?" he inquired, turning the Dream Catcher over in his hands, admiring its delicate beauty.

"In a way. This belonged to my parents. They had it, and most of the other items here in their home."

"Oh," he said, handing it back to her, "They collected the artifacts and passed them on to you?"

Cody paused, taking a deep breath. "They were in our home because we lived on the reservation. My parents were full blooded Sioux. I grew up on the Pine Ridge Reservation in South Dakota."

Fancy's eyebrows went up, quite involuntarily this time. He didn't know quite what to say.

She laughed. "Well, what did you expect? I'm not going to take your scalp, you know."

Fancy laughed and felt himself turning red. "I'm sorry, I've just never met a real Indian before." He shook his head. "You see, once I saw this movie with Kirk Douglas. I think it was called "The Long Rifle". It had the most beautiful girl I had ever seen playing an Indian girl or woman and I fell in love with her. You're a dead ringer for her. My brother and I must have seen that movie six or seven times before it left town." *Boy, it feels hot in here* he thought.

"I'm flattered. Did you and your brother fight over her too?"

"I don't think so, but we both thought she was beautiful."

After a few more minutes of small talk Fancy looked out the window and noticed it had gotten dark all of a sudden. Tomorrow was going to be a busy day and he thought maybe he'd better get going. The last thing he wanted to do was overstay his welcome. "Listen, I'd better get going. This has been wonderful. Thank you so much for inviting me. Its been great."

"Thank you so much for coming. I just hope you haven't been bored. Let me get you some cake to take with you. Young lady, you get going on thse dishes."

"Okay, mom," smiled Amanda.

As they walked out to the car, Fancy said, "Thanks again for everything. It couldn't have been a better day. It just went too fast. And that cake, wow..." Pausing, he looked at Cody and plunged ahead. I sure would like to see you again. I hope I'm not being, uh...."

"Bold," she answered for him, smiling.

"Yeah, I guess that's what I mean. I don't want any flash in the pan kind of thing. The thing that sailors are known for if you know what I mean." He felt himself getting hot again in spite of the cool night air.

"If I get any time this week, could I take you out to dinner or something—Amanda too, of course."

She looked up at him, not answering for what seemed like a long time. "Yes, I'd like that—a lot. Please, call." Then she shook his hand and walked back toward the house.

She was still standing by the front door as Fancy drove away. Like Bagger, Fancy could have made it back to San Diego without the 240.

Fancy walked in the big yellow house to find Bagger, Poncho, and Big Wave sitting around the kitchen table. "Hey, what's up guys?" he said as he set the cake on the table, noticing for the first time it was a whole cake.

"We should be asking the questions," grinned Poncho. "Such as, where did you get that and can we have a piece? It looks homemade."

"It is and you can, just make sure to leave me some. That is great cake, let me tell you."

"Which leaves the big question unanswered," said Bagger. "Come on, come clean to your friends."

Fancy shook his head and smiled. "At the air show," he began, and related the whole story to a disbelieving Bagger and friends.

"Gator," said Big Wave, shaking his head, "you've only been here less than a week. Man you're an operator."

"Damn, this cake is great!" said Bagger, with a full mouth. "This woman must be as ugly as sin to be able to make a cake like this."

Smiling, Fancy got up. "I won't even try to describe her. Right now I don't even know the words. You'll just have to see for yourselves. I've got to get some shut eye. Remember, leave me some of that. Hey, Bagger, how was the service?"

Turning serious, Bagger said, "It was moving, it brought tears. I had to get up and say a few words. Man, that was hard, one of the hardest things I've ever had to do, and I just barely knew the guy. Promise me I won't have to do that for any of you."

Fancy nodded in the affirmative. "See you in the morning."

"Is it my imagination, or is he floating just a little bit?" commented Big Wave, as Fancy disappeared out of the kitchen.

# 6

Monday morning found the pilots and RIOs of VF-124 jammed into their ready room. Everyone could feel a little more tension as the day for the deployment drew closer, although no one knew exactly when that exact date would be. Commander Robinson brought everybody to their feet as he entered the room. "As you were!" he commanded. "Good morning. I'm glad to see everyone here this morning, especially the det we sent up to Nellis. For those of you who didn't know, there was a mid air between an F-5 and one of the Eagles last week. As sorry as I am, I'm damn glad it wasn't any of you."

Now, you're probably all wondering about our schedule this week. *Enterprise* has left Alameda, the catapults are fixed and she's ready for us to get back to doing what we do. Today is dedicated to touch and goes. We need to get back in the groove and get everybody qualified. That'll be ten day traps and six night traps. I want that out of the way by Thursday afternoon—latest. Any questions so far?"

"Who'll do the first traps on the boat?" asked Hunter Schott.

"I want to get all the folks who were at Nellis requaled first. Everyone else got some touch and goes last week. Some of us even went out to St.

Nick (San Nicholos Island, off the coast of Southern California). "We'll head out to the boat first thing in the morning. The maintenance troops spent a good part of their weekend tweaking the birds and getting them ready. Make sure you let them know you appreciate it. Also thanks to the people who were at the Air Show. Admiral Smith got a lot of positive feedback. After we finish up here and you're suited up, the FOD walkdown should be finished and we can get going."

Lt. Commander Baldon, the senior LSO (landing signal officer) would like to say a few words. Badrod, it's all yours."

"Morning, gentleman," growled Badrod. The short, fireplug, of a man was not happy about being up this early and he was letting everyone know it. His short grayish hair seemed to be actually bristling as he strode to the front of the room. People who didn't know Badrod thought he must be mad at the world 24 hours a day, seven days a week. Those who knew him well however, knew him to be one of the kindest, most thoughtful men they had ever known. He had been known to literally give the shirt off his back to those who were in need. Most important—if you needed to get back aboard on a dark, moonless night, with a pitching deck, and high winds—Badrod was the man you wanted on the platform at the back of the boat.

"This morning you're going to be using 24 R. The winds are going to be negligible today so there won't be much of a problem getting down, but that's not going to help getting you guys back in the groove. Fly the ball just like you're going to be hitting the boat. I'll be on the platform, just like on the boat working with my crew. That's going to include a nugget. He's going to be getting a great deal of the work today. Any questions? Good." Before anyone could open his mouth, Badrod was marching out of the room.

"Well," remarked Killer, "I'm glad that he does realize that we do know it all."

"Man," croaked Moose Milwood, "they think they're some kind of Gods sometimes."

"They aren't," responded Commander Robinson, "but on those dark and stormy nights they might have God-like qualities." Nobody said anything, but the up and down movement of almost everyone's head said it all.

Fancy thought to himself that out the five thousand plus men on a carrier, LSOs were some of the very few that could definitely make a difference in whether people lived or died.

LSOs are pilots themselves, mostly junior officers. Most volunteer for the position, but when there is a shortage of volunteers, a few get assigned to it. Those getting the assignment seem to possess the right mix of flying skill and personality. The position itself has so little going for it. They spend hours exposed to cold, wind, and wet—often far into the night. By the time they're finished, the mess is closed. In addition the responsibility is far greater than any other job open to junior officers. Finally, thought Fancy, and for most of us this is the key, they generally fly much less than their squadron roomies.

That might be an interesting career move he mused to himself. Shuddering, he immediately rejected the thought.

The rest of the briefing was dedicated to plane assignments, order of take off, the nuts and bolts of what would be happening. Fancy and Mirabal were tasked with twenty touch and goes. Upon completion of the last one they would head out over the Pacific and rendezvous with an S-3B Viking to practice tanking. After that, ten more touch and goes. Not a bad way to spend the day.

Walking out to the flight line with Bagger, Rhino, Killer, Poncho, Animal, and Big Wave, Fancy remarked, "It looks like it's going to be a great day. Is the weather generally this good out here?"

"We get some overcast in the winter, spring, and early summer, but it's generally pretty thin. Fallon's nearly always clear, but man, it gets cold up there in the winter. How does this compare with Oceana?"

"There's a lot of rain, clouds. Some of those big thunder bumpers go way up," answered Fancy.

"Do I detect a certain spring in your step, Gator. You seem pretty chipper today. Could it be that a certain member of the female persuasion could have something to do with it. Come clean, you need to let your wingies in on important things, you know."

"Actually," said Fancy, arriving at his assigned aircraft, I was just looking forward to getting back into the air. But, now that you mention it…" he replied, his voice trailing off.

"Uh-huh," came back Animal, "I recognize that smitten look from my first marriage."

"Hey, it has more to do with flying than anything. Even the mundane bounces look good. Come on, Rhino, let's pre-flight the bird."

They were assigned to Desperado 201. After the quick walk around with a senior CPO, they climbed aboard and started running down their checklists prior to engine start.

"How's it look back there, Rhino?"

"Looks pretty good. Everything's here and ready to come on line."

Fifteen minutes later they were in the air headed back to Miramar, after making a circuit that took them near the Mexican border, ready for the first bounce of the day. Fancy's eyes were darting over the instruments then to the horizon beyond. Ahead of him he could see Big Wave's plane just settling over the fence. Make sure the gear, flaps, and, double-check that the tailhook are all down. "201, Tomcat, ball, four point seven," he announced quietly, there by confirming his identity, his sighting of the glide slope, and how much fuel he had on board, measured in pounds. They had four thousand seven hundred pounds of JP-8. Fancy liked to hit the boat with about 3000 pounds, but this would do for today.

Badrod was right, with no cross wind there wasn't going to be any problem getting down. He watched the Fresnel lens. The orange colored, movable light, or meatball was perfectly centered, confirming that he was on the glide slope.

As he felt the big fighter touch down on its main gear, he brought the nose gear down and immediately pushed the twin throttles all the way forward, stopping just short of the afterburner detents. He felt himself being pushed back into his seat as the plane accelerated and in just a few seconds they were climbing out. Fancy slapped the gear handle and felt the landing gear retract back into their wells.

"That was smooth, babe, real smooth," commented Mirabal.

"Thanks, I wish they were all that easy." He retarded the throttles as they came up to altitude. As he looked to his left he could see Poncho's plane just touching down, and behind him Bagger just lowering his landing gear.

After their twentieth touch and go, Fancy and Mirabal were vectored out over the city of San Diego to the azure blue waters of the Pacific. It was a brilliant, clear day and it seemed to Fancy that he could see almost to the ends of the earth. "Rhino," Fancy called after they had been cleared feet wet, "any sign of that S-3? We're going to be on fumes in a few minutes."

"Come to 260 degrees and climb to 10 grand."

The Tomcat's nose came 260 degrees at the same time they arrived at ten thousand feet. Just coming out of a turn and settling on the homestretch leg of a race track course, was the S-3B of VS-29, the Dragonfires, tactical call sign Bugs. The Dragonfires had been named the best S-3 squadron on the Pacific Coast last year.

"Bugs, this is Desperado 201 coming up your six. We're hoping to get a little gas. How do you read me?"

"We read you loud and clear, Desperado. Say your fuel state."

"Desperado 201 is at just under 1000 pounds."

Fancy watched the refueling probe come out of the starboard well. It was a piece of cake, he thought, to refuel since the probe was at such a convenient place and angle. He watched the S-3 unreel the hose with the basket on the end, and could now make out the circular red lights that defined the basket.

Easing the throttle forward just slightly he brought the tip of the probe closer to the basket that had stopped unreeling.

"Desperado, we're all set, you can plug in now."

"Roger, Bugs." Fancy eased the the refueling probe toward the basket, which, he noted, was remarkably stable. The end of the probe disappeared inside the basket, and Fancy eased the throttles forward just a hair to make a solid connection and push the hose into the form of an "S", signaling the S-3 that they could start the flow of gas. Much to his dismay, and discomfort, the red datum lights remained red.

"Bugs, uh I'm still looking at red lights."

"We hear you Desperado," came the disembodied voice from the S-3. "Give another nudge, maybe you're not seated firmly enough."

"Roger," said Fancy, as his heart began to beat a little faster. He didn't want to shove his nose into the end of the S-3, so he took a deep breath and eased the throttles slightly ahead. The lights remained red.

"Bugs, we're still lookin' at red lights," he returned, trying to keep his voice calm. Something that was getting difficult to do. Seven hundred pounds of fuel was not enough to go around the block, much less back to Miramar.

"Okay, Desperado, back out and let's try it again. We'll recycle everything on our end."

"Roger." He eased the Tomcat back enough to disengage, but not too far to use up precious fuel plugging in again.

"Desperado, plug in one more time. Give it a good shot."

"Coming back in, Bugs," answered Fancy. As he eased the plane toward the basket, he said, "Rhino, go to Guard and see if there's another tanker out there."

"Okay, boss." Switching channels on his radio, Mirabal called, "This is Navy Tomcat, Desperado 201 approximately 155 miles west of San Diego. We're attempting to tank and are having little success. Give us a steer if you can help out. Again, this is Navy Tomcat, Desperado 201 in need of tanker support."

Fancy realized he was sweating while at the same time he felt oddly cold. He put the refueling probe right in the basket on the first try. Again the datum lights of the basket remained a defiant red. "Damn," he muttered to himself.

"Any luck, Rhino?" he asked trying to keep his voice calm and steady. "Bugs, these lights are still red. Can you try transferring fuel, just in case it's just he lights and not the whole system?"

"Desperado, we're giving it a try right now. We don't show any fuel flow."

"Well, I'm out of ideas and it looks like luck," growled Fancy. "Have you…"

"Gator, I'm getting somebody on Guard. Change frequency."

"Bug, going to Guard and I'm going to stay plugged in."

"Roger, Desperado."

"This is Desperado 201. I'm experiencing a refueling emergency."

A new voice boomed into his headset. "Desperado, this is Runner one-one, KC-10, outward bound from March. We have you and your buddy on the scope. We're at your five o' clock, descending to 10,000, at twelve miles."

Fancy felt a tremendous weight lift from his shoulders. "Roger, Runner one-one. Looking for you on our starboard side. Rhino, did you copy that?"

"I sure did." His voice sounded more calm. Nothing like the possibility of a blue water divert to get the juices flowing.

"Bugs, we have a KC-10 coming to the rescue. Let's stay connected until we've got a visual and he's in position."

"Roger that Desperado."

Watching the fuel gauge winding down immediately got Fancy's attention again and he twisted around in his seat to see if he could catch a glimpse of the KC-10. "Rhino, keep looking for him and I'll try not to cause any more complications up here."

Rhino chuckled. "I think I've got a visual. Yep. Man that thing is big. He's about, uh, a mile and a half back about 500 feet, high."

"Desperado, Runner one-one, we have you in sight. Moving into position now."

Fancy took a quick look and saw the military version of the McDonnell Douglas DC-10 floating down and almost pulling even with their plane.

"Bugs, let's disengage."

"Roger, Desperado. We'll pull off to port and climb to 11,500."

Fancy eased the Tomcat away from the S-3, retarding the throttles slightly to provide a safety margin for disengagement, while he kept the Extender in sight out of the corner of his eye.

The Extender pulled ahead as Fancy pulled over and aft of the bigger plane. Looking up he could see the boomer or boom operator looking down at him through his plexiglass window on the bottom of the plane. He felt an urge to wave, but thought better of it.

"Desperado," came the crisp, cool, professional voice of the boomer, I'm unreeling the hose. Wait for my command to plug in, please, sir." Immediately the hose and basket began to unwind from the fuselage of the plane.

"Okay, Desperado, plug in and let's do it."

"Thanks, Runner," said Fancy as he eased the throttles forward, plugging into the basket, and then easing the probe in a little further. Immediately the datum lights changed from red to green."

"We have green lights, Runner."

"Roger, Desperado, commencing refueling now." Fancy felt and smelled the JP-8 start to flow. Nothing had smelled that good in a long time. He eased the throttles forward to compensate for the added weight of the fuel coming on board.

"Desperado, we can give you 4,500 pounds. We're meeting some F-15s coming in from Hawaii."

"That's fine Runner. We're much obliged. We'll make it right. What do you guys drink?"

"Desperado, don't worry about it. We're glad we could help. We show you've got 4,500 pounds. Unplug and pull off to starboard, please."

"Roger that, disengaging to starboard," replied Fancy, as he retarded the throttles and moved the stick to the right. Holding the plane in a shallow right hand turn he headed back to Miramar.

They flew in silence for few minutes after confirming their position and their intention to return to Miramar and complete their last ten bounces. "That was a little closer that I normally like to cut it," said Fancy as he let out a long sigh.

"Hey, I'm sure we could have dead-sticked this beast all the way back to Miramar. I have complete confidence in you and in this airplane." His voice almost sounded like it was back to normal.

"I'm beginning to be a huge believer in jointness," chuckled Fancy.

"Me too, but I don't envy those tanker guys and what they have to put up with," returned Rhino.

Fancy knew what was coming, but he decided to bite anyway. "What do they have to put up with anyway?"

"Say you have a kid and another kid in school asks him what his dad does for a job. The kid has to say my dad passes gas." Mirabal laughed at his own joke.

Fancy chuckled, mostly at Mirabal for telling one of the oldest jokes in the world.

"Seriously, Gator, how close was it?"

"You don't want to know. I'm not that sure anyway. I stopped looking at the gauge, figuring I'd just fly it until something happened either way."

Desperado 201 taxied into the parking place under the direction of a senior enlisted man. He cut the engines and raised the canopy. Just another day in Naval aviation, he thought as he stretched and released his koch fittings. He stood and prepared to climb down. What a great way to make a living, he mused. Have a great time, scare the wee out of yourself, be on the verge of throwing up, etc…

Once he was on the ground, Mirabal jumped down beside him. "Another great day. You feel pretty good about hitting the boat?"

"You bet. You ready to go with me?" he grinned.

Mirabal clapped him on the shoulder, "To hell and back, compadre. But let's not try to go that far, okay?"

"Okay," said Fancy. "That was as close as I ever want to go."

Upon entering the ready room they encountered Commander Robinson entering the room at the same time. "How'd everything go today? No problems I hope?"

"The bounces went fine—no problems there. It got kind of exciting when we tried to tank with the S-3 though."

Robinson stopped quickly and turned around. "How so?" he asked.

"We found the S-3 and made the hook up just fine. The problem being, they couldn't pass the gas." He heard Rhino stifle a laugh.

"Oh," said Robinson, grinning himself. "What happened next?"

Fancy quickly related their tale of woe.

Robinson thought for a moment at the conclusion of the story. "Somebody was in the right place at the right time. I'll let them know we're grateful. Nice work—and you got all your bounces in today? I'm impressed." He smiled and continued his trip to the front of the room.

Rhino looked at Fancy. "We're done for a while. Do you want to grab something to eat? All of a sudden I feel like I'm starving."

"Sure, I've got that same feeling. Let's go."

"Gator," asked Big Wave, "did you have any kind of religious experience after the frab up with the S-3?" They were all sitting in the white wicker furniture on the large, open front porch. The Pacific sparkled in the distance.

Fancy took a swallow of his cream soda. Pausing, he answered, "No, but I'm sure glad that KC-10 was where he was. I'll tell you, it definitely got my attention. The blue suiters were really professional. Man, they came down to us, put us in position, passed the gas, and we were back in business. It turned around that quick. Mirabal was really with it too."

"You seemed to have been a good influence on Rhino," remarked Poncho. "When he got here he was such a wiseass. Nobody much wanted to fly with him. He was always getting passed around."

"I've had no real problem with him, although we did have to get a couple of things straight. Once that happened, we've become a real team." Fancy shrugged and stood up.

"I think I'll call it a night. See you guys in the morning."

"Do you feel you're ready to hit the boat?" asked Bagger, who had been strangely quiet during most of the evening.

Pausing at the doorway, Fancy turned to face the group. "Yeah, I feel ready. You've seen one carrier, you've seen 'em all." He grinned and continued back into the house.

Big Wave shook his head. "He's a pretty cool customer. Rhino told me that it was a real close thing. He came about that close," he said, using his thumb and forefinger held closely together, "to parking that big beast in the water."

"What else could any of us do?" chipped in Bagger. "You either get right back up or you better turn in your wings. There's no in between. How do you guys feel about tomorrow?"

"I'm good to go," smiled Poncho. "Wave, you okay?"

"You betcha. I like the challenge. You know better than to ask. Bagger, you've been pretty quiet this evening. How about you?"

Bagger took a deep breath, holding it in for several seconds. "I'd like to say I'm as ready as I've ever been, but it's just not the truth."

He paused again, under their steady gaze. "To be truthful, ever since I met Wendy, I'm looking at things a little bit different." He sighed again. "Hey don't look so serious. I'll be there."

Fancy brought the F-14 along the *Enterprise's* starboard side. Bringing the stick to the left he rolled into a nearly vertical left bank. Out of the side of his eyes he could see condensation flicker above the swept back wings like white fire. Under the drag of the five-g turn, the air speed rapidly began to bleed off from 400 knots to the desired 150, the wings automatically starting to move from their fully swept back position. He noticed the inflatable g-suit snapping tightly around his legs, forcing the blood back into his upper extremities. His eyes darted from the blur of instruments to the horizon and back again.

Parallel to the carrier, Fancy rolled level. All right, he thought, check the speed, dirty up, put the gear and flaps down and double check that the tailhook is down. In anticipation he lifted himself slightly up from his seat, twisting and adjusting his posture and the feel of the seat pad on his thighs, a nervous gesture he habitually went through each time he got ready to trap on the boat.

On the landing signal officer's platform near the stern, on the port side of the ship, the hook spotter examined the F-14 through a pair of powerful binoculars, ignoring Bagger's F-14 on short final. Ropes of vapor stream from its wingtips. As Bagger roared by the platform and successfully trapped, the LSO takes a quick look to see which hook it caught.

"203, gear and hook down," called the hook spotter.

At the same time the phone talker shouted, "Foul deck!"

Badrod Baldon, the controlling LSO, turned to the writer and shouted over the din going on around him on the deck and in the air, "A little long in the grove, a little stopped rate of descent, in the middle, a little high in close. OK-3 wire."

203, Tomcat, ball, two point eight, Fancy radioed, confirming his identity, his sighting of the glide slope indicator, and his fuel state.

"Roger, ball," Baldon acknowledges.

Rolling into the grove, Fancy noticed that whatever smoothness there was in the flight thus far had been replaced by a series of sharp jolts. With a series of swift small control movements he juggled the luminous amber ball on the edge of the port side whose alignment with the row of green lights told him he's on the glide path. Aware of the sound of the two engines, and continually jinking up and down, he continues the movement of throttle and stick to stay there. The ship loomed ahead, the deck looking more wide than long. No distractions now he reminded himself. Meatball, lineup, angle of attack. Now instead of waiting for the ball to tell him what to do, he nudged it just to the top and center where he could best see it move, playing it cat and mouse, mastering rather than following with deft movements of the stick. The last fifteen seconds seemed to last for minutes as the carrier grew larger.

"Foul deck!" called the phone talker. "Foul deck!"

Badrod held his arm aloft, a signal to the air boss in the island that he knows the deck is obstructed. He can hear the fluctuating engines of the Tomcat as the gray blur started to take shape and grows in size.

"Clear deck! Gear set, 740, Tomcat!" The arresting gear will be set for the 74,000 pound plane and the deck is clear. Badrod lowers his arm and glances at the televised image from the flight deck centerline camera. He squeezes the press-to-talk button on the telephone handset he holds to his left ear. "Right for lineup."

Fancy felt his mouth go dry. Par for the course he thinks. A quiet voice floats in the center of Fancy's head, calmly giving him a tiny correction to make. He had allowed himself to drift a few feet to the left of centerline. Five seconds to go—five difficult seconds, as he nears the end of what he thinks of as a funnel where deviations in the path of the 37 ton plane are measured in inches. The deck seems to be rising on a swell as he descends. Although he is at the ramp, he seems headed for a point far down the deck. Another quick correction for lineup, wing down, wing up, just a few degrees in a split second—the deck rushing toward him. Again the soft voice of Badrod sounds in his headset, but with the slight hint of warning: "powWERR" as the wheels meet the deck, actually feeling the plane rolling over the 3-wire and then the 4-wire, his hand automatically pushed the throttle to full power.

Amazingly the plane slowed and a seemingly massive force, gentle at first but building fast, dragging his body forward, the plane coming to a stop, throttles, after to going to full afterburner, coming back to idle.

Badrod turned to the writer, "Pitching deck. A little high all the way, a little line up left in the middle, OK-3" Killer's F-14, is already in the grove.

Rhino's voice comes up. "Nice, Gator, real nice."

"I appreciate the vote of confidence. One down, nine to go." What was left unsaid was that the last six had to be at night.

Once the hook runner had disengaged the wire from the tailhook, Fancy was directed forward by the taxi director's signals toward the port bow catapult—Cat Two. Rhino made sure the radar was in stand-by and inertial navigation aligned.

Purple shirted enlisted men dragged a hose to Desperado 203. They would hot fuel the plane while the engines were running.

"I'm never crazy about fueling this way," grumbled Rhino.

Fancy grunted in response. "Yeah."

"Takeoff checklist," Fancy directed, as he ran through his own list. It all came back without conscious thought as he followed the director's signals. Rogering the weight board, flaps and slats to takeoff position, etc...

Rhino grunted, "Roger, that."

With another 4,000 pounds of fuel, Fancy once again moved forward under the direction of the yellow-shirted taxi director. They moved back of the jet blast deflector. Bagger's plane moved into position and the JBD raised out of the deck to block their view. Sixty seconds later Bagger's plane was flung off the bow and the JBD sinks back into the deck. Fancy advanced the throttle to move up to the catapult.

Now it was their turn as the JBD came down and they were directed forward. He eases the throttles forward and the big Cat moved forward. The plane seemingly eager to move into position.

With the signal to release brakes, given with one hand and a sweeping motion below his waist with the other, giving the signal to the catapult operator to ease the shuttle forward with a hydraulic piston, all the slack was taken out of the nose-wheel tow launching mechanism. Now that they were on the catapult he flicked a switch on his right, making the plane's nosegear compress, or as it looked to someone looking at them from the deck, the plane seemed to be kneeling. The spring housing over the strut descended fourteen inches, making the plane seem ready to pounce. This would give it a leap at the end of the three-hundred foot, two and a half second launch when the sudden steam thrust abruptly halted at the end of the deck and the housing sprang back up to lift the nose into the air. Every little bit helped. There was the fimiliar jolt as the green-suited hookup man, wearing his Mickey Mouse ears and goggles, fastened the plane to the shuttle. He felt the thunk as he released the brakes and pushed both throttles forward to the stops. Without looking at the engines he could feel them spooling up. Looking at the instruments, RPM, exhaust gas temperatures, and fuel flow—everything right where they should be as the engines came to full power.

The Tomcat vibrated like a living thing as the engines sucked in massive amounts of air and slammed it out the exhausts.

"You, ready?" Fancy asked Mirabal, as he rested the heel of his left hand against the throttles.

"I'm right behind you, babe," came the calm reply.

Fancy chuckled to himself.

The taxi director was pointing to the shooter, or catapult officer, who was ten feet up the deck. The shooter was twirling his fingers and looking directly at Fancy, waiting.

Oil pressure for both engines right where they should be. Hydraulics—right on. Fancy moved the stick back and forth and checked the movement of the stabilator in his left-side rearview mirror on the canopy rail. With his right hand he saluted the cat officer. The shooter immediately returned it and glanced up the cat track toward the bow as Fancy put his head back into the headrest, with his right hand behind the stick

Fancy saw the cat officer lunge forward and actually touch the deck with his right hand

Within two heartbeats the catapult was fired. The acceleration was tremendously violent.

In two and a half seconds it was over. Fancy was conscious of being swept over the bow and they were out over the glittering sea.

Fancy let the trim rotate the nose to nine degrees up as he slapped the gear handle, while at the same time sweeping his eyes over the HUD taking in the attitude reference on the vertical display indicator, the VDI, the altimeter—120 feet and going up, the rate of climb, positive, airspeed 160 knots and accelerating, no warning lights. He was able to take in these welcome bits of information without conscious thought, just noting them somewhere in his subconscious and putting it all together as the airplane accelerated and climbed away from the ship.

With the gear in the wells and locked, he raises the flaps and slats. The big plane continued to accelerate as Fancy stopped the climb at five hundred feet, while running the nose trim down slightly. Going through two hundred knots, 250, 300, 350…and still accelerating.

At 420 knots Fancy eased the the throttles back slightly. As five miles came up on the DME (distance measuring equipment) he pulled the nose up steeply, dropping the left wing. As he eases the throttles forward again the plane leapt away from the ocean in a climbing turn. Scanning the sky for Bagger's plane that had preceeded him.

He had roughly 3,000 thousand pounds of fuel left, oops not right, four thousand pounds now, about 500 pounds to burn off before he had to land again in fifteen minutes.

*I want to burn if off, but not waste it*, he thought as he pulled back on the throttles, coming up to five thousand feet. He put the plane in a gentle left hand turn, at 260 knots, that would allow him to orbit the ship on a five mile circle.

Looking to his left he could see Bagger on the other side of the ship, level at the same altitude, and turning on the five mile arc. Fancy steepened his turn slightly to cut across above the ship and rendezvous with Bagger.

Fancy pulled up and got on Bagger's bearing line, easing in some left rudder thereby lowering the nose so he could see Bagger out on the forward right quarter of the canopy. Joining up took a little finesse when coming in on the lead's left because the pilot the plane of the joining aircraft could easily lose sight of the lead plane. If he went a little high, or if he let his plane fall a little behind the bearing line—being sucked, they called it—and attempted to pull back to the bearing, the lead would disappear under the wingman's nose and he would be closing blind. Being unable to see at any time, but especially now, was a situation filled with danger for everyone concerned.

Fancy concentrated and stayed glued to the bearing. When he was fifty feet away from Bagger's plane he lowered the nose and crossed behind and under Bagger. As he emerged on Bagger's starboard side in parade position. Bagger looked over and gave him a thumb's-up.

Bagger's RIO gave them a frequency shift and they made two more orbits of the circle and then started down.

As they descended Fancy noticed the patches of sunlight and shadow. Every now and then a shaft of gold would play on the planes and make the sea below glisten. *Better concentrate on what you're doing*, he thought to himself.

The plane felt good—very responsive and tight. He concentrated by moving the plane a few inches forward or back on Bagger, feeling one hundred percent in control. When it felt just right he moved on the bearing line so that the wings tips overlapped, stopping when he could feel the downdraft off Bagger's wing, holding it there for a few seconds just to prove he could still do it. Making a minute movement with the stick he moved out to where he belonged.

*This is as good as life gets,* he thought. *Flying is the best part of living and carrier flying is the best living of all.*

Seemingly glued together the two Tomcats came up the Enterprise's wake at an altitude of eight hundred feet. There were two other planes in the pattern with their gear down, so Bagger delayed the break. His RIO kissed him off and Bagger dropped his left wing and pulled. Fancy watched Bagger turn away and he started to count. When he reached seven he brought the stick to the left and pulled while at the same time reaching for the gear handle, slapping it down, then the flaps.

Coming level at three G's, he could feel the gear coming down, flaps and slats—3,100 pounds of fuel. Just about right he thought.

Coming up on the ninety, on speed exactly with a three o' clock angle of attack...there's the meatball on the Fresnel lens. Cross the wake, roll out, coming in to the angled deck. Watch it Be ready for the little burble from the island and the tendency to roll to the left, the infamous Dutch Roll. Keep the power on; ease back just a tad. Keep that ball in the center.

The main gear crunched down into the deck, the nose gear coming down harder than Fancy usually liked, he shoved the throttles to the stops, the speed brakes closed with the throttle mounted switch. Bringing the stick back the big fighter shot up the angled deck and leaped into the air.

On the downwind he lowered the gear and hook, checking that his harness was locked. Usually he flew with it unlocked so that he could lean forward if he wanted or just have a little wiggle room in his seat.

The interval between Fancy and Bagger was good, and Bagger trapped on his first pass just as he reduced his power at the 180-position. Down and turning, on speed, looking for the ball crossing the wake, wings level and reducing power, adding a little power for the burble, he watched the lineup and flying the ball.

The Tomcat swept across the ramp and slammed down into the deck. At the same time he pushed the throttles full forward feeling the tailhook catch a wire, and then coming to a full stop.

As he felt the plane roll backward, he pushed the hook up button and added just a little power to taxi out of the gear, while the yellow-shirted director gave him the come ahead signal.

They lined up waiting for catapult two. He checked the gear and flap settings, then the fuel, before once again bringing the plane into the shuttle. Things were coming automatically to him now, things he knew how to do—well, things that made everything else other than flying worthwhile.

Throttles up…the salute—and bam, they were off to do it again. Leaving the gear and flaps down, he flew straight ahead until he saw Bagger pass him on the left going downwind.

Banking for the crosswind turn he grinned to himself, briefly noticing the shaft of sunlight that played across the plane. All worthwhile he mused again.

After another trap they were directed once more to stop near the island of the carrier. With the engines running, the plane was once more refueled for another hot turn around. Opening the canopy he removed his oxygen mask. His face, hot with sweat. Wiping away the wetness he watched other planes making their approaches.

There was a strange silence if you could call the howl of jet engines, the slam of the catapult, and every so often the sound of the radio. Being on the flight deck of an aircraft carrier was the loudest place on earth, yet at the same time so very pleasant.

It only took a few minutes before the purple-shirted fuelers were finished and Fancy gave them the cut sign, a slice of the hand across the throat. Closing the canopy he put on his mask, took off the parking brake, engaged the nose-wheel steering, and advanced the throttles ever so slightly to follow the director's signals into the queue to wait for the cat.

After ten traps it was over. Long before Fancy was ready. Again he was day qualified. At the direction of the director he taxied to the porch near Elevator Four. With his helmet still on he climbed down from the plane. A plane captain came up and after a quick conference on the state of the plane, he and Mirabal walked across the deck, down a ladder to the catwalk, then down into the first passageway leading into the 0-3 level, just under the flight deck.

"We, I mean you, did real well."

Fancy turned, stopped and answered, "We did real well. I appreciate the way you handle everything in the back without a lot of unnecessary chatter. Concentrating on the job at hand is so much easier without having to comment or answer stupid questions, so I appreciate that. You're a pro Rhino and I like flying with you."

Mirabal beamed. "Thanks, man, that means a lot. What do you say we grab a slider and something to drink. This part of the job always makes me real thirsty."

"My thoughts exactly."

After a quick hamburger, quite a bit of drink to slake both their thirsts, and then a trip to the head, Fancy was sitting in the back of the ready room completing some paper work when Badrod Baldon came through with an LSO from one of the F-18 squadrons. Consulting his notebook, Badrod said, "Not bad Fancy, you did pretty well. The touch-and-go was good and then you had nine OKs and one fair, all three wires.

Fancy found himself at a loss for words. He felt he had done well, with maybe four or five OKs, but nine. OKs were perfect passes. He managed to stammer, "Which pass was the fair?"

Badrod once again looked at his notes. "Uh, it was the seventh one. The captain was chasing some wind and put the helm over a little. You went a little low and were lined up a little too much on the left." Grinning, he slapped Fancy on the shoulder, "Try harder next time, okay?"

An hour later he and Mirabal were strapped in, ready to go after the six night traps. As he looked out over the flight deck, he noticed a little bit of light in the western horizon and, he noted, a clear defined horizon. He hoped the light would hold and their first shot would be a "pinky" or a twilight shot. A pinky was just fine with him.

Still looking at the sky he noticed that the cloud cover was thickening. He guessed the base at about seven to eight thousand feet. The wind was out of the northwest and seemed to be blowing a little harder than it had been earlier, which was good. With a stronger wind, the ship would not have to steam as fast to get the thirty knots of wind over the deck. Every mile upwind would take the ship farther off shore and farther away from any bases he might have to divert to, the fewer of those miles the better.

Experience told him that carrier quals had some frab ups, and there was always a chance he might have to divert. Maybe that wouldn't be so bad, he might get a chance to call Cody. No, better not to think about shore, Cody, or anything else.

Mirabal came up on the ICS, "Everything looks okay back here, how about the front end?"

"Okay," Fancy replied.

"Are there any changes you want or need for tonight?" asked Mirabal.

"No, let's keep it simple. You handle the frequency changes and I'll do the transmissions."

"Roger, that," came the easy reply.

"Let's do it, takeoff checklist." Mirabal began reading off the items and Fancy checked off each item with the appropriate response. A few minutes later the engines had spooled up smoothly and they were taxiing toward the cat.

The F-14 on the cat in front of them, Fancy thought it was Killer's, seemed to be having a problem with the nose-tow. There was a conference going on around the nose of the plane, but nothing seemed to be getting done.

Fancy felt the tension start to build. The sky was starting to darken. Instinctively he began to go over what he would have to do if the cat didn't work as advertised, otherwise known as a cold cat shot. That's when the catapult didn't deliver enough power to throw the plane off the ship. Then he thought about engine failure, not likely, but something to keep your mind occupied. He ran his hand over the emergency jettison button. If he had to act, his actions would have to be sure and quick. No fumbling, no trying to remember what to do, just do it instinctively with no hesitation. Besides, Fancy knew, any real problems always cropped up at night.

Glancing at the sky he noticed that it was darkening fast. The group around Killer's plane was still screwing around with it. *Come on* he thought, *if you don't get something done, were going to be shot off here and it will be like being shot into an inkwell at midnight.*

After what seemed an eternity, though he realized it must have been a few seconds, he smacked the instrument panel in disgust, addressing the group working on the problem in front of them. "For cryin' out loud, stop dickin' around. Let's shoot or get off the cat. Jesus!"

As if a prayer had been answered, he noticed one of the senior enlisted men striding down the deck motioning for the F-14 to indeed be taken off the cat.

As soon as Killer's plane was rolled back out of the way, Fancy eased the plane forward, hearing and feeling the thump as the shuttle was moved forward, easing off the brakes, adding full power, cycling through the controls, checking the flaps, slats, and finally the engine gauges. Time to go.

Instead of saluting as he would have done in the daylight, Fancy flipped on the external lights in a salute to the cat officer. Placing his head back into the rest, with it inclined just enough to see the instrument panel, wham, they were shot into the sky. It was a pinky, not very pink but pink enough.

He felt himself being pushed into the seat as the G's increased. Then they were airborne.

The engines pushed them up at an eight degree nose up attitude, instruments okay, as he reached for and slapped up the gear handle.

Feeling the gear coming into the wells and everything looking, and more importantly, feeling good, he keyed the radio transmitter and said, "Desperado 203, airborne."

"Roger 203," came the disembodied voice of the departure controller, from Air Ops deep inside the ship. "Climb to six thousand then hold on one-three-five radial at sixteen miles. Your push at one seven after the hour."

"203 up to six, then hold on the one three five at sixteen, roger." Moving his left thumb from the radio button to the ICS, he opened his mouth to say something to Mirabal, but then thought better of it, as he felt the flaps and slats retract into their position.

As they climbed to sixteen thousand the night enfolded them. Their world ended at the canopy, only the wingtip lights would give any illumination and that would be faint at best. Besides, the wings were swept back and Fancy would have to twist and turn to see them anyway and he wasn't going to be doing much of that. Now he was on instruments making the TACAN needle go to where it needed to, holding the rate-of-climb steady, making the compass behave, keeping the wings level. After a few minutes he decided enough was enough and he engaged the automatic pilot. Naturally, it decided to go south and refused to engage.

Shaking his head in disgust, he felt for the circuit breakers, hoping one had just popped, but of course there was no such luck. He tried it three more times before he swore to himself.

"Gator, anything wrong?" queried Mirabal.

"Ahhhhhh, the auto-pilot's gone south," he replied in disgust. "No biggie."

"Keep the faith, big guy," Mirabal encouraged.

They hit the hold fix, sixteen miles on the one three five radial. Once they were established inbound he pulled the throttles back until he was showing only 1,800 pounds of fuel flow for both engines an hour, giving him an air speed of 220 knots. This would give him max conservation of air speed.

Hit the fix, turn left and go round and round, this time with the tailhook up. This first pass would be a touch-and-go, a practice bolter.

At exactly seventeen minutes after the hour he hit the fix for the third time, popping his speed brakes and pushed the nose down. There was another F-14 holding at five thousand heading inbound a minute in front of them.

Keying the mike: "Desperado 203 inbound at one seven state seven point six."

"Roger that, Desperado, continue inbound."

Arriving at five thousand, Fancy brought the nose up slightly to lessen the rate of descent, at the same time calling on the radio, "203, platform."

"Roger, 203, switch to button 8."

Rhino changed the frequency as Fancy watched the TACAN needle and made any corrections to stay on the final bearing inbound. At 1,200 feet and ten miles he dropped the gear and flaps, slowing the plane, stabilizing at 120 knots. Rhino read off the check list as Fancy verbally rogered each item.

With seventy-five hundred pounds of fuel, he toggled the main fuel dump and let 1,000 pounds bleed into the night air. If everything went as planned he should cross the ramp with 6,000 pounds, the maximum fuel load for an arrested landing.

Fancy reached over and adjusted the rheostat on the angle-of-attack indexer. This was a small group of lights on the left canopy bow in front of him, showing his airspeed that showed him a little slow. He would like 128 knots and he was at about 126, just a smidgen, he thought as he eased the throttle forward just a touch.. The indexer showed 128, okay.

Straining, he could just make out the ship. Not that it was recognizable as a ship. It only showed up as an assortment of white and red lights. Now he could see the outline of the landing area and the drop lights down the stern that would help with his lineup. The ball on the side of the landing area that would give him his glide slope was not yet visible.

"203, you're approaching glide slope, call your needles," came the metallic voice of the controller.

Those needles were cross hairs in a cockpit instrument that was driven by a computer aboard the ship. The computer contrasted the radar-derived position of the aircraft with the known location of the glide slope and centerline. It would then send a radio signal to a box in the plane, which positioned the needles to depict the glide slope and centerline. The system is called the ACLS, or automatic carrier landing system. Fancy still had to fly the plane, though in theory the plane could be landed automatically. Like most pilots, Fancy placed his faith in himself.

"Down and right."

"Disregard. You are low and slightly left, 203, slightly below glide slope, lined up slightly left. Come right a tad for lineup, on glide path, on glide path..."

Upon hearing the on-glide path confirmation he eased out the speed brakes and concentrated intently on his instruments. Now he had to hold a six-hundred-foot of descent rate, hold the heading, hold the airspeed, and keep the wings level. Finesse was now the name of the game.

He could see the ball now as the controller's voice told him to come left and then come right.

Making the corrections he could see by the drop lights that he was a little left of where he should be. Except for a quick glimpse straight ahead he kept his eyes on the heads up display.

"203, three quarter miles, call the ball."

Glancing ahead he saw that he had the meatball centered between the green datum lights. Lineup looks good. Fancy keyed his mike and said, "203, Tomcat ball, six point oh."

"Roger ball. Lookin' good," came Badrod's calm voice.

The ball moved in relation to the green reference or datum lights that were arrranged in a horizontal line. When the yellow meatball in the center moved up, you were above glide path. When it appeared below the reference line, you were low. If you got too low, the ball turned red, kind of a blood red. If that didn't get your attention of what could be impending doom, you were in the wrong place, at the wrong time, in the wrong business. Seeing a red ball meant you had to climb immediately higher on the glide slope. If you didn't the ramp was waiting to smash you and your plane to bits.

If the glide slope wasn't enough to worry about, the lineup was even more so. The landing area on the ship was only 115 feet wide. The wing span of the F-14, fully extended was 64 feet. Add to that the planes, on both sides of the deck, that were parked with their noses along what was called the foul lines, narrowing the deck considerably.

While monitoring his air speed, something else that was critical, the angle-of-attack indexer was a huge help. Any variation in his air speed affected his descent rate, thus messing up his control of the ball. A good way to kill yourself was to run out of airspeed at the ramp.

Fancy's eyes were moving constantly as he monitored the meatball, angle-of-attack, and lineup. As he got closer to the ship he dropped the angle-of-attack from his list and concentrated on keeping lined up, keeping the ball centered. Crossing the ramp he kept his eyes on the meatball flying it to touchdown.

Since this was a touch and go, when the gear made contact with the deck he thumbed in the speed brakes and pushed the throttles all the way to the stops. He could hear Bad Rod callling "Bolter, bolter, bolter," in the off hand chance he was forgetting to advance the throttles or to positively rotate to a flying attitude as he shot off the edge of the angled deck.

The engines were at full power as the Tomcat left the deck and vaulted into the air into the charcoal black night. Easing the stick back until he had ten degrees nose up attitude, checking for positive rate of climb. He brought the gear up and continued to accelerate, bringing the flaps and slats up, showing 195 knots. Now, all he needed was the six traps.

Upon reaching 1,300 feet, he was directed by radar control to level off and turn downwind, just the reciprocal or opposite of the ship's course, showing 220 knots. Reaching for the hook handle he brought it back down. "Hook down," he muttered to himself.

"What did you say, Gator?" asked Mirabal.

"Nothin', just talking to myself," he answered as he scanned the instruments.

"Whatever works, babe."

He thanked the controller, silently, for putting him on an eight mile groove, which Fancy thought was just about perfect. Bringing the wings level, he dropped the gear and flaps. Retrimming the plane just slightly she actually seemed to fly herself with just the tiniest amounts of inputs to the stick, and he found himself able to concentrate on the airspeed and altitude control. This had to be precision flying, get sloppy here and you died.

"203, approaching glide slope. 203, up and on glide slope. Three quarters of a mile, call the ball."

"203, Tomcat ball, five point two."

At the same time in Air Ops, located deep in the bowels of the ship, an enlisted man wrote 5.2 in grease pencil on a Plexiglass board. Beside that he then wrote, Fancy, 203. The notations were written backward so that the air officer, the air wing commander, and any one else on that side of the board watching the monitors, could read the data.

At the present time the display on the monitors was presented by a camera buried on the centerline of the flight deck, pointing aft and up the glide slope. As they watched they could see the lights of Fancy's plane in the center of the crosshairs that indicated the proper glide slope and lineup.

Up in the superstructure or island was Pri-Fly, the realm of the air boss. It was fairly quiet now since all the air traffic was being controlled by radar and radio from Air Ops. Even so the two enlisted men behind the air boss's chair were engaged. The taller of the two held a pair of binoculars pointed up the glide slope. Immediately upon seeing the approaching Tomcat, he identified it and sang out, "Set seven four zero, F-14." Regardless of the plane's advertised fuel state, the arresting gear was always set at the maximum trap weight.

On his left side another sailor made a notation in his log and repeated into a sound powered telephone, "Set seven four zero, F-14."

Reposing in his raised easy chair, the air boss could hear the radio transmissions. By his nod they knew that his eyes and ears agreed with them, that there was an F-14 on the ball with a trap weight of 74,000 pounds.

In the arresting gear engine rooms located under the flight deck at the rear of the ship. Sailors sat in each of four rooms, connected to Pri Fly by sound powered phones. Upon receiving the information from Pri Fly the men began to spin wheels that set the metering devices of their particular arresting gear wire. As this was accomplished they sang out in order, "One set seven—four- zero F-14…"

As soon as the last engine operator had reported his engine set, the talker in Pri Fly called, "All engines set, seven four zero, F-14." The air boss immediately rogered the information.

Directly aft of the island, on the fantail, located on the starboard side of the catwalk area, a sailor was stationed to retract the arresting gear engines once they had been engaged. When the fourth engine was reported set, he shouted to the arresting gear officer who stood above him on the deck, right on the starboard foul line. "Sir, all engines set, seven four zero, F-14."

The gear officer looked up the glide slope identifying the F-14. Glancing up the deck he noted that the landing area was clear with no aircraft protruding over the foul lines and there were no people in the landing area. Immediately he squeezed a trigger switch on the pistol grip that he held in his left hand.

The switch controlled a stop-light twenty feet aft of the landing signal officer's platform on the port side. Badrod Boldon saw the red light go out and a green light appear. He knew that the deck was clear and he called out, "Clear deck!" This call was echoed by the other LSOs on the platform.

Amazingly enough this whole cycle had taken only fifteen seconds and the ship was now ready to recover Fancy's F-14. Now all he had to do was fly it to the much coveted three wire.

Working the stick and throttles he plowed into the burble of air from the ship's superstructure. The F-14 jolted and he jammed on some power then immediately took it back again as he hit the calm air over the aft part of the ship.

His eyes glued to Fancy's plane, Badrod shuffled into the landing area. Against his right ear he held the headset connecting him with the ship's radios. In front of the platform was a televison monitor, called the PLAT, or pilot landing assistance television, which he glanced at occasionally to make sure the plane was lined up and in the grove. Even though he could talk to Fancy, he had nothing to say. The F-14 was coming in right on the money.

Fancy could still see the yellow ball as the wheels kissed the deck. Immediately he pushed the throttles right to the stops while at the same time he could feel the hook catch and he could feel himself being thrown forward against his harness straps. It only took two hundred and sixty feet for the plane to come to a complete stop.

Bringing the engines back to idle he could feel the plane being pulled backwards by the rebound of what he hoped was the three wire.

Twenty feet in front of them was the gear runner signaling with his wands to put the hook back up. Upon seeing the tailhook coming up he waved one of the wands in a huge circle to signal the arresting gear operator in the aft end of the ship to activate the engine and take the wire back.

Fancy noticed that the F-14 that had just landed ahead of him was sweeping back his wings to the seventy-two degree position and was taxiing out of the landing area. He goosed his throttles a little to move the big plane up the deck to make way for the next plane.

Badrod, on his platform, turned to one of the other LSOs and said, "Give him an OK Three. He was a little lined up to the right at the start."

The other man wrote in his logbook: 203, OK3 (LRATS).

Immediately they got ready for the next F-14 already in the grove, looking for the clear deck light to come on.

Again, they were on the pointy end of the boat, sitting behind the JBD, waiting for the F-14 on Cat One to do its thing. The last one. Fancy wiggled in his seat trying to get comfortable, becoming aware of how tired he was. The previous five landings had gone well, but he wanted to get this last one over with. He forced himself to look over everything carefully, flaps out, slats too, roger the weight board, ease forward into the shuttle, throttles up, brakes off, cat grip up, one last look at the gauges, fuel flow, RPM. Light on and wham! They were once more hurtling down the deck off into the blackness.

Nose up, gear up, still climbing.

Everything went well until they leveled off at 1,300 feet and turned downwind, directed by the controller. Holding at 260 knots until he was told to dirty up, which he did at the same time he turned on the base. He mangaged to lose a hundred feet while he was trimming, slowing and trying to maintain altitude. Mirabal cleared his throat. I deserved that, Fancy thought to himself. This is the big leagues and I'm supposed to be able to do this crap in my sleep, he chided himself.

Finally he was able to call the ball. No matter how hard he tried he just couldn't seem to get stabalized. Every correction seemed to be too much. He could feel the plane wobbling up and down on the glide slope going from too fast to too slow. Crossing the ramp, with not quite enough power he settled for a two wire.

After they had taxied out of the wire and were directed to a parking area, he shut down the engines with what he figured was the last of his energy and will power. Raising the canopy he was grateful for the rush of cool sea air. Forcing himself he pried his body out of the plane and plodded across the deck.

Mirabal, seeming not the least bit fatigued came up beside him. "Another exciting day in the Navy. I don't know about you, but I'm glad that's over. You okay?"

Fancy shook his head to clear some cobwebs. "Other than the fact that my fanny is draggin', I'm okay. Honestly though, I couldn't do it again tonight. Man, I'm beat."

"I hear you. I was just along for the ride and I'm tired. You did all the work. You did it pretty well too."

"Thanks. That last pass was a bad as it gets. I just couldn't seem to get everything working together. At least we're back to the bird farm in one piece, though, no thanks to me."

"Don't be so hard on yourself. If this was easy, everybody could do it."

After a session with the LSOs, and a discussion about this last pass, Fancy and Mirabal headed for their stateroom. Until they joined the ship for good this would be their temporary home tonight.

Mirabal was first through the hatch when they had finally located their home away from home. There were two bunks, one on top of the other, a desk, chair, and all the charm of someone's old garage. Mirabal heaved himself into the upper bunk and sighed deeply. "Home sweet home."

Fancy unlaced his steel-toed boots, wiggled his toes to see if he could still feel them and flopped into the lower bunk. Never, he thought, had a Navy rack been so welcome.

Mirabal leaned over the edge of his bunk to say something to Fancy. Before he could get the words out of his mouth, he was met by the gentle snores of his pilot. Shaking his head he lay back down, smiling. *You really earned it tonight, you realy did.* It was only a few moments later that he joined his friend in a blissful sleep.

Fancy was vaguely aware of someone shaking him. For a few seconds he wasn't sure where he was. Opening his eyes, it all came back. Looking up the arm of the enlisted sailor he grumbled, "Thanks, I'm tactical. What's up?"

"Sir, Commander Robinson wants all pilots and RIOs in Ready 3 at 0800. It's 0715 now, sir."

"Okay, thanks. Rhino, you awake?"

"Yeah. I wonder what's up?"

"Beats me. We'd better get moving."

After a quick shave and a quicker shower, Mirabal and Fancy walked into Ready Three. Fancy started to look around for Bagger. Not seeing him, he and Mirabal took two seats near the back. "Do you see Bagger anywhere?" he asked, again looking around the room.

"No, he probably tried to grab something to eat."

Fancy felt the pangs of hunger starting to assert themselves and wished that he had grabbed something. There was coffee, but it never went down very well on an empty stomach—make that a very empty stomach.

Any thoughts about eating were interrupted by the arrival of Commander Robinson. Robinson was dressed in his green bag and looked tired. "Stay seated," he said as he walked to the front of the room.

"Good morning. I trust you all slept well, I know I did. First of all I'd like to congratulate all you who qualified yesterday. For those of you who did not," he said icily, "I want to finish up today. Poncho, Killer, and

Animal, due to problems with the deck or their planes were not able to get qualed. Gentleman, as I have just stated, let's get it finished today.

"For those of you who have qualed, you'll be heading back to Miramar. You'll be taking back planes that have any minor problems that can be attended to back there. Once you're back, go see Chief Tomsha and get any paperwork finished up. When you've got that done you have until Friday at 0800 to get any other personal affairs in order. We're due to be back aboard on Friday by 1100 hours. Any questions?"

Even though two hands went up, Robinson just plowed ahead. "If you haven't heard, there's going to be a visiting Congressional delegation on board to see a little demonstration of what we can do. It will be mostly an F-18 show. We'll put up four planes to cover the Hornets."

"Do you know who's going to fly the four planes yet?" asked Poncho.

"I haven't made up my mind who the other three will be," answered Robinson with his ear-to-ear grin, partially answering Animal's question.

"Anything else? If not, your plane assignments are on the board in the equipment room. If you haven't eaten, grab something quick and be ready to launch by 0930."

Fancy rose, eager to get something to eat. Robinson's voice dashed his hopes of getting anything quick to eat. "Gator, I need to see you for a minute."

Fancy turned and walked to the front of the room. He waited while Robinson said something to Matsen. Matsen nodded to Fancy and then walked out of the room.

"Good morning, sir," he said, hoping this would only take a minute.

"Morning, Fancy. How'd it go last night?"

"Things went pretty well, sir. My last pass was nothing to write home about. I"ll admit it, I was pretty beat by the time we finished."

"Thanks to my many many spies aboard, I know you did just fine, and about everybody's last pass was not that great, I know mine wasn't."

Anyway, that's not what I wanted to talk to you about. I know you must have been looking around for Bailey?"

"Uh, yes, sir, I was. I figured he must be grabbing something to eat. His stomach sometimes rules his good sense."

"No, he's in his stateroom, getting some extra shuteye, by my orders."

"Sir?" questioned Fancy. This didn't sound good.

"He had a bad time last night. On his fifth trap, he had two bolters and then got a case of vertigo. Finally, he was able to get it down. When he did, he came to see me right away. Seems like he's thinking of turning in his wings."

Fancy blanched and let out a deep breath. "Shoot, sir, we've all had our turn in the barrel. Is he really serious about it?"

"He was last night. I'm hoping you can talk to him and get it straightened out. I'd hate to lose him, he's really turning out to be one of the better pilots in the squadron. No one else knows about this, although there may be some suspicions because he did come to see me."

Fancy paused. "Why do you think I'm qualified to get him back, sir?"

"You two have a little history. I know he thinks a great deal of you. He didn't seem to be very receptive to what I had to say last night. Give it a try, please. I really don't want to see him do anything he's going to regret later."

Before he could answer, Fancy's stomach rumbled. "I'll do my best, sir."

"I know you will, Gator. Have a good flight back."

"Thank you, sir."

As Fancy headed for the dirty-shirt wardroom, he didn't feel hungry anymore. He knew Bailey was too good a pilot to let one bad night get to him. He wondered what else it could be.

He found Mirabal and sat down beside him, his tray piled high with eggs, sausage, and toast. Even thought he didn't feel as hungry as before, he knew he had to eat to stay sharp. Getting stupid wasn't an option.

"Everything okay with the skipper?" asked Mirabal.

"Yeah, I'll tell you about it in the plane."

Mirabal raised his eyebrows, nodded, and continued eating.

After a quick bite they found their plane, Desperado 203, chained down and waiting for them right by the island. They would be taking off first, followed by Bagger in Desperado 208. A senior chief and a younger enlisted man were just finishing buttoning up the plane.

"Morning, sir," said the the senior of the two. Fancy looked at his name tag. It said Rugani.

"Morning, chief. How's she look?"

"She's fine, except for the auto pilot, sir. Other than that she checks out perfect."

Fancy smiled and started the walk around. As he was peering in the port side engine nozzle, he noticed that Bagger and his RIO, Walrus Carpenter, were coming up the catwalk.

"Hey, Bagger, how's it goin'?" he asked, trying to keep his voice light.

Bagger grinned, weakly. "Today's okay, so far. Last night," he shrugged, "was a bitch."

"What happened?"

"My first four traps went okay, but on number five…" He shook his head. "Two bolters and then I didn't know which way was up, down, sideways, or what. I was really screwed up. Hell, I scared the crap out of me and I don't know if Walrus wants to fly with me anymore. Notice the gray hairs he now sports."

Walrus Carpenter grinned, and said, "As long as I've flown with you, that was your only bad night. I'm in it for the long haul, you know that." He slapped Bagger on the shoulder and walked over to their plane.

"Did you see Robinson this morning?"

Fancy nodded. "We talked in the ready room. No one else was within earshot. He wants me to talk to you."

"Did he tell you what I said to him last night?"

"Yes."

Bagger shrugged. "Man, last night I was ready to give it all up, but…"

"But, today's a new day, right?"

"Something like that. I don't know."

"Let's get off this birdfarm, get squared away with Chief Tomsha and talk about it—if you want to."

"I do. Let's get to it." Bailey turned and walked over to his plane, with, what Fancy thought was the familiar spring in his step.

Fifteen minutes later Fancy was rogering the weight board and eased the plane into the shuttle. He felt the nose-two bar drop into the shuttle slot and came off the brakes, adding power at the yellow-shirt's signal.

He could feel more than hear the engines spooling up. There was another small jolt as the hydraulic arm shoved the cat pistons into tension, taking all the slack out of the hold-back bar. Only the shear-bolt was holding them back.

He went to full power while at the same time taking one last quick look at the gauges. "Rhino, you ready?"

"Gator, I'm good to go."

As the powerful engines sucked in the air and then blasted it out the exhausts against the jet blast deflector, he could feel the plane straining and vibrating to get off the deck. Once more he took a glance at the panel and guages—all warning lights out. He saluted the cat officer.

With one last look at the island, then a glimpse up the catapult into the morning sky, in a fencer's move he lunged down and almost touched the deck then quickly came up to a point.

At the exact instant the catapult fired. The G's threw him into the seat.

The sudden acceleration stopped as they came off the cat. Nose coming up, airspeed okay, angle of attack, right on. He slapped up the gear handle, wings were level. All was right with the world.

Pushing through 180 knots he brought up the flaps and slats. They were going through 2,500 feet still accelerating. Fancy squirmed a little in his seat. *One fine day he thought, one fine day.*

"Desperado, 203," called out Bagger.

"203," answered Fancy.

"I'm coming up on your starboard side."

"Roger that 208, nice to have you."

Fancy looked over to his right and and saw Bagger slide up almost even with them about 100 feet away. He wondered if the sight of his Tomcat was sending shivers up Bagger's spine like it was his.

Bagger moved in closer with all the precision of a surgeon. Fancy could see Bailey and Carpenter clearly now. He turned and gave a salute in acknowledgement.

"Desperado, 208, you're lookin good. Let's level off at 16,000."

"Roger 16,000," answered Bagger.

At 16,000 feet the planes leveled off with Bagger still on Fancy's starboard side. It always made Fancy feel good to fly a good formation. Precision, that's what it was all about.

"Rhino, how's everything looking on the scope?"

"Uh, there's some traffic at eleven o' clock at twenty, on roughly our course. Looks like commercial, probably headed to Lindbergh. Otherwise it's unusually quiet."

Fancy knew things could change in a hurry and he kept up a constant scan. Good old Mark I eyeballs, he thought.

Twenty-five minutes later they were on the ground and had turned the plane over to Shrader who promised to get the problem of the broken automatic pilot fixed post haste. He seemed embarrassed that anything had gone wrong with **his** plane.

Once they had checked with Chief Tomsha, and found out, much to their relief that they were all squared away, and as far as the Chief was concerned, they were ready to deploy.

An hour later they were sitting on the porch of the "big yellow house", Bailey with a beer and Fancy with a soft drink, the two men watched the waves roll in. They had been sitting, taking an occasional sip of their drinks but saying little.

Finally Fancy broke the silence. "What happened last night. It seems Robinson is pretty worked up, he feels he might lose a great talent."

"Last night…" Baggers voice trailed off and he shook his head as if he were trying to brush away some cobwebs or bad memories. "Things just went delta sierra. I was on the fifth trap and to tell you the truth, the first four hadn't been all that wonderful. The first bolter didn't bother me too much, but after the second one I began to wonder if it was me or the plane or…"

"Robinson mentioned vertigo after the second bolter."

"After I came off the deck after the second one I couldn't tell which was which. Carpenter really came through. He told me the instruments were functioning okay. If it hadn't been for him, we'd both probably be at the bottom of the Pacific."

After a long pause, Bagger continued. "Once we were on final I began thinking."

"About what?"

"Living. Wendy. Kids. The Navy. I don't want to kill anybody, myself, Carpenter. You know."

"Yeah, I know. But you did get down in one piece. You walked away from it."

"It was close. When I saw Badrod, he didn't say anything, he just held up his fingers like this." Bagger held up his hand with his thumb and forefinger almost closed. "I went to see Robinson right after that. He said he wasn't going to take my wings just then. He thinks I need to think about it, mull it over, you know."

"And, have you thought it over?"

"I've been back and forth with it. Sleep didn't seem to be an option last night. What do you think?"

"It doesn't matter one bit what I think. This is something you'll have to live with. What would you tell me?"

"Shoot, I'd tell you to stick it out, hang in there."

"I thought you'd say that. That's what I hope you'll do. You're too good a pilot to do anything else—and I'm just not blowing smoke I hope you know that."

Bagger looked at Fancy for several seconds. "I've got to admit that when I came up on deck this morning everything did look a little better, a lot better in fact. But…what if things go bad again. What if I can't hack it?"

"We both know that things will go south again. The bottom line is that we do what we have to do at that particular time. Have you ever spent any time worrying about it before?"

"No," answered Bagger, "and I don't want to start now."

"Like I said, you're a good pilot. You know what you're doing up there. There are no guarantees. There's no such thing as luck up there. We make our own by working harder or getting smarter. Besides can you see yourself doing anything else in the Navy?"

Fancy knew Bagger was back when he said, "What do you mean good pilot! Man, I'm a great pilot!."

"That's what I meant to say," replied Fancy. "What do you say I give Cody a call and if she's willing, we could all go get something to eat?" He was relieved he hadn't said what he had been thinking, "What would Rowdy Kobyashi have said?"

"You don't want me tagging along, do you?" asked Bagger. You're not going to have that much time with her?"

"That's okay. Let me give her a call."

The phone rang four times before it was picked up by an answering machine. Fancy felt his heart drop. After the beep, just as he started to deliver his message, Cody's voice broke in. "Hello, Dan?"

"Hi, it's me. I'm glad you got there in time to pick up the phone. I was wondering if Bagger and I could come up and take you out to get something to eat. Amanda too, of course." He felt like he was back in high school trying to get a date with the prom queen. His mouth felt dry and his stomach was starting to do flip-flops. Could this be love he wondered?

"I've been home with a sick girl. Getting something to eat sounds wonderful, but I'm not sure Amanda is up to it, she's running a fever and has been in bed all day. Of course, once she knows you're coming she'll probably feel better."

"I noticed there was a fast food place on the way. How about if we pick up something there and bring it up?"

"I think that would work out. Remember, we've got plenty of drinks," she said with a lilt in her voice.

"Okay then, we're on our way. Anything in particular you'd like us to pick up?'

"Burgers and fries go over real well in this house. It's often a sure cure for what ails someone I know."

"We'll see you in a bit then," said Fancy with an obvious eagerness in his voice as he hung up the phone.

"Man, I thought I drove fast," Bagger grinned as they walked up to the front door.

"It wasn't that fast was it?" smiled Fancy sheepishly.

"Oh no, no sireee," continued Bagger. "Then of course, there was the weaving in and out of traffic. And then," he looked at his watch, "there is the new record from San Diego to Carlsbad. No, you weren't driving fast, that 240 was flying."

Just then the door flew open and Amanda was standing. there in her pajamas. "Hi," she beamed. "Mom, Lt. Fancy's here!"

Cody appeared from around the corner, wiping her hands on a towel. "You don't have to yell, young lady. I'm not deaf and I'm only in the next room."

"Sorry, mom."

"Come on in, Dan." Again she extended her hand. Fancy took it and felt his heart race.

They stepped through the door and Fancy made the introductions. After they had shaken hands all around Fancy and Bailey carried their contribution to the kitchen. "I hope you like burgers, Amanda?"

"Oh, yeah, I love 'em. Are they from that place just off the freeway. Those are the best!"

"That's the place," answered Fancy. "Your mom says you're not feeling so hot. Maybe you should be in bed."

"I've been there all day and honest, I'm feeling better. Besides those burger smell good."

Fancy looked up in time to see Cody wink at him, grin, and nod an *I told you so*.

Amanda turned to Bagger and said, "Are you Bagger? Gator, uh Lt. Fancy has told us all about you."

Bagger looked at Fancy and asked, "What exactly did you tell these young ladies?"

Fancy, feigning innocence, said, "Just the truth, nothing but the truth."

"Come on in and sit down. I'll get some plates and we can eat."

"Sounds good, let me help you," said Fancy as he moved toward the cupboards. "I'll try not to break anything."

Cody grinned, "That's the last thing I was worried about."

After they had eaten, Fancy was glad of two things: one that he had bought extra burgers, and, that he was here. He couldn't take his eyes off Cody. Every time he saw her she seemed…right. If this was love, it sure felt a lot different than it had with Janice. He couldn't put it to words, but the feeling was different, good, but different.

Amanda was sitting there trying to look happy and well, but she was not succeeding. Fancy thought that she looked a little green around the gills. "Amanda, would you, or your mother mind, if I carried you back to your bed. You don't look so good."

Cody reached over and felt her forehead with the back of her hand. "Young lady, you still feel pretty warm to me. Would you like to walk or ride back to your bed?"

"Oh, mom," came the somewhat weak reply, "I don't want to go back to bed, I'm okay, really."

"Walk or ride?" her mother replied.

Amanda, knew when she was beat, "A ride would be just fine."

Fancy got up, and picked her up, putting her on his back piggyback style. Amanda shreiked in surprise and delight. "OOHHH Mom!"

"Watch for low bridges, we're headed for the bedroom. By the way, where is it?"

"Just down the hall, then turn right."

Amanda and Fancy disappeared down the hall, accompanied by what Bagger thought was an imitation of an F-14. Amanda's delighted cries seemed to make the flight back to bed a successful mission. Bagger gazed after them and then looked at Cody who was still following them down the hall with her eyes.

She turned. "He's quite a guy."

"Yes, he is. He's one of those one in a million, I think."

"Why do you say that?" she asked.

"Well the very fact that I'm here with him. I know that he really wanted to see you before we leave. I had a bad night last night on the boat. In fact is was so bad that I was seriously contemplating turning in my wings. The skipper wouldn't take them, I hope he hasn't changed his mind," he chuckled and paused.

"Go on."

"I just hope I'm making sense. Anyway, he took time to talk to me this morning. He didn't rush it, didn't try to b.s. me. I'd pretty well decided to keep my wings, but he solidified it. This cruise will be tough enough and going with him will make it a little bit easier, at least for me.

"Is he a good pilot?"

Bagger leaned forward, looking around to make sure no one was sneaking up on him or listening. No, he's not good, he's great, one of the real great ones. He's in that upper one tenth of everybody who flies in the Navy, as far as I'm concerned. The thing is, it doesn't go to his head. There are so many big egos in this business, but not Fancy. He just lets his flying do his talking—period.

"In addition, he's a great guy to have as a friend. You know he's going to be there for you, no matter what. When the going gets tough—you know he'll be there until the sun goes down. Loyalty is something he takes very seriously."

She nodded slowly staring off into space. "I sensed that about him, but it's always nice to hear it from someone else. Have you known him long?"

"We met at Pensacola in flight school. He kind of stood out even then. After we graduated we were assigned to different squadrons. He got married. They lost their baby. His loyalty maybe got misdirected, according to him. The marriage went south and he kind of lost his way for awhile. Then he got, by his own admission, a second chance. Maybe in more ways that one in that arena," he grinned.

Cody just smiled.

Fancy cleared his throat as he entered the room. "She wanted to know what it was like to be on a carrier so I started to tell her. I must be a boring story-teller because she was asleep by the time I started to tell her about my second trap," he laughed.

Bagger winked at Cody and replied, "That's what you get for being so good at what you do. Good thing I wasn't telling her about last night, she'd be having nightmares right now."

They all laughed.

"Listen," said Bagger as he jumped up from the table, "let me do up these dishes while you two take a walk or something." Looking at Fancy he continued, "I might need the practice in the near or far future."

Cody showed him where all the dish washing things were and after checking on Amanda, who remained fast asleep, they walked out the front door. "We'll be back soon," she called to Bagger who was up to his elbows in soap suds.

"You youngsters take your time," he called in his best old folks voice. "And more importantly, don't do anything I wouldn't do."

Fancy shook his head as they headed down the driveway.

"He's nice," said Cody. "I'm glad you brought him."

"He had kind of a rough night so I figured he could use the diversion. I'm glad you didn't mind."

They walked in silence for a few minutes before Fancy said, "I hope the burgers were okay?"

"They were fine. Amanda hijacks me to that place as often as she can."

"I was really glad when you picked up the phone, I really dislike talking to a machine."

"As a matter of fact I screen all my calls. My ex-husband has an irritating habit of calling every now and then and I don't like to talk to him."

"Tough divorce? I'm sorry, that's none of my business, I don't mean to pry."

"You're not and yes, it was. Very messy. Paul was abusive and I..." her voice trailed off.

They kept walking. "Anyway, he was very unhappy that I wanted a divorce. He accused me of all kinds of vile things—none of them true."

"Abusive in what kind of way?"

"He hit me—just once but that was more than enough and I knew from all I had read and heard it wasn't going to get any better, so I opted out before things got really bad. Things weren't going that well before the blow was struck. He was terribly jealous and possessive."

"Did you live here when all this happened?"

"No, we lived in Redondo Beach. That's up the coast in Los Angeles. We both worked for the Southern California Edison Company as engineers. That's where we met. After the divorce I was able to get a job down here with San Diego Gas And Electric, at a slight raise in pay. You probably noticed that big stack across the lagoon on the way up. That's where I work making sure everybody has what they need in the way of electricity."

"I can't say that I'm disappointed that you're a divorcee, to be honest with you."

"I can say that I'm pretty happy about it myself right now," she answered turning away for a moment. "You must think I'm terrible."

"No, not at all! I'm glad you're happy and away from that guy. He can't be much of a man. A real man never hits a woman. I learned that from my Uncle Don."

"Your Uncle Don sounds pretty smart to me. Is the rest of your family that smart?"

"I think so. We're probably all pretty boring, but all my aunts, uncles, cousins, etc…are good people. I hope you get to meet them sometime."

"I hope I do too."

"What about your relatives. Where are they? How did you get from…"

"The reservation?"

Fancy stammered, wanting to kick himself for sticking his nose where it probably didn't belong. "There I go again, I don't mean to pry, I guess I'm just naturally nosey."

"Don't be silly. You know, most of the men I've met only want to talk about themselves and let me know how great they are or think they are. Nobody ever asks about me or my relatives. I'm impressed."

Fancy felt himself blushing. "I've wanted to know ever since I met you, to tell the truth. I'd like to know all about you."

She began slowly. "My folks were among the very few of my people who didn't drink, take drugs, or abuse their kids. They ran a store—more like a trading post really. In fact they probably lost a lot of business because they didn't stock any liquor. Anyway they worked hard, put away all the money they could for my brother's and my education. They realized that the only way for us to have a future was to get off the reservation. Getting a good education was the ticket out. By their labor of love they saved enough to pay for partial tuition at the University of South Dakota. My brother and I were only a year apart and it helped that we were able to win partial scholarships, as well as be there together. We kind of formed our own support group. That was the hardest thing I had ever had to do—leave home and live among the white eyes. There were so many adjustments to make."

Without realizing it himself, Fancy had taken her hand and gave it a little squeeze. When he realized what he had done he let go of it as if it had been a white hot metal rod. "I'm sorry, I didn't mean to be forward or disrespectful." *Geez,* he thought, *what next, am I going to break out in great big zits?*

"Stop being sorry," she bantered. "If I hadn't liked it I would have let go." With that, she took his hand and continued to walk.

"What kind of adjustments?"

"Mostly just being away from home. I was so homesick for most of that first year. Then I made some friends in the dorm and everything started to fall into place. I hit the books and did pretty well, even made the dean's list."

"The next year my brother Scott arrived and things went really well for both of us.

"Where's Scott now?"

"He graduated with a degree in Marine Biology. He got to make one trip out to the west coast with a class and he was hooked on the ocean and everything in it. He lives in Hawaii and works for the state trying to keep everything the way it should be, as he puts it."

"How did you get into engineering?"

"Math always held my interest when I was growing up. My parents kept us away from the riff raff on the reservation by making sure our teachers in school always kept us challenged. At first Math was hard for me, especially the multiplication tables. When I had learned them, everything just seemed to fall into place for me."

"Multiplication tables?" exclaimed Fancy.

"Yes, and just like that I took off like a rocket."

Fancy shook his head. "If only I had known, I would have learned them earlier."

"Just before I graduated there was a job fair at the university. It seems I was just what Southern California Edison was looking for: a woman, a minority, and someone who was willing to relocate. I went out to Los Angeles, went to work, met Paul, and you know the rest."

"What about your folks? Do you see them very often?"

Cody took in a deep breath. "They're both dead—drunk driver. He survived—they didn't."

"Unbelievable, just unbelievable," Fancy murmured. "I'm sorry. I guess I just take my folks for granted. They've always been there and you just never know, do you?"

"No, no you don't," she said turning away and dabbing at her eyes.

"I didn't mean to, I'm..." he faltered. Boy, he thought, *I'm so smooth.*

"Hey," she said, "don't get down on yourself. You weren't driving the car that killed them. Come on, let's go see how Bagger is doing."

Bagger was doing just fine. He was stretched out on the living room floor, fast asleep. His snoring seemed to rattle the blinds on the windows.

"Bagger! Bagger, wake up!" Fancy insisted.

"What? Where am I? What the hell?" he croaked as he jumped up, still partly asleep.

Fancy and Cody both tried to stifle their laughter. When Fancy was unsuccessful, they both came unglued. It was a good way to end the day he thought.

After saying good-bye to Amanda, the three of them walked down to Fancy's car. "What are you going to do with your car while your gone?" asked Cody.

"Uh, there's a big warehouse just off base. I was planning on leaving it there."

"I'd be glad to keep it in our garage if you like. It's a three car garage with only one car. Amanda and I could take care of it, start it once in awhile, that sort of thing."

Fancy nodded. "I'd be glad to pay you for your trouble. At least I wouldn't have to worry about it."

Indignantly she drew herself up and announced, "You will not! It would be our pleasure, after all we've got almost a life time supply of cream soda. I'd say that makes us more than even."

Fancy put up his hands in surrender. "I'd really appreciate it, thanks. Let me give you a call and we'll see when I need to bring it up."

She stuck out her hand to again shake his, but this time she reached up and brushed his cheek in a quick kiss. Fancy involuntarily put his hand to his cheek. "I'm never going to wash my face again," he vowed.

She smiled, "Call me as soon as you know about the car."

The drive back to the big yellow house was made at a considerably slower speed. "Gator, I notice you keep rubbing your cheek. Is it okay? You want me to drive?"

Fancy stopped rubbing his cheek and looked at Bagger. "Well, what did you think?"

"She's a very striking lady. Very beautiful, charming, a real lady, and she's crazy about you. I think Amanda is a little young for you though."

Fancy punched Bagger playfully in the arm. "Could you please, extend your opinion a little farther up the family line?"

"Oh, Cody? Yeah, she's okay too," joshed Bagger. "Seriously, she's something else. Classy, very classy, and yeah, I think she kind of likes you too. I guess she's kind of turned your world upside down?"

"You can say that again, but don't. I wonder if you leave a car in someone's garage, if that means we're going steady." He smiled, turned on the radio and started to beat the time to Anita Baker's *Sweet Love*.

Coming through the door of the big yellow house, Bagger and Fancy found Poncho and Big Wave in a frenzy of activity. Seabags and suitcases were strewn about in various stages of packing.

"What's goin' on, guys?" asked Bagger. "How come you're getting all your stuff packed now?"

Poncho looked up from stuffing some underwear into his B-4 bag. "We got a call about half an hour ago from Chief Tomsha. Seems like they want us launching for the boat by 1300 tomorrow."

"I thought you were supposed to finish qualifying today?" continued Bagger. "What happened to that?"

Big Wave came in with some freshly pressed uniforms. "I don't know. We were on deck doing the walk around and they just shut everything down and told us to report back to the Ready Three. Robinson told us there had been a change of plans and we would qual on the way to Hawaii. Said he couldn't tell us anymore than that, because he didn't know what was going on either, word just came all the way down from CINCPAC."

"Maybe we should take care of that car business tonight," drawled Bagger. "I bet we have to be back at the base by 0800."

"I bet you're right," sighed Fancy as he headed for the phone.

He dialed the number, having to start over once. Slow down he told himself. "Hello, Cody. There's been a change of plans…"

Five minutes later he came back into the living room. Bagger looked up. "Are we going up there right now or are you going up by yourself, or…"

"She said she would come down, there's a neighbor that will bring her down she thinks. If she can't do it that way, she's going to call back and if she doesn't in the next few minutes, that means she's on her way. I guess I better get my stuff out. Of course it's mostly already packed anyway," he muttered.

"I hope this means the sooner we leave, the sooner we get back," croaked Poncho.

"Yeah, right," said Big Wave. "Remember, this is the Navy. You know, see the world and all that jazz, being a presence in the four corners of the world."

"You mean," asked Bagger in mock horror, "that this just isn't a sight-seeing cruise. I'm shocked, truly shocked."

Poncho threw a stack of underwear at Bagger, connecting with his face. "You have just destroyed my faith in the human condition, Bagger. I was so looking forward to this."

By the time Cody, and her neighbor, Mrs. Green, arrived, the packing was pretty much finished. The four pilots were sitting on the front porch looking out across the Pacific. Fancy got up off the steps and walked down to Cody's car. "Where's Amanda? I hope she's not worse, I could have brought it up."

"She's fine. In fact she wanted to come, but I insisted she get some rest. This is a note she wrote, but you have to promise not to open it until you're on the the carrier."

"Mysterious. I love mysteries and tell her it will be the first thing I do after I land."

"She'll be so relieved. I had to promise her it was the first thing I'd talk to you about. Only then did she agree that she did indeed need some more rest. You've been so good for her, Dan. It's hard to believe how hard she's working in school."

"Make sure she knows her multiplication facts. It's the key to success," he replied. "And I'm not making fun of anyone either."

"I hope not," she said. "Listen, Amanda is going to miss you and so will I.

"I've never been much of a writer, but I'd like to write to you and Amanda if that's okay. You know, I'll need to check on how she's doing and all."

"I hope the 'and all' includes me," she added.

A long silence followed as they both looked at each other. "The 'and all' definitely includes you. You know we've just met, but somehow I feel like I've always known you. To tell you the truth, before the airshow I hadn't been this happy for a long time. Here's the address where Amanda or you can drop me a line. I'd like to know how she's getting along."

She took the slip of paper and put it in the pocket of her jeans. "Maybe Amanda will let me slip a note into her letters, which she definitely wants to write. Amanda writing, that's something new." She shook her head. "Seems like you have made quite an impression on the whole family Lieutenant. Please, be careful—take care of yourself, Dan."

Again she took his hand, but this time they both leaned forward, in what Fancy thought was the best kiss of his entire life, short, but oh so sweet. Then she was gone. "There she goes with my car and my heart," he sighed to himself as he watched the taillights disappear up Ocean Blvd.

"Well babe, what are you going to miss more, the car or…" coaxed Big Wave.

"No contest, Wave, no contest," Fancy said, as he turned to go back in the house.

The four flyers walked into VF-124's ready room. They were surprised to find that they were among the last of the squadron to arrive. Robinson and Matsen were already at the front of the room talking quietly. Fancy gave him an okay sign with his thmb and forefinger and pointed to Bagger as he slid by and sat down. Robinson smiled and nodded and then went back to his discussion with Matsen. He also noticed Doc Su was sitting in the front of the room with another officer he hadn't seen before.

Fancy sat down heavily. In a moment Moose Milwood sat down beside him. "How goes it, Gator?" he rumbled. "You ready to go to sea?"

"I'm good to go. How 'bout you?"

"I'm ready, good and ready. After that cluster on the boat, I hope they're ready for us. I was not impressed by the way things were going on the flattop."

"What was the skinny? I thought things went okay. Of course by the time I got that sixth trap, I wasn't exactly clear-headed."

"Personally, I thought the deck force was moving way too slow. I know that bird farm came from the east coast, so maybe that's the reason." He shrugged. "No offense, but I think we do it better out here."

"Gentleman, I need your attention," announced Robinson. "By now you're probably wondering why we're rushing things and why we didn't quite finish the carrier quals. As a matter of fact so was I. This morning I have some answers for everyone." Gesturing toward the new officer, who started to get to his feet, he introduced him. "This is Lt. Commander Coleman. He's from Admiral Ballard's staff. Commander Coleman."

Lt. Commander Coleman was tall, wore glasses, and his prematurely graying hair made him appear older than he probably was. "Good morning, gentleman. Admiral Ballard sent me over here to bring you up to speed and let you know why we've sped things up."

He turned to the world map hanging on the wall back of him. Taking a pointer he put the point on Taiwan. "As you have probably noticed, this part of the world is heating up. The Chinese are particularly tweaked about the Taiwanese President', President Lee, visiting his alma mater's graduation ceremonies, even if his son was graduating. As a result, the Chinese have begun to move large numbers of troops, ships, and planes into the region across from Taiwan. They have informed the Taiwanese that they will be conducting live fire exercises, including missiles. No one expects too much to come of this, except they also are moving significant numbers of landing craft into the same area. If that isn't enough," he said moving the pointer to the Korean peninsula, the North Koreans have increased their military presence close to the DMZ. This is surprising, since they they're trying to get economic help from the South Koreans and the United States. Any questions so far?"

No hands were raised and he continued. "With our commitment in the Persian Gulf, we seem to be a little short on carriers. We want Enterprise and her battle group to add some muscle in this area," he announced, again tapping the map with his pointer. "Again, we don't expect the Chinese or the North Koreans to do much except posture, but then again, we can't be a hundred percent sure either."

Robinson stood up. "I want you to make sure you're already to launch at 1300. Enterprise wants to start recovering aircraft no later than 1500. That should give everyone time to get out to the boat with time to spare."

Moose nudged Fancy and just grinned. "Time for some fun and games," he whispered.

"Unless there's anymore questions or problems, I'll see everybody out on the flight line at 1240. Bagger, I need to see you for a minute."

Fancy got up, stretched and watched Bagger move toward the front of the room. He was glad that little episode was over with. Then he wondered if it would ever happen to him. Anything is possible he thought, as he knocked on the door frame as he passed out into the hall.

As he emerged from the building he noticed the base was in full swing with engines being started, and planes taxiing toward the active runway. A C-130 caught his eye as it touched down and started its roll out. He noticed that its tail showed it to be from Nellis. Wouldn't that be something? he mused as he turned around after hearing someone call his name. The caller was Bagger.

"Gator, wait up!" Bagger strode up with a huge grin on his face.

"I take it everything is okay with you and the Skipper?"

"Oh yeah, maybe Matsen is a little disappointed, but we're okay. He said as far as he was concerned, that was the end of it. Matsen kind of gave me a look, but I think he was just screwin' around. Let's grab something to eat unless you have something you need to get squared away."

"No," Fancy answered, "I'm good to go, we're going to have to walk though."

"That's okay with me. We're going to wish we could walk somewhere beside the flight deck of that carrier all too soon."

As they headed toward the Officer's Club, an enlisted man called out to Bagger, "Lt. Bailey, there's a call for you from the tower."

"The tower?" Bailey asked with a puzzled expression on his face. "I don't think I know anybody who works up there."

"Maybe it has something to do with that C-130 I saw recovering a few minutes ago."

Bagger's face brightened, then fell again. "Nah, that would be just too good, but I'll check it out anyway." He turned and walked back in the building.

It didn't take but a very few seconds before he came flying back out, calling to Fancy to help him find some transportation. "She's here, can you believe that?"

"Miracles happen," grinned Fancy. "Let's grab the Caddy."

Fancy followed Bagger, who by now was moving close to the speed of sound. He was fussing with the ignition switch as Fancy pulled open the passenger's door.

"Why don't people leave the damn keys in here like they're supposed to. Man...," he grumbled as he touched various wires together. Finally, the car rumbled to life. Bagger jammed it into gear and headed for the transient aircraft parking area.

"I didn't know you could hot-wire cars. Is there no end to your talents?"

Bagger grimaced. "You work around here long enough and you pick up all kinds of useful and some not so useful skills. I do what I need to do. Can you believe this. This is so great!"

"How do you think she managed this?" asked Fancy.

"Dunno, but I'm glad she did. I called her last night after you hit the rack. She gave no indication she'd show up here though."

Bagger brought the big black caddy to the rear ramp of the C-130. It had been dropped and some equipment was being unloaded. Rowdy Kobayashi and Razor Dodson were supervising the operation. Almost before the car was stopped Bagger was out, running over to the two female pilots.

By the time Fancy had walked up, Bagger was hugging the diminutive Air Force pilot. "Morning Cassie, how you doin'?"

She smiled and turned to greet him. "I'm fine, not as fine as they are though," she said jerking her thumb toward the still embracing pair. "How have you been?"

"Can't complain," he answered. "Boy, did you surprise him. He lit up like a Christmas tree when he heard from the tower you were here. How'd you manage this anyway?"

"The plane was scheduled to come, but we weren't. After Bagger called last night, Wendy made a couple of calls, one to Winkleman. The rest, shall we say, is now history, or something."

By now Wendy Kobayashi had disengaged herself from Bagger's long encompasssing arms. "Hey Gator, nice to see you again."

"Nice to see you too, Wendy. I just wish Bagger could work up some enthusiasm though."

"This is so great," laughed Bagger. "I just can't believe it. After I got off the phone last night, I thought it would be six months before I would get to see you." He immediately hugged her again, lifting her off her feet and twirling her around and around.

"Put me down, I've got to fly back sometime today!" she laughed, shaking herself free.

Reluctantly he put her down, but managed to keep hold of one of her hands. "Listen, we've got some time before we have to take off. Are you on any kind of strict schedule?"

"Before we go back to Nellis, we have to go down to Luke Air Force Base. The 64th is going on the road and we're taking some communications gear down," Razor said, gesturing with her thumb towards the interior of the cavernous C-130. We're expected at Luke by, she looked at her watch, 1530 at the latest."

"We were headed for the O' Club to get something, but how about if we head off base to that place up Miramar Blvd., you know…" He gestured toward the civilian side of the base.

"Don't look at me," said Fancy, holding up his hands. Remember, I'm the new guy here."

"Let's not waste time driving around, isn't there a place we can get something quick?"

"Ah, the messhall is probably our quickest bet. Is that okay with you, ladies?"

"Sure," said Rowdy. "Is that our transportation?"

"Great isn't it?" beamed Bailey.

"That is definitely classy," grinned Wendy. "Positively classy."

The time passed all too quickly, particularly from Bagger's point of view, and they found themselve again standing by the C-130. Cassie said good-bye to Fancy and Bagger and said she better begin the preflight for their flight to Luke. Fancy said he'd walk back to the Gunfighter's hanger, and after saying good-bye to the two pilots he trudged back up the road.

"I'm so glad you were able to come. Man, I was so surprised this morning. Thanks for making the effort," Bagger said, holding both her hands as they faced each other.

"Listen," he said. "There's something else I need to tell you."

She cocked her head. "Go ahead, I'm all ears."

He sighed and took a deep breath. "The other night when we were trying to finish up night quals I had a bad night. I had two bolters and then got a bad case of vertigo. Things got a little hairy and I had a real tough time getting back on deck."

"How bad?" she asked seriously.

"It was bad enough that I went to the skipper and talked about turning in my wings."

"Obviously you didn't, what changed your mind?"

"Probably a combination of things. I like what I do, but probably the main reason was I didn't want you to be disappointed in me."

She took a step back and looked up at the tall Texan. "I don't want you to make any decisions based on what I'm going to think. You know your own mind."

"Wendy, you've become a big part of my life right now." Suddenly, he knelt down beside her on one knee. "I've done a lot of thinking and I want to be with you for the rest of my life and beyond. I want to grow old with you."

Wendy Kobayashi took a certain amount of pride in the fact that she was very rarely taken by surprise, but this was one of those times she had been overtaken by the tide of events. Her first impulse was to laugh, but she saw that Scott Bailey was completely serious. "Is this a proposal?"

Bagger, who was as surprised or even more so by what he was doing blurted out, "Yes, yes it is. Will you marry me?"

Wendy shook her head. "You know, you're the guy that my parents warned me about."

"How's that?" he asked, still on bended knee.

"You're not a Mormon, it's too sudden, I don't know that much about you, and, yes, I will."

Bagger sprang to his feet. "You will?" he asked in an astonished voice. "You will?"

"Yes, but…" her voice trailed off and she shook her head.

"You're not going to change your mind are you?"

"No, but you've got to promise to come back safe and sound, you big lug."

"Oh man oh man!" shouted Bagger, literally jumping up and down for joy. "This, this is the greatest day of my life."

"We both owe Winkleman, big time. Listen, I really want you to be careful, big guy," she said as she looked up at him. "I know that must sound silly, because I know what you do is dangerous."

"It's what we do," he reminded her.

She smiled. "I'll get to Luke and its 10,000 foot runway. You're going to a carrier, with what 265 feet?"

"270, but who's counting."

"What a luxury. Be careful anyway, we've got some mountains to climb when you get back. I'm going to miss you, in fact that started when you left Nellis last week." She reached up and gave him a kiss on the lips, then turned and walked to help with the preflight for the C-130. Suddenly she turned. "Mrs. Wendy Bailey. Has a nice ring to it, don't you think?"

"Nice?" he shouted back, I think it sounds just right." He immediately reversed direction and loped back to her side as he fished around in his pocket. "I put these in my pocket this morning and I have no idea why I did, until now." He brought out a pair of gold wings. "This is the pair of wings I got when I graduated from Pensacola. I don't have a ring, but, ah, could you keep these until we can pick one out?"

"Sure, nothing would mean more to me right now," she said, as she pecked him on the cheek and walked to the waiting C-130.

Fancy and Mirabal had just finished their own preflight when they heard the unmistakeable sound of the C-130's four turbo props, climbing out, headed for Luke Air Force Base in Arizona. Looking over towards Bagger's Tomcat, he saw Bagger following the plane until it was swallowed up by the Southern California haze.

Fancy and Mirabal completed their walk-around and Fancy strolled over to Bagger's plane just as Bagger was about to climb the boarding ladder. "Bagger!"

His friend turned and dropped back down to the ground. "She made a pretty nice take off, didn't she?"

"It looked good to me. Say, since were the last two to launch today, what say we make a little detour up the coast?"

Would this 'little detour' be by way of Carlsbad, huh?"

laughed Bagger.

"It wouldn't be much out of our way and we've got some time to play with. How about it?"

Bagger appeared to give the idea long and deliberate thought before he nodded in the affirmative. "Uh, Gator, would you be my best man?"

Fancy screwed up his face in puzzlement. "Best man, don't you have to be engaged first?"

"I just got through asking her. She said yes. Can you believe that?"

"Just now?" Fancy asked, surprise ringing in his voice. "You mean when you were talking to her by the 130?"

"That's it. I don't quite believe it myself yet."

Fancy stuck out his hand. "Congratulations, Babe. I'd be proud to stand up with you." Fancy shook his head. "What is it about California, the water? What? Everything happens so fast out here. By the way, what did you use for a ring?"

"You got to admit, Gator, what ever it is that's happened, it's for the better, don't you think? And, I used my wings. I just stuffed them in my pocket this morning for no absolute reason I can fathom."

"It is, in my best guesstimation," sighed Fancy. "Are you game for a little detour?"

"Si, let's do it."

Fancy slapped him on the back, turned and walked over to Desperado 207. Mirabal looked over the edge of the canopy rail. "Lt. Bailey seems pretty happy. What's going on with him?"

"He just got engaged a few minutes ago, " said Fancy as he climbed up the boarding ladder and swung himself over the edge of the cockpit.

Mirabal laughed, "Leave it to Bagger to keep things stirred up one way or another. Is it that little Oriental gal from Nellis, I saw the C-130 with the Nellis tail code?"

"She's the one. Captain Wendy Kobayashi, call sign, Rowdy."

# 7

Fancy watched as Bagger's plane started to rumble down the runway. As his plane broke free from the runway, Fancy pushed the throttles forward to the stops and felt himself pushed back in his seat as his reward. Tingles pushed their way up his spine. He felt ready and confident for whatever the next several months held in store.

As soon as the two planes went feet wet, Bagger flying lead, climbed to 5,000 feet and continued a shallow right hand turn until they were parallel to the coast.

"Desperado, 203, do you know where that big stack is along the beach at Carlsbad?"

"207, not exactly, but I think I'll be able to pick it out. I"m going to start a gradual descent so we're at 500 feet by the time we get to Carlsbad. Why don't you fall back a little bit more so when you see me go to zone five you'll know we're there. Keep your eyes peeled for traffic from Palomar airport. Down this low they should be no problem, but…"

"Roger that, Bagger," he answered as he retarted the throttles and fell back of Bagger's plane. It was a beautiful, clear day that was just made for flying. The tingles returned.

What took thirty minutes to drive from San Diego took only a few seconds before Carlsbad was beneath them.

"Desperado 207, I've got the stack in sight. Going zone five now."

"Roger, 203." Fancy saw the two pinpoints of light emerge from the tail of Bagger's plane as he went to zone five afterburner.

Fancy pushed the throttles forward, past the detents and he felt himself pushed back in his seat as the afterburners kicked in. The big Tomcat accelerated and as the stack flashed by he pulled the stick back and at the same time did a series of three hundred and sixty degree rolls as they followed Bagger up into the Southern California sky.

Cody Thorn had just come out of the master control room, after working out a small pwer surge problem, and was walking back to the building where her office was. As she normally did she looked out over the water and down the coast. She heard and felt the passage of Bagger's plane as he blasted past. Fortunately, she kept looking down the coast and was able to pick up Fancy's aircraft as he screamed by. She watched the variable geometry wings sweep back as the plane picked up speed and climbed in a series of rolls up and out of sight. Somehow she knew that the second plane belonged to Dan Fancy. "Come back safely, Dan, I miss you already," she murmurred to herself as she followed the plane until it was swallowed up and lost to sight.

Before they knew it they were in the marshal stack waiting their turn to land. The flight out to the carrier had been fun. The plane was working as advertised, and the air was uncommonly clear.

"Strike," Fancy radioed the controllers sitting front of their radar scopes in a darkened room inside Enterprise. "Desperado two zero seven, checking in on Mom's 260. Sixty. State five point three."

With that short radio transmission he had let the carrier, mom, know that he was at the 260 radial emanating from the carrier, sixty miles away and with 5,300 pounds of fuel left, a very important piece of information, Fancy reminded himself. The plan was for everyone to do a touch and go and then land. He watched Bailey roll in on his approach.

After Bagger made his touch and go, Fancy completed his circle in the stack and started in toward the Enterprise. At three quarters of a mile he radioed 207, Tomcat, ball, four point nine."

As soon as he felt the plane's wheels come in contact with the deck he pushes the throttles forward and they roared off the deck.

"Looked good, Babe," called Mirabal.

"Thanks, good job on the checklist. It was short and concise, just what I need."

After the touch and go the landing turned out to be a piece of cake, at least that was the way it looked and felt to Fancy as he rolled backward to rid the plane of the wire and looked to the yellow shirt for directions as to where they would be directed to park.

The F-14 is controllable and graceful in the air, but once on the deck, it can seem like more of a cow on a wet kitchen floor, or in this case the rolling and pitching deck of the carrier. If things don't go right a plane can go over the side killing the aviators inside before they can eject.

At the yellow shirt's directions he pushed the throttles forward to move the plane toward their parking space. As they gathered momentum Fancy pushed his feet against the tops of the rudder pedals to put on the brakes in order to turn at the direction of the yellow shirt. Absolutely nothing happened, the brakes were not grabbing. Things had gone south in hurry. Without the brakes they could go over the side when the ship pitched and or rolled. Fortunately, there was only a slight swell. Crashing into parked plane could touch off a fireball.

The word eject raced through his mind. Ejecting on the busy flight deck was dangerous at best. Even though they had zero-zero ejection seats there was still enough danger to want to choose another option.

They could land in the water right next to the ship and get sucked into the massive propellers. Or if they ejected as they went over the side they could be slammed into the side of the carrier. If they were lucky enough to come down over the ship they could be run over by a plane landing or even get ingested into a plane about to take off.

"Rhino," he said, as calmly as he could, "we've got no brakes."

"I hate it when that happens. No brakes are a definite drag," he said chuckling at his own joke.

Fancy figured he was either the coolest guy in town or he just didn't understand the situation. He turned on the landing and navigation lights and dropped the tailhook to let everyone on deck, as well as the Air Boss, know that there was a runaway plane on deck. Keeping the Tomcat's engines at idle and in a righthand turn he was surprised by how fast the plane moved around the deck. Cutting the engines would lead to electrical loss and he figured he needed that to work the radios to keep in contact with those outside who were now working to save the plane.

Other options that raced through his mind were crashing into the JBD, or the jet blast deflector. Again the thought of an explosion ruled that out. Right now he was grateful that Enterprise had a new nonskid surface. They needed every edge.

On the deck of the Enterprise, Senior Chief Mark Watson, thirty-eight, realized that something was going to have to be done and quickly or the plane, and quite possibly the crew, might be lost. He and his young deck crew would have to do something and do it fast. In awe he watched his crew of youngsters do everything they could think of to capture the runaway plane. Airman Apprentice James Chad, just nineteen, and on his first cruise, scrambled under right wing and threw a chock under the right main gear wheel. The massive plane ran right over it. Aviation Boatswain's Mate First Class Charles Reynolds threw it under the wheel again. At the same time Aviation Boatswain's Mate Second Class Joel Swenson threw another chock under the left main gear wheel. Inside the Tomcat Fancy and Mirabal heard the thump—thump as the plane ran over them. Almost at the same instant Swenson and Reynolds realized that the chock would stay under the wheel if they kept them there with their feet. Taking the risk, each planted his feet against the beam of the chock. Miraculously the chocks held and the plane rocked to a stop. Immediately one of the blue-shirted tractor drivers rushed his vehicle with its long yellow tow bar into position at the nose of the plane. Immediately he was directed by one of the yellow-shirted directors to tow the plane to its parking place. Blue shirts quickly chained it to the white stars of steel bars, called pad eyes, buried in the deck. The pad eyes looked like divots chopped out of a golf course.

Although it had seemed to Fancy that they had been loose on that deck forever, the elapsed time was only sixty-five seconds. After shutting down the engines, he undid his koch fittings, raised the canopy, and climbed down to the deck. For an instant he felt like kneelling down and kissing it.

Mirabal dropped down beside him. His eyes seemed a little larger than usual, otherwise he seemed none the worse for wear. "Well, Gator, we've dodged another of the bullets that makes what we do so very interesting."

Fancy just shook his head. Immediately he sought out the enlisted men who had literally saved the day. Shaking hands with each of them he thanked them effusively while getting their names. Making a mental note to do something for each of them. He then ducked under the plane to see if there were any tell-tale signs of what made the brakes malfunction. Seeing nothing he straightened up and started to walk across the steel deck to the ladder that would take them down to the O3 level where they could put their gear away.

Before they arrived at the ladder, an officer, who Fancy had never met before rushed over to them. Lt. Fancy, Captain Bedley would like to see you, right now."

"Hey he probably wants to congratulate you on how well you handled the emergency," said Mirabal as he continued down the deck to the ladder.

Fancy knew that could be the case, or he could be in for a royal butt-chewing. You never knew which way it would go in this business. He didn't know Bedley and began to sweat again as he headed for the island and the captain's solitary splendor.

When he reached the bridge he noticed that Bagger was standing by the big upholstered chair, where Captain Bedley was sitting, looking out over the deck. Fancy looked over at Bagger, who just gave a little shrug and said nothing.

"Lt. Fancy, that was good work out there, congratulations," he said as he turned his chair to face them. Fancy couldn't tell how tall Bedley was, but he was drawn immediately to his blue eyes, that right now seemed to be shooting laser beams at the two aviators. He knew there must be something besides the runaway.

"Thank you, sir. It was the deck crew that deserves all the credit. Lt. Mirabal and I just sat there and watched it unfold. They did a heck of a job, sir."

"Yes, they did," Bedley answered, still not smiling and keeping the angry eyes on the two pilots.

"We've had a communication from Miramar. It seems that two planes, two jet fighters, flew by a power generating plant located in the city of Carlsbad."

Fancy swallowed and fixed his gaze over Bedley's head out toward the flight deck. He was tempted to give only name, rank, and serial number. Thoughts of plausible stories raced through his head, but they were dog squeeze and he knew it. A firm, 'wadn't me' probably wouldn't do it either.

After several to many uncomfortable seconds he started to open his mouth to say something. What, he hadn't the faintest clue.

Captain Bedley filled in the blank. "It seems there was a very distinguished gentleman conducting some kind of inspection of this particular plant. He used to be a," he looked at a piece of paper he held in his right hand, "a Major in the California National Guard. He identified the planes as two F-15s."

Fancy's wanted to catch Bagger's eye, but decided against it.

Finally Fancy spoke. "Sir, you can just never tell what the Air Force will do. They seem to have very little discipline. The very idea of…doing what, sir?"

"Buzzing the generating plant, gentleman."

"Yes, buzzing the generating plant, sir. A disgrace, a real disgrace, sir," he nailed the sir at the last possible breath.

Bedley fixed them with a hard stare, fingering his walrus type mustache, as he did so. "Well, gentleman, I know if it had been Navy fighters they would have come in lower and faster, much too fast to be identified. Getting my drift gentleman?"

"Yes, sir," they sang out in unison.

"Now get out of here before, I receive any more communications," he growled, as he slapped the paper with his left hand.

With that the two pilots wheeled around and marched out into the sunshine that once again seemed clear and bright.

"Holy cow!" exhaled Fancy. "We lucked out."

Bagger let out a great deal of stored up air and leaned up against the bulkhead. "What do they expect of a National Guard puke and probably a staff weenie to boot. What would he know about fighter pilots."

They headed back to below decks while warily checking their six every few steps. As they rounded a corner and headed for Ready Three, they ran into Mongo Matsen coming the other way. He did not look pleased.

"Ya ta he, XO," greeted Bailey. "How goes it?"

"Ya ta he, yerass, Bagger! That's two!" he snarled, holding up his hand with two fingers extended. "One more and I'm going to stake you out and pour honey all over you, and call in the aardvarks! You savvy?" With that he stomped past them headed toward the flight deck.

Bagger looked over at Fancy and shrugged his shoulders. "Man, talk about a royal case of the redass. What do the aardvarks have to do with anything?" he laughed.

"Bagger, I'll square it with him and tell him the whole deal was my idea. I'm sorry, man," said Fancy shaking his head.

"Hey, don't worry about it. He won't stay mad for long, especially after he sees me qual tonight. I heard he and Lt. Andrews, the FASO Lt. Andrews, are no longer an item. Maybe that's the problem." Laughing to himself and muttering something about 'aardvarks', Bailey headed for Ready Three.

Bagger went out that night and made everybody happy by snagging six straight OK-3s.

When Fancy reached the room he and Bagger would inhabit for the next six months he pulled the letter from Amanda out of his flight pocket. Unfolding it he started to read.

> Dear Lt. Fancy,
>
> I'm really glad you and my mom met. My real dad wasn't very nice to her. When I see you together she seems very happy and I know you wouldn't be mean to her like he was. I hope you come home safely.
>
> Yours truly
>
> Amanda
>
> PS Don't tell my mom but I'd really like you to be my dad someday.

He reread it and felt a lump start to crawl up in his throat. He was fighting back a lump in his throat when Bagger walked in.

"Let's go get something to eat. Hey are you okay? Did you get some bad news? What's up?"

Fancy shook his head and held up the letter and then stuffed back in his pocket. "No, just some really good news. Give me a minute."

0800 found the squadron assembled in their new home away from home, Ready Three. It was a rectangular room, with large leather chairs arranged in eight rows. The front of the room was dominated by a large map of the world, with several other regional maps rolled up at the top. On the right hand side of the room was a TV whose camera was buried in the center of the flight deck duplicating the view in Pri Fly. The Green Board was on the left side of the room, letting everyone know how they stood within the squadron as far as landing grades went. At the present time Bagger, thanks to his six OK-3s the previous night, was number one. Fancy was number two.

Ratchett Robinson came in and went directly to the front of the room, after clapping Bagger on the shoulder as he went by. "Good morning, gentleman. I trust that you have found our accomodations satisfactory."

The catcalls, boos, and groans let him know that everything was less than satisfactory.

"I'm so sorry to hear that. Believe me, I'll take it up with Captain Bedley. Interestingly enough he's already met two of our illustrious pilots and even invited them up to the bridge for a one v. two."

Fancy squirmed in his seat but decided it was a good time to lay low. Bagger, by his silence, had decided on the same course of inaction.

Mongo Matsen, seated behind Robinson, again held up one hand with two fingers extended and mouthed the word "aardvark". Bailey poked Fancy in the ribs, said nothing, and shook his head.

"As you know there will be a visiting Congressional delegation coming on board tomorrow. The Wing will be putting on a firepower demonstration, otherwise known as blowing holes in the ocean. Our contribution will be to fly a simulated MiG sweep ahead of the F-18s, who will be actually dropping some live 500 pounders. Just prior to the bombs going off, we'll let fly with one Sparrow and one winder. We'll shoot the winder at a flair, dropped by one of the S-3s. That pronouncement was met with sighs of relief. "After the helos dip and do their thing and the Vikings drop some sonobuoys, we'll streak by with another four planes in a diamond formation doing our best to imitate the Blue Angels. Concluding the show, two F-14s will fly down either side of the ship and go supersonic."

Before the last syllable of the word supersonic was out of Robinson's mouth, hands and calls of "Who's going to shoot? Who's going to fly the diamond?" came raining down upon him.

"Commander Matsen, would you please, let the good people know who will be flying tomorrow and of course later today in the rehearsal?"

Matsen stood up and picked up a piece of paper off the rostrum. Clearing his throat, he paused for dramatic effect. "Flying the simulated MiG sweep will be our esteemed leader, on his wing will be Killer, number three will be Poncho and number four on his wing will be Big Wave. Killer will shoot the Aim seven. You'll never guess who gets to shoot the 'winder?"

Robinson stood up, smiling. So much for any guessing.

Matsen continued, "In the diamond I'll fly lead, with Animal number two. Number three will be Gator with Moose on his wing. Making the pass on the port side of the ship will be Gizmo and on the starboard side will be Elvis. Rainman and Fuzzy will be the back up for the supersonic flyby. Gooey and Jammin' will back everybody else up." There were groans of protest, but, of course, many less than before.

Robinson remained standing and moved to the front of the raised platform as Matsen sat back down. "The demonstration is set for 1300 hours tomorrow. The wizards at Point Magu are going to try and get a drone out this far in order to give the Aim-7 something to lock onto instead of just shoot it off over the wild blue yonder. Our launch for the rehearsal will be at," he said looking at his watch, " 1200. Planning will commence after we finish here."

Burners belched fire and mighty jets slipped the surly bonds as the "Foxtrot" flag flapped in the 30 knot wind that Mother Nature and Captain Bedley had arranged for the 1300 launch. Clouds of steam boiled out of the catapult tracks as the deck crew in their brightly colored jerseys carefully choreographed the dance of the jets on the huge flight deck. *Funny how big it looks in the daylight*, thought Fancy. He thought back to yesterday's practice where everything had gone so well.

*I wonder if that means things won't go well today? Well, I'm ready* he thought.

"Rhino, how goes it back in the pit?"

"Excuse me. My office, is ready, willing and able," came Mirabal's prompt reply. "I love these kinds of days. Your, our, defense dollars at work, a great many defense dollars at work," he continued. "All these Congress Persons here to observe the handiwork of their industrial constituents and the brave American boys who make it all work. I mean spending a day being sucked up to on an Enterprise type yacht, eating "chow" with the boys, and then watching some major league fireworks. Not too bad in my humble estimation."

Fancy chuckled in reply and eased the big Tomcat up to the catapult.

Since timing is everything in these kinds of things, a great amount of time had been put in that morning. Clocks had been hacked and potatoes counted—everybody was honed and ready for the big day.

The launch had gone like clockwork. Everyone was in the air when and where they should be, much to the dismay and disappointment of those four pilots who were now climbing out of their planes, relegated to fill the roll of spectators.

Mongo Matsen had them in perfect position at their 7,000 foot roll-in point ready to start their shallow dive that would bring them by on the portside of the ship.

Everyone had seemed serious this morning. It would be, of course, very bad form to punch some kind of hole in the ship, for there was a long tradition of interesting occurances at these type of shows. One time a photo F-8 Crusader that had completed a half Cuban eight, popping out flash bombs had smacked into an F-4 Phantom coming the other way. There were also tales of other aircraft that had smacked into one another or the water. It was one thing to be dead, but quite another to look bad.

However, the day was going like clockwork. Matsen and the rest of the planes in the diamond had watched the rest of the air wing do their thing, were now monitoring their radios and just waiting for their turn.

The F-18 leader called inbound and switched "hot". Their formation was impeccable, with the F-18s flying their bomb run steady and level. Something that would never happen if the you-know-what hit the fan. Each plane seemingly glued to the others in the formation.

"Stand by, stand by," their fearless leader called, prepping his wingies to drop their bombs on his call. Matsen and the rest of the diamond rolled into their run, still lagging behind and slightly higher than the F-18s.

"Pickle, pickle, pickle," hollared the F-18 lead, and then an impressive number of 500 pounders fell off the four planes.

Unfortunately, two of the five hundred pounders had the very bad manners to blow up almost immediately as they came off the hard points of Ace two and three. Right away fuel, in large amounts started streaming from the wings of the two planes.

"Yaaaaa! Ace Two is hit!"

"Yaaaaa! Ace Three is hit!"

Fancy's first thought was "Neato, just like the Big War." Quickly his eyes got all squinty as he guided his pipper right on Ace Two.

Quicky the once impeccable formation of F-18s deteriorated and then disappeared in a haze of JP-5. Frantic radio calls quickly followed.

Meanwhile the Congress Persons were cheering wildly thinking this frab up to be part of the show. The F-14s continued their roll-in and roared out of sight, miraculously not running into the F-18s who were now trying to decide whether to eject or try to make Point Magu. Luckily, the two F-18s had just enough fuel to reach Point Magu, but without even enough gas to even leak on the runway.

After the rest of the wing had recovered successfully, Fancy saw Ace lead in the passageway by Ready Three. He told him how lucky they were to have the F-18s on board and even more important to give tone to what otherwise would have been just an ordinary show. He added that the very impressed Congress Persons would probably buy them a couple of new planes.

Ace Lead adjusted his ascot, favored by the Hornet drivers, and considered shifting his weapon systems from air-to ground to air- to- Fancy smack'im-in-the-mouth-mode.

"You dirty, lousy, stinky, cheating rat!" he snarled, making a fist and pulling it back, ready to strike.

"Yes," retorted Fancy, adjusting his squadron baseball cap, "And isn't it pretty to think so?" And then he spun around on his heels and walked off to Ready Three.

While Ace was left fuming, Fancy continued his journey to Ready Three when he saw the same officer who had informed him of his audience with Captain Bedley approaching. He looked impecable in his khakis, pressed to perfection. Fancy suddenly felt somewhat grubby.

As the two officers approached, the staff weenie, as Fancy liked to think of them, stopped and inquired, "Lt. Fancy?"

"That's me," Fancy replied, just knowing he wouldn't have to make another trip to the bridge again. Immediately his belief was dashed.

"Captain Bedley would like to see you on the Bridge, a.s.a.p."

"What? Are you sure it's me he wants to see?"

"If you're Lt. Dan Fancy, he wants to see you, immediately, if not sooner."

"I suppose that means I can't change," Fancy pleaded, feeling grubbier and grubbier by the second. *Is that me I smell?* he wondered.

"If you'll follow me, Lt, I'll take you right up."

Fancy pursed his lips, shook his head resignedly, and growled, "Let's get it over with. Have you any idea what this is about?"

"I'm just the messenger," the officer volunteered.

Three minutes later Fancy found himself standing outside Captain Bedley's cabin. The marine sentry stepped aside as he saluted briskly.

Fancy and the staff officer returned the salute. The officer, who had introduced himself as Lt. Bill Crockett. Crockett rapped smartly on the door. Upon hearing, "Enter," from inside, he opened the door and stepped aside as Fancy entered.

Captain Bedley was standing by his desk. Seated at the desk was Fancy's former father-in-law, Congressman Randy Cross.

Fancy came to attention and announced, "Sir, Lt. Fancy reporting as ordered."

"At ease Fancy, relax. I believe you know Congressman Cross?" said Bedley.

"Yes, sir, I do." Fancy stammered.

"I'll leave you alone. Congressman, if you need anything at all, just hit that button on the desk. Lt. Crockett will help you with anything you might need."

Cross stood and reached over with his hand extended to Bedley, who shook it and left the room. He then extended his hand to Fancy. The handshake was firm. "Dan, how are you, it's good to see you. It looks like you've been busy?"

"Yes, sir, it's really good to see you. I was flying number two in the diamond. I imagine Captain Bedley wasn't too happy with the way the bombing went, I know the CAG won't be pleased."

Cross grinned. "If there's one thing I learned flying off these birdfarms is that whatever can go wrong most often will. I understand both planes made it to Magu safely, so outside of a few red faces and cosmetic damage to the Hornets, no harm done. This is a dangerous business. I hope my colleagues take that message back to Washington. Here, sit down, damn it's good to see you," he said as he gestured to an easy chair.

Fancy sat down, luxuriating in the soft chair. "Thank you, sir, this feels pretty good, compared to the F-14."

"Somehow," Cross continued, "I don't think you're ready to trade seats?"

"No, sir, I'll keep that seat, thank you."

Cross smiled and interlocked his hands behind his head. Fancy noticed that even though he had put on a little weight and the face was starting to show some jowels, his eyes still said he could climb in a plane and turn and burn with anybody.

"How's your new squadron working out, son. From what I could see their part of the show went well and they, you, looked sharp."

"It's great, sir. Commander Robinson runs a tight ship. The guys are a good bunch. I knew a couple of them from flight school. They've made me feel welcome and even useful."

Cross nodded and smiled. "That's good, I'm pleased and happy for you."

Fancy opened his mouth to answer when the door opened and his ex-wife came in.

*Marvelous,* thought Fancy, *just marvelous.*

He stood up, much too surprised by the turn of events to say anything.

"Hello, Dan, its good to see you," she said. "Dad offered me the chance to come at the last minute. I hoped I would get to see you."

"Uh, it's nice to see you. How have you been?" he managed to get out. "This is quite a surprise." What an understatement he thought.

Her father cleared his throat. "It's nice to see you both."

"You look well, Dan. It looks like the change of scenery has agreed with you."

"Yes, things have been working out pretty well. I"ve been pretty busy getting caught up. Right off the bat we had a detachment go up to Red

Flag. Luckily, I got to go." He stopped and an awkward silence fell upon the room.

Congressman Cross broke the silence. "Are you looking forward to the cruise, Dan? Six months can be a long time and it could be longer the way things are going in certain hotspots around the world. It seems that we have a very violent peace."

"I'm looking forward to it, sir. You know, new plane, new squadron. VF-124 is pretty squared away. I'm excited. Of course in six months I might not be quite as gung ho as I am now." He shrugged his shoulders.

He turned to his former wife. "You look great, Janice. What have you been up t? Great was definitely another understatement. Janice Cross was a gorgeous woman. Tall, thin, with a figure that turned heads everywhere she went. Even in jeans, a simple white blouse, and a blazer, she looked elegant. Her long black hair was in some kind of a braid. She was indeed beautiful. No doubt she would be a topic of conversation on the Enterprise and the cruise had just started.

"I got a job with a company that finds top executives for Fortune 500 type companies, in D.C. It's pretty exciting, there's a great deal of travel mixed with some research. It seems I'm always in an airport going or coming. There's a lot of interesting people out there."

Fancy smiled. At one time that conversation would have brought on some jealous thoughts. Funny, he thought to himself, it's absolutely no problem now.

Again a silence enveloped the room. Fancy wished he could be done with this and get back to the squadron.

"Listen," said the Congressman, "I'm going to duck out to the bridge for a few minutes. "I'll let you two get reacquainted."

After the door closed Fancy shifted uncomfortably in his seat. For the first time in a long while he was at a loss for words.

Finally after what seemed like several minutes he mustered, "Where are you headed after you and your dad leave here?"

"We'll go back to San Diego. I think Dad has a couple of speeches to give and then we'll both go back to D.C. I'm taking a little vacation time."

"Your dad looks good, although he's put on a little weight. I bet he could still climb in a Tomcat and do more than hold his own."

"Every once in a while he'll drive over to Maryland to one of those little airports and rent a plane. He says that's enough."

After another long pause Janice broke the silence. "You've met someone else, haven't you?"

Fancy felt himself start to turn red and he squirmed in his seat. "Uh, well, yes, I have. We met at the air show at Miramar as a matter of fact."

He saw her eyebrows involuntarily raise and he knew what she was thinking. "She's a fine person, you'd probably like her. I'm sure after you met her you would agree she's not one of the air show groupies."

"You didn't waste much time did you?" came the icy reply.

"Jesus, Janice, you're the one who walked out, remember! I didn't set out to get even. It just happened."

"Is she going to understand how you can love a plane or a squadron more than a person!" Janice snapped, sparks seemingly ready to jump out of her eyes. "How is she going to feel when you're not there when she really needs you?"

Fancy felt the anger building somewhere inside his chest, spreading like a Japanese fan throughout his body. Instead of saying anything he might regret and knowing this was an argument he could never win, he stood up. "I'm really sorry we're having to replay this scene. I hope you have a good trip back to Washington."

Turning on his heel, he reached for the door. Before he could grasp the handle, the door opened and her father was there ready to enter. "I can see that I probably made a mistake, Dan. Way down deep I've been hoping both of you have grown up somewhat and you could get back together. Now, I realize I was sadly mistaken. Dan, I hope the cruise goes well. Give me a call when you get back."

Fancy took his extended hand. The return grip was firm and friendly. "Thank you, sir, I'll do that. Have a good trip back to Washington."

Breathing a sigh of relief, he walked past his ex-father-in-law and headed back to Ready Three knowing that part of his life was now completely behind him.

Arriving at Ready Three he found Bagger, Killer, Matsen, and Ratchet Robinson rehashing the afternoon's demonstration. "Fancy," smiled Robinson, "you're getting to be a regular in the rarified air of the bridge. What gives anyway?"

Fancy paused, not quite sure how to answer. "Uh, well, my father-in-law, or I guess my ex- father-in-law so to speak, is with the visiting Congressional delegation. He just wanted to say hello."

"What's his name, there were several congressman in the delegation? Anybody we might know?" querried Matsen.

Fancy turned toward the coffee machine and muttered, Congressman Cross, Randy Cross."

"The Randy Cross!" exclaimed Killer. "Same guy that bagged five MiGs in Vietnam?"

Fancy found himself the center of intense scrutiny. "Yeah, same guy," he said, trying to keep it light and no big deal.

Robinson was getting ready to open his mouth to say something, when Big Wave came through the hatch and proclaimed to the denisons of Ready Three, and probably the entire ship, "Man, oh man, you should see the babe traveling with that visiting congressional delegation. Wow! This is one great looking woman. You should see the rack on her. She is somethin' else."

As Big Wave went on and on, Bagger, who was standing behind Fancy, was waving and gesturing at Big Wave desperately to get his attention to shut him up.

Big Wave paused, looked at Bagger, and said, "Bagger, I know that's Gator. What's the matter?"

Bagger stopped quickly as if someone had pulled the plug on an electric toy. "Big Wave, that, that…"

"Babe," interjected Fancy. "She's a babe, right Big Wave?"

Big Wave looked from Bagger to Fancy and back again, a puzzled expression spreading across his face. "Yeah, what's goin' on?"

"Wave," said Bagger, "she's Gator's former wife. Cngressman Randy, yes, that Randy Cross, is his former father-in-law."

Big Wave's mouth started to move, but nothing emerged except a great deal of stored up, stale air. "Geez, Gator, I didn't know…I'm sorry," he shrugged and tried to melt into the deck.

"Wave, there's no problem. She is a babe. Do you want me to introduce you?"

"Are you kidding? Ah, she's probably way over my head. She is one attractive lady, though."

"You'd probably have to give up your life as you know it in the Navy. Her dad's the Ace, but she can't understand how somebody could be attached to an F-14. Seriously, she has a lot of good qualities. She's bright and funny, but…"

Robinson, sensing Fancy's growing discomfort, growled, "We'll reconvene the dating game when we get back to CONUS. In the mean time, let's get on with the business at hand."

"By the way, Gator. I saw Ace, of the F-18 squadron. He wasn't thrilled with your critique of their performance today. Let's all lay off those guys. This is going to be a long cruise and we can't afford to have any, shall we say schisms, develop. We've got to work with these guys."

"Sorry, skipper," Fancy smiled. "I'll tell him I'm sorry."

"Just stay away from him for now. They've all got a royal case of the red ass right now. Now about our part of the show…"

They paused as they felt the great ship heel over, her sharp bow biting into the Pacific swell, headed west. The cruise, Fancy felt, was now really underway.

# 8

The Enterprise sailed west across an empty restless ocean. Flight operations had been curtailed for a day or so while the ship's crew and air wing got squared away doing routine maintenance on the ship and planes. Fancy tried to get up on deck as much as he could during the respite. Some of the crew he knew, seldom, and in rare instances, never came out to see the light of day, spending their days in their working spaces, their berthing spaces, or the mess deck. He felt he would go crazy if he wasn't able breathe the salt air, feel the wind on his face, and get some sun.

The second time he came up after finishing up some paper work as Assistant Maintenance Officer, he spotted a school of dolphins. Indeed, it seemed as if the whole ship, paused while the sleek mammals frolicked off the port side of the ship. They seemed unimpressed by the Enterprise's relatively slow speed, and after a few minutes they pulled away from the ship.

Strolling down the deck toward the bow he made conversation with various crew members going about their duties. He seemed naturally drawn to the planes—even the helos. Invariably he would stroll toward the bow of the ship. Standing between the catapults he let the brisk wind take away all the below-deck smells.

As the Enterprise continued her journey to Hawaii life aboard quickly assumed its natural rhythm, which was dictated by over two hundred years of naval tradition and regulations. Everybody worked, meals were served, the laundry ran night and day. General quarters was sounded at 13:30 every afternoon by the PA system coming to life and announcing: "This is a drill, this a drill. General quarters, general quarters. All hands man your battle stations. Go up and forward on the starboard side and down and aft on the port side. General quarters."

All the pilots, RIOs, and BNs reported to their ready rooms while the damage control parties fought mock fires and delt with flooding, nuclear, chemical, and biological situations. In the various ready rooms the aviators took NATOPS exams, listened to lectures, and generally bored each other. Often each pilot was called upon to deliver a lecture and Fancy found he didn't mind too much. After all he was talking about his passion, flying.

After the ship secured from general quarters, everyone scattered throughout the ship to do paper work, which, Fancy, decided there would never be an end.

There were two wardrooms where officers could eat. The formal wardroom on the main deck, right beside Ready Five, where uniforms were required or the dirty-shirt wardroom up forward in the O-3 level between the bow catapults where flight suits and flight deck jerseys were permitted. Reality dictated that the formal wardroom was the domain of the ships company who were not aviators. Only occassionally did members of the air wing decide to eat there. It was here that the evening movie was shown.

Movies for the air wing usually took place in the various ready rooms. It was here that whistling, shouting out (often ribald) instructions to the characters, throwing popcorn at the screen, and at each other, took place. If a flyer didn't care for the movie he could always wander to another squadron's ready room where he would be welcomed, if he could find a seat.

Those aviators not interested in watching the movies that were offered could be found in their staterooms engaged in a card game, talking, listening to music, or writing letters home. Even a thirsty fellow could find a drink. As long as one did not appear in the ship's common areas smelling of liquor, no one seemed to mind.

Fancy, having seen most of the movies being offered their third night out decided to write to his folks. When he had located some paper and sat down at the small gray desk, he surprised himself by starting the letter—Dear Cody,

> This is our third day out on our way to Pearl Harbor. The Enterprise is making only about 20 knots. As big as she is, she can go faster, but since the escorting frigates and destroyers were starting to take a beating in the heavy seas, we had to slow down. I was told the sea has been kicked up by a storm, that we would call a hurricane, but is called a typhoon in the Pacific. That's amazing since this storm was centered almost two thousand miles away from us.
>
> I'm rooming with Bagger. He's over in one of the other squadron's ready room watching a movie. It's so odd to be by myself on the ship. It's somewhat of a luxury, what with over five thousand men on the ship.
>
> I hope Amanda is feeling better. Tell her I read her letter and we both have the same hopes. She'll know what that means.
>
> Due to the heavy weather flight operations have been curtailed and we've been studying and listening to letures. Tell Amanda learning never ends. I gave a couple of lectures and didn't seem to put anyone to sleep.

We had a little problem after we landed the other night. Seems the brakes stopped working after we had landed and were being directed to our parking place. Lucky for us a couple of guys on the deck were able to get a chock under the main gear and get it stopped.

He paused in his writng, marveling at how easy the words had spilled onto the paper. Usually writing a letter was just this side of getting a root canal for him. He continued.

I've been thinking about you—a lot. Life is strange. Just when I had decided not to get involved with anyone—there you were, and I'm so glad. I didn't think I could fall in love so suddenly. I always figured, based on past experience that it kind of crept over you, like a warm feeling on a summer day. You, and Amanda, have been in my thoughts and I'm finding that very comforting.

Love,<br>Dan

He stood up suddenly, surprised at what he had put down on the paper. He reached for it, intending to rip it up. Thinking again, he quickly addressed an envelope. After another few minutes he had the letter to his folks done and was walking to the ship's post office to mail them.

On the fifth day out the seas abated, the skies cleared, and best of all, thought Fancy, flight operations were resumed.

He even welcomed the cool rubbery feeling of the oxygen mask. They were at twelve thousand feet paired up with Poncho Barnes, flying a simulated MiG Cap out in front of the Enterprise. The very fact that the nearest MiG was probably over ten thousand miles away bothered him not in the least. Although what they might find were planes from the carrier Kitty Hawk, returning from her deployment.

"Rhino, is there anything out there?"

"Gator, the gee whiz boxes and scopes show absolutely nothing. Are you bored up there?"

"Are you kidding, when I fly I'm never bored, especially after having to suck rubber for four days. I was starting to get a little edgy."

"I hear you. I'm so glad to be away from the paper work, at least for a little while."

Fancy looked off to their left watching Poncho's plane. They were in a 'loose duce' combat spread. He could see Poncho and his RIO. Poncho must have seen him watching and gave him a pumped fist, which he returned in kind. Taking a deep breath he squirmed aroud in his seat while at the same time rotating his neck.

"Gator, I've got something. Looks like a flight of two, probably F-18s, at ninety miles, at uh, ten thousand. Come to two six zero and they'll be on our nose."

Fancy brought the Tomcat to two six zero. His own display confirmed what Mirabal had just told him.

"Desperado, 207, we've picked something up. Have you got the same package?"

"Roger that, 201. We have a flight of two, lose combat spread at two six zero, at ten thousand. They're right on our nose. Wigs picked them up at probably the same you guys did."

"207, let's stay head-to-head with them. Rhino, what's the distance now?"

"Still on our nose, distance at a little under 80 miles, 201."

"Okay, Poncho, let's spread out and start to jink and weave, we don't need to present any kind of predictable target."

He heard Poncho chuckle. "Roger that, 201."

Man, Fancy thought to himself, I didn't need to remind him of that. But then again, maybe he did. Take nothing for granted.

Fancy and Poncho continued to close with the two F-18s, who had also spread out and had begun to climb.

"Two six zero, twelve, distance seventy miles," said Rhino in a calm cool voice.

"Roger, that."

"207, let's go head to head with them, blow through and see if we can find the carrier. We can shoot the 'Great White Hope' when we're in range and as we close shoot the 'winder."

"207 copies and agrees 201. Let's shoot the 'Winders, then get down on the deck after we've acquired the Hawk. How's your fuel?"

"207, fuel is good, we've still got some left in the centerline. How you?'

"201, centerline is just finishing, we're good."

"Roger, 207. Rhino, can you pick up the carrier?"

"No, not yet…"

"Desperado 201, this is Eagle two five. Do you copy?"

"Eagle, two five, I copy five by five," replied Fancy. He had been momentarily startled by the voice of Eagle two five, the E2C carrier's AWACs plane.

"Desperado 201, after you blow through the Hornets come to course two three five. The Hawk will be about fifty miles away at that point. We have no other traffic in the vicinity at this time. We'll keep you aprised."

"Roger that, Eagle two five, fifty miles at two three five. You copy, 207?"

"207 copies, 201."

"Gator, they're still on the nose, distance forty-five miles. They've climbed to 12."

"Let's bring it up," he said as he brought the nose up, while advancing the throttles. "We'll go to 14, Poncho and keep 'em low."

"Roger that, 201."

"Range, thirty-five miles and closing. They've come up to 14," reported Rhino.

It was going to be hard to get a visual in the somewhat murky skies, Fancy thought to himself.

"Thirty and closing, still at 14," said Rhino.

Fancy felt himself straining to acquire the F-18s visually, although he knew that wasn't going to happen just yet.

They were just in range of the two AIM-7M Sparrows they were carrying, and he got the first indications that they were in range with a slight growling tone from the missile.

Now their RAH gear was going ape. Kitty Hawk's battle group knew that they had company.

"Rhino, I'm getting a tone on the Hope. I'd shoot that sucker now and disrupt their thinking just a little and then get closer and shoot the 'winder." Now the tone was stronger indicating the missile had the F-18 locked up.

"Range twenty-two miles."

It seemed to Fancy that the closer they got, the calmer Rhino's voice became, which helped him stay steady and focused.

At eleven miles he could use the AIM-9L Sidewinder, his favorite weapon of choice, if he couldn't use the M61A1 Vulcan 20mm Gatling gun.

The tone from the Sparrow was stronger now and Fancy could visualize it coming off the rail.

"Fourteen miles," called Rhino.

Fancy continued to strain to pick up the F-18s. The radar picture was comforting but he liked to see his prey.

Now he could hear the rattlesnake-like growl from the Sidewinders. They were good to go.

Glancing out of the corner of his eye he could see Poncho's plane out about a quarter of a mile, closer than they would be if this was the real thing.

Just as he was deciding he could shoot the 'winder he picked up the F-18s coming on strong at roughly their altitude. "I've got 'em visually, Rhino, here they come."

In almost the blink of an eye the four planes flashed past each other, much too close for Fancy's comfort and he heard himself gasp in surprise.

Immediately he brought the Tomcat to a course of two three five and lowered the nose to get down on the deck. By the time those Hornets got turned around they would have picked up the carrier and paid it a visit.

Now all the threat warnings the Tomcat possessed were going ballistic, giving Fancy a very uncomfortable feeling. It was nice to know that they were on your side, but nevertheless…

"207, let's go down to a hundred and fifty feet. As soon as we get a visual we'll go bow to stern. I'll go down the port side you take the starboard We can go outboard and rendezvous at 11 on fifty-five degrees and we'll beat feet back to Enterprise."

"Roger, 201. Taking it down the starboard side, joining up at 11 on fifty-five degrees."

Fancy took the plane down to one hundred and fifty feet above the gray-blue waters of the Pacific. Everything was just a blur as they passed over one of the escorting frigates of the Kitty Hawk's battle group.

"Gator, there she is, come left one degree and we can go right down the port side. Range is just under six miles."

Fancy eased the stick over and held it there when he heard Rhino grunt his satisfaction. Another larger ship came and went. He thought he could see some of her men gaping up at them as they raced by.

The gray mass of the Kitty Hawk suddenly appeared out of the haze. Out of the corner of his eye he saw Poncho alter his course. In just the blink of an eye, it seemed to Fancy, they were passing down the length of the huge carrier. After clearing the air space around them Fancy racked the fighter around in a tight right hand turn and stroked the afterburners to zone two to take them up and home. If this was the real thing he and Poncho would have stayed low in order to present the worst possible target. Since it wasn't the real thing he felt it was time to get back home and count it as a successful mission. As they pulled up and away from the carrier he caught a glance of an F-18 climbing up at them at their two o'clock.

Immediately Fancy rolled to his right to put the threat on their nose. Getting a good tone from the starboard AIM-9 he knew he could have shot him down. Of course he could have been on the receiving end of the Hornet's own missile too he reckoned. However, he wasn't going to give anyone the benefit of a doubt.

"Man, that was fun. Do you think we can do this tomorrow, Gator?"

"That'll be fine with me," he replied, suddenly feeling very thirsty.

"That was nice the way you picked up that Hornet. I was just going to open my mouth when you turned into him."

"I was lucky. I was just barely able to pick him up out of the haze. Do you think he could have gotten off a shot at us?"

"It's a good bet and I'll wager that when he traps he's going to be bragging about getting us. But, we're on our way home in one piece and that's all I'm going to worry about."

"That's the way I feel too."

At eleven thousand feet Poncho had joined up on their port side. Fancy turned and gave him a thumb's up.

In return Poncho pumped his fist up and down and then flashed a victory sign.

"207, look me over and then I'll do the same for you."

"Roger, 201, coming from your left."

With that Poncho dropped back and underneath Fancy's plane just to make sure everything was there and there would be no surprises.

"201, you look good, everything is there and I see nothing leaking."

"207, hold your position and I'll do the same for you."

"Roger, holding."

Fancy eased back on the throttles and felt the plane sink slightly. Easing under Poncho's plane he could see that everything looked just as it should and he came out on Poncho's starboard side. Advancing the throttles ahead just slightly he pulled even and gave him another thumb's up. "Lookin' good 207, let's go home. Is your fuel okay?"

"201, we're at about, uh, 7,000 pounds. We're okay."

"207, that's about what we show."

The flight back to the Enterprise was uneventful. Fancy did note that the sky was blackening and there was more turbulence than when they had launched.

At fifty miles Fancy radioed the ship. "Strike, Desperado two zero one. Checking on mom's 55. Fifty, state five point four."

"Roger, Desperado, continue. be advised of heavy rain squalls over the ship."

"Terrific," he mumbled to himself. "Did you copy that, Rhino."

"Yeah, I heard. The end of a perfect day."

At ten miles, Fancy repeated the call and was told to continue and was again advised of the rain.

As if on cue he felt the Tomcat move in the turbulent air and rain began to pelt the canopy. He thought he could actually hear it beating on the canopy. You're wandering he told himself. Get focused. He squirmed in his seat trying to pick out the carrier.

The turbulence and rain increased. Straining he looked for the ship that should have been visible by now.

"Man, it's coming down razor blades and cannon balls," said Mirabal.

"Razor blades?" Fancy answered in surprise.

"Exactamundo. That's much harder than mere cats and dogs Sounds much more macho, don't you think?"

"Yeah, definitely," replied Fancy, now willing his eyes to pick the carrier out of the gloom.

Fancy checked his speed one more time and dirtied up the airplane, *gear, flaps, and hook* down. Double check that the hook was down, he reminded himself.

"Call the ball, 201,"

Fancy paused. There was no ball to call. He felt like he had been dropped into an inkwell. Then in the wink of an eye he could see the drop line and then the ball.

"Roger ball, 201 Tomcat, four point eight."

Miraculously, the ball is centered. Fancy, aware of a series of small jolts deftly makes the corrections, keeping the ball centered. Upon contact with the deck he shoves the throttles forward and feels himself thrown against his harness. Down one more time he receives the signal to move forward into the parking place.

As he was shutting down the engine he noticed that the rain had stopped and the sky was beginning to clear. After raising the canopy he unhooked and climbed out. Once on the deck he waited for Mirabal to join him. "Talk about timing. Can you believe things can change so fast," he said as he gestured at the now rapidly clearing sky.

Mirabal stretched, put his hands on his hips and rotated his back. "I didn't think it would quit as fast as it did, much less start to clear this fast."

Poncho and his RIO, Dave Yates, joined them on their trek across the deck. "We did some good work out there today, wouldn't you say, Gator?" he said, grinning his All-American good-looks grin.

Fancy put his hands up to give him a high five. "As a matter of fact, yes, I think we did some very fine work. Did the rain squall give you any trouble when you recovered?"

"I had a little trouble picking out the ball. Man it was black up there, then we just seemed to pop out of it and there she was."

After taking off their gear they headed for the Dirty Shirt wardroom. Fancy inhaled several glasses of fruit punch. It seemed that he was always thirsty when he returned from a hop and today was certainly no exception.

As they were about to get up, Commander Robinson came in. "Ahh, the intrepid warriors have returned. Nice going on finding and giving our regards to Kitty Hawk."

"There weren't any problems were there, Skipper?" asked Fancy, while he looked around in anticipation of another visit to the CAG or Captain Bedley.

"No, she reported that two Tomcats had found her. Of course they said you were both shot down way before you reached Kitty Hawk."

"That's what we figured they'd say. The fact was the RAH gear was going ape so they probably had more than a few good shots at us," responded Poncho.

"Rhino, I'm glad I found you. I'm going to need a RIO this afternoon. Charley Mejia had to report to sickbay. We're going to run some intercepts against some F-18s. We'll plan on launching at 1300. Any questions?

Before Tony could open his mouth, Robinson said, "Good, I'll see you on deck at 1230."

Mirabal sat there with a hamburger ready to be put in his mouth. Shaking his head, he said to the retreating Robinson, "Thanks for askin' me, skipper. I'm good to go any time." He finished taking a bite of the burger while at the same time glancing at his watch. "Man, I'd better hurry, I've only got twenty minutes and I better hit the head before I go back up to the roof."

He got up, gathered up his metal tray and smiled. "I'll see you all later."

"Don't embarrass me, Rhino. I've been telling the skipper how good you are."

Turning to look back over his shoulder he replied, "I'll uphold the honor of the team. See ya later, babe."

Fancy watched him until he had turned a corner and was out of sight. Picking up his own tray he started toward the waste can to deposit the leftovers.

"Gator," called Poncho, "where are you off to? You're not scheduled to fly again today are you?"

"Uh, no, not today. I've got a whole pile of paperwork to go through and I want to get it behind me before anymore comes my way. I'm going to stop by Ready Three and then retire to my palatial cabin and get going on it. I'll see ya later."

"That reminds me what I need to do too. Catch you later," called Poncho, as Fancy turned and headed to Ready Three.

By the time Fancy had settled in and had made a fair amount of headway through the mountain of papers enveloping his small desk, Ratchet Robinson and Tony Mirabal were pitting Desperado 211 against the F-18s of Squadron VFA-83, the Rampagers.

Mirabal noted that while the skipper was good, he thought, no, make that- he knew, Fancy was better. Robinson had more than held his own against the two F-18s but on the last merge they had been sandwiched. If it had been the real thing, they'd would be so much burning JP-8 burning on the surface of the ocean. Fancy, Mirabal figured, would have gotten at least one of their tormentors.

The two F-18s, were low on gas, as they were too often wont to do and had started their return to the ship. Robinson, not being too happy about the way the last encounter had gone was putting the plane through a series of rolls and turns.

Unknown to either of the two aviators a tiny crack had developed in one of the turbine blades in their starboard engine. The crack had started when a screw had fallen out of one of the E-2Cs during the early morning launch. It had lodged in one of the tie down points on the deck. When one of the F-18s had started to taxi to Cat One, the screw had been blown out and had been ingested in their starboard engine, where it hit one of the turbine blades, starting the small crack.

As Robinson brought Desperado 211 out of a bat turn- the blade shattered. Almost instantaneously Mirabal and Robinson felt the plane shake and then begin to vibrate as the engine began to tear itself apart.

"We've lost an engine, Rhino," said Robinson, a definite edge in his voice.

The plane began to pitch up. Robinson was able to get the nose down—barely before it started to come up again and yaw to the left.

"Eject! Eject! Eject!" Robinson called.

Mirabal was just barely able to get his arms at his sides and the back of his legs against the seat before they were blown out of the stricken plane.

Mirabal felt a tremendous force hit him right in the ass. There was a tremendous acceleration for what seemed like only a few seconds. Then he started to fall.

When the parachute opened it did so with a sudden jolt that surprised him. Out of the corner of his eyes he caught sight of the plane going down like a ton of bricks with flames and black smoke coming from the aft portion. Finally, after what looked like a last gasp effort the nose pitched up and then straight down and it went into the water. After the large splash there was only foam to mark the plane's demise.

He twisted around in the harness looking for Robinson. Taking off his mask and throwing it away he continued to search the sky for Robinson. There he was, below, and almost directly behind him.

Glancing down he saw the angry water coming up to meet him which brought him back to the business at hand. It was hard to judge how high he was. Pulling a lever on the left side of his seat pan he watched as his life raft dropped below him, tethered to the seat itself. As it fell away it opened and inflated when it reached the end of its restraint. *Well, it looks like I'm at the end of my rope,* he thought, grinning at his own stupid joke. When he saw the raft hit the water he decided he was going to release the Koch fittings and drop into the water, hopefully close to the raft. Without taking his eyes from it he felt around for the CO-2 cartridges and inflated his life vest. When the vest inflated he felt that maybe, this was one he was going to win.

Mirabal was grateful for the safety training day that happened every time the ship left port. Part of that exercise had every flight crewman hanging from a harness in full flight gear from the ready room ceiling, blindfolded. Each man had to touch and identify each piece of gear he was wearing and then run through the proper sequence for ejections over water and land. Now everything was just sort of on automatic and he could just do it and not have to dwell on when and how.

When the life raft hit the water he reached up to release the Koch fittings on his harness located near his collar bones. They held the parachute shroud lines to his harness. Nothing happened. They were stuck, jammed or both. Before he got the word he was thinking out of his mouth, the water was there to greet him. Barely getting his mouth and eyes closed the cold sea water consumed him. Now he had to get those fittings to work. Maybe the shock of hitting the water did the trick because when he toggled them they worked. The parachute started to drift away to the…east? He realized he was gasping for air. Now, where was the raft?

Realizing the line was wrapped around his left leg he started to pull the raft toward him while at the same time trying to swim toward it. At last the raft was in front of him. All that remained was to get in it.

Kicking as hard as he could he tried to push one side down and slide in. All he got for his effort was to have it squirt out from under him and he suddenly found himself under water.

The size of the swells was not helping any either. When he was about to try it again another swell hit him and forced the raft out of his grasp. He figured if he swallowed much more sea water he was going to sink and wouldn't need the raft.

After the seventh try he got lucky and a swell actually helped lift him up and into the raft. He laid there feeling more tired than he had ever been in his life.

Taking stock of his situation he realized that he was still wearing his helmet. At first he was tempted to chuck it overboard, but then thought better of it and decided he'd better keep it. *I can always throw it, but I won't be able to get it back if I do need it. Besides I'd just have to pay for another one,* he grumbled to himself.

After laying there for a few more minutes gathering his strength he carefully sat up as straight and high as he could to look for Robinson.

All he got for his effort was a vast expanse of empty ocean. Robinson was nowhere to be seen.

Fancy was just getting up from his cluttered desk when Big Wave and Bailey came through the hatch without so much as a knock. The minute Fancy saw Bagger's face he knew something was up.

Before he could open his mouth to ask what was up Bagger said, "It looks like the skipper and Rhino have gone down. They just dropped off the screen."

"Did they get any kind of call off—Mayday or anything?" Fancy asked as he felt his heart start to pound a little quicker.

"If they did no one heard it. One minute they were there, the next they weren't," answered Big Wave, his face more serious than Fancy ever remembered. "They were about 175 miles out, you know running through some ACM with the two Hornets. The Hornets started to run low on fuel and headed back. The last radio transmission said Ratchet was going to follow them in just a few minutes later." He shrugged his shoulders and then his whole body began to sag. "Shit."

"They're getting ready to launch an S-3 and the rescue helo," said Bagger.

"That's it?" Fancy asked incredulously. "Where's Matsen?"

"He was up in Pri-Fly when the word came in. Then he talked to CAG for a minute or two and came down to the ready room. That's how we found out."

Fancy studied his two friends for several seconds. "Do you think they'll let us join in the search. Jesus, I can't just sit here and do nothing," snapped Fancy. "I'm going to see what's going on. You comin'?"

Fancy was out the hatch before either of them could open their mouths.

Mirabal lay back in the raft watching the clouds. Sitting up every few minutes he looked for Robinson. Whether it was the corkscrewing motion of the raft or the fact that Robinson was missing he felt his stomach start to contract and he threw up over the side. The wrong side; the wind blowing most of it back in his face. Gagging and then looking at his watch, he saw that it was full of water and had stopped. *Just great. Can things get any worse? Of course they could,* he told himself. *Here he was in the middle of the Pacific with his ass in six inches of water. Marvelous, just marvelous. And people actually pay to come to this part of the world for fun.*

Deciding that feeling sorry for himself was not going to carry the day, he started to take stock of things. Everything seemed to be there—including his radio. Why hadn't he thought of that before? Being careful to make sure it was fastened to his vest he made a tentative call. "Skipper, skipper, are you okay?"

He was pretty sure the radio was working and called again. "Skipper, it's me Rhino."

He was just about to call it a day and save the batteries when he got a weak reply. "Rhino, is that you?"

"It's me. How you doin'? Are you hurt?"

"I hurt all over, but everything seems to function. How about you?"

"I feel pretty good except for being wet. The accommodations are definitely not as advertised in the slick brochure." He heard Robinson chuckle. Weakly he thought.

"I can't see you, Skipper. Can you blow on your whistle to help me get a fix on you?"

"All right, let me see if it's still attached. Yeah, here it is."

Mirabal tried to will himself to listen hard. After a few seconds he heard a few weak blasts of the whistle. He just couldn't seem to get the direction. "Skipper, keep blowing. I can hear you, but I can't tell which direction to look."

Again he heard the whistle, a little stronger now. He kneeled in the raft and almost fell out for his efforts. Trying again he did a quick three sixty. There! Was that a helmet over to his left? Yes, it was!

Carefully sitting down facing the direction he had spotted Robinson, he radioed him again. "Skipper, I think I saw you. Are you still wearing your helmet?"

"Affirmative on the helmet. I'll keep blowing."

Kneeling again, he gingerly scanned the direction where he thought Robinson was. Nothing but empty sea. Balancing against the swells and the motion of the raft, he kept looking. There he was about a hundred twenty-yards away! The whistle seemed to be fading.

"Skipper, I'm going to start paddling toward you. Keep up the blowing every twenty seconds or so."

"Roger," came the distant voice.

Kneeling down in the direction he wanted to go, he started to paddle towards Robinson.

Fancy meanwhile was in Ready Three. Matsen had stepped out and Fancy felt himself getting impatient and irritated. He began to pace.

Matsen walked back into the room, his face grim. "I guess you heard?"

"Yeah, what's being done and when can I launch?"

"They've just launched the S-3. They're going to hold the helo for a few more minutes."

"What are they saving it for!" fumed Fancy. "Jesus. You didn't answer me, when can I launch?"

"Launch, what do you mean launch? You're not going anywhere."

"That's my friend out there. I owe him, not to mention Robinson! What are we supposed to do, just sit here and…" His voice trailed off. He realized that his voice was rising and last time he checked, Matsen was senior to him. And none of this was his fault.

They stood there eye to eye, neither of them quite knowing what to say next.

Fancy broke the awkward silence. "Listen, I've got to fly anyway, why not just vector me out where they went down? An extra set of eyes. How could that hurt the situation?"

Matsen stared at him for minute and realized that Fancy wasn't going to back off. He liked that, knowing it could be him in the water some day. "It's not our call. CAG will decide who goes out and looks and who doesn't."

Fancy expelled some stale air and put his hands on his hips. "How about if I talk to CAG?"

Matsen felt himself getting hot under the collar. "Look, why don't we just let the powers-that-be work this out. You know everything that can be done—will be done."

"Sir," said Fancy coming to a semi-attention stance, "I respectfully request permission to talk to CAG."

Gritting his teeth he said, "Permission granted, but I'll be going with you. We might as well get both of our asses in a sling."

Mirabal felt like he was on a treadmill. Despite all the paddling he had done, Robinson seemed to be no closer than he had been. Worse, the sounds of the whistle appeared to be getting weaker. It was also getting darker.

Once more he kneeled upright and stretched himself to see as far as he could. There was Robinson, maybe a little closer, he thought. Crouching low and making large sweeping motions as he tried to close the gap, he took another quick look and resumed paddling. "Skipper, don't give up and keep that whistle going. Don't give up!"

Darkness was falling rapidly now. Mirabal got out his survival light, triggered the light, and stuck it to the Velcro that was glued on the right side of his helmet. "Skipper, put your survival light on your helmet! Can you hear me. Put your light on your helmet!"

The sound of the whistle stopped. After what seemed like an eternity he saw the beam of the survival light stab out into the darkness. Even better Robinson was closer, maybe only twenty yards away. With renewed energy he put everything he had into closing the gap. *My mother told me there'd be days like this,* he thought to himself.

Just when he thought his arms would come out of their sockets they were next to each other. His breathing was coming in great ragged breaths as he reached out and pulled his raft next to Robinson's.

Fancy and Matsen headed for the bridge where the CAG was watching the ongoing recoveries of the rest of the Air Wing.

"Are you sure you want to do this?" grumbled Matsen as they entered Pri Fly.

"You bet. Why the hell not?"

Captain Jeff Van Gundy was perched in a large leather chair. Fancy didn't know anything about him, but if looks could talk, he was going to be a tough nut to crack. He could see that he was a tall man, with iron gray hair cut short, almost like a Marine's boot camp cut. He sat ramrod straight and Fancy wondered if he slept at attention. His uniform was sharp and crisp. He turned and eyed the two intruders into his domain.

"Good afternoon, sir!" said Matsen as they both came to semi-attention on the left side of his chair.

"Afternoon, gentleman. What can I do for you?"

"Sir, this is Lt. Fancy. His RIO was flying with Commander Robinson this afternoon."

Van Gundy, rubbed his chin and his eyes seemed to bore holes in Fancy.

"Are you the Fancy that was in the Tomcat that lost the brakes?"

"Yes, sir. The deck crew saved that plane and Lt. Mirabal and myself. They really took the bull by the horns and saved our bacon." Fancy shifted uncomfortably from one foot to the other, wondering whether he should go on or just shut up. He decided to shut up.

"They did a splendid job, that's for sure. And yes, they did save your bacon. Now what brings you up here?"

Matsen took a deep breath and said, "Sir, Lt. Fancy wants to launch and add another set of eyes to the search for Commander Robinson and Lt. Mirabal."

"Sir, I'd really like to help. I think I can be useful in the search for the Skipper and, like Commander Matsen said, my RIO, Lt. Mirabal."

Van Gundy, sighed, stood and stretched, arching his back. Fancy noted that he was tall and on the slim side.

"We've launched an S-3, and there's a frigate headed to their last known position. It's going to be dark in about ten minutes. There's nothing you can do right now, but I appreciate the offer."

"Sir, I need to be out there. He's my friend. We can't just leave him out there!"

Fancy felt Matsen's hand on his arm as he tried to get him to back off.

Van Gundy shook his head. "Like I said, Lt. Fancy, there's nothing you can do right now. We're not going to leave them out there. Everything that can be done, is being done." He sat back down and turned the chair away from the two officers in a sign of dismissal.

"Come on, Gator, let's go."

"No, goddammit! Sir, please! Even if they just hear the plane, that could make a difference. They'll know they're not being left!"

"Gator, it's time to leave," said Matsen with steel in his voice.

Shaking lose of his hand on his arm, Fancy took a step toward Van Gundy's chair.

"Sir…"

Van Gundy turned and fixed him with steely blue eyes. "Lieutenant, you better take Commander Matsen's advice. As I said, there is nothing you can do right now." The last words were said in very measured syllables, as if he were talking to a petulant child.

Matsen once more took his arm and tried to steer him toward the hatch and back to Ready Three.

Once more Fancy shook off the hand and he heard Matsen curse, not so softly under his breath.

"Sir, if that was you out there, wouldn't you want as many eyes out there as possible?"

The CAG came out of his chair as if he had been shot from a gun. "Lieutenant! Haven't you heard a thing I've said?"

"Yes, sir, I heard every word. I should be out there."

Van Gundy looked past Fancy to Matsen as if to say, "What's with this dufus?"

When he felt Matsen take his arm he allowed himself to be led toward the hatch.

"Lieutenant Fancy," said Van Gundy, still trying to control his anger. "At first light, you may launch for a routine Combat Air Patrol. Your sector will be in the general vicinity of where we think they went down. If you come up empty, I don't want to see you back here asking to go one more time. Understood?"

"Yes, sir," Fancy barked, "Thank you, sir." But in his heart, he knew he'd be back here in a heartbeat if he wasn't successful in the morning.

It was completely dark when they got the two rafts together. Mirabal used lengths of parachute shroud he kept in the pocket of his vest to lash them together. Mirabal had arranged the rafts so that his feet were toward Robinson's head. He shined his light over Robinson to see if he should be administering first-aid. He looked okay but seemed to be holding his side.

They lay quietly for several minutes as their breathing slowly came back to normal. Robinson looked pale and it looked like he had some plexiglass cuts on his face.

"How do you feel, skipper?"

Robinson managed a feeble grin. "Not too bad, considering. My side hurts. I came down pretty hard. This is one fine mess."

"You know they'll send people out to search, skipper. We won't be here long." Mirabal tried to keep his voice positive and upbeat.

"Yeah, they'll be looking for us. How about turning out that light?"

Mirabal quickly switched off the light. He couldn't believe how dark it was. There were some stars out but that did nothing to alleviate the darkness around them. Reaching for one of the two baby bottles he took a healthy swig. The water tasted good, in fact he couldn't remember when anything had tasted so good. *I'm never going to take water for granted again,* he thought.

Mirabal took off his helmet and set it between his legs. He ran his hands through his hair and rotated his neck, wishing he could stand up and stretch. If he stretched now he would kick Robinson right in the teeth.

Something seemed to bump the raft and Mirabal jumped. Sharks! He reached for the Beretta. He felt reassured just having the automatic in his hand as he peered through the darkness.

"What have you got your gun out for?" whispered Robinson.

"I felt something bump the raft. If it's a shark I want to get in the last word."

He heard Robinson chuckle. "With our luck you'd probably shoot a hole in the raft. Besides the bullets lose their punch when they hit the water."

Mirabal shook his head and grinned at himself in spite of how miserable he was beginning to feel. He put the automatic back in its holster and reached down and made sure his survival knife was still there.

Water continued to spill into the raft which got his butt wet, which made his flight suit act like the wick on a candle and funnel the dampness to his upper extremities which was making him cold. Maybe just thinking about the mechanics of what was happening was making him colder. Better not to think he thought and laughed at himself again.

"What's so funny?" Robinson asked.

"I was thinking about what was making me cold and I figured if I didn't think about it maybe I wouldn't be so cold."

"Are you okay? You're not flippin' out on me are you?"

"No, I'm here in mind and body for the long haul, no pun intended. Seriously, I'm okay, just a little damp."

"Me too. Don't worry, we're going to get out of this. Let's make sure we're lashed together. I know you don't want to spend the night paddling around looking for me. And if I didn't mention it before, thanks, I really appreciate it."

"Just keepin' the faith, skipper. I know you'd do the same for me."

"Bet your ass I would. I think I may have a couple of cracked ribs and I don't believe I'd be able to paddle very far. I've been trying to think how I hurt my side. Guess I blacked out when I hit the water. Either the chute didn't deploy or…" he said, his voice trailing off.

"Anyway," he continued after a few seconds, "I can't taste any blood, so I don't think I nicked anything internally."

They checked to make sure the rafts were securely lashed together and settled down hoping to get some sleep and pass the night.

Fancy had gone right back to his cabin after talking to Van Gundy. Maybe talking was too bold a statement, he mused. He laid out his gear so he could be up at first light. Laying down on his rack he tried to imagine what it would be like to be out there—alone, wet, scared, wondering what, if anything, was being done. He turned on his side trying to get comfortable and will himself to sleep. *I haven't been this anxious for time to pass since I believed in Santa Claus and wanted that Lionel train for Christmas.*

After tossing and turning for what seemed like hours he turned on the light and sat up and looked at his watch. All of twenty whole minutes had managed to pass. He got up and sat down at his desk and started a letter to his folks.

Dear Mom and Dad,

"We're on our way to Hawaii. I can't help but think of all the people who have been or would like to go there. Right now I'm wondering about my RIO, Tony Mirabal, who is probably sitting on a life raft hoping someone is going to find him, and our skipper…

Pushing himself back from the desk and stretching he glanced at his watch and was surprised at how long he had been writing. Oddly enough he felt happy and at the same time pleased with himself. Stuffing the several pages of the letter into an envelope, he addressed it and set it aside. When he flopped down on the bed he closed his eyes and was instantly asleep.

"Sir, sir," came the far off voice. "Sir, Commander Matsen says takeoff is set in forty-five minutes, at 0600."

Fancy opened his eyes and immediately sat up slamming his head into the overhead bunk. Rubbing his head, Fancy growled, "Okay, I'm tactical. Thanks."

Yes, sir, your welcome," answered the retreating voice.

Rubbing his now sore head, Fancy rolled out of the bunk, made it up, and got dressed.

Breakfast, in the Dirty Shirt Wardroom, was some scrambled eggs stuffed between two pieces of bread and some coffee.

Making his way to Ready Three he found Matsen sipping a cup of coffee. "Morning, Sir."

Matsen turned, looked him up and down and replied. "Morning, Fancy. You ready to go?"

"You bet. I had a little trouble getting to sleep, but once I did…"

"I hear you. All right, you did understand what Captain Van Gundy told us yesterday. This is it."

"I heard what he said, sir."

"Yeah, but did you understand it?"

Fancy nodded in the affirmative, while crossing his fingers behind his back, something he hadn't done since he had wanted something from his older brother. He remembered it hadn't worked then and he had spent some time in his room thinking about being honest.

Matsen extended his hand. "Let's make this count for something." Fancy grasped the outstretched hand and nodded, turned and headed for the equipment room.

As they reached the flight deck, they were greeted with the sound of the launch of an S-3, with an E-2C spotted immediately behind the

JBD. Fancy walked over to Desperado 201 and immediately started the walk around. He was immediately joined by Shrader.

"Sir, I'm sorry about Commander Robinson and Lt. Mirabal. I'd sure like to be going with you to help out."

"Thanks, Shrader. If you've done your usual good job on this plane, that will be a big plus for me. One less thing to worry about if I know the plane is one hundred percent."

"It is, sir. I've been over everything two times. She's ready to go."

"Thanks, Shrader."

Charley Mejia joined them on deck. "Morning, Fancy. Let's go find some wet aviators."

Fancy looked over the RIO. He carried his helmet in a bag and had some charts in the other. He was shorter than Fancy and wore his hair longer than most of the other pilots and RIOs. His stocky build filled out his green bag nicely. He was handsome in a rugged sort of way.

"I thought you were sick. Are you sure you feel up to this?"

He saw Mejia stiffen and start to open his mouth. He immediately regretted saying anything.

"I'm fine and I'm good to go. Anything else you need or want to know?" he said taking a step closer, his eyes flashing.

"I'm sorry. You look just fine to me. Let's go do it."

The launch went as smooth as a baby's backside and after they checked in with the E-2, they headed for the CAP station about 175 miles due west.

"Desperado 201," called Matsen. "Let's find the S-3 that's already out there in the general vicinity where they think they went down. Then we can fan out from there."

"Sounds good, 204. Is there a helo out there too?"

"201, that's affirmative. Their call sign is Hasty 2. It's a SF-60 from Enterprise. The crew opted to land on one of the Frigates and spend the night on board. They launched just before we did."

Fancy felt better knowing there were other assets being used. He felt all the better for being out here.

It wasn't long before Mejia picked up the S-3 and the helo. "Fancy, we've got company. Come right ten degrees and they'll be at our 12. Range is 50 miles and closing."

"Thanks. Coming right." As if they were welded together the two big fighters came to a heading of 280 degrees."

"201, let's start a descent to five hundred feet."

"Roger, 204, coming down to five hundred. Toons, can you raise that helo for me?"

"No problem."

In five seconds he was speaking to Hasty 2. "Hasty two, this is Desperado 201. How goes it?"

"Desperado 201, we haven't seen diddly. Not so much as a piece of wreckage or anything," came the deep voice of the helo pilot. "Are these guys friends of yours?"

"Roger that, Hasty. Say do you have any flares on board?"

After a momentary silence, "Yes, yes we do."

"How about if you drop a couple of flares, lit of course, just to check which way they might be drifting. Could you do that?"

"We can do that Desperado," came the same voice, although now tinged with puzzlement.

"Desperado 201, where did you come up with that idea?" queried Matsen.

"204, I don't know. It just kind of seems like a good idea. This is one big ocean. I figured we had to start somewhere. I hope I'm not out of line?"

"201, I don't have anything better up my sleeve. Let's go with it."

"Roger, 204."

"Desperado, 201, we're kicking out two flares—right now. We'll hover and start to track them and then give you a heading."

"Thanks, Hasty, we've got a visual on you now."

Fancy could see the SF-60, now hovering over the water. As he set up an orbit above the helo he saw the flares come out the side door of the helo.

"Desperado, it looks like the flares are drifting on a heading of, uh 260. I'll rotate around so they're on my nose."

"Desperado 204, shall we go to a loose combat spread and try a heading of 260?"

"Like I said, Gator, it's the best plan I've heard. Coming to 260 and I'll drift out to a half to three quarters of mile. Let's keep it at 500 feet."

"Roger, 500 feet at 260," Fancy replied, wondering if they had a snowball's chance in hell of finding anything.

Mirabal had awakened with a start just as the sun was beginning to assert itself on the far horizon. He shook his head, marveling that he had gotten any sleep at all, although he remembered waking up several times during the night to check on their lashings and to make sure Robinson was still with him. So far, so good.

"Skipper, skipper, are you still with me?" he said, reaching over and gently shaking the still form of his CO.

"I'm awake, no thanks to you. How are you doin'?"

"Considering everything, I'm okay. I could stand to be warmer and I could use a big steak and some eggs, but…" he grinned.

Mirabal reached for one of his water bottles and offered Robinson a drink. He was surprised when Robinson shook his head no, and reached for one of his bottles. After taking a quick drink he passed the bottle over. "Try this, it will warm you up."

Mirabal took a short drink and felt the liquor spread a little warmth throughout his body. "Is this what I think it is?" he asked, gasping a little at the surprise taste.

"Brandy, I never leave home without it. You never know when it's going to come in handy. And, it looks like this was one of those times," Robinson grinned.

"You seem to be feeling better, Skipper."

"I do, I don't know why, but I do. Getting to sleep last night must have done the trick. I'm stiff and my side still hurts, but, hey, I do feel better."

Mirabal got out his survival radio. It looked a little damp and he decided to give it a try. "This is Desperado 211. Anybody out there. We're temporarily grounded, but anxious to get back in the game." He shook his head when he received no reply. After another few minutes of fruitless calls he stowed the radio.

Robinson looked over at Mirabal who seemed a bit dejected when his call was not immediately answered. "Don't worry, they're out there. They'll be coming."

"I know they will, I just want it to happen now. I've always been impatient."

Robinson chuckled and stretched, offering him another drink of brandy.

Fancy, alternately looking left then right as they skimmed across the surface of the seemingly endless ocean, wondering how far they could have drifted or even if they drifted this way at all. Flying at this altitude used up fuel quicker that he liked but they had no choice if they hoped to spot anything at all.

The two aviators quickly warmed as the sun climbed over the horizon. Mirabal put his helmet back on partly to provide some shade and partly to get it out of the way. Upon hearing the sound of an aircraft jet engine he almost tipped over the raft. "Skipper, do hear what I hear? That's an F-14 or my name's not Tony Mirabal." He ripped the helmet off his head in order to locate the direction of the plane.

Robinson likewise strained to hear and locate the direction of the plane. Unfortunately, the sound faded away as the plane turned away from them. "They're out there. It's just a matter of time now."

Mirabal balled his fists and was tempted to throw his helmet in what he thought was the direction the plane was headed in. "Man, I hope so. What's the saying so close, yet so far."

Rhino started to fish around in his survival vest. "I want to make sure those flares are handy," he said as he felt them in the pocket of his vest.

"Let's try the radio again. They should be listening for us by now," Robinson said as he brought out his survival radio. "This is Desperado 211. Say again, this is Desperado 211. We just heard an F-14 so we know you're in the vicinity."

Do you think it's working, Skipper?" asked Mirabal, who by now had his own survival radio out.

"I have a funny feeling about it. I'm not picking up any static or anything. These things are supposed to be pretty reliable and I don't think I hit that hard."

Rhino put the radio up to his ear. After listening for a few seconds he held it out in front of him and gave it several shakes. The rattling noise from inside gave him some indication that all was not well with his gear either. He passed it over to Robinson who also gave it a shake.

"I'd definitely say something is wrong with this. At least mine doesn't make any noise when I shake it around. I"ll try your batteries and see if mine could be the problem."

After a few minutes of working with the radios, Robinson had the batteries changed. "This is Desperado 211, say again Desperado 211. Anybody out there? We heard the sound of a plane a few minutes ago."

"At least I'm getting some static now. I think its working," said Robinson with hope in his voice.

Fancy felt that his eyes were being drawn to the fuel gauges as much as they were to the surface of the ocean. It was hard not to focus on them the way the fuel seemed to be eaten up. Of course at this low altitude what could he expect. He lowered the nose a tad and dropped to four hundred feet. Might as well make this count for something he figured.

"Gator, I just heard something on Guard. It sounded like the last syllable of Desperado and then two -one-one. It sounded real weak.

Fancy keyed his mike and at the same time switched to Guard, the emergency frequency. "Desperado, 211, this is Desperado 201. Give me a call so we can start to get a fix on you. say again, this is Desperado 201 calling Desperado 211. Two-one-one, give a call."

"What do you think, Toons? Are we headed in the right direction?"

"Gator, if I had to bet, I'd wager that call came from behind us. I have no safe or sane reason for believing if that's right, but it's just a feeling."

"Are your hunches usually pretty good?"

"Actually they are. I was going to marry this babe I met in Florida. Great lookin' gal, smart, sexy, the whole package. Still I had this nagging feeling about her that I just couldn't shake. Turned out she had a terrible cocaine habit and was seeing somebody else on the side. So, yeah, I trust my intuitions most of the time."

"Desperado 204, what do you say we reverse course and retrace our pattern? Did you hear that call on Guard?"

"Negative on the call on Guard, Gator. Why do want to reverse course?"

"Toons got what he thinks was a call from two-one-one on Guard and he thinks it sounded like it was from behind us. Gut feeling."

"Okay, Gator. Let's scissors and come to course zero eight zero."

"Roger, Mongo, zero eight zero," Fancy answered as he put the big fighter into a gradual turn to port. He watched as Matsen turned toward him and then passed to their port side a hundred yards separating the two planes.

"As soon as they came to the reciprocal course Fancy instructed Mejia to get back on Guard and radio every minute.

When the F-14 had passed out of their hearing range, Robinson and Mirabal tried to cheer each other up. Liberty in Hawaii was discussed as were other possible liberty ports such as Hong Kong and Australia. The silence however, fell about them like a shroud and soon both men lapsed into a discouraged silence.

"Desperado 201, how you doin' on fuel? We're starting to get to that point."

Fancy glanced at the gauge, not liking one bit what he saw, or in this case, what he didn't see. "Ah, we're at about, uh 5,800 pounds." Fuel was being consumed at an alarming rate even though the turbo-fan engines were pretty fuel efficient at low altitudes. Still 5,800 pounds meant they had little time left.

"That's just about what we've got," answered Matsen. "Did you hear anything else on Guard?"

"Negative, we're calling out every minute, but I guess you can hear that."

"Yeah, I'd give anything for an answer, any kind of answer."

Fancy was just ready to respond when Toons came up and almost screamed, "Gator, Gator! I just heard something. It was weak, but I'll bet the farm that we're headed in the right direction!"

"Mongo, did you catch that? Toons just heard something on Guard."

"No, we didn't. Damn it all anyway. I'm glad somebody has their ears plugged in, cause, I sure don't. What did he hear?"

"XO, I just heard the numbers two-one-one. although it was weak, it sounded a little stronger than the first time I heard it. Sounds like somebody's batteries are going south and maybe there's a loose connection in their radio. It faded in and out real quick."

"Okay, let's drop down to three hundred feet. We'll stay on Guard and keep calling, while you listen."

"Roger that 204, dropping to three hundred."

The sun was now beating down unmercifully and Mirabal was thinking about how long his water would last. He wanted more than anything to take a drink but resisted the temptation not knowing how much longer he would have to make the little bit of water last.

After finally deciding that one small draw wouldn't hurt, he had just put the nipple of the baby bottle in his mouth when he heard the unmistakable sound of a jet engine, and, he surmised, that engine was one of two belonging to an F-14. *It's Fancy*, he thought to himself.

"Skipper, skipper," he whispered, not wanting to lose the sound again, "do you hear that?"

Robinson perked up and the look in his eyes told Mirabal he wasn't the only one tuned into what he now considered the sweetest sound in the world.

"Skipper, I'm going to fire one of these flares." Reaching for the flare, he pulled it out of his vest pocket, pointed it skyward and fired. The flare arched up quickly into the deep blue sky.

"Gator, how we doin' with the fuel?" called Mejia, concern etched in his voice.

"Forty seven hundred pounds, babe. We're good for another few minutes. *A very few minutes.*

After a very few minutes Fancy heard the words he had been dreading: Desperado 201, we gotta get out of here. We're at Bingo fuel in about a minute."

Fancy turned in the direction of Matsen's plane and saw the flare as it reached its apogee and started its fall back into the ocean. "Desperado 204, did you see that? That was a flare. I'm coming left. That's got to be them!"

Trying to keep the spot where he had seen the flare, Fancy racked his plane around and headed for what he hoped were two people in a raft.

"It's coming this way!" shouted Mirabal. Reaching into his vest pocket and took out another flare. In his excitement to launch the flare he almost shot it into the water.

"Calm down, Rhino. Be careful with that thing!" Robinson demanded. He felt the same excitement, but somebody had better remain calm. He also reached for one of his flares.

"There's another one! Did you see it?" Fancy was shouting now, unable to contain himself. Bringing the Tomcat slightly to starboard the flare was just starting to fall back toward the water. He was rewarded by the sight of another flare that was close, really close, he figured. Retarding the throttles slightly and then lowering the flaps, as he thought of it, just a tad, he didn't want to shoot past his squadron mates in the water.

"Gator, did you see that flare? We're close."

"Bet your ass I did, 204. We're close, the trick will be now to pinpoint their location. I hope they'll fire one more flare."

Almost in concert with Fancy's plea, Robinson pointed the flare skyward and pushed the button on the tube that would fire the flare. He was rewarded with—nothing. Throwing the useless flare tube over the side of his raft he yelled at Mirabal. "Rhino, get your signal mirror out, the damn flare went south!"

Both men reached frantically for their signal mirrors, the lowest of low tech solutions to their plight.

Mirabal tried to make himself calm down. Sitting down in the raft he pointed the mirror in the direction of what were now the strong sound of jet engines—heading their way.

Fancy and Matsen had slowed their planes and were literally just hanging in the air as close to stalling the planes as was humanly possible without crossing what was now a very thin line.

Robinson saw one of the planes first. "There they are, at your six, Rhino!"

Mirabal, in his rush to turn around almost fell out of the raft. "I see 'em. There they are! Yeah!" Immediately he fell back in the raft, which had taken on considerably more water in the last few seconds, and concentrated on signaling their rescuers. "Come on, guys, over here, come to papa," he muttered to himself. "Come on, look this way."

Fancy strained in his harness trying to see his comrades in arms. A glance at the fuel gauges told him that he better see something—quick!

"Gator, there they are. One o' clock, one o' clock. Look!"

Fancy picked up the raft, guided by the reflections of the two mirrors. "Mongo, they're at one o' clock." Bringing the plane in a tight ninety degree bank he set up an orbit around the raft straining to keep the raft in his sight and at the same time fly the plane.

"Hasty 2, Desperado 201," called Mejia, "we've spotted them. Have you got a fix on us?"

"Roger, 201. This is Hasty 04. We've taken over from zero two. We're about ten minutes away from your posit. The frigate Underwood will be headed toward them. They're about, uh, an hour and fifteen minutes from your guys. Great job."

"Thanks, Hasty. We're starting to run a little low on fuel, but we'll hang around until we're sure you've got them sighted and ready to pick 'em up."

"Roger, 201, we've got a pretty good fix on you and them. Don't run yourself too low. We've only got room for so many people in here ya know," replied the voice from Hasty 02.

Fancy guessed he must be from Alabama or Mississippi. The voice was calm and delivered in a rich, slow southern drawl. The voice alone had a calming effect on Fancy, who, with every glance at the fuel gauges realized he had very few reason or pounds of fuel left to be calm.

"Desperado 201, it's time to head on back to the boat. That helo is about five minutes out."

Fancy was tempted to argue the point. With success well within their grasp he didn't want any last minute foul ups to spoil what was now looking like a sierra hotel day.

"Roger that 204. How about one more orbit just to be on the safe side?"

"Fancy, you really know how to push it don't you?"

Fancy brought the plane around. The two men and their raft wagging the wings as he headed to join up with Matsen.

Seeing the two plane head away from them gave Mirabal a momentary stab of panic. Then he realized that if that is indeed Fancy, he wouldn't leave unless help was on the way. He knew Fancy would never break the faith.

Mirabal followed the two planes until they were out of sight. Looking at Robinson he croaked, "This calls for a celebration don't you think, Skipper? Do you want some of my water?"

"I think the water would hit the spot right now. I'm betting the helo must be no more than five minutes out, otherwise they wouldn't have left."

"That's what I figure. In fact, do you hear what I hear?"

The unmistakable thrump of rotor blades perforated the air. Mirabal reached for the remaining baby bottle and handed it to Robinson who took a healthy swig before handing it back. Before Mirabal had drained the bottle, the SF-60 was starting its final run in to pick them up. He could see one of the swimmers standing in the door ready to jump in and assist them getting into the hoist. Funny, Mirabal thought, I've never thought of helos as especially attractive. Hasty zero two was the most beautiful thing he remembered seeing in a long time.

About the time Robinson and Mirabal were being wrapped in blankets and offered some coffee Fancy and Matsen had leveled off at 2,000 feet. The fuel gauges seemed to be leaping out of the instrument panel sending their urgent message of the plane's fuel state.

"Homeplate, this is Desperado two zero four on Mom's 240. State is one point six." Matsen tried to keep his voice calm, but was afraid his voice was coming out an octave too high. "We could sure use a steer to the nearest tanker."

"Desperado 204, tanker had to return to homeplate with an engine problem. Right now we have to move some airplanes around to launch the spare. The alert five went down with a nose wheel problem."

"Roger that," confirmed Matsen disgustedly. "201, did you copy that bit of good news?"

"Good news comes in bunches doesn't it?" gibed Fancy with a sigh, vowing not to look at the fuel state until he was on deck and had shut down the engines, while at the same time retarding the throttles a little. *Can't hurt* he thought.

"Toons, what's the distance to the carrier?"

"I've got 'em about seventy-five miles—well within gliding distance, right?"

"Oh, definitely. We have a glide ratio of say, two to one," reckoned Fancy with a chuckle.

The two planes flew toward the carrier in silence, each pilot and RIO alone with their own thoughts and concerns.

When Mejia announced they were within twenty-five miles Fancy almost stole a glance at the fuel gauge, but managed to resist the temptation.

At ten miles Fancy was almost giddy with anticipation. Somehow he knew they were going to make it—one way or another.

"204, what's your fuel state?"

"Gator, you don't want to know. It's less than 800 pounds."

"Well, Babe, that's a lot less than I've got, you better recover first," telling what was one of the biggest untruths of his life.

"Strike," he radioed to Enterprise. Desperado two zero one checking in on Mom's 235. Eight, state zero point 900."

"Desperado 201, you're second to recover."

"Roger strike, second to recover," he answered calmly while watching Matsen start to line up for his final approach. Maybe final was too strong a word in this case he thought.

"Okay, Toons, let's go over the checklist, we're only get one chance today."

"Roger checklist, Gator."

Once again after going through the checklist, Fancy began twisting and turning, trying to get comfortable trying not to look at the fuel gauges. This was going to be tight. He hoped Mongo had made a perfect pass and the deck would be clear. Well, too late to worry now. Sighing to himself he went through the twisting and turning routine once more.

"210, Tomcat, ball, fumes," Gator called.

"Roger ball," came the cool, calm voice of Badrod Baldon. *Man, he's way too high,* thought Baldon as he picked out the Tomcat that had rolled into the groove. *What's goin' on here?*

As Fancy rolled into the groove, the starboard engine flamed out and he was just able to make the correction before the plane started to yaw in the direction of the now silent engine. A heartbeat later the port engine ran out of gas. *Thank God I anticipated that* breathed Fancy to himself. *One thing I hate to see is altitude above me.*

Baldon realized what had happened. "He's flamed out. Oh shit, come on, Gator, you can do it."

Fancy felt the normal smoothness of flight disrupted as he made a series of small corrections to bring the ball down to line up with the row of green lights. At least he was on glide path. Bringing the stick back slightly the ball stays aligned.

Baldon, standing on his platform realizized there was not much he could do. Bringing the microphone up to his lips, he wanted to tell Fancy to add power, but realized that would be futile. "Looking good, Gator. Keep'er coming, you can do it."

The deck was rising on a swell. He allowed himself to make a tiny correction to bring the plane to the left. *Thank God she's still responding.* He held his breath as they crossed the roundoff and he felt the wheels slam into the deck and found himself thrown forward into his harness as usual Automatically he pushed the throttles all the way forward. Shaking his head he pulled the throttles back to the idle position.

"How ya doin', Toons?"

"You won't mind if I get out of here and kiss the deck will you. That was some piece of flying, man. I think we may have made a little bit of history here. Deadstick. Unbelievable."

Raising the canopy, he was greeted by Shrader's face who had a look of total disbelief on his face. "Welcome back, sirs," he said looking toward the rear seat where Mejia was unhooking and preparing to get out. "Nice to have you back."

"Thanks, Shrader, glad to be back. Any word about Commander Robinson and Lt. Mirabal?"

"We just heard that they were picked up successfully. They had to go to the Underwood to refuel, then they're flying directly back here."

"Great," grinned Fancy, as he handed his helmet to Shrader, who climbed down to the deck. Fancy motioned for Mejia to give him his helmet and climb down. He grinned as Mejia did indeed bend down and kiss the deck. After the gesture he turned and gave Fancy a thumb's up.

Throwing the helmet down to Mejia, Fancy climbed down, somewhat stiffly and arched his back. As much as he loved to be in the air, it wasn't a bad feeling to feel the solid steel deck beneath his feet.

Retrieving his helmet from Shrader and letting him know there was nothing wrong with 201 that 16,000 pounds of fuel wouldn't cure, he walked toward the ladder that would take him below deck. As he passed the nose of the plane, he gave it a loving pat on the nose. "Good job, baby, good job."

Fancy raced down to the equipment room and hung up his gear. Animal Schott and Big Wave were suiting up as he entered. "Gator," called Big Wave, "we heard the good news."

"Way to go guys," said Animal as he came over and shook Fancy's hand. "I was beginning to think that maybe this cruise was going south in a hurry. Who spotted them anyway?"

"They launched a flare and Toons saw it. Lucky for us they launched another one right after and we just motored on over to where they were.

Man, that ocean just seemed to be getting bigger and bigger the more we looked. Whoever invented that flare," he sighed shaking his head, "really made a difference today."

"That flare makes no difference unless there's somebody there to see it," drawled Big Wave. "You guys did some good work out there. I hope if that ever happens to me, you guys will come lookin'."

"If we don't find you, Wave, can I have your boards?" joked Animal.

"We heard they had to go to the Underwood to pick up some fuel and then they were going to be flown here," said Big Wave. "Don't tell Mirabal, but I'll be really glad to see that little wise ass."

"Hey, don't bust my RIO," interjected Fancy. That guy is good at what he does. Mejia did a good job today, but I tell you, Rhino's better."

Hanging up his gear, Fancy said, "I'm going to grab a quick shower and change." Looking at his watch, he said, "I want to be on the roof when they land. I'll see you guys later."

Thirty minutes later Fancy watched the SH-60 Seahawk touch down. By the time he had walked over to the helo, Mirabal had bounced out of the helo. A stretcher carrying Robinson came out next. Fancy was relieved to see Robinson raising his head and looking around. Captain Van Gundy moved through the now gathering crowd of multicolored shirts of the deck crew.

"Ratchet, how are feeling? You look pretty good for somebody who's just had some time off, cruising around the Pacific," he smiled as he grasped Robinson's outstretched hand.

"Robinson grinned his ear-to-ear grin. "Oh yeah, it was just a walk in the park. Uh, make that a cruise in the park."

Mirabal strode over to where Fancy was taking the reunion in. "Thanks, man. I can't believe how good it made me feel to hear and then see you guys. I was starting to get worried."

"How'd you know it was me?" queried Fancy.

"I just knew—you know about keeping the faith. There was no doubt in my mind it was you."

Smiling, Fancy grinned and said, "You better let Toons know how grateful you are, he spotted the flare you guys shot off. We were just about ready to head back to the boat when he saw it. The second one was really the one that got us over there as soon as we did. Hey, you know, Mejia's pretty good. He really knows his way around that back seat."

"He's not as good as I am though, is he?" gasped Mirabal grasping his chest in mock horror.

"Well, he's pretty good," said Fancy, barely containing his glee. "But, no, he's not as good as you are. It's really good to see you, in one piece no less. How rough was it?"

"That ejection was the most violent thing that I've ever gone through. Bam! We were out of there. The seat and chute worked as advertised. Getting into the damn raft was a chore until I finally figured it out. I don't know how long I paddled before the Skipper and I finally got together. I thought my arms were going to fall off. Do they look any longer?"

"As a matter of fact they do. You do look like a knuckle dragger."

Mirabal clapped Fancy on the back and they continued their trip down to the ships infirmary.

Just as they reached the ladder to go below deck, Van Gundy walked by and said, "Fancy after you get Lt. Mirabal squared away in the infirmary, I want to see you."

"Yes, sir, should I come now, sir."

"No, but make it quick," he commanded and marched back to his throne in Pri-Fly.

"What's that about," asked Mirabal. "I bet he wants to tell you what a great job you guys did."

"Uh," muttered Fancy, "I'll just have to see. What was it like out there during the night?"

"Besides dark. I thought I felt something bump the raft—thinking shark, right?"

"That would be my first guess," amplified Fancy.

"I got my gun out and was ready to defend our two raft fleet. Ratchet persuaded me to put it away lest I blast a hole in the raft."

"A cooler head prevailed," speculated Fancy.

"Wetter anyway," retorted Mirabal. "After that it wasn't too bad. We even grabbed some Zs."

Fifteen minutes later Fancy was reporting to Van Gundy in Pri-Fly. As Fancy entered the room, Van Gundy as if on cue, turned his chair around to face him. "Fancy that was a brilliant landing. I've only seen one other dead stick in all the years I've been in the Navy. That was some great flying."

"Thank you, sir. I was just lucky to be almost back before she flamed out."

"Which brings me to reason why you're here. Why in the hell did you let yourself get so low on gas. That almost cost us another plane, not to mention a crew."

"Sir, I didn't know we would be without tanker support. They're usually there when we need them." Mentally he kicked himself for such a lame excuse.

"Not exactly a hundred percent guarantee. You know that!" Van Gundy was steamed.

"Sir, I thought the risk was worth it. Even so it was probably pure luck that we spotted them. I'd do it again, sir."

"I bet you would. When we get to Pearl, you're confined to the ship. Mister, you had better start thinking of the big picture instead of just winging it! Understand?"

Fancy, figuring he had already said too much, paused to let his rising anger cool down, and was about to say "yes sir", when one of the enlisted men walked up behind Van Gundy with a message. The CAG read it once and Fancy thought he saw him take in a sudden breath. Van Gundy read the message again. Not saying anything he handed the message to Fancy. Animal and his RIO had gone down.

Despite two days of intensive searching not a trace was found of the plane or the two men.

As if Mother Nature had decided enough was enough, the day after the search was finally called off for Animal and his RIO, bad weather hit the battle group ending anymore flying for the immediate future.

Right after the memorial for the two aviators, Robinson called the entire squadron of 350 enlisted men and officers together in the hanger bay. He had already spent some time talking one on one with some of the pilots and RIOs. Still looking somewhat pale and favoring his ribs which, luckily for him, were only badly bruised. First he reassured everyone that the loss of two planes and one crew was a fluke. He urged everyone to put the accidents out of their minds and get back to work and be willing to work hard. Stressing that there was no evidence of faulty maintenance in any of the crashes, although admitting not knowing what downed the two planes. Closing, he said, "I have nothing to offer you but more hard work. It's not going to be easy, but that's why we're all here. If it was easy everybody could do it, and we all know that's just not the case."

Immediately after that meeting he called the officers together in Ready three. Standing at the podium he spoke to the assembled aviators. "I need to know," he began, "if there is anyone here who feels that they cannot go out and give their full concentration to flying or even fears it. Come and see me so we can talk about it. Or, if you feel the need, go to the Chaplin," he said very softly, almost pleadingly. This was no fire and brimstone or a challenge to anyone's manhood. It seemed as if he was more of a healer, inviting anyone who had lost his nerve because of the accidents to hand in his wings before he killed himself, or worse, someone else.

Each man lost himself in his own personal thoughts, yet all were much the same. They knew that turning in your wings is a very extreme move for any Navy pilot. For the rest of his life he would be held in contempt by the aviators he once flew with. In their view, he'd quit in the middle of the game because he was afraid of getting hurt. He'd be saying their way of life was not worth dying for. This particular fraternity could not judge him rationally or judge him brave for giving up his wings.

As they would see it the aviators who keep flying until they are killed, become gray, or are grounded are stupid or cowardly. This fraternity is afraid to try to do something else with their lives; so they keep letting themselves get catapulted off the end of the boat to see if they can get back aboard two hours later.

The squadron sat in silence at the end of Robinson's remarks. Fancy wanted to take a look at Bailey to see if Robinson's words had had any effect on his friend. He willed himself not to look.

After the meeting Fancy and Mirabal headed out the hatch to get something to eat. As they made their way out, Bagger caught up with them. "You guys going to get something to eat by any chance?"

Mirabal answered for them both before Fancy could open his mouth. "You bet. This kind of meeting always make me hungry. Grab a bite with us."

Fancy fell in step with Bagger. Mirabal plowed ahead talking to one of the other RIOs.

"What did you think of the meetings, Gator?'

I like the way the Skipper laid it on the line. We can't afford to feel sorry for ourselves. The hard part of the cruise is still ahead of us. Shoot for that matter the whole cruise is still in front of us. Are you having any second thoughts? I know he made me think about some things."

"No, I'm still good to go. If anything I feel more committed than ever. Flying is something I really love. If I quit I'd be kicking myself forever."

"What if somebody did decide to pull the plug. How would you feel about him?"

"Well if you mean would I hate him or any of that bullshit, I wouldn't. I've got friends that don't fly and I like them. Probably, I'd feel sorry for the guy, but I could never disassociate myself from him.

Besides, I can really empathize with somebody who could or would make that decision. Life is too short."

"Say, what did CAG want with you?"

"First he patted me on the back for the landing and then he kicked me in the butt for cutting it too fine. He wants me to stay aboard ship and make sure nobody steals it while everyone else hits the beach." Fancy sighed. "It was worth it, but I was really looking forward to seeing some of the islands."

"That stinks. Hey, I'll keep you company."

"You will not. You haven't been here before have you?"

"No, but it's no big deal."

"Sure it is. Get off the ship and then come back and tell me all about it. You never know I might want to come back there on a honeymoon or something in the future."

"What?" blurted Bagger. "Is there something in the works that I don't know about?"

Fancy smiled, "No, but you just never know."

# 9

Five days later the Enterprise entered Pearl Harbor.

Pushing back his chair Fancy surveyed the almost finished pile of paperwork that seemed to have devoured the small gray steel desk. He had seen Bagger, Poncho, and Big Wave off the ship almost as soon, it seemed, as she tied up at the pier. After his friends had gone, promising to bring him back a souvenir, Fancy had spent some time looking at the historic harbor.

As he wandered to various parts of the ship he ran into Doc Su, the flight surgeon.

"Doc, I thought you'd be one of the first ones off the ship?"

"Good morning, Lt. Fancy. I would have thought the same about you?"

"Actually the CAG thought I should stay on board and finish up some of the squadron paperwork."

Su raised his eyebrows in surprise. "Oh, I thought after you brought your plane back aboard so well he would be very pleased with you. That's a shame. Have you been here before?"

"No, but it's a place I'll come back to someday. Even here from the ship I can tell it's a pretty exotic place. How about you?"

"Fortunately, I have visited here several times. It is a very beautiful place. My wife and I came here on our honeymoon. Since that time I have been captivated. We have managed to visit all the islands. At least the ones people are allowed to visit."

"Do you mean there are some islands you can't visit?"

"Yes, the island of Niihau is privately owned and visitors, up to now, have been discouraged, although I understand for a price, picnickers are able to eat on the beach of the island, but go no further."

"How long have you been married, Doc?"

"Thirty-five years in November. I'm so surprised at how fast the time has flown by."

"Are you married, Lieutenant?"

"Was. We've been divorced for about six months now." Fancy shrugged not knowing what to say next.

"I'm sorry it didn't work out, Lieutenant."

"Well, maybe it was for the best Doc. She wanted me to quit the Navy, go to work for the airlines." His voice trailed off.

"I didn't mean to pry, Lieutenant. It's really none of my business."

"That's okay, Doc. No problem. Listen, it's good to see you. I better get going on the pile of work CAG sent down. Are you going ashore?"

"Yes. I have someone to see and then I'll go."

"Have a good time Doc, I'll see you around, " he said as he turned to go to his stateroom.

Finishing up the last of the reports and other trivia, Fancy dug around in the papers he had brought aboard. Finding the small spiral notebook he was seeking, he flipped through the pages until he came to a phone number.

Robinson had been the bearer of some good news when he brought the paperwork, telling Fancy he could get off the ship and go no further than the end of the pier. During his walk around on the deck he had noticed that there was a bank of phones at the end.

As he walked down the pier toward the phone bank, Fancy noticed how warm it was. Not hot, but just pleasantly warm. He had no desire to walk in the shadow of the Enterprise.

Depositing a quarter in the first phone he came to he dialed Scott Thorn's number. On the first try it was busy. After trying two more times without success, on the fourth try the phone was answered. "Good morning. Is this Scott Thorn?"

"Good morning, and yes, it is."

"Uh, my name is Dan Fancy. I know your sister, Cody. She gave me your number and asked if I would give you a ring when I got here."

"Cody, huh. How is she?" His voice had taken on a decidedly guarded tone, not unfriendly, exactly.

"She and Amanda are fine, just fine."

"Are you at the airport? Do you need a lift to your hotel or anything?"

"Actually I'm at Pearl Harbor. I'm in the Navy on the carrier *Enterprise*. We just pulled in this morning."

"Oh, you're in the Navy. How did you meet my sister?" Again the guarded tone.

"She brought Amanda down to Miramar for the annual air show. Amanda showed a great interest in the plane I fly and I was giving her a sort or private tour and then…"

"What kind of plane do you fly?" The voice was decidedly friendlier.

"The F-14D, the Tomcat. I'm in VF-124, the Gunfighters."

"Fighters, huh. I bet that's a challenge?"

"At times it can be, sometimes it's more than that. We lost two planes and two men between San Diego and Pearl."

"I'm sorry to hear that. After an awkward silence, he continued. "Are you and Cody seeing each other?" The voice was again guarded or was it protective?

"She was kind enough to invite me up to a cookout. I don't know if you could call it going together. She's keeping my car in her garage until this cruise is over."

"Oh, I see," he responded. Again there was a silence.

"Listen, the only thing we've done is shake hands three times, one peck on the cheek, and a better kiss the night she took my car back to her place. If you're wondering how I feel about her, I'm definitely in love with her and I think she feels the same way about me."

"I want you to know that I don't want to see her hurt again. That prick she was married to before ought to be drop-kicked around the block and I'd like to do the kicking."

"I hear you and I agree one hundred percent. She's special and I would never do anything to hurt her or show any disrespect, believe me."

"I hope not. Say are you going to get, uh, what do they call it—liberty?"

It was Fancy's turn to pause. After a deep sigh he said, "That's why I'm calling you, I'm sort of confined to the ship."

Upon hearing the chuckle at the other end of the phone he felt himself start to turn red.

"Confined to the ship. What did you do, piss in the punchbowl?"

"It was nothing that serious. I cut it a little close fuel-wise a few days ago and the CAG was not pleased."

"Did you say CAG?"

"That is Captain Jeff Van Gundy. CAG stands for Commander Air Group. It's a term that goes back to World War Two."

"Hmmm, sounds like a serious kind of guy?"

"Believe me, he is, especially where his airplanes are conerned. Say, are you busy today? I'd like to talk to you in person. Could you take some time off? I could show you around the ship if you like?"

"Hey, I'd like that. I've never been on a ship that big before. Let me call my boss. I'm sure he won't mind. Besides I've been working some long hours lately and I probably got a little comp time stored up. Give me the number you're calling from and I'll call you right back."

After a few minutes Scott called back and confirmed that he could get some time off. Fancy, after inquiring about getting someone on to the base, told him where to park and what to do to get to the carrier.

Almost an hour later Fancy watched Scott Thorn pass through the gate guarded by two large Navy enlisted men. It didn't take a genius to tell that the man coming toward him was an Indian—a very large Indian. Fancy figured he must be at least six five, two hundred and fifty pounds. He wore blue jeans, a t-shirt, and running shoes. His black hair was worn in a pony tail and his black eyes rested above a hawk nose. *I bet this guy has no problems getting a date,* Fancy thought.

"I hope you're Dan Fancy," the man said as he extended a hand. Fancy noted that the hand was huge and the grip hearty but could probably shift to excruciating in the blink of an eye.

"Guilty," Fancy answered, hoping he wasn't appearing too surprised at Thorn's appearance.

"Man, this is one big ship," he announced with a sweep on his arms. "How many people are on it?"

"They tell me it's around, maybe a little over 5,000 men and about eighty planes."

"That's impressive. Thanks for inviting me. It was worth all the hassle they put me through at the main gate. I guess they can't be too careful."

"I guess not in today's world." Fancy decided that he liked Scott Thorn. He had an easy going manner and asked some very intelligent questions about the ship right off the bat.

After a few minutes Fancy asked, "Would you like to come on board and take a look around?"

"Oh, yeah, I sure would. I've never been on anything even remotely this big before."

After a call to the Officer of the Day, on the bridge, from the Junior Officer of the Day, Fancy was granted permission to bring his guest on board.

Once on board Fancy and Thorn walked around the crowded flight deck, with Fancy pointing out the different planes and their particular missions. Again he was impressed by Thorn's questions and his interest in what went on on board the carrier.

Before he knew it two and a half hours had passed. "Are you hungry by any chance?" he asked Thorn.

Now that you mention it I am. Is there anywhere we can get something to eat. I'd like to buy your lunch. This is so interesting."

"How about it if we put your tax dollars to work. We can go down to the dirty shirt wardroom and grab something."

"Sounds good to me."

Getting to the dirty shirt wardroom took longer than usual because Thorn had more than a few questions. Nothing escaped his piercing black eyes.

After getting some hamburgers and drinks they found a seat, which wasn't hard, with so many of the crew taking advantage of being in Hawaii.

"I'm glad your boss could gave you the time off today. It's been nice meeting you."

"It wasn't hard, uh, I'm kind of the boss. I had to make sure my guys were clear on what they had to do today."

"What is it exactly that you do?"

"I work for the state of Hawaii. My job is making sure the islands stay as pristine as possible. It seems to get harder every day. This is the destination of choice of a whole bunch of people. Which is good in some ways and bad in others. So much of the economy is tourism. Agriculture is being edged out by golf courses and hotels."

"I know I'd like to come back here some day. It's so beautiful even the little bit I could see from the ship. It even smells good," he said, pushing his empty plate away.

"It is a beautiful place. I can't imagine living anywhere else now. Maybe when you come back I can show you around. Each island is so different and unique."

"I'd really like that," Fancy said. "My appetite has definitely been whetted."

The two men stood on deck looking at the various planes. Thorn asked, "Which plane is yours?"

"We're not assigned a particular plane. Very seldom do you ever fly the same plane two days in a row."

Thorn looked at his watch. "I've probably taken up too much of your time. I guess I better hit the road."

"Nonsense, I've enjoyed meeting you. Your sister thinks a great deal of you; she was very complimentary."

"Cody's a terrific lady. She's smart, tough, a great mother. Being her closest relative, I'd like to know what your intentions are. I really don't want to see her hurt again. I hope you're not offended, but…"

Fancy held up his hands in front of him. "Believe me, I would never do anything to hurt Cody in any way, shape, or form. When we met, I was coming off a divorce and all the attending baggage that goes with that. My wife and I lost our baby daughter to Sudden Infant Death Syndrom. If that wasn't enough, I was drinking—a lot. Luckily I had an understanding commanding officer back in Oceana and he transferred me out here. Kind of like a second chance. Getting involved with someone was the fartherest thing from my mind. Then there she was at the air show. I have nothing but honorable intentions toward your sister. However," he said after pausing, "I'm in love with her and like I said before, I think she feels the same way about me."

"You know, I hope she is. I get a really good feeling about you. She went through a lot with that jerk she was married to. Did she tell you he abused her?" Thorn replied, his black eyes seeming to bore holes in Fancy

She told me he hit her once and she left."

"That's Cody. This asshole really did a number on her. She managed to get away, but spent a week in the hospital, then she left. The really bad thing, if that wasn't enough, was that Amanda had to see the whole thing."

Fancy felt himself getting angry. "I wouldn't mind going a few rounds with this guy myself."

"Cody wouldn't let me even get near this guy. She was afraid I was going to kill him, which I was. I've got a friend who works for United Airlines. He says he can get me a ticket on a moment's notice to get to LA if she needs me. Next time I "talk" to the guy and then tell her about it if there's any problem."

Fancy imagined what that would be like and made a mental note never to get Scott Thorn the least bit upset at him."

"Extending his hand Thorn said, "I hope you have a safe cruise. You never said it but it must be pretty dangerous at times."

Fancy shrugged. "There are times when you need to marshal all your powers of concentration."

Digging in his pocket he fished out some money. "Say could you do me a favor and buy something for Amanda and Cody. I was going to get something and send it, but…"

"I'd be glad to. Anything in particular you have in mind?"

Fancy held up his hands and shook his head. "Not really. Any suggestions?"

"Yeah, let me take care of it, okay? I'm going to call them tonight and tell them I met you and let them know something is on the way."

"Thanks, I'd really appreciate it," said Fancy extending his hand.

After they parted Fancy watched Thorn until he had gone through the gate and was out of sight. *Man, that guy is big,* he thought as he rubbed his hand, now aching due to the hearty parting handshake.

As soon as Thorn was out of sight Fancy decided to get in a little exercise by jogging the length of the flight deck. After falling twice because he hadn't watched for tie-down cables, he found his rhythm. After five circuits of the deck he stopped. With sweat running down his face and body and his breath coming in ragged gasps he rested with his hands on his thighs promising to do more jogging and maybe even get down to the weight room. If and when he returned to Hawaii he wanted to come back in some semblance of shape, wondering at the same time if Cody worked out. Looking again at the phone bank at the end of the pier he decided he might as well ask her.

Looking at his watch he calculated the difference in time and decided it might be a little early to call. Besides, after jogging he could probably use a shower he decided.

Dressed in a pair of fresh shorts, t-shirt, and his jogging shoes, he once more departed the ship armed with all the spare change he could find, and walked down the pier toward the phones. He saw Doc Su come through the gate and walk toward him. "Hey, Doc, how goes it? Did you see anything interesting this afternoon?"

"Indeed I did, Lt. Fancy. I spent the afternoon at the Bishop Museum. If you ever get the chance it's well worth your time. Even though I've been there several times before I always seem to find something that is new and interesting or old and still interesting."

"I'll make a note of it, Doc. I'm not ashamed to be seen in a museum."

The diminutive man looked questioningly at Fancy as if wondering whether he was being patronized.

Fancy caught the look and continued. "No, Doc, I mean it. I wouldn't tell you that if I didn't. Thanks for the tip. Maybe we can get together and you can fill me in on some other places to see."

Doc smiled. "Lieutenant, there are a great many places to see and things to do and I'd be glad to let you in on some of my favorites. Right now I have some paperwork to finish. I'll see you later."

"Okay, Doc, I'd really like that," Fancy said as he turned his attention once again to the phone bank.

*I bet the phone company makes a mint off this single bank of phones* he thought as he fed coin after coin into the phone. Finally he was rewarded with a dial tone and at last with—a busy signal.

*Must be Scott,* he thought.

After waiting for a few minutes he repeated the process and again received a busy signal. This time the phone didn't return all his change. He hoped he would have enough.

*Third time has got to be the charm* he figured as he started to pay off any debts the phone company might have incurred in the last few minutes.

When he heard the phone make connection he breathed a sigh of relief. After several rings he heard the phone pick up and listened to the recorder message of the answering machine. Amanda, he concluded, sounded very mature for her age.

"Hello," came Amanda's voice.

"Hi, Amanda, How are you?"

"Dan! Mom, it's Dan!" she shouted. "Guess what? My Uncle Scott just called and he said he got to come to the ship and see you. He's so lucky!"

"I'm fine, thank you," smiled Dan to himself.

"Oops, I'm sorry. How are you? What's Hawaii like?"

"Well, right now I'm at Pearl Harbor. What I can see of Hawaii looks pretty neat. Uh, is your mom handy?"

"Oh, sure. Here she is."

"Hello, Dan. How are you?"

At the sound of her voice he was at a momentary loss for words. "Ahh, I'm…I'm fine. It's so good to hear your voice." He couldn't believe how good. "How are you?"

"I'm, well I should say, we're both fine. I just got through talking to Scott. He told me he spent part of the day with you. That was awfully nice of you to ask him out to the ship. He was really excited about it."

"It was nice of him to come. I really like him—he seems like a pretty good guy."

"He is."

"That is one big guy though. Boy, I wouldn't want him irked at me. He was very intent on what my intentions were about you are." He chuckled.

"He didn't?"

"Yes, he did and I can't say I blame him."

"Oh, I'm so embarrassed."

"Don't be. If I had a sister like you I'd ask the same questions."

"And, Mr. Fancy, what did you tell him?"

"The truth—nothing but the truth," he teased.

"Yes, what is the truth, as you see it?"

Taking a deep breath he plunged ahead. "I'd really like to come back to Hawaii—with you, and Amanda of course. Have you ever been here?"

There was a long pause on the other of the phone. Thinking he might have lost the connection he blurted out, "Cody, Cody are you still there?"

"Yes, I am. No, I've never been there, but I would sure like to go someday." Another long pause. "I would never travel anywhere with anyone unless I was married though."

"Oh sure. Yes, that would be the only way. I didn't mean…That is…"

She laughed. "I know you didn't and I hope that was what I think it was."

Fancy felt himself break out in a sweat. "It was, it really was. I love you, Cody, I really do. This is…"

Before he could complete his sentence, the a mechanical voice told him his time was up unless he put in some more money. Fishing around frantically through his pockets for some more change. Finding nothing, he shouted, "I'll write, Cody, I'll write!" Hanging up the phone he found himself the object of several bemused looks from passing sailors as he hung up the phone.

Walking back to the ship he mused that he hadn't asked whether she worked out or not.

After paying Robinson a short visit in sickbay, went back to his room and settled down with his portable CD player and a compilation of, as he thought of them, oldies and moldies.

He was awakened later that night by a weight on his chest and then by someone kissing him. Sitting up suddenly slamming his head on the bunk above his, he was startled to find a small white puppy now sitting in his lap. "What the hell…?" His own voice startled him.

"Hey, Gator, what do think, is that a cute dog or what?" said Big Wave.

"This is a dog!"

"Of course it's a dog. I just told you that. Isn't it cute?" continued Big Wave, who by the smell of his breath and his somewhat slurred speech, must have had one or two too many.

"I know it's a dog, the question is, what is it doing here and who does it belong to?"

"It's mine. Who do you think? It's a great dog. Smart and…"

"You better get it off this ship. Matsen will tear you a new one if he finds it."

"I'm not going to get rid of it. We're going to keep it, right, Poncho."

Fancy looked around big Wave and saw that Poncho must be even more hammered that Big Wave. He was slumped on the floor in the corner, fast asleep. "Yeah, I can see Poncho is going to be a big help. What are you thinking about? Where did you get it?"

"Poncho and me headed over to the North Shore to check out the surf. Some of the locals were picking on it, kind of using it for a football. We kind of persuaded them, shall we say, to let it alone and we brought it back. We just couldn't just leave it there, you know."

Fancy shook his head. "How did you get it on board?"

"Oh, that was easy. One of the F-18 drivers had a golf bag. I just put him in the bag. No sweat."

Bagger burst through the door. He took in the scene before him and blinked in amazement. "That's a dog!"

"Of course it's dog. Haven't you ever seen a dog before. Geez."

Bagger looked at Fancy. "Am I missing something here? Man you better get that thing out of here."

Poncho woke up and mumbled, "What thing?"

"The dog, you know the dog, you and Big Wave brought on board," said Fancy, shaking his head again.

Poncho blinked in surprise. "We did what! Big Wave, what did we do?" he said, emphasizing the word we.

"Don't you remember, North Shore, local dudes, pickin' on the dog?"

Poncho put his head in his hands. "It's coming back. Then we took him, it, whatever, to the bar. The free drinks. Oh yeah, I remember, I think. There were those babes, they thought the dog was so cute…"

"I don't think it was just the dog they were interested in, Poncho," sighed Big Wave.

Poncho smiled and stood up. "Well, compadre, what are we going to do with this dog?"

"Keep him, what else?"

"You guys better decide quick, because the "Big E" is pulling out pretty quick, that's what I was coming to tell you."

"What's up?" asked Fancy.

"Evidently the North Koreans are causing some problems around the DMZ and have even harassed some airliners flying between South Korea and Japan."

The news of the unexpected departure seemed to quell everyone's enthusiasm. The small puppy had made itself at home in Fancy's lap and had gone to sleep.

"How did you find out about what was happening, Bagger?" queried Big Wave, who by now was looking at the puppy in a whole new light.

"Moose and I were walking down the main drag, uh, Kalakawa Ave. I think. Anyway, this Shore Patrol truck comes rollin' down the street with a loudspeaker instructing anybody from the Enterprise battle group to report back to their ships, immediately. So Moose and I caught a cab back here. We saw Killer and brought him back too. It was kind of like The Big One, you know, World War Two."

"How did you find out about the North Koreans?" asked Fancy.

"We came through the gate, down by the end of the pier, down by the phone banks, and Matsen was coming through going the other way and he gave us the word."

"Did he say anything else?"

"No, just what I told you. Well, one more thing. Anybody who doesn't make it back before we pull out, will be put on board the *Gettysburg* and she'll catch up to the battle group."

An uneasy silence settled over the aviators. Finally, Fancy broke the silence. "It doesn't make sense to me why North Korea would stick its chin out like that. If any country needs to curry some good will in the world, it's North Korea. Whoever is calling the shots over there is not playing with a full deck."

The sudden knock at the door startled everyone. Fancy grabbed the dog and tried to put it behind him but the squirming animal was having none of it and was able to wiggle away from him. Before Fancy could recover the wayward animal, Killer Stevens opened the door and stuck his head in. "I suppose.... That's a dog. Gator, what are you doing with a dog?"

"Of course it's a dog, Killer, haven't you ever seen a dog before. I can't believe one small dog is such a big deal."

Killer paused, raised his eyebrows in disbelief, and shook his head. "Anyway, I suppose you guys have heard about the recall and getting underway. Matsen asked me to tell you there's going to be a meeting in Ready Three in ten minutes. Gator, what is that dog doing here?"

Fancy looked at Big Wave and Poncho. "I know this is hard to believe, but it isn't my dog." He nodded his head in the direction of Big Wave.

Killer laughed, "Wave, you've really done it this time. What are you going to do with that thing?"

Big Wave, drawing himself up to his full height, stated, "For one thing it isn't a thing. And we're going to keep it, right Poncho?"

Poncho, realizing things had gone south in a hurry, nodded his head in the affirmative, while his eyes seemed to be pleading for help from his fellow aviators.

"You better call him Short Round, cause he aint going to make it all the way on this cruise. That's for sure."

"We better get to that meeting and see what's going on. Wave," said Fancy, handing over the dog.

Short Round promptly showed appreciation by taking a whiz on Big Wave.

"Oh, man," howled Schwartz. "How could you do this to me after I saved you from those jerks? Oh, man!"

Amid the hoots of laughter the men filed out and headed to Ready Three.

Matsen was standing in the front of the rapidly filling room. Robinson was seated by the lectern looking a lot better, thought Fancy, than he had earlier in the day.

"All right. Let's get quiet. Skipper, they're all yours," ordered Matsen.

Robinson stood up stiffly. "As you know the Enterprise and her escorts will be putting back out to sea, sometime within the hour. It seems as if the North Koreans are flexing what little muscle they have. There have been troop movements toward the 38th Parallel, bringing some of their front line units up to within ten miles, and in some cases even closer." He paused, looking at some notes. Continuing he said, "There have been five instances of commercial air traffic between Japan and Korea being shadowed, quite closely in some instances. Independence is in the yard having some work done. So, for right now we're it. The State Department feels the situation won't escalate much beyond what's going on now. It's hard to figure out the North Koreans. All the spooks, DIA, CIA, NIA—everybody is in agreement that there is a real crisis brewing there in terms of the North Koreans just being able to feed themselves, let alone mount any kind of push to the south. They really need the help and good will of the rest of the world. Our job, of course, is to provide a presence—to let them know we're interested. Any questions?"

"Skipper," drawled Killer, "are you going to be with us. How are you doin'?"

Robinson grimaced. "Right now, as far as I know, I'm going. Van Gundy hasn't signaled I won't."

Holding his ribs he continued, "I won't be flying for about two weeks. Doc Su feels my ribs need the rest. But, we'll see. Of course if I'm not in the air, I'm not pulling my share of the weight. I hope this won't be a problem for you or the squadron?"

Heads shook in the negative telling Robinson what he had hoped for, but had not counted on."Flight operations will commence thirty minutes after we clear Pearl. We're getting two planes that were left here by Kitty Hawk. That's the good news. The bad news is that they are A+s. Eventually two more Ds are scheduled to catch up to us. When, I don't know."

"That leads me to my next order of business. Killer, you and Poncho get your gear, and head over to Ford Island. The two planes have been tweeked and they're ready for us to take delivery.

"Aye, aye, Skipper," said Poncho, as he and Killer got up and started toward the door.

"Have a doggone good flight," called out Bagger.

Poncho turned and shot him a look, then grinned and went out the hatch.

Fancy and Bagger stood on the flight deck as Enterprise headed down the channel toward Mamala Bay and the open ocean.

"Kind of gives you the shivers," said Fancy softly.

"Yeah, it does. I never cared much for history in school, but being here where so many other ships headed for war…"

"I used to watch that program, ah, you know the program with the good music?"

"Victory At Sea? I used to watch that. In fact I had some of the music from that program."

"Me too," continued Fancy. "After a while I only watched it to listen to the music. It makes me feel kind of funny, you know, being in a place where real history was made."

The two friends stood in silence as the sweet, fruity, pungent smell of the land fell away and the salty taste and smell of the ocean enveloped them. Without a word they turned and headed below decks to get ready to fly.

Thirty minutes later Mirabal and Fancy were completing their walk around and pre-flight inspection of Desperado 205. Fancy had taken more time than usual making sure that all hatches were securely buttoned and everything that was hung on the plane such as missiles and drop tanks were secured. Jumping up into the starboard engine intake he flashed a light down the intake as far as he could see, repeating the process on the port engine intake. Everything seemed to be in order and he felt satisfied that he had looked at everything he could. Shrader had followed him around, who in turn was followed by Mirabal and the three men were satisfied the plane was ready to go.

Mirabal had been especially thorough not wanting to have to punch out again, at least in this lifetime.

"Gator, she looks good-to-go to me. What do you think?"

"Ummm, looks good. Shrader, any problems from the last flight that haven't been looked at and fixed?"

Shrader shifted uncomfortably. "Sir, there was a little hydraulic leak on the port side main gear. It's still there, but there is no perceptible loss of fluid. We also looked at TCS which went out on the last flight. We changed a box and it's working perfectly. Other than that, she's in tip-top shape."

Fancy nodded and smiled. Shrader was so serious, but that made him feel better. He liked someone who took his job, especially this job seriously. "Thanks, Shrader. I, uh, we, appreciate your thoroughness. It sure makes it a lot easier to sit on the pointy end of the boat and know you've done your job." He reached out and shook Shrader's hand.

Shrader smiled and returned the handshake. "Thank you, sir, and I'll pass that on to the rest of the men."

Fancy nodded and turned to climb the boarding ladder steps that fit flush with the fuselage once they were in the air. "Let's go flying, Rhino."

"I'm right behind you, Gator."

Shrader followed Fancy and Mirabal up the ladder and gave each of them a hand in strapping in. Fancy reminded himself that he needed to be careful, very careful in the light of the recent mishaps. Wiggling around in the seat, mindful of the Martin-Baker GRU-7A ejection seat beneath him, a potential life-saver in case things went south. He continued to check the shoulder and lap harnesses, then snapping in the leg restraints, making sure his legs were firmly up against the seat in case he had to punch out. *No sense leaving them in the cockpit if it ever comes to an ejection* he thought. Finally, he connected the hoses and wires that hooked him into the plane. Gesturing to Shrader, who was now in front of the plane, Fancy yanked the pins out of the ejection seat. It was now armed and ready. Catching sight of the yellow handles above his head and between his legs, he knew they were hot and that he could be in for a wild ride if the occasion arose.

"Rhino," he called to Mirabal, to make sure the intercom was working, "how's everything in the pit?"

"Pit! You're referring to my office, the nerve center of this aircraft a pit! The very idea!" Mirabal replied in mock horror.

"Seriously, you okay, no second thoughts? Believe me, I might be having some."

"Gator, I'm ready, very willing, and of course you know, very, very able. Really, I'm good and even looking forward to going up."

"I know, but I don't want you to be doing something that goes against the grain."

Mirabal, choking back some momentary anger, realized Fancy had to know about his state of mind and was glad Fancy had enough confidence in himself and in him to ask. "I appreciate your thinking, Gator, but I'm definitely ready. Anyway, everything is in alignment and good-to-go."

He knew alignment was vital. In effect it would tell the F-14's internal navigation systems literally where on earth they were. *It's a big ocean* Fancy thought, thinking back to their search for Robinson and Mirabal. *Knowing where you are is at least useful.*

Fancy flipped a switch and the big canopy whirred down over them, putting them in a world apart now. The canopy slid down and forward, sealing out some of the flight deck noise. The momentary peace did not last for long as Fancy, after notifying Mirabal, started the engines.

The plane seemed to come alive as the engines spooled up. His eyes ran over the instrument panel and down the check list item by item. Outside the "blue shirts" were breaking down the plane, unfastening the chocks and chains that tie the bird to the deck. A "yellow shirt" flight director appeared under the nose of the plane and signaled for him to release the brakes. Fancy's heart began to beat a little faster in anticipation.

Using the tips of the rudder pedals and precise throttle movements, Fancy moved the plane up to the catapults on the bow. They will be the first F-14 off the deck. He watched the JBD lower. Goosing the twin throttles just a tad he taxied into position as crewmen scurried around and under the plane.

Even though he couldn't see what was going on he knew they were hooking the nosewheel to the catapult shuttle. The plane was being connected by the nosewheel to a giant steam-piston, which when activated would throw them off the pointy end of the boat, *without going to afterburner* Fancy remembered once again. He liked that idea of more fuel in the air and less used on the deck, he liked it a lot.

At the yellow shirt's signal, Fancy started to advance the throttles slowly to run up the engines. While the engines were coming up Fancy went through the mandatory flight control checks, moving the stick back and forth, left and right, stepping on each rudder pedal. One of the crewmen on the deck watched the appropriate control surfaces moving on the plane and confirmed that they were working as advertised. After a few more checks the crew finally cleared from under the plane. The catapult officer in his yellow jacket and helmet waited patiently for his salute. It was time.

From a standing start the F-14 made the 300 foot run to the edge of the deck at 148 knots just as it was flung into the air. Fancy felt the welcome feeling of being pushed back into his seat. *No pain, no gain* he muttered to himself. Now the acceleration was not nearly as perceptible after the violent cat stroke, the airspeed seeming to crawl lazily upward. As he slapped the gear handle he felt the landing gear begin their short trip into the wheel wells. Next the flaps slid back in, as he put the fighter in a right hand climbing turn. Another few seconds and he retarded the throttles slightly to save even more fuel.

"Good shot," crackled the radio.

Mirabal, always on top of things, radioed the air boss, "Desperado 205, airborne."

Out of the corner of his eye Fancy caught the new frequency being dialed in on one of the radios. Mirabal was back and he certainly wasn't idle back there. Fancy grinned to himself.

The Carrier Air Traffic Control Center, CATCC, came up on the radio, telling Fancy to take a heading of two-seven-zero at angels 12, or twelve thousand feet. Advancing the throttles the Tomcat comes to altitude with an effortless grace.

Sensing more than seeing, Desperado 203, with Moose Milwood slid up to starboard. Moose gave them a thumbs up and then slid out to a combat spread about four hundred yards away and stepped up about a hundred feet.

The CATCC radioed the two planes to climb to twenty thousand feet.

"What's on the scope, Rhino?"

"Right now, nothing. It's absolutely empty for one hundred miles."

Out of sheer exhilaration Fancy rolled the plane three hundred and sixty degrees.

"That was fun. What brought that on?"

" Dunno, it's just nice to not be sucking rubber anymore. Sorry, I should have warned you."

"No problem, it takes more than that to get to me. I eat this stuff up.

"Desperado 205, everything okay over there?"

"203, everything is just perfect, couldn't be better."

"Roger that," croaked Moose.

"I remember," said Fancy, "when four hours was an eternity."

"Hey, four hours can still be a long time. These seats are definitely not first class, you know," replied Mirabal. "Believe me, I'd love to get up and stretch."

Fancy sighed. "I could stay up here all day and all night."

After four hours and one refueling Desperado 205 had turned, somewhat reluctantly, back toward the carrier. For Fancy the time had literally and figuratively flown by.

Desperado 205 came to Marshall. Marshall is a stack of airplanes ten miles back of the carrier waiting their turn to land. Since Fancy had taken off first they were among the first to get to "push time". When push came Fancy took the plane away from the stack and headed for the carrier. Since the day was clear and visibility almost unlimited a visual pattern was being flown. Coming up on Enterprise's starboard side he dropped the tailhook while flying at about a thousand feet on the upwind leg. Passing the carrier he made a hard ninety degree turn to the left while at the same time crossing the carrier's bow. This is called the "Break". Now a hundred knots slower and two hundred feet lower, he again made a ninety degree turn and began the downwind leg. Now lower and slower, moving parallel to the carrier in the opposite direction, he could see the boat out of the corner of his left eye. Slapping the gear handle and lowering the flap he dirtied up the plane. About two miles behind the carrier he pulled tightly through another ninety degree turn through the base leg and slid into the final approach, just over a mile behind the carrier. *Now the fun begins* he thought.

Fancy began to set his rate of descent and angle-of-attack in order to get down that magic three-degree glideslope that would terminate on the flight deck with a three wire. The ILS (Instrument Landing System) needles on the HSI monitor centered on the panel lit up. This was the set of drifting crosshairs that told Fancy he was slightly left of center and a little above glideslope. Fixing the problem with deft movements of rudder and throttles. Too soon the glideslope was there at just under a mile. Now get that angle- of- attack just right, little throttle. *I wish this was as easy as it sounds when I'm explaining it to someone. Change one and the other changes too, so I'm correcting the first without upsetting the second . In additon this balancing act has to be done in the light of the delay of engine windup, shifting winds, and that fast approaching deck. No problem. Just a lot of little ones.*

"Desperado 205 slightly left, on glidepath, three quarter mile, call the ball," came the disembodied voice of the approach controller.

Things were happening fast now. Now he was searching for the "meatball", the light, that would tell him whether he was high or low in these last few seconds. With less than twenty seconds left to touchdown he called the words everyone was waiting for.

"205, Tomcat, ball, three point one."

Badrod acknowledged, "Roger, ball. A little high, off on power, a little right."

Three things now dominate Fancy's mind, meatball, lineup, angle-of-attack, meatball, lineup, angle-of-attack…

*The meatball and Badrod will keep me on glidescope; lineup will keeps me from veering right or left off the deck or even worse, into the parked planes. Angle-of-attack will keep me from smacking the round off first instead of the deck.*

"On glidepath, lookin' good, drifting left, don't go left, keep it coming…" Badrod's cool voice floated through his headset.

*Meatball, lineup, angle-of-attack..* The carrier grows quickly and the corrections seem to be bigger and bigger. Slightly left, but the glidescope is right where it should be. Here comes the ramp…

The wheels smacked the deck bringing Fancy forward against his restraints. Slamming the throttles forward into military power, just in case the tailhook didn't engage. In the blink of an eye the fighter had gone from over one hundred knots to zero. Before he knew it a yellow shirt was in front of the plane signaling him to retard the throttles. He sensed the green shirt beneath the plane disengaging the hook from the wire, already getting ready for the next recovery. After retracting the hook, he was directed forward in order to be placed in a parking place. *Boy, I enjoyed that* he thought as he took his oxygen mask off and prepared to raise the canopy.

That night the flight is repeated with another successful trap. At 2300 hours Fancy hi the rack and fell asleep immediately. For the next ten days the routine repeated itself as the Enterprise raced across Pacific toward Korea.

# 10

On the eleventh day the Enterprise and her battle group found themselves off the coast of Japan, specifically off the island of Kyushu. During the night they had passed through the Ryukyu island chain. The ship would turn to the northeast and pass through the Korea Strait into the Sea of Japan.

Fancy dropped to the steel deck of the Enterprise. It was the end of a long day. Snagging a two wire was at 2330 was not, Fancy figured, the perfect end of a day, but at least it was satisfactory just to be down in one piece. For one of the first times since he had joined the Navy he wished he didn't have to fly the next day. Even the irrepressible Mirabal had little to say. "Man, I don't know about you, but my tired old fanny is really draggin'. If somebody offered me a day off I would seriously consider it."

"Consider it! Hah! In a heartbeat. I'm just plain whipped and I don't care who knows it."

In the equipment room as they divested themselves of their gear, Big Wave, who had landed a few minutes ahead of them greeted them with, "Hey, did you guys hear about the day off tomorrow?"

"You're shittin' me," growled Fancy. "That's not a nice thing to do to someone who's as beat as I am. I might let it out that there's a dog on this boat."

"I'm not kiddin' you. Admiral Blue figured we needed a day to catch up with ourselves. Somebody said he asked Van Gundy if we could use a day. I guess Van Gundy didn't miss a beat and said yes we could."

"Hmmmm," yawned Mirabal. "What's the catch? There must be some catch?"

"No catch," grinned big Wave. "The maintenance guys won't get quite the same deal. They're going to be working on the birds. Once we hit the Sea of Japan we start all over again."

Fancy allowed himself to sink to the bench, running the length of the room, allowing the welcome news to wash over him like a cool ocean wave. Just thinking about it started to rejuvenate him. "Wave, I was just kidding about the dog."

"I know, I'm tired too. Is this great news or what?"

"You better believe it!" shouted Mirabal as he jumped in the air shooting an imaginary jump shot.

Fancy was amazed at what kinds of things popped out of peoples' rooms and from the numerous nooks and crannies of the ship. Moose Milwood had a rubber inflatable wading pool as well as a palm tree. It had been Fancy's job to blow it up. Killer Stevens had brought two more just like it. The warm morning found a good percentage of the squadron sunning and soaking in their oasis. It seemed that Fancy was the only one in attendance without his own beach chair or lounge. The other squadrons seemed to be as equally well equipped as the Desperados. From the bow of the ship the smell of hot dogs and hamburgers cooking on a barbecue wafted back over the deck. In one fell swoop the Enterprise had gone from a warship to a party boat—and no one seemed to mind.

Dress went from bathing suits to various lengths of shorts. T-shirts were the order of the day, with many bearing slogans and logos. On the way up to the deck Fancy noticed an F-18 driver with one that said: "If you're not a pilot you're not shit". Big Wave had one on that proclaimed: "Kill 'em all, then let God sort 'em out". Many of the squadron personnel had on the official squadron shirt emblazoned with a tough looking Tomcat, carrying a six-shooter, standing in front of an F-14, with "Any Time Baby" stenciled across the front. *That might be a good present for Amanda* he thought. *Why not Cody while I'm at it. Geez I miss her.*

"This is the life," said a very relaxed Killer. "This is why I joined the Navy—to travel and see the world."

"Think about that, Killer," croaked Moose. "Here you are on a ship with, what, five thousand other guys? Are you kidding me?"

"Listen, this steel beach party is just what we needed," Killer shot back. "Besides, there's got to be some liberty somewhere in the near future. And as to the five thousand guys—it's a small price to pay, having to look at all your ugly mugs. You just make me appreciate the female of the species all the more."

Moose just shook his head as if to say, "I give up."

Fancy, dressed in a pair of old faded blue jogging shorts, and what he thought of now as a very plain white t-shirt, yawned and stretched out on the towels he had lugged up from his room. "I wonder how much this deal with the North Koreans will play with any liberty that might come our way?"

Bagger answered that question as he walked up behind Killer's chair and tipped him backwards to the deck. "I was just talking to one of the ship's officers, the guy works in communications. He heard that the closer we've gotten, the less aggressive the slopes have become. Maybe once we hit the Sea of Japan, they'll decide it's just not worth their effort. Stupid sons of bitches anyway. What could they hope to accomplish besides just pissin' off most of the world."

Even though the same thoughts had been said over and over during the past several days, everyone nodded their ascent.

"Where's Short Round?" asked Mirabal, directing his question to Poncho, since Big Wave had drifted off to sleep.

"He's in our room. That little beast got a hold of Wave's cover and practically chewed it to pieces," he laughed, gesturing to the now snoring Schwartz. "Wave was ready to pitch him over board for a minute."

"How long are you going to keep him on board?" questioned Fancy, propping himself up on one elbow.

"It doesn't look like he' going to get very big. He must be some kind of toy dog, you know like a toy poodle, something like that. Wave wants to keep him."

Bagger shook his head. "I heard Matsen talking to the XO of the helo squadron. This guy was back of the fantail this morning and found a shiny brown log on the deck. He was asking Matsen if he had seen any dogs on board. Of course Matsen said no, in no uncertain terms and said he better not find one."

"Wave and I took him back there and he did his thing. Neither one of us brought anything to pick it up in, and I sure wasn't going to pick it up in my hand. We heard somebody coming and we had to beat feet back to the room. If any of you guys come across any plastic bags, steer them our way, okay?"

"What do you think now, Killer?" snickered Mirabal, "Poop patrol?"

"Like I said," deadpanned Stevens, "this is the life, at least for today."

The rest of the day was spent lazing around the deck, visiting other squadrons, and swapping truths and embellishments. Fancy had, what he considered, one of the best "sliders" he had ever had, when he had wandered up toward the bow and was convinced to try one of the helo squadron's hamburgers. He was even persuaded to have a second.

With his hunger and thirst satisfied, he wandered back down to his stateroom and started a letter to Cody.

Dawn found the Enterprise heading into the Sea of Japan. Fancy and Mirabal, Bagger and Carpenter would launch at 10:30 hours, relieving Matsen and Killer who were among the first to launch that morning.

Fancy, who had been up early and had watched the 0700 launch of Matsen and Killer, had gone to the cavernous hanger deck and had found his "mount" for the day, Desperado 208. He and the plane captain, a young enlisted man by the name of Joe Richardson, had gone over the plane from stem to stern. There were no problems or anomalies with the plane.

Fancy had watched while the red-shirted ordinance men had rolled out and loaded two AIM Seven Sparrows and two AIM 9-M Sidewinders. He would have preferred to leave the AIM Sevens on the ship and take two more "'winders". After the missiles had been loaded he watched closely as the 20mm shells were loaded the M61A1 Gatling gun. Its six barrels could spew out a lethal dose of 6,000 rounds per minute. Before they had been loaded, Fancy noted that the shells were clean and did not appear to have any dents or other indentations that could cause a jam—probably at the worst possible time.

About the time the last shell had been loaded, Mirabal appeared out of the maze of aircraft, parts, and men. "Morning, Gator. How's she look?"

"The plane captain and I have looked at everything we can open or peer into. She looks good to me. No gripes."

Mirabal went over and opened several panels so he could get a look at the APG-71radar. After borrowing a flashlight and scrutinizing the maze of black boxes and wires, he grunted, nodded in the affirmative, and closed up the panels. He then climbed up into his "office" and, after a few minutes returned to the dirty gray steel deck. "I'm happy. She looks good to go." Richardson seemed to breath a sigh of relief.

Satisfied with the state of the plane they walked back to Ready Three. Robinson, looking quite pleased with himself, was in the front of the room studying their operating area in the Sea of Japan.

"Morning, Skipper," said Fancy. "How are you feeling"?

Robinson turned around and, as Fancy thought of it, the "grin" spread across Robinson's face. "Mornin' Gator, Rhino. Doc Su cleared me to fly this afternoon, so I couldn't be any better. One more day of suckin' rubber and I think I'd be ready for a section eight."

"Hey, that's great, Skipper," Mirabal said, as he reached to shake Robinson's hand, as did Fancy.

"Sounds like the North Koreans have come to their senses," Robinson continued as he gestured toward the map. "There haven't been incidents in the air or along the DMZ. However, they do continue to send aircraft out over the Sea of Japan. That in itself is not unusual, but what is, is the fact that they're coming way out. Much farther than usual."

"What are they flying out that far?" queried Fancy.

"Just about everything in their inventory—Mig 21s, 23s, and 29s. Maybe even SU-27s. That's not confirmed though.

He turned back to the map and pointed to a spot just below the 39th parallel. "The intel weenies say they're operating out of here's a place called Kojo. Fancy, aren't you TARPS (Tactical Aerial Reconnaissance Pod System) qualified?"

"Uh, yes, sir, I am." Fancy felt a surge of adrenalin move through his body. He liked flying TARPS missions. When he was with VF-84 he had flown quite a few TARPS missions and, if he did say so himself, did more than an adequate job. "Are we going to take a look at Kojo, Skipper?"

Robinson turned back toward the map, taking a few moments to study it again. Turning back toward the two men, he grinned, "You just never know. We received a communique from CINPAC double checking our capability. In your spare time, you better go down to the Intel shop and look over the maps and any information they've got down there."

"Good as done, Skipper. I'll…we'll get on it right away." He could feel Mirabal beaming.

"You guys better get suited up. Don't you have a 10:30 launch?"

"We're on our way, see you later, Skipper. Anything new about ROEs (rules of engagement)?"

Robinson frowned. "You know the drill, if they decide to do something stupid, and fire first, then take 'em out. These guys are really squirrelly, so be on your toes."

Fancy was amazed by the transformation that had taken place within twelve hours. Wading pools, palm trees, and barbecues had been replaced by the lethal weapons of war. They walked down the deck toward Desperado 208, that had just been brought up from the hanger deck on the port side elevator. He had jammed his helmet on just before he had stepped on deck. The noise, even with his helmet on was almost overwhelming. The ear splitting sounds of engines being started, planes taxiing, and taking off made conversation impossible. All communication was done by sound powered telephones or, in most cases, by hand signals, making the ship look like a mime's paradise. Make that a colorful paradise. Yellow-shirted plane directors, purple-shirted refuelers, green-shirts and brown worked purposeful ballet to launch and recover the planes of the air wing. If a civilian or someone not familiar with the workings of a carrier were to view the same thing Fancy was looking at he would see nothing but what appeared to be mass confussion.

Reaching the plane he and Mirabal made another walk around with Richardson. Again nothing was amiss and they climbed the boarding ladder and proceeded to strap in.

The launch went perfectly—if you consider being crushed into the seat perfect. Cleaning up the plane as soon he was able to lift his arms, flaps in and gear up, the Tomcat began a shallow left-hand turn designed to bring them to a course of three five zero. CATCC directed to climb to an altitude of 16,000 feet. This would put them roughly parallel to the coast of South Korea just north of the thirty-seventh parallel. The sky was broken into splotches of white by clouds forming above them.

Bagger, flying Desperado 200 slid into a position that put them off to port about three hundred yards out and slightly stepped up above Fancy. Both planes were now bobbing and weaving in order not to produce a predictable flight path.

"Desperado, two zero eight," came Bagger's laconic voice, "we're here and we're ready."

Fancy grinned underneath his oxygen mask. "Glad to have you, Bagger. You're looking good."

"Rhino, anything on the scope?"

"It looks like we have contact at zero two zero, at uh, seventy-five miles heading away. Probably commercial traffic."

For the next forty minutes the two planes continued north. Bobbing, weaving, climbing, and descending, the sky remained empty.

Fancy was just about to say something to Mirabal when Rhino beat him to the punch. "Gator, I've two bogeys at three four zero, eighty miles, at 10 angels, and climbing."

"Roger that. Coming to three four zero, we'll keep 'em on our nose. Good time to put them on TV."

Rhino muttered his ascent. "I've got a fuzzy picture. They're flying somewhat of a welded wing. They could be, uh, Mig 21s, I think. Yeah, I'm sure they're 21s. Range is seventy miles, they've climbed to about twelve thousand feet, and…still climbing."

Again Fancy tried to will his eyes to zoom out the now sixty some miles to pick the Migs out of the sky. Patience had never been one of his strong points.

"Bagger, we'll close and keep 'em on our nose."

"Roger that, Gator," answered Bagger as he slid a little farther out to port.

It seemed to Fancy as if time was starting to compress, he seemed to be operating in slow motion.

"Fifty miles, fourteen thousand feet, they're picking up speed. Uh, looks like they've punched off their tanks," continued Mirabal.

The four planes continued to race toward each other at over nine hundred miles per hour. Fancy continued to jink and weave while all the time keeping the oncoming Migs at their twelve o' clock, while at the same time climbing to keep the North Koreans low.

"Twenty-five miles, almost seventeen thousand feet. Whoa, they're turning. Yeah, they're reversing, turning tail."

"Damn! grumbled Fancy. "I was hoping we'd get eyeball to eyeball with them. Shoot!"

"Bagger, let's close on 'em!" Fancy fumed as he pushed the throttles forward. The big fighter immediately leaped ahead and started to close the distance on the Migs.

"We're with you, Babe," responded Bagger.

When the Tomcats had closed to fifteen miles, Fancy sighed and called the chase off. "Okay, no sense in pissin' people off unnecessarily. Let's go home guys, comin' to starboard on one seven zero."

"Roger, one seven zero, headin' back to the bird farm. Hey, that was fun. Why do you think they turned tail?"

"Dunno, they punched off their tanks, maybe they were getting low on fuel."

"Or they got as close as they dared," lamented Bagger.

"I'll vote for that theory," interjected Mirabal.

The flight back to the boat was uneventful. Traffic was heavier inbound to the boat. They picked up South Korean F-16's, on the TCS, but didn't get close enough to make a visual sighting. Two of the Enterprise's F-18s were spotted outward bound. Fancy wanted to bounce them but thought better of the idea. Once the juices had started flowing, it was hard to turn off the adrenalin.

Arriving ten miles behind the Enterprise at the Marshall, he noticed as a COD, C-2A Greyhound, depart the stack and begin its final approach to the ship.

Soon it was their time to land. "Let's make it look good, Bagger."

"Roger that, Gator. Let's burn some of this fuel off."

Fancy grinned. That was just fine with him. Preparing for the break they screamed down the starboard side of the carrier at four hundred plus (with the emphasis on plus) knots. With wing swept back, Fancy knew they looked good. Just before he saw the numbers on the forward part of the flight deck, Fancy snapped the plane into a sharp ninety degree bank pulling firmly, but smoothly on the stick. Five—Gs into the crosswind leg. He put out the airbrakes to get a little more deceleration; the wings started to come forward automatically. Keeping an eye on the boat he pulled, not as hard, into another ninety degree turn putting two zero eight into the down wind leg at 270 knots.

At 150 knots gear out, flaps down, and don't forget that large metal hook back there.

The base leg came up quickly and they turned to their 180. One more left turn to cross Enterprise's wake. Now one more smooth turn to the left and they were on final. The rest of the approach went so smoothly it was more like a training film. Fancy felt he an the plane were melded into one piece of machinery. If things got any better, Fancy couldn't imagine things getting any better.

After a short conference with the plane captain, he and Mirabal walked across the deck. Once again he noticed the C2A Greyhound. An engine was being unloaded and, much to his delight, bags of mail. It surprised him, because up to this minute he hadn't been thinking about anything but flying. At least, he thought, he had his priorities straight.

Just before they stepped on the ladder to go below, Killer and Poncho appeared on their way to man up for their afternoon launch. "Hey guys, how'd it go?" asked Killer.

"Pretty routine—if you call a couple of Migs coming up for a look see. We closed to about, oh, twenty-five miles. They decided to head back home. Then we closed on them to about fifteen miles and then headed back."

"In that case, they're not as dumb as they seem," announced Poncho. "Actually, I hope we get to see a Mig or two up close."

"Right," chimed in Killer, "at their six and we're closing to gun range, right, Gator?"

Fancy smiled. "Just so you see them first. Hey, you guys have fun out there."

"Always," decreed Poncho.

After getting out their gear, they headed for Ready Three where they found Matsen, Robinson, and two new faces.

"Gator, Rhino, we heard you had a contact?" said Robinson as he turned toward them.

"A couple of 21s, climbed out, got to within twenty-five miles. They turned and headed for home. We pursued and closed to fifteen miles before we headed back."

Robinson pursed his lips in thought. "Anything else? Anything unusual?"

Fancy and Mirabal looked at each other and shook their heads. "Not that I can think of, Skipper. Rhino?"

"No, Skipper. Well, they did punch off their tanks and it wasn't long after that they did a one-eighty."

Robinson nodded his head and turned toward the two new officers who were all ears to the attendant conversation. Dan Fancy, Tony Mirabal, Gator and Rhino respectively," continued Robinson, this is Tane McClure, Stash, and our new RIO, Colin Miller, call sign Bones."

Fancy extended his hand and shook both men's hands. For the first time he noticed how young they looked. McClure was tall, blond and well built. Miller was shorter, blond, and had a ready smile. He sensed both men would meld well with the squadron.

Matsen stepped forward and interjected, "They've just completed the RAG (replacement air group) course. They're fresh out of Miramar."

McClure and Miller seemed to blanch somewhat with the revelation that they were FNG (fucking new guys) or Nuggets.

"Welcome to the Desperados," said Fancy as he finished shaking Miller's hand. "You'll like it here. Lots of good people here that fly and maintain the birds."

Fancy figured that he shouldn't mention that they were replacing two pretty good people. That bit of information would come out soon enough. "Where are your rooms?"

McClure told them and Mirabal chimed in, "Hey, that puts you right close to where all the action is. Welcome to the squadron."

After a few more minutes of small talk Fancy and Mirabal started to leave to go to their rooms. They had another flight that night. Fancy wanted to clean up any paperwork that had accumulated and freshen up. As they turned to go out the hatch, Robinson motioned to see Fancy alone for a minute.

"Listen, Gator, these guys came out of the RAG with some pretty good marks and recommendations. But…I want you to take McClure under your wing and show him the ropes. You know how these first cruise jitters can be. Can you do that for me?"

"No problem, Skipper. When is he scheduled to go up?"

"He's got to get qualed. We're going to try and get that in today. We'll schedule the two of you for day after tomorrow just in case there's a problem with the qualifying."

Fancy nodded. "Okay, sounds good to me."

When Fancy got back to his room, Bagger was coming out. "Hey, there was a letter from Rowdy and a big thick one for you postmarked Carlsbad, California. You happen to know anyone in that neck of the woods."

"I gather your letter contained nothing but good news?"

Bagger brought the letter out and ran it under his nose. "The best, man. She signed it 'I love you'. That is so great. I love it!"

"Well, I wish you'd show a little enthusiasm," Fancy grinned and he playfully punched his friend's arm. "Where you goin'?"

"After reading that letter, I realized I was starving. You want to come?"

"Sure, let me get out of this green bag. I'll be right with you, and I'll tell you about the Migs we saw."

"Migs!" replied Bagger. "You did—really? Man, I wish I'd been there. What were they?"

"Two twenty-ones. We got no closer than fifteen miles though. They turned back toward what I guess was their home drome and we chased them for a few miles."

Bagger shook his head. "That's somethin' else."

Five hours later, and several readings and rereadings of Cody's letter, Fancy and Mirabal sat in Desperado 205 waiting to launch. As he waited for the JBD to come down Fancy noted the brilliant full moon and cloudless sky. If ever there was a night for flying he thought, this was it. "Some night, huh, Rhino?"

"Yeah, it doesn't get any better than this. It looks like I could reach out there and grab that sucker."

The JBD came down and Fancy was directed by the yellow-shirt, signaling with his wands, to move forward to the catapult. Two minutes later they roared off the ship into the moon lit sky.

Fancy loved to fly at night. As he thought about it he wondered why he felt that way. As a kid he had never been afraid of the dark, even though his older brother had tried time and again to scare him. Maybe it was just a carry over from his childhood.

Desperado 204 moved easily to Matsen's Desperado 210. Matsen was off his forward starboard quarter, stepped down and about six hundred feet out in front of him. Both planes were flying with their anti-collision lights on, since they weren't in any type of wartime scenario. They had been directed by the duty E2C AWACS to climb away from the ship to an altitude of eighteen thousand feet on a course of zero four five.

"204, any problems?"

"Negative, two one zero, everything is up and running as advertised. How about you?"

"Two one zero is good to go."

For the next four hours the two planes flew out ahead of the carrier—bobbing, weaving, and jinking through the night sky. Fancy was surprised at the many contacts they picked up on radar. At one point flying within four miles of what they identified with the TCS as a 747.

When it was time to return to the ship the two Tomcats made a gentle turn to starboard making sure they wouldn't be turning into any commercial traffic. The remainder of the flight was uneventful—almost too routine Fancy felt, not that they had any kind of choice as to what might happen when you climbed into one of these big metal beasts.

Fancy wasn't scheduled the next day. After he had cleared some paperwork off his desk he went up to the "roof" to watch McClure get his day trips. Bad Rod Baldon was the controlling LSO working the landings. Also on the platform, on the port side of the ship, were four other officers working with him as well as two enlisted men. "Here, Gator, put one of these on," he said, as he motioned to one of the bright orange vests lying nearby. "What are you doing out here?"

"I just thought I'd see how the nugget, McClure was making out. How many traps has he got?"

Badrod took a quick look at a notebook supplied by one of the other officers. "Uh, he's got four. Looks pretty good, one two wire and three OK Threes. He's doin' okay, no problems. I think he's in the groove now, right behind this F-18."

Fancy looked at the sky beyond the stern of Enterprise and was able to pick out the F-18 on final. He heard Badrod say, "Roger, ball." He heard the engines changing pitch as the pilot made changes with his throttles. In no time at all the Hornet had crossed the ramp and caught a three wire. Badrod was making comments to one of the officers. He would be talking with the pilots later.

Putting on his sunglasses he again squinted into the hazy blue sky. Almost immediately he saw the F-14 materialize out of the dirty blue sky. McClure seemed to be coming in on a rail. Then he started to sink slightly and he heard Badrod tell him, in a very calm, almost soothing voice to add power. The Tomcat came up and then down as McClure worked the ball.

Badrod held the "pickle", controlling wave-offs above his head. Baldon told him, calmly, to keep it coming, back off on power, and then McClure was across the ramp and snagging a three wire. "Little high on final," he told the writer and then immediately got ready for the next plane, an EA-6B Prowler, the electronic jamming plane that Fancy had always considered the Cadillac of airplanes. After watching several more planes, he thanked Badrod, and after a break in the recoveries, dashed across the deck to go below.

Heading directly for Ready Three he found Killer, the new RIO Miller and Big Wave watching the landings on the monitor that was in the front of the room.

"Gator, how you doin'?" asked Big Wave.

"Good. I was just up on the roof with Badrod, kind of getting a look at our new guy getting his six day traps. He looks good."

They turned back to the monitor as they watched an F-14 recover. At that point Robinson walked in. Since he had been back on flight status his mood, always pretty good to begin with, was even more upbeat. "Gentleman, as you were," he smiled as he walked up to the group and glanced at the monitor. "Gator, was that you back there with Badrod a few minutes ago."

"Yes, I just wanted to take a look, get a feel to see how he was doing. He made one recovery while I was up there. Looked pretty smooth. Badrod seemed pleased."

"Are you ready to go up with him tomorrow for some ACM?'

"That's the plan skipper. I was going to get together with him after he finishes up his day traps and before he goes up tonight. He's still scheduled for tonight isn't he?"

"Yeah, he is. He should be able to get some rest and probably launch at sundown. His first launch should be a "pinky".

"After you get things squared away with him, or before, why don't you motor on down and take a look at the TARPS pods I got a feeling we may be hauling them out pretty soon."

"I thought things had pretty well calmed down?" put in Killer. Ever since Gator's encounter with those two Migs, we haven't even had a distant sighting."

"Things have been pretty quiet. They seemed to have pulled back from the DMZ. There haven't been any provocations of any type. Scuttlebutt has it that we'll be leaving the Sea of Japan soon. How soon, I don't know. Van Gundy has called for a meeting with all squadron commanders and executive officers, so maybe we'll know more then."

Fancy and the other pilots continued to watch recoveries and shoot the breeze. In forty minutes McClure entered Ready Three.

"Stash, you looked good up there. It looked like you've been doing that forever," said Fancy as he turned toward the new man.

McClure grinned, obviously pleased with the compliment. "Thanks Gator. That LSO should get the lion's share of the credit. He's good, had me in the groove, and on the deck as smooth as a baby's butt."

Gator, Killer, and Big Wave, didn't say, but they were impressed with the fact that McClure hadn't come back with a big head."

"Stash, the Skipper wants us to touch base before we launch tomorrow for some ACM. How about we grab a bite to eat and go over some things?"

"Great," said McClure with real enthusiasm, "I'm so hungry I could eat a horse or just about anything else with four legs."

Before Fancy and McClure could get out of the hatch Matsen walked in. It only took one look to tell the assembled aviators that he wasn't in a good mood. "Has anyone seen Bagger?"

"XO, I think he was headed down to the barber, I saw him about thirty minutes ago," answered Killer.

Matsen shook his head. "There's a dog on this ship and I'll bet my next liberty he's got something to do with it. One of the CPOs slipped on some dog shit on the fantail. He's about ready to hang somebody and I bet that somebody is Bagger."

Doing his best to suppress a rather large smile that was building, Fancy asked, "Why would it be Bagger, XO. There's over five thousand men on this bucket. Why him?"

"Because I just bet it is," Matsen fumed. "Who else would pull a dumbass stunt like this." Matsen shook his head. "It's Bagger, it's got to be."

As if on cue Bagger walked through the hatch, sporting a fresh haircut, and unfortunately, a big smile. "Ya te ha, XO, Skipper, everybody."

"Bagger," snarled the fuming Matsen, "what do you know about there being a dog on this ship?"

"XO, who else would pull something like bringing a dog on board, besides me."

Matsen furled his bushy eyebrows and narrowed his eyes. Looking as pleased as a meter maid who has just seen a parking meter run out, he nodded in the affirmative. "Uh huh, I knew it was you. See what did I tell you guys."

Bagger stood there, the grin just getting bigger, and to Matsen, more irritating by the second. "Actually, XO, the dog, the alleged dog, that is, is not mine. How could you think it was mine. I'm so crushed," he said, as he feigned a wounded look. "Just crushed."

Matsen stared at Bagger for a few seconds. "But, you know something about it, don't you?"

Keeping the extremely hurt look on his face, Bagger continued to shake his head in the negative. "XO, what can I say?" With that pronunciation, he suddenly grabbed Matsen's head between his hands, pulled it forward before Matsen realized what was going on, and planted a sloppy, wet, kiss on his forhead.

"Jesus, Bagger, what the hell do you think you're doing. Do you want me to put you in for a Section Eight!" thundered Matsen, desperately wiping off the offending wetness.

Before Matsen could go completely ballistic, Robinson, who was trying hard not to come apart laughing himself, took Matsen's arm. "Come in, Mongo," injected Robinson, let's grab something to eat. I've got a couple of things I need to go over with you." With that he steered his angry executive officer out of the room. Before he disappeared, he turned, looked at the pilots, and winked before he disappeared out the hatch.

Bagger turned to Big Wave. "I hope you appreciate what I'm going through, Wave?"

"Oh, I do, Bagger, I do," Schwartz deadpanned. The new RIO, Miller, just stood there, wondering what he had gotten himself into.

The next morning found Fancy and Mirabal pre-flighting Desperado 200. They had started on the port side in front of the cockpit. Fancy and Mirabal had come to the conclusions that two heads were better than one. Fancy worked his way around the plane clockwise while Mirabal walked around the opposite way in a counter clockwise path. Meeting back at the boarding ladder they pronounced the plane good to go.

They watched McClure and his RIO, Lt. Commander Merrick, the third most senior officer in the squadron. It was common policy to place new pilots with more experienced RIOs and vice versa when the occasion arose.

"She looks good," said Mirabal.

"Solid," returned Fancy. "You ready to have some fun?"

"Always, babe, always," grinned Mirabal.

Thirty minutes later and Fancy called, "Fight's on." The two F-14s, which had been headed away from each other now turned and began searching for each other. Fancy brought Desperado 200 around in a gentle left hand turn. As they came around he couldn't, at first, pick out McClure. Then, just as he was willing his eyes to give him something, he picked out a speck that had to be McClure's plane. The first engagement, they had agreed, was to be guns only. He know he would have only a few seconds before he could open up with his gun camera in a head-on pass, with a combined closure rate of 1,000 to 1,100 miles per hour. He hoped this looked like an easy kill to McClure.

Before McClure could come into range Fancy started climbing in a right hand turn presenting the belly of his plane to his opponent. As he had hoped, McClure started to turn to the right and bring his nose up. Fancy was still too far away for any kind of shot. Desperado 200 seemed to be pulling away from the fight and McClure started into a level turn so that when Fancy rolled out, he'd be low and at Fancy's six.

Instead of rolling out when he was at McClure's one o' clock he reversed his turn and dove on McClure. Fancy had traded about a hundred knots of airspeed for 2,000 feet of altitude. By flying slower he was able to make the sharp turn. McClure, trying to upset his tracking solution, turned toward Fancy. The very second he did Fancy reversed his turn, again presenting the belly of the F-14 to McClure. Now McClure was worse off than before because he couldn't bring his gunsight to bear on Fancy's Tomcat for even a snap shot, even if he had been in range, which he wasn't by a long shot.

McClure, believing Fancy might be turning away from the fight, continued his turn toward his opponent. Just when Stash thought he might be back in the game, Fancy reversed again and he then realized he could be on the end of what could be an angled shot. Slamming the Tomcat into zone five full afterburner, pulling the big plane up and to the left, hoping with his higher airspeed, he could could gain a height advantage. Too late he realized he didn't have squat; he had pulled too tight, lost any airspeed advantage, and had gained very little altitude—and worst of all—couldn't find Fancy. "Merrick, can you see him?"

Merrick, who had been trying desperately to keep an eye on Matsen answered in the negative. "No, I lost him on his last turn."

The next sound that McClure heard came from his headset. "Bang, bang, bang, you're a mort, Stash." Startled by the sudden turn of events he looked in the rearview mirror and saw the nose of Fancy's Tomcat in a perfect gun kill position less than 700 feet behind them. It had been less than ninety seconds since the fight had begun.

For the next forty-five minutes Fancy gave McClure every advantage and whipped him seven out of eight times. It would have been eight out of eight but McClure had to call Bingo fuel and had to call "Knock if off", in order to get back to the ship. As they joined up to head back to the Enterprise, McClure, found to his utter disgust that he had nearly twenty minutes less fuel than his opponent. *Just perfect* he thought, *just perfect*.

Fancy sat on the table in the front of the room in Ready Three. McClure, Mirabal, and Merrick sitting in the front row. McClure had his head down and was not a happy camper. Finally he looked up and said, "How did you do it? How did you whip my ass? Was you plane specially configured? Of course it wasn't." Running his hand through his hair he stood up and then sat down heavily in the padded chair.

Fancy thought he looked like a whipped puppy.

"How did you do it? Damn, we're both flying the same kind of plane. I did pretty well, if I do say so myself during the RAG course. I just can't understand it. What do I have to do get better, much better?"

Taking a deep breath, Fancy said, "For one thing I didn't whip your ass, I whipped y our mind. All you could think of was getting your guns on me and keeping me in sight."

McClure looked bewildered. "Well, that's the cardinal rule isn't it, never lose sight of your opponent?"

Ignoring the comment, Fancy continued, "You're giving up way too much energy when you maneuver." He watched McClure's face and saw it change from anger to bewilderment. This was what he had wanted to see. Now they could talk about what had happened, depending on whose point of view.

Picking up two red and white airplanes, called fighter sticks he proceeded to recreate each encounter during the flight pointing out McClure's errors in as much detail as he could without grinding his ego into the ground. As he talked about each encounter he used the terms red or white airplane rather than the pronouns you and me.

McClure, to his credit, Fancy thought paid attention and seemed to be taking it all in without feeling sorry for himself.

"I'm following what you are saying, Gator, but how did you know my airspeed and G-loads? How did you get position on me without going to burner, or did you? And how did you keep me in sight even when you turned away from me?"

"Good, you're asking the right questions now. First of all, I'm going to know my opponent's airspeed and G-load just due to being more experienced that you are. I've got a lot of hours in Tomcats and it paid off today. Second, and you've probably figured this out by now, your wing sweep is a give away. I didn't have to go to burners because I was able to ease into my climbs and turns and didn't yank into a lot of unnecessary G-loads that slowed me down. Last, and probably the most important my backseater was in the game keeping you in sight. Don't waste a valuable asset like that. Another pair of eyeballs is just invaluable; I can't stress that too much."

Fancy watched Merrick and Mirabal nod in the affirmative. "Think of us as an integral part of the weapon system," said Merrick.

Picking up the sticks again, Fancy resumed, " I kept calculating your airspeed, turn rate, and G-load in my head so I knew where you'd be when you rolled out. Even when I turned away it was never for more than ten seconds."

"How did you know or not know that I would continue the turns?" McClure asked.

"You became predictable in the first sixty seconds. The only time you weren't was when you called 'bingo fuel' and called it off, so you did do something right."

"Geez, I figured the only thing I did right was land the plane without bending or denting anything. Did I do anything else right?"

Pausing, Fancy said, "After the seventh engagement you accelerated down and away from the fight." "Yeah, I was positioning for reattack," nodded McClure.

Fancy sighed, "Then you were not doing the smart thing. You made the right move for the wrong reason."

McClure pursed his lips and then let out a lot of stale air. "You were close to getting my ass again, so I tried to get away while gaining enough airspeed to come back at you. What's wrong with that?"

"The smart thing would have been to keep on going and not even think about the reattack."

"What?" McClure demanded.

"By then you should have realized that you had met a superior tactician who was going to kill you, it was time to disengage and live to fight another day. If there has been one thing I've learned in this business is that a good pilot, a really good pilot, is one who uses his judgment to avoid bad situations—situations that will get you killed.

"I don't run from fights."

Fancy couldn't help but laugh, remembering back to when he had first arrived at the Jolly Rogers. "You sound just like I did, and so many other guys who've come through here and I'll tell you the same thing I've been told and learned the hard way. There's just no point in sticking your pecker down the gun barrel to pee on the bullet just to prove you have what it takes." Fancy stood up and stretched. "Listen, if you don't have position and you can't get it, if you don't have airspeed and can't gain it, it's time to get the hell out of Dodge. Period."

"That isn't what I've been taught. That's pussycat stuff."

Fancy sighed again. "You're trying my patience. You ought to know by now you can't fight without ammunition or gas in your tanks, and so it is with getting the tactical advantage. Gain the damn advantage is what I'm trying to tell you. It's as vital as fuel or ammo. If you damn well can't gain it, haul ass and get back to the boat so you can figure out what it is you need to do to get another crack at them the next day."

Putting his hands on his hips, he continued his commentary. "I've learned, the hard way that your ego can help you or get you killed. Think of it like fire. It can cook your meals, smelt your steel, or kill you most unpleasantly. As a fighter pilot you've got to have the right mixture. Enough to go into a card game confident that you can whip anybody's ass, but not so much ego that you won't fold when you have a bad hand."

Again Fancy moved the fighter sticks. "I'm here and he's there. Of course I don't have a direct reading of his airspeed but I know pretty much what he's done on the last thirty degrees of turn. I can see his nose and guesstimate pretty accurately how fast he's going, his rate of turn. I can keep looking at his nose to see where he's going and what he can do; and I know that he's motoring along at about 250 knots and within ninety degrees of turn and with that G-load, he'll be down to about 180 and if he continues to do that, he will have dumped all his energy. Now, just suppose he thinks about the bad spot he's in and decides to act—even then I know that the only other thing he can do is unload, ease out of his turn and then he's going to be right here. I'm basing my decision on the data I've taken in. I conceptualize the fight and act."

Fancy felt himself getting wound up now and plunged ahead, warming to the subject. "Bring your nose down across here, then up, a roll, a pirouette, now pull, down here, back across and then pull into the vertical, cross here, back over the top. Over the top, unload roll, pull, bam, you're getting there. Now get down—fast." He moved the sticks, white plane after the red plane from a height advantage. "Nobody cares if you're upside down, right side up, or sideways. An unload is an unload is an unload. And, you can't turn when you're pulling. Unload, roll, pull, if you've got to pull five, six, seven Gs, when you're fighting the airplane, you're doing it wrong."

McClure again ran his hand through his hair trying to take it all in.

"Keep your smash up so you can maneuver. You learn to fight fast in this plane. Once you get slow, wrap it up—because you're going down.

But—go fast and you can use the vertical. Go straight up, fighting all the way. Energy to burn. I love the vertical even though everybody is using it. You just have to be more aggressive about it and use it first."

"Again," Fancy said, gesturing to Merrick and Mirabal, "these guys can make or break you. Make them part of the team. I just can't emphasize that too much."

"I hate to admit it, but it's really hard to fly with someone else in the plane. But, I know that's ego talkin'. You're right and I know it."

"Now you're thinking. Let's go get something to eat. I'm starved."

Robinson who had slipped in and had taken a seat in the back gave Fancy a thumb's up as the four men headed out of Ready Three.

The Enterprise spent the next three days on station in the Sea of Japan. Robinson had told the squadron that on the fifth day they would leave the area. Enterprise had continued to cruise northeast and had just crossed the forty-first parallel. Air ops had been going well, meaning no accidents or loss of life.

Fancy and Mirabal were manning the alert five aircraft, sitting on Enterprise's starboard catapult. In fifteen minutes they would stand down and Big Wave and his RIO would trade places with them. The weather had turned colder and Fancy figured that as long as he wasn't going to be flying, it wouldn't be bad to get something hot to drink and turn in early. "Rhino, you awake?"

"Just barely, Gator, just barely. Man, I'm going to have to start wearing something warmer. It's starting to get a little chilly."

Fancy was just about to mention something about the cooler weather when he felt the ship heel sharply to port.

"Oh, oh," he cautioned Mirabal, "Bedley's lookin' for some wind. Let's start going down the checklist. We're going to launch."

Almost as if on cue, the 1MC came to life. "Prepare to launch the alert five aircraft! Prepare to launch the alert five aircraft!"

Immediately the deck seemed to come alive with activity. He sensed rather than saw the cat crewmen taking the rubber seal out of the catapult shot. Steam wisped skyward from the open slot, leaking from some fittings somewhere in the cat. They kept the slot sealed in between launches to help maintain the temperature in the eighteen inch tubes.

Fancy decided it wouldn't be a good idea to begin thinking about all the things that could go wrong on a catapult launch. He wondered what dickhead had decided the planes needed to be parked on the cat. No doubt it was just to make the pilot watch the steam escaping and think about dying.

The plane rumbled to life as the port engine started to spool up, followed immediately by the starboard engine. Two minutes later Fancy rogered the weight board. Everything was in the green and looked good. Fancy was glad to be flying. He couldn't allow himself to think about anything else. There was a small jolt as the hydraulic arm shoved the cat pistons into tension, taking all the play out of the hold back bar.

Scanning the instruments one more time he shoved the throttles into full power. "Ready, Rhino?"

"Ready. Really, really, really ready! I'm right behind you."

Fancy felt the vibrations as the engines gulped in air throwing it out the back against the JBD. He flicked the exterior light master switch on, the nighttime equivalent of the salute to the cat officer.

Again, sensing rather than seeing, he knew the cat officer would be taking one more look at the deck in front of the plane. Then in one sweeping motion he brought his yellow wand down in a lunge that came down all the way down to the deck.

Immediately the catapult fired and the Gs forced them back in their seats. Fancy reached for the gear handle and slapped it up.

Again he sensed rather than saw Big Wave in Desperado 201 sliding into position on their port side and slightly behind them.

The plane was accelerating well and climbing. He keyed the transmitter. "Desperado 205 airborne."

"Roger Desperado 205," called departure control. Bend it on around to two- niner- zero and squawk a ten thousand; contact Echo 2. Keep your radar in standby." Echo 2 was the duty E-2C Hawkeye AWACS plane.

Before Fancy could say anything he noticed the radio frequency was being changed. Rhino was on top of things in his "office" as usual. Fancy nudged the throttles forward as they climbed out.

"Echo 2—this is Desperado 205 at ten thousand. What have you got for us.?"

"Stand by 205," came the metallic voice from the E-2.

"Desperado 205, leave your radar in standby. We'll be feeding you info over JTIDS (joint tactical information distribution system)."

"Roger, radar is in standby, Echo 2."

"Desperado 205, continue climbing to 32 angels. We've got a situation developing. Uh, there's a Philippine Air 747 inbound from Alaska, headed to Taegu, South, Korea. Evidently they've had some trouble with their navigation system and have strayed close to the coast of North Korea. They finally sorted things out and started to turn away from the North Korean coast when two MiG-29s came up to take a look and they're trying to crowd the airliner, edging them into their airspace."

Fancy paused for a moment. "And..."

"And, you get to see if you can discourage the slopes, uh make that the North Korean Air Force, from doing, shall we say anything rash."

"Roger, nothing rash. ROE (rules of engagement)?"

"You go weapons free if you are fired upon first. You know the drill?"

"Roger on the ROE, thanks, Echo."

"201, you copy the situation?"

"Copied sitrep, Gator, we're here and good to go."

Several minutes later they were at thirty-two thousand feet. Fancy leveled off and took a quick look at his radar presentation that was being relayed to them from the E-2C AWACS.

The second he thought he had picked their targets out of the murk, Rhino called them out. "Gator, I've got something big and two somethings' small. That's got to be them. We're, uh, fifty miles on their six and about two thousand feet below them."

Fancy felt the big cat leap forward as he pushed the throttles clear to the stops. The HUD confirmed their course and he could pick up the jumbo jet and the two smaller MiGs. "The pilot of that jumbo is doing a good job of slowing things down. That must be nerve wracking as hell to have those guys drifting just off your wing."

"He or she must be one cool customer. I wonder if the passengers have figured out what's goin' on?"

"Let's hope they're enjoying the movie."

"Wave, when we get close I want to be low and at their six. Slide over and you take the guy on the right and I'll try to get the guy's attention on the left. We'll light 'em up when we get in position. Rhino, let's go to GUARD."

"Roger GUARD, Gator," came the calm reply.

"Roger, Gator, sounds like a plan. Moving to your starboard, I'm going to slide right under you now to your starboard."

Another three minutes brought them close enough for Fancy to pick out the red and green navigation lights of the 747. Keeping his eyes moving from side to side he was able to pick out the darker and smaller shapes of the MiGs. Luckily they seemed to be about seventy-five or so yards off the big plane's wings. *Not too crowded* thought Fancy. *Could be worse Man this could be just like shootin' fish in a barrel—only easier.* The left hand MiG was right in the center of the gunsight. *Just a little pressure on the red button and you're gone, bud.* "Wave, let's light 'em up on three...One, two, three..."

"Good evening," he said at the same time Mirabal took the radar out of standby and he switched to guns. "We would like to thank the North Korean Air Force for the fine job of escorting this big piece of aluminum overcast out of harm's way. We'll be taking over now at the request of the Philippine government."

Fancy wondered if there would be any reason to send some laundry to the cleaners when these guys landed. He also couldn't believe that they had been able to sneak up on them without their ground controllers saying something. Knowing that the E2 would keep them apprised and that the Alert 15 planes must have been launched, gave him a myriad of satisfaction and assurance that nothing would be coming up on their six as they had just done to the MiGs.

"Philippine Air, this is United States Navy aircraft at your six and stepped down. We would like you to come to course one seven zero. Please, commence your turn in thirty seconds."

For a few seconds, which seemed like an eternity to Fancy, the five planes continued on their course. Then when he felt his thumb start to caress the red button on top of the stick which would bring the gun to life, the MiG on the port side of the 747 went to afterburner and accelerated away from the big passenger plane. The jumbo started to come left in a gentle left hand turn and soon settled on course one seven zero.

He was startled by the female voice that came through his headphones. "Thanks, Navy. This is Captain de Leon of Philippine Air. After Tailhook I thought I'd never want anything to do with you guys. I've had a sudden change of heart."

"You're welcome, glad we were in the neighborhood." Fancy hadn't attended the infamous 92 Tailhook, but decided this wasn't the time to mention it.

"Philippine Air, we'll escort you into South Korean air space if that's okay with you? We'll just stay out about five hundred yards at your altitude," he said, matter of factly.

"Navy, that will be just fine with us. Thanks again. We'll begin to descend for landing in about ten minutes," Captain DeLeon responded professionally.

"Roger, ten minutes to let down, Philippine Air."

The ten minutes passed uneventfully and at about the time the 747 started to let down for what would be just a slightly late landing, they found themselves in South Korean air space. "Desperado, 201, let's head back to the bird farm."

"Desperado 201 thinks that's a good idea. You lead we'll follow."

Fancy brought the Tomcat around in a hard left turn and headed back to the Enterprise.

The flight back was uneventful and even, Fancy thought, quite beautiful.

"205. Tomcat, Ball, 2,800 pounds," he called out as they picked out the datum lights at three quarters of a mile from the ship.

"Roger, Ball," came the acknowledgement.

*Ummm, that's not Badrod working tonight,* he allowed himself to think as he worked on keeping the lights centered to stay on glide path. *Speed, centerline, glide path. That's all I need to concern myself with,* he reminded himself. *Stick to basics and fly the plane and everything works out.*

Robinson and Matsen were in Pri-Fly and noted that Fancy was flying what they thought of as a textbook recovery.

As he felt the wheels slam onto the deck he shoved the throttles all the way to zone five afterburner and, unexpectedly slowed and then picked up speed again. Before he could blink he knew that they must have had a hook skip or where the tailhook for some reason managed to skip over the three wire he wanted to snag.

"Uh, oh," he said to himself. "Rhino, you still with me?"

"I'm here, What happened, you think we had a hook skip?"

"Must be," Fancy growled as he brought the gear up and the flaps in. At least they were flying and everything seemed to be normal.

Robinson and Matsen turned to each other and gasped as they watched Fancy roar off the deck—a trail of fire from the afterburner showing the way.

"They've lost their hook!" came the voice of the Air Boss. "Jesus, can you believe that. They snagged the three wire, pulled about fifty feet of it out and then they lost their hook. Unbelievable!"

Fancy now knew it was more serious than a hook skip when he tried to bring the tailhook back up. *There's nothing to bring up.* "Rhino, I think we've lost the hook."

"What!" You've got to be kidding, but I don't think you would be—would you?"

"Noooo, I wouldn't. Believe me."

"I believe you. Any ideas?"

"Desperado 205," came the voice of departure control. "You've got a problem. You're up there and your tailhook is sitting here on the deck next to the mule it hit. The hook's okay, but I think the mule might be a mort."

"How does she fly. Anything in the red or control problems on anomalies?"

Fancy appreciated the attempt at humor. This was no time to turn sour and inward. "Sorry about the mule. The plane seems fine. She responds with no problems. Nothing is in the red. What do you want us to do?" Knowing there were only two choices he wanted all the advice he could get. Eventually, fuel would be critical. Decisions had to be made—now.

"We're going to leave it up to you. We can rig the barrier and you can bring it in, or you can punch out next to one of the destroyers. It's your call, 205."

"Rhino, you copy?"

"I heard it loud and clear, what do you want to do?"

"Babe, I'm going to leave it up to you for a change. You've been in the water so…"

"Let's go for the barrier. You know what you're doing."

"I appreciate the vote of confidence, but are you sure?"

"Yeah, I'm sure, let's go for it."

Fancy took a deep breath. "Strike, this is Desperado 205. We're going to put her on the deck. How long will it take you to rig the barrier?"

"205, we'll have it up in ten minutes or less. How's your fuel?"

Fancy looked at the gauges. "Uh, just under 2000 pounds, lets call it 1900 pounds."

"Roger 1900 pounds. Okay, go to Marshal, burn off as much fuel as you feel comfortable ."

"Strike, I'm going to burn all but a couple of hundred pounds off—'till she's about to flame out."

"Roger, burn off, Desperado. Good luck."

"Gator."

"Yeah?"

"Thanks for letting me have some input. I appreciate it. Is this what you want to do?"

"Yes, I feel like I have more control over my, uh our destinies. Does that make me a control freak or something?"

"Probably, but who gives a rip."

The two men flew in silence. Fancy mused how the night had gone from beautiful to delta sierra in a matter of a few seconds.

They flew out past what would have been the Marshal area and turned on final. Since only the E2 and they were still in the air there didn't seem to be too much urgency to their situation. *It would be very easy to get complacent,* he thought to himself. *Definitely, not a time to get complacent.* He never thought he would be happy to see the fuel gauge ribbons wind down as rapidly as they were.

Once again they carefully went through their landing check lists. Fancy had to chuckle to himself when it was time to put down the tailhook. *We're creatures of habit* he smiled to himself.

"Tomcat. Ball, less than 300 pounds I'd guess."

"Roger, Ball," came Badrod's voice, giving Fancy a sudden burst of confidence.

"Speed, glide, centerline," he muttered to himself as they closed to within a quarter mile of the ship. He could make out the general shape and of course the lights and drop line.

At the last minute he took the plane a little high and came back on the throttles.

"Little high, Gator, bring'er down..." breathed Badrod softly.

Then they were over the roundoff, slamming on to the deck and into the barrier that stopped them as surely as if someone had reached out and grabbed them. Fancy had deliberately not looked for the barrier and had not seen it before they plowed into it. He was grateful for that bit of foresight.

In no time at all the crash crews were swarming over and under the plane looking for any spark that might ignite the now still Tomcat.

Fancy unhooked his oxygen mask, twisted his neck around and started to unhook his Koch settings. Immediately he was being helped by one of the crash crew who had scrambled up the crew boarding ladder and the steps that were created when someone pushed in on them.

"Are you okay, sir?" the man asked.

"I'm fine, considering," he replied as he took off his helmet and handed it to the sailor, who then inquired about Mirabal. Dropping Fancy's helmet down to one of his buddies he did likewise with Mirabal's helmet and then dropped to the ground.

When Mirabal had joined him on the ground they walked around the plane. Fancy was surprised that the plane looked as good as it did. The nose, housing the radar and other electronics, had a large crack in it and would need to be replaced. Underneath the nose the damage was more extensive with the chin pod housing the TCS (television camera system) and the Infared Search and Tracking (IRST) just barely hanging on the plane. The leading edge of the wings also looked a little the worse for wear he noticed.

Fancy whistled. "So much for the chin pod." Turning to Mirabal, "It doesn't look too bad, considering..."

"Considering what? Man, compared to the cost of a new plane or even a Class A. Jeez…" his voice trailing off as he ran his hand over the hanging pod, and shaking his head. "That was a Sierra Hotel recovery as far as I'm concerned."

"Fancy, that was as pretty a landing as I've ever seen," said Robinson as he walked up behind the gathering group of sailors and aviators. "Gator, this one will show up all over the fleet. Nice work," he continued as he shook Fancy's hand.

"Thank's, Skipper. Badrod had us lined up and in the groove, except for the tailhook not being there, it was pretty routine."

"As routine as landing on a moving piece of steel can be," piped up Mirabal. "Let's look at where our hook was supposed to be."

Pushing their way through the crewmen they made their way to the rear of the plane where even more men had gathered to look at the plane.

"That is hard to believe. Man, look at that," Fancy heard a pilot, whom he recognized as a pilot from one of the F/A-18 squadrons. "This should never happen."

Looking at the arresting hook attachment point, he could see, at least from his somewhat limited viewpoint, that there was no rust evident. It looked like, he thought, just a broken toy.

"How'd it look when you did your Walk Around, Gator?"

Fancy shook his head. "You know, as far as I can remember, it looked fine, normal, nothing that drew my attention to it."

"You did look at it?" asked Robinson.

"Yes, I did, Skipper," answered Fancy, with a definite edge in his voice.

"Easy, Gator, I had to ask. I've got no problems with that."

"Skipper, we both looked at it. There was just nothing that was out of the ordinary. I gave it a shake and I saw Gator do the same thing. If there was something to see, we would have seen it."

Robinson clapped them both on the shoulder. "Don't worry about it. You guys did a hell of a job getting it down in one piece, more or less. Come on, I'll buy you some coffee."

For the next ten days the *Enterprise* cruised closer to the coast of Korea in the Sea of Japan. The North Koreans seemed to have lost all interest in drawing any kind of negative attention to themselves. The intelligence community passed the word that units of the North Korean Army had quietly withdrawn all of the units they had moved south from their bases in the north in the area near the DMZ. Naval units of their navy were reported tied up at their docks, with all their subs, accounted for. On the tenth day after the incident with the MiGs and the 747, the word was passed that *Enterprise* would head south out of the Sea of Japan and the crew would be given liberty in Singapore.

# 11

The ship was moving through the East China Sea, five hundred miles north of the island nation of Taiwan. Fancy had just flopped down on his bunk after a morning flight and some ACM with Stash McClure. *McClure is getting a lot better or I'm getting worse* he thought to himself, as he tried to rub the kinks out of his neck. He was just about to close his eyes to grab some shut-eye when there was a knock at the door. Before he could reply to the knock the door opened and Big Wave and Poncho slid in, slamming the door quickly behind them.

"And to what do I owe the pleasure of this visit?"

In reply, Poncho reached inside his jacket and hauled out Short Round. Immediately the squirming dog was deposited on Fancy's bunk. He immediately crawled up on Fancy chest, licked his face, turned around, and settled down for a nap on his stomach.

"Don't tell me, Matsen's hot on your trail and I was the nearest place of refuge, right?"

Poncho and Wave did their best to look innocent and hurt at the same time.

"Of course not. It wasn't Matsen," said Poncho. "Actually, it's the Master At Arms. We were returning from the fantail, when he almost caught us."

"Yeah," continued Wave, "Short Round really likes it back there. If we get back there just after they've tested an engine, there's hardly anybody around for a while. But today…"

Short Round, raised his head, yawned, and put his head back down.

Fancy shook his head. "How much longer do you think you can keep hiding him?"

"Indefinitely," shrugged Poncho. "Besides, the squadron needs a mascot. Why not Short Round?"

"I tell you who'll be the mascot. It'll be your ass when Matsen nails it to the wall," smiled Fancy, rubbing the dog behind his ears. His efforts were rewarded by a sigh and then the dog rolled over on its side and settled in for the duration.

At that moment Bagger came through the hatch. "Ya te ha, compadres," he said, as he threw two letters down next to Fancy. "Hey, Short Round. How you doin'? You're a good boy," he said as he bent down and scratched Short Round behind his ears.

"Did you get anything?" asked Fancy.

"Oh yeah," he grinned, drawing two letters out from his shirt. Dramatically, he drew the letters under his nose. "Oh yeah!"

"By the way," Bagger continued, "the Skipper's called a meeting at 1400."

"Did he mention what it could be about?" inquired Poncho.

Shaking his head in the negative, "Nupe, just said he wanted everyone there at 1400. If it's any big thing I think we'd be meeting right now."

Fancy sat up picking up the dog as he did so. "All right, boy, it's time for you to hit the road." Handing the squirming puppy to Poncho, he got off his rack checking his trousers to see if there was any tell-tale dog hair. Anybody want to grab a bite before the meeting?" he asked the group of aviators.

He was met with enthusiastic nods in the affirmative. Just as Poncho was reaching for the door to check the passageway to make sure it was safe to spirit Short Round to Poncho and Big Wave's room, there was knock on the door. Poncho turned suddenly and handed the dog to Big Wave who in turn handed it to Bagger, who quickly gave it back to Fancy. As Poncho opened the door Fancy put the dog behind him.

"Hey, guys," smiled Mirabal. "I just wanted to let Gator and Bagger know there was a meeting at 1400. What's going on, you guys look guilty as hell about something?"

As if he had been cued, Short Round poked his head out from behind Fancy and gave a short, sharp bark, as if to say, "This is so humiliating being passed around like this."

"Oh, I see why," grinned Mirabal.

"We know about the meet, Rhino. We were just going to grab a bite to eat," put in Big Wave. "Want to come?"

"Sure, let's go," returned Mirabal, as he backed out into the passageway. "The coast is clear."

Once in the passageway the group took furtive looks up and down the passageway and slunk along like a bunch of naughty schoolboys trying to put something over on their teacher.

By the time they had eaten and gotten to Ready Three, they found the room full, finding the only empty seats in the undesirable front row. Robinson was at the lectern with a map of the coast of China, the East China Sea, and the Taiwan Strait.

"Uh oh," sighed Mirabal, as he eased into a chair, "what do you think that particular map means?"

"Dunno, guess that's why were here though." responded Fancy, sliding into his own chair.

"Good afternoon, gentleman," drawled Robinson. The room became silent as the talking died away. Picking up a pointer hanging from the side of the map, he tapped the most populous country on earth, China.

"Gentlemen, yesterday afternoon, the Vice-President of Taiwan flew quietly to the United States to visit his son who has come down with a serious illness. Almost immediately Chinese on the mainland went ballistic. They're claiming that constitutes a violation of the status quo and that the United States is recognizing Taiwan over them." After waiting for the ensuing murmur to die down, Robinson continued. As you know, or maybe you didn't, Enterprise is scheduled to transit the Strait of Taiwan en route to Singapore. The Chinese, mainland China, is making its displeasure known at the highest levels. In addition they are extending the military exercises that they have been conducting. Our government is of the mind that we will continue our transit as planned. While the powers that be feel there won't be any serious problems with the People's Liberation Army or Navy, or whatever, Van Gundy, Admiral Blue, Captain Bedley, and whomever else has any input, feel there could be some close calls with some of their guys getting up close and personal with us, pushing the proverbial envelope"

"Skipper," drawled Killer Stevens, "what's the deal on keeping the Chicoms away from Enterprise?"

"We'll be in international waters, but, the Chinese claim territorial waters out to two hundred miles. We expect them to come out and take a look at Enterprise. Of course we're going to provide an escort service. This'll be a great chance to work on intercepts against some folks who might be, somewhat aggressive and even a little hostile If they happen to find us, which I expect they will, we want them to carry the message back that they'd be in a world of hurt before they ever get over the ship."

"They'll probably be staging from Little Woody Island, as well as from bases on the mainland. Little Woody Island is part of the Paracel Islands. Unlike the last time there was tension between Taiwan and the mainland Chinese, our government is not going to back down from our lawful right of passage in the Taiwan Strait, or anywhere else for that matter."

After letting the message sink in for a few seconds he continued. "As of right now, and of course you know how quickly things can change, there is no special flight schedule. We will continue flight operations as usual. Any more questions?"

"Is Singapore still on the schedule for a port visit?" croaked Moose, his deep voice sounding like it was coming from the bottom of a deep well.

"Singapore is our next port of call as far as I know. No one has mentioned anything to the contrary. But…"

"Yeah, we know all about the 'buts'", groused Moose.

"If there's nothing else, I want everyone to start going over recognition cards. Your Mark I eyeballs will always be your best bet if things start to get hairy. Fancy, have you checked out the TARPS pod lately?"

"I was down looking at them day before yesterday, Skipper. Both of them look like they're in good shape. The enlisted guys have been running checks on them every four days and they check out one hundred percent. Do you think we'll be getting to use them?"

"It's not official, but yeah, I think we're going to use them. Stay on top of them and be ready."

"Right, Skipper."

*Enterprise* and her battle group continued to move through the East China Sea. Normal flight operations continued, with no sightings of anything but normal airline traffic. The People's Liberation Army (Air Force) seemed to be sticking to their mainland bases. However, the People's Liberation Army, (Navy) seemed to be taking an active interest in the *Enterprise* battlegroup.

Two days later Fancy and Bagger were on routine Air Combat Patrol out in front of the battlegroup when their threat receivers began to light up like Christmas trees.

"Gator, we're being painted by, uh looks like Top Can radar, a type found on Chinese Navy destroyers and frigates. So far they're just looking, they haven't done anything hostile yet," came Mirabal's nonchalant voice.

When the RWAH gear had given its ominous warning, Fancy had automatically started to bob and weave even more than he and Bagger had been doing. "Bagger, we could probably glow in the dark."

"Roger that, Gator. We' ve got 'em at thirty-five miles at one nine zero. Why don't we take a look?"

"Why not. Let's come to one nine zero and gradually go down to uh, nine thousand feet."

"Desperado 202, coming left to one nine zero, going to nine angels in a gradual descent, " answered Bagger, as the two planes came to their new course.

Fancy saw the new numbers come up on the radio as Mirabal changed frequencies to let the Enterprise in on what they were doing. *He's a pro,* thought Fancy.

The two Tomcats quickly ate up the miles between them and the Chinese ships. The closer they got the stronger the indications they got from their RHAW gear. Because it was a very clear day, with visibility almost unlimited, Fancy was able to pick out the ships almost as quickly as the radar was able to give him what he was looking for. "Bagger, two o' clock. It looks like four ships."

"I see 'em, Gator. Looks like an oiler, maybe two frigates, and something larger, possibly a destroyer."

"Roger that, Bagger. They're sure in a pretty tight formation. Maybe they were taking on fuel from the oiler."

"That's my guess. Do you want to go lower and get a better look?"

No, let's not give them any reason to get pissed off. Let's go back to eighteen angels on course zero one five."

"Roger that, Gator, course zero one five, going up to eighteen grand."

Fancy noted the change in the broad band search radar from the Chinese ships to that of the much narrower and higher pitched sound of a fire control radar. The Chinese were painting both planes and could shoot if they so desired.

"Maybe we pissed 'em off after all, Gator?" said Mirabal.

"Gives you kind of a creepy feeling doesn't it," Fancy responded. "Maybe we should go down and give them a good looking over."

"I'm right behind you," chuckled Mirabal.

Fancy considered his options. He hated to seem to be running away, but there was no sense in creating some kind of international incident with the Chinese.

"Nah, let's go home. Like I said, no sense in gettin' these guys all bent out of shape." With that said he bent the plane around and started climbing to eighteen thousand feet.

The flight back to Enterprise was uneventful. Both planes caught three wires. Unfortunately for the four aviators the debrief took an hour and a half. After looking through the briefing books, it was decided by the intel weenies, as Fancy thought of them, that there had been two frigates of the *Hulnali* class. The largest of the three warships was a type 052 *Luda* II class destroyer. The oiler was identified as the *Nancang*.

Fancy went straight to his room and flopped down on his bunk. Before he could decide whether to get cleaned up or just get some sleep, Bagger came in. "Well, that was something. How did you feel getting lit up like that. I don't mind telling you that it made me a little uncomfortable and I didn't especially like it."

"Me neither," answered Fancy with a yawn. "You know it's times like that that makes me miss the A-6. We could have made a dent and tickled those ships with the Gatling gun, but that's about it."

"Yeah, no matter what we've said about the Intruders, you couldn't beat them for getting the job done, especially a job like that. Those guys are really going to be missed."

"You better not let the Hornet drivers hear you say that. They think they can do it all."

"I'm not questioning their cajones, mind you," continued Mirabal, "but you know what we'll really miss?"

"Their experience?"

"Exactly. When they disestablished all those A-6 squadrons so many of those pilots and BNs went somewhere else or had to leave the service. That's a lot of experience to lose, especially in so short a time."

"You know when we're on the roof, it seems so strange not to see any of those ugly planes, but I agree, they're definitely going to be missed," sighed Fancy, settling down into his bunk. "What are you going to do, sleep or go to Ready Three"

"I'm torn, but, I think I'll hit the rack for a while then go to Ready Three for the movie."

Fancy nodded in the affirmative then closed his eyes and was almost immediately asleep.

Fancy was awakened an hour later when Bagger reached down from his bunk and shook him awake. "Gator! Wake up. Let's get cleaned up and head for Ready Three. I want to see the movie."

Fancy stretched, yawned, and grabbed Bagger's arm, giving it a pull. "I'm tactical. Give me a minute to get the kinks out. What's so important about this particular movie?"

"You're kidding. Didn't you hear what it's going to be?"

"No, what's the big deal anyway?"

"Demi Moore. "Strip Tease." Wouldn't you call that a big deal?"

"Uh, no, I would not," Fancy suggested as he sat up and swung his legs over the side of the bunk.

"Well, I would, so let's get a move on, okay?"

As they walked into Ready Three Fancy was struck by how good it felt to be part of the squadron. Looking at Bagger, who immediately drew an evil eye from Matsen, he was glad Bailey had made the decision that he had. After talking with Killer Stevens and Poncho for a few minutes someone put the tape in the VCR and the movie started.

Two hours later he still wondered what the big deal was about "Strip Tease". The best part of watching the movie was listening to all the ribald comments that everyone felt free to call out and advice that was given to all the parties concerned in the movie. Most comments were of a very explicit sexual nature. The advice and comments were better than the movie he figured.

When the lights came on and everyone started to file out, he found himself next to Moose, who had been very liberal in the advice that he had given out. "Man," the diminutive pilot said, "I can't believe that movie didn't win all kinds of Oscars. She is one fine piece of work."

"We noticed that this is probably your all time favorite," chided Fancy.

"Is she married?"

"Yeah," said Bagger, "to Bruce Willis I think."

"She should ditch him and come with me," croaked Moose.

"Right," laughed Fancy. "Just what have you got to offer her by the way?"

"Besides me," said Moose, as he drew himself up to his full height, "there's this magnificent yacht. What more could she ask for?"

"I just can't believe she'd turn you down, dude," said Big Wave, trailing behind them. Beside's you're a Navy pilot, what more could she ask for.

"Did you guys hear the one about the mouse. She tells her girlfriend that she's dating a bat. The girlfriend says, 'You're dating a what? Why that's nothing but a moth with wings and so ugly.' She says 'Well, yes, but he is a pilot, isn't he'?"

The joke was met with hearty guffaws all around.

Poncho put in, "You know after the crash of a DC-10, the FAA ordered the operators to ground the plane until after the investigation results."

"Oh the FAA, when they die and bury me face down in the tall tall grass, so the FAA can kiss my ass," sang Big Wave in his best off key voice.

"You better believe we need some liberty in Singapore," growled Moose, "in the worst way possible."

The Tomcat started to sink slightly as fuel was transferred from the S-3 Viking to Desperado 200. Fancy eased the throttles forward to compensate for the extra weight being taken on board. Stash McClure had just taken on a full load and was off Fancy's starboard side. It had been an extra ordinarily rough flight so far, and Fancy was using every bit of his skill to keep the big fighter from falling off the basket. Finally, they were topped off and Fancy eased the plane back and away from the S-3.

Once they were away from the tanker Fancy pushed the throttles forward and brought the stick back as he and McClure climbed to altitude. The plane continued to move around as they hit another pocket of rough air.

"Gator, I can't remember when we've been bounced around this much for this long. I just hope I don't toss my cookies."

"That makes two of us, Rhino. Desperado 211, let's climb to twenty-five grand and see if things smooth out a little bit."

"Roger, climbing to 250. Man, this has been one rough ride."

Once they had climbed to twenty-five thousand they found that the ride smoothed out, but only slightly.

"Desperado two zero zero, this is Echo Four," came the disembodied voice of the controller on board the E-2C AWACS plane.

"Roger, Echo Four." Desperado 200. What's cookin'?"

"Come to course two two zero and continue on your present altitude. You're going to be looking for what we think is a TU-95."

"You gotta be kidding. A Bear?"

"Roger that, Desperado."

"Well, Rhino, what do you think of that?"

"I think it's cool," replied Mirabal as he worked the control stick between his legs and punched buttons above his radar. The stick was focusing the plane's radar beams on different sectors of the sky.

"Bring her left two degrees," he instructed Fancy.

"Stash, you with us, okay?"

"We're here for the duration," came Stash's voice, a little bit higher than Fancy remembered it.

"I've got him, Gator. He's at 150 miles on our nose, just slightly lower than we are. He's probably making about 500 knots. Man, can you believe the return we're getting on this guy."

"He's one big dude," said Fancy as he glanced at his own scope. The radar cross section was bigger than he had seen in a long time. *Damn,* he thought to himself, *the only problem we've got on this plane is that the TCS* (Television Camera System) *is down.*

"Desperado two one one, is your TCS up?"

"Two hundred, it's up and functioning perfectly. You should see the picture we're getting. Remarkable."

"Stash make sure you get some good tape, the intel guys will be falling all over you if you don't."

"Lights, camera, action, shooting tape." McClure's voice had come down an octave and he sounded like he was enjoying this as much as Fancy was.

At over a thousand miles per hour closure rate it was only a few minutes before Fancy was able to pick out the huge bomber visually. "That is one big plane, a regular piece of aluminum overcast."

"I'll take your word for it, Gator. I've never seen a return this huge."

"Just wait until you see this beast."

"Stash, you slip into the shooter's position at his six. We'll take a look at what's up front."

"Roger that, Gator.

The two Tomcats passed down the port side of the huge bomber. Immediately after they passed the Chinese plane, Fancy racked the plane around and converted the head-on intercept, turning in and joining smoothly off the left wing of the Chinese plane. *This is one pretty plane* he thought to himself. Looking the plane over he noted that it looked like it had been polished to a high gloss. He also noted the large in-flight refueling probe on the starboard side, just forward of the cockpit. Making the conversion he had also noted the twin guns mounted aft of the tail. Other than those two guns, he couldn't see any other defensive armament. There were no missiles hanging off the wings. Four big turbo prop engines with counter rotating props were moving the huge plane along at over 485 knots, over five hundred and fifty miles per hour. What did catch Fancy's eye were the antennae and some funny bulges about half way down the fuselage right where the bomb bay should be.

Glancing over at the plane he saw the Chinese pilot looking them over. He waved and the Chinese pilot waved back. Dropping back he could see a large bubble, from within which was a crewman watching him. Again he waved. Instead of waving back the man held up what looked like a poster. Easing the plane in closer for a better look he saw that it was the centerfold of a men's magazine.

"What's this guy up to?"

"Dunno," came Rhino's reply, "but he does have good taste, doesn't he?"

Feeling an air stream creating a Bernoulli effect, which brought the Tomcat in closer than he felt was comfortable, Fancy eased the plane back off the wing and forward again. The Chinese pilot seemed to be laughing at something.

"You got your camera with you by any chance, Rhino?"

"Negative, and I even was thinking of bringing it."

"I'm going to drift back and take another look at those antennae and bulges on the fuselage."

"Okay, I've got some paper and a pencil. I'll do a rough sketch. Maybe the intel guys will be able to make something out of it."

Retarding the throttles slightly, Fancy let the Chinese plane pull ahead of them. As it did so Fancy let the plane drift over and then under the bombe,r giving them a good look at the bulges and antennae.

"Desperado 211, let's trade places. Keep that tape rolling and see if you can get a shot of the belly of his fuselage."

"Trading places, Gator," came the reply.

As Fancy's plane drifted back to three quarters of a mile he marveled at how big the TU-95 looked. It still looked huge from where he sat.

It wasn't long before the three planes had flown over the the Enterprise Battle Group. The Chinese plane did not come down from altitude and after- over flying the carrier, turned back on a reciprocal course. After escorting them for a hundred and fifty miles away from the carrier they headed back to Enterprise.

Much to their displeasure, the high winds they had been encountering had dropped down to the surface of the ocean. The Air Boss came up on the radio to tell them that they had fifty-seven mile an hour winds over the deck. In addition to the high winds the cloud layer was dropping rapidly. Definitely an unusual condition.

"Hey, good news come in bunches, doesn't it?" he said to Rhino.

"You know what's coming next don't you," replied Mirabal. "They won't be able to launch the rescue helos because of the high wind over the deck."

Sure enough, that was the next bit of good news, telling them as well that the frigates and destroyers would have a hard time picking them up from the water due to the rough sea state.

"Do we really need this information? Jesus." It was time to really pay attention to his instruments. Oddly enough he felt calm and even relaxed.

McClure went down the chute first and snagged a two wire.

"Desperado two zero zero, two point one, Tomcat, ball." The F-14 was now really being buffeted around by the high winds.

"Power, bring it up a little," came the voice of the LSO. "Power, bring it up," he repeated.

Momentarily the ball disappeared from view and then popped into a view again.

"Drop your nose. Easy 200."

Bringing the nose down slightly and seeing that he was lined up perfectly he was right over the ramp almost before he knew it. "Geez, what a lucky break!" Fancy shouted into his mask, as he shoved the throttles all the way to the stops. Then realizing he wasn't decelerating one bit, they were off the deck almost before he could blink.

"Bolter! Bolter! Bolter!" shouted the LSO.

They were in the air and back into the low clouds almost before they knew it. Fancy figured instinctive flying was what saved them. Hook skips are somewhat infrequent occurrences. Fancy was thinking that he couldn't duplicate that landing or luck in a hundred years. Fuel was now a concern. Although the low fuel state light had not come on, he knew it was only a matter of time, with enough fuel left for one, maybe two passes.

Surprisingly enough the second landing was a duplicate of the first, with the exception that they caught the two wire, just behind McClure who had also snagged a two wire.

The ceiling was now so low that when they watched the tapes there was only seven seconds between the time his plane came out of the overcast until touchdown.

The intel guys were more than happy with Mirabal's drawing and McClure's tape, and they were able to do a reasonably thorough evaluation of dimensions and capabilities of the Bear's reconnaissance capabilities.

After they had finished with the intelligence people, and changed out of their flight gear, the four aviators made their way to Ready Three. They were surprised to see the room almost vacant, except for Matsen who was looking through some papers.

"Hey, XO, how goes it?" called Mirabal.

Matsen looked up. His face broke into a grin when he saw the four men. "Ah ha, the Bear Hunters are back. That must have been something to see?"

"That was one huge airplane. I've seen a lot of pictures of that plane, but they sure didn't prepare me for the real thing. That's an impressive piece of work, gushed McClure.

"I hope I get to see one," returned Matsen. "You guys missed some excitement here for a change though."

"Oh, what happened? Is everybody all right?" asked Fancy, almost afraid to hear the reply.

"Oh yeah, no problem with anybody on the ship or the battle group. You know those Chinese frigates and destroyers you spotted the other day?"

Fancy and Mirabal nodded in the affirmative.

Matsen continued, a huge grin spreading across his face. "Well, they decided they were going to rip right through the battle group. They came charging through us bold as you please. Naturally, we went to General Quarters when they were picked up by the E-2 and a frigate out in front of the battle group. When they were almost abeam of us, they trained one of their main guns on us. I guess that really pissed Admiral Blue off, and he was pretty bent out of shape. He had the whole battle group illuminate these idiots. They must have figured their world was going to come to an end because they radioed, 'Are you trying to start World War Three?' I guess Blue radioed back, 'If we are, you'll be the first to know it.'" Matsen started to laugh as he shook his head. "What a bunch of assholes, can you believe that crap?"

Gesturing toward the PLAT screen he said, "That was a nice job coming out of the soup. I've haven't seen conditions that bad for a long while. I was talking to one of the senior chiefs and he said they used to put toilet paper under the wires to hold them up a little higher when things got a little hairy. Maybe we should try that again?"

"Pretty crappy way to run a Navy, don't you think XO," laughed Mirabal. "I just couldn't resist that. It was just too easy."

Matsen added his laughter to everyone else's.

The incessant banging on the door brought Fancy out of a dream where someone was selling his car—without his permission. Shaking his head in order to clear the cobwebs he heard Bagger grunt, "Go away!"

Struggling out of his bunk he made his way to the door and opened. Standing outside the door was an enlisted man, poised to knock again. "Good evening, sir. Commander Robinson wants everybody in Ready Three in ten minutes, sir." Looking at his watch, he continued, "Better make that eight minutes, sir."

"Thanks," muttered Fancy, closing the door. "We're up."

"Did he say what I thought he said," growled Bagger as he lowered himself to the deck. "Now what?" he said stretching, while grabbing for his trousers at the same time.

"Beats me," said Fancy. "Man, it's twenty-three thirty. It seem like I've been asleep for a long time."

"You know what they say about time and having fun," said Bagger, buttoning up his uniform shirt. "Now, where are the bleeping shoes and the bleeping socks. Now, why didn't I think of that?" he said disgustedly, looking at Fancy, who had put on his flight suit.

"You missed a button."

"Thanks. You figure we're going flying?"

"Gotta be the case. Let's go. One of us has to be wrong."

Arriving at Ready Three they found, despite the fact that Bagger had taken the time to change into his green bag, they were, surprisingly enough, almost the first ones there. Killer came in right behind them, yawning.

"What's the word? Do you guys know what's happening?"

"Nupe," answering Killer's yawn with one of his own. "We were hopin' you would."

"I got no clue. Heck, I was on my way to man the alert five bird, when I was told to get down here."

Moose, Poncho, Big Wave, Mirabal, and Matsen all came in together. If Matsen knew anything he wasn't talking, and continued up to the front of the room. By the time Fancy had sat down the rest of the squadron had filtered in and had found seats. Everyone wanted to know what was going on. Matsen held up his hands and shrugged his shoulders to let everyone know he didn't know either.

Two minutes later Robinson came through the hatch and made his way to the front of the room. "Stay seated," he commanded. Grinning from ear to ear he turned and faced the squadron, putting several papers he had been carrying atop the small beat-up table beside him.

Still grinning he asked, "Does anybody know why we're here?" After letting the catcalls and comments die down he continued. "Admiral Blue, evidently a little more than pissed off at the way the Chinese came through our formation yesterday has decided to mount a Sierra Strike, albeit a practice strike, against those ships. He thinks no-notice drills are the way to go. We're going to launch at zero three-thirty. Our job will be to provide a MiG sweep, a TAR Cap, and of course, cover their egress so nobody gets on their six in the way home. We're to find their ships and then pull off to the southeast. The F/A-18s, will put some live ordinance in the water, probably some buoys the sub will release. If there are no questions I'll tell you who is going to do what this morning."

Mirabal nudged Fancy. "We want the MiG sweep, right?"

Fancy just grinned and nodded.

Robinson went on. "We're planning on using every plane and I've been assured by the wrench turners that every plane is up and good to go. XO, Poncho, Moose, and Gizmo, you take the MiG sweep. You'll launch at 0300. Big Wave, Killer, Rainman, and myself will take the BAR Cap. Gator, Bagger, Stretch and Stash will be the spares and cover the egress. You'll launch at 0330."

Looking at Gator, Mirabal couldn't tell whether he was disappointed or happy about their part in the strike. "You disappointed?"

"Hey, you know everything balances out one way or another." He shrugged. "We'll cover that egress like the pros we are, right?"

Mirabal grinned and gave him a thumb's up.

Because they were the spares for each division, Gator made sure he and Mirabal knew what those divisions' parts in the strike were. After making sure they knew each of the planes' frequencies, wingmen, and place in the flight. That task completed, they got together with Stretch Gerlicki, Bagger, and Stash to work out their particulars. Once he was satisfied with their part in the overall plan he and Rhino spent a few minutes reviewing the whole operation. When they were both satisfied, they grabbed a quick bite and then went to don their flight gear.

After suiting up Gator and Bagger walked up to flight control to look at the cardboard cutout to find where their plane was parked. As he spotted Desperado two zero two's parking slot, he noticed that it was beginning to rain. The drops were just starting to run down the bomb proof windows of flight control. *Another something wonderful* he thought to himself. Gesturing toward the window he nudged Bagger. "Starting to rain."

Bagger shook his head and put his finger on Desperado two zero five. Frowning, he pursed his lips, exhaled, and shrugged. "Join the Navy, see the world, shit your pants."

Turning for the hatch that led to the flight deck, he opened it and was greeted by a blast of cold air laden with rain. Putting on his helmet he walked out the hatch and onto the flight deck which was already busy with planes being moved and refueled, as well as ordinance being loaded.

Their bird was parked on Elevator Four. Since the tail was sticking out over the water, Fancy took special care to watch his step. He also noticed their load out of four Sidewinders and four Sparrows. *Loaded for bear,* he thought. One slip and he would wind up in the water. Mirabal joined them and they started their walk around. Fancy put his clear visor down to keep the rain out of his eyes. He realized the rain drops, driven by the wind, had been stinging his eyes.

When it came time to check the ejection seat he took special pains to count the pins carefully two times each. He resisted the temptation to hurry it up and get in the cockpit and get the canopy closed. Hanging on with one hand he felt that the motion of the ship was magnified. Finally satisfied he hoisted himself in the cockpit. Mirabal was right behind him.

Knowing the plane captain was right behind Mirabal, Fancy looked to his left to see who it might be tonight. Sharader's face popped up over the canopy rail. "Tough night, Sir," he said as he helped Fancy hook up the oxygen, made sure the leg restraints were right, and snapped the four Koch fittings into place. Finishing with Fancy he repeated the procedure with Mirabal. Giving them one final check he closed the canopy.

Immediately he checked the gear handle, armament switches, and arranged the switches for engine start. Again he resisted the temptation to hurry things. Just because he had done this many, many times before he slowed himself down to make sure it was done right. The rain seemed to have intensified.

Now came the hard part as far as Fancy was concerned: the waiting, something he had never been very good at.

Looking out over the deck he marveled at the activity that to an outsider, would seem like chaos. In the absence of light he watched the colored wands of the yellow shirts. Engines were being started. Things were beginning to happen as 0300 rapidly approached. Glancing at his watch he saw that it was 0250.

First to take off were the S-3 Vikings which would act as airborne tankers. They would refuel the somewhat short legged F/A-18 Hornets. Next came the two EA6 Prowlers to provide electronic counter measures, as well as shoot the HARM missile at any radars that threatened the strike.

After the F/A-18s were launched, at precisely 0300 the first Tomcat was launched. "That's Matsen," he said to Mirabal.

"Yeah," replied Mirabal, somewhat glumly.

Fancy chuckled to himself but said nothing.

Seven minutes later the strike had been launched and a strange calm came over the deck.

An E-2 taxied toward Cat Three, the waist catapult. Through the gloom Fancy could make out the cloud of water that was lifted from the deck by the two turbo prop engines. The JBD came up and Fancy could hear the low moan of the engines as they went to full power. The wingtip lights came on and a few seconds later the plane accelerated down the deck and was flung off the ship only to be swallowed up by the night an instant later.

Now that his eyes had adjusted to the night he could make out the blue-shirted enlisted men coming toward the plane to break down the chains that held them to the deck.

Once the chains had been taken off one of the mules backed up to the plane and a tow bar was attached. They were towed to Cat Two on the bow. In order to save fuel they would start engines this side of the JBD. Fancy was sure they would be towed. What with the rain, limited visibility, and a slick deck, he figured the odds of being towed were increased in their favor. He was wrong and was given the signal to start the engines.

Both engines came on-line and everything settled down into the green. "Good alignment," Mirabal reported and signaled to Shrader to pull the cable that connected them to the ship's inertial navigation system.

The JBD came down and they taxied onto Cat Two. *If the truth be know* he thought to himself, *this is the toughest part of Naval aviation. Being flung off the pointy end of the boat into a night blacker than the inside of a cow is definitely not my favorite part of flying.* Wrestling the fear into the far recesses of his mind he turned his attention to the task at hand. Scanning the instruments one more time...all okay.

Turning on his exterior lights the shooter saluted the cockpit while he kept giving the full power signal with wand in his left hand. Fancy figured he was waiting for the bow to reach the bottom of its plunge into a trough between the swells.

Suddenly the shooter leaned forward and touched the wand to the deck. The deck must be rising. Immediately the plane shot forward.

No warning lights, rotate to eight degrees, airspeed good, he slapped the gear handle up.

"Positive rate of climb," Mirabal reported.

They climbed out quickly to twenty-one thousand feet. Flying in this weather wasn't much like flying at all. It seemed to Fancy that the world ended where the canopy began.

At this altitude they were above the clouds but there was enough turbulence to keep the plane moving around. Looking to his left he strained to see if Stash had joined up. The air was clear and the visibility was excellent and he was able to pick up Stash's plane five hundred feet off his port wing. *So far so good. Stash was coming along very nicely.* Fancy always had thought that making a night rendezvous was among the toughest things to do, especially for a nugget. As it was he was fighting a slight case of vertigo. *Yes, sir, he was coming along very nicely.*

"Departure, Desperado two zero two, switch to strike and climb to two five zero feet."

" Roger, Desperado two zero two, switching to strike and climbing."

He brought the stick back slightly and advanced the throttles, climbing out to twenty-five thousand feet.

"Desperado two zero two, this is Echo six zero two," came the voice of the controller in the E2-C. "Come to course three two zero and maintain present altitude. It looks like the Chinese have sent out a couple of Bears. It looks like there about, uh, two hundred miles out."

"Roger, Echo, coming to three two zero, maintian present altitude." Fancy then heard the same controller order Bagger and Stretch to continue their heading and altitude to cover the strike force.

"Desperado two zero six, did you copy, okay?"

"Roger on the copy, two zero two," Stash answered matter of factly.

"I think I've got something," said Mirabal. There at one hundred eighty miles. Looks like they're descending back into the clouds."

"We'll stay up here. No sense trying to take them head on in the clouds."

"Why tempt fate?" came back Mirabal with a chuckle. "Uh, it looks like they've leveled off at about eighteen thousand feet. Range is now one hundred sixty-five miles. Too bad we don't have a couple of AIM 54s."

Mirabal was referring to the Phoenix missile that had a range of over one hundred miles.

Fancy glanced at his own radar scope and noted the two dots coming toward them. The turbulence, he noted, had not let up.

"Range one hundred fifty miles," called out Mirabal, "and closing. I always wanted to say that."

"Are we living out some boyhood fantasy?" questioned Fancy.

"Exactamundo! I am, babe! The wily Communists coming toward us, loaded, if you will excuse the expression, for bear. We're all that stands between them and the destruction of the free world. Just like that movie, oh what the hell, oh, High Noon. You know Gary Cooper, the bad guys in black hats. You know?"

"Yeah, I know. I just never thought of High Noon before," answered Fancy, smiling to himself.

Easing the throttles forward a little, he called, "Desperado 206, let's pick up the pace a little and see what these guys have on their minds."

"Roger that, 202."

A few minutes later they had descended and closed on the two Chinese planes and had taken up station at their six. The two Chinese planes were flying in the clouds about a quarter of a mile apart.

"Hey, these guys aren't bears! Jesus, they're Backfires, TU-22s!"

"I can't believe these guys are plowing through the clouds like this. Did they actually think we couldn't find them in this soup?" muttered Fancy more to himself than to Mirabal.

"They can run, but they can't hide," returned Mirabal.

"206, you stay back here, I'm going to creep up and see if these guys have anything anybody might have to worry about. Let's make sure the TCS is up and functioning."

"TCS is up and functioning," responded Mirabal.

Fancy advanced the throttles slightly and the big fighter accelerated bringing them up closer to the two TU-22s. He had gone to missiles and was getting a strong tone from the Sidewinders. Deciding to take a closer look at the plane on his left he moved the stick slightly to port and advanced the throttles. At about that time the cloud cover seemed to evaporate and he could make out the big plane quite easily. Working the throttles with a deft touch Fancy brought the plane up and out to the left of the Chinese jet. As with the Bear, it was bare metal and seemed to have been polished to a high gloss. Looking at the sleek plane he noted that, like the F-14, the TU-22 had variable sweep wings which were presently swept at about 30 degrees.

Advancing the throttles again he drew up across from the cockpit and could see the pilot looking back at him. After flying alongside the plane for a couple of minutes he could make out the bulbous radar dome in the nose of the plane. *Hmmm, definitely ruins the lines of the plane* he thought to himself. *The Ruskis can sure make some pretty planes.* Taking a long look he could see that there was a huge missile in what would have been the bomb bay. "Looks like they're packing some heat, Rhino."

"Man, that is one big mother hanging out of that bomb bay. Looks like they're getting in some practice on the battle group."

"Just from the size of that mother they probably would have launched a while ago. Oh, oh, looks like he's turning. Stash, close on us, they're turning, looks like they're going to reverse course."

"Roger, closing on you, 202."

Fancy backed off another five hundred feet as the two TU-22s slowly came around and reversed course. He and Stash followed them around, retarding their throttles and letting the big planes pull away from them.

"206, let's trail them for a little ways just to make sure they're headed back to where they came from."

"Roger that, 202."

"Boy, that was a surprise," said Fancy. "I thought only the Russians had those. Must be selling hardware to the Chinese."

"Must be," replied Mirabal. "Their return didn't show any difference from the Bear we saw the other day. Same big cross section."

"I wasn't criticizing, I was just thinking out loud. Those were some big missiles they were carrying. If I remember right, and I saw what I think I saw, they must have been SA-6 Kingfish, air to surface missiles.

"Yeah, they've got active radar terminal guidance. If we would have taken out the plane they probably wouldn't have guided."

"Did you see us being tracked by the rear gunner?"

"Sure did."

"I definitely made note of that one as I came up to look them over. If I had to, I'd use a 'Winder if we had to get in close."

"Good choice," sighed Mirabal. "Looks like they're definitely headed back to where they came from."

"Two zero six, time to head back to the bird farm, unless you'd like to chase these guys."

"202, we've seen enough. We sure thought they were Bears too. Were those missiles hanging off the wings?"

"That they were. Probably SA-6 Kingfish."

"That'll give the Intel guys something to chew on."

"Okay, 206, we're going to head home, let's come to one four zero."

"Roger, one four zero, 202."

Settling in on their new course they found themselves again enveloped in clouds with a steady rain pelting the plane. Even at four hundred plus knots there was a film of water on the canopy.

He was distracted momentarily by a lightning flash directly ahead of them. Turbulence was also increasing. He was about to tell Stash they were going to see if they could climb out of the soup when there was a tremendous flash accompanied by a loud bang. Fancy thought it sounded like someone had struck the plane with a large hammer. They had been struck by lightning

Momentarily blinded by the bright flash he blinked his eyes furiously trying to get back his vision. Another few moments of rapid blinking and he began to be able to make out the instrument panel. Thank God they still had electrical power.

He flinches as there was another bright flash, though this one didn't seem as close. "How's everything back there, Rhino?"

"Not good, I think the radar is down for the count," came the curt reply. "I'm working on it, but, yeah, it's out. We must have been hit in the nose."

"Desperado 206, looks like we took a lightning strike. We're okay except for the radar."

"Two zero two, we saw it. You looked like a Christmas tree."

"206, you take the lead and we'll follow you home."

"Roger, taking the lead, 202 You want to climb back to 25 grand and see if we can get out of this?"

"Let's give it a try, 206."

Unfortunately, things were as bad at twenty-five thousand as they were at the lower altitude. Fancy hung on Stash's wing concentrating as he hadn't in a long time. Lose Stash and they would be swimming for it. He took solace in the deep breath he could draw. The oxygen tasted cool and rubbery, and strangely enough, reassuring. Around them the sky was strobed constantly by the lightning.

Surprisingly, at least to Fancy, the rest of the flight to the Enterprise was uneventful. They had been guided back to elevator three and were immediately lowered to the hanger deck. Once they were chocked down and had climbed down to the hard steel deck they immediately walked to the nose of the plane. The radome had a hole in it about the size of a fifty cent piece with black edges where the material had actually melted.

"You know, if I were flying with anyone else," said Mirabal, trying to hold back a smile, "I'd say that we're jinxed."

"What do you mean," said Fancy defensively.

"Things just seem to happen to you."

"To me! Last time I checked, there were two of us in this plane," Fancy shot back, holding up two fingers and putting them under Mirabal's nose.

"Like I said, if I were flying with anyone else," laughed Mirabal. "Come on let's get this debrief over with."

Fancy shook his head and followed Mirabal toward the equipment room. He turned and took one last look at the wounded plane. The hole in the nose looked huge from where he was standing. "Rhino!"

Mirabal turned, and looked at Fancy with a quizzical look on his face. "What?"

"You know the only reason I fly off this boat don't you?"

"I thought, that you just loved flying."

"Nope, I just do it for the great dental plan we get."

Mirabal laughed. "Well, I just do it for the great food you know."

The debrief took an hour and a half. Once again the intelligence troops were happy as well as somewhat surprised that the Chinese had TU-22s.

*Enterprise* and her consorts continued through the Taiwan Strait. Almost every flight by the ship's squadrons resulted in a meeting with TU-95s or TU-22s. In every instance the Chinese planes turned and retreated in the direction they had come from.

In a briefing, four hours after Fancy's encounter with the Backfire, one of the intelligence officers, Bobby "BB" Braxton told the assembled pilots and RIOs that the Chinese had acquired some TU-22s and had made some improvements to the avionics and had reengined the planes with a more powerful variant of the original Kuznetsov NK-144 engine. The missile, he told his attentive audience, was no doubt a SA-4 Kitchen, three of which could be carried on short range missions.

"The Russians," BB went on, "are hurting for hard currency and will sell to anybody right now. Don't be surprised to see SU-27s and MiG 29s."

Moose raised his hand. "BB, are there going to be any other surprises?"

"Moose, your guess is as good as mine. The Chinese are spending a great deal of money to upgrade all aspects of their military. Right now they have the second largest economy in the world. They intend to be a major player not only in Asia but elsewhere as well." Shrugging his shoulders, he continued, "In other words don't be surprised at what you might see. As far as their flying out toward the battle group and then turning around when they're intercepted, we think they're going to school on us just as we're trying to find out about them. Several of you have reported lots of antennae on the TU-95s, and we figure they're gathering information electronically and otherwise. Keep your heads and energy up."

Fancy heard Moose growl, "Give me kinetic energy any day and I'll take his potential energy and shove it up his ass."

Fancy chuckled in reply.

# 12

The battle group had cleared the Taiwan Strait and had entered the South China Sea. "Desperado two zero zero," this is Echo six one three, come to course two seven zero. Looks like we've got some visitors inbound. Two TU-22s and it looks like they've got an escort of two fighters. Probably they came out of their base at Heifang. Range is one hundred fifty miles at one six zero feet."

Fancy, taking a quick look out at Moose, brought the F-14 around in a tight turn and settled on course 270. Moose settled in on his port side, both planes slipping into a loose deuce formation. That way they would be able to cover each others' six.

"Okay, Moose, are we picking up anything?"

"Yeah, bogeys at one hundred thirty miles and closing fast. They're low."

"Moose, you got your TCS up and running."

"Roger on the TCS, Gator."

The six planes were closing at a rate of nearly a thousand miles an hour.

"Fifty miles, I've got some dots." called Mirabal, three minutes later. "These guys are really movin'!"

"Dash Two, let's pick it up a little, when we convert you take the guys on the right."

"Rog, guys on the right," answered Moose.

"Gator, they're padocked I could shoot all six right now." "What do the fighters look like? Have you got any kind of decent picture?"

"Yeah, I do. The big mothers are definitely TU-22s. Uh, the fighters don't appear to be MiGs."

"Oh?"

"Definitely not MiGs."

By this time Fancy and Moose started to rack their planes around in order to convert to the Backfire's six o'clock. The Chinese planes maintained their course. As Fancy and Moose settled in at their six o'clock, the Chinese planes instead of reversing course started to accelerate. The two fighters eased out further from the now accelerating bombers.

"Oh oh, looks like they're playing a new game," Fancy called out, at the same time advancing his own throttles. "Let's not let them get out of range, Moose."

"Roger that," responded Moose.

Fancy and Moose closed to within a quarter mile of the Chinese planes. "You were right, Rhino. Those aren't MiGs. I think they're J-8 IIs."

"Could be, I can't tell from this angle, but they are definitely not MiGs. TCS is rolling."

"I want to close and get a better look. Moose, I'm to close on the fast mover."

Easing the throttles forward, the F-14 was able to move closer to the Chinese fighter, easing into the Chinese plane's seven o' clock position. The plane was fairly big, with a single tail, swept wings and a long nose, painted sky blue, with the side number, 81891 in red under the cockpit. The nose was painted black. Two fuel tanks hung off both wings and there were two missiles outside of the fuel tanks. Easing his plane forward he could see the pilot twisting around in his seat in order to get a better look at him. His face was hidden under a dull blue helmet and the obligatory oxygen mask. Fancy then noticed some kind of a ventral fin under the engine nozzle. The canopy, Fancy thought, did not offer a great rearward view due to the long slender bulge that ran from the back of the canopy to the vertical stabilizer.

Almost as if on cue the Chinese planes started to turn to starboard and reverse course.

Fancy was still looking at the Chinese fighter when he was astonished to see the canopy come off the plane followed a split second later by the ejection seat as it rocketed the pilot and the seat he was strapped into out of the plane.

"Fancy was almost too shocked to say anything for several seconds as he watched the seat fall away and pea soup green parachute deploy. "Moose, the left hand fighter guy just ejected!"

"You didn't shoot him did you?"

"Are you kidding. He's got a good chute."

Taking his eyes off the pilot who was now swinging back and forth under the canopy of the parachute, Fancy caught sight of the Chinese plane flying straight and level. Just before he shifted his eyes back to the now descending pilot, the Chinese plane exploded.

"He must have had some problem, the damn plane just blew up, Rhino! Moose, did you see that?"

"I saw it go off the scope, Gator. Are you sure you didn't slip a missile up his tailpipe?"

"I'm sure," Fancy chuckled. "Let's follow him down and make sure he's okay. Rhino, make the call, let's let the battle group know what's happened."

After a few seconds Mirabal responded. "The E2 is relaying the message. What are we going to do?"

"I think we should stick around and make sure the guy is in his raft or what ever it is he's got."

"Desperado 200, let's let him swim for it. These guys wouldn't give a rip about us."

"Desperado 209, we don't know that and I don't want to find out, but I think we should at least make sure he's okay."

"Roger that," came the reluctant reply.

Fancy, who had been keeping an eye on the dangling pilot rolled the F-14 into a ninety degree left hand turn and started to circle the falling Chinese pilot in a constant descending left hand turn. At five hundred feet he saw the pilot hit the water and the parachute start to crumble like a broken toy. His thoughts immediately went back to FASO training at Miramar. He could only imagine how the man in the water must feel.

"Gator," called Moose, "he's in the water. Can you see him?"

"I see him, Moose, it looks like he's trying to get into a raft. Let's go to GUARD to see if he's got a radio."

"Moose, you stay on GUARD, and we'll let the E2 know that he's in the water."

"Echo six one three, the Chinese pilot is in the water and it looks like he's okay." Mirabal, as usual, was on the ball.

"Desperado 200, what's your fuel state?"

"Echo, we've got, uh, 4200 pounds."

"Desperado, the Stump has launched a helo. ETA is about twenty minutes. The powers that be don't think the Chinese have anything that can get to him. We're going to get him out of the water. CAG wants you to hang around and direct the helo to his location."

"Roger that Echo. We'll keep him in sight and pinpoint him for the helo."

"Moose, is your fuel still good?"

"We're at 5,100 pounds. We're okay."

"Moose, let's go to a thousand feet, we've got good visibility and we can conserve a little fuel."

"Okay, let me go down first and let him know we're here and on his side."

"Good idea, Moose."

As Fancy put the plane in a gentle climb, while maintaining a sighting on the downed pilot he saw Moose fly over him wagging his wings back and forth and then start to climb.

second Fancy wondered what he had done wrong. Van Gundy extended his hand, "Nice work out there today, Fancy."

"Thank you, sir," answered Fancy, wondering whether the CAG was talking about the TU-22 or the downed pilot.

"You did good, Gator," continued Robinson, extending his own hand. "Get rid of your speed jeans and report back to the roof. One of the helos is going to take you guys over the Stump. Seems like the Chinese pilot would like to thank you in person. Are you up for it?"

Fancy looked at Mirabal, who shrugged as if to say why not. "Aye aye, sir, give us five minutes." He and Mirabal hurried to the equipment room to rid themselves of their helmets and g-suits.

Ten minutes later they were on one of the ship's helos headed for the destroyer Stump. Moose looked over at Fancy and and shook his head back and forth. Fancy knew what he was thinking, *I wouldn't want to fly one of these things either.* After the relative smooth quiet flight in the Tomcat, Fancy felt uneasy with the shaking and noise of the engine, directly over their heads, somewhat distracting and irritating. He also realized that he felt uncomfortable when someone else was doing the flying.

As they disembarked from the SH-60, he almost fell as he climbed out on the rolling pitching deck of the destroyer. Mirabal caught him before he fell. "Whoa, Gator, take it easy! Good thing the ocean's not too rough."

"Man, there's a lot of movement on one of these things," he said, as they were led through the hanger of the destroyer.

"Makes you appreciate the Enterprise, doesn't it," laughed Moose.

"Bet your ass it does," put in Moose. "I'll take big any day, the bigger the better."

Coming out of the hanger, they were met by a Lt. Commander. "Afternoon, welcome to the Stump. I'm Commander Terry, the exec. You the guys that kept watch over this guy?"

"Afternoon, sir," said Fancy as he extended his hand. "Yes, we saw him eject and watched the nylon letdown. How's he doing?"

"He's fine, pretty anxious to meet you. Follow me. He's in my cave."

After following Terry up a deck and down a passage way they arrived at Terry's room. Terry gave a sharp rap, opened the door, and went in, followed by the four aviators.

Fancy hadn't thought much about what the Chinese pilot would look like, but he was not prepared for the man they met. As Fancy and the other entered the small room, the Chinese pilot got up from the bunk he had been sitting on.

Immediately Fancy was drawn to the height of the man who now faced them. *The man looked more like a linebacker than a pilot,* Fancy thought. He also had a magnificent handle bar mustache. His hair was close cropped and he was wearing what was probably a set of Terry's khakis, which, appeared to Fancy, were at least two sizes two small.

Terry nodded to the man and said, "Gentleman, this is Pilot First Class Hai Feng, People's Liberation Army, Air Force."

"Most people call me Henry," the man said in perfect English.

The surprise must have registered rather obviously on all their faces.

"UCLA, class of 90," he continued, smiling at their surprise. "Maybe you were expecting pidgin?"

"Uh, I didn't know what to expect, to tell you the truth. What happened up there? Your plane looked fine and all of a sudden you were out of there."

"My fire warning light came on and my experience with the J-8 is when that light comes on it's time to step out."

"I saw the plane explode after your chute deployed, so you sure made the right decision."

"I would like to thank you for covering me and waiting until the helicopter arrived. I thought I was going to be out there for a while. Our Air Force does not have the rescue capability you guys have. I sure appreciate it. I have a wife and a son who will also be grateful."

Moose, looking a bit sheepish, injected, "We were glad to be in a position to help."

Mirabal cleared his throat. "I spent a little time in the water between the U.S. and Hawaii, so I kind of know how you feet. That ocean seems absolutely endless when you're sitting in a raft."

"Yes," answered Feng, "I was feeling pretty bad when I hit the water. When I saw your planes orbiting I was hoping there was a helicopter coming. When I heard it I started to shout, 'Over here, over here,' when they were probably three minutes away."

"Were you born in the states or did you just go to school there," asked Mirabal. "Honestly, I was real surprised when you started to speak."

"I could see that right away. I went to the states to study engineering at UCLA. Played a little intramural football and basketball."

"So how did you wind up in the Air Force?" asked Tom Bui, Moose's RIO.

Feng grinned and then laughed out loud. "I was majoring in aeronautical engineering and," laughing again, "I saw the movie Top Gun. I was hooked. I managed to take some private flying lessons through the school. When I returned to China I was able to put my tiny bit of flying experience to good use for my country. I would give anything to fly the F-14."

"Ahh, MTV goes to war," laughed Fancy.

"Exactly," beamed Feng. "I must have played that CD a million times. Drives my wife crazy every time I put it on."

"Where did you meet your wife?" asked Cheese.

"I met her at Burbank airport where I took the flying lessons. She looks a little like Pam Anderson, you know the babe on Bay Watch. I'd show you a picture but I don't carry it with me when I fly, although I'm starting to rethink that."

"How does she like living in China?" asked Fancy.

"She seems to like it very much. Jan is very good at picking up new things and she's picked up the language like you wouldn't believe. She remains somewhat of a curiosity, however." He grinned, "My fellow squadron members certainly like to be around her."

"I bet they do," croaked Moose.

"You said you were flying a J-8?"

"Yes, the J-8 is a plane that was developed entirely in China. It's no doubt a generation behind the F-14, but we've learned a great deal and are working on several promising projects. The J-8 is a good plane, not a great plane but a good solid plane, when it doesn't catch fire that is."

"How he's getting back to the mainland?" asked Bui.

"We'll pulling be out of the battle group after you guys helo back to Enterprise and we'll take him to Hong Kong."

"Hong Kong!" said Mirabal increduously. "Are you guys going to get some liberty there?"

"It looks that way, we'll be there for about forty-eight hours."

After a few more minutes of small talk, the men shook hands, said their goodbyes, and were helicoptered back to the Enterprise.

As they walked across the steel deck Fancy turned to Moose. "Moose, would you still like to let that guy swim for it?"

Moose, shaking his head, smiled sheepishly, "Ahh, I didn't really mean it. You know…I was just talkin'. You should have seen the look on your face when he stood up and started to talk."

"You could have knocked me over with a feather. I couldn't believe it. UCLA? I was more than surprised."

"Shoot," said Mirabal, "I forgot to ask him how he managed to get his oxygen mask on with that mustache. He seemed like a pretty good guy to me."

"The truth is you only see another pilot after you start to talk," said Moose. "I liked him."

"Good thing we didn't tell him that you thought he should swim for it," chimed in Cheese.

"Cheese, you disappoint me. You're supposed to stick with your bubbas."

Cheese clapped him on the shoulder. "You did notice, Moose, that I didn't mention one word. Not one word."

"Good thing too," smiled Moose. "Come on, I'll buy you dinner, I'm starved."

Whether it was coincidence or the Chinese being grateful to get their pilot back, no one knew, but the Chinese quit sending out any kind of plane or ship to keep an eye on the battle group. The *Enterprise* and her escorts headed toward Singapore.

When they were a day's sailing from the now much desired liberty port, air ops were halted. Fancy and Bagger were jogging on deck on what had turned out to be a beautiful warm day.

Ducking around one of the S-3s, they met Poncho and a puffing red-faced Big Wave coming the other way. Stopping under the wing of the S-3, Poncho beamed, "Hey did you guys hear where the squadron is going to be setting up our Admin?" An Admin was the party headquarters when the members of the squadron got liberty.

"No, we haven't heard yet. Where?" wheezed Bagger.

"Raffles, you know the world famous hotel? You have heard of it haven't you?" asked Big Wave.

"Well sure I have," exclaimed Bagger indignantly. "You think I just fell off the the turnip truck or somethin'?"

"The thought never crossed our mind, right, Wave?" needled Poncho.

"Gator, are you going to be able to get off this floating funny farm this time?" queried Poncho.

"As far as I know. I know I don't have a dog to worry about. Where is the little beast?"

"In our room. Wave put him in one of the cabinets."

"You've got to get rid of that thing. You're going to wind up with your ass in a sling if you don't. Worse yet, Mongo's going to put my ass in a sling just on general principals even if he catches you guys with the mutt. You got any plans in that direction by chance?"

"Mutt, what do you mean mutt? He's a champion, man," spluttered Big Wave. "But you're right. The Master At Arms almost caught us yesterday. You guys got any ideas?"

"We could probably find him a good home in Singapore. There must be some kid that would like a dog," chided Fancy.

"In Singapore? Are you kidding? The Chinese eat dogs. Don't they?" accused Schwartz.

"I don't think people in Singapore are Chinese. I think they're Malaysian."

"Malaysian—Chinese, I bet they eat dogs too," grumbled Poncho. "But you're right, we've got to get it off the boat. It isn't good for the dog and it's not going to be good for us if Matsen catches us. We can take him off the same way we got him on and we'll see what happens."

As Bagger and Fancy continued their jogging, Bagger asked, "Have you ever heard of Raffles?"

"Never heard of it. Couldn't be too bad could it?"

*Enterprise* and the rest of the battle group dropped anchor in the outer harbor a third of a mile off shore. Fancy and most of the rest of the Gunfighters were standing on the flight deck waiting to get on board one of the four launches that would take them ashore. Pilots and enlisted alike were dressed in their whites. Without the movement of the ship, there was no wind over the deck. Even though it was 0730, the heat was already starting to build. Nobody seemed to mind. Everyone was anxious to get off the ship and see something besides other sailors and gray paint. Off in the distance they could see skyscrapers jutting into the sky.

"You lookin' forward to this, Rhino?"

"I can hardly wait. This is really makes everything we put up with worthwhile. Can you believe that skyline. It looks more like New York than I would have thought any Asian country would look like."

"It sure is hot," said Fancy glancing at his watch, "and it's not even eight in the morning yet."

"You gotta figure we're only one degree north of the equator, so it's bound to be pretty warm."

"It's going to be beyond warm pretty soon," said Fancy as he wiped his brow with his arm.

Doc Su came up beside the two aviators. "Good morning, gentleman. It looks like a splendid day to go ashore."

"Any day is a good day to get off the boat, Doc. You ever been here before?"

"Yes, once before when I was attached to the *Kitty Hawk*. It's a most interesting place. You'll be very impressed. In fact it is made up of the main island and fifty-five smaller islands. It's not as large as Hong Kong, but is a very crowded country with more than eleven thousand people per square mile."

"Well, one thing that impresses me is the fact that if you're caught with drugs, the penalty is death. Isn't this the place that kid was cained because he did some kind of vandalism?"

"This is the very place Lt. Mirabal. They are very strict. In fact even chewing gum is outlawed."

Mirabal raised his eyebrows. "They definitely don't screw around. I wonder how that would work in the states?"

"Sometimes I wish we could find out," said Bagger. "But, it'll never happen, at least not in our life time."

After a twenty minute launch ride they found themselves on Cliff Pier ready to see the sights. "Let's go find this Raffles, see what it's like and then take a look around, what do you say?" invited Bagger.

"Let's do it, sounds good to me," answered Fancy, as he started to walk toward one of the many cabs parked by the curb at the head of the pier.

During the taxi ride to the hotel the three aviators sharing the cab could only gawk and point at the very metropolitan city. Raffles turned out to be a beautiful white hotel that looked like it had come right out of a thirties movie. Their room was spacious and, most important, Fancy thought, air-conditioned. After changing into civilian clothes, exploring the room and the grounds of the hotel, Mirabal, Bagger, and Fancy set off to get in all the sight—seeing they could squeeze into two days.

Thirty-two hours later Fancy fell back with a sigh of relief on the king size bed in the second of two bedrooms of their suite. Bagger had already collapsed on the other bed. "I don't know about you pardner, but I feel whipped. Is there anything we haven't seen?"

"I don't know and I don't care right now. Man, this place is warm!"

"Warm? Warm? That is not even close to being the understatement of the year. Besides, it's not the heat…"

"It's the humidity that gets you every time," finished Bagger as he closed his eyes savoring the air conditioning washing over the two pilots like cool ocean water over two beached whales.

"Ahh, this is the life, I could get use to this," sighed Fancy.

"Me too, this kind of life could get to be addictive. It feels funny laying here though.

"Oh, how's that?" questioned Fancy, who couldn't think of anything but laying on a comfortable bed, in a room that was cooled to the point of being almost arctic in temperature.

"You do notice that this room is not moving around and it's so quiet. I love that."

"Yeah, now that you mention it," groaned Fancy, as he stretched, "the quiet part is great. All that noise on the boat is something you just get used to and you don't think about it much, until there's no noise."

Mirabal came to the doorway. "Are you guys going to go down to get something to eat pretty soon?"

"I was thinking of having room service send something up, but, yeah, I'm going down. How 'bout you Gator?"

"Closing his eyes Fancy sighed, "I want to go down and call Cody. What are we sixteen hours ahead?"

"On the west coast? Yeah. I noticed when we came in with all those clocks at the front desk."

"That makes it one thirty in Carlsbad. Maybe I'll wait awhile and let her get her beauty sleep."

"Like she needs it," grinned Bagger who ducked the pillow Fancy threw at him. "Come on, let's get a move on."

Thirty minutes later the three men arrived on the main floor of the elegant hotel. Fancy was mesmerized by the many languages and cosmopolitan atmosphere. As he turned around to catch up with with his friends, he bumped into a man in a Philippine Air uniform. Extending his arm to keep the man from falling, he said, "Whoa, excuse me. Didn't mean to knock you down."

"It's okay," the man returned. "There's certainly a great deal to distract one's attention."

Fancy was about to return to his original course when he spun around on his heel, almost knocking the man down again. "Geez, I'm sorry, again. I just thought of something. Do you know a Captain DeLeon? I think she flies seven forty sevens."

"This is a small world," the man said. "You wouldn't believe who I flew into Singapore with?"

"You're kiddin' me?"

"No. In fact," he said looking at his watch, "she had to meet with some of our maintenance people, and she'll probably be here within an hour, I would say."

Fancy shook his head disbelief. "Will you see her when she arrives?"

"The man shrugged his shoulders and shook his head. "Probably not. I'm going to get out of this uniform and go out with some other members of the cabin crew."

"Well, if you do see her, could you tell her Desperado 205 is here, and would like to meet her."

"Will do and you are…?"

"Dan Fancy, I'm in the Navy. I fly off the Enterprise."

The two men shook hands and Fancy hurried to catch up with his friends.

"Having a little trouble with situational awareness, compadre?" laughed Bagger as Fancy joined the two men at the bar.

"Looked like it didn't it?" grinned Fancy. "I almost knocked the guy down twice, but you'll never guess who he flew in here with?"

"He's wearing a Philippine Air uniform," said Mirabal, so it must be the pilot of that 747 that was being 'escorted' by the MiGs."

"You're so clever, oh mighty, RIO. That's right. Small world, huh?"

Little by little the rest of the squadron began to filter into the bar area of the hotel. Fancy, Bailey, Moose, Killer, and Mirabal were standing at the far end of the ornate bar admiring the palatial surroundings of the room. Moose, taking a long pull on a beer, observed, "This is one beautiful domicile."

"Domicile? Domicile!" chided Killer. "Moose, you're going uptown on us. Domicile?"

"Listen, you guys could use a little class. I mean, we are, by order of Congress, officers and gentleman."

"In that case," exclaimed Poncho, "a person of class and good upbringing, not to mention an officer and gentleman, should buy the next round. Am I right, gentleman?"

"You're right! Of course you're right!" came a chorus of aviators.

"Barkeep!" declared Moose, spinning around on his heel toward the bar, "Set 'em up for my esteemed squadron associates!"

As the bartender delivered Fancy's soft drink a group of men in uniforms came to the door of the bar. Pausing briefly to take in their surroundings they came through the door and headed directly to the bar. Moose standing on the far end, drinking his beer moved down to give them room. Upon closer inspection of the men's uniforms he saw that they were Australian.

One of the men, a drink in hand turned to survey what was going on around him. He was fairly tall. His blond hair was short and neatly combed. At first glance he seemed handsome. On closer inspection one could make out a scar in the left hand corner of his mouth which made him appear to be sneering at everyone and everything. Fancy looking at his rank saw that he was a full commander. "Bloody room is filled with bloody fucking Yanks."

Moose turned to take a brief look at the man, looking at Fancy, he shrugged his shoulders, raised his eyebrows, and moved away from the Aussie toward Fancy.

Mirabal, who had been looking toward the door of the bar said, "Hey, there's someone in a Philippine Air uniform, Gator. You think that could be her?"

Fancy turned quickly to see what Mirabal was looking at and in doing so bumped into Moose, who in turn collided with the Australian spilling his beer over his pristine white uniform. "Bloody hell! What's the matter with you, you bloody dwarf!"

Moose, as surprised as anyone, said, "Whoa, I'm sorry."

"Sorry, sorry!" spluttered the now agitated officer, wiping off his uniform.

"It was an accident. Let me buy you another beer," apologized Moose, extending a linen napkin.

The enraged Australian was having none of it and slapped the napkin away and out of Moose's hand. "You simple-minded bastard, get away from me!" he snapped. "Bloody ignorant yank!"

Shaking his head Moose countered. "Listen, it was an accident, I'm sorry. Let me pay to have your uniform cleaned."

"Just like a bloody Yank, think you can buy your way out of anything don't you? Stupid bugger."

"No, actually I don't, but I would do it to be polite and because it might be the right thing to do. After all we are allies aren't we?"

"Technically, yes," the man snarled. "But as far as I'm concerned, you and every other bloody yank can go straight to bloody hell. I ought to break you in two but that would be too easy. I'd probably get in trouble some how, seeing that there isn't much of you to begin with."

"Well, don't let that stop you, if you think you can," retorted Moose, who had finally had his fill. "One more crack like that though and I'll pound your inconsiderate head so far up your ass you'll need to drop your pants to say hello."

The big Aussie suddenly drew back his fist. Just as suddenly before the fist could move toward Moose's face, it stopped, seeming suspended in air. Fancy had moved over and had grabbed the man's balls. As Fancy squeezed the Australian's eyes started to bulge.

"Like my friend said, he's just trying to do the right thing. If you don't want to take advantage of his offer, that's fine, but let it go either way. If you understand and agree, but can't talk, nod your head," said Fancy in a low, quiet voice, giving the man's privates another sharp squeeze.

The nod of the head told Fancy that he definitely had the man's attention. "If you'd like to stay, no problem, or if you want to go, that's certainly no problem either. We don't want any trouble. Do we understand each other?"

"Yes," squeaked the Australian, his voice about four octaves higher than it had been when he entered the bar.

Fancy released him and took a step back. His friends, now only realizing that something was happening, started to gather around him.

Giving Fancy a dirty look, he mustered all the dignity he could, saying, "Come on, mates, let's get the hell out of here. This used to be a rather good place to drink."

After the Australians had left, Moose extended his hand. "Thanks, Gator."

"I know you could have taken him, but I didn't think it would be worth all the hassle with the guys in the head shed. Let me buy you another beer."

After one of the best steak and lobster dinners he had ever had, Fancy made his way to the lobby. Finding a secluded corner with an ornate old time phone, he sat down in a plush wing chair and dialed Cody's number in California. He felt bad that it was still early in the morning there, he decided to call anyway. After several rings a slumberous voice answered. "Hello."

Until then, he really hadn't processed how much he missed her. "Cody, it's Dan. I'm sorry to…"

"Oh, Dan, I'm so glad you called."

"I know it's really early there, but I haven't been able to reach you at a decent hour. Anyway, how are you?"

"Oh, I'm fine, much better now. It's so good to hear your voice…I've really missed you."

Feeling his knees go slightly weak, he managed to stammer, "I've missed you too, so much. I'm calling from Singapore, can you believe it? Can you hear me all right? How's Amanda?"

"Just like you're next door, and she's fine. It's unbelievable you're so far away. You sound so close."

"This is a fascinating place. Boy, sometime I hope we can come here and see it together. It's a beautiful place and I understand the shopping is great."

"Umm, I can hardly wait. How is everything going? You must be doing something right," she laughed, "you got off the ship this time."

"I tried to stay on the straight and narrow. It's great being off the boat. I'm calling from a hotel named Raffles. Have you ever heard of it?"

"Yes, I have. I've seen some pictures of it. It looks like something in a thirties movie."

"That was exactly my thought when I climbed out of the taxi."

After a few more minutes of idle conversation, Fancy was about to say goodbye when he spotted Poncho and Big Wave passing through the lobby with the golf bag containing Short Round. Suddenly an idea tore through his mind. "Cody, would you like to do a favor for Poncho and Big Wave?"

"Well…sure, what is it?"

"When Enterprise was in Hawaii, Poncho and Wave rescued a puppy from some of the locals and brought it back to the ship. It's kind of been the squadron's mascot, but it's getting to be a real hassle for them hiding it out. Dogs aren't exactly welcome on ships mind you." He heard her chuckle.

"Anyway, Shortround, as we dubbed him needs a home. How would Amanda like a dog. He's pretty cute and probably won't get much bigger than he is now. In fact, now he fits in a golf bag, and he's house, uh, make that boat trained. So…"

"I bet you could sell ice to the Eskimos. Sure, Amanda would love a dog. It might be good for her to have a little extra responsibility and have to think of someone else's needs. Do I get to come and get it?"

"Oh, I wish. That's what I've got to work on now. If I can solve that little problem, is it okay if I call you back?"

"You better, sailor or I'll never forgive you. I love you."

"Oh, Cody, I love you so much. I just can't believe how much I've missed you. Hopefully, I'll be talking to you after a while."

Sighing, he hung up the phone, wondering what it would be like to come home to Cody every single night. A sliver of doubt crept through him. Maybe the Navy as a career wasn't for him after all. Chastising himself and thinking this was no time in the cruise to let himself get distracted he headed back to the restaurant.

As he was coming abreast of the elevators a tall, attractive women exited the furthermost elevator. Deciding to take a chance he caught up to her as she walked toward the front entrance. "Excuse me. Excuse me."

The woman turned, looking at him skeptically. She was a very striking woman and Fancy figured she must have been hit on more than a few times by strange men. "Yes," she answered, somewhat cooly.

"Uh, you don't know me, well you do, kind of…I'm Desperado 205."

For a moment a puzzled look crossed her beautiful face. Then she broke into a smile. "Navy, F-14, North Koreans. I certainly do remember you. How are you?"

"Fine, and it's very good to meet you. One of your crew told me you were staying here, I hope you don't mind?"

"Certainly not. It's really good to finally put a face with that most welcome voice. I wasn't sure where or if I would be landing. I"ll never forget that night," she said, shaking her head. "Listen, I'd love to buy you dinner. Are you busy right now?"

Fancy paused. "Uh, well, uh, I was going to ask you to do me a favor."

"Name it, what can I do for you, within reason that is," she said.

Taking a very deep breath, Fancy decided the best course of action would be to just plunge ahead." "Our squadron, that is two guys in our squadron managed to smuggle a dog on board when we were in Pearl Harbor. The heats on and they need to get the dog off the boat." Pausing again trying to gauge her reaction and seeing the beginnings of a faint smile he figured he might be looking at a kindred spirit.

Rushing on, "What I was wondering was do you fly into L.A. and could you possibly get this dog there. If you could I have someone who could take it off your hands."

Pursing her lips and twisting her mouth around from a frown to somewhat of a grin, "You must live right because after we fly back to Manila, my next flight is to LAX. I'll be in Manila for two days though." With that a huge grin spread across her face and she tried in vain to keep from laughing. Finally, when she could contain it no longer she began to laugh."

Fancy, starting to see the humor in the situation, started to laugh too. Bystanders and passers by alike, turned their attention to the two people laughing, until they were both doubled up with laughter. Fancy felt as if he might collapse right there in the floor.

Mirabal, coming out of the restaurant saw Fancy and a very attractive woman laughing their heads off. Knowing who the woman must be he walked over. Fancy put out his arm to steady himself. Finally pulling himself together he turned toward Mirabal. "Lt. Mirabal, this is Captain DeLeon. Captain DeLeon, this is my good friend and RIO, Tony Mirabal. He's the guy that got us where we needed to be so expediently that night."

Rhino stuck out his hand, looking for any kind of engagement or wedding ring, "It's very good to meet you, Captain DeLeon. That was quite a night wasn't it?"

"Janelle," she returned, extending her hand, "and yes it was a night to remember. Thanks to you two though, I'm here to talk, and, maybe even laugh about it. I suppose you're part of this conspiracy with the dog?"

Rolling his eyes and chuckling to himself, "Oh yeah, the whole squadron except the XO is in on it."

"Captain DeLeon, uh Janelle, has agreed to help us out of this situation."

"Oooohhhh, I wondered what was so funny. I kind of figured that's what you two were talking about."

After a few more minutes of small talk the final arrangements were made. It was decided that the dog would have to be kept in the golf bag to be put aboard the 747 for the trip back to Manila.

True to her word, DeLeon bought them dinner, or more accurately she bought Mirabal another dinner. When Fancy walked out of the restaurant he left a completely stuffed Mirabal and Janelle DeLeon at the table engaged in conversation.

Making his way to the phone he called Cody again. "Good morning again," he whispered into the phone, when she answered.

"Good morning again to you," she said sleepily. "It's still nice to hear your voice. I'm glad you called back."

"Well, it looks like you have a dog—for better or for worse. On second thought let's make it for better. I think you'll both like him. "Its coming by way of Manila…"

After giving her the whole story he found himself trying to find a way to stay on the phone longer. "I don't want to hang up. I really miss you."

"Dan, I can't tell you how much I miss you. After we finish I'm going to sit down and write you a long letter."

"I'll have something to look forward to. I'll write too. I love you." Reluctantly he clicked the receiver while holding on to the phone, trying to keep her close to him for a minute longer.

*Enterprise* weighed anchor twelve hours later, setting a course for Australia, sailing southeast between the islands of Sumatra and Borneo, part of the populous country of Indonesia. Two hours later Fancy and Mirabal were blasted off cat two into a cobalt blue sky.

"Landing checklist," said Fancy, picking out the ship as a speck on the horizon. They went through it quickly and perfunctorily, not cutting any corners but not dragging it out either.

"Ball, three point oh," said Fancy.

"Roger Ball," came the reply from the ship. Fancy recognized Badrod's voice.

Centering the ball and with just a little dip he worked the landing centerline to the right working the throttles in minute, sure moves not wanting to over control the plane. If working the throttles were an art, Fancy felt himself one of the masters at that moment. Not bragging he reminded himself but having confidence and a surety that made him feel good. Getting things just right the ball stayed centered, the lineup was on target, and the angle-of-attack was out of a text book…and they caught the three wire.

Walking across the steel deck they met Moose and his RIO coming up to the deck to man the alert five plane. "Guess what?" growled Moose, as he stopped in front of them.

"What's up, did Matsen finally find out about the dog?"

"Much worse. We've reversed course, we're headed for the Gulf."

"I noticed the ship was headed one hundred eighty degrees from the time we took off. I just thought the wind had shifted and they were hunting for wind over the deck," sighed Fancy, removing his helmet and running his hand throught his hair.

"What's the deal? Is Saddam Insane starting to screw around again?" asked Mirabal. "I bet that llittle bit of good news went over big?"

"Not much was said, but a lot of faces got real long in a big hurry. I don't think it's really sunk in yet, especially since we had some pretty good liberty in Singapore. Captain Bedley came up on the 1MC and made the announcement to the whole crew."

"They should rename *Enterprise* Nine One One," yawned Mirabal. "So far we've been jumping from one hot spot to another."

"Seriously," said Moose, "I'd rather be out here with a purpose instead of just flying around the flagpole. It makes the time go faster, at least for me. Don't tell anybody I said so though." He shrugged, raising his eyebrows.

"Did the skipper call a meeting?" asked Fancy.

"No, when we saw him just before we come up to the roof, he said he didn't know anything, other than what Bedley's announcement told everybody."

"Good," said Fancy, "I'm going to get some paperwork cleared up and then I'm going to hit the rack."

"Come on Cheese, we'd better man up or we'll be hearing about it. See you guys later," said Moose as he and Cheese walked toward their plane.

As they took off their equipment and put it away, Fancy paused, and looked at Mirabal, "What do you think about what Moose said, about being on the tip of the spear so to speak?"

"That's what it's all about, it's what we've trained for, yeah, I'm kind of glad to be going to the Gulf. If there's one guy I'd like to kick right in the ass, it's Sadam. The guy's a jerk of the first order. Who knows, maybe we'll get a chance to put some hurt on him."

Fancy nodded in the affirmative. "You know when Moose told us, I was glad, but I thought at the same time, maybe I was going off the deep end. I could really care less about going to Australia, not that it's a bad place or anything, but I want to be where the action is."

Mirabal smiled. "Well, for whatever it's worth, I don't think you're weird, at least not too weird, I mean after all you're a pilot, you know, you could have been a RIO, but…" he continued, clapping Fancy on the back.

The squadron gathered around Matsen by the CAG bird, hoping to hear what was going on and why they were suddenly headed for the Gulf. "XO," called out Bagger, "why the sudden one eighty away from Australia?" Bagger, for one had really wanted to visit the land down under.

"Our crony in Iraq, well maybe that's not a good choice of words, seems to be moving a great many of his troops around, especially Republican Guard units. In the north, while he hasn't exactly gone after the Kurds, he' doing a lot of posturing, threatening, harassing in a lot of ways. What really has the wheels concerned is the sudden build up of his air force. It seems that he's been able to acquire quite a few MiGs and SU-27s."

"I thought Russia wasn't going to sell any more hardware to him?" interjected Killer.

"Clever bastard that he is, he got them through a third party—India. India bought newer models and sent the older units on to you-know-who. It's reported that he's paying some disgruntled former East German pilots to bring his guys up to snuff. Hussein says he just wants to fly pilgrims to their home towns as they come back from Saudi Arabia."

"Yeah, right, how many "pilgrims" can you get in a MiG," chided Stretch Gerlicki, holding up two fingers on each hand to form quotation marks.

"What Saddam's guys are up to is flying right up to the fence of the No-Fly Zone and even crossing it when the cover is thin or nonexistent. As you know in the past we've rushed troops over there when things start to get crazy, but I guess it's gotten expensive and they don't want to send people half way around the world if he's just bluffing."

"And if he's not bluffing?" asked Bagger.

Matsen grinned, his dark face seeming to light up. "We'll be the first to find out and then get to do something about it."

It was quiet as that bit of news was mulled over.

"We're going to go up through the Strait of Malaca and into the Indian Ocean. When we hit the Indian Ocean, most flying, excepting the helos, will cease flying. Two reasons: we want to give the maintenance troops time to bring the birds up to snuff and you might recall at this time of year winds in the upper atmosphere carry a fine silt from the Indian subcontinent that just raises ned with the engines. When we get resupplied in a few days, we'll be getting a significant number or AIM-120s." (The AIM-120 AMRAAM or Advanced Medium Range Air-to-Air Missile gives the F-14 the capability of precision medium range attack against airborne targets. It is replacing the AIM-Sparrow.) Heads bobbed and there were murmurs of approval at that news.

"This little breather will give everyone an opportunity to study NATOPS manuals as well as coming up to speed on the AIM-120. Alert 5, 15, and 30 aircraft will be manned continually as we cross the Indian Ocean."

"A Persian Excursion," said Poncho as they started to jog the length of the flight deck.

"How do you feel about goin', Poncho?" asked Fancy.

"I'm up for it," replied Poncho. "Australia would have been nice, but I'm for getting down and dirty if we have to, and to be honest, I hope we have to."

Mirabal and Fancy looked at each other and laughed.

Two days later Fancy and Mirabal sat in Desperado 200, the alert five bird. Fancy looked at his watch for what was probably the two hundredth time. *So close yet so far* he thought to himself. Squirming around trying to get more comfortable he wished he had brought something to read. "Rhino, what did you bring to read?"

"Ah, it's called *Spencerville*."

"Who wrote it?"

"Guy named Nelson Demille. I've read a couple of his books, he's pretty good."

"Where did you get it?"

"Ship's library. Actually they have a pretty good selection. I'm almost done, do you want this when I finish?'

"Sure. What's the plot?"

"Guy retires from a job in Washington, comes back to the family farm in Indiana, gets involved with the ex-girlfriend…"

"Okay, I get the picture. Let me have it when you're finished."

After several more minutes of silence, Fancy, asked, are you finished yet?"

"No, not yet. Getting restless up there?"

"Yeah, you could say that. You never told me how you wound up in the Navy, what's the story?"

"Brilliant person, picked by the Navy, you know the rest."

"Uh huh, like I said, what's the real story?"

"My parents came to this country from Puerto Rico just after they got married. They lived in New York for a while. My dad had a chance to work with an uncle in Philadelphia in his deli. They moved to Philadelphia and my mother became great with child, me. When my dad's Uncle Benny decided to retire to Florida, he sold the place to my dad. He was so proud to have his own business. By the time I hit junior high the neighborhood had changed somewhat for the worse and I started running with some of the bad dudes. I started scamming my folks, staying out late, stupid things."

"When did your folks find out?"

"After a friend of my dad's caught one of my friends shop-lifting and my name came up, even though I wasn't there. There was a beat cop that came into my dad's deli almost everyday for lunch or coffee. My dad told him about what happened and he started to take an interest in me.

Naturally, I knew everything and paid not one ounce of attention to him." Mirabal paused.

Resuming, he said in a voice that had more emotion than before, "One night, and this was after I had hit high school, I came down with a bad cold and my mother insisted that I spend a Friday night, no less in bed. I was so sick, I didn't argue much. My so-called friends decided to try robbing a liquor store a couple of blocks up the street. This officer, Officer Bentene, walked in on them and was shot and killed by a guy, who I had thought was my good friend, Georgie Swan. My dad was just sick about it. He made me go to Officer Bentene's funeral, made me speak to his widow and four kids. I went home and threw up for about two hours. It didn't take me long to figure out which way I wanted my life to go. Georgie Swan and the three guys that were with him are still in jail and will probably be there for the rest of their lives. I went back to school with a vengeance the Monday after the funeral. I went to Temple University in Philadelphia. There was a Navy recruiter on campus one day and, shall we say, the rest is history."

"Did you want to go to flight school?"

"Oh yeah, but I just didn't score high enough and my eyesight wasn't quite good enough. At first I was disappointed, but I like what I do. You know I thought that was really classy the way you introduced me to Janelle, uh Captain DeLeon. I really appreciated it. It meant a lot to me, believe me."

Fancy chuckled, "I was just telling her the truth and I meant everything I said. It looked like you two were hitting it off pretty well. Is there anything happening there?"

"I don't think so, we exchanged numbers and addresses, but I don't think anything's going to happen. If it does, I wouldn't mind, but I'm not that hopeful."

"Like I said, we're a team." Fancy looked at his watch. "Five more minutes, we're not going anywhere today. Nuts."

"Desperado 200, this is Echo 613. The helo is about twelve minutes out, we have you and 209 on the scope. You're clear for three hundred and sixty degrees. It looks like the remaining fighter and the TU-22s are headed to Heifang."

"Gator, why do think the guy punched out. Was there any sign of fire, smoke, or anything?"

"No, he was just motoring along and all of a sudden there went the canopy followed by the ejection. I was stunned. He was looking good until then."

"I think I've got the helo on the scope. Scorpion 613, I'm picking you up on the scope."

"Desperado 200, I think we can see you. Why don't you come down and lead us to the guy in the water. That will save everybody some time."

"Scorpion six one three, I have you in sight. I'll come down your starboard side."

"Roger, starboard side, Desperado 200."

"Rhino, keep him in sight. I'm going to go down his port side, convert to his six and pass up his starboard side."

"I've got him, Gator."

As Fancy rolled the plane into a left hand turn he lowered the flaps, put out the boards, and retarded the throttle. The F-14, it seemed to Fancy, was just hanging in the air as they came down on the SH-60F. As they passed over the downed pilot Fancy thought he saw a circle of yellow around the raft. *Looks like he's okay and doin' something to help himself,* thought Fancy as he climbed up to join on Moose.

"What do you say Moose, shall we call it a day?"

"Desperado 209 thinks we've put in a good day's work, let's head for the barn. They've almost got him in the helo."

Reversing his course and climbing Fancy could see that the helo was already headed back to the destroyer it had launched from.

As Fancy climbed down from Desperado 200 he and Mirabal were met by Captain Van Gundy, the CAG and Ratchet Robinson. For a

The Enterprise and her battle group charged into the Indian Ocean. Flight operations, except for anti-submarine operations by the helicopters, stopped. The maintenance troops went to work with a vengeance. Big, little, and even anticipated problems were fixed. Planes that had no problems were washed and shined. Many of the planes looked as if they had just come out of the shop at North Island.

Fancy put down the NATOPS, stretched, yawned, and worked out the kinks in his neck. Picking up the manual put out by the Hughs Corporation he started to refresh his memory about the AMRAAM, or AIM-120. The manual referring to it as the fastest, smartest, most deadly missile in use by any country in the world. When they had been at Coyote North, he had heard one of the Air Force pilots compare the shooting down of an enemy plane with the AIM-120 to "clubbing baby seals, one after another…whomp…whomp…whomp". It was referred to by most fighter pilots as the "Slammer". It was the replacement for the AIM-7 Sparrow, sometimes called the "Great White Hope" meaning the pilots hoped it hit something. He liked it because it had the same "fire and forget" capabilities of the Sidewinder, but with greater range and speed, as well as reliability. The Sparrow had neither the brains or the energy for sophisticated maneuvering, so it was easy for a skilled pilot to evade the missile.

As Fancy read on, he was glad the program to continue development of the missile hadn't been killed, as had almost happened on several occasions. At Mach 4, the "Slammer" was fast enough to chase down anything in the air.

"Hey, Gator, there isn't going to be a test on that is there?" questioned Poncho, as he came in and flopped into a chair across the aisle.

"There's only one test that I can think of and that's the one when I go boresight on a bad guy. If this thing works half as good as advertised, it's a winner."

"I was talking to some ordie folks a couple of days ago, and, from what they say, it more than works as advertised. It's already got kills over

Iraq and in Bosnia. Shoot if the blue-suiters can get it to work…" he smiled, as his voice trailed off.

"You guys glad to be rid of the dog?" asked Fancy.

"To tell you the truth, yes and no. I kind of miss the little guy, but I don't miss sneaking around, trying to keep him hidden, I don't miss that at all. I don't know what we were thinking about," he said laughing and shaking his head.

"I think he's getting a pretty good home, and shoot, you can come and visit him."

"Yeah. That was pretty lucky getting that babe to get him to L.A. It looked like she and Rhino were getting pretty chummy. Is Rhino going into pursuit mode?"

"He doesn't think anything will come of it, but if it does, he won't be at all disappointed."

"Rhino's a good kid. I hope it works out for him. I'm going to go jogging. Want to come?"

Fancy shook his head, "Thanks, but not right now. I'm going to write a couple of letters and clean up some loose ends."

"Right, see ya later."

Flight operations resumed as the Enterprise headed northwest into the Arabian Sea and the Gulf of Oman. The heat became taxing to the deck crews, with a preview of what was to come. Fancy and Mirabal had just landed and were divesting themselves of their flight gear. Robinson and Charley Mejia entered the somewhat malodorous room. "How'd it go up there this morning, guys?"

"It felt really good to get back in the air. The visibility is unlimited. That's the good news. On the other hand, it's hotter than blue-blazes. I feel like I'm part of a shish-kabob. Those guys on deck should be getting some kind of bonus."

"Did you hear what happened to Stretch Gerlicki, this morning?" asked Mejia as he reached for his speed jeans.

Rhino and Fancy looked at each other, shaking their heads. "No, what happened?" queried Mirabal. "I saw him last night during the movie and he looked fine to me."

"He was in the weight room working out. Whoever was supposed to be spotting for him turned away when somebody asked him a question. The weight got away from Stretch and fell on his chest and throat. He's got some busted ribs and and a crushed, uh, trachea, I think that's what Doc Su said."

Mirabal shook his head and pursed his lips. "What's the prognosis?"

"Doc Su thinks *eventually* he'll be all right. The key word of course being eventually. The Greyhound took him off," said Robinson looking at his watch,"about forty-five minutes ago. He'll go to the United Arab Emirate and from there back to the states."

"That's a tough break for Stretch, no pun intended of course," said Fancy. Do you think we'll get a replacement?"

"I know we will. CAG told me there's someone on the Lincoln who wants to stay and has volunteered to join our merry little band."

"Who is it," asked Mirabal, shaking his head.

"He must be some kind of crazy mother-grabber," put in Mejia as he shucked on his survival vest.

"CAG didn't say, but I can hardly wait to meet him, I'll tell you that," said Robinson, picking up his Nav bag. "Come on Toons, let's get going, we're burning daylight here." Robinson grinned his ear to ear grin, winked, and walked out. Toons shaking his head started to follow.

"Hey, Toons, did the COD plane that took Stretch off happen to bring any mail?"

"It did and I think Bagger picked up a couple of letters for you. Last time I saw Bagger he was running an envelope back and forth under his nose, savoring it, he said. See ya."

Later that evening Fancy was laying in his bunk doing some savoring of his own when Bagger barged through the door and flopped down beside him.

Fancy brought his legs up to give Bagger a little more room.

"Oh, fuck me," groaned Bagger. "Oh, man oh man."

"One, you're not my type. And two, we haven't been out that long, have we?"

Bagger grinned and shook his head. "I had a great flight. Recovery was just like out of a text book at P-cola. Perfect lineup, glide path, etc…So they attach us to a mule and they pull us over to the elevator on the starboard side. The blue-shirts chain us down and we're lowered down to the hanger bay. The handlers attach a spotting dolly and break down the chains to get her off the elevator into the bay."

Fancy interrupted, "How come you're takin' it down there?"

Bagger ran his hand through his hair. "The kid that was supposed to ride it down. He got sick or hurt his foot or something, anyway I said I'd do it. After all, I didn't have any place to be, so…Anyway, there I was and the director signals me to release the brakes. So I do and about that time the ship starts a lazy roll to starboard. Naturally, the spotting dolly is no match for that big mother and she begins to slide toward the deck edge of the elevator." Pausing, shaking his head, and sighing Bagger goes on with his tale of woe. "Man, everybody starts to yell 'Chocks in! Brakes on'! Everybody is starting to get real concerned, including me. This poor kid that's the director is trying to move the plane around as carefully as he can, but with the slight starboard list and slow rolls he's havin' problems. I'm releasing and reapplying the brakes and this spotting dolly just can't hack the course. Whistles are screaming and the chock walkers can't place those blocks in the way of the plane that is starting to pick up a little speed with each roll of the dammed ship. In short we're heading for the edge of the elevator."

"With all this applying and reapplying of the brakes the brake pressure is depleted from all this use and abuse and I'm pumping the brake accumulator furiously to regain some pressure. Finally, someone had the sense to call in the cavalry in the form of a tow tractor. Man, I could feel the main gear top the deck edge coaming. By now I'm thinking about the possibility of a cold, dark swim. After the plane was stopped momentarily by the coaming, they got the tow tractor hooked up and eased us back into the bay." Finishing his story, Bagger sagged back onto the crowded bunk and closed his eyes.

"Another E ride, babe. Just think they pay us to have all this fun. I don't know about you, but I wouldn't miss it for the world."

Bagger opened his eyes, while squinting at him suspiciously. "If this is your idea of fun—you've got to get out more. You must have gotten the letters that came in on the COD?"

Fancy withdrew the two letters from underneath his pillow. "Yeah, thanks. I understand you got some too?"

Bagger smiled. "Yes, and she's still hot for me. Nothing but good news from CONUS."

"That was bad news for Stretch, huh?" he continued. "Geez, that must have smarted," he continued rubbing his throat.

"Yeah, talk about a freak accident. I guess it's going to be a long recovery."

"Cody said she got the dog. Amanda decided he answered to Shorty better than Short Round."

Getting up, Bagger walked over to the small wash basin and splashed some water on his face. "I bet that mutt doesn't mind what they call him as long as he doesn't have to do any more traveling. That thing's been all over the world. Come on, let's grab something to eat, I'm starved."

Maybe, thought Fancy to himself, it's the power of suggestion. He had always heard that this part of the world was hot and he certainly felt that way right now. Poncho and he had been launched just before dawn to provide part of the combat air patrol that would see Enterprise through the Strait of Hormuz. Even though he had the air conditioning cranked to the max, he felt like he was burning up. could be nerves he murmured to himself.

"Rhino, do you feel hotter than normal?"

"Nupe, I feel okay, maybe even a little on the cool side. Of course that air is turned up quite a bit."

Fancy squirmed in his seat trying to get comfortable and trying to itch the middle of his back. At last satisfying the itch he looked off to his port side and picked up Poncho's plane, Desperado 204. If the navigation gear was on the ball they should be at precisely 26ºN 57ºW, with the United Arab Emirates and Oman to port beyond Poncho's plane and Iran off the his starboard wing. He remembered what the CAG had told them yesterday about the possibility of seeing Iranian F-14s. There were, Van Gundy had cautioned, some still flying. They had been bought by the Shah of Iran before he had been deposed. Fancy wondered how on earth the Iranians had kept them flying. Talk about a maintenance nightmare.

As the two planes weaved and jinked through the brilliant blue sky, Fancy marveled at the amount of shipping he could pick out from their altitude of 19,000 feet. Equally amazing was the amount of traffic in the air. "How's everything lookin', Rhino?"

"Lots of commercial traffic, especially coming out of Iran. Could be some military traffic further inland, but they don't seem to heading in our direction though."

"Dash Two," Fancy called looking in Poncho's direction. How are things looking over there?"

"Desperado 209, everything looks and sounds pretty quiet. Man, this is one crowded part of the world though."

"Roger that. Let's stay sharp."

"Roger that, 209."

After another few minutes of bobbing and weaving through the searing air their isolation was interrupted. "Desperado 209, this is Echo six one two."

"209, Echo. We read you five by five."

"209, it appears we've got some activity. It looks like we've got two bogeys climbing out of the air base Jaghdan. So far they're still inside Iranian airspace at, uh, 060. Come to 060 and put them on your nose."

"Coming to 060. Dash Two, you copy?"

"Dash Two copies."

"204, let's throttle back a little. We definitely don't need to go feet dry in this part of the world."

"Roger, 209."

"Rhino, you picking up anything?"

"Not yet. Wait, wait…Maybe…Yeah, yeah I think I've got 'em. Two dots at 060, that's got to be them. They're at 75 miles at 14 grand, still climbing. That's definitely them. Seventy miles at fourteen five and still coming. TCS on and, wow! One's an F-14 and I think the other is an F-4. Sixty-five miles at 15."

Fancy continued his present course, now picking out the two Iranian planes on his own radar screen. Even though he and Poncho had throttled back the four planes were closing at a rate approaching a thousand miles an hour. He was also aware the Iranian coastline was getting uncomfortably close. "Poncho, we've either got to throttle back or turn away from the coast."

"Roger that, Gator."

Now Fancy could see the brown smudge on the horizon that was Iran.

"Fifty miles at 17 grand and still coming," reported Rhino. Fancy appreciated the calm with which he delivered the information.

"Dash Two, let's reverse hard, to port and extend out before we wind up over Iran. We'll go hard for two minutes and then reverse back into them. Echo six one two, we're going to reverse for two minutes and then reverse back into them. Keep us apprised."

"Roger on the reversal 209," came the tinny answer.

"Coming to port, 204." Fancy racked the Tomcat around in a hard break to port.

Rhino, with all his might, tried, successfully, to keep his blood from pooling in his lower extremities. He heard himself grunt as he was pushed down into his seat; and they came out of the turn and then felt the acceleration push him back into the seat. "Uhhhhh…" he continued as things started to get gray. Then almost as quickly as he could swallow they were out of the turn. Everything came back in color and in focus. Giving his head a shake he scanned his instruments. Everything was okay and in the green.

"Desperado, they're still coming and they've gone feet wet. You're extending out and away from them. They don't seem to interested in getting too close."

"Roger, six one two."

"Okay, Poncho, let's see what these guys want to do. Coming left now!" Again Fancy brought the big plane around in a tight turn, possible, Rhino thought later, tighter than the proceeding turn.

Willing his eyes to come back into focus, Rhino said, "I've got 'em! Come right three degrees, at 14 miles. See 'em?"

At first Fancy couldn't see anything. Then the two Iranian planes seemed to leap out of the blue sky and into focus. The plane on the right was an F-14. For a split second he felt frozen not quite believing what he was seeing.

"We'll take 'em head on down the port side, Rhino. I've got a good tone on the 'winders. Geez, 'winders nothin', we could gun him!"

In a flash the four planes shrieked past each other. Immediately Fancy reversed again in order to put the two Tomcats at the Iranian's six.

"Come left, come left!" Rhino grunted as they came out of the hard left turn.

Fancy pushed the throttles to full military power just short of going into afterburner. The fighter leaped ahead and the tone from the AIM-9 Sidewinders started their lethal growl in his headset. He was amazed that the Iranian planes were taking little, if any evasive action. "Dash—Two, this seems almost too easy."

"I don't mind easy, but this seems a little much," replied Poncho. "My 'Winders want to go in the worst possible way."

"Desperado 209, remember these guys have every right to be out here," mandated the voice on board the E-2. "Unless you detected anything hanging off their weapon stations…"

"Uh, we couldn't determine if there was anything on the weapon stations. Dash Two—any thing you noticed?"

"Are you kidding? Check out our closing speed? Give me a break!"

No sooner had Poncho finished his chronicle than Rhino broke in, "It looks like it's a mute point, it looks like they're reversing course."

Fancy picked up the two Iranian planes visually and confirmed Rhino's observance as they came around in a lazy right hand turn, lowering their noses, picking up speed, and disappearing from their sight.

"Nice job, Desperados, we'll see you back at the farm."

"Thanks, Echo, Desperado headed back home."

"Well, Rhino, what did you make of that little encounter?"

"Kind of bizarro, we've had some easy firing solutions. That one was like looking in the mirror. Our evil twin."

Fancy chuckled, "It was strange. Something I don't want anyone else to see either. We're not exactly stealthy or easy to miss."

"Roger that. This should be an interesting couple of months and this is just the first day. Where did the Iranians get their F-14s anyway?"

"Same place we do. Bethpage. The Shah knew a good thing when he saw it. He actually made the decision to buy the Beast over the F-15. I think it cost him, or his country, something approaching two billion dollars for around eighty planes. The way I heard it there was an actual flyoff between the two planes. Two pilots from Grumman just stole the show from the Eagle and I guess after it was over, the Shah came right out of the stands where he was watching and went right over to the F-14 and just ignored the Eagle. Naturally the Air Force whined and pouted about how the Navy cheated and put the Shah in danger. Actually, the two Grumman pilots did fudge a tad, but…"

Rhino laughed out loud. "Did Iran get all eighty planes?"

"I'm not sure, it was probably pretty close. I guess they built one of the finest air bases the world had ever seen, somewhere in the desert. It covered around fifty square miles. Aircraft revetments were enormous and overbuilt. Repair and maintenance facilities just really superb, just first class all the way. But…"

"But what?"

They had a big weakness. Their pilots came from the elite upper class and were generally considered really good. The maintainers were highly trained and considered pretty good. The big weakness were their RIOs. Since the U.S. Air Force didn't employ RIOs in their Phantoms, the Iranians didn't either. Their guys in back (GIBs) were all pilots who knew something about radar and the geometry of making interceptions. Naturally, the key word was "something". Their knowledge went from brilliant to abysmal."

"Just the opposite of the way it is in the Navy of course," Rhino chided.

"No doubt about that," grinned Fancy, as he raised the nose slightly. "Anyway, the pilots were veterans of other planes, mainly F-4s and they were said to range the spectrum from dangerous to brilliant. The RIOs didn't have the educational background the pilots did and their performance wasn't near as high. I guess in many cases there was some real animosity between the pilots and RIOs. There was never a real effort to make the crew concept work. The RIOs were just second-class citizens."

"Did they see any combat?"

"Yeah, I think they had ten, eleven shoot downs of Iraqi aircraft. But, they were also used as kind of a mini-AWACS plane. They'd use 'em to vector other Iranian planes, particularly against low flying planes trying to use the mountains to mask their approach. Just think how much better the radar is now compared to the late 70s. Pretty amazing."

"How'd you find all this stuff out?"

"Ah, you know, read about it. Back at Oceana there was a Captain I got to know that made a couple of deliveries to Iran. He said that base Khatami was just awesome."

Glancing to his left he could see Poncho, realizing that while he had been talking, how often he had scanned his instrument panel, as they returned to the ship. Bringing the nose down slightly he found that they had arrived at the marshal stack. Four planes were ahead of them, one plane going down the chute to land every sixty seconds. Four minutes later they pushed over for their turn to land.

"Tomcat two zero nine. Two point four. Ball" Less than thirty seconds later after catching the three wire, Fancy was taxiing forward, directed by a yellow shirt. *Piece of cake,* he thought to himself. *I wish I was flying tonight.*

As they were about to go below deck to get rid of their flight gear they met Robinson heading the same way. "Just the guys I was looking for. Be ready for a 0615 launch. We're going to Saudi Arabia to get a briefing. Any questions?"

Before Fancy could open his mouth to answer, Robinson turned on his heels to go in the opposite direction. "Good," he called back to them. "See you at 0415 in Ready Three."

Fancy and Mirabal looked at each other, smiled, shook their heads and continued on their way. "Boy, I'm glad we had that conversation," mused Mirabal. "I feel so much better now that I'm really in the information loop."

# 13

Fancy and Mirabal trudged across the steel flight deck to where Desperado 207 was parked. Reveling in the silence of the flight deck. The lack of noises and, what seemed to many outsiders, confusion, was a welcome respite. They would be the second and third planes launched. Upon reaching the plane Fancy put his helmet bag and knee board on the port side intake and began to circle the plane clockwise while Mirabal went in the opposite direction looking for wrenches, parts, leaks, torn metal, looseness, or breaks in the flaps or other control surfaces, bruises on the tires, or other anomalies that could otherwise ruin their day. As Fancy completed his walk around he noticed for the first time that his name, as well as Mirabal's, and call sign had been painted just below the canopy rail. Mirabal joined him as Fancy pointed upward. "Hey, does this mean we've arrived or what?"

Mirabal followed his pointing finger and grinned. Nodding he said, "I guess so. Looks like it belongs to me."

Fancy looked over toward Robinson's plane and noticed that he was watching the two men. He gave them a thumb's up and climbed the boarding ladder into the cockpit.

Fancy climbed his own boarding ladder. Settling into his seat he pulled the pins for the ejection seat and stowed them. Reaching for the rear and lap safety harness connections he buckled them together. Then he twisted the oxygen hose into its socket and snapped the leg restraints into their fittings. (The leg restraints hook in above the ankle and are anchored to fittings just off the floor of the cockpit. These restraints are designed to keep your legs from being amputated by the edge of the cockpit should your legs shoot out in front of you in case of an ejection.)

Mirabal, who had climbed up after Fancy was already strapped in and was starting the pre-takeoff checklist. Completing the checklist, Fancy started the engines as the green shirts began breaking down the chains holding the plane to the deck. Yellow shirts then directed them on the waist catapult where they went over another list of checks. Saluting the launching officer to signal he was ready to be shot off the boat, he took a deep breath, scanned the instrument panel one more time, and then placed his head on the headrest with just the slightest downward tilt, to give him a view of what was in front of him in addition to the instrument panel.

"Here we go," he announced to Mirabal.

With a wham, rattle, zoom, and then with what seemed to be absolute quiet they were off the end of the boat in less than two seconds.

Fancy wondered if his eyeballs really flattened out because he could hardly make much of anything out. Relaxing slightly, knowing they were airborne he noticed the dirty blue water of the Gulf and then searched for Robinson's plane while pulling up and to the left. Through the haze he caught sight of Ratchett's plane and immediately shoved the throttles forward and pulled the stick back. Within a minute he was settled in on his port side about even with his port wing.

"Echo, six one three, Desperado, two zero zero checking in."

"Desperado 200, you're cleared for the beach. Good day."

"Thanks Echo, cleared for the beach, thank you. Climbing to 160."

"Roger, 160, Desperado."

Fancy eased the stick back and advanced the throttles while glancing at Robinson's plane as it started its climb to sixteen thousand feet.

"Dash Two, let's go to combat spread. Keep your head on a swivel."

"Roger that Desperado 200."

Again Fancy was amazed at the many ships' wakes headed, it seemed, in all directions in the Gulf.

It wasn't long before they passed over the peninsular country of Qatar, then over the Gulf of Bahrain. Fancy could look to starboard and see the tiny country of Bahrain. He'd heard it was often referred to as the Switzerland of the Middle East.

As they flew into Saudi Arabia, the city of Az Zahran was visible to his right. Keeping one eye on his HUD and keeping that same eye on Robinson's plane, he looked down upon bright green circles of vegetation much like one might find in parts of the United States. *That's a lot of irrigated land* he thought to himself. *Food here must really be expensive.* Beyond the coastal farms they started to pass over numerous drilling and refining sites.

In no time at all they had passed what would be considered civilization and entered into what Fancy thought of as the most desolate piece of real estate he had ever experienced. "Geez, Rhino, can you believe this place? This gives a whole new meaning to the word desolate."

"I never thought I'd see a place that made the Mojave Desert look like a garden spot, but this is it! Unbelievable!"

The land was empty of any kind of vegetation, scrub or even cactus. There were no geographic features to provide any kind of geographic relief which was so familiar in the States. Fancy thought it seemed even more forbidding as it stretched from horizon to horizon without a let up. Twice they flew over tiny encampments, otherwise there was no break in the view for what seemed hundreds and hundreds of miles.

"Desperado 200," the voice boomed in Fancy's headset. "This is Deep Star."

He heard Robinson respond to the Air Force AWACS plane orbiting to the north of them.

"Deep Star, Desperado 200, flight of two at 160 angels."

"Desperado 200, you're going to be picking up some company presently. There are two Saudi F-15 at one four zero angels at your seven."

Reflexively Fancy twisted around in his seat as far as the restraints would let him. He was unable to see anything and the RAH gear was otherwise silent.

In another three minutes of his eye Fancy caught sight of movement from the corner of his left eye. Almost immediately the movement became an F-15. Coming to altitude the Saudi pilot eased his plane over toward Fancy's plane. Picking out Robinson's plane, he noticed the Saudi's wingman coming up on it's port side. Looking back toward the F-15 he began to feel a little uncomfortable as the F-15 moved in even closer. "I'm not crazy about this guy getting so close, Rhino. I hope he knows what he's doing.

Coming in closer still Fancy could pick out details of the Saudi pilot under his bubble canopy. As if on cue the Saudi pilot waved.

Fancy waved back, hoping the F-15 would give him a little more space.

After flying along side the two Navy planes for several minutes the Saudis stroked their burners, extended out, and climbed out of sight.

"Welcome to Saudi Arabia, Gator. How do you like it so far?"

"They seem friendly enough, but man, this is the most desolate piece of the world. It's almost surreal."

"Surreal? You're going to give fighter jocks a bad name if you use those big words you know," chortled Robinson. "I've got a feeling we're going to be doing some low level work. How 'bout we get in a little practice?"

"Dash Two likes the idea," answered Fancy.

Robinson's RIO switched frequencies and Robinson requested the change in altitude which was granted. "Gator, we're cleared for five hundred feet. How's you fuel state?"

"Ummm, 'bout 8500 pounds, Skipper."

"That's just about what I've got," answered Robinson, who was showing a little under 6800 pounds. "Let's take 'em down, Gator."

Fancy waited until he saw Robinson's nose start to drop and he pushed the stick forward and advanced the throttles. "Here we go, Rhino."

"I'm right behind you, Gator," replied Mirabal as he reached for the bar above his radar. He knew from experience it could get rough at 500 feet.

As they lost altitude and gained speed the air got rougher and the ride became a little bit more exciting. The hot air coming off the floor of the blistering desert floor tended to push the big plane upward. Fancy felt himself using a little more muscle to keep the plane at 500 feet. Blasting along at 500 knots indicated air speed, the world outside the canopy passed in a brown blur. He felt exhilarated as he and the plane seemed to become one. Most pilots didn't like to fly low, but Fancy thought he was a better pilot the lower he got. While it took his attention, he wasn't buried in the cockpit, thanks to the HUD and his own ability to scan the world outside the bubble of his canopy, as well as jinking and juking to present an unpredictable target. *Like it or not* he thought, *I better get used to it because it looks like this might be the name of the game for this tour.*

"Dash Two, we'll be recovering in ah, about five minutes. We're cleared straight in, let's make it look good, coming up one zero angels."

"Roger 10 angels," answered Fancy as he brought the plane up five hundred feet. The plane, he noticed, seemed to float very quickly to one thousand feet.

Two minutes later they were lowering their gear and had been cleared to land at the Royal Saudi Air Base at Qiba.

As Fancy and Mirabal touched down they were directed off the runway toward a refueling area, where they would refuel with the engines still running. Once they had taxied to a stop they safetied their ejection seats and raised their hands so the refueling crew could see they wouldn't be touching anything they shouldn't. Mirabal had already put the radar in standby. Fuel was being transferred from large rubber bladders.

Waiting for the refueling to be completed Fancy strained in his seat to look around at the Saudi Base. From what he could see the base was large. He could see F-15s, F-16s, A-10s, C-130s, C-141s and just taking off the biggest plane in the Air Force inventory, a C-5 Galaxy. Two KC-10s waited their turn on the taxi way to take off. Four Saudi Arabian F-15s recovered almost before the C-5 was out of sight. "What do think, Rhino?"

"We're not in Kansas anymore, Babe. Did you get a load of that runway. I couldn't believe it when we turned off the runway. I took a look expecting to see the end of it. Man, that thing just keeps going and going. If they can't get off the ground, maybe they just drive into Iraq."

"That's got to be the longest runway I've ever seen, no doubt about it. Looks like we're ready." Fancy eased the throttle forward and they followed Robinson's plane, being led by a jeep, away from the refueling area to what looked like to Fancy, a transient aircraft parking area. Directed into a space where they were chocked. Shutting down the engines, Fancy raised the canopy. An Air Force enlisted man climbed up and took his helmet after helping him out of koch fittings.

Climbing down he was sure that he must be in the jet blast of a taxiing plane and he looked around for the offending plane. A quick glance around and he realized there was no plane.

Rhino dropped down beside him and immediately started his own pursuit of what seemed to be jet exhaust.

"Me too," Fancy grinned. "I thought a plane was taxiing by. Amazing, makes Nellis seem like an oasis."

Mirabal laughed. "I bet I could fry an egg on the ground. Whoowe, this is one hot place."

They walked over to Robinson's plane where almost immediately an Air Force van arrived and picked them up. Mercifully, it was air coditioned.

The Naval aviators were whisked across the vast flight line to what looked like a semi-permanent building with only the number 204 stenciled in bold black numbers above the doorway. Emerging quickly from the van they made their way through the door. An Air Force enlisted man rose from his desk. "Good morning, sir. Welcome to Qiba. Colonel Mladenik is expecting you. Would you care for anything to drink?"

Robinson paused, "Well, we've been at sea for some time, you wouldn't have some beer, would you?"

The airman seemed to squirm a bit before he answered. "Sir, unfortunately we don't. The Saudis are really firm about alcohol. I can scare up some soft drinks though."

Robinson grinned. "Soft drinks will be fine, son. Is it always this hot here?"

"Actually, no sir, it isn't; it can and does get hotter."

Robinson threw him a sympathetic look and shook his head in regret.

"If you'll come this way, gentleman, as I said Colonel Mladenik is expecting you." Getting up he walked over to an office door, knocked, paused a second, and then opened the door. They entered a somewhat sparse office and were met by a Lt. Col. in an Air Force flight suit.

The tall, blond woman wearing the flight suit wore the wings of a Command Pilot. Rising and coming around her government issue steel desk, she extended her hand. "Good morning, gentleman. Welcome to Saudi Arabia." Smiling she shook each of the fliers' hands with a firm handshake. "I'd ask if it's hot enough for you, but..." Her voice trailed off as her comment was met with laughter from the Navy aviators. Motioning to some metal folding chairs she motioned for them to sit down.

"For obvious reasons I know you're eager to get back to the Enterprise. Obviously, we're glad to have the Enterprise in the Gulf. I should also say we're really glad to have those EA-6 Prowlers. Saddam's starting to play games again."

Robinson shifted in his chair. "We've heard that he's flying pilgrims back and forth and around to various places."

Mladenik snorted in disgust. "If small arms, triple A, SAM components, etc…qualify as pilgrims, I suppose he is." She rose and walked to a map of the Gulf region. "In addition to the fixed-wing flights there have also been helicopter flights in Saudi Arabia at various places along the border. They claim they're just picking up the pilgrims and dropping them off at their various villages. They're a clear violation of the no-fly, no-drive zone."

Fancy kept looking at the wings she wore on her flight suit. *Maybe I've been at sea too long,* he thought as he shifted his attention to the map.

"As you know the no-fly zone has been pushed up to the thirty second parallel. JSTARS, AWACS, and satellite intelligence show a whole bunch of activity between the Iraqi air base at Al Kut," she motioned with a pointer she had picked up, "and the Iranian base at Ahvaz. They fly into Iran above the thirty- second parallel and then south to Ahvaz. Sometimes they fly back from Ahvaz by way of air space below the the no-fly boundary."

"M'am," Fancy raised his arm slightly, " I thought that Iraq and Iran hated each other's guts?"

"That's another interesting bit of the puzzle. Most of the intel guys believe they've put aside some of their differences. They definitely hate us more than they hate each other. In addition to that bit of good news the intelligence weenies have picked up radio transmissions that suggest Russian and probably former East German pilots are working in both countries to train and bring the pilots of both countries' air forces up to speed ."

"These guys are probably disgruntled former pilots who either didn't get paid or have seen a chance to make some big bucks or dinars. There is no evidence that the Russian government is behind any of this— although they've sold both countries a significant number of MiG-29s and SU-27s."

Fancy glanced at Mladenik and wondered what kind of aircraft she had hours in to get those Command Pilot's wings. *I've definitely been away too long.* Fancy mused about how serious the Air Force Colonel seemed to be. When she spoke she seemed to squeeze each vowel out of each word as she spoke.

"Have the Iraqis come over the no-fly zone?" asked Robinson.

"They make a dash up to the thirty-second parallel and depending on how we're deployed, they'll cruise along the fence or cross it until we start to pick them up; then they'll high tail it back across. Simply put, they seem to be getting bolder."

A silence settled over the room as the Navy fliers let that information sink in. Fancy glanced at Mirabal, who also seemed focused on the Colonel's wings, and wondered if he was thinking the same thing he was: *I hope they come across and I hope we're there when they do!*

A knock at the door broke the silence. The young airman entered carrying soft drinks. As the refreshments were passed around Robinson glanced over at Fancy and grinned while raising his bottle in salute.

"Sorry I can't offer you anything stronger, gentleman," remarked Mladenik, as she left the map and walked to her desk. Sitting down, she paused while the refreshments were finished.

When I mentioned your EA-6Bs, I should also have mentioned that your TARPS capability is going to be used a great deal. As you know the Air Force does not have the reconnaissance capability we had with the F-4s. Right now Enterprise and your TARPS pods represent all the reconnaissance in the theater."

Robinson grinned again. "Speaking for Enterprise and VF-125 we stand ready to take up the slack. Right, Lt. Fancy?"

"Yes, Sir," Fancy said, sitting up a little straighter.

Gesturing toward Fancy, Robinson continued, "Lt. Fancy here is one of our TARPS experts. We'll bring back any photos that are needed."

Fancy felt himself turning red and squirmed uncomfortably in his seat. He felt like a schoolboy being called on in class. *Good thing I know the answers,* he thought.

Mladenik turned and looked at him. Frowning she said, "Another bit of good news," and she paused thoughtfully while she pondered her next words, "is that if anyone goes down in Indian country, there won't be an all out effort to get you back. Right now the assets just aren't available."

Fancy's eyes met Robinson's. The look he passed back told Fancy that this wouldn't be the case if he had any choice in the matter.

"How about the SAM threat?" asked Robinson.

Mladenik sighed and leaned back in her chair. "We've picked up everything from SA-2s, SA-3s, SA-6s, and we know they've got a lot of SA-7s. Probably everybody and their grandmother have one within arm's reach. If that wasn't enough, the French have sold them quite a few batteries of their Roland system. Answer your question?" she smiled, running her hand through her blond hair.

Robinson laughed out loud, shook his head and replied, "I think that about covers it. Are they shooting any of this stuff or just lighting people up?"

"Every once in a great while they'll let loose with an SA-2, but whenever they do, it never even comes close. They probably shut down their radar immediately after launch and the thing never guides."

"Maybe they're not as dumb as they seem," interjected Fancy. "Who in their right mind wants a HARM down their throat?"

After another few minutes, the briefing came to an end. Shaking hands again the Navy fliers left Mladenik's office.

As they walked down the hall Fancy and Mirabal turned at the sound of a familiar voice. "Hey, Gator, is that really you?"

Turning they saw they were being hailed by Colonel Winkleman.

"Good morning, Sir. This is a surprise."

"It was a surprise for me too. It seems that my predecessor had a bit of a sexual harassment problem and got shipped home. Anyway, I'm here with the First Tactical Fighter Wing. Kind of a dream come true for me. What are you doing here anyway?"

Fancy heard Robinson quietly clear his throat. "Ah, excuse me Sir. Colonel Winkleman, this is my CO, Commander Robinson and his RIO, Lt. Mejia. I think you remember Lt. Mirabal?"

"You bet. How are you, Lieutenant?"

"Just fine, Sir. It's good to see you again."

There were handshakes all around.

"How long have you been here, Colonel?" asked Robinson.

"Ten days, but who's counting. Guessing from your appearance here, Enterprise must have just arrived on, what do you guys call it? Camel Station? Welcome to the Gulf."

"We were just briefed by the S-2, Colonel Mladenik," said Fancy.

"She's a sharp cookie," replied Winkleman. "Listen, I've got a meeting with my squadron commanders," he said looking at his watch. "Is Bagger with you or is he still on the ship?"

"He's back on the boat. He'll be sorry he missed you," said Fancy.

"He sure managed to sweep Wendy Kobayashi off her feet in a hurry. She seems pretty happy about the whole deal."

"Well, I know he is," replied Fancy. "Every time he gets a letter he seems to be in a state of euphoria for a couple of days."

"Listen, I've got to get to this meeting, our tail code is FF, we'll probably be seeing you over Iraq. You guys take care. Commander Robinson, Lt. Mejia, it was good to meet you. Gator, Rhino, take care. Tell Bagger hello for me."

"Will do Colonel, it's good to see you."

Just as Winkleman was about to turn to leave, Robinson called, "Colonel, in this briefing with Col. Mladenik, we were told there would be no all out attempts at rescue if anyone went down. What's your take on that?"

"Personally, I think it's bullshit. If any of my guys wind up on the ground, I'm going to do anything I have to in order to get them out. There aren't that many assets in place but I'm asking for more and I'll use those to the max if need be. How do you feel about it?"

"For once, the Navy and Air Force are in perfect agreement. Let's just hope we don't have to worry about it. Nice meeting you, Colonel."

As they walked over to the two Tomcats after being delivered to the transient air craft parking area, Robinson turned to Fancy. "Well, what did you think about no all out rescue attempt if anyone goes down?"

"Not much. It seems to me that's a huge mistake to let that word out. Morale could take a real nose dive."

"That's what I think. I don't think Van Gundy would disagree either. I hope you know how I feel about it?"

"I do, Skipper. No question as far as I'm concerned."

"Good, let's get out of here and back to the ship and check out the TARPS pods."

The flight back to the ship was uneventful.

Falling in step with Robinson as they walked across the deck of Enterprise Robinson stopped. "Gator, as soon as you get out of your gear, get down below and check out the TARPS pods. I know I've threatened before, but the real thing's going to happen. If I put you on the spot back there, it's only because I know you can hack the course." Clapping him on the shoulder, Robinson continued across the deck.

Calling back to them he said, "Be ready for a 0600 launch. I know for a fact that you're going to be touring Iraq."

Turning to Rhino, Fancy responded, "Want to come down with me and we'll see what's going on with the TARPS pods?"

"Sure, why not. Looks like we'll be seeing a lot of those babes."

"Have you ever flown any TARP missions?"

"Just a couple of times, once with the Skipper and once with the guy whose place you took."

"How did you like it?"

"Wasn't bad. They're going to draw some attention though."

"Yeah," grinned Fancy. "That's part of the benefits package."

"So, how was your visit to Saudi?" interrupted Killer, as he and Bagger came out on deck to preflight their planes.

"Not bad. Man, it is one barren place though. Makes Nellis look like a garden spot. You'll never guess who we ran into."

Bailey laughed. "This is not even a great place to visit, let alone live here. I don't know about you, but I've started my count down already. And, who did you run into?"

"Colonel Winkleman, you know, from Red Flag."

"Really?" gasped Bagger. "Uh, did he say anything about Wendy?"

"She's still crazy about you, if that's what you're looking for. Any mail?" pursued Fancy, preferring not to even worry about counting down yet

"I got two letters, but I didn't see one addressed to you. Maybe it hasn't all been sorted yet." He shrugged, looking like someone who got caught with his hand in the cookie jar.

"Yeah, maybe that's it," said Fancy, feeling more disappointed than he hoped he was letting on. "We'll talk to you later. Don't bend the birds."

Thirty minutes later Fancy and Mirabal were deep in the bowels of the ship in the room where the TARPS pods were kept. There were three of the pods, and the CPO who was responsible for maintaining them said they were going to get one, maybe two from the Lincoln when she left the Gulf.

"Chief, it looks like we're going to be using these big mothers quite a bit. Are they ready to go?" Fancy knew full well that they were, and had been ever since they had left the States.

"Yes, Sir, they're ready," replied the Chief, used to dumb questions from pilots. He knew they had to ask.

The TARPS pod was large at almost seventeen feet long and a hefty 1,750 pounds. It was carried on the number five weapons station. It contained a KS-87 two position camera for vertical and forward oblique pictures. In addition there was also a KA-99 low altitude camera that gave a sideways panoramic view. Completing the package was an AAD-5 infrared imaging camera used at medium and low altitudes. Fancy thought the whole system was one of the best engineered packages he had ever seen. Whoever designed it had included a lot of bang for the buck. There was little demand on the aircraft's power supply. It was almost a perfect match of plane and system to his way of thinking.

"Chief is this the one that's going in the morning at the 0600 launch?"

"This is the one, Sir." Looking at a slip of paper, he continued, "Two zero zero has been brought down off the roof and my crew is going to load it and check it out. Two zero zero won't be taken back to the roof until just before you preflight the bird, sir."

"Thanks, Chief, I guess I better find out where we're going in the morning. Any word on where we're goin'?"

"No, sir, they don't tell me anything except get it ready and get it on the plane. Good luck tomorrow, Sir."

Smiling, he and Mirabal turned and headed for Ready Three. As they walked through the hatchway, Fancy saw that Robinson and Matsen were scrutinizing the map in the front of the room. Glancing at the TV monitor he watched an F/A-18 snag a three wire on the PLAT. Continuing to the front of the room Matsen turned toward him.

"Gator, Rhino, looks like you, the TARPS pod, and me are headed for a place called Badrah." Turning back toward the map he poked his beefy finger at a place, that looked to Fancy, like it was on the border with Iran. Upon closer inspection he saw that it was to the south east of Iraq's capital, Baghdad.

Continuing his on-the-spot briefing, Matsen traced the route from Badrah back into the Gulf. "Our launch time has been moved up to 0500."

Nodding his head, Fancy stepped closer to the map. "What are we going to be looking at?"

Turning back toward the map, Matsen said, "This is a place the U.N. inspection teams have had no success in getting a peek at. They suspect that on the outskirts of town there could be a plant where they make chemical weapons or at least produce some of the compounds or chemicals that would go into such weapons. The Iraqis claim it's just a fertilizer factory. Of course that's what they claim about a lot of places. Trouble is, they have no land to grow anything to use all of this," as he held up his fingers making quote signs, "fertilizer capacity."

For the first time Fancy noticed a three-ring binder laying open on the table. Looking closer he could see photos of what looked like a medium sized city. Several locations on the photograph had been circled. Several maps of Iraq were also on the table.

Speaking for the first time Robinson asked, "Is the pod ready to go?"

"Yes, Sir, they've finished checking it out and they're going to bring 200 down from the roof and load and check it again."

Robinson nodded approvingly. "Okay, why don't you and Mongo start to work out your ingress and egress. You'll have support from the EA-6B and of course from the E-2s. It looks like the powers-that-be want us to get our feet wet ASAP. If you look carefully," he said flipping through the notebook until he came to the page he was looking for, you might notice the place is quite heavily packed with triple A and you're going to be in range of several SAM sites on your way in and out. They must really value their fertilizer."

They all smiled and Rhino asked, "Have they opened up with guns or missiles as far as we know?"

"The guys from the Lincoln, that's where Van Gundy has been, say no, but they're being lit up on the way in and out. It's not for very long, just enough to let us know they can see us," smiled Robinson. "I'll see you 1600," he said as turned to leave. "I've got to go see CAG and tell him what we found out on our little jaunt. Oh, by the way, Lincoln is leaving for CONUS today. She should be passing close aboard between 1400 and 1430. You may want to take a look."

"Right, Skipper. Thanks, probably at about that time we could use a little break, right XO?"

Matsen shrugged. "Sounds about right to me. Let's get goin'."

For the next hour Matsen and Fancy planned their ingress starting with large scale maps and then going to progressively smaller ones. There were even several photographs, taken by previous missions and two that had been taken from satellites. Their egress, they figured should just be a one-eighty of their way in. There was no use in trying to get fancy at this point they both figured. After agreeing on the basics of their mission, each pilot, with his RIO, retreated to a different part the room to commit to memory the most vital parts of their flight. At 1410, Fancy felt ready and ready for a break.

"XO, do you want to head up to the roof and take a peek at Lincoln?"

Matsen shook his head no, and pointed to a pile of paperwork on the seat beside him.

As Mirabal and Fancy stepped out on the steel deck, Fancy was struck by the relative silence that had settled over the ship. No planes were being launched or recovered. It was he thought, like the calm before the storm. Walking across the deck to the port side of the ship, he saw the elevator as it started its descent to the hanger bay with Desperado 200. Things were already in motion. He also noticed a good many of the crew that normally weren't part of flight deck operations on deck.

Looking towards the bow he could see the Abraham Lincoln about half a mile away. Even at that distance she looked massive.

When the two ships were abeam of each other, the *Enterprise's* crew heard a roar come from the *Lincoln* and he could make out many of her crew waving and shouting as they passed.

Mirabal sighed, "That must be a good feeling, if nothing else to put this heat behind them. They sound really happy."

"They sure do." Clapping Mirabal on the back, "Don't look so glum, it'll be our turn before you know it."

Mirabal took a deep breath. "I'm okay. Besides, I like being here. We're going to do some good work."

They watched as the *Lincoln* disappeared from sight and 1MC announced the commencement of flight operations.

At 1600 Robinson looked up from the papers he had been shuffling and addressed the assembled squadron. "Gentleman, may I have your attention, please. Beginning in one hour, we will represent the lone carrier in the Persian Gulf. I trust that many of you witnessed and probably heard *Lincoln's* departure. By all accounts *Lincoln* and her air group did a sensational job while they were here. Captain Van Gundy has already expressed his desire that we do even better. And…I expect the Desperados to be leading the way. I've been very proud of what this squadron has accomplished so far on this cruise in spite of the bumpy beginning."

"As you know, Gator and I spent some time in Saudi Arabia this morning getting the word from the Air Force. By the way, Colonel Winkleman, who some of you met at the Red Flag prior to departure, said to say hello."

"As most of you know, our primary mission is to enforce the No-Fly Zone and provide theater photo reconnaissance."

Pausing, Robinson waited for the squirming and murmuring to die down. "The terrain we will be flying over will be dry, hot and unforgiving. There's all kinds of snakes, spiders, and biting bugs. If you go down, the people you can expect to encounter will be indifferent at best and downright mean at the worst." Again he paused and waited.

"When we're done here I want each of you to double check your survival gear. An item that is being added to your gear is this chart." Robinson brought out a chart and unfolded it. "This is intended for use if you have to navigate to a safe area. Naturally, American know-how lets this thing be used for other collateral uses, conveniently delineated on the chart. These include using as a blanket, a way to catch rain water, a flotation device, a bag, a splint for a broken wrist, and I'm not kidding about this, a plug for a sucking chest wound. Personally, I wish I had a whole bunch of these and some late night TV time."

Waiting for the laughter to die down, Robinson held up another item. "This, I believe, could prove to be more useful. It's called a blood chit. This thing is pretty durable and has an American flag. Down below, in five languages, no less, Turkish, Farsi, English, Arabic, and Kurdish, is a promise to reward anyone who presents a numbered corner of the chit, or the aircrew, that he had aided an American flyer. No one said if this can help with a sucking chest wound."

Mirabal nudged Fancy. "You know what a sucking chest wound is don't you?"

Fancy shook his head in the negative.

"It's nature's way of telling you to slow down," he chuckled.

Fancy, shaking his head, smiled in spite of himself.

"That's the good news. The bad news that we got this morning is that there just aren't the men and assets in place to go all out on rescues. However, Captain Van Gundy and Colonel Winkleman agree that we'll scream, yell, and do everything possible to get anybody out."

"What can we expect if we are captured?" called out Poncho.

"I suppose it would depend on who gets you. Military—civilians. Perhaps torture, starvation, rape, death…The intel guys know what has been done to Iranians and Kurds. Who knows how they're going to treat westerners especially since we kicked their asses in '91 and have been a constant pain in one way or another since then. I wouldn't expect great treatment."

Unless there are any other pressing matters, check the flight schedule, check your gear, and get ready for…" he paused for dramatic effect, "this great adventure."

Fancy awoke to the soft chime of his watch. Straining his eyes to make out the illuminated dial he saw that it was indeed 0330. Stretching, he sighed to himself and swung his legs over the side of his rack to the floor, that even at that hour of the morning was warm to the touch. Bagger mumbled something in his sleep and thrashed around, and again fell silent. Groping his was to the small steel desk he fumbled with the small goose neck lamp, turning it away from the sleeping Bagger. Pulling on some shorts and grabbing his toiletries he made his way to the common head for a quick shower and shave.

Forty-five minutes later after a quick breakfast and an even quicker conference with Matsen he and Mirabal were walking around Desperado 200 which had just arrived on the roof from the hanger deck.

"Let's be real thorough today, Rhino. We're in the big leagues now."

"Yeah, I'm ready to slam one over the fence. How about you?"

Fancy paused before he answered. He felt a knot in his stomach as he hung his helmet bag on the boarding ladder. He knew it wasn't from the quick bite to eat. It was fear. *This is what I've trained for and I'm good at what I do. So why am I feeling this way. I sure as hell don't want to let anybody down.* Taking a deep breath he answered, "I'm ready—but to tell you the truth I've got a few butterflies."

"Oh, man, I'm glad you said that," said Mirabal shaking his head. I must have tossed and turned half the night away. I don't think I really got to sleep last night. Something tells me though we're not the only ones. A reality check tells me this isn't just going to the office."

They both turned as Matsen and his RIO walked by. "Morning XO," called Mirabal. "You all set?"

Matsen walked over. "I'm about as ready as you can get. How about you guys?"

"We're ready, XO, we're ready," laughed Fancy. "Let's get after them." They mounted the ladder.

After watching an E-2 and an S-3 Viking, from which they would top off from after reaching their assigned altitude, they were directed to Cat 2. The launch, at precisely 0500 went flawlessly. However, the next ten seconds sent the mission south in a hurry.

As Fancy brought up the landing gear he noticed that the horizontal display was flickering. Before he could comment the tactical information display was doing the same thing.

Opening his mouth to say something he heard Mirabal, say, (rather calmly he thought at the time) "Gator, I've got a fire back here." Fighting an urge to say, "You're kidding, right." He knew Mirabal was not kidding. Sweeping the instrument panel he noticed the HSD and TID were still flickering as was everything else, but the big red lights that would tell him there was a fire remained out.

Flames were coming from the right side of the TID from behind the rear-cockpit instrument panel into Mirabal's cockpit. Instinct took over and Fancy immediately shut off both generators, but decided to leave the stability augmentation system switches engaged as well as the corresponding circuit breakers in. Gently he began a turn back to the ship.

"Rhino, is the fire out?"

"No," came the resounding answer, still calm, but maybe pitched higher this time.

With the generator off the cockpit got dark in a hurry even though the sky was beginning to lighten to the east. Reaching for his flashlight he scanned the instruments again. "Any luck?" Fancy said, twisting around in his seat as much as he could muster.

"No!" Mirabal shouted back.

*Geez, this plane is the fastest thing in the fleet and we can't outrun a fire in the cockpit,* he grumbled to himself.

"Can you see where it's coming from?" he shouted, twisting in his seat again.

"It's hard to see anything when you're being barbecued!" came the reply. "Uh, I think it coming from the TID. Hey, I think it might be going out!"

Taking a chance and waiting another thirty seconds, Fancy brought the generator back on line, even though there was some residual smoldering from the insulation around the wiring.

"Does it look like it's out for good?"

"Yeah, yeah, it looks like it, yeah I'm pretty sure it's out," groused Mirabal, who's voice had come down an octave.

With the instrument lighting back on, Mirabal immediately got on the radio to declare an emergency.

Selecting RAM air in order to clear the cockpit, Fancy secured the ECS and brought the cabin pressure down.

As he started to descend he then started to dump fuel in order to get down to the maximum trap limit. Mirabal then inserted the marshal frequency into the front radio just in case the fire flared up again. The controllers calmly vectored them in to the final bearing in order to recover.

Fancy felt the initial adrenaline rush starting to wear off. It was now time to concentrate on good basic aviating and crew coordination. He would have to fly the best pass he could muster with manual throttles, minimal instrument lighting, and only the approach light for the LSO to see.

At one mile they were in the home stretch. The ball started rising and Fancy wrestled with the throttles to pull off the right amount of power.

The LSO quickly responded, "Deck's going down, power, power."

Nudging the throttles forward slowly as the deck came back up, good enough for an OK-2 wire.

As the stricken plane rolled out it was immediately surrounded by the crash-salvage crew throwing chocks under the gear and giving the shutdown signal. *Man, I don't have to see that signal twice* he thought, bringing the throttles to off and safing his ejection seat.

Once on deck they scrambled away from the plane and watched the crash crew do their thing as they swarmed over the Tomcat.

Looking at Mirabal, Fancy restrained himself from laughing out loud. Rhino's green bag looked singed and his nomex gloves were definitely blackened. "Geez, you weren't kidding about being barbecued, were you?" The laugh could be held back no longer.

"Well, I'm glad you thought it was funny! Man, my fun meter was pegged to the max!" Then he laughed too. "Woowee," he continued, shaking his head. "Join the Navy, see the world, catch fire, shit your pants."

"You didn't?"

"No, but I'm never going to make fun of anyone who does, believe me."

"How long do you think it was from the time you called fire, until we climbed out of the plane?" he asked Mirabal.

Shrugging, Mirabal shook his head, "Ten minutes, an hour, maybe longer, it seemed like forever. How long?"

"Would you believe less than two minutes? Talk about time compression. It sure seemed like a lot longer than that to me."

Thinking back to an earlier conversation, Fancy in the most serious voice he could muster commented, "Boy, I don't know. Every time we go up, something happens. Maybe you're just a…"

before he could finish he burst out laughing at seeing Mirabal's face fall.

Taking one more look at the plane, they both laughed and walked across the deck.

Before they had gone five steps, the CAG, Captain Van Gundy and his RIO emerged from below deck, clad in their flight gear. Van Gundy did not look like a happy camper.

"Morning CAG," said Fancy.

Without smiling, Van Gundy stopped short of the two men and proceeded to look them over from head to toe before he spoke. "Are you guys all right? Mirabal, you look a little singed around the edges."

"I'm okay," Mirabal answered. "Gator did a great job of getting us down in one piece."

Looking them over once again, Van Gundy continued. "CENTCOM is going ape because we couldn't fulfill the mission. Koontz and I were the Alert 15, but the pod for my plane had a systems failure and the backup for that one is still being unpacked and put together. What a cluster!" he said, fairly spitting out the words.

Fancy and Mirabal looked at each other, wondering if they were being blamed for the failure of the mission.

"It's just bad luck all the way around, don't worry about it, We'll get it going. Come on Earth Man, let's see if the plane checks out. See you guys later."

After stowing their flight gear they headed back to Ready Three. As they entered the room Fancy noticed a man sitting in the back of the room. He appeared somewhat overweight. Fancy also noted that he was wearing what appeared to be a black jogging suit and some kind of sandals.

Robinson was in the front of the room looking at the map of Iraq. He turned as Fancy and Mirabal continued to the front of the room.

"Hey, hey, you guys had an exciting few minutes this morning. Everybody okay?"

"Rhino's going to need some new gloves and maybe a new green bag, but we're good to go. Right partner?"

Mirabal nodded his head in the affirmative.

Running his hand through his hair, Robinson smiled and said, "I just got a call from the maintenance troops. They said there was a circuit card in the TID that shorted out, caught fire, and then melted two bundles of wire on the left side of the TID. That caused most of the smoke. You guys did a hell of a job getting back on board. Nice going."

"Thanks, Skipper," replied Fancy. "We saw CAG on the roof. It seems like nothing is going right this morning."

"CAG is not a happy man—as you may have gathered. They're probably going to have to take the pod off your plane and put it on his. He should probably launch in twenty minutes—if nothing else goes wrong."

"It looks like you'll be flying that same mission tomorrow morning. Stash will be your wingie. Take the rest of the day to catch up on any paper work or whatever. You'll launch at 0430 in the morning."

"Right, Skipper, 0430 to Badrah."

As they headed out of Ready Three Fancy had another opportunity to look the visitor over. His black hair framed a face with the blackest eyes Fancy had ever seen, and dominating his face was a large hooked nose. For the first time Fancy saw that he was holding an enormous cigar.

As they passed out of the hatch Mirabal whispered, "Did you get a load of that stogie that guy was holding. Shoot, if it was any bigger he could pole vault with it. Must be one of the tech reps from Grumman, what do you think?"

"Beats me, I've never seen him before. He could have come in on the COD."

"Hey, could you direct me to where I could get a cup of coffee?" a voice addressed them from behind.

Turning, they saw the man who had been sitting in the back of Ready Three. "Uh, we're headed for the Dirty Shirt wardroom. Feel free to tag along."

"Thanks, I could use a good cup of java."

"I don't know how good it will be, but it's usually hot," interjected Mirabal. "Are you with Grumman?"

The man stopped. "No, I just came over from the *Lincoln*." Sticking out his hand he continued, "Steve Valdorama, Joker. I was with VF-2, the Bounty Hunters. Man, everybody I've met so far seems to think I'm with Grumman or some other tech rep. What gives?"

Fancy and Miabal looked at each other, both trying to suppress smiles. "Uh, could be the uniform," sniggered Mirabal.

Valdorama stopped as if he had run into a door. "Oh, yeah, well I guess that could be it," he smiled back, his black eyes flashing as the grin spread across his face. "I was just coming out of the head from shaving and showering when I got the word to get up to the roof to the helo that was going to deliver my carcass over here. Naturally, I got here and my gear didn't."

Introductions were completed in the Dirty Shirt wardroom over coffee and breakfast.

"I take it you guys had a little problem after you launched this morning?" probed Valdorama.

Fancy shrugged and rubbed the back of his neck. "Yeah, luckily it was a small problem, although I don't think Rhino," he said gesturing at his RIO, "thought so at the time. He handled it. I don't think I could have been that cool-headed. Honestly, the thing I fear most of all is fire and burning to death," he continued, shaking his head.

Valdorama took a long look at the men across from him. Most of the pilots he knew would have made some kind of smart ass remark at the expense of their RIO. Fancy respected his RIO and wasn't afraid to let him know it. Immediately he knew he would fit in and he knew he liked these two.

Taking another sip of coffee Valdorama asked, "So, what are the Gunfighters like? I've heard some pretty good things—even if you are from the left coast."

Fancy pursed his lips. "I'm pretty new myself. I transferred from VF-84 just before the cruise started."

Valdorama's eyebrows shot up. "The Jolly Rogers, so you're not exactly from the left coast?"

"Not exactly. This is a hell of a squadron as far as I'm concerned. These guys are squared away and have all their shit on the same page," he said holding a steady gaze with Joker's black eyes.

Valdorama held his gaze. "That's what I heard. I'm going to like it here."

There was a pause before Mirabal asked, "Why in the world did you volunteer to spend any more time out here? I thought I'd see some raving lunatic when we heard you were coming."

Chuckling, Valdorama took another sip of coffee and pushed his chair back. "I don't know what you heard, but I was only on Lincoln a month before Enterprise showed up. I was going through that dumb ass FASO training when I got up out of the pool, slipped and put my hip all out of joint. That was just before the cruise started and I got left on the beach to rehabilitate. Man I was pissed off. Believe me I wasn't always this heavy; it was a while before I could start the physical part of the rehabilitation. It's no secret I love to eat and I just got a little out of control. I had to do some fast talking even to get out to *Lincoln* for that month."

Fancy leaned forward on the table pushing his coffee and plate out of the way. "What was it like over Iraq? You see any MiGs?"

Running his hand over his face and through his jet black hair, Valdorama leaned forward. "There were MiGs and probably SU-27s, and some French Mirage F-1s. They'd make a run toward the fence, the 32nd parallel, then split—s for the home drome."

Pausing, Valdorama leaned even closer and lowered his voice. "The Intel Shop on Lincoln was pretty squared away, even if you wonder sometimes about military intelligence. For the most part they gave us some pretty good info. One thing that made an impression on everybody two weeks ago was that the Iraqis were looking to shoot down a western plane, more specifically a Navy plane. It seems that Saddam himself has put a bounty or offered a reward for anyone of his guys that brought down a western aircraft." Shifting in his seat and grinning broadly he continued. "Naturally, they get a lesser amount for an Air Force plane, and even less for anybody else. Welcome to Dodge."

There was silence for a time as the three fliers pondered the information. "Where is this good info coming from?" queried Mirabal.

"Where does any of it come from?" said Valdorama. "Sometimes I think they make it up, but they seemed pretty serious and confident about this."

After another pause he continued. "You've probably guessed that my ancestors came from this part of the world. My grandfather came to California from Lebanon. Most people think that Arabs or other people from this region are just a bunch of camel jockeys, don't know shit and aren't honest. From first hand experience working' with my grandfather, my dad, and their friends, I can tell you that's a bunch of crap. Saddam is one cagey bastard. We've probably noticed he's still around while the guy that was responsible for kickin' his ass is giving speeches to Rotary Clubs in the U.S. He's smart enough to put aside his problems with the Iranians. Personally, I think he's up to something—even if it's just movin' troops around and keeping us, the Saudis, and everybody else in this region stirred up. He just gets points for still being in power."

After letting that sink in Valdorama stood up. "Hey, it's nice meetin' you guys. I think I better round up my gear so I don't have to answer any real hard questions about the big beast. See you later."

After he had retreated out of earshot Fancy remarked, "Funny, I thought his call sign might be Fridge. Seems like he'll fit in here pretty well."

Mirabal nodded, "Yeah, I like him. Wonder how he got the call sign Joker?"

At 0415 the next morning they began to find out. Finishing their walk-around of Desperado 206, Fancy had just climbed in and had finished strapping in when he heard Mirabal utter a loud curse. "Damn, somebody tossed their cookies in here. Judas Priest! Give me a rag so I can wipe it up. Jesus!"

The young enlisted plane captain was mortified and scurried down the boarding ladder to find a rag, screaming at his underlings to get him a rag and ask who threw up in the plane?"

Before too long Mirabal's cursing had turned to laughter. "Hey, Gator, look at this," he said, holding up what looked to be someone's last night's dinner. "It's not real," he said tossing the disgusting looking object into Fancy's lap."

Tentatively Fancy picked it up and laughed. "You think it could be anybody we know?"

"It wouldn't surprise me one bit. We'll have to do some investigating, but I don't think we'll have to look too deep. That's funny."

*At least it is now* Fancy thought to himself.

Fancy breathed a sigh of relief to himself as they pulled away from the S-3 Viking after taking on a full bag of fuel. The launch and refueling had been text book perfect. *A good omen.* Stash McClure was positioned off his starboard side.

"Desperado 207, everything in the green?"

"Everything is in the green and we're good to go, 206."

Fancy felt good with McClure on his wing. He had proven to be a quick study, and was open to criticism and advice. Now he was more than holding his own with the rest of the squadron and seemed to be making progres. He and Mirabal had had a tough time taking two out of three ACM engagements the last time they had flown together.

"Desperado 206, this is Echo six one two. You copy?"

"Desperado 206 reads you loud and clear Echo six one two."

"206, you're cleared to 250 angels. Contact Igloo White on button 4. We show only friendlies in the area. Good luck. Six one two out."

"We copy six one two."

"Dash Two, you copy?"

"Dash Two copies, five by five."

Fancy advanced the throttles slightly and brought the stick back. Even with this slight advancement of the throttles the big fighter seemed to leap ahead as if straining at an invisible leash, eager to get on with the business of the day.

A quick check with the E-3 Sentry AWACS plane confirmed that there were only friendly aircraft in the area.

Once they were at twenty-five thousand feet Fancy could make out the land mass that was Iraq. As soon as they were over land Fancy clicked his mike two times to let Enterprise know they had gone feet dry. Radio silence would be the order of the day until they went feet wet again.

"Rhino, everything working back there?"

"You mean all these little dials and lights, and stuff?"

Chuckling Fancy answered, "Yeah, all that good stuff back there."

"Everything is where it should be. I'm thrilled. When we went feet dry the town we passed over was Al Faw so I know we're pointed in the right direction. This little gizmo that has the screen shows there's nothing in front of us."

Fancy recognized that he felt a great deal different than he had yesterday. He felt calm, no butterflies, no doubts. Glancing to his right he could see McClure bobbing and weaving through the brilliant blue sky.

As they proceeded on a northwesterly course of 345 he looked down at the Iraqi country side. At first he was surprised at how much different it was than Saudi Arabia. While it was barren and dry it didn't seem to be the wasteland that Saudia Arabia had been. There were towns, green fields, clusters of oil rigs, even, he imagined, an oasis.

"Gator, that river must be the Euphrates."

"Yeah, must be. Amazing, at one time that was just something in my seventh grade geography book. I wish I would have paid better attention in some of those so called boring classes. *The cradle of civilization,* he thought to himself. *Just a blue line on a page and here I am flying over it. It's been there forever. Imagine all that's happened since it began its flow to the…the Tigris and that will flow into the Persian Gulf.*

"Gator, I was just thinking I wish I would have paid better attention in school. It doesn't seem that long ago I was trying to memorize that stuff for a test. Gives you kind of a funny feeling doesn't it?'

"You must have been reading my mind. I was just thinking the same thing. Yeah, it does give me a funny feeling. What is is Yogi Berra said, 'Deja vu all over again?'" *I better knock this tourist crap or I'm going to get to see Iraq from the ground, not something I'm anxious to do.*

"Hmmmm," whispered Mirabal, "it looks like they want us to know they know we're here. There's a Top Palm radar that's painting us. That means an SA-2 battery, just where the intel guys said it would be."

Out of the corner of his eye Fancy could hear his own RHAW gear give a weak response to the Iraqi radar. They were just looking and hadn't locked them up—yet.

Three minutes later the Top Palm had given way to a Top Can, meaning an SA-6 SAM battery. Definitely the greater threat. But as before the threat faded as they passed over the city of Al Hayy. Another six minutes and they would pass by the city of Al Kut.

"McClure was still off his port wing about a six hundred yards out.

"Okay, Rhino, we're going down and coming to three five eight."

"Right behind you, Gator," came Mirabal's calm voice.

They had been asked to get the pictures from between fourteen thousand and twelve thousand feet—depending on weather conditions and the clouds. *No clouds and the weather would not be a factor.* The RAW gear was quiet—*too quiet*—he contemplated, suddenly ill at ease the farther they flew into Iraq.

Running his thumb over the red button on his stick he saw the outskirts of Badrah rapidly coming up. He activated, a little late he thought, the cameras. The RHAW gear remained mute, making him feel more uncomfortable than if it had been going crazy. Then they were over the fertilizer complex. With cameras still rolling he rolled the plane into a steep 90 degree bank and reversed course, expecting at any time for the sky to erupt in missiles and triple A. McClure slid above him and was now on his starboard wing. Fuel was no problem—for the present—and instead of climbing they put their noses down and went to full military. The RHAW gear stayed quiet. *This is too easy and it's too quiet.*

"What do you think, Rhino, seemed awfully quiet to me. Is there anything on your gear?"

"Nupe. Looks like they're laying low. Besides, I'll take quiet—and we're not home yet. And…"

"And what?"

"We may have spoken too soon. I've got bogeys, at uh forty miles at angels twenty, they're on our nose."

"Keep an eye on 'em," Fancy said, using the fingers of his right hand to change the switchology from the TARPS pod to his AIM-120 missiles, and flipped up the Master Arm switch.

"Bogeys closing, thirty miles. Ahh, they're Hornets."

Fancy eased his thumb off the red button. "They're a long way from home. Probably low on gas too—they always are."

Mirabal chuckled. F-18s were known for their short legs.

After they had passed beneath the two Hornets, Fancy eased over toward McClure's plane and pointed up, and then held two fingers. They would now climb to twenty thousand feet.

After another thirty-five minutes Fancy clicked his mike once to let Enterprise know they were again feet wet. The rest of the flight and the recovery were again almost text book perfect.

Immediately after they had snagged a three wire, they were directed to the elevator on the starboard side of Enterprise where they were chained down and struck below to the hanger deck. Fancy considered that to be the scariest part of the day so far. He could only trust the yellow-shirts so far he figured.

After changing out of their flight gear and into their khaki uniforms he and Mirabal had a quick debrief and then made their way below to the photo shop where the pictures would be developed and the intel troops would pour over them.

A lieutenant j.g. and assorted enlisted personnel were starting to look at the long strip of film coming out of the developing machine. Foster had what looked like a small magnifying glass in his hand and was bent over the developed film looking at the first of the pictures.

Looking up he said to Fancy, "This must be your work. From what I see so far they look pretty good. I do notice that you may have turned on the camera a little late." The statement was made as a fact with no reproachment indicated.

Fancy shrugged. "I thought I was a little late too. I'll work on it."

Foster again bent over the photos squinting into his glass. Muttering to himself he stood up. "Want to take a look?"

"Sure, thanks," said Fancy taking the glass from the outstretched hand. Bending over one of the frames he squinted into the glass. At first he saw nothing. Taking the glass away from his eye he looked at the picture again. Bringing it into focus he began to make sense of what he was seeing. The pictures were remarkably clear and even from that height he could make out cars, people, even what must have been animals. Nothing he saw looked the least bit threatening however.

He stood up and nodded at Mirabal. "Sure," Foster nodded back.

Mirabal looked at a new picture that had just come out of the machine. He moved the glass around on the frame.

As Mirabal squinted through the glass, Foster asked, "Did you see anything that was unusual—out of the ordinary…?" his voice trailing off.

Fancy rubbed his eyes and shook his head. "We got painted by a couple of SAM sites, only briefly. I thought they would be looking at us a lot harder. I mean it was a really easy up and back," he shrugged.

Foster pulled on his lower lip and nodded.

"These are really clear and sharp, but I don't see anything that's worth the trip—at least so far," mused Mirabal, again scanning the new pictures rolling out of the developer.

Foster grinned. "This is only what you shot first. There's probably nothing much on the first few dozen frames. We'll be up all night looking. You never know what's going to show up—it might be that one in a million something that somebody in the head shed is looking for. Why don't you come back later, say in two hours then you can see what the fertilizer factory looks like."

"Thanks, I'll probably do that," replied Fancy.

Making their way back to Ready Three they again saw Valdorama, wreathed in cigar smoke, but now dressed in his uniform. Fancy noted that, like himself, he was a lieutenant, not that it mattered to Fancy.

Valdorama looked up from the NATOPS manual he had been reading. "Ah ha. The intrepid warriors return to the home drome. How'd it go?"

Shaking his head Fancy replied, "Piece of cake. We got painted by a couple of SAM sites, just where the intel guys said we would, but other than that it was a real milk run. I'm not complaining mind you, just noting the information. Actually, it seemed too quiet, too easy. That's just my gut feeling."

"I don't know about you, but I trust my instincts more than anything," he said patting his ample midriff.

"Maybe Saddam knows the first team is here," put in Mirabal. "You said he wasn't stupid."

"Yeah, but I also told you about the bounty he's got on our collective heads, and that's on pretty good authority." Shrugging, Valdorama smiled, "Let's both stick with our gut feelings, Gator."

Fancy looked into the coal black eyes. "I hadn't planned on changing my ways now. Rhino, you can be the optimist for both of us."

Looking a bit chagrined, Mirabal hesitated and then said, "I was always taught to defer to my elders and those wiser than me. Don't worry about me."

"I don't, Rhino, I don't, but…"

"But what?"

"Nothin', geez let's not go too far off the deep end. This was only our first mission."

After Mirabal had departed to parts unknown, Fancy sat down by Valdorama. "He's the best. I couldn't believe how calm he was when that fire broke out the other day. I really feel good when he's back in the pit."

"Good RIOs are hard to find. I've had a couple that just drove me nuts. Here was this one guy that couldn't make it through flight school telling me what to do and when to do it. Unbelievable."

"So," Fancy inquired, "how'd you wind up driving a Tomcat?"

"Women."

"Women?"

"Bet your ass. I grew up in Laguna Beach, it's south of Los Angeles about 80 miles. Some buddies of mine were going up to the air show at El Toro, a Marine Corps Air Station. They told me there would be all kinds of women there."

"And?"

"And, there were. The Blue Angels flew that afternoon—really awesome performance."

"So, the Blue Angels inspired you?"

"No! I told you it was the women. After they landed they came down to where everybody was standing, you know back of the yellow tape guarded by these jarheads. Anyway, these guys come down to this line and you know who got the autographs. The babes. Right then I started thinking."

Fancy stared at him with no comment.

"Well, in high school, up till then I couldn't get a date or even a girl to look at me. In school I'd just laughed my way through without even cracking a book hardly. I checked my friendly local recruiter to see what it might take. He suggested I try Navy ROTC. So I got real serious about school, especially math, which the recruiter said I'd need. My parents just about had a heart attack, they couldn't believe I was finally following their advice."

"My dad was so glad because of the drug problem in Laguna. Lots of drugs there. In fact he told me one day he'd rather kill me than see me mess up my life with that stuff. If you knew my dad, you'd know he was dead serious about it."

"Anyway I got into UCLA, the ROTC and basically worked my butt off. I got into flight school and then we found out the whole class except for about five people would be going to helos. I couldn't believe it. But I lucked out and was one of the two that didn't get to be helo driver."

How'd you get here?"

"'Bout the same way. I went to Syracuse."

"Like it?"

"Yeah. Some day I might even get good at it. Who knows?"

Valdorama looked at Fancy for a good long time. "I've been talking to some of the guys, Bagger, Poncho, Killer, the midget Moose, Big Wave...They all said the same thing. You've got it together."

Fancy smiled. "You know as well as I do, don't believe anything you hear and and only half of what you see. I'll see you later. When do you go up?"

"I'm going to sit the Alert Five in an hour and then I'm flying with the XO to Badrah in the morning at zero dark thirty."

"See you later then."

"Count on it."

# 14

Over the next two weeks Fancy flew two more missions to Badrah, one mission to Al Salman, carrying the TARPS pod and three missions where he escorted the TARPS plane. Each of these missions proved to be almost identical to the first mission to Badrah. It was fast becoming the consensus of most of the squadron that the Iraqis didn't have the cajones to challenge the Western aircraft—particularly Navy planes. Fancy and Valdorama weren't buying it.

Fancy looked off his port wing and saw that Big Wave was right where he should be—five hundred yards out and stepped up about three hundred feet. He and Big Wave had drawn what everyone considered the most boring of any of the possible missions, escorting a high value unit or HVU. The unit being an EA6B Prowler. This particular Prowler was providing electronic jamming for an F/A-18 division (four planes) patrolling the fence or 32nd parallel or no-fly zone. As the F/A-18s they would make sure the Hornets weren't being followed by any Iraqi aircraft. Although there were numerous "targets" or aircraft out in front of them, none of them, at the time, were Iraqi planes.

At present they were nearly sixty miles southwest of the Iraqi city of An Najaf. To make matters worse, during what was considered a whisky delta mission the weather had turned sour and there was considerable turbulence, along with clouds going from the deck to over thirty thousand feet.

"Dash Two, how you doing?"

Big Wave, as if gathering his thoughts, finally answered. "Oh, just peachy-keen. Now I know what a yo-yo feels like. Jesus, it's hard to hold'er down. I've never been tossed around like this. Tanking is going to be really exciting—I can hardly wait for that."

Fancy, taking a quick look at his own fuel gauges realized that time was fast approaching. As soon as the Hornets were out of the area the EA6B pulled a 180 and headed back to Enterprise. Having been on station for nearly four hours the Tomcats would need fuel to get back to the ship.

Looking at his kneeboard, Fancy noted that the Hornets would be heading home and passing underneath their position in ten minutes. He knew where and at what altitude the tanker, in this case an Air Force KC-135, could be found. Fancy had to agree with Big Wave about being tossed around like a chip of wood on a storm tossed sea. This was as bad as he had ever flown in. Not impossible but extremely uncomfortable.

As the Hornets headed back to the Enterprise (knowing they would need to refuel too but closer to the ship) the EA6B turned toward *Enterprise*. As Big Wave and Fancy turned to their new heading the turbulence got worse.

Once the KC-135 had been spotted Fancy pulled up and under the tanker's tail. Since the KC-135s were used primarily to refuel Air Force planes, Fancy thought of them as somewhat makeshift. They had been put together to refuel Navy planes that used the probe and drouge method. At the end of the boom was the refueling probe, that was plugged into the receiving aircraft by an Air Force enlisted man laying down and looking out a plexiglass window. In order to get more bang for the buck, a hose and basket had been added to the refueling probe and the receiving Navy planes had to plug into the basket they normally used. The hose with the basket attached, trailed out about nine feet. It neither extended nor retracted. At the point where the basket was attached to the hose, there was a heavy steel turnbuckle. If things went south the turnbuckle could slam into the canopy with the force of a steel wrecking ball leaving the pilot in a world of hurt.

Fancy eased his plane up to the basket that was moving around in the turbulence. On his second try he was able to stab the basket and push the probe in the required two feet to begin the flow of fuel. Between the fumes of the fuel and the constant buffeting, Fancy wondered if he was going to be able to keep his last meal down.

Fancy eased the throttles forward as he felt the plane begin to sink under the weight of added fuel. The plane was moving around and it took all his concentration in order to keep his connection to the tanker.

At last, the fueling was complete. Fancy disengaged and let the tanker pull away from him. Fancy eased over to starboard and Big Wave moved into position to begin receiving fuel.

As he watched Big Wave slide into position he noticed the turbulence was increasing. Big Wave missed the basket on his first try. *Come on Wave, take a deep breath and put that mother in there. You can do it.* Another miss and yes, the turbulence was definitely getting to be a factor.

Fancy twisted around in his seat, rotating his neck, while willing Big Wave's probe into the basket. The moment he looked back toward the KC-135 the resounding sound of cursing shot through his helmet. "Shit, Goddammit, fuck, damn…" and continued for what seemed like an eternity.

"Dash Two, what's the matter? You copy?" He was rewarded by more cursing.

Finally, "That Goddamn turnbuckle nailed us! Jesus! For two cents I'd put some twenty mike-mike into that tanker! Damn!"

So much for radio discipline.

"Wave, has the canopy got a hole in it?"

"Lead," came a somewhat calmer reply, "no, but the damn thing looks like the inside of a spider web."

"Can you complete refueling, Dash Two?"

"Right now, I think not; completing refueling is not an option."

"All right, Dash Two, take a deep breath, give it another try. Do you think descending to a lower altitude would help?"

"No, Lead. I want some altitude if..." he let his voice trail off.

"Understood, Dash Two."

Fancy watched as Big Wave backed off, then came forward to make the connect.

"I've got fuel flowing," came Wave's voice, about two octaves lower than on the last transmission.

Just as he was about to say something to Mirabal, a voice blasted through his earphones. "Desperado 207, this is Igloo 605."

Despite the ringing in his ears Fancy managed to reply, civily he thought, "Read you loud and clear, Igloo." *With emphasis on loud.*

"Desperado, we're tracking two fast movers that have taken off from Al Kufah. They're definitely over the fence and it looks like they're headed your way. Come to three three zero. They're at 120 miles and climbing from, uh, angels 12."

As he brought the Tomcat around Mirabal commented, "Well, a MiG at your six is better than no MiG at all."

Fancy grunted from the g forces that were threatening to push him down into one corner of his cockpit. Settling on three three zero, he asked, "You got 'em?"

After just the slightest of pauses Mirabal came back. Yep, two fast movers, climbing at 100 miles angels 14. I smell MiG 29s. Still comin' hard!"

Fancy found the two fast moving dots on his own radar display. *Ninety miles. What are these guys up to?* he wondered.

"Eighty-two miles and closing, angels 16," said Mirabal. "We've got them on collision."

"Still just the two?"

"Only two, Gator. Geez, don't they know they're outnumbered. Dumb shits," he murmured. "Seventy miles. Come port, uh, 10."

Fancy came left.

"Speed is 500 knots, sixty miles, angels 16, they've leveled out."

"Rhino, looks like they're increasing speed."

"Looks like it."

Fancy advanced the throttles and the big plane plunged ahead like a hunting dog released from its leash.

"Forty-five miles, still at angels 16, speed 530 knots."

At thirty miles Fancy flipped on the Master Arm Switch and selected the AIM-120 Slammer. He didn't want any distractions if things got ugly.

"Jesus!" came Mirabal's startled cry, "The lead guy has just launched! Unless they have something new, they're way out of range!"

"Popping flares!" declared Fancy. "He's jinking into us! Fancy, after checking that the Master Arm was in the on position, he ran his thumb over the red button on the stick as he rolled into a barrel roll just in case they did have something new, keeping the MiGs on their nose.

"Fifteen miles. Let's shoot these guys!" grunted Mirabal.

"I've got no tone! No tone!" Fancy muttered back.

And then—suddenly—there was a tone or a sound more like the sound of rattlesnake indicating the AIM-120 had acquired the target. Fancy squashed the red button and for an instant thought that they had a dud. An instant later the Slammer had dropped from its station on the port wing and was streaking away from them.

They were rewarded by the site of a of a puff of dirty gray smoke, not the dramatic explosion so often seen in the movies. The Slammer in all its lethality had done its job.

"Holy shit!" breathed Mirabal. "You got him! It looks like his buddy has reversed and is leaving the area. Man oh man. AMF baby!"

"We got him."

"Right, that's what I meant."

Fancy decided against any further pursuit but continued to keep the MiG on the scope as it rapidly accelerated away from the conflagration that had been his wingman.

As Fancy brought the fighter around in order to head back to Enterprise a strange silence settled over the plane and for a few minutes they flew with only the "Indian night noises" (sounds a plane makes in flight) were the only sounds that accompanied them.

Finally, after what seemed an eternity Fancy asked, "Did you see a chute?"

"Negative on the chute, Gator. I don't think the guy got out."

"Neither do I," he responded. "Neither do I."

They flew along in silence until they had crossed the coast back into the Persian Gulf.

"What do you think that guy was thinking about, launching at that range?" inquired Fancy who felt he had to say something to break the silence.

"Well, you know you've got a Tomcat coming straight down your throat. Right there that's got to set the pucker factor of—say about eight. He knows the home team hasn't got much to show for its effort, or lack there of since they were dukin' it out with Iran. The guy must have figured blast away and hope for the best."

"Mmmm," murmured Fancy. "Did you see any sign of the missiles he fired at us?"

"I can't be sure. When you went into the barrel roll I lost it for a few seconds."

"Sure happened quick. I'd always envisioned this big rolling, banking, breaking dogfight."

"I'll take it any day," laughed Mirabal.

"It's funny, I don't feel like I thought I would. I mean the only reason we put up with a lot of this garbage is to one day get a MiG."

"Would you feel better if there had been a chute?'

"Could be. Yeah, I think I'd feel better. I guess."

Thirty minutes later they had recovered on board *Enterprise*. As they climbed down from the plane Fancy became aware of a cheering crowd gathering around them. Bagger was the first member of the squadron to get to them. Immediately he engulfed both aviators, one in each of his long arms and drew them into an embrace.

"Oh man! You guys did it. This is so great!" he thundered. "Babe, I'm so proud of you! If it couldn't be me, Gator, I'm glad it was you!"

Fancy felt by now that he was in more danger from Bagger than he had been from the MiGs.

"Jesus, Bagger, Fancy hissed, "you're going to break my ribs!"

Bagger seemed not to have heard and managed to squeeze even harder, while twirling him, and now Mirabal, who he had managed to get in his grasp, around in a tightening circle. The crowd continued to swell. Just when Fancy thought they might be crushed by the ever growing group of sailors, the sea of men started to part and the crowd grew noticeable quieter.

The CAG and Captain Bedley came through the sailors like two sailors headed for the nearest bar on a long deserved shore leave. Van Gundy extended his hand and shook. Fancy thought he was happier and possibly more human than he had ever seen him.

"Fancy, Mirabal, congratulations! You both did a fantastic job. Sierra Hotel all the way!"

Before Fancy could answer Van Gundy had grabbed Mirabal's hand. "You've made us all proud, nice work!"

Bedley immediately took Fancy's hand in his own great paw and shook it until Fancy felt like a pump being primed by someone who was dying of thirst. "You men have made the whole ship proud. Of course you probably have no idea how everyone feels." As if on cue the crowd of sailors roared their approval. Van Gundy raised his arms to encourage the crowd to another cheer.

After a few seconds of pandemonium, Van Gundy motioned for quiet. "Lieutenant Fancy, could we get you to say a few words?"

*Like I have a choice?* Fancy thought. After clearing his throat, "We were very fortunate today, we were in the right place, at the right time, with the greatest airplane in the world."

There was a roar from the crowd, mostly from the Tomcat maintainers Fancy figured.

After waiting for the noise to die down he continued. "Every man on this ship deserves some of the credit for what happened up there today. Believe it or not we do know and appreciate what people do on this ship to make sure these planes can launch, carry out the mission, and, like today…" he let his voice trail off amid the cheers of the assemblage.

"Lieutenant Mirabal," asked, actually more like an order, "would you like to say something," smiled Van Gundy Fancy almost had to laugh at the look of panic that spread across his friend's face.

"Uh, well, hey, thanks, we couldn't have done it without all you guys." He stopped, looking for all the world like he hoped the deck would swallow him up.

Bedley motioned for the gathering to quiet down. "I hope that I can get a first hand account of what happened today. Right now these guys probably want to get out of the gear and relax a little."

Fancy smiled and nodded in the affirmative. Waving one more time he and Mirabal made their way below to divest themselves of their flight gear. Below decks they were congratulated and pummeled by those troops who had not been able to make it up to the flight deck.

After a thirty minute debrief with the intel troops Fancy was able to make his way to his cabin, where he slumped down on his rack. Falling back he sighed and closed his eyes.

Almost immediately the door flew open and Bagger charged through the hatch.

Hoping to save himself from being suffocated, Fancy sat up and held up his hands protectively. "Whoa, man. My ribs can't take any more. Man, I didn't know you were so strong."

Bagger hardly slowed down. "I'm just so stoked! It's just…Geez, I don't know…Everybody just feels great about what happened."

Fancy kneaded his forehead with his thumb and forefinger, realizing for the first time that he had the mother of all headaches. Running his hand through his hair he leaned back on his rack.

"You don't look like you're happy about this. You okay?"

Pursing his lips and letting out a great deal of air Fancy moved his head around trying to get the kinks out of his neck. "There was no chute. As far as Mirabal and I know, the guy didn't get out." He shrugged, frowning.

"So?"

"So, when I launched this morning I just didn't figure on taking anyone's life. You know, we, I, all of us, want to shoot the MiGs, but you know…"

"I'll tell you what I know, and without any apologies, I'm glad you're here and they're not celebrating in Baghdad. He wouldn't be losing any sleep if you were so much scrap metal in the desert. Would he?"

Fancy held up his hands and shook his head. "I don't know, but I doubt it."

Bagger smiled and nodded in the affirmative. "Exactly. That guy had his chance. He blew it and paid the price. Case closed."

Fancy couldn't help but smile. A serious Bagger was almost too much to behold.

"Did any mail happen to make it our way?" Fancy said, glad to be changing the subject.

"Yeah, I think I saw some bags comin' off the COD. What do you say we get some food. Air combat makes me hungry."

"Makes you hungry?"

"Exactamundo. If I ever get a MiG, there won't be enough food to satisfy me for days, yeah days. I'm starved, come on, let's go."

"You go ahead, I'm not very hungry right now. I'll catch up to you after a while."

"All right, I can see you'd rather not talk about it, but I hope I get a first hand account of what happened?"

"You will, I promise," smiled Fancy as he sank back on his rack. Although he felt drained, sleep wouldn't come.

Twenty-four hours later Fancy wasn't sure he was any less tired. Since he wasn't scheduled to fly until that night, he had been "invited" to have lunch with Captain Bedley. He and Mirabal had hiked up to the rarified air of the Captain's cabin and had lunch not only with Captain Bedley, but also Admiral Blue, and Captain Van Gundy. There was very little eating and a great deal of recounting the events of the previous day. Both he and Mirabal had been glad to beat a retreat after ninety minutes of rehashing the "incident" as Fancy was beginning to think of it.

Walking back to Ready Three Miralbal shook his head and remarked, "Well, that went well didn't it? I can't believe I actually had lunch with an Admiral and a Captain, uh Captains. Amazing."

"It wasn't too bad was it? I mean after all they seemed pretty genuine, pretty down to earth."

"Yeah, Van Gundy even chews with his mouth open. My mother would have been all over him if that meal had taken place at my folk's house, captain or not."

As they walked through the hatch into Ready Three, Fancy felt relieved that everyone in the room had heard the details and he wouldn't have to relive, what he had come to think of, as the "incident" one more time.

Bagger turned to greet them, smiling and holding out two letters. "Hey, hey, hey, two for you."

Fancy managed to have enough decorum not to snatch them out of his hand. "Thanks. These are just what I needed," he sighed, hardly daring to look at them, fearing they might not be what he really was hoping for.

Looking at the first letter he frowned, noting his mother's writing. Any other time…Shoving the first letter under the second letter his heart gave a jump as he saw the return address. Looking more closely at the writing he saw that although it said Thorn, the writing definitely was not Cody's although the address was that of her house.

Eagerly tearing the envelope and removing the letter, he began to read.

Bagger turned toward Fancy just in time to hear his friend gasp and then lose all the color in his face as if someone had turned on a faucet to drain a hose. Fancy seemed to go limp and put his hand on the bulkhead to steady himself. Bailey started toward him.

"Jesus, Gator, you're as white as sheet, what's the matter?" As Bailey looked at his stricken friend he could see his mouth was trying to work but no words seemed to be able to make their way out.

"Is it a 'Dear John'? What is it?"

Reluctantly Fancy extended a visibly shaking hand and Bagger took the letter. Bailey felt his own legs go weak and felt his own color sink to his lower extremities. "No, oh no, God no…" was all he say.

By now most of the conversation in the room had dropped off the scope and every aviator in the room was looking at Fancy and Bailey. Mirabal made his way over to his friend. As long as he would live he would never forget the look on their two faces. Bailey, now also unable to articulate his thoughts nodded at Mirabal and then at the letter. Fancy nodded back in the affirmative.

Still looking at his two friends Mirabal took the letter and began to read. When he came to the word shot, he shook his head as if trying to clear it and reread it. Somehow he managed to get through to the end. "Jesus Christ…This can't be. Oh, Gator…" he whispered, running his hands through his hair. "I'm so sorry…"

*That sounds so lame , it doesn't even begin to cover it* he thought, reaching out without thinking to put his hand on Fancy's arm.

By now a silence had fallen over Ready Three like a terrible shroud. Robinson looking up sensing that something was wrong, scanning the assembled men. It was like a tomb—just an overwhelming silence. Chills ran up his back as if someone had dropped ice cubes down his shirt. *What in the world could shut down this mob?*

"Rhino, what's the matter here?"

"Skipper, Gator just got a letter…"

"I can see that!" Robinson snapped. "Is it a Dear John?"

"No…"

"Well?" he asked, wondering just why he wasn't talking to Fancy, but in truth, Fancy didn't look at all well, and Bailey didn't look much better.

Mirabal paused, wishing he were somewhere, anywhere else. Swallowing and pausing again, but also sensing Robinson's growing impatience. "Gator, uh Lt. Fancy was, uh is…going with a lady back in California. A couple of weeks or ten days ago, I'm not sure, someone broke into her house and shot her and her daughter. The daughter's about ten years old. This letter is from her brother."

"Are they…?"

Mirabal fumbled with the letter. "Ummm, yeah, no, uh, they're both alive. The mother was shot in the head. She seems to be in serious condition. Her daughter, Amanda, was shot in the back and may be paralyzed from the neck down."

"Jesus! Fancy, are you okay?" Robinson regretted the question as soon as it was out of his mouth. *Sure, he's just swell. Judas Priest, what a dumb-ass thing to say.*

"I'm sorry," he continued, "of course you're not okay."

Fancy by now looked slightly better, starting to regain some of his color and looked, Robinson thought, only slightly better than death warmed over.

Fancy was aware of where he was and who was around him, but he felt as if he was in a world where time and motion had been slowed down. His arms felt like two lead weights that threatened to drag him down to he knew not where. From somewhere deep inside him he could feel his stomach start to churn and then someone had grabbed a nearby wastebasket and the lunch he had enjoyed with the brass came up. Other hands helped him to a seat. Putting his head in his hands be leaned over hoping to clear his head. Surely if he just waited a few minutes he would be awake, dressing for the next mission. In his heart he knew it was not a bad dream.

Robinson squatted in front of him. "Listen, I'm going to take you off the flight schedule for a couple of days."

Attempting to get to his feet Fancy, breathing hard managed to hold up his hand in protest. "Skipper, I can…"

"Bull shit! I want you to jog, go to the weight room, the Chaplain, what ever…"

"I can hold up my end, Skipper. I'm okay, really."

"Yeah, yeah, I can see that. Listen, I don't know your, your…"

"Fiancee."

"You're not okay. I'm not okay with this and I don't even know her! Got it?"

Fancy could see that Robinson had made up his mind and was not going to give an inch." "Okay, Skipper."

"Now that we've got that ironed out, get out of here and get some rest. And take Bagger with you, he looks as bad as you do."

Putting his face closer to Fancy's, "I'm so sorry. It sounds so weak, but I really am. Now, get out of here."

Fancy wasn't sure how he and Bagger managed to get down to their room. Things seemed out of focus, so disjointed, so unreal. Everything seemed to be a blur going in slow motion. He sagged down on to his bunk and closed his eyes. Bagger shut the door and leaned against it shaking his head.

"I'm, I'm…" Bagger began. "This just doesn't make any sense. No sense at all. Who in the hell would do something like that?"

"Her ex. I caught that much from the letter." He extended the letter back to Bailey.

Scanning the letter and mumbling to himself, Bailey screwed up his face as he read and then reread the letter. "Yeah, it says her ex had been calling and had even showed up once at her house. She didn't want to worry anybody so she didn't say anything to you because you had enough on your mind as it was."

"What's her brother like."

"For starters he's big. Real big and he really cares about his sister. Her ex is in a world of hurt if he ever gets his hands on him and somehow I think that's a real good possibility."

The two men continued to stare at the letter; each hoping beyond hope that it was still a bad dream, but knowing it wasn't.

"What are you going to do for the next two days?"

"I don't know. There's absolutely no reason I shouldn't be flying."

"I think there's every reason. You should have seen the color drain out of your face. No, Ratchett's right, you need to sort things out, get your thoughts together. For once I'm glad you're not flying next to me."

At first, Fancy felt a well-spring of anger rise within him and he stiffened.

"Think about it. Would you want me to be on your wing if this had happened to me?"

Fancy relaxed and lay back down on his rack taking a deep breath. "Okay, you're right, Skipper's right, shit—that bastard!"

For what seemed the first time in hours Bagger forced a grin. "That's one of the many good things about me. I'm usually right." He wasn't quite fast enough to duck the pillow that hit him in the face.

For the next two days he ran, lifted weights, and spent a good deal of time on the fantail of the ship watching the wake of the great ship and trying to make sense of what had happened, wondering if he had somehow caused the tragedy.

Finally, not knowing exactly how he had arrived, he found himself outside the office of the Chaplin.

The sign on the hatch said Commander J. Deverich, Chaplin. Pausing before the door he heard what he thought was someone hitting something. Raising his hand he knocked on the door.

"Come in!" came the immediate response.

Fancy opened the door. He saw a short, powerful looking man busy working out on a speed bag hanging in one corner of the small gray spartan office. The man paused long enough to motion Fancy to come in, then he went back to committing mayhem on the bag. Sweat flew off him as he kept up a continued battering of the bag. Finally, he stopped, breathing heavily. Facing Fancy he smiled and extended a meaty paw. Fancy looked into gray eyes that seemed to sparkle at some unheard joke. His bald pate was ringed by a fringe of black hair. There didn't seem to be much of a neck and his powerful shoulders seemed to blend into his head. Standing only slightly over five feet he seemed to be nearly as wide as he was tall.

"Lt. Fancy, I've been expecting you."

Fancy felt a firm but not an excruciating handshake. Regaining his hand he said. "Why?"

"Do you realize every member of the Gunfighters over the last two days, have dropped in here or by the chapel, asking me to put in a good word for your fiancee. I figured it was only a matter of time before you showed up. Please, sit down."

Fancy dropped into a green, somewhat battered government issue chair. He shook his head. "I'm…"

"Lost?"

"I guess that's a good a way to put it as any. There's just no sense to it. I'm so angry one minute—then just…I don't know."

"Something like this always leaves more questions than answers."

Deverich rose and walked back toward the speed bag. "Personally, I'd like to go five or six rounds with the son of…uh the poor misguided soul that did it." Immediately, he unleashed a series of blows on the bag that sounded like a heavy rain on a tin roof. "Professionally, I'd like to look into his soul and find the reason someone would commit such heinous crime; then I'd like to save him." More blows rained down on the bag.

"Of course you're probably wondering why God would let something like this happen to…?"

"Her name is Cody, Cody Thorn. She's one of those rare people who's made the most of her life, to really raise herself up from some pretty humble beginnings."

Deverich gave the speed bag one more ferocious wallop. "Sounds like love to me. How long have you known her?"

"We met at the air show there at Miramar, before we left on the cruise. She's just a terrific person, mother, human being…Most of our courtship has been done through letters or the couple of times we were able to connect on the telephone."

Deverich fell heavily into his swivel chair. "Do you blame God for this?"

Fancy rubbed his temples and gave a huge sigh. "No, I don't think so. I was raised to believe we—uh people had free agency. God doesn't sit around and pick and choose what happens to who. Of course, I'm no expert."

Deverich leaned back in his chair, clasping his hands back of his head. After a moment's pause, he smiled. "Of course most people think I am. I do know that God loves us all—even those bas…uh sad souls whose actions cause others so much pain and suffering. Personally, I think those people who can get over the rage and desire for revenge help not only themselves but those people who have been directly affected."

"I can understand that and I can even embrace it, really doing it is something else."

"I went up to the bow last night after flight ops had wound down. At one point I had decided to resign. I mean why am I here if someone I really care about can't be safe in her own home. What's the point. Who needs me more?"

Deverich glanced at the wings still attached to Fancy shirt. "Can I assume you've reached a decision about that?"

Fancy glanced down at his gold wings and ran his hand over them. "As I stood there feeling sorry for myself I remembered how hard I had to work for them. Even though Cody would support that, I think she would be kind of disappointed if I did turn in my wings. She's a fighter and I think she'd want me stay the course, so to speak."

After a lapse of several seconds Fancy went on. "But I really don't want to be a hazard to anyone else in the squadron. Getting someone killed because my head isn't where it should be, I've thought about that quite a bit. It makes me wonder about whether I'm any better. I took a life. I…"

Deverich nodded his approval. " As far as you being like the poor sack of sh.. uh,…fellow that shot your friend, there's absoluteiy no comparison. It could have gone his way. You know that. Don't put any extra baggage on yourself. Your job out here is tough enough. How can I help you?"

" Geez, I don't know. We'll, I think you already have."

"Oh?"

The two men stared at each other.

"I guess I just needed to talk about it, verbalize with someone apart from those people who have been close to me on the ship. Somehow, I just feel some of the weight has been lifted off of me. I really appreciate your time, Sir."

"That's why I'm here. Don't be a stranger, I just love to talk you know."

Fancy stood up and extended his hand. "You really know how to work that speed bag. I'm impressed."

"Boxing got me through school. Boston College, class of '85. I managed to win a few more than I lost."

"Thanks again, Sir. I really appreciate it."

"You're welcome, and like I said, drop in any time. By the way, congratulations on the MiG. That really gave the whole ship a lift."

"I guess I will be back. There was no chute, the guy didn't get out as far as I know. That kind of bothers me…"

"I would think it would to some extent, even if he fired first. No matter how hard we train, humanity can't be programed out of most people. Like I said, I love to talk or just listen."

Fancy extended his hand and then headed for Ready Three.

Deverich listened to Fancy's receding footsteps. *Strange, no, not strange, different. A pilot who's not so full of himself that he can worry about someone else's life — even someone who tried to kill him. Different, definitely different.*

When Fancy walked into Ready Three most of the squadron was present sitting or talking several knots of men. The conversation died momentarily then picked up again. Several of the pilots and RIOs nodded at him and then went back to their conversations. Just as he was about to head over to where Killer, Poncho, and Big Wave were leaning against the bulkhead, Robinson entered the room behind him.

"Gator, how are you doing?" Putting his hand on his shoulder and giving it a squeeze, he continued on to the front of the room.

"I feel pretty good, Skipper. When do I get to go up again?" he asked his retreating back.

"Tonight, you and Valdorama. All right you animals, let's get seated."

Standing impatiently at the front of the room he waited until the room was quiet. "We've gotten some information, regarding Gator's shoot-down the other day. I'm not sure how this information was obtained, but it's supposed to be pretty accurate."

The assembled aviators moaned in protest. Too much intelligence had proved to be grossly inaccurate or just plain wrong.

Waiting for the commotion to die down he continued. "On what is good authority, and it was strongly hinted that this information came from someone on the ground close to this situation. Anyway, the wingie of the hombre that Gator shot down was taken directly from his plane, tried in about fifteen minutes and then shot right in front of his wife and young son."

Valdarama, sitting down the row from Fancy, leaned forward and looked down the row. After their eyes had met, Joker nodded and leaned back in his seat. Fancy felt himself break out in a cold sweat.

Robinson let the silence hover like a dark cloud for several moments. "I don't know about you, but I'm wondering what kind of people would do something like that. It does tell me that these bozos are definitely serious about bagging a western aircraft, particularly a Navy plane. As far as I'm concerned they've thrown down the gauntlet. We need to make sure we've got our heads on a swivel and our shit on the same page."

"Skip, what about the ROEs? Do we need to let them shoot first?" called out Valdorama.

Looking slightly annoyed, Robinson massaged his right temple. "I've talked to CAG, and he's talked to Admiral Blue. They both feel if you feel that you're in any kind of danger or situation, take 'em out, and they'll back us up all the way."

The murmurs of approval rolled through the room, and several of the aviators gave high-fives to those men sitting close to and around them.

A smile broke out on Robinson's face as he again waited for the noise to die down. "Poncho, will you close the hatch, please."

After the door was shut he continued. "What I'm going to tell you now will go no further than this room. Understood?"

Before Robinson could begin the hatch opened and Matsen walked in and sat down. At the sound of what could be someone loudly passing gas he shot to his feet, turning red as he did so. Leaning back down he brought the red whoopee cushion up chest high. "Bagger, I'm gonna have your ass for this!"

After the laughter died down, Killer called out, "XO, Bagger launched two hours ago."

Finding nothing but innocence in the sea of faces, Matsen sat down still clutching the whoopee cushion. "Bagger had to have something to do with this," he muttered.

Robinson shook his head. He knew Matsen wasn't as outraged as he seemed and as far as he was concerned they could use all the tension breakers they could get.

Again, Fancy looked down the row and caught Valdorama's eye. Valdorama just winked and went back to giving his full attention to Robinson who had just pulled down a map of Iraq.

"Again, I want to emphasize that what I'm going to tell you must not leave this room. I don't want it discussed anywhere but here when we've secured this room. I hope I'm perfectly clear on this."

After waiting for any questions or comments, of which there were none, he continued. "As you know, we've been doing a lot of TARPS work around Badrah. Two days ago I was briefed by Admiral Blue. Badrah is a legitimate point of interest and we're going to be going back there time and again. However," he turned and pointed to a spot east of Badrah on the map. "this is Al Ritt. As you can see it's within five kilometers of the border with Iran."

Pulling down another map, one with what looked like a satellite photo attached he continued. "East of the town are these two hills. Intelligence has strong reason to believe that some kind of cave which already exists is being enlarged on this hill right here." He pointed to the hill on the right.

"What CENTCOM and every other agency that has an interest in this part of the world wants us to do is keep a discreet eye on this place. Specifically, when we go to Badrah they want us to, and these are their words, egress to the east over Al Ritt and then expend film. However, we've got to make sure that these are random passes, no pattern whatsoever and only once in a great while when we do go to Badrah. As you might have guessed, it is probably pretty difficult to get people in this part of Iraq or Iran. Satellites will continue to be used but we are very definitely an important piece of the big picture."

Letting the information sink in for a few moments and hearing no questions or comments Robinson moved forward. "In spite of the somewhat aggressive moves put on by the Iraqis, the wheels in the 'Puzzle Palace' have decided to pull out some of the Air Force and Army units they sent over when the Iraqis were moving troops around. They don't feel the Iraqis are in any shape to make any serious moves."

After the groans and catcalls had died down Robinson smiled his entire face smile. "Now for the really good news." The room became as silent as a tomb. "CAG says we're going to be running the COD down to Bahrain once a week to give everyone some time off this bird farm." This welcome bit of good news got everyone's attention in a big way. Robinson had to wait a good three minutes before the din even started to die down.

Bahrain is a very small island nation located down off the eastern coast of Saudi Arabia it was barely thirty miles long and only eight to ten miles wide. In the early 70s the island gained full autonomy from the British having been a protectorate of that late great country. It is ruled by a family, headed by an Emir. Its economy had once depended on oil but now focused on banking and commerce having earned the reputation as the Switzerland of the Mid East. While still an Islamic state the people and the government are more relaxed than those nations surrounding it. Alcohol was not forbidden and because of this the tiny country attracts a great number of tourists from neighboring countries.

"Gee, I didn't think anybody would want to go," crowed Robinson.

"Hey, Skip," queried Valdorama, "who gets to go first?"

"Joker, I haven't decided, but it will probably be the people with the most seniority with the squadron or, who have a pressing need to go. I understand," he beamed, "that they have a first class phone system with easy access to the states." Turning toward where Fancy was seated, he winked.

"Don't worry, everybody's going to get a chance to go. If there's nothing else, make sure you check the flight schedule. And for sure, make sure you don't say anything about Al Ritt. If there's nothing else…"

Fancy stood up. "Uh, Skipper, uh everybody, I just wanted to say thanks for…well…, you know, support. I talked to the Chaplin and he let me know about…well…you know…I appreciate knowing that when the chips are down…"

"Gator!" bantered Valdorama, "You know when the chips are down the buffalo is empty. And Gator…"

"What?"

"Your fly is down."

Fancy felt himself turn red. He checked and found nothing amiss. Shaking his head, he regained some of his composure. "Thanks, guys."

Completing their preflight Fancy swung himself over the canopy rail and settled in. Taking a deep breath he savored the smell and feel of the cockpit, realizing for the first time how much he had missed it. Running his hands over the instruments he reassured himself that he hadn't forgotten anything. Shrader appeared and helped him to strap in. Pulling his helmet on he felt almost as if he had come home from a distant place. *This is where Cody would want me* he thought. Bowing his head, for the first time in a very long time he uttered a prayer for her and Amanda's continued recovery. The tear that rolled down his cheek surprised him but he didn't brush it away, vowing at the same time to be the best possible husband and father he could be no matter what. She'd never have to worry about being safe again. *First*, he thought *I better take care of business right here.* Taking a deep breath he felt a calm come over him reminding him of the time he and his dad had been fishing and the sun had come up warming his chilled bones. Right after that he had caught his first fish.

"Gator, it seems like a long time since we strapped in. It feels pretty good to me. How about you?"

"Yeah, it seems like a long time ago. I'm good to go."

"I never figured otherwise."

After a few minutes of going over their checklist, Desperado 201 was ready. As they were waiting for engine start up Mirabal came up on the intercom again. "I was talking to one of the FAGs (fighter attack guys) last night. He was tellin' this story about an A-7 driver who had been up most of the night over Route Pack Six in 'Nam. The guy is pretty well thrashed and it gets to be recovery time. He flies the pass, gets the cut and manages to bolter. Everybody is yelling 'Bolter! Bolter!' Naturally, the guy is zoned out and he goes dribbling down the deck and manages to stumble off the deck. Finally, he manages to wake himself up and rolls over on his back. Realizing this is not a good situation, he takes off some power, rolls it back over, getting lower by the second and heads off into the distance, blowing spray all the way."

Being it's so dark nobody on board was able to see any of this and after a few minutes, this calm voice from the CATCC comes up and says, 'Flasher 301, when comfortable, climb to 500 feet and turn 130 degrees for the bolter pattern.' Of course there was complete silence. Once more the guy in the CATCC comes up, 'Flasher 301, when comfortable, climb to 500 feet and turn to 130 degrees.' More silence. By now CATCC is getting bothered and calls Flasher 301 for a radio check and Flasher answers, 'Loud and clear!' Once again the CATCC says, 'When comfortable, climb to 500 feet and turn 130 degrees for the bolter pattern!"

"Flasher comes back and replies, 'You said to do all that stuff when comfortable. Well, pardner, that ain't going to be tonight!'"

Fancy burst out laughing. And the more he laughed the funnier the story became. Soon tears of glee were rolling down his face. "Jesus, that's funny," and he started to laugh again. Finally, he was able to stop, his sides literally hurting from the effort. A minute later they started the engines.

After the last chain had been removed, the wand of the yellow-shirt motioned them forward to the starboard cat, rolling over the lowered JBD.

Not being able to see anything but almost feeling it he knew the nosewheel was being connected to the catapult shuttle.

*Not being able to see anything is a misnomer* he thought to himself.

"Gator, am I imagining things or is it one dark night out there?"

Straining his eyes Fancy couldn't even make out the end of the ship. "I can't recall a night as dark as this. It's definitely not our imaginations. Brother…"

"It's kind of an ominous feeling. What does it make you think of?"

Smiling to himself Fancy replied, "Well, this plane and every component on it was made by the low bidder."

Mirabal chuckled. "Now there's a comfort."

After watching an F/A-18 blast off into the murk, and at the yellow-shirt's direction, he advanced the throttle slowly while making the requisite flight control checks by moving the stick forward, backward, left, and right while stepping on each rudder pedal, while an enlisted man on the deck watches the control surfaces moving on the plane and confirms that they are working. The catapult officer waits for the flash of the lights.

Two seconds later the catapult fires and the feeling of being squashed back in the seat almost feels good. At 146 knots they leave the ship behind and are immediately swallowed up by the pitch-black night.

Mirabal, ever on the ball, lets the air boss know everything is well. "Good shot, two-oh-seven is airborne." Then he reset the radio frequency.

"Desperado two-oh-seven, come to a heading of three-zero five at angels 16." commands the CATCC.

"Roger, heading three-zero-five, to angels 16." Fancy advanced the throttles and eased back the stick toward his stomach. Sensing, but not seeing, he knows Valdorama is off to his port side. *Somehow it feels just right.*

Tonight they would be flying along the thirty-second parallel westward from the Iraqi city of An Janaf westward to the Saudi border and then back to the east, then repeating the pattern. Most of the pilot and RIOs felt this was definitely a "borex" or a boring exercise. If the Iraqis hadn't shown much of a threat during the day, they had shown absolutely no initiative when the sun went down. There hadn't even been any sightings of Iraqi helicopters along the Saudi border.

As they arrived at sixteen thousand feet Fancy looked out over the vast expanse of water and land where the Persian Gulf ended and the country of Iraq began. Kuwait was on their port side as they went feet wet.

Clicking his mike once to let the ship know they were over land he was able to make out small pinpoints of light that passed quickly beneath them.

Taking a deep breath he allowed himself a moment or two to savor being back in the air, tasting the familiar flow of oxygen, the dull glow of the lights of the instruments, and the Indian night noises of the plane itself as it streaked toward the 32nd parallel.

"Gator, uh, shouldn't we check in with Big Eye?"

"Yeah, we should have done that three minutes ago. I was just enjoying being back. Sorry."

"Hey, no problema, babe."

"Big Eye, this is Desperado 207 checking in with a flight of two, heading three-zero-fve at one six angels."

"Roger, Desperado 207, maintain heading and altitude. There's a flight of two F-16s, Pintail flight, on course zero-nine-zero at angels 21."

"Roger on heading, altitude, and the two electric jets, Big Eye. Dash Two, you copy?"

"Dash Two copies," came the crisp reply.

An Janaf was a fairly large city and it was well illuminated. "Dash Two, lets come to two-six-zero."

"Coming to two-six-zero, 207."

West of An Janaf the Iraqi landscape was swallowed in a sea of darkness.

"I've got dots at, umm seventy miles, at twenty-one thousand. Looks like the Vipers."

After passing underneath the F-16s they continued westward with nothing in sight or on radar. "Pretty quiet, Rhino."

"Quiet, but I can live with it."

The two Tomcats flew westward to the Saudi Arabian where they reversed course and climbed to twenty-one thousand feet. When the F-16s turned west and they would drop to sixteen thousand feet.

They flew along in silence for several minutes. Fancy chuckled out loud to himself when he thought of the joke Mirabal had told just before they had launched.

"What's so funny, Gator?"

"Oh, I just thought of the guy being asked to recover when he felt comfortable. Cracks me up. Who ever feels comfortable?" and he snickered again.

"Hey, it's nice to hear you laughin' again. I don't know if I could ever laugh or even smile again after getting that kind of news. It makes me sick. Who'd do something like that anyway?"

"After I screwed up enough courage to read the letter again, I learned it was most likely her ex-husband. At least that's what her brother believes."

"No, that, that…"

"Couldn't be? Yeah, it could and I think he's right, which means the guy is in a world of hurt."

"His own kid?"

Fancy shook his head. "Well, they pull some guy out of his plane, give him some kind of kangaroo court, shoot him in front of his family. Anything's possible, so yeah, I can see it. I just hope I wasn't the cause of his going over the edge."

"Her brother's pretty protective, huh?"

"That just starts to cover it. Believe me, he's someone you want on your side. He talks the talk and walks the walk."

"I'm pullin' for them both, Gator, I really am."

"I know you are and I appreciate it. Right now that's what I want too. Strangely enough, I'm thinking more about that than I am any kind of retribution against the asshole that did it."

"That's probably the best way. I don't know if I could do that, I get enraged just thinking about it. Oh oh, I've got two dots at eighty miles at one six angels."

Fancy glanced at his own display and picked up the two F-16s.

"Dash Two, how's everything?"

"Peachy. We've got the Electric Jets at seventy-five miles. And…Hey it looks like one of them is dropping down. Do you see it?"

Looking back at his radar display Fancy could indeed pick out one of the planes that seemed to be losing altitude. "Rhino, what do you make of that?"

"Beats me. There didn't seem to be any kind of missile launch, I don't think he's been hit."

"Desperado 207, this is Big Eye. You copy?"

"We read you loud and clear, Big Eye."

"207, Pintail Lead has lost his engine and it looks like he's going to have to punch out. Have you got them on your scopes?"

"Big Eye, we have them at sixty-five miles, with one plane definitely losing altitude. He's at about eight thousand right now," said Fancy, watching his display with one eye and his HUD with the other.

"Big Eye, he's punched out just east of Ka id. We can pick something in the air, and the plane is just going off the scope, yeah its gone in right now. We'll set up a Res Cap."

"Roger Res Cap. Pintail Two will head for the tanker. The Saudis have a forward base at Badanah. There's still a detachment of CH-53s there. We'll get them moving to your position."

"Dash Two, you copy?"

"Dash Two copies Res Cap," answered Valdorama, with what Fancy thought was an eager voice.

"Joker, lets pick up a little smash and go down to base plus three. (Base was seven thousand feet so they would go to ten thousand feet.)

"Roger, base plus three."

"Rhino, lets pick up Pintail Two. No sense getting up close and personal."

"I've got him. He's at base minus five, uh, looks like a racetrack pattern, uh, about twelve miles east of Ka id."

"I guess it's too much to hope that the camel jockeys haven't got anything near there?"

After wrestling with his chart, Mirabal came back. "Actually, Lady Luck might be smiling on this guy. The Iraqis have got something about thirty miles north of Ka id. If this chart is right it's an infantry battalion. Probably they have some kind of transport though. Of course they may not get the word right away. And, there are no, or supposed to be, no guns or missile sights."

"Pintail Two, this is Desperado two-oh-seven, we have you on the scope. What's the situation?"

"Desperado, Pintail One lost his engine. Looks like it just quit and he's punched out. I have not been able to establish any kind of contact with him."

By now Fancy could make out something burning on the ground that marked where Pintail Lead had augured in.

"Pintail, we'll set up Res Cap until you hit the tanker and get back."

Somewhat reluctantly, Pintail Two came back. "Roger, heading for the tanker. Desperado?'

"Pintail?"

"Take care of this guy, he's a good friend."

"We will, Pintail, we will."

"Dash Two, you set up a race track at twelve thousand and keep an eye out for any uninvited visitors. We'll get down in the weeds and see if we can raise Pintail Lead."

"Roger, Lead, going to twelve."

Dropping the nose and retarding the throttle a little Fancy dropped down to fifteen hundred feet. What was left of the F-16 was burning fiercely. Outside of that he could see or hear nothing.

Switching to Guard he took a deep breath and called, "Pintail Lead, this is Desperado two-oh-seven, presently above your plane. Do you read?"

Nothing.

Fancy brought the plane around and reversed their course once again flying over the burning plane, that was now starting to burn itself out. "Pintail Lead, this is Desperado two-oh-seven. Do you copy, Pintail?" Again the ominous silence. The only thing Fancy could hear was the sound of his own breathing coming through his oxygen mask.

Coming back over the plane once more he saw that there was only the tiniest trace of flames. "Pintail, this is Desperado two-oh-seven. Do you copy? Pintail, do you copy?" *Come on Pintail, come up* he pleaded to himself.

After two more futile orbits around the area of the crash, by now the fire was out, there was no response. Having retarded the throttles as much as he dared, the big fighter was just above stalling speed. Fancy wanted to preserve as much fuel as possible.

"Desperado two-oh-one, how's your fuel?"

"Two-oh-seven, we're good at about fifty-five hundred."

Fancy knowing they were light on fuel because of the low altitude they were tooling around at. "Okay, Dash Two, I'm a little light, I'm going to make another two orbits and then we'll trade places. I'm gettin' zilch from the ground."

"Roger that, Gator."

"Pintail Lead, do you read? This is Desperado two-oh-seven. Pintail Lead, click your radio if you can't answer." *Come on you can do it. Just click the friggin' button. Do something.*

"Okay, Rhino, we're going a little lower. Keep your ears open."

Fancy flew out a little farther from the spot where the plane had crashed, now showing up as a hot spot on the FLIR (forward looking infrared radar). "Pintail Lead, this is Desperado two-oh-seven. Give us a call or a click or a flare. Come on Pintail, we need to know, you can do it."

Fancy was just about to give up the Air Force pilot for dead when a weak voice came through his his headphones.

"Desperado, this is Pintail Lead."

Fancy's heart gave a thump and hung fire scarcely believing what he was hearing.

"Pintail, good to hear from you. We were almost ready to believe the worst. How're you doing?" He tried to keep his voice calm and reassuring.

"I must have hit harder than I thought. It seems that I'm in one piece, more or less." The voice, though weak, seemed coherent.

"Do you hear or see anything on the ground that would indicate the Iraqis might be close or coming?"

"Besides the ringing in my ears, the only other thing I can hear is you. Never thought I'd be glad to hear a Tomcat."

Fancy chuckled. "Can you move or get around?"

"I think so, Desperado, maybe not real quick though."

"That's okay. There seems to be an Iraqi infantry battalion north of your position. We don't know if they're on the ball or not, so it'll be a good idea to keep your ears open."

"No problem, Desperado, ears open and tuned."

"Rhino, give Big Eye a call and check on the progress of those helos."

Before they could complete another orbit Rhino came back, "Gator, the helos are in the air and have crossed the border. They're about ten minutes out. Big Eye wants to know if we can stay in the area until the rescue is completed?"

Running his eyes over the fuel gauges Fancy sighed and replied, "Yeah, it'll be tight, but we'll stay. Any chance they can push a tanker this way?"

"Dash Two, you copied all this?"

"Dash Two has copied. Ready to come up?"

"Dash Two, we'll extend out to the east and climb to 12 grand."

"Roger, Gator, we'll go out to the west and descend to fifteen hundred."

Fancy advanced the throttles slightly and headed east while bringing the nose up slightly to get to twelve thousand feet.

"Gator, Big Eye says they are going to push a KC-135 this way with an escort of no less of two F-16's."

"That makes my day," he said as he glanced at the fuel gauges, that were definitely showing the effects of the low altitude at which they'd been flying.

Prying his eyes off the fuel gauges, he scanned his radar display. "Rhino, I've got two slow movers and two fast movers headed this way, at about twenty miles."

"I've got 'em. That's one good looking display."

"Roger that…"

"Gator", came Valdorama's voice. "Pintail lead says he thinks he can hear the sound of engines. He can't tell how far off they are, but they're definitely headed this way."

"Have you got any kind of heading?"

"Right now he only hears the engines, can't tell exactly from what direction."

"Rhino, get those choppers' attention and tell them to pour it on; we may have company. We'll take a look to the north of Pintail."

Fancy brought the Tomcat to a course that took them north of the crash site. "We're going to be depending on the FLIR, Rhino, I hope it can pick up any engine signatures. We'll have to get down in the weeds."

"I'm right behind you, babe. Let's take'r down."

Pushing the stick forward, they descended to five hundred feet. Fancy, praying to himself that he had remembered correctly the charts showing no hills in this part of Iraq. *No time for self doubts now.*

"There they are! There they are! Damn!" he growled much too loudly. "Man, they're only about four miles away. How'd they get here this fast?"

"Dunno, could have been in the area."

"Joker, we've got company out here about three to three and a half miles, headed to your direction. How's that helo doin'?"

"Twelve miles, give or take a few yards."

Taking a deep breath, but not caring, or at this point, daring, to look at the fuel gauges, he breathed, "Rhino, we better slow them up." Then thinking but not saying *and I hope they don't have any hand -held SAMs.*

"Rhino, I'm going to use the gun."

"Talk about the Wild West!"

*Actually* , Fancy thought, *this is only going to be the third or fourth time I've actually fired it. Great! Hell of a time to practice.*

Setting up for his pass, he noticed that the six or was that seven vehicles had spread out. He could now make out the heat signatures of men sitting in the back of what must be jeep-type vehicles.

He was glad the systems on the Tomcat made firing and hitting something with the 20mm Gatling Gun a "no brainer" – if you kept your cool. Picking out the vehicle that seemed to be in the lead, he put the reflective gun recticle illuminated in his HUD on the intended target. As they came within range, automatic cuing would appear, and all he had to do was "pull the trigger". If the recticle was centered over the target, then the twenty millimeter rounds would hit. The gun was deadly and accurate.

Feeling the hair on the back of his neck start to stand up under his helmet, he closed the range and squeezed off what he thought of as a short burst, and then started his pull-up, dumping off flares as he did so.

"Rhino, did you see anything?"

"No, I didn't."

"Coming back around again, he repeated the procedure, though this time diving on the target a little more steeply.

After another short burst, Rhino yelled, "You got one, he's burning!"

"Coming around once again Fancy could indeed see something burning and the rest of the vehicles seemed to be stopping. Fancy could glimpse little white blobs moving away from the larger white blobs.

Popping some more flares, he came back and made one more pass, setting another vehicle on fire. "I think they've got the point. Anything from the helos?"

"They've recovered Pintail, and are just now departing the area."

"Good deal, let's join them and find that tanker."

Fancy vowed never to make fun of the Air Force again. They had only been outward bound for only a few minutes when they picked up the KC-135. Another few minutes and they were coming up on the six o' clock of the big plane. Off to either side were two F-16s, just in case.

"Desperado 207, this is Creek Party Tankers, understand you could use a little fuel?"

"Creek Party, you've got that right."

Since Fancy had spent the most time at low altitude and was lower on fuel, he slid into position first. The boom was lowered and the basket on the end of the boom was lit up with a circle of red lights. Just as he plunged the refueling probe into the basket and saw the red lights go from red to green, the port engine, flamed out.

As calmly as he could he told Creek Party of their situation: "Creek Party, I've just had both engines flame out. Can you dump your nose and we'll do a little tobogganing?"

The decidedly calm voice that answered him replied, "No problem, Desperado, dumping the nose now and commencing to give you some gas."

The big tanker gently went to a nose down attitude and Fancy felt the fuel start to flow into the Tomcat. Pausing to get his head straight, he started up the restart procedures and was rewarded after what seemed an eternity, but was only a few seconds of the low rumble of the port engine spooling up, and after another few seconds the starboard engine came on line. "That was close," he said to no one in particular.

"Creek Party, we have both engines on line." Adding power to compensate for the fuel being taken on he maneuvered the stick in order not to fall off the basket. After taking on 2,000 pounds he disengaged and let Valdorama plug in and top off. Following Valdorama back to the basket, he topped off.

Just before backing out of the basket, the voice of the tanker pilot came through his headphones. "Desperado, thanks for stickin' around back there. We all appreciate it."

"Creek Party, it was no problem—and thank you!"

Joining up in a loose combat spread the two Navy planes turned to the south and back to the Enterprise.

After trapping without incident on Enterprise, Fancy waited for Mirabal to clamber down. "Hey, Babe, nice goin' up there today, tonight, whatever the hell it was. You did good."

Mirabal stepped back in disbelief. He still wasn't quite used to pilots who went out of their way to share the credit and or glory. "Thanks, I was just trying to hold up my end of things."

"Yeah, well, you sure did more than…"

"Wow, what a night! That was more action in one night than I had in the time I was aboard Lincoln! Man, that was fun! You guys are great to work with!" Valdorama emphasized his point by putting his arms around Mirabal and Fancy, already having produced a massive black cigar. He was waving it around somewhat like an orchestra conductor would wave his baton.

*Not again*, groaned Fancy to himself. Disengaging himself from Valdorama's enthusiastic embrace.

"It was nice workin' with you too. I hope I get the chance to do it again," Fancy replied, making sure he could take a deep breath.

As the four men started to walk to the edge of the deck and onto the catwalk to go below, Shrader came up behind them. "Uh, Lieutenant, there's something you might want to take a look at on your plane."

"Oh, yeah, let's take a look."

Together, they walked over to Desperado 207, now chained down and the wings fully swept back to 72 degrees. Shrader directed them aft to the port horizontal tailplane. Shining his hooded flashlight he directed their attention to several holes about the size of fifty cent pieces.

"Fancy put his finger in one of the holes in the gray skin of the plane, He pulled his finger out and taking Shrader's light he shined it into the hole, noting that the hole went clear through.

"I never even felt anything, did you, Rhino?"

Mirabal looked at the holes, and like Fancy, put his fingers into one. "Never felt a thing, not a thing. Hmmmm…"

Valdorama and his RIO, in the meantime, had walked over to their plane to see if they had been hit.

Fancy shook his head. "Thanks, Shrader. Can you get it patched up okay?"

"No sweat, Sir, as soon as the last plane is aboard, we're going to strike her below. She'll be up for tomorrow's missions."

"Thanks, Shrader, I, uh, we appreciate all your hard work. Nothin' happens without you."

Shrader beamed and headed back to check out the rest of the plane.

As Valdorama rejoined Fancy and Mirabal, he fell in step with them. "I guess we dodged the bullet that time, there doesn't seem to be any extra holes. So you didn't feel anything?" He sounded somewhat disappointed.

"Nothin', had no clue. I guess no news is good news," replied Fancy, shaking his head. "Was that pick-up by the helo as smooth as it sounded?"

As they headed down the ladder to the equipment room, Valdorama broke into laughter. "It was kind of funny, though. The helo is just about on final, when the guys on the helo started to ask the four questions, you know mother-in-law's maiden name, favorite baseball team, you're first lay, you know, all that shit. Then they start to repeat it all over and ask the guy if it's really him, you know. Finally, the F-16 driver has had it up to here," he continued, motioning to a point above his head. "He's really pissed off and more than ready to get on that helo and he says, 'Fuck yes, it's me! Who the hell do you think it is, the Hills Brothers' coffee bean buyer?' That just cracked me up!"

Fancy and Mirabal laughed and they headed into the equipment room to get rid of the sweaty flight gear.

By the time Fancy was through with the debrief with the Intel Troops, he was more than a little tired. As he entered his room he could see from by the light from the passageway the inert form of Bagger laying on his bunk, snoring softly.

Figuring it was too much trouble to wake him up and reclaim his rack, he slipped off his steel-toed boots and slipped out of his green bag, which had been traded in for the more current desert tan model. He tossed it over the back of the desk chair, and climbed up into Bagger's rack. In mere seconds he was out cold.

Morning came quickly and with a jolt. Fancy felt someone shaking him, not too gently, awake. "Jesus, take it easy, will ya!" he growled. "I'm tactical!" Rolling over he found himself looking eyeball to eyeball with his roomie.

"This better be good, pard, I'm beat."

"Well, maybe I should have waited until later," Bagger teased as he stepped back, waving a letter in his right hand. "I'll just let you sleep."

Fancy momentarily forgetting where he was, reached out and made a grab for letter. Bagger was too quick and the only thing he accomplished was to launch himself out of the upper bunk and onto the floor.

"Hey, nice recovery, Gator. OK-3 all the way," he howled and he danced around the pile of blankets and and the thrashing form of his roommate. "Wow!"

Struggling to his feet while trying to disengage himself from the gray government issue blankets, succeeded only in winding up on the floor again. "Show me the damn letter!" he shouted.

"Okay, okay, don't get your shorts in a bunch," Bagger chortled, as he handed him the envelope.

Eagerly he snatched it from Bagger's outstretched hand and ripped it open. Feeling as if he were on pins and needles he began to read.

Bagger, with the greatest of restraint, waited somewhat like an eager puppy on a leash, watching Fancy as he poured over the three pages. After finishing the letter, he immediately flipped back to the first page and started to reread it.

"Well? What's the deal?"

"Just a second.," Fancy continued reading. Coming to the last page he sighed and leaned back against the bed. Rubbing his eyes with his thumb and forefinger, he shook his head.

"Well?"

"Man, I just don't know. Life…" He shook his head again, looking at Bagger who seemed ready to explode. "Scott, that's her brother, says it looks like Cody is going to be okay. If you can call being shot twice, okay?"

"Twice?"

"Yeah, once through the chest, just missing the heart and once through the cheek."

"Jesus, the heart?"

"It couldn't have been any closer he says. That's just one part, the biggest part of course, but…"

"Keep going. What about Amanda?"

Frowning, Fancy took a long look at the letter. "Right now, she's paralyzed with a bullet lodged next to her spine. In two days from now, if

I'm computing right, they're going to try to remove the bullet. A doctor that is a friend of her boss, is going to do the operation. He's supposed to be about the best there is. He works at, uh, Scripps. Is that a hospital or something?"

"Scripps is north of San Diego. Definitely a major league place. This guy must be pretty good."

"Man, I hope so. Anyway, if things don't go as planned, she won't be any worse off than she is. This doctor seems to think he can do it and she'll regain all movement."

The two men stared at each other for several seconds, digesting the information; Fancy trying to imagine the risks and the chances of success.

Bowing his head and then looking up, sighing, and moving his head around continued, "It just gets stranger though."

"How so?"

"Remember, how could you ever forget, the dog?"

"Short Round," laughed Bagger, shaking his head. "Who's ever going to forget that crazy dog?"

"For one, I won't. Evidently, Amanda, for what ever reason, was sleeping in her mother's bed. Short Round must have heard this guy come in or break in and must have woke both of them up. They were out of the bed when they were shot. Scott figures if they had been asleep, he would have killed them both, they wouldn't have had a chance. None."

Bagger let out a lot of stale air. "Damn, what if...?"

"Exactly, what if Poncho and Big Wave hadn't brought him on board, if the North Koreans had reacted differently with that 747, if we hadn't met the KAL pilot in Singapore. If, if, if...Damn!"

"I still don't know," growled Bagger as he jabbed a fist into his other had, "how somebody could do that, much less her husband. It's just beyond me."

"I just hope I didn't trigger this. I don't know if I could live with myself."

"Look, she's got a right to a life. Falling in love with someone else is no reason or excuse. You just can't blame yourself. I'm not going to let you."

Fancy had to chuckle at how serious Bagger was.

"Well, I'm not, dammit!"

"Okay, okay, let's put our efforts to getting her, I mean them, well."

"That's what we'll do," he said leaning down to give a high five to Fancy.

Bagger stopped, looking both serious and guilty. "Listen, I've got to get something off my chest. When that first letter came, I felt bad, but I was thinking I was so glad it wasn't Rowdy. I feel so low; what an asshole thing to think. Man, I'm so sorry. I hope you know how I feel about Cody."

Fancy stood up and punched his friend on the arm. "That's probably a natural feeling. You know, that would probably be my first reaction. Nobody wants disaster to strike someone close to them." He shrugged. "What we need to do is take care of business, and make sure we get our tired old butts home in one piece."

Before either one of them could say anything there was a knock on the door. Bagger, closer to the door opened it. "Sir," said the enlisted man waiting outside, "Commander Robinson says the COD plane is leaving for Bahrain in thirty minutes and he says he wants you on it, along with Mr. Fancy, Sir."

"Thanks, pal, you just made my day. Did you hear that? Man, let's get packing before someone changes their mind. Forget that, let's just get up to the roof and get in COD!" said Bagger as he slammed the door shut, his face one huge grin, while pumping his arms in the air and doing a sort of victory dance. "Yesssss!"

"You know, you should try and show a little enthusiasm about this whole deal. You're so subdued," laughed Fancy as he reached into the tiny closet to get a fresh uniform.

For as long as he could remember Fancy hadn't especially liked to ride with someone else. Letting someone else pilot the plane he was on was much harder. Even though he relished the idea of getting off the boat and getting to a phone, it still bothered him. Nonetheless, strapping himself into the seat of C2-A or COD (carrier on board delivery) plane, backwards no less, he could hardly wait for it to launch.

Forty minutes later he and Bagger walked down the ramp of the C-2A into the stifling heat almost taking their breath away. Again he thought they had parked too close to another plane. After a quick look around he realized that Bahrain was just as hot and maybe hotter than it had been in Saudi Arabia. A sign welcomed them to Shaikh Isa, Royal Bahrainian Air Force Base. Right away Fancy started to recompute the time from Bahrainian time to west coast time in the United States. *It's 10:30 here...and it's sixteen hours ahead of the Gulf so that makes it...4:30 a.m. there. I'd better not wake anybody up. Yes, I will, Scott will probably answer the phone.*

Spotting a bank of phones at the end of the building, Fancy started to quicken his pace, jogged, and then ran full tilt toward them.

"Gator!" Bagger called, "let's find some inside! We're going to cook out here!"

The running proved for naught, a sign informed him they were out of order and more phones could be found inside the door around the corner.

Bagger finally caught up to his friend as he almost tore the door off the hinges trying to get inside.

"Gator, I wish you'd try to show some enthusiasm. You're so shy and retiring."

Spotting the phones Fancy skidded to a halt at the first one in the group, oblivious to the stares of the men and women working there. Picking up a phone with one hand he started to dig through his pockets trying to locate the slip of paper that had Cody's number on it. Not finding the paper immediately he momentarily panicked as he hurriedly checked his pockets again.

As Bagger walked up he bent down and picked up a small piece of paper by Fancy's right shoe. "You looking for this, by any chance?" he said as he straightened up extending his hand.

Mumbling a thanks, Fancy then tried to find some change, but just managing to drop it all over the floor.

By now several people had stopped what they were doing and were looking intently and somewhat amusedly at the two fliers.

"Wait, just wait. Please, allow me," he said. Picking up several of the coins he pushed Fancy away and took the receiver. What's the number?"

Turning the paper right side up he gave it to him. Bagger put in a coin, listened and then inserted several more coins while pointing at the change on the floor, then pointing towards the phone. Punching in the numbers he beamed as he handed the phone back to Fancy.

After several rings Fancy was startled when the phone was picked up and a voice on the other end said, "Hello."

"Ah, ah," was all he was able to stammer.

"Hello, say hello," Bagger urged, wondering how someone who was cool enough to shoot down a MiG could turn to jello making a simple phone call.

Bagger breathed a sigh of relief as Fancy managed to finally say hello.

"Hello, this is Dan Fancy. I'm calling from Bahrain. How are Cody and Amanda doing? I hope I didn't wake you." All this was shouted nearly at the top of his lungs and delivered machine gun fashion.

By now more people were watching and some were laughing out loud.

"Easy, Gator, they can hear you. You don't have to yell, you'll break his eardrums."

After the initial shock and pain in his ears had subsided Scott Thorn answered. "Dan? Wow, this is a surprise. Where are you?"

"Bahrain, at a place called Shaikh Isa, it's a Bahrainian Air Force Base. We're just down here until about 1600 hours."

"It's good to hear from you. Cody and Amanda are still in the hospital. It looks like Cody can come home in about a week. They're going to operate on Amanda day after tomorrow."

"A week. Is that good? How is she?"

"She's doing well physically. Mentally, she's down about Amanda. We both are."

"What's the prognosis for this operation? Is this guy that's doing the operation pretty good?"

"Doctor Tomlin believes it will go just the way everyone wants it to. This guy is one self-confident person who believes in his ability. According to what we've read and been told, he's the top guy in the nation and probably the world."

"Scott, I'm so sorry about this. Is this my fault?"

"Hell no, it's not your fault! Her ex had been giving her a lot of problems before this happened. Cody being Cody wasn't going to burden anybody else with her problems. He had made some threats but she never told me, you or anybody else. Sometimes she's just too independent for her own good."

"Is she able to take any calls at the hospital?" Fancy felt himself holding his breath.

"Right now, I can't think of any better medicine than to hear from you, with Amanda going to have surgery and all. Yeah, by all means, call her. Here's the number."

Again Fancy fished through his pockets for a pen. "Wait, just a minute, Bagger, have you got a pen or pencil?"

Frantically Bagger repeated the process coming up empty. Rushing over to an Army enlisted woman he asked, "Could I please borrow a pencil?"

Rushing back to his friend he motioned for Fancy to read him the number as he copied it down.

"Scott, it's really good to speak with you. I'm so sorry about your sister and Amanda. Have they caught him yet?"

"No, not yet, but I intend to look into matters when everybody is up and on their feet again. I hope they don't get to him before I do as a matter of fact." The voice had hardened and Fancy shuddered, almost feeling sorry for Cody's ex-husband.

"Listen, why don't you give Cody a call. Whoa! Wait a minute, it's only ten minutes to five here. They won't put you through for at least another three hours.

Trying to hide his disappointment, Fancy answered, "That's when I'll call then. In the meantime Bagger and I will go into Manama. I understand rings and jewelry are their speciality. I want to get the biggest engagement ring I can find. And, Scott?"

"Yeah?"

"Will you give your sister away?"

"I'd be proud to." After a pause, he went on. "She's been told that she may have a pretty bad scar on her cheek and she was kind of worried that may affect how you feel about her."

"The only thing that matters to me is that she and Amanda are alive. That's the *only* thing."

"That's what I figured and that's what I told her. I hope I didn't mess with your head by letting you know what had happened. You struck me as the kind of guy who would want to know and could deal with it."

"To say the least I was shocked, but I'm glad you let me know. I wouldn't want it any other way."

"That's what I thought. How are you doing out there? Pretty hot place I bet?"

"You wouldn't believe it. I was in Saudi and just like here I thought we had parked by a plane that was taxiing by or was just starting up. Gives a whole new meaning to the word hot, believe me."

"I do. Give me a call later if you have a chance."

"Will do, thanks for answering the phone. Say, we're going to be running guys down here every few days or so. Uh, would you mind if they called and got an update. They're great guys, and…"

"That'd be fine, no problem. If I'm not here, I'll leave a message on the machine they can listen to."

"Geez, thanks, Scott. I really appreciate it. I'll talk to you later."

Fancy put the phone down and turned just in time to see the crowd that had gathered quickly try and resume their normal activities. "What's that all about?"

"It was quite a sight, you know," he chuckled. "Come on let's go see the sights of Manama."

"I want to buy a ring. Are you still willing to be my best man?"

"Does a chicken lay eggs? Does a bear live in the woods? Do I have a thing for Rowdy Kobayashi?"

"I'll take that as a yes. Say, I've been so wrapped up in my own problems. Do you want to call Nellis?"

"I do, but I don't think I'd get anywhere. But on the other hand, it might be the best time before she fires up the Herk for the day."

Twenty minutes later after they had scrounged change and had made the call, catching Rowdy and Razor at home, the two men literally waltzed out the gate and were hailing a taxi.

Bagger, who was literally dancing, seemed ready, willing, and able to make it into Manama without the taxi. "Man, it was so good to hear her voice. I am so happy!"

Upon leaving the gate area for the U.S. Military, they were besieged by various drivers offering them the cheapest rates and fastest service into town. Bagger picked a scruffy little man with a huge mustache and what looked like an early Beatles haircut, who promptly introduced himself as Modi. He promptly led them to a jeep Cherokee, that looked to be in mint condition.

Holding open the rear door he said in flawless English, "Gentleman, thank you for riding with me today. Do you have any special destination in mind?" Before either man could answer, Modi had shut the door, returned to the driver's side, slid in between the wheel, started the engine, and mercifully had the air-conditioner up and running before either Fancy or Bailey could reply.

"I'm looking for an engagement ring for my fiancee. Can you recommend a place to start looking?"

"Indeed I can, Sir," he replied stroking his mustache. "It just so happens my cousin, Kamran, has his own shop. He makes his own jewelry in fact and is well known as not only a very talented jeweler, but also a very honest one. Would you be interested in starting there? However, you do not have to feel any obligation because you ride with me."

Looking at Bagger, Fancy shrugged. "What do you think?"

"Let's go with Modi's cousin. Modi?"

"Yes, Sir?"

"Before we get there could we stop for something to drink. I'm about parched."

"Of course. If you reach behind your seat you will find an ice chest, please, feel free to help yourself. I am, I'm sorry to say, only permitted to carry soft drinks."

"That's fine, because that's all I need. Thanks."

"My pleasure, Sir." Putting the car in gear they headed for Manama.

On the way in to Manama they found out that Bahrain meant "two seas" in Arabic and is named after the largest island in the archipelago with an area of 676 square kilometers. The population being, on a good day Bagger figured, 516, 444. About the time Bagger was about to say enough already, they had arrived in the city.

Manama looked anything but a third world country. The rows of very modern looking office buildings clung to the waterfront area and could have been picked right out of any modern country in the world. There was an efficient hustle and bustle about the city.

As Modi drove he kept up a running commentary about the many 'cousins' he had that worked in various buildings. "My friends," he said, "I am going to take you to my cousin Kamran's shop in what we call the

Souk. The Souk is in the old part of the city and what many Bahranians consider the real, how do you say, *soul* of the city."

Both men strained to take everything in. This, at least to Fancy's way of thinking was what a Middle Eastern country should look like. There were countless stalls with fruit, vegetables, spices, and other local produce on display. As they pulled up to a modest looking storefront, Modi slipped the Jeep into a space that Fancy would never even have thought about using—and made it look easy.

"Come, gentleman, this way to some of the finest jewelry in all the world."

As they departed the car, they were assaulted by not only the heat but the heady aroma of the fruits, nuts, spices and countless other substances that were being sold. Modi led them to the front door and held it open while they scrambled in. The air conditioning was a blessed relief from the inferno outside.

The shop was taken up almost completely by display cases of jewelry of all types. Fancy hardly knew where to start looking. From the back a tall, dignified, bespectacled man walked toward them extending his hand to Modi.

"Greetings, Cousin. It's good to see you again."

"It's good to see you again, Cousin. I would like you to meet my new acquaintances, Lt. Fancy and Lt. Bailey of the United States Navy. Lt. Fancy is on a mission of great importance. He is looking for a special engagement ring for his fiancee."

"Gentleman, it is very good to meet you. Welcome to my humble shop. I shall do everything I can to accommodate you. Please, come this way. We can start over here."

They followed him to a display case with what looked like several hundred rings. He felt overwhelmed by the sheer numbers. "That's quite a selection. I'm not sure where to begin."

"Does your fiancee have any special hobbies or interests?"

Fancy scrunched up his face in thought. "Well, she likes the ocean, the beach, that kind of thing."

"Ahh, that's a start." Pausing for a few seconds, he moved quickly and slid the door of the case open, reached in, and withdrew a velvet box.

Taking the box from Moussa Zahab's extended hand he opened the box and Fancy saw what appeared to be a sizable diamond surrounded by what looked like three fish. Picking up the box he saw the fish were really three dolphins forming a circle around the diamond. The dolphins were exquisitely formed. He liked it immediately. "That's beautiful. I really like that." Turning it one way and then another, he tried to imagine what it would look like on Cody's finger.

"Go ahead; take it out of the box, Lieutenant."

Gently removing it, he examined it more closely. The more he looked at it, the better he liked it. "Bagger, what do you think?"

Bagger took it from Fancy and held it up to the light, turning it this way and that. "This is something. Man, this is a work of art."

"Think she'll like it?"

"I don't see why not. This is one beautiful piece."

"Lieutenant, please, feel free to look further," Moussa-Zahab said, gesturing to the shop. "If you don't find anything, I can maybe make something to your special order and liking."

Modi and his cousin withdrew to a far corner of the shop where they continued a quiet conversation.

As hard as he tried, there was not another ring in the entire shop that Fancy liked as much as the three dolphins, as he had come to think of it. He kept coming back to it.

"Mr. Moussa-Zahab, you have so many beautiful pieces of jewelry, but I can't seem to find anything quite as beautiful as this," he said, holding up the 'three dolphins'. "This is the one I really want."

"Thank you, Lieutenant. I feel honored that you have decided to make a purchase from my humble abode."

Fancy was almost afraid to ask the next question. "Umm, how much is it?"

"Lieutenant, it is $700, U. S."

Letting out a gasp of surprise, Fancy quickly looked at Bagger, who was also raising his eyebrows.

"Lieutenant, this is beyond your, how do you say, budget?"

"No, no, definitely not. This is such a beautiful ring I thought it would cost me much more. I'm very happy." Fancy thought he saw a momentary look of disappointment, but it quickly passed.

"I am so pleased that you are happy. I'm sure your lady will find it to her liking. You may, of course, bring it back if she is not."

Fancy grinned and reached for his wallet. He considered it the best $700 he had ever spent.

After thanking Modi's cousin they walked out into the blazing heat of the day. Modi had them in the Jeep and the air conditioning cranked up before they could break a sweat.

"Gentleman, where may I take you?"

Looking at his watch, he felt disappointed at the slow passage of time, much like a sixth grader watching the clock on a Friday afternoon. "I would really like to find a phone to call the states. My fiancee is in the hospital and I haven't talked to her since she was admitted."

Fancy saw that Modi wanted to know the circumstances but was too much a gentleman to pry. "I am so sorry to hear of her and your misfortune. I hope her stay will be very short."

After a few minutes Fancy gave him a thumbnail version of the story. Modi nodded gravely and repeated his hope that Cody's stay would be short and wondered to himself what kind of a barbaric land America was anyway.

"Let me take you to the Forte Grande Diplomat Hotel. It offers you a wonderful view of the coast and the food in the restaurants are absolutely marvelous. And of course, there are many places you can telephone from within the hotel."

"Any cousins that work there?" asked Bagger.

"Unfortunately, no, not at the present time, but I can personally vouch for the hotel."

The Forte Grande Diplomat welcomed the two fliers with open arms. Modi dropped them off at the main entrance, promising to pick them up in time to get them back to Shaikh Isa in time for the flight back to the ship. As they walked through the front entrance they headed immediately to the front desk and got directions to the nearest phones and restaurant.

After a delicious meal in the Hunt Club restaurant Fancy found himself pacing near one of the house phones. The assistant manager had directed them to an area of the hotel set aside for businessman. Fancy was surprised to see an array of fax and copy machines as well computers. He was grateful the hotel would put the call through for him and he would reimburse the hotel.

When the phone gave a soft ring he reached for it and then paused, suddenly at a loss for words. After another soft chime he picked up the receiver. "Hello, Cody?"

"Dan, is it really you?"

"You bet it is! It's so good to hear your voice. You'll never know how much I've missed you. This is probably going to sound corny, but, how are you—really?"

"Well, I'm feeling much better now. You can't believe how much I've been wishing I could hear from you. Where are you? You can't be calling from the ship can you?"

"I'm in Bahrain. It's a small country south of Saudi Arabia. We're in the capital, Manama."

"How long will you be there?"

"The flight back to the ship leaves at 1600, uh four o' clock. Listen, I didn't disrupt anything did I? I just couldn't wait any longer to call. Oh, God, I miss you."

" I miss you too. What's it like there?"

"It's hot, you wouldn't believe how hot it is. We're, uh Bagger and I, are at a hotel called the Forte Grande Diplomat. It's a beautiful place."

"How did you know where…Oh, you must have talked to Scott."

"Yeah, as soon as we got off the plane, I made a beeline for a phone."

"Geez, Cody, I'm so sorry. When I got Scott's letter I just about passed out. I still can't believe what happened. It makes me so angry sometimes I…I just hope it wasn't…"

"Paul had been making some threats before we met. Believe me, I never thought he'd go so far. I'd gotten a restraining order and figured that would be the end of it."

"How's Amanda doing? Scott told me they're going to operate day after tomorrow."

"She's doing great, considering everything. There's no doubt in her mind the operation is going to be one hundred percent effective. She's even bothered she might be getting behind in school. Boy, did you ever have an effect on her," Cody chuckled.

The sound of her laughter almost brought Fancy to tears. He had never heard anything so beautiful or so welcome. "Could you do that again?"

"Do what?"

"Laugh, just laugh. That sounds so good."

She did manage a laugh that made him laugh too. "Hey, you won't believe what Bagger and I did before we got to the hotel.?

"Oh, and what would that be?"

"I bought what I think, is the most beautiful engagement ring in the world for the most beautiful girl in the world."

There was a silence on the other end of the phone. "I'm probably going to have a terrible scar on my cheek. Are you…? I don't want you to feel obligated or feel sorry for me."

"Like I said, it's for the most beautiful girl in the world—bar none, and yes, I'm sure, more than sure, one hundred and ten percent sure. My mother always said, 'it's a person's inner beauty that counts' and my mother's never ever wrong. I've seen your inner beauty and that's all that matters to me."

"I love you."

The three words sent a chill up and down his spine and he felt weak in the knees. "Cody, I love you! I love you now and I'll love you forever."

"I'm so glad, because I love you too. I can hardly wait until you're home. And, what does this ring look like. I can hardly wait to wear it."

Fancy gave her a vivid description.

"Now I'm really anxious," she sighed. "It sounds beautiful."

"It is and I think you'll like it. It's somethin' else, it really is."

"I don't doubt it! I know it is."

There was a long pause, each knowing that the conversation was coming to an end.

"Well, it looks like they're here to do their morning poking and prodding. This must be costing you a fortune."

"I have no idea and I don't care one bit. I'll let them get on with getting you better. Please, tell Amanda I love her and am pulling for her. In fact you can tell her the whole squadron is—for both of you."

"Oh, that reminds me. Some of the guys will be coming down here from the boat every couple of days. Is it okay if they give you a call or give Scott a call just to see how things are going?"

"That would be great. I'll look forward to it."

After another few minutes they each agreed to hang up at the same time—albeit reluctantly.

The nurse who had entered Cody's room as the conversation was winding down was amazed at the progress her patient seemed to have made in the last twenty-four hours. She seemed to be absolutely glowing. *Whoever was on the other end of that phone ought to be bottled. They could make a mint,* she thought to herself.

As Fancy hung up the phone he gave a huge sigh. "Sounds like you've had a huge weight lifted from your wide shoulders, compadre? How is she?"

"She sounds great, she'll probably be going home within the week. Naturally, she seems to be worried about the scar she's going to have on her cheek. Big deal! Man, you sure find out what's important when the chips are down."

"And you only had to come half way around the world to find out what it is. You Bozo! What's the matter with you anyway?" Bagger danced out of the way as Fancy made a half-hearted grab for him.

"Come on, they've got a huge pool. Let's buy some trunks and cool off."

"Yeah, lets!"

The remainder of the day was spent in or by the pool. After they had exhausted themselves in the water, each of the fliers went horizontal enjoying the opportunity to sleep without the din from the routine of the ship.

# 15

Twenty-four hours later Fancy felt he had never been away. He and Bagger were flying at eighteen thousand feet on a course of zero nine zero just south of the Iraqi city of Al Hayy, just below the thirty-second parallel.

"Bagger, I've got some dots at eighty miles. You see 'em?"

"Dash Two, I have 'em. Looks like a pair about seventy-five miles, at angels 20. They're legal, just on the other side of the fence. Maybe we can reel 'em in a little closer."

"Desperado 200." The voice from the ship's E-2C AWACS pierced their headphones. "You've got some company headed your way."

"Roger that. Desperado 200 has them at 65 miles at angels 20. "We're going to keep them at our twelve o' clock," answered Bagger, who was flying lead.

"Dash Two, you copy?"

"Dash Two copies," answered Fancy, sliding out to Bagger's port side, while moving the stick back toward his stomach and then forward, trying to present as poor a target as possible.

"Gator, I've got us being painted by Palm Top fire control; looks like an SA-6 site. He's just looking right now."

Now Fancy could hear the sound of the radar in his headset. "Bagger, I'm getting a Palm Top looking us over."

"And, it's getting stronger. Maybe the dots and the SAM sight are looking to get even."

"That's a good bet, Dash Two."

"Fifty-five miles and it looks like they're descending, Gator. Jesus, did you see that?"

There was some ugly black bursts of flak off their port side.

"Bagger, looks like these idiots are looking for a little pay back." Fancy tried to keep his voice even and calm. He doubted he was doing a very good job of it. As he looked to his left there were more bursts, not any closer but definitely keeping pace with them.

"What do you figure, Gator, 37 millimeter?"

"I hate to tell you this but I have no clue. Well, no, I think I read that 37 millimeter is white. As black as it is, that's probably 58 millimeter. This is a first for me." Fancy was aggressively working the stick and rudder pedals moving the Tomcat up and down and from side to side to present the worst possible target.

Almost as soon as it had started, the flak stopped or they had flown out of range. "Bogies are at forty miles and have changed course; they're now twenty degrees off and continuing to swing out, twenty-five degrees off angle now," reported Mirabal. "It looks like they're reversing course. Yup, that's what they're doing."

Fancy breathed a sigh of relief. "I wonder what that was all about?" he mumbled to himself.

"What'd you say, Gator?"

"Nothin', just wondering what that was all about. I'm thinking you might be right about me being a jinx. We, I, us, whatever, seem to draw attention whenever we're up here."

"Keeps things interesting," chuckled Mirabal. "You've got to admit there's not too many dull moments."

"Just hope it doesn't get too interesting. I think there are some angry people down there."

"Dash Two," called Bagger, "it looks like the Bogies have reversed; let's go for five more minutes and then we'll have to head back to the boat."

"Roger, five more minutes, Lead."

Five minutes later they began to reverse course as Fancy swung his head to the left. His heart almost stopped as he saw in that instant, and would be forever frozen in his memory, the most beautiful plane he had ever seen. It was a MiG-29 in what he figured was a forty degree dive coming at them from their nine o' clock position. Fancy figured he must have rolled over from thirty or thirty-five thousand feet, pointing that gorgeous plane in a thundering dive. He was really moving. For the first time in a long time Fancy felt he was standing still. As it streaked past, just off their wing tip, Fancy caught sight of the most masterful paint job he could imagine. The plane was painted shades of blue in a scalloped pattern with the peaks of the scallops pointing toward the top of the aircraft, in a shade blending in beautifully with the sky.

"Jesus!" was all Mirabal could utter before it was gone.

Fancy was tempted to stroke the afterburners to zone five and give chase, but realizing immediately that it would be futile.

"Dash Two, what the hell?" demanded Bagger. "Somebody must be looking out for us. Damn!"

"Lead, ten to one that guy's not a camel jockey."

"No shit! Man! I'm going to be laying awake tonight wondering why he didn't take one or both of us out!"

The flight back to the *Enterprise* was made in relative silence, each pilot realizing they would have to keep their heads on a swivel or they were going to pay the ultimate price.

"I don't know how we missed this guy," lamented Commander Mike "Dick" Trazi, commanding officer of VAW-125, the Air Wing's E2-Cs. "Echo 612 was on station. It must have been headed west or just turned to course 270 when that guy made his appearance."

Trazi had come down to Ready Three after Fancy and Bagger had debriefed. Robinson had asked him to come down after hearing what Bagger and Fancy had told him about the beautifully camouflaged MiG.

"That's a first rate crew on board and all the whistles and bells are working as advertised." Trazi shrugged and shook his head in disbelief. "It could be that you were just out of range or he started down out of range. You guys know that if we see anything at all, we'll tell you."

"When is six-one-two due to recover?" asked Robinson, who had absolutely no hint of a smile today.

Trazi glanced at the clock on the bulkhead. "They've got another hour on station, uh 1630 they'll be on deck."

"I'd like to come over and visit with them for a few minutes, Dick, if you don't mind," requested Robinson.

Trazi shrugged again. "Ratchett, you know you're always welcome, no problem."

"Look, Mike, I just want to talk to your guys on the scopes and see what their recollections are. This isn't about being pissed off at anybody or passing blame. You guys do a terrific job and believe me, there's no loss of confidence in you or your guys. And, I think I'm speaking for Bagger and Gator," he continued, gesturing toward his two pilots, "when I say that." Bagger and Fancy nodded in agreement.

"Commander, all the way back to the ship I was more concerned with my failure to spot him than with your guys, believe me," Fancy said extending his hand.

"Hey, you know if there is a problem on our end, we want to find it and make sure it doesn't happen again."

"We know, Dick," said Robinson as he extended his hand to Trazi. "I'll come over after they've recovered, okay?"

"Sure, Ratchett, I'll see you later."

After Trazi left, Robinson turned to Bagger and Fancy. I think I can probably get more information if I go see those guys than if you do. It must have been exciting to get up close and personal with the MiG?"

"Considering the position we were in..." Fancy said shaking his head and gesturing with his hands to approximate the angle and position of the MiG. "Why he didn't shoot is something I'll always wonder about."

Maybe his maintainers hadn't quite got the job done right," interjected Bagger. "I'll bet you anything that pilot had round eyes, fair skin, and blond hair. The Iraqis have probably brought in these ringers, but guess who still maintains the equipment?" And, we all know the hardware they've gotten from the Russians, or whoever it comes from aint that great to begin with. Or," Bagger laughed, "He just couldn't believe his eyes and was laughing so hard he couldn't get the switchology right and he just blew his chance. Right now, I really don't care. The only thing I care about is that I'm here talkin' to you two."

Robinson ran his hand through his hair. "The feelings likewise, but if there is a problem on anybody's part, I want to find out about it."

Fancy, although he didn't say anything, agreed with Robinson. *Leave nothing to chance,* he thought to himself. *It's just not good for your health and well being.*

Two nights later Enterprise had come off station and was cruising along the coast of Qatar, making just enough headway to create the hint of a breeze over the deck. Fancy and Mirabal had flown five missions, including one to Badrah, without one hint of aggressive actions on the part of the Iraqis.

Captain Bedley had ordered the ship to stand down and a steel beach party was underway. Even though the sun had been down for almost two hours the deck was still radiating heat from the day's unrelenting sun and the daily launching and recovery of planes.

VF-124 was gathered in a semi-circle near the bow of the ship. Stash McClure, because of his junior status had been designated squadron chef and was flipping hamburgers on a make do grill. Fancy leaned back in his beach chair, the only other purchase he had made in Bahrain, just before they had caught the COD plane back to the ship. He was savoring the news that Poncho had brought back that afternoon from

Bahrain. The operation had gone well and it looked like Amanda would regain most if not all body movement. All seemed right with the world once again.

Joker was puffing on one of his immense cigars, leisurely blowing smoke rings into the warm night air. After sending a prodigious sized spiral, he leaned back in his chair and gestured with his stogie towards the departing Poncho who had been dispatched to get some more soft drinks.

"What's with this guy, Poncho?" Joker gestured to the retreating Poncho. "You know he's almost too good lookin'. Is he gay or somethin'?"

Big Wave sat up straight, his jaw set, and Fancy, although he couldn't see for sure, imagined his eyes boring holes in Joker, while at the same time making sure his Master Arm switch was on, while getting ready to go to fist-to mouth mode. "In a word, no, and I hope I don't have to say that again."

"Easy Wave, don't get your skivvies in a bunch. I was just askin'. You see guys that attractive and you know…"

"No, I don't know. What I do know is that he's one of the most decent people that you'll ever meet, and next to me, the best pilot on this bird farm. Man, if I was that good lookin', and we do agree on that, I'd be stickin' my face in front of a mirror every chance I got. Poncho doesn't do that."

Big Wave paused. "I remember one night at the Club at Miramar, you know one of those nights we called Big Wednesdays, when all kinds of babes and women come to party and hang out with the pilots, and" he smiled, tossing a glance at Mirabal, " and occasionally the RIOs. It's always been kind of a tradition and a big midweek party. Anyway, this sorority from U.C. San Diego or San Diego State come on board."

"It was U C San Diego," proclaimed Killer, as he sat down in Poncho's vacant chair.

"Yeah, that was it. Well, anyway they were having what they called 'Pig Night'. The whole sorority comes and they bring some poor soul who desperately wants to be a part of that scene. They brought this girl who was a little overweight and sort of homely. If she could get a pilot to take her home she would get to join the sorority. Naturally these babes are swarming around Poncho like flies around a picnic. He sees this girl sitting by herself and he wanders over and starts talkin' to her. One thing leads to another and he asks her to dance and buys her a drink. Finally, someone else tells him what the hell is going on and he gets really pissed. For the rest of the night he didn't leave her side; bought her drinks, walked her out to the flight line, shows her the greatest time ever and, takes her home. What's more he makes sure he sees her again on campus. Just bent these stupid sorority babes all out of shape."

"Did she get to join the sorority?" asked Joker, blowing another large smoke ring into the night.

"Well," continued Big Wave, "after that she kind of lost interest in her so called friends and sorority sisters. When she graduated she invited Poncho. He went, met her folks, the whole nine yards."

"Wasn't that kind of leading her on though?"

"He told her he wasn't looking for a girl friend or a relationship right then, you know he was pretty honest with her."

Joker sighed, "Jesus, sounds like he's a Boy Scout or something."

"Listen, he is a straight arrow kind of guy, but if there's fun to be had or if things go sour, he knows all about keepin' the faith, believe me."

"He and Wave smuggled this dog on board when we were in Hawaii. He thought that was a riot, at least for awhile, to stay one step ahead of the Master-At-Arms and the XO," chuckled Fancy.

"Who wants another burger?" called McClure who was getting sick of cooking and hoped nobody did.

Just to keep the nugget in his place, everybody, of course, wanted at least one more burger. McClure gave a disgusted snort and turned back to his cooking vowing never to cook or eat another hamburger again in his life.

After everyone had stopped giving advice and letting Stash know how much they enjoyed his cooking, the squadron broke down into smaller groups with the conversation ranging from planes to women and then back to planes.

Joker moved his chair around to form a group with Fancy, Big Wave, Killer, and Bagger.

"Well boys, we better savor moments like these."

"Oh?" uttered Mirabal who had moved to the group. "Why so? You mean leaving the Gulf will break your heart. Joker, you've got to get out more. Get a grip."

Puffing on his cigar Valdorama sighed, blowing out another ring. "No, I mean carriers like the Enterprise, F-14s, even those little toys, the F-18s. Sooner, I suspect, rather than later, they'll all be replaced."

"By what!" snapped Big Wave. "The Super Hornet? What a joke."

"You know, I wish it was going to be the Super Hornet, big a joke as it is." Shaking his head he continued. "Nope, it'll probably be some version of the TLAMs (Tomahawk land-attack missile) and probably conventional air-launched cruise missiles."

Hoots of derisions rained down upon Joker's ample shoulders.

"Yeah, that was my reaction at first, too. But think about it. A cruise missile strike has certain advantages over strikes by aircraft. For instance, does anyone see any replacement on the far horizon or at all for the A-6? No. The missile becomes both the bomb and the bomber and that does more than eliminate the need for the bomber. It also eliminates the need for any other aircraft to support the bomber, not to mention collateral damage."

Pausing and taking another puff Joker smiled. "When the air wing went to Strike U at Fallon, we were getting ready to come to the Gulf. The last exercise was a classic Alpha Strike, you know a typical Navy defense style of attack of thirty aircraft. Only four were going to be dropping any bombs," he said gesturing with his cigar. "Four planes!"

"You know how it goes. We burned the midnight oil staying up nearly all night hatching this little miracle, getting done just in time to grab something to eat before we briefed and manned the birds. Then it was another two hours before we even started the engines. After we got them started and taxiing, more or less on schedule, eight planes dropped out for various discrepancies. The lead started his take-off roll, hit an owl, aborted, and shut down right there on the runway."

"There we were, the entire strike package lined up from the hold short line clear back to the transient aircraft parking just waiting for the lead to get towed away. Somebody, we're not quite sure who it was, keyed their mike, probably by accident, and just blurted out, 'Is anybody left in this goat-rope who's actually going to the target'?"

"Anybody we might know?" chuckled Fancy.

Smiling somewhat smugly, Joker continued. "Realistically, I bet this strike could have been conducted with less than thirty missiles. Plus, we wouldn't need the carrier to launch or recover them. That makes the Beltway Cowboys happy because there won't be any air crews shot down, or more importantly, hostages to be paraded before the TV cameras and beamed into the living rooms of America."

Valdorama was getting really warmed up and his audience sat back, knowing sooner or later he would make a mistake and mudsuck himself. When that happened they would immediately jump on his misguided logic.

"The money is just not going to be there. We can keep platforms like cruisers, destroyers, big old ugly bombers and lose a carrier or two and save some real money. There's some big bucks to be saved over the thirty year life of a carrier, not to mention the air crews and technicians that won't have to be trained. Then kick in the price of an over blown aircraft program and you are definitely talking a crud-load of money. Maybe enough to fix Social Security and Medicare combined. At least that's the idea a lot of the bean counters are sure to jump on."

"What about stealth?" croaked Bagger.

"What about it? You're surely not thinking of the A-12 are you?"

"I know it's been canceled, but…"

"But is right. Back at Oceana some junior surface warfare officer jumped up from his nap and proclaimed, 'That's outstanding that that project has been canceled! That pig was a total money sump. We can do the exact same mission with the TLAM and get off watch in time for mid-rats.'"

There were chuckles from the assembled group, that had now grown substantially.

"If this moron had checked his six he would have probably rethought that remark because there was another officer in the room who happened to be an attack pilot. He spins this guy around and gets right up in his face and snaps, 'That's just the kind of moronic comment that perfectly illustrates the typical 15 knot, ignorant, black-shoe mentality!'"

"Naturally the black-shoe takes issue with that bit of rhetoric and he says, 'Oh, really. Tell me three important strike capabilities the A-12 would have given the Navy it doesn't already have with TLAM?'"

"This attack puke fires back, 'That's easy. It was a hundred times sexier, and a thousand times more expensive, and I was gonna fly it!'"

The assembled pilots and RIOs roared with laughter and agreement, even if the guy was an attack puke.

"Joker," put in Fancy, "the cruise missiles we have today have some serious limitations such as not being able to fly in the rain, dust and fog causes them problems. The next generation has to be a whole bunch better."

"Right!" shot back Joker. "From what I hear they've already corrected a whole bunch of those failings. I don't know if they can make a cruise missile that will do everything a stealth bomber can do, but they can come very close. Hell, if we can cover the requirement for deep, precision strikes with a cruise missile we, they, whoever, could scrap stealth bombers."

"What about tactical situations? The jar heads will go nuts if they don't have air support when they go over the beach," said Poncho who rejoined the group by dumping Killer out of his chair. "The Bad Guys aren't going to be intimidated by threats and especially threats they can't see."

"Say the Bad Guys gets this really bright idea and decide to roll his armor into…uh, the country of Friendly during the World Series. His brain trust decides it's doable and they can roll in there during the seventh inning stretch and two hours later the country is theirs. They figure the only thing in their area is a sub and TLAM can't do diddly against moving tanks. The threat of knocking down Bad Guy's power grid deters him not one bit. There we are up the proverbial creek without a paddle: we either wimp out or have to mount a massive operation and drive out the Bad Guys."

Joker nodded in agreement. "Like I said there's improvements on the way and I don't mean the far future. It's not impossible that these improvements would include hitting moving targets from a sub launched TLAM. Bad Guys might think twice before they rolls those tanks and sit back and watch the rest of the series."

"In other words Joker, we're not out of business quite yet?" said Robinson from the edge of the group.

"Not yet, Skipper, it's a little way off, but we can see it from here."

A week later, with the steel beach party now a distant memory, Fancy fell back on his bunk. Tired as he was he pulled a letter from inside his "tan bag". Although he had only had it in his hands for less than thirty minutes it looked as thought it had been through the wringer. Pulling it out of its envelope he read it again relishing what he imagined had to be Cody's scent, as well as the words, particularly the last three. It was hard to believe that eight letters could make him so euphoric. Amanda was up and beginning to get around, albeit somewhat slower than normal and would be sent home by the time the letter had reached him.. Cody was home, and was being tended by Scott, who also sent his regards. Bagger would be interested in the fact that Rowdy Kobayashi had come to visit and check on her progress.

Just as he was about to raise his tired bones off the rack Bagger exploded through the door. "What a day! Man, those ragheads shot a missile at us!"

"Obviously they missed. Where'd they shoot from?"

"We were on our side of the fence, just southwest of Al Diwaniyah at about twelve grand and lo and behold they locked us up and shot, bam, just like that!"

"What'd you do?"

"Pulled many g's to the right and went into a barrel roll, and started to look for the next one."

"Only one?"

"Yeah, just one, which was one more than I'd ever like to see—ever."

"How close did it get?"

Bagger screwed up his face. "Half mile, maybe a little closer. Man, that's scary when you can see 'em, even if it is for only a split second. Walrus's eyes were as big as saucers after we recovered."

"You sure look happy. Maybe we're going back to Bahrain?"

"No," said Fancy, waving the letter. "Cody's home , Amanda is starting to get feeling back and has even taken a few tentative steps, and is probably home by now. Rowdy dropped in for a visit. Said she had fallen for some Eagle driver."

Bagger's face fell for a half second. "Ha! That'll be the day. She knows a stud when she meets one. Fell for an Eagle driver my ass!"

Fancy laughed out loud. "That was pretty nice of Rowdy. According to this, it sounds like they really hit it off."

"Cody obviously has good taste, present company not withstanding. Is her brother still there?"

"Uh, yeah, he'll be there until they get her ex or he gets him, and I'm not bettin' on the cops."

"I'm surprised the idiot is still on the loose. Talk about a dufus," said Bagger shaking his head.

"I can't imagine anything worse than to have Scott Thorn comin' after you. He's a dead man and probably knows it Probably headed across the border."

"What are you up to now?"

"I'm going to go horizontal for a while, catch some zzzzzs, get some paperwork out of the way, and write a letter to Cody, not necessarily in that order. You?"

"I'm goin' to get somethin' to eat, then drift down to Ready Three to see what's cookin'."

Over the next five days eight more SAMs tried their luck against the Navy planes. It was decided by the folks in the head shed that the F-14s would team up with F/A-18s to shoot HARM anti-radiation missiles if the Iraqis wanted to continue to shoot at the American planes. Fancy and Mirabal were scheduled to launch at 1600 hours to patrol along the 32nd parallel. Or as Fancy liked to think of it trolling for SAMs.

As Fancy came on deck after the final brief with their wingman from VFA-81, the Sun Liners, he walked over the steel deck to Desperado 207. He noted that the plane had been washed and looked slightly out of place among all the other planes on deck. It had spent three days in the hanger bay undergoing an engine change. As he drew near he noticed the small Iraqi flag painted on the port side. Next to it was the outline of a truck. Shaking his head he smiled. Not, he figured, that he had much to smile about. After a morning test hop on another F-14, being assistant maintenance officer did have its perks, he had had to wade through a mountain of paperwork. After that he had decided to shave and had managed to cut himself not once but twice. Then due to some problem with the hot water he had managed to just about scald himself before the water went 180 degrees and turned to ice water. After managing to get out of the shower alive and stem the bleeding he had put on his "zoombag" and then as he pulled up the zipper it stuck, refusing to slide up or down. Solving that problem, after a liberal dose of colorful language, and on the way to he managed to scrape his right shin over the combing as he went through one of the water tight door ways. More colorful language. Thinking his problems must be over as he came on to the sweltering deck only to discover he had shaved only one half of his upper lip. Curiously, that bothered him the most. He kept running his hand over his lip trying to will away the unwanted whiskers.

"Hey, Gator, how you doin'?"

Fancy turned and at the same time took a step backwards. As he started to open his mouth to reply he backed up into one of the tie-down chains and was sent sprawling to the deck.

"Did you have a nice trip?" laughed Rhino, as he extended his hand to the now thoroughly brassed off Fancy. "Graceful, very graceful."

"I'm so happy I've provided several moments of mirth for your enjoyment," growled Fancy as he was pulled back to his feet. "Jesus, can anything else go wrong?"

"Oh, I can think of about a jillion things even before we get off the deck."

"Hell, I can think of two jillion before we get off the deck. Come on, let's look this thing over. At least it looks like it belongs to the Navy."

Noting Shrader hanging back wondering if he should make his presence felt, Fancy called, "Shrader, did you wash this plane? It looks great!"

"Yes, sir. Well, not just me. The jarheads wanted to put some of the brig rats to work and I happened to be in the right place at the right time to get a lot of free bodies."

"Is she up?"

"Yes, Sir! We changed the port engine, fixed the gripe on the stick inputs, and changed the fire control module. She's up and ready, Sir."

Twenty-five minutes later Fancy was sitting in the cockpit wondering if someone had sprayed new car smell and was about to make that comment to Shrader when he noticed Mirabal still standing on the deck looking for all the world like he was sniffing at something.

Shaking his head he pulled on his helmet and started to look at his takeoff check list. When he looked again Mirabal was starting to climb the boarding ladder.

Fancy was still trying to rub away the stubble under his nose. Shifting around in his seat he decided that Moose must have flown this plane the last time it was up. If he put the canopy down now something would have to give and that something was his neck and head. Cranking his seat down he grumbled about the seat and the condition of things in general.

"Gator, everything okay up there? Did you say something?"

"Yeah, just great. No, I was just talking to myself, trying to get comfortable. You got a razor back there by any chance?"

"A what?"

"Nothin'. Forget it. You squared away?"

"We're good to go. Let's do the checklist. The nose is cold and I'm ready!"

"You sound particularly chipper today," said Fancy as they completed the checklist for take off.

"Do you know what the ideal Air Force cockpit crew is?"

"No."

"A pilot and a dog. The pilot is there to feed the dog, and the dog is there to bite the pilot in case he tries to touch anything."

Before Fancy could reply, Mirabal was laughing uproariously at his own joke.

"Do I detect Joker's fine hand?"

"Oh yeah. How do you know if you have an Air Force pilot at your party?"

Fancy sighed. "How do you know?"

"He'll tell you." More laughter. Is that funny or what?"

Fancy smiled to himself, trying to hold back the laughter he felt coming. He didn't know which was funnier, Mirabal's jokes or Mirabal laughing as he told the jokes.

"What do Air Force pilots use for birth control?"
"Birth control? I give up."
"Their personality." Much more laughter.
This time Fancy couldn't contain his laughter.

When they both got themselves more or less under control it was time to start engines.

Both engines were up and in the green as Fancy scanned the instruments one more time. Upon seeing that everything was working as advertised, he glanced to his left and Shrader gave him the signal that the chains holding the plane to the deck had been removed. A yellow-shirt began directing him forward to the port catapult. As they pulled up to the JBD an S-3 was thrown into the air. The JBD came down and Fancy eased off the brakes and advanced the throttles and the big plane lumbered to the catapult where he swept the wings forward. Again he felt, rather than saw, them being hooked up to the catapult by the greenies. Taking off the brakes, he went to full power, cycling through the controls, checking the flaps, slats, and engine gauges. At last it was time.

Fancy gave a thumbs up, fired off a sharp salute at the Cat Officer and put his head against the seat rest. He tilted his head down ever so slightly so he could keep an eye on the instruments. Then they were off. A minute later the F/A-18 that they would escort came off the deck and joined up to Fancy's starboard side. Their wingman was the commanding officer of the Sunliners, Commander Tony "Lu Lu" Lee. Before they went feet dry the F/A-18 would top off its tanks. Fancy shook his head thinking one more time about one of the criticisms of the Hornet—its short legs.

The strike controller cleared them to 20,000 feet. The sun had been hidden by the moisture in the air but when they went through 8,000 feet it immediately reasserted itself.

At 20,000 feet Rhino reported their arrival. "Boy, that controller sounds bored. Man, no enthusiasm at all."

"What's he got to be enthused about? Encased in all that steel. I sure wouldn't trade places with him," Fancy answered, bringing the throttles back so they were conserving the maximum amount of fuel. Commander Gray's F/A-18 off to their starboard side seemed to be hanging motionless in the clear cobalt sky.

"Desperado 207, the Texaco is 20 angels at ten miles. Slide in first and top off and then we'll do the same," came Gray's disembodied voice. It wasn't a suggestion.

"Roger that, Gypsy 302. Dead ahead at uh, eight miles, we'll plug in first."

"Gypsy 302 copies."

"Sounds like he doesn't much like working with us," commented Mirabal.

"Ah, you know. They feel inferior. They've got to pump themselves up somehow."

Mirabal chuckled. "Come right a tad and we'll be right at the tanker's six."

"What's a tad?"

"Oh, you know, just a skosh."

"That clears it right up, thanks."

"De nada, anytime."

They took their gas without any trouble and had backed out and were watching Commander Gray plugging in to the tanker.

"That was as smooth as a baby's butt," observed Mirabal. "At least it looked smooth to me."

"He made it look easy."

"Hey, you know how many pilots it takes to change a light bulb?"

"Ha! Gotcha! Just one. He plugs it in and the world revolves around him."

They both laughed as Gray came off the tanker and they headed northwest. Mirabal let *Enterprise* know they had gone feet dry when they crossed over the beach at Al Faw. Immediately both planes began to jink and weave as they entered Iraqi airspace. At least technically it was. The Iraqis had ceded it to the Americans in 1991, under some duress of course.

"Despera…2…let's…kee…eyes…."came Gray's voice crackled through Fancy's headphones.

"Say again, Gypsy 302. Your last transmission was broken up."

The reply from Gray's plane was not much better, but the message came through. "He's pretty broken up. Are our radios okay, Rhino?"

"As far as I can tell. I think we're being jammed."

"Well they're doing a good job of it."

"Desperado 207, this is Big Eye. Are you receiving?"

"Loud and clear, Big Eye."

"You're coming in weak and breaking up."

"Roger that, Big Eye, it looks like the Iraqis are jamming today."

"Desperado, be advised we have bandits airborne on their side of the fence. It looks like four MiG-29s. They're at 19,000 feet, at 90 miles, in a race track pattern around Nippur."

"Gypsy 302, do you copy the four MiGs?"

"Gyp…30…cop.." came the reply, strong but broken up."

At the same time Fancy heard the unmistakable warble of a search radar in his headphones. "Uh oh, good news comes in bunches."

"Sounds like a Palm Top," responded Mirabal. "They're just lookin'."

The radar signals became stronger as they approached the 32nd Parallel. As they turned westward on a course of 270 the RAW gear started to give off even stronger indications that the Iraqis were indeed looking at them—hard.

"De…207…it…loo…like…they're getting…to sho…" The rest of the transmission was lost but its meaning was not.

"Oh oh, that's a fire control radar and it's got us painted and Gypsy's right, they're about ready to…"

As Fancy glanced to his port side he saw the huge plume of dust as a missile was launched from the other side of the 32nd parallel. It looked like only one, but that was enough.

"Desperado 207, I'm going to shoot the HARM."

Evidently the jamming had stopped because Gray sounded as clear as a bell.

As Fancy rolled into a barrel roll he remembered the MiGs. *Where the hell were they?* he wondered. "Rhino, where are the MiGs?" *So much for situational awareness* he groused to himself.

As he rolled inverted his question was suddenly answered as two MiG-29s flew between the two Navy planes on an opposite heading. Out of the corner of his eye he caught a glimpse of the SAM as it went ballistic heading up into the empty sky. *I love those HARMs. I might even change my feelings about Hornet pukes.* The threat of the HARM had caused the Iraqis to shut down their radar, meaning their missile had no guidance.

"Gypsy 302, you've got bandits passing down your right side!" Immediately, Fancy pulled down to the left into a low-side yo-yo. If it was successful he could cut across a circle in the vertical plane to turn inside and gain an advantage over the two MiGs.

At the same time he heard, "Desperado 207, Gypsy 302 has got fuel transfer problems!" Gray sounded pissed and embarrassed at the same time.

"Extend out to the south Gypsy. We'll try to keep these guys occupied!" He flipped the Master Arm switch to on.

As Fancy bottomed out and had started back up he had picked up a lot of speed. He also noticed that the MiGs had gone into a left hand turn. Seeing one of the MiGs against the cool blue sky for a background he was getting a good tone from his Sidewinder indicating that it had acquired the target. Fancy mashed the red button on his stick. Immediately, the AIM-9M leaped off the rail and streaked after the

MiG. The missile tracked perfectly then nothing seemed to happen. *Missed dammit!*

In the next instant the MiG exploded in a dirty black breath of smoke and airplane parts. The missile had tracked perfectly and had flown right up the MiGs tailpipe. *Now they're going to be really pissed*!

"We got one!" grunted Mirabal as he was pushed back into his seat.

Fancy brought the big fighter into a highside yo-yo to keep his advantage on the other MiG.

"Bogeys at 9 o'clock!" called out Mirabal.

*Well, at least I know where the other two are now.* Fancy pulled hard and turned into them causing them to overshoot the F-14.

"Goin down, Rhino," he said, as he pulled into a low-side yo-yo in order to get into a position to reattack the first MiG. "Rhino, don't loose those two guys!" He knew Mirabal would keep his head on a swivel, but he had to say something.

Fancy figured if he traded a little height for speed he could close the horizontal distance hopefully taking him into the MiG's blind spot. And it looked like the MiG driver wasn't keeping his head on a swivel. The first MiG was right where Fancy knew he would be. Getting another good tone from the AIM-9M, he fired the second Sidewinder of the day. This one seemed to hang on the rail a little longer than the first one and then it came off the rail in a brilliant flash and started to track.

"Gator, MiGs at eight!" shouted Mirabal.

Out of the corner of his eye Fancy saw their noses light up as they fired their cannons at them. *Buck fever* he thought, *they're out of range.* However it was still a little unnerving to see their noses light up like Christmas trees even as their shells were falling short.

"Coming left, Rhino!" he called, breaking away in a sharp negative-G roll. He hoped he hadn't put Mirabal to sleep as he brought the plane back up in a high-G pull up. *I've gotta get to the weight room. My arms feel like two tons of lead.* He heard Mirabal grunting to himself in his pit, trying to force the blood that was seeking refuge in his lower extremities back to his vital organs.

He saw the second pair of MiGs now headed west. Pushing the throttles past the detents he went to zone 5 afterburner and felt the big ship accelerate sharply toward the retreating MiGs. "Come on, Baby, let's close it up." As if responding to his command, the Tomcat began to close in on the MiGs. Again the good tone and he fired his third Sidewinder of the day. The MiGs tried to turn into them. Sensing that the Sidewinder was going after the right hand MiG, Fancy turned his attention to his wingman.

Coming out of zone five Fancy realized he was going to over shoot the MiG and would become the target. Pulling up into a high-speed yo-yo he managed to stay behind the MiG who was now in a tight left hand turn. "Takin' her up, Rhino!"

"I'm right behind you babe. That MiG that was headed to the right took the 'Winder of the port wing. Blew it right off. Holy shit, that's three! I've got the MiG! Hard left hand turn. He wants to play!"

Fancy pulled the stick back into his gut. As he reached an altitude roughly a thousand feet above his opponent he brought the stick to his right and rolled inverted while at the same time bringing the plane back down. Straining in his straps he rolled his neck trying to keep his eyes on the Iraqi plane. As the plane started to build up ahead of steam he switched from missiles to guns. He could see the MiG through the top of his canopy as he seemed to hang in his straps. The MiG was right there. *Guy wasn't paying attention. Thought he lost me.*

As they roared down, the MiG-29 grew larger and became centered in the gunsight. Mashing down the red button once again the 20mm Gatling gun spewed out a deadly stream of 20mm shells culminating in a collision at the MiGs canopy. Fancy pulled hard and to the right as the MiG desintegrated.

"AMF! AMF!" (adios mother fucker) Mirabal shouted. "Whoowee! Talk about Shit Hot!"

"Easy on the eardrums, babe," Fancy panted, realizing for the first time how tired he felt. His arms and neck ached, and he felt himself breathing hard. He quickly scanned the instruments, making sure everything was where it should be. It was and even the fuel looked okay.

"Jesus, Gator, do you know what you've just done. Four MiGs! Four of 'em. Man, I am so pumped!"

"Desperado 207, we have two more MiGs airborne. Bearing 090 at one-eight angels. They're definitely headed your way."

"Well, you know what they say," chimed in Mirabal, a MiG at…"

Fancy finished the thought as he reefed the big fighter around to meet the new threat. "…your six is better than no MiG at all."

"Bogeys, 50 miles, at one nine angels, and comin' hard."

Taking a quick stock of their situation Fancy observed that he had one AIM-9 left and the Vulcan. *What I wouldn't give for a Slammer right now or even an AIM-7, the Great White Hope.*

"Forty miles at 20 angels," reported Mirabal calmly and professionally.

Fancy saw the two dots on his own radar display. The three planes continued to fly towards each other. Neither the MiGs nor the Tomcat showing any signs of giving way.

"Twenty miles, still at two zero angels. Hey, they've launched. Man, that's a little extreme. Whoa, they're starting to turn away. That's it, that's what they're doin'! They've turned tail."

Fancy throttled back to conserve fuel. As he watched his scope he could see as the two missiles ran out of fuel they started a one way trip to the ground.

Fancy brought the plane around and started to head back for the Enterprise. "I hope those two things don't land on some poor farmer's head. I wonder what they were thinking?"

"Those poor guys must have been worrying about what happened to their buddies and then they had to worry about what was going to happen to them once they reached the home drome. It could get ugly for them either way. I'd probably rather take my chances on the ground though."

"Desperado 207, it looks like you've got a clear road back home. Nice work up there. That was something to see on the scopes. We'd sure like to know what you guys like to drink?" came the voice from the E-3 Sentry, Big Eye.

" Thanks. How 'bout a case of Dr. Pepper?"

"Dr. Pepper? Hey," came the unbelieving voice. "If that's what you want, that's what you'll get. Nice going, Desperado. You've sent Saddam a message."

"Thanks, Big Eye. Desperado is heading for the farm. Say, uh, did Gypsy 302 make it back?"

"Gypsy 302 made an emergency landing in Kuwait. Probably pissed the Kuwaitis off somehow," came the sarcastic reply.

For the second time that day Fancy eased Desperado 207 behind an S-3B. Plugging into the basket he advanced the throttle slightly as soon as the red lights went to green and the fuel began to pass between the two planes.

As soon as they had taken on 4,000 pounds they disengaged. "Thanks, Texaco we appreciate the service."

"Desperado, it's our pleasure, believe me. We've never tanked a MiG killer before, let alone one that got four in one hop. Nice goin' we're proud of you."

"Thanks, Texaco. We also know it's a team effort. See you back at the ranch."

"Count on it, Desperado. The Dr. Pepper is on us."

"Word gets around real quick doesn't it, Gator?" chortled Mirabal.

"We live in a marvelous age, Rhino. A marvelous age."

"Well, hey, I've got two dots, at umm, 60 plus miles at 22 angels headed our way. I'll bet the farm they're Turkeys."

"Let's hope so. We're just about Winchester." (out of ammunition)

"Yup, TCS shows two Tomcats at 50 plus miles, still at 22 angels."

"Desperado 207, this is Desperado 200. We have you at forty plus miles. How you doin'?" came the voice of Ratchet Robinson.

"Desperado 200, we're good for another round if that's what Saddam wants."

"Gator, that doesn't surprise me a bit. Shit hot work up there today."

"Thanks, Skipper. We kind of got it right. Mirabal kept me on the straight and narrow."

Robinson chuckled. "Desperado, we'll pass to your port side. Who knows, maybe we'll get lucky tonight. By the way, you better provide something other than just a straight-in approach when you get back to the ship. That whole big boat is just goin' nuts."

"Good hunting, Desperado 200. We'll try."

The three planes continued toward the merge. At four miles Fancy could pick them out of the darkening blue sky. They had to be friendlies, they had their anti-smash lights on.

The three Tomcats flashed past each other in what seemed like a split second. Quickly Fancy turned in his seat as much as he possibly could but the two planes had been swallowed up in the murk, their anti-collision lights now turned off. Fancy felt a chill pass up his spine.

Badrod Boldon stood on his platform. "Lucky for me I had the duty or I would have had to use my authority to usurp somebody's getting to land this guy," he said to no one in particular."

Fancy had asked for and had received permission for a break at the numbers. As they roared down the starboard side of the *Enterprise* he rolled the Tomcat to his right 270 degrees and then to his left and the plane crossed the carrier's bow right across the number 65 painted on her flight deck. Bringing the stick to his left again they tore down the port side of the ship. In an instant the ship was left behind, just a chip on the endless sea. Gaining some altitude he brought it left again until they were on their final approach.

"207, Tomcat, ball, four point six," he reported as soon as he had the glide slope indicator in sight.

"Roger, ball," Badrod acknowledged.

Fancy concentrated now, keeping the amber ball aligned with the row of green lights.

Badrod could now hear the the sounds of the jet engines as they changed in pitch as Fancy worked to keep the ball centered. "Right for lineup. Keep it coming, Gator."

With eight seconds Fancy made a series of small corrections as he saw the deck coming up on a swell: wing up, wing down. Now they're over the round off.

"Power," scolded Badrod lightly.

The sound floated through Fancy's helmet as he felt the mains crunch onto the deck. Pushing the throttles all the way forward, he felt the plane starting to slow, and his body dragged forward by the momentum.

Badrod, turned to his writer saying," Pitching deck. A little high, little lined up to the left in the middle. OK 3."

Following the directions of the yellow-shirt plane director he eased the throttles forward and taxied forward where he was directed to cut the engines. As the big General Electrics wound down he raised the canopy. A strange silence had fallen over the deck where the norm was a cacophony of sounds, smells, and movement. The pungent sticky air of the Gulf and a slight smell of kerosene brought a surreal feeling to him as he lifted himself out of the cockpit. He felt the presence of someone as he landed heavily on the deck. As he turned Shrader's smiling face greeted him.

"Congratulations, Lieutenant. It looks like I'll get to paint some more Iraqi flags on her."

Opening his mouth to reply Fancy became aware of the movement of many men. Looking around he saw what looked like the whole deck crew, the purples, greens, yellows, reds, and whites, making a veritable rainbow of men, as they crowded in closer.

"Thanks, Shrader. You were right, she was up and ready to go. She's the star of the show today."

"Whoa, what have we here?" smiled Mirabal as he vaulted to the deck. "Man, I hope nobody's in the pattern."

Voices from the crowd fell around and upon like rain, congratulating them on the four kills. Hands reached out to touch them and shake hands. Fancy was aware that the entire crowd was made up of enlisted men.

Making their way, slowly through the throng of men, they reached the edge of the flight deck. Turning, Fancy motioned with his hands for quiet. "First of all I'd like to thank you. I also hope there's nobody in the pattern."

The crew cheered and laughed at the attempted humor.

"I really never thought in my wildest dreams that I'd get this kind of greeting—again. Thanks to you, and I mean all of you, plus the guys below decks, we were able to score…"

Wild cheers erupted again.

"Anyway as I was saying, that big beast," he continued, gesturing back at Desperado 207, "and everything on it, worked as advertised. Everything. All of those hours you put in really paid off. Those 'winders came off the rails and tracked like you wouldn't believe. The Gatling put the shells right where they would do the most good, or harm, depending on your point of view. You guys and everybody else on this ship had a part to play in what we did up there. Thank you." With more cheers ringing in their ears they continued off the flight deck and headed below.

He wasn't sure if he felt relief or mild disappointment as he and Mirabal headed toward the equipment room to rid themselves of their flight gear. He told himself it was relief while at the same time remembering his sore ribs after the first "celebration". "Rhino," he called to Mirabal as they made their way along the narrow passageway, "what were you doing on deck before we launched? It looked like you were trying to pick up the scent of something."

Mirabal stopped and turned. "Actually I did pick up the scent of something."

"What?"

"You'll laugh."

"Probably, but tell me anyway."

"Nah, you'll think I'm nuts."

An enlisted yellow-shirt brushed by them, offering them congratulations.

"Come on, I know you well enough to know you're not exactly crazy."

"See, I told ya you would," continued Mirabal as he turned and started to walk again.

"Hey, I was just kidding about the crazy part. Come on what gives?"

Mirabal turned once again. "Okay, but don't laugh, all right?"

"Scout's honor, I promise."

Mirabal studied Fancy's face, looking for the slightest hint of a smile. Seeing none, he paused. "Now don't laugh."

"I won't, and this better be worth it."

Pausing, while another yellow-shirt squeezed past them on his way to the flight deck, Mirabal took a deep breath. "When I was standing there I smelled MiGs."

Fancy studied his friend while at the same time stifling an urge that threatened to make him break out in full fledged laughter. "MiGs?"

"MiGs. I just knew we were going to get close to some. I knew it just as sure as you're standing there."

"You smelled 'em? What do they smell like?"

"Burning kerosene," he said seriously, studying Fancy's face for the slightest reaction.

" Burning kerosene? Burning kerosene! Let's see. We're on a carrier. There's lots of planes. Why wouldn't you smell burning kerosene," marveled Fancy. "And why didn't you let me in on it?"

Mirabal shrugged, "I don't know. The only thing I could think of was MiGs. Just as sure as I know, the, the…the island is up on the roof, I just knew it. I could just imagine saying, 'Hey, Gator, guess what…?'"

Fancy shook his head, still trying to choke down the laughter. "Listen, next time, if there is a next time, let me in on it, okay?"

"Sure, why not?" Mirabal smiled, looking like an errant teenager caught making out with a popular cheerleader at a school dance.

Shaking his head Fancy continued on to the equipment room. Suddenly stopping, he turned once more to face Mirabal. "It's going to take forever with the debrief. Geez, those guys can be slower than molasses in the dead of winter. Man!"

Divesting themselves of the bulky survival equipment and g-suits they decided to continue to Ready Three. No one had been around to tell them any different. As they exited the room they were met with a sight neither of them would forget for the rest of their lives. Lining the narrow passageway it seemed that every last man who wasn't flying was lined up forming a trail of men that probably stretched all the way to Ready Three. In front of the assembled Air Wing were Matsen and Commander Gray.

Sticking his hand out Gray said, "I hope you know I wanted to stick around. When I dumped the centerline tank, the check valve stuck in the open position."

Before he could say anything else Fancy took his hand and shook it. "Commander, you don't have to say a thing. I have no doubts in my mind and when things can go wrong they will."

Gray smiled and slapped him on the back. "Thanks, Fancy, I appreciate that."

"No problem, Sir."

Fancy, looking around, was sure the ensuing commotion could be heard all the way to Saudi Arabia. Shouts and calls of, "Way to go! Gunfighters forever! Fighter pilots do it better…" and on and on.

As he and Mirabal made their way through the ebullient gauntlet of fliers, hands were shaken and backs slapped It seemed everyone just wanted to touch them in some way. *My body just won't take any more shoot downs* Fancy decided to himself. *This is worse than pullin' eight on rnine G's.*

Just when he thought his body was going to cave in to the celebration, they reached Ready Three, they were met by the nonflying Gunfighters and they were treated to another round of shouting and back slapping.

Valdorama, with another giant cigar in hand, seemed to be leading the revelry. "Jesus Christ, four, count 'em four!"

Just as he seemed about to put Fancy in a bear hug, Fancy put his hands up in self defense. "Whoa, big guy. My body can't take much more celebrating."

Valdorama threw back his head and laughed and then grabbed him anyway. "Gator, you're too funny. Man, do you realize what you've done?"

"Won't be too funny when I die right here in Ready Three from fractured ribs though."

Valdorama turned him loose and the celebration continued. Almost magically a large sheet cake arrived. It was decorated with the representation of a MiG in the middle of a gun sight and what looked like 20mm tracer shells impacting on it.

Amid the din Matsen got close to Fancy and shouted, "Intel said the debrief can wait a while. Congratulations, you guys did a hell of a job up there!"

"Thanks XO!" Fancy shouted back.

The revelry continued without let up for the next ninety minutes. Fancy thought that he must have shot his wrist watch off his left arm at least fifty times as he replayed the action over Iraq for his squadron and all the members of the Air Wing that could squeeze in and out of Ready Three.

Turning around he saw Poncho and Big Wave enter the room. "What the hell is goin' on here? Man you can hear shouting and yelling clear up on the roof. Somebody said somebody got a MiG", declared Poncho to the assembled throng.

"What gives? Who was it?" solicited Big Wave.

"Somebody did!" shouted someone in the front of the room.

"Did you guys talk to Cody?" demanded Fancy.

"Sure did. Who shot down the MiG?" returned Poncho.

"Well, how was she?" How did she sound? How long did you talk to her? How's Amanda?" grilled Fancy.

"Hey, I asked first," came back Poncho. "Mirabal and I did. Now how is she?"

Fancy noticed that both Ponchos and Big Wave's eyes were getting bigger. Turning he caught Stash McClure holding up four fingers with one hand and pointing at Fancy with the other.

"Four?" asked Big Wave incredulously. "Four?"

"Yeah, now what did she have to say?"

Poncho shook his head, his eyes seeming to glaze over. "She's doin' fine. Amanda is, is…uh, she's making progress a lot faster than anyone even hoped. They're doin' fantastic. Four?"

"Anything else?"

"That's the gist of it. I can't remember word for word. How'd you get four?"

"We got lucky. Come on there's got to be more?"

"No, well yes, they're doing great. Cody's going to have plastic surgery within the next couple of days?"

"Day after tomorrow?"

"That's right, isn't it Poncho?"

Poncho nodded in the affirmative while shaking his head and mouthing four over and over.

Fancy really felt that he had something to celebrate now and he breathed a great sigh of —relief? No, it was more like a feeling of peace and the four MiGs had nothing to do with it. He turned back to the celebration knowing he really had something to celebrate.

The party began to wind down when the realization started to hit home that a good many of fliers and crew had early morning launches. Slowly, but in a steady stream the room and the attending passageway started to empty as pilots, RIOs, and other crew members drifted to their rooms to grab some much needed shut eye.

Fancy let himself fall into one of the big leather chairs. Looking over at the PLATT screen he noticed the lack of activity on the flight deck. Letting himself reflect on the now past festivities for a few moments he looked up at Bagger who was still in an animated conversation with Walrus Carpenter, Mirabal, and Joker Valdorama who was still making his points with his cigar. "Hey, does anybody want to grab some fresh air?"

"Sounds like a good idea to me," said Mirabal casting a sideways glance at Joker's stogie. "A real good idea."

A few minutes later the four men could be found standing on the bow of the Enterprise. Flight operations had subsided for the moment and the only movement on the deck were planes being moved and respotted for the resumption of flight operations. The lack of activity and most of all, noise, made the ship seem almost unreal. The heat had abated somewhat and it was merely just plain hot.

"Well, Gator, you've had quite a day for yourself," said Valdorama.

Fancy nodded toward Mirabal. "We've had quite a day."

Mirabal said nothing but he didn't have to, the ear to ear grin said it all.

As the warm breeze washed over them they fell silent, each with his own thoughts.

"Gator," said Joker finally, "how you dealin' with all this?"

"You mean compared to the funk I fell into when we got the first one? Hell, it's a whole different situation. To be honest, I've been thinking more about what Wave and Poncho told me about their conversation with Cody. Let's face it, I've had it easy compared to what Amanda and Cody had to go through."

"You don't sound bitter or angry anymore about what happened?"

"I'm trying not to, but if I think about it long enough…"

"Feels pretty nice up here doesn't it?" said Bagger trying to steer the conversation in another direction, sensing his friend's discomfort.

"You know what feels good is the fact that we have only one more week on station and then it's adios Camel Station and hello CONUS," exalted Bagger, "and not to mention, hello Wendy Kobayashi! Yes! Yes! Yes!"

Everyone laughed at Bagger's obvious pleasure.

"Say," said Bagger, "how long were you guys engaged with the MiGs?'

Fancy, shaking his head, looked over at Mirabal. "I don't know, must have been under two minutes, ninety seconds, what do you think, Rhino?"

"It was just over seven minutes."

"What? It couldn't have been that long. Seven minutes! How do you know?"

"I remember taking a look at the clock on my panel just an instant before we made visual contact. When it was all over I remembered to check the time again. It's interesting that you thought it was over so quick. To me it was a hell of a long time, I was surprised it was only nine minutes. It really seemed a lot longer than that to me."

Fancy pursed his lips, held his breath, and finally let out of lot of stored up air. "Geez, I wonder how two people in the same airplane can experience the same perception of events and yet come out of it with such different feelings. Time passing or not passing. That's something that never fails to bewilder me."

"You know the whole engagement kind of reminded me of a day I had in Little League?"

"Oh, how's that?"

"One day we had to play two games. I remember the ball that whole day just looked so big—more like a basketball than a baseball. Man, I just hit everything, something like nine for ten, maybe it was even ten for ten in the two games. Today…it just seemed like I had the big picture. You know where everything and everybody was going where they would be…Talk about situational awareness. I don't know but it just kind of was there—only in spades. Almost unreal."

"Well, you were pretty busy and for most of those nine minutes I was just hangin' on and trying to keep the MiGs in sight."

"I guess that's the difference, but I don't want you to think for one instant that you didn't contribute today," Fancy said forcefully.

"Thanks, I appreciate that. Listen, I'm beat. I'll see you guys in the morning. Nice goin', today, Gator," Mirabal responded.

"Yeah, me too," said Bagger and Joker, almost in the same breath.

"You did good, babe," said Bagger as the three of them walked off.

As the sound of their footsteps faded into the night Fancy turned around facing the enveloping blackness of the night. He listened to the sound of water being pushed out of the way by the *Enterprise's* enormous bow as the great ship made her way through the night. After a time Fancy took a deep breath, turned and headed for his room.

Coming in to the dark room he removed his flight suit without turning on the light. Making sure Bagger hadn't collapsed into the lower bunk he lowered himself in and stretched out.

Closing his eyes he expected sleep to come easily. Of course it did not. Turning from one side and then to his other, sleep refused to come. Finally, realizing his tossing and turning would eventually wake Bagger he turned over on his back and listened to make sure he was asleep. Hearing deep breathing and an occasional soft snore he carefully raised himself off the rack and felt his way to the small desk. Pulling out the metal chair he sat down and reached for the small desk lamp. Turning the light away from where Bagger was sleeping he turned it on. Pulling out the drawer he withdrew a piece of paper and a pen.

Dear Cody and Amanda,
It's been quite a day. The best part of it was
when Poncho and Big Wave came back from Bahrain and
told me they had talked to you on the phone…

When he finished the letter he returned to his rack. This time sleep washed over him like a tidal wave.

# 16

The next week seemed to stretch out forever. When Fancy and Mirabal did get to fly, the missions turned out to be standard CAP (combat air patrol) that seemed to keep them tethered close to the ship. The George Washington, the carrier that would replace them, would be a day late in relieving them due to heavy weather in transit. And as Bagger had reminded them more than once, Big George was probably a dollar short too.

On what was promised to be their last day on Camel Station, Fancy and Mirabal were sitting in Ready Three. Technically, they were manning the Alert 15 aircraft. Because of the heat they were allowed to sit in the relatively air conditioned comfort of Ready Three in their flight gear. Bagger and Stash McClure were scheduled to fly the last mission that would actually take squadron aircraft inside Iraq, a TARPS flight that would take them to Badrah and close to the border of Iran.

Matsen and Robinson walked into the room, took a look at the PLATT, and then walked over to Fancy and Mirabal.

"I just got through talking to the Intel guys. One of those MiGs you guys shot down was piloted by someone who was blond and blue-eyed, probably a former East German by the name of Willi Phistenhammer. By all accounts he was supposed to be one of the East German's better pilots. He's been around, seeing service in North Korea, Afghanistan, Vietnam, even to India as an IP."

"How do they find this stuff out?" asked Fancy.

"Beats me. We must have somebody on the ground somewhere. I don't think they could do all that with satellites and recon flights." He shrugged his shoulders. "You guys ready to go home?"

"I've got an ulterior motive, but I think Rhino would like to stay."

"If Gator is going to stay, hey, I'll be glad to. I mean this is one of the garden spots of the world."

"You never got to go to Bahrain did you, Rhino?" asked Matsen.

"Nup, XO, I never made the Freedom Bird, but I don't want you to stay an extra day so I can go. I'll make liberty there on the next cruise."

Robinson opened his mouth to say something when the 1MC announced: "Man the Alert 15. I repeat, Man the Alert 15."

"I wonder what that's all about?" asked Rhino. "So much for an easy day in the shade."

As they made their way to the deck Fancy also wondered. Part of him thinking *Too bad you've got to go one more time,* while another, larger part was saying, *Good deal, who wants to sit when you could be flying.* Wondering which voice mirrored his true feeling, he and Mirabal arrived on deck to the heat and pandemonium of flight operations.

Although they had pre-flighted the bird before they did another quick walk around just to make sure. Everything seemed solid and ready to go. As Fancy put his foot on the bottom rung of the boarding ladder Robinson came up behind him and tapped him on the shoulder.

"Stash has had an on board fire, something that happened to you guys. They're on their way back and the fire seems to be out. The Alert Five nav gear has gone south. You can probably hear Joker swearing and kicking his bird."

Robinson stared hard into Fancy's eyes for what seemed a long time. "Listen, I didn't want you to have to go North again. If for any reason you don't want to, you've more than earned the right to say so. Okay? And, I'm not questioning your manhood in any way."

"I know, Skipper. I'll go. Besides, it beats sittin' around. Rhino, you ready?"

Mirabal who had been close enough to hear the brief conversation said, "Bet your ass. Let's go."

Robinson nodded. "That's what I thought you'd say, but I figured I owed you."

Fancy nodded and climbed the ladder and settled himself in Desperado 207's cockpit. As the Koch fittings were attached he knew this was where he wanted to be. There wasn't the slightest doubt, no doubt at all.

The pre takeoff checks went quickly and the F-110s rumbled to life. Fancy lowered the canopy and they were ready. Mirabal has the Navigation gear aligned and is working on the avionics' test procedures. The yellow-shirt plane director was giving signals as he advanced the throttles and they pulled out of the parking space moving over the deck being passed on from one yellow-shirt to another. As Fancy glanced to his left he noticed what must have been Joker's plane being pushed back toward the elevator to be taken down to the hanger deck. Joker and his RIO were no where in sight. The JBD had already been lowered and they moved across onto catapult one.

At another yellow-shirt's signal Fancy advanced the throttles. Another set of hand signals and he ran through the requisite control checks, moving the stick forward, back, and to either side, while stepping on each rudder pedal. Again hand signals lets Fancy know they were working. As the crew members cleared from under and around the plane the Cat officer, in his yellow jacket waited for Fancy's salute.

In the blink of an eye after the salute Desperado 207 made the 300 foot run to the edge of the deck and they were airborne at 150 knots.

Gear up, flaps in, while Fancy climbs in a shallow left hand climb. "Good shot," the radio crackled. "Desperado 207 airborne."

"Desperado 207, come to three-three-five and climb to angels 15. Texaco should be on your nose," commanded the Carrier Air Traffic Control Center.

"Coming to three-three-five and angels 15," responds Fancy, who by now was quite tickled to be flying and more than happy with the way the plane was responding.

"Gator, I've got Texaco and Desperado 204 at twelve miles dead ahead."

Two minutes later the duty S-3 tanker and Desperado 204 emerged from the somewhat murky sky. Bagger was just coming off the basket and was moving out to the right. *Perfect timing*, Fancy thought as he moved in toward the basket that he now saw was moving around quite a bit. *Well, that's not perfect*, he thought as he made one stab toward the basket and missed and then another, missing that one too. *Maybe the loadmaster is flying that pig*. Taking a deep breath and trying to relax, he eased the throttle forward and plugged in. The red lights went from red to green and his nose told him the fuel had begun to flow.

Refueling complete he brings the plane off to the right. "Desperado 204, we've got a full bag and we're good to go."

"Roger that, Desperado 207. Let's go to angels 27."

"Copy angels 27." The throttles are pushed forward while at the same time the 'pole" is brought back and the two planes begin to climb to twenty-seven thousand feet.

At 27 thousand the sky was a brilliant blue with unlimited visibility. "I think I can see Baghdad. Boy, talk about being able to see forever."

"Baghdad? I think I can see San Diego," fantasized Mirabal.

"Ah ha, do I detect a little channel fever, Rhino?"

"No, you don't detect a little—you're detecting a lot, babe, a lot."

By now they could see the land mass that was Kuwait and Iraq. "We're feet dry," crooned Fancy as they crossed over the beach.

The mission profile called for a low level ingress and egress. Somebody up the line decided the pictures needed to be taken up close and personal. They would stay at altitude until they reached the 32nd parallel and they had passed to the west of Al Hay. Once they had put Al Hay behind them they would drop down on the deck picking up some smash in the process.

"Gator, you still good to go?"

"Everything's in the green babe. We're good to go."

Fancy was off Bagger's starboard side out 200 hundred yards and stepped up 500 feet. They were able to keep an eye on each other's tails.

Fancy took a huge intake of oxygen and adjusted the air-conditioning. After a few minutes of wiggling, twisting and adjusting he finally felt somewhat comfortable. Comfortable of course, being a relative term. Both planes moved up and down as well as sideways like two boxers shadow boxing. Unfortunately, it would take only one "punch" to declare someone a winner.

"Hey, did you hear about Santa Claus and the FAA?" inquired Rhino, after they had been in Iraqi territory for a few minutes.

"The FAA and who?"

"Santa Claus."

"No, I didn't hear about it."

"Well, last Christmas just as it was getting close to the deadline for the big night, Santa opened up the mail and there was a letter from the FAA. He opens it up and reads that he's up for recertification. Naturally, this couldn't come at a worse time."

"So he details some of the elves to get the sleigh shined up, the bells polished, the reindeer brushed, the whole nine yards."

"Finally, the FAA guys shows up and he sees the weight and balances charts are up to snuff, the log books are in order, everything looks really good. The guys says, 'Let's take'er up. I'll be right back.'"

"Santa gets in the sleigh and the FAA inspector comes back and climbs in and he's got a shotgun.

"Santa asks, 'What's that for?'"

"The FAA guy gets this huge grin on his face and says, 'On takeoff you're going to lose an engine.'"

Fancy shook his head and grinned under his oxygen mask. "Another one of Joker's?"

"Nah, Badrod Baldon told that one in the Dirty Shirt Wardroom this morning at breakfast."

"Badrod, huh? That's pretty funny."

"Desperado 207, you ready to get down and dirty?"

"Roger that, 204. Down but not necessarily dirty."

"Let's blow the external fuel tanks as soon as the fuel is used up."

"Roger that," replied Fancy.

As Fancy looked to his right he saw Bagger lower his nose. He did likewise pushing the stick forward feeling the plane pick up speed. A split second later he heard the chirping of a search radar.

"They're just looking. Sounds like a Palm Top, SA-6s."

As they rocketed over the barren landscape that was Iraq the sound faded for a few seconds and then it was back, stronger as they built up speed in their shallow dives.

"Angels 15," said Fancy.

Al Kat came and went in a split second as the two planes came to a course of 345 degrees. Fancy punched off the two external 360 gallon fuel tanks. The plane seemed to give a shake as the tanks came off, seemingly relieved of the extra burden.

At 1,000 feet they leveled out for a few seconds. Now there was a definite sensation of speed. The ride was also getting rougher as the heat from below tried to push them up. Fancy, out of the corner of his eye was cogniscent of the ground rushing by, roads, an occasional car, houses, and out buildings all passed in a blur.

Fancy brought the stick back slightly as they roared over the top of a small hill. He gasped to himself as they blasted right over the top of an Iraqi Army mechanized column. They must have been warned a few seconds before the arrival of the F-14s because some of the vehicles were dispersing off to either side of the road. Seeing muzzle flashes from small arms Fancy involuntarily started to duck down and behind his instrument column. *Now there's a good place to hide* he smiled to himself. *They'll never see me there.* "Jesus," he muttered to himself.

"What did you say, Gator?"

"Nothin', just trying to find a good place to hide up here."

"I thought I saw muzzle flashes," returned Rhino. "Let me know if you find a good place."

Fancy pushed the stick forward once again and they went down to 500 feet. The outside world was just a blur and they went hurtling down the side of a small hill. Fancy hoped it was masking them somewhat. *Hope in one hand and spit in the other.* His hopes were dashed as he caught sight of what looked like red and green golf balls on the end of lighted ropes coming toward them. "Bagger, ZSU-23s!"

""Yeah man, look at those suckers! This is just like the Big One!"

Both planes were maneuvering against the guns trying to throw off their aim. Luck and skill seemed to be with them as they left the Iraqi guns in their wake.

"Badrah, 20 miles, come right two degrees."

Now there was more chirping in his ears indicating a SAM battery was looking at them. Look was all they could do because they were under their minimum guidance altitude.

Somebody must have forgotten to tell the Iraqis that because the sound changed from a search radar to that of a fire control radar. Fancy thought his heart must have stopped when he saw the dust plumes from two missiles being fired. Coming out of the dust and debris of the launch they did their best to guide onto the two Tomcats, but the Navy planes were just too low and the missiles, after what looked like five or six course corrections, went ballistic and passed from their view. Fancy breathed a sigh of relief and turned his attention to the guns.

"Forget the SAMs, Bagger, the guns are the bigger threat!"

"You got that right, Gator!"

"Twelve miles, come a little left."

Fancy moved the stick to the right and then back as they topped another hill.

"Perfect. Ten miles."

Now Fancy pushed the stick forward and they dropped down another hundred feet. The plane bucked, pitched, and shook in the thick, hot, desert air. "Come on, Baby. This is a piece of cake."

More golf balls on bright red ropes again floated up toward them. Again, they were left behind and Fancy worked the stick and rudder pedals in a series of furious but controlled movements presenting the worst possible target he could.

"Six miles."

"Four miles," came Mirabal's calm voice.

Now there were more guns firing at them: the ZSU-23s, 37mm, and those of larger calibers desperately tried to swat them out of the sky. Fancy decided he didn't want to look down to see the muzzle flashes of rifles and automatic weapons being fired at them, probably people laying on their back and just shooting straight up into the air.

At two miles he started to pump out chaff and flares. The fire seemed to be more intense and most of it seemed to be above them. Then they were racing across the grounds of the complex they had been sent to photograph, at least they hoped that's what the Iraqis would think.

Coming off the target both planes brought their noses up slightly as if they were going to climb to a safer altitude. An instant later both noses came down and they dropped to 300 feet "Comin' right," he announced to Rhino. At the same time Fancy rolled the streaking plane to the left 270 degrees and then bent the stick to the right. The maneuver seemed to throw the Iraqi tracking off momentarily as they reversed course even as the high Gs tried to squeeze Fancy and Mirabal down into the bottom of their seats. Now Bagger's cameras on board the

TARP pod should be rolling, *Taking pictures of what only God knows is there,* grumped Fancy to himself.

"Desperado 204 has been hit," came Bagger's detached voice. "Shutting down the starboard engine."

Sensing things would only get worse at this altitude Fancy called, "Bagger, let's get off the deck as soon as we get by that hill on our right."

"Climbing after the hill."

As the hill streaked by both planes started a gradual climb to a higher altitude.

"Gator, the temperature on the port engine is starting to climb a little. When we hit ten thousand how about looking me over."

"Roger that, Bagger. Goin' to ten thousand."

After an excruciatingly slow climb, of what seemed like hours, but was only four minutes they reached the desired altitude. Fancy moved over and slid under Bagger's plane. As he came out from under on the starboard side he moved above and back of the stricken Tomcat.

"Bagger, you've got some holes right under the engine, looks like you're losing fuel, and…" he paused.

"And what?"

Fancy felt the sweat start to run down his back and he felt a cold chill sweep over him at the same time. "And it looks like there's an SA-7 stuck in your tail feathers."

The SA-7 Strella was a shoulder fired surface to air missile comparable to the American Stinger. Although it was reported not to be as good as the Stinger, this one had certainly worked fairly well.

"Well, shit, good news comes in bunches," snapped Bagger.

"Bagger, if it was going to explode, I think it would have done so already."

"You're probably right."

"How's the engine temp on the port engine."

"Uh, it's working it's way up."

"All right, let's get some more altitude, we're sitting ducks here." The chirping of the Palm Top search radar was again evident in his ears.

In Desperado 204 Bagger squeezed his grip on the stick and advanced the throttles, bringing the stick back slightly. *I better not get greedy and try for it all at once*, he thought.

Fancy watched Bagger's nose come up slightly and duplicated the process in his own cockpit. "That a way, Bagger; let's ease into it."

"Rhino, what do you think the strongest part of this plane is?"

"Better be the wing box," he replied. "Why?"

"How about the very front of the canopy?"

"They're made to resist bird strikes while you're making high knots. What are you thinking?"

"I'm thinking he's going to have to shut down that engine any time and we're going to have to push him."

"Do what!" sputtered Rhino.

"Push him."

"Yeah, that's what I thought you said. Just how are we going to do that?"

"If he drops his hook we can come right up under him and gently make contact with our front canopy and his hook. Then we can just push him home."

"Well, sure. No problem, just push him home, why not?"

"You're with me?"

"Of course, like I have a choice?"

"I'll call it off if you say so."

*Sweet mother of God*, contemplated Mirabal, *I'm sure I'm going to call it off. Push him home!*

Taking a very deep breath, "Sounds like a plan to me. You think we can do it?"

"Piece of cake."

"Bagger, drop your hook."

"What?"

"Drop your hook." Fancy watched as the tailhook came down. "Rhino, get on the horn and let the powers-that-be know that we could use a little help."

The two planes were now at 15,000 feet. "Gator, this looks like as high as I can get her to go. The temp is just about in the wrong place."

"All right. Now, listen to me. I'm going to push you out of here. Just before you've got to shut down the port engine, let me know. I'm going to slide back and then put my nose under you, then come up and make contact with your hook and the front of my canopy. Mirabal has assured me it's one of the strongest parts on this plane."

"You've got to be kidding!" responded Bagger, knowing he wasn't kidding the least bit and he hadn't heard him use the word try. He was just going to do it. *Just like that.* "This wasn't Mirabal's idea was it? Because if it was…"

"Don't worry about who's idea it is, just remember it's going to work."

"Rhino, shut down the radar. No use taking a chance on frying them before we get them home.

"The nose is cold," reported Mirabal.

"Walrus," asked Bagger, "what do you think?"

"I think we're out of ideas and engines," responded his RIO who was just now remembering his mother had told him there would be days like this. Well…maybe not quite like this.

"If you've got to communicate with another plane, use a closed fist for yes and an open hand for no. Fingers can indicate numbers. We'll go the the field at Al Jarah in Kuwait. You set?"

"Gator!" Mirabal interrupted. "Have them get their survival radios out. We can use those to talk back and forth. Range definitely won't be a problem!"

"Did you copy that, Bagger?"

"We copied. Great idea, Rhino." *There it was again; the word try never entered the conversation.* "Sure, we're set, I guess."

"Okay, Babe. Let me slide behind you and move up under you. Tell me just before you cut the engine."

"Will do. And Gator."

"What?"

"Thanks."

"No problem, you'd do the same for us."

"Terrific idea, Rhino. Man, you were way ahead of me. That was some great thinking about the survival radios! Just great!"

"That was the easy part, Gator."

Fancy let Bagger drift out in front of them and deftly brought his plane to Bagger's six. With the gentlest of movements he eased the throttles forward until the long nose of the Tomcat was directly under Bagger's plane. His tailhook was about four feet away directly level with the front of their canopy.

"Shutting down the port engine—now," reported Bagger.

Fancy noted that Bagger's plane wasn't losing any altitude yet and he eased his plane forward and let Bagger's tailhook settle on to the front of his canopy. Again he eased the throttles forward and the two planes joined together as one and started the long trip home.

Fancy glanced at his own temperature gauges. They looked good. Then he looked at the fuel gauges. Not so good. He looked away. *I'd better concentrate on one thing at a time. Besides there's nothing I can do immediately about the fuel situation.*

In the meantime, right after shutting down the engine, both Bagger and Walrus had wrestled around and had taken their survival radios out. "Desperado 207, come in 207, come in, please." commanded Bailey. "Christ, I hope these batteries are okay."

"When's the last time you checked them, Bagger?" asked Walrus.

"Not too long ago, I think. Desperado 207, come in." There was no reply.

Fancy looked up at Bagger's plane. The holes in the fuselage seemed bigger. Any fuel that was left had already leaked out. Sneaking a quick look at the temperature gauge he saw that it had crept up slightly but had seemed to have stabilized.

"Rhino, you handle all the radio traffic and I'll see if I can get us to Kuwait."

"Like I said, Babe, I've got the easy part."

Raising his own survival radio to his lips he called, "Desperado 204, come in please. Desperado 204."

"We copy, 207," Walrus replied. "Everything looks good up here. I can't believe how quiet it is though."

"Nice to hear your voice, Walrus. Gator, the survival radios work. I'm in contact with them."

"Great, let's go easy on the batteries, just in case."

Rhino needed no reminding of what "just in case" meant.

"Rhino, see what you can get us in the way of a sitrep."

"Sitrep coming up."

A minute later Rhino was back with his report. "Gator, the duty E-2C is going to pass information over JTIDS (joint tactical information display system). Killer and Poncho are headed our way and they've launched Big Wave and Mongo. The EA-6B is coming toward us to jam. Tanker support is also being sent this way. That's the good news."

"What's the bad news?"

"The Iraqis have launched at least two planes out of Al Mussayyib and they're headed this way."

Fancy looked down at his radar display, now being passed from the E-2C Hawkeye. He could see the symbols of the planes as they moved toward them. It could be close.

"Shall I pass all the news up to Bagger?"

Fancy hesitated. "Sure," he finally said. "I'd want to know what was happening."

"204, we got a sitrep. We're going to have some company. Killer and Poncho are headed our way, as well as the EA-6B to run a little interference for us electronically. The ragheads have launched a couple of their guys from Al Musayyib."

"There was a pause of a few seconds. "Gator, Bagger says get while the getting is good. "They're more than willing to take their chances on the ground."

"Ask him how he'd like an Iraqi jail and some huge guy named Abdul wanting to snuggle up to him every night?"

After another few seconds. "Gator, Bagger says the jail part might not be so bad, but Abdul, no way."

"That's what I thought he would say. Tell him we'll stick around a while longer."

Seeing that the temperature gauge wasn't moving he thought about trying to gain a little altitude. Then, figuring that he might need the fuel more than he probably would the altitude he resisted the temptation.

"We're just south of Al Hay, Gator. We can almost see the Fence from here," reported Mirabal.

Fancy at that moment was more interested in the two dots at their five o' clock position. Seeing the two symbols that were moving toward their two o' clock gave him confidence this just might work out after all. Those two dots were much closer and moving faster than the Iraqis were.

"I've got Killer and Poncho at twenty miles and coming hard," Rhino exalted. "Come on guys!"

At the same time Fancy heard the sound of a search radar probing the sky. In another minute the higher warble of the fire control radar shot through his headset. *Great, just great.*

"They're going to launch, Gator."

# 17

Fancy's heart began to pound in his chest like a triphammer. *It was one thing to risk your own life, but here you are putting three other lives on the line for what? Well, no one said life was easy.*

Suddenly, the chirping of the fire control radar was silenced. "Hey, looks like they're more worried about the Prowler than they are about bagging us. They really shut it down real fast. Those missiles aint going nowhere but down."

"Not fast enough for me," breathed Mirabal. "Killer and Poncho are at eight miles. Bad guys are still coming hard; they're at twenty-five miles."

"Desperado 207, this is a flight of two Tomcats coming up on your…" Killer stopped in mid sentence. "Holy…Jesus…"

In the blink of an eye Killer and Poncho had blown by their two brethren, not quite willing to believe what they had seen in the blink of an eye.

"Desperado 207," came the somewhat unbelieving voice of Poncho Barnes, " We'll see what these guys from Al Musayyib are up to. Man, I saw that, but I sure as hell don't believe it."

"We're glad to have you join the party, Poncho. If you don't mind we'll just keep motoring on south."

Fancy's eyes were again drawn to the fuel gauges. *Better not to look.* Then he looked again at the SAM that was now part of Bagger's plane. *That's going to make a great trophy for the squadron. Much better to think positive at a time like this.*

"Gator, we're about two minutes away from the Fence. There are two dots coming fast, must be Big Wave and Mongo."

After a long two minutes Mirabal announced, "Okay! We've crossed the Fence."

"That's progress," answered Fancy. He forced himself not to look at the fuel gauge. Engine temp was okay, but had moved up a little. Gradually, they were losing altitude but not enough to matter he figured. *I'd better trade altitude for fuel.*

"Rhino, have Bagger try and bring his nose up."

Mirabal relayed the message and they seemed to stabilize at just a little over 13,000 feet.

"Yeah, that's just what we needed. We're looking good."

The two planes continued their course with a silence enveloping both cockpits. Mirabal, who didn't like to go too long without some type of conversation going finally broke the stillness. "Gator, if you don't mind my asking, how in the hell did you come up with this, this…"

"Concept?"

"Whatever you want to call it."

"I was reading somewhere, could have been the Hook magazine. I can't remember exactly where. Anyway, these two F-4s were coming back to Thailand after hitting a target in North Vietnam. Both planes had been hit and were losing fuel, one was about to flame out. No way were they going to make it to the tankers. This guy named Bob Pardo, flying the second plane and also losing fuel, decided rather than bailing out over the North he could push his wingman using the Phantom's tailhook."

"These were Air Force planes?"

"Yeah, but they were built with tailhooks just like the Navy Phantoms. After they joined up, one of Pardo's engines caught fire and he had to shut it down. They flew for another eight or ten minutes on one engine. They were hoping they could get to the tankers but it didn't work out. They had just crossed the North Vietnam—Laos border when they realized they were going to have to bail out. When they punched out they were pretty widely separated but all four were eventually picked up, thanks to the "*Jolly and Sandy*" support they got. Happy ending. Funny thing is, they weren't able to get back together for about 22 years when some congressman read about it and got them together. Pardo and his back-seater got a late Silver Star out of the reunion."

"Too muckin' fuch," said Mirabal. "Well, well, looks like we've got some company."

Fancy looked to his left and saw two F-14s slide into position about two hundred yards out.

One of the planes moved in for a closer look. Fancy could see both the pilot and RIO shaking their heads. "Desperado 207, that is something to see. Man oh man, I wish I had brought my camera."

"Nice to see you, Mongo, you too Wave."

"I'm going to slide back and get some video on the TCS. People aren't going to believe this unless they see it."

Mongo moved his plane back and commenced to roll film from all possible positions.

Big Wave moved in next. "Is that what I think it is sticking out of the back of Bagger's plane, Gator?"

"Yeah, that's what it is."

"Mother Fletcher," Big Wave groaned. He immediately moved his plane out and away from Bagger and Fancy.

As Mongo moved to their right he asked, "Fancy, are you trying for Al Jurah?"

"Roger that. Anything closer?"

"No, I think that's the best bet. What's your fuel state?"

Fancy paused, "Uh 'bout 3500 pounds, maybe a little less. *Definitely, make that less.* He could lie with the best of them.

Presently, they were joined by Killer and Poncho. The two Su-27s from Al Musayyib had decided they had business elsewhere and had done a 180 well inside the 32nd parallel.

The six planes continued toward Kuwait. "Gator," Mongo announced, "the border's coming up in ten minutes. It'll be another eight or nine minutes to Al Jurah. How do you want to work this?"

Fancy stole another glance at the fuel gauges. They could make it— barely. "Let's start a real gentle left hand turn and get lined up on the runway at Al Jurah while we've got some altitude to play with. How's the weather there?"

"Unlimited visibility and winds are negligible. The Kuwaitais are going to shut down the field in about five minutes and will have crash crews standing by."

Mirabal was relaying the information to Bagger as the plans unfolded.

"When we're about three quarters of a mile from the numbers, I'm going to cut my speed and pull off to the right. As soon as I pull off, Bagger will blow his gear down. What do you think, anybody got any other ideas?" Nobody did.

"Mongo, what about that tanker?" inquired Fancy, trying to sound as nonchalant as he could. Did his voice sound an octave higher? He hoped not.

"Texaco is flying a loose formation off to starboard. What do you want to do with him?"

"How about he joins up with us as soon I leave Bagger. I'll slide over and grab some gas." He could hear Mongo chuckle.

"That bad huh. Well, we've come this far. We might as well play this all the way out. Can you make it?"

"Sure, piece of cake." *A very thin piece…*

Taking his own survival radio for the first time, "Bagger, we're going to start a real gradual left hand turn to course one-two-zero, and get lined up on the runway at Al Jurah. Right after we come to one-two-zero, we'll start a gradual descent. At three quarters of a mile, blow down the gear and I'll turn you loose. You're going to have to call the field as soon as you can. Visibility is somewhat limited back here."

"Roger that, gradual left hand turn to one-two-zero. How you doin' on fuel?"

"Okay," he answered, trying to fight the rising tide of concern that was making its way up his throat. Bagger had been doing some calculating too.

"207, we're across the border."

"Roger, border."

"Okay, Bagger, here we go, real gradual turn." Taking a deep breath he nudged the throttles forward as he moved the stick to the left.

Slowly the two planes settled on their new course. Fancy felt the perspiration roll down his back as he gingerly kept the two planes together. The air was rougher, and Bagger's plane moved up and away from them. Fancy gingerly let the F-14 settle back down on their windshield. The air was more disturbed as they got lower. His right arm began to ache. *Come on, just a few more minutes.*

"Gator, I've got the field in sight."

"207, Al Jurah is at three miles, you're cleared for a straight in approach. Texaco is to starboard at half a mile, and they're ready to tank just after you disengage."

"Roger that, thanks, Mongo."

"Two miles, looks like we're a little high."

"Gripe, gripe, gripe," replied Fancy, feeling some of the tension drain away. "I want you to have a little something to play with."

"Mile and a half."

"One mile."

"Okay, Bagger, you're on your own." Immediately he retarded the throttles, dropped his nose, and moved to starboard. That was when the port engine, starved for fuel, flamed out.

Fancy took a hurried look just in time to see Bagger's gear come down. Looking to his right he saw the S-3, it's hose and basket already out starting to move to their front.

He knew he was only going to get one chance to stab the basket. "Cross your fingers, Rhino, this is going to be close."

Holding down an urge to go for the basket, he made himself count to ten and then moved the throttles forward and put the probe right down the middle. The lights went from red to green and the starboard engine died.

"Texaco, we have a little situation back here. Both engines are out. You're going to have to give us a little tow until I can get them started."

"Roger on the tow, a little toboggan ride."

The ground started to rise to meet them as the fuel came on board, Fancy, fighting the impetus to rush, made himself deliberately and intentionally go through the engine restart procedure. His efforts were rewarded when the port engine rumbled back to life. Seconds later the starboard engine followed suit.

"Texaco, both engines are back on line. We're back in business."

"Roger that Desperado 207. We just got word that Lieutenant Bailey is safe and sound on the ground at Al Jurah."

Four minutes later when the refueling was completed Fancy pointed the big fighter toward the sky, stroked the afterburners to Zone Five and did a series of aileron roles.

Leveling off at 12,000 feet he shouted, "Man, that felt good!"

Mirabal, who was sure at more than one time during the mission his heart might have to be jump-started could only murmur his agreement.

As the yellow mule shoved Desperado 207 into its parking space Fancy pulled off his helmet and red skull cap. Pulling off his Nomex gloves he ran his hand through his damp hair. He breathed a sigh of relief as the continuing business of launching and recovering planes went on without interruption. He listened for a minute listening to the creaks and groans of the plane as it cooled off. It too seemed to be relieved to be back on deck.

As he climbed down the boarding ladder he watched as the C-2A Greyhound COD plane was launched off the number two catapult. Looking back at Mirabal who was tidying up his "office", he quipped "Bet I know where they're going," he said as he jerked his thumb at the fast disappearing plane.

"I'd hate to be Bagger if Chief Tomshaw is on board. He's not going to be happy about the holes in that plane. On the other hand, he does have a plane to be pissed off about. Either way, he's going to be all bent out of shape." He hoisted himself out of the cockpit. "Let's get done with the Intel guys, I am so hungry not to mention thirsty."

Looking down at Fancy he smiled and shook his head. "That was some great flying today. Man, someday I'll be telling my grandchildren about this. Thanks for letting me be a part of all this."

" Oh, like you had a choice? Hey don't get all sentimental on me. You more than held up your end, especially today. Don't ever sell yourself short. It's been a team effort—everything that's happened. There's no way I could have pulled that off by myself. You really made it happen." Fancy shrugged and smiled. "Come on pardner, I could use something to eat too."

*Somehow you probably would have found a way,* Mirabal thought as he climbed down. *You would have found a way. I'd bet money on that.*

Two hours later Fancy flopped down on his rack. He had counted on the session with the intelligence specialists. The forty-five minutes with them had passed fairly quickly. What he hadn't counted on the hour and fifteen minutes with the Tech Rep from the Grumman Corporation. It might have been longer except they had the tape from Mongo's TCS to look at. Frank Royce, a former Navy fighter pilot, had been more than impressed, less so with Fancy's flying and more so with the performance of Desperado 207. Fancy agreed all the way with his assessment about the plane. Closing his eyes he immediately dropped off to sleep.

It seemed like only a few minutes had passed when Fancy was awakened by something pressing on his chest. Trying to come out of the fog he seemed to be in and trying to make sense out of whatever it was that had found a home on his body. "What the hell..."

"Gator, you awake?" came Bagger's voice cutting through his befuddlement.

"I am now, thanks to you." Running his hand along the cylindrical object. "What is this anyway?"

"Can I turn on the lights?"

"No, let's leave 'em off and play Twenty Questions!"

"I'll take that to be a yes."

Fancy shut his eyes and then opened them and looked at the object of his curiosity. "Jesus, what are you doing with this?"

"Pretty cool, huh. How often do you get this close to a SAM?"

Fancy gingerly sat up and carefully rolled the Strella down on to his lap. "Hey, I saw more of this baby than I ever really wanted to, believe me." Looking at his watch and being surprised that he had been asleep for nearly four hours.

"Did you just get back?"

"'Bout fifteen minutes ago. What do you think?" Bagger said, gesturing at the inert missile.

"It definitely belongs in the trophy room. Does the squadron have a trophy room? Not very big is it?"

"We do now. Nope, it isn't too big. I was wondering what would have happened if it had exploded."

"You've got to get out more, man."

Both of them laughed at the absurdity of the situation.

"I owe you big time, Gator. That was real precision flying, hell that was great flying. No doubt about it, man I owe you..."

"You owe me nothing. You would have done the same thing if things had been the other way around."

"You know I would have rung my hands and covered you when you would've had to punch out. I never would have thought of pushing, the tailhook...the whole thing."

"Well, it was an Air Force idea. I just happened to remember I'd read it somewhere and the plane did the rest."

"Yeah, sure! That was all you! And I just want you to know how much I appreciate it. I really owe you."

Fancy smiled. "You'll do anything?"

"Anything."

"Then take this thing off of me ."

"What should I do with it?"

"Let's mount it over the fireplace."

The *George Washington*, one of the Navy's newest carriers, passed the Enterprise. The scene on the Enterprise was one of stark contrast from when she had come on station. The port side of the huge carrier was lined with what seemed to Fancy most of the crew. Catcalls, advice, and just plain expressions of happiness were being shouted across the quarter mile that now separated the two ships. Not much was coming the other way.

"What a difference a few months can make," observed Mirabal.

"It went a lot faster than I thought it would," said Bagger as he watched the Washington pull away.

"Something about busy hands," smiled Fancy.

The three aviators were standing on the port side elevator watching the Washington and change of station ceremony. A few minutes earlier Van Gundy and Ratchet Robinson, along with the CAG from Washington and his wingman had flown between and parallel to the two ships. When they were amidships Van Gundy and his wingman had stroked the burners and had pulled straight up into the somewhat hazy blue sky, and then recovered, while the two planes from Washington had continued north to fly their first mission into the No Fly Zone.

"You know, in a way I kind of envy those guys—at least the guys that are doin' the flying."

Fancy and Mirabal looked closely at Bailey. "I suppose you'd like to stay for another couple of months?"

"You've got to admit, Gator, that the flying was pretty good. Man, if you would have stayed the Iraqis might've run out of MiGs."

Fancy laughed. "I'm sure there's more than enough to go around."

"Hey, before you guys take off I wanted to ask a big favor from each of you."

"Sure," answered Bagger, "anything you need, babe."

"Count me in too," said Mirabal.

"I talked to Father Deverich about Cody and I'm getting married as soon as we get back to San Diego. He's pretty sure we can do it right away. I'd really like you guys to stand up with me, you know, be my best man, uh men. It would mean a lot to me."

Both men extended their hands and congratulated Fancy. "Thanks for asking me, I'd be honored," announced Mirabal.

"Count me in," declared Bagger.

"Well, I know you guys want to take off and get home or to Nellis, so we're thinking of having the ceremony in that little base chapel the day after we get back. What do you think?"

"Great," said Bagger. "Let me write Wendy so she can make arrangements to be there too. Yeah, it's a swell idea."

"My folks will still be in Philadelphia. A day won't matter at all to them. Thanks for asking me."

"Thanks, guys, I really appreciate it."

Taking one more look at the *Washington*, that was now hull down on the horizon they headed below to take care of paperwork and other squadron business.

The *Enterprise*, the oldest of the nuclear powered carriers, was also reputed to be one of the fastest, if not the fastest ship in the Navy. Three and a half weeks of steady steaming found her and the rest of the Battle Group east of the Hawaiian Islands. VF-124 was gathered in Ready Three. The purpose of the meeting was to decide which pilots and RIOs would fly off the ship and into Miramar ahead of the rest of the ship and its company.

"All right you guys, let's settle down and get this over with." Robinson was having a difficult time getting and keeping everybody's attention. "Knock it off or I'm going to invoke executive privilege." The room suddenly and completely fell silent.

"You all know the drill. We'll pick from the straws, that my esteemed executive officer," he nodded toward Matsen, "is holding. Long straws get to go, short straws ride the ship to Alameda. That should keep the moaning and bitching from the losers to a minimum." Of course he knew it would not stop any moaning or bitching at all. Who ever didn't get to fly off would swear all the way to his deathbed that he had been robbed, but nobody had any better ideas and the drawing got under way.

He had forgotten or had just ignored the fact that this was the way it was done in most squadrons. If he had to ride in with the ship, the wedding was at least three days off from the time the first F-14 left the ship. Well, nobody said life was fair.

When Joker pulled the first short straw, he began to feel somewhat optimistic. When everyone who stepped up to draw a straw out of Matsen's hand wound up with a short straw he began to smell a rat. Everybody with a short straw just seemed a little too well adjusted to that fact. Four more people drew with the now predictable results.

Finally it was his turn. Taking a deep breath he moved to where Matsen was standing and picked one. He was not the least bit surprised to find he had a long one. Looking around he saw the smiles on the faces of the squadron.

"I smell a rat here. What's going on?"

Robinson, with his ear to ear grin, stepped forward. "If anybody's earned a first ride home, it's you." As Fancy started to open his mouth in protest, he held up his hand. "Don't give me a hard time. This is something we all talked about and everybody, and I mean everybody, agreed on, for once. We all know about the wedding and we want to make sure it comes off as scheduled. The maintenance troops have worked their collective butts off and they're promising that every F-14 is going to be able to launch—even 204," he smiled, nodding at Bagger. "Make sure you let them know you appreciate all that work. They've really gone the extra mile, as they've done for this whole cruise."

"I don't know what to say."

"Good," put in Matsen, "you don't have to say anything."

"I do. It's just that I...I don't have the words right now. But thanks, guys. This really means a lot—more than you'll ever know, believe me." He remembered something from one of his English Lit. classes, something from Shakespeare about *"this band of brothers"*. It seemed to be on the tip of his tongue when his thoughts were interrupted by Killer clapping him on the shoulder. "I hope we're all invited?"

"Of course you are—everybody is. I was kind of reluctant to make a huge deal out of it because I know some people want to get away from San Diego as soon as possible."

"Are you kidding, all these guys want to be there, believe me."

Fancy, of course by now, did.

# 19

When the Enterprise was a thousand miles from the coast of California she changed course slightly in order to get more wind over the deck to launch the first of the planes that would be returning to their bases. The F-14s with their long range would be the first to launch. Fancy and Mirabal had completed two walk-arounds an hour before they were even supposed to report to their aircraft.

During the past several days there had been rumors that the squadron might be disestablished in the next round of budget cuts. One rumor had it that the Enterprise might be taken out of commission. Another rumor was that the next time the Enterprise sailed there would be no F-14s on board, replaced with another squadron of F-18s.

"What do you think about all the scuttlebutt that's been going around the past couple of days, Gator?"

"I think it's just that—a bunch of rumors. None of it came from Van Gundy or the skipper. No matter what we just have to roll with the punch or punches. That's one thing you can always count on in the Navy, there's always going to be some floating around. It's that way from the minute I signed on the dotted line."

# 18

When the Enterprise was a thousand miles from the coast of California she changed course slightly in order to get more wind over the deck to launch the first of the planes that would be returning to their bases. The F-14s with their long range would be the first to launch. Fancy and Mirabal had completed two walk-arounds an hour before they were even supposed to report to their aircraft.

During the past several days there had been rumors that the squadron might be disestablished in the next round of budget cuts. One rumor had it that the Enterprise might be taken out of commission. Another rumor was that the next time the Enterprise sailed there would be no F-14s on board, replaced with another squadron of F-18s.

"What do you think about all the scuttlebutt that's been going around the past couple of days, Gator?"

"I think it's just that—a bunch of rumors. None of it came from Van Gundy or the skipper. No matter what we just have to roll with the punch or punches. That's one thing you can always count on in the Navy, there's always going to be some floating around. It's that way from the minute I signed on the dotted line."

"That's the truth. We were always waiting for the "word", whatever the hell that was. Movie, no movie, liberty, no liberty," Mirabal laughed. "The Navy runs on rumors; they fuel the beast."

"Mornin', Gentleman."

Fancy turned. "Morning, Skipper."

"Well, it looks like a magnificent day to go flying. What do you think?"

"Couldn't agree more, Sir," said Mirabal. "The weather guessers say we'll have perfect weather from here all the way to Miramar."

"Great way to end a cruise. The way things started out, I was beginning to wonder."

"It was hard losing Animal that way," agreed Fancy.

Robinson stared out over the open ocean. Barely visible on the horizon was one of the escorting destroyers. "You just never know what's going to happen when you go down to the sea in ships. I think of all the ships that have sailed just since I've been in the Navy. Man, some of the things that've happened to men, planes, ships…" He shook his head.

"I'll never forget my first cruise with VF-51. You guys probably don't remember the old Midway. She was forward deployed in Japan. Man, everybody thought I had lucked out; seems like she was considered a lucky ship—Midway Magic was kind of her unofficial slogan. We were flying Phantoms because she was too small to handle the F-14s. Mrs. Murphy was alive and well. If anything could go wrong it did. We had just started flight operations. The first plane that was launched, an A-7, just dribbled off the end of the boat; the plane got run over by the ship, pilot was never found. All kinds of stuff like that. Funny thing was, I didn't have one single problem, not one. Everybody was so glad when that cruise was over. It probably went down as the worst six months any carrier ever had over that period of time without some kind of catastrophic incident. We've been very fortunate the past six months."

"Skipper, there's been a lot of scuttlebutt going around about the squadron being disestablished, Enterprise being cut up for razor blades, all kinds of stuff. Do you know what's going on?"

"Well, Rhino, I'm sure of one thing. The Gunfighters are not going to be disestablished nor is the Enterprise being scrapped. What I do know is that when we start this whole process of getting ready for the next cruise, and I don't know who will or won't be back, we'll be working with a new TARPS pod and that's going to change the way we do business."

"Oh, how's that?"

"Imagine you and Bagger take off as a section. One plane with the TARPS, but it's fitted with a digital imagery camera taking the place of the KS-87 serial frame camera. You've still got your air-to-air weapons and two laser guided. Bagger's got a LANTRIN (Low Altitude Navigation and Targeting Infrared for Night) targeting system, air-to-air missiles and two more laser guided bombs."

As Mirabal and Fancy nodded their interest Robinson continued. "The great thing about the digital camera is that you can transmit real time pictures back to the ship or just anywhere they need to be sent, hell, even to another plane. Both of you will be able to view whatever it is you're taking on a 25mm viewfinder. What you wind up with is just about the perfect strike fighter. We've got range and payload, and we're able to find the target, fight our way in, and of course out."

"Sounds pretty exciting," nodded Fancy. "I wouldn't mind being part of something like that. How many of the guys do you figure will be with the squadron after the workups?"

"Hard to tell right now. I know Mongo probably won't. I'm pretty sure he'll get his own squadron. Other than that I don't want to speculate."

Checking his watch Robinson nodded toward his plane. "'Bout time to man up, I'll see you guys at Miramar." Clapping Mirabal on the shoulder he strode away to his plane.

"And to think at one time the cry was, *not one pound for air to ground*," smiled Mirabal at Robinson's retreating back.

"Times are a changin', Babe. What do you think about it?"

"In for a dime, in for a dollar. What the hell, can't be too bad lugging all that iron around."

"Yeah, we could find some way to make it exciting. Let's go home."

After another quick walk around, just to be sure, Fancy climbed the boarding ladder and eased himself into the seat, checking first to make sure Joker hadn't left any kind of a calling card. An eager enlisted man named Ketsdever helped him strap in. Preflight checks went smoothly and without a hitch. After lowering the canopy he started the port engine and it spooled up without a hitch. The starboard engine refused to start. *Well that's just par for the course* he thought to himself as he worked through the process once again, taking his time and doing everything deliberately and by the book. Nothing. "Damn!" he muttered.

"We got a problem?" inquired Mirabal.

"Dunno, how 'bout we launch with one engine?"

"That bad, huh?"

After trying once more he slammed the instrument panel with his left hand. "Jesus, I can't fucking believe it!"

"Mrs. Murphy is alive and well."

Fancy looked up and to his left in time to see Shrader and Chief Tomshaw heading their way.

A few seconds later Shrader had plugged in his headset. "Shrader, what's wrong with this plane?" he asked more sharply than he intended to. He could just imagine Shrader blushing with shame and it probably wasn't even his fault.

"I'm sorry, Sir," came the chastened voice. "Could you please shut down the port engine. The Chief thinks he knows what the trouble is."

Reluctantly he shut down the engine and raised the canopy. Shrader and Tomshaw disappeared from view. He could sense if not feel panels being opened up. By this time Robinson had been launched off the number one catapult followed by Killer. In quick succession Poncho, then Matsen were blasted off the front of the boat. He saw Bagger taxi across the lowered JBD.

*Come on Chief, do some of that magic mechanical shit.* Bagger was launched next, trailed immediately by Big Wave. One of the tractors or mules rumbled over the deck, pulling one of the long yellow tow bars, turned and backed toward them. "Can you believe this shit!"

"Sure, I believe it. Don't give up on the Chief and Shrader though."

Joker Valdorama and Stash McClure taxied forward, the port JBD came down and Valdorama rolled over it to the catapult. A few seconds later McClure joined him on the starboard cat.

Squirming around in his seat Fancy felt the anger start to creep up from down around his ankles. By the time Joker and Stash were mere blips on the horizon, the anger was in his throat. "God damn it! Shit!" Moose and Gizmo moved up behind the JBDs. Rainman James, on whose wing Fancy was to fly, started to move.

The plan had been to launch all the F-14s. They would join up, do a fly-by and scoot for San Diego. Fancy could see it going down the drain. The anger continued to build. More yellow-shirts started to move toward them. Someone Fancy couldn't see must have motioned them back, because they stopped, waiting in a group like a bunch of dandelions. Rainman James rolled over the lowered JBD, was hooked to the cat and launched.

After another few minutes the Gunfighters roared overhead with a sound and sight that sent tingles up and down Fancy's back. They disappeared to the east. Figuring the game was lost he had just started to take off his helmet when Shrader appeared out from under the plane, tethered to it by the wire on his headset. "Sir, we've just about got it licked. It'll be another three minutes the Chief says."

"Well, how about that, Rhino?"

Trying not to show the immense sense of relief he was feeling, Mirabal answered, trying with all his might to keep his voice as casual as possible, "Never bet against Chief Tomshaw. I wonder what the problem was?"

"Don't know and I don't even care right now as long as it's fixed. The three minutes turned out to be five, but now nobody was counting. Tomshaw came out from under the plane and signaled them to start the port engine. It rumbled to life and thirty seconds later, its up to then lifeless brother did the same. Another few minutes showed that everything was where it should be and they were ready to go. Heaving a sigh of relief he followed the yellow-shirts' directions and they moved up to the starboard catapult. One minute later, after another check of the controls and the sharpest salute he could muster, they were thrown off the boat. As soon as Fancy could once more focus on the instruments, he slapped the gear handle, the wheels came up into their wells and Desperado 207 climbed into the clear blue sky. The *Enterprise* soon became just a speck behind them.

"Man, I didn't think we were going to get off today." By now the Enterprise had disappeared from view altogether. As they reached 19,000 feet Fancy trimmed the plane up and started to look at his radar display just in case they had managed to close the distance between them and the rest of the squadron. The scope told him what he already knew but it never hurt to be sure.

"Like I say, never bet against the Chief. Maybe it's a good thing we didn't know what the problem was."

"Ignorance is bliss?"

"That works for me," laughed Mirabal. "Well, some of the time anyway. Are we going to play catch up?"

"I can't think of a reason not to. We've got a full bag of fuel and we're traveling light with no missiles."

"Hey, hey, let's motor on home then."

Fancy pushed the throttles to full military power. The big fighter, seeming to share in the urgency of the moment, leaped ahead pushing them both back into their seats.

Four hundred and twenty-five miles off the coast of California, Mirabal called out, "Oh yeah, I have a large formation at seventy-five miles, 19 angels, course zero four zero, heading away. It's my very educated guess that we've found our guys."

"I very much concur with your very educated guess."

"Desperado 201, this is Desperado 207 at your six at, uh, sixty-five miles and closing."

"Howdy boys. I was worried you were going to miss the homecoming. Welcome to the party," came Robinson's laconic voice. "Slide in on Rainman's port side and we'll head for the barn."

Another few minutes found the squadron in sight. Picking out Rainman's F-14 proved to be no problem and Fancy brought Desperado 207 on his left side. "Rainman James looked over at the new arrival and gave them a thumbs up. Fancy returned the gesture in kind, grinning beneath his oxygen mask.

The fact that they were really back was brought home to them when Fancy caught sight of the dirty gray blanket that hung over the edge of the land. "Smog."

"What'd you say?"

"Smog. I never thought I would be glad to see that gray crud, but right now it really looks good."

"We've been away much too long."

"Listen up Gunfighters." Robinson's voice made it clear that this was not a polite request. "Remember, we just want to get these beasts on the ground. No hotdoggin' or any other bullshit. We've come to far to screw around now. We'll be feet dry in two minutes and we'll just make a straight in approach. Any questions?" Before anyone could answer, "Good, see you on the ground."

"You know I've never seen this many F-14s in the air at one time for, geez, I don't know if I've ever seen a whole squadron in the air at once. How about you, Gator. Have you ever seen this happen?"

"Yeah once, but it was only a squadron of seven when we came back from the Med on the Vinson. You know what they say when you see a whole squadron of Turkeys in the air at once."

"Yeah, it means we have one hell of a maintenance team."

"We sure as hell can testify to that," replied Fancy, noting the fact that they had just gone feet dry.

The squadron made their landfall over the city of Imperial Beach. Before long they had passed over San Diego Bay, National City, the city of San Diego itself. Finally, just north of the small city of Santee, Fancy smoothly brought the big plane to a course of two-one-zero. The squadron was now spread out in a line astern formation, lined up like toys on a store shelf.

Fancy started to twist and squirm; rotating his neck. All of a sudden he couldn't seem to get comfortable.

"You nervous, babe?"

"No, yeah, I guess so. I don't know. Damn, I hope I've still got the ring."

"You do. I saw you put it in your pocket right after you showed it to me—for about the millionth time I might add."

Taking his hand off the throttles Fancy sighed with relief as he reached down and patted the pocket in his flight suit, feeling the ring box.

"Desperado 207, you're cleared for a straight in approach. Winds from the southwest. Welcome home."

The voice from Miramar's tower startled him. Reaching for the gear handle he lowered the gear. "Three down and locked." *Fine time to have my head up my ass. Not a good time.*

In the distance he could see James touch down and start his rollout. Seconds later they crossed the Fence and the mains were kissing the ground and they started their own rollout. Holding the nose up Fancy let the big fighter slow down and then gently lowered the nose. Using the rudder pedals for brakes he slowed the plane down even more until they were barely rolling. Reaching the turn out he moved the throttles forward while holding down the right rudder pedal. At the same time he moved the wings back to their fully swept position of 68 degrees and, at the direction of an enlisted man, pulled up beside James's plane.

"That was pretty smooth, compadre."

"If I can't do a halfway decent landing by now on something that isn't pitching and rolling, I better find an easier line of work," Fancy replied as he shut down the engines. In the distance by the large hanger that proclaimed the base: Fighter Town U.S.A., he could see a crowd of people behind a yellow rope.

He raised the canopy and took in a deep breath of air, not minding one bit that it was thick with the smell of JP-8 jet fuel. Taking off his helmet and skull cap he ran his hand through his damp hair, standing up as he did so. Dropping his helmet down to the enlisted man that had guided them to their parking place, he climbed down the boarding ladder and dropped to the ground.

As he turned to say something to Mirabal he noticed his RIO nod in the direction of the hanger. Before he could get fully turned around to look he was almost knocked off his feet by someone or something crashing into him.

"Dan! Dan! I'm so glad you're home! Is this your plane? Can I look inside? What are all those flags and pictures on the side? Oh, I'm so glad your home. Are you really going to marry my mom tomorrow?" All this in a torrent of words raining down on Fancy like a machine gun gone mad in the space of ten seconds.

Kneeling down as he tried to gain his balance and composure he looked Amanda in the eyes and as his own eyes began to mist up, he hugged her to him. "Amanda, it's so good to see you. I can't believe how you've grown—and how fast you can move."

"How do you feel?" he asked again holding her at arms length

"I'm fine—good as new. Heck, I think I'm better than new, right mom?"

Fancy felt his heart hang fire. Slowly he stood up and turned around.

"Well, Squirt, better than new is a stretch since you were pretty wonderful before."

He wanted to say something but the words couldn't seem to make it past his throat.

He felt a small hand on his back trying to push him toward the beautiful woman that stood only an arm's length away. His body felt like he was pulling 7 g's as he tried to raise his arms and take a step. "Cody…I…I…"

Finally, he managed to take a step and Cody melted into his arms. He had no idea that she was so strong. Her arms felt like iron bands around his neck. For an instant he was afraid he might be hurting her. "Are you okay, I'm not…"

Releasing her hold on him enough to move back, she looked up into his face and shook her head, and then pulled him tightly to her again, murmuring, "I'm so glad you're back. I've been so anxious." Catching him by surprise she pulled his lips to hers.

The clapping, cheers, and whistles caught them both by surprise. Coming out of the embrace like two naughty teenagers they saw the squadron, along with their friends and members of the squadron in a cirlce around them.

"Gator," croaked Moose, "if you had taken any longer to kiss her, I was going to do it myself and take her away from you. Moose Milwood, Cody. It's nice to finally meet you. He hasn't begun to do you justice.."

"Moose, it's so nice to finally meet you. Dan's written me lots about you."

"He did? I didn't know he could write."

One by one the pilots and RIOs of the Gunfighters introduced themselves. Fancy could only stand and smile, despite some of the comments, as the squadron filed by.

"Cody," said Robinson, the last member of the group to introduce himself, "I'm so glad to meet you. When we received word of your misfortune, I thought we might be losing a pilot. I've never seen anybody go so pale so fast. It's easy to see now why he was so concerned. There's not even a word that comes close to what he must have been feeling." Jerking his thumb at the assembled aviators, "Despite what you've heard from some of these jokers, you're getting quite a man—in every sense of the word. But I'm sure you know that."

"Thank you, Commander. Yes, I know he is, in every sense of the word."

While the introductions had been going on, Fancy had been fishing around in his "green bag" for the ring box. At last he was able to get it out, surprised at how much his hands were shaking. Finally, seeing his chance he opened the box while pulling Cody toward him. "I'd like to ask you something."

With a twinkle, or was it a tear, in her eyes, she said sharply, "Yes."

"Yes?"

"Yes, you can ask me anything."

"Would you mar...?"

"Yes, yes, yes, a thousand times yes!" She nearly sent him to the ground when she leaped into his arms.

At that moment all over the base personnel looked up from whatever it was they were doing when they heard the pandemonium set by the cheering and clapping that was given off by the returning pilots and RIOs of the Gunfighters.

With trembling hands he placed the ring on her finger. "Oh, Dan, it's even more beautiful than I imagined, it's just perfect! Amanda, look."

"It's great, Mom. Dan, can I look in the plane now?"

Amid the last bit of cheering and laughing at Amanda's interest in the plane, the group of men started to drift off to their own wives, lovers, and friends.

Mirabal, sensing Fancy's difficulty at taking care of his soon-to-be-daughter's needs and staying with his soon- to- be- wife, stepped up. "Come on, Amanda, let me show you around. I'll even let you sit in my "office", the most important part of this plane."

"Wow, what a homecoming." Fancy, realizing he was still holding Cody's hand, brought it up to his lips. "You've made me so happy. It's hard to believe I'm here with you."

"You better believe it, sailor, because I'm not going away—ever."

"That's just fine by me."

Hand in hand they strolled back to the plane just as Amanda was moving from Mirablal's office to the front seat. "Dan what are those flags and drawings on here? Are they supposed to be here?"

Looking upward at her eager face he shrugged and looked at Mirabal for help. "Rhino just shook his head, "You're on your own, Babe."

"Well, yeah, they're supposed to be there."

"But what do they mean?"

"The five Iraqi flags are for planes we shot down."

Amanda's eyes grew larger. "Mom, I told you it was Dan. I told you!"

Answering Fancy's inquisitive look, Cody smiled and kissed him on the cheek. "Don't you know?"

"Uh, no, know what?"

"You two have made the news, TV, magazines, everything. There have been stories about Iraqi planes being shot down after violating the No-Fly Zone. No names of pilots or even the squadron was mentioned, only the fact that they were from the carrier *Enterprise*. As soon as Amanda heard the first words about it she was telling me that it had to be you."

"See, Mom, I knew it, I knew it! What about the picture of the two trucks? One of them looks like a tow truck!"

"We just kind of helped somebody out." Fancy tried to make it sound casual just as if he had helped someone change a flat tire.

"Come on, Gator," chimed in Mirabal.

Two sets of eyes seemed to be boring holes in him, waiting expectantly.

"We just kind of pushed Bagger's plane out of Iraq."

Mirabal shook his head in disgust. "You know that's just like saying the flight to the moon was just routine. It was the most awesome display of flying I or anybody else has ever witnessed. It was just awesome. I'll be telling my grandchildren about that. Talk about precision flying, awesome, just awesome."

"He's exaggerating a little."

"Bull…." Mirabal checked himself just in time.

"Listen, you have to remember, just whose idea was it?"

"Well, it was the blue-suiters…"

"Right. If I hadn't read about it," he said turning to Cody, "it just wouldn't have happened. I probably wouldn't have thought about it."

Mirabal, behind his back, was shaking his head in the negative.

"How could you push somebody in an airplane," demanded Amanda, who was looking all around the plane questioningly.

Fancy and Mirabal looked at each other. Come on, Gator, tell 'em how you did it."

"I'll tell you how we did it." Holding up his hands and gesturing for Amanda to climb down, he said, "Come on down and I'll show you."

Walking around to the rear of the plane, he gestured toward the tailhook, then grabbing it and gave it a shake. " Bagger got nailed on our last misssion and lost an engine. Before he lost his second engine we had him put down his tailhook. After that it was just a matter of getting close, and bringing our plane up close so the hook was up against the front of our canopy. The plane did the rest. We just motored on home, well, to Kuwait. Bagger greased it in and we flew back to the carrier. Simple."

By now Cody was looking at him with a look of awe on her face. Mirabal just shook his head.

"That's so neat, Dan. Can we go look in the cockpit again?"

"Sure, let's go."

Amanda tore past them and was trying to climb the boarding ladder to get back in the plane. Mirabal once again went to her assistance.

"Amanda, I think it's time to get down now. You don't want to wear out our welcome."

"Oh, Mom…" she implored looking to Fancy for help.

"Cody, she's fine. Let me continue the tour. Besides, it'll give you two a chance to get reacquainted."

"Thanks, Tony, but…"

"No buts. I don't have any place I need to be. It's my pleasure, really."

As Amanda continued her climb, Fancy and Cody, hand in hand strolled a short distance away from the plane.

Taking Cody's hand he brought it to his lips. "Listen, I hope I'm not rushing you into anything. I want this to last forever. But I don't want you to feel rushed or pressured. If you want to wait…"

With her free hand she put her forefinger on his lips. "You're not getting cold feet are you?"

"No, no way. I just don't want to get things off to a bad start."

Putting her arms around his neck and looking him straight in the eyes, "If I could, I'd go to the preacher right now. I love you more than I can ever tell you. I knew it at the air show, and when you first came up to the house and I know it now."

"Being a Navy wife isn't easy. As soon as our thirty day leave is up, we start to get ready for the next deployment. It means I'll be gone sometimes for weeks at a time before we deploy again."

"Do I look like a wimp to you, sailor?"

"Not from where I'm standing."

"Case closed. There's no way you're getting rid of me—ever."

Fancy hoisted himself up on the foam rubber raft and almost managed to arrange himself on the raft before it shot out from underneath him and dumped him back into the water. After another try and some loss of dignity, he finally managed to arrange himself to lay face up on the raft. Looking into the warm desert sun he smiled at Cody and mouthed the words, "I love you."

Cody, with Amanda curled up asleep beside her, laughed and first pointed to her eye, her heart, and them him, echoing his words back to him.

As he drifted around the pool he marveled at what had transpired in the past 48 hours. The wedding ceremony had gone off without a hitch. Writing thank you notes to those who had helped make it a perfect day would take some time. Cody had surprised him when she mentioned they needed to go to Lindbergh Field to pick up his parents. There was no doubt that she and Amanda were going to be accepted into the family. The squadron had arranged to fly them to Palm Springs. Once there a limousine had whisked them to this beautiful house with its own private pool where Amanda had exhausted herself swimming. His parents had offered to entertain Amanda while Fancy and Cody went on a brief honeymoon. At first he had been tempted, but thinking it through, he wanted to start out as a family and he had absolutely no regrets as he watched the two people who mattered most to him.

Hearing it before he saw it, he watched a small turbo prop plane climb out of the local airport. For a moment he wondered if staying in the Navy would be the best thing for him and his new family. Could he keep his edge if he had others to worry about? If he knew other people's happiness now depended on him? As the small plane faded from sight and sound he realized he would have to take it one day at a time.

Just as he was about to say something to Cody, he heard the deep throated roar of jet engines. The two F-14s passed over the desert hideaway, and even at an altitude of over 5,000 feet, he could feel their power right through the water and the raft. He strained to keep sight of them as long as possible. Moving the raft around he saw Cody smile and nod in the affirmative. He smiled and nodded back.

Printed in the United States
5246